VALORIAN'S LEGACY

Books by Mary H. Herbert

Dark Horse
Lightning's Daughter
(Published in an SFBC omnibus edition as *Valorian's Children*)

Valorian

City of the Sorcerers
Winged Magic
(Published in an SFBC omnibus edition as *Valorian's Legacy*)

Valorian's Legacy

City·of the Sorcerers
Winged Magic

Mary H. Herbert

50 YEARS SFBC FANTASY

Published by arrangement with the author.

Visit the SFBC at http://www.sfbc.com

ISBN 0-7394-3304-0

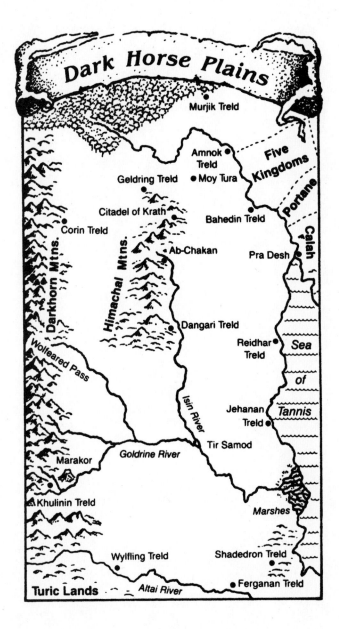

Dark Horse Plains

Murjik Treld

Amnok Treld

Moy Tura

Geldring Treld

Five Kingdoms

Citadel of Krath

Bahedin Treld

Portane

Corin Treld

Calah

Ab-Chakan

Pra Desh

Darkhorn Mtns.

Himachal Mtns.

Dangari Treld

Reidhar Treld

Sea

Wolfeared Pass

of

Isin River

Jehanan Treld

Tannis

Tir Samod

Goldrine River

Marakor

Khulinin Treld

Marshes

Wylfling Treld

Shadedron Treld

Turic Lands

Altai River

Ferganan Treld

CONTENTS

CITY OF THE SORCERERS

For my parents-in-law,
Richard and Helene Herbert,
with thanks for all
of your love and support.

PROLOGUE

The bright morning sun streamed in golden bars through the branches of the old gray cottonwoods that grew scattered around the abandoned clearing. The light dappled the long, untrampled grass and sparkled on the Isin River, which flowed nearby. Its heat warmed the early breeze.

Lady Gabria felt the sun's warmth on her shoulders as she waded out of the shallow water and climbed the bank. She drew a deep breath full of the scents of sun-warmed grass, wildflowers, and the cool smell of the river. She wiped some mud from her bare feet, then dropped the hem of her long split-skirts and walked slowly into the large open space between the trees.

Gabria wasn't sure why she had come here today. It had been years since she'd felt the painful stir of memories that used to bring her to this place. She glanced back downriver to where she could see the large clan camps clustered around the riverbanks. Once again the eleven clans of Valorian had traveled across the wide-flung realm of the Ramtharin Plains to come together at the sacred Tir Samod for their annual summer gathering. Once again, out of deference and a little fear, not one clan had pitched its tents in this shady, pleasant clearing by the river.

Gabria's shoulders shifted in a slight shrug. Not that it really mattered. No one had forgotten her family—she had seen to that—and if the clanspeople wished to avoid this place where the Corin used to camp so many years ago, that was a choice she could understand. After all, the massacre of her family and clan had been totally unprecedented in remembered clan history. It was a tragedy that still reverberated through the collective consciousness of the people of Valorian.

Gabria walked deeper into the clearing. It felt so strange to be here again. The area had changed over the years, yet she could still see in her mind how this clearing had looked twenty-five years ago when her father and brothers were still alive.

She gazed from place to place, looking past the weeds and trees to the shadows in her memory: of faces, objects, and laughter long remembered and still loved.

Something caught her glance near a huge, old tree—a single grave mound adorned with a spear and helmet. A faint smile lifted her mouth, for she could see now she was not the only person who had come here recently.

The spear was new; the helmet gleamed from careful polishing. The grass and weeds had been pulled away from the mound where fresh dirt had been piled to renew its sunken height. Gabria didn't need to guess who had performed that simple task of respect. Pazric, the man who had long ago moldered into the earth beneath the spear, had once been her husband's close friend.

Gabria stared at the grave, unwilling to tear her eyes away. The mound reminded her of another much larger grave far to the north in Corin Treld. The smell of turned earth, the soft rattle of the helmet as it swung gently in the morning breeze, the gleam of sunlight on the polished haft of the spear—they were all the same.

She stood in place, unmoving. The breeze teased a wisp of pale gold hair that had come loose from the plait coiled on the back of her neck. Despite the sun she shivered—from an old fear, a new apprehension, or perhaps from the touch of bitter memories, she didn't know. Her skin quivered at the strange chill that seeped into her, and her heart began to bang painfully in her chest.

The sunlight seemed to wither to a pale yellowing light that threw the world around her out of focus. Gabria tried to force her eyesight back to normal, but the visual images faded out of her reach and sank into a dim, opaque fog that surrounded her like a shroud. In just a moment the sunlit morning had vanished, obscured in mist and silence.

Gabria's breathing quickened. She stared in surprise at the place where the burial mound had been, even though she could not see anything through the veil of gloomy fog.

Fog. There had been fog at Corin Treld the afternoon that . . . The thought intruded into her mind with a stunning comprehension. Gods, no, she whispered silently. Not again.

Fog is coming in, she heard a familiar voice say. It was Gabran, her twin brother. She tried to turn, to see him in the mist, only to hear more voices faintly call nearby.

The herds are in.

Everyone is here, Gabran called again. *Wait! What is that noise?*

Unknowingly, Gabria's fingers clenched, and her nails dug into her palms. Her face was bloodless. From the other side of the river, along the flatlands to the south, a horn blew a loud, clear blast, and the sudden sound of hoofbeats came faintly on the breeze. Gabria's body shook with a violent tremor.

Taleon, get Father! she heard Gabran call to another brother. *I must find Gabria. There are horses coming. It sounds like a large troop.*

The noise of hoofbeats grew louder, pounding in her ears like thunder.

Oh, my gods, they're attacking us! Gabran shouted somewhere in the grayish mist. Shrieks and cries and screams of pain echoed around Gabria. Frantically she reached out to her family. She knew in a part of her mind that this event had happened twenty-four years ago and that the Corin clan was dead and buried in their mound. She accepted, too, that this was only a vision, similar to one she had had before. But nothing could alleviate the feelings of grief and helplessness that raged through her, as fresh and painful as ever.

They are burning the tents. We must get to Father. Where is Gabria?

"I'm here!" the clanswoman cried to the unseen voices. "Gabran, I'm here."

Gabria? Where are you? I've got to warn you! Her brother's voice grew louder as if he had heard her and was searching through the heavy fog to reach her.

"I'm *here,* my brother," she answered desperately.

All at once his voice changed to grief and anger. *No! Father is down. We must stand and fight. The women and children could run, but it is too late. We are surrounded by horsemen. Fire everywhere. We cannot see in this smoke and fog. Oh, gods,* Gabran groaned over the furious sounds of killing. *I know that man with the scar. These men are exiles! Medb sent them. He swore to kill us, and he has. The cowards, they're bringing lances. Oh. Gabria, be safe.*

"No! Gabran, come back!" Gabria screamed. Her brother's voice rose to a cry of agony and died into silence. The other noises vanished, too, leaving Gabria alone again in the fog. She stood rooted in place, too stunned by the vision to move.

"Gabria?" a voice said beside her.

She started so violently she would have fallen if a pair of hands had not caught her and gently steadied her. The fog in her mind swept away as quickly as it had come. The sunlight and Gabria's sight returned with blinding clarity. The sounds of the river, the wind in the trees, and the distant clan gathering filled the aching void of silence.

"What's wrong? Are you all right?" the voice said again.

A long moan escaped her as she leaned into the familiar, comforting shoulder of her old friend, Sayyed Raid-Ja. She felt the chill slowly leave her body. "I'm well enough," she said sadly into the woven linen of his blue tunic. Lifting her head, she came eye to eye with him.

Sayyed, the son of a clanswoman and a Turic tribesman, had been disowned by his father when he revealed his talent to wield magic. He had come, young and eager, to find Gabria and learn her sorcery, and he had stayed with the clans to be her friend.

Thankful for his solid presence, Gabria tried to smile.

The worry eased only a little from his face, and his hands remained firmly on her arms. He was short for a Turic, so his black eyes were level with her green ones. For a moment he studied her keenly. "What happened?" he demanded. "You looked like you were about to faint. Your face is as white as a winter moon."

Gabria hesitated before she answered. "I saw something—or rather heard something—out of the past," she said slowly.

Sayyed's swarthy face, darkly tanned from years of sun and wind, creased into a frown. He knew her well enough to recognize the tightly controlled tension in her expression and the reasons that sometimes brought her to this clearing. "The massacre?" he asked.

She nodded, her gaze leaving his to wander to a place only she could see. When she did not reply, Sayyed gently prompted, "I remember you told me about the first time you had the vision."

Gabria barely moved her head. "This time though, I didn't see anything. I just heard it."

Suddenly a horn blared again in the distance, and the faint staccato of hoofbeats echoed in the air. Gabria visibly winced. Tears filled her eyes at the ghostly memories.

"They're racing on the flats this morning," Sayyed said softly.

The clanswoman let go of Sayyed's arms and rubbed at the ache beginning to throb in her temples. Forcefully she brought herself back to reality. She was the daughter of a chieftain, the wife of a chieftain, and a sorceress—she was not a weak-kneed girl to be brought to weeping by the memories of an old tragedy.

Turning her back on the clearing, Gabria made her way down along the riverbank. Sayyed kept pace beside her, satisfied that the worst seemed to be over. Color was returning to her face, and her stride was steady.

"Why did you come here today?" he asked while they walked along the bank. "What brought on that vision?"

"I don't know," Gabria replied loudly over the rush of the shallow rapids. "I was looking for Kelene. She was supposed to go with me to visit the Reidhar camp. There is a little boy they think has the talent for magic, but he is too frightened to try his power. Kelene is so good with children; she always wins them over."

Sayyed's smile was knowing and rueful. "But you couldn't find her," he said.

"No. She's off somewhere with her horse, I guess."

The man cocked an eye toward the distant racing flats where he could see the crowds that had gathered for the day's racing. He had a very good idea where Gabria's daughter Kelene had gone. But that still didn't answer his question of why Gabria had gone to the clearing, and she seemed to be in no hurry to explain.

Together they climbed down the bank and waded across the Isin, Gabria silent and pensive, Sayyed respecting her reticence. Once on the west bank, they walked downstream toward the second river, the Goldrine, which joined the Isin in a series of easy rapids. The focal point of the clan gatherings, the sacred island of the Tir Samod and its crowning temple of standing stones, lay in the middle of the rivers' confluence. On an arrow-shaped point of land directly across from the island was the council grove where the huge chieftains' tent was being raised for the upcoming meetings of the council.

Gabria paused in the shade of an old cottonwood to watch as the men around the tent began to hang the clan banners: gold, brown, indigo, green, black, yellow, gray, purple, orange, light blue, and maroon. One by one they were hung to catch the breeze until only the scarlet banner of Clan Corin was missing. One tent pole was always left empty in honor of the slaughtered clan.

The sorceress stared sadly at the empty space among the banners. "He was trying to warn me," she murmured as if to herself.

Sayyed was startled. "What?"

"I think Gabran was trying to tell me something. I only heard the sounds of the massacre this time. I couldn't see anything in the fog. But I heard him say, 'I've got to warn you!' He'd never said that before."

"Warn you about what? The massacre? Lord Medb?"

"No, not those. He didn't say anything like that in my first vision when I was trying to confront Lord Medb." Gabria hugged her arms close to her sides and tried to ignore the headache that was now pounding like a drum. "What did he mean? Why now?" she wondered aloud.

"If you were anyone else I'd think you were suffering from the heat or too much wine. But your visions always seem to have significance," Sayyed replied.

Gabria smiled slightly. "If only I knew what it was."

"Maybe it's a premonition taking the form of some disaster familiar to you," he suggested.

The clanswoman's face looked bleak. "You could be right."

A familiar shout cut across the grove, and the two people turned to see Lord Athlone come around the back of the council tent and stride toward them, a young boy at his side.

Gabria's pulse quickened as it always did at the sight of her husband. After twenty-three years of marriage, she still adored him. She watched while he approached, his hand on the shoulder of their youngest son.

At forty-six, a life span that brought many clansmen into old age, Lord Athlone was still in the prime of his power. Tall, muscular, and solid, he wore his unspoken authority as easily as the sword at his side. He was chieftain of Clan Khulinin, the largest and most powerful clan on the plains, and he held the unique position of being the only chieftain who could wield magic. Twenty-four years ago, when clan law strictly forbade the practice of sorcery and clan society was taught to abhor it, that talent would have condemned him to death or exile. But many things had changed since Lord Medb and Gabria resurrected the old arts of magic. Now Lord Athlone tread a careful path between the growing acceptance of sorcery in the clans and the suspicion and prejudice against it that remained.

Cheerfully the lord chieftain greeted his friend and brushed a kiss on Gabria's cheek. She smiled at the tickle of his mustache and at the humor in his dark eyes.

"Hi, Mamma. Hi, Sayyed," her son, Coren, piped up. "I've been helping the men set up the tent!"

Athlone said, "I didn't expect to see you this morning. Have you been to the Reidhar camp already?"

Gabria shook her head. "Not yet. I can't find Kelene." She kept her expression bland and decided to tell him about her vision in a quieter moment.

Athlone made an irritated noise. "Puppies have more sense of responsibility than that girl. Is she ever going to grow up?"

No one bothered to answer, since the question was one they had all asked at some time in the past few years. Of the four children Gabria had borne, their oldest daughter, Kelene, had always been the most challenging. Unlike her oldest brother, Savaron, and her younger sister, Lymira, Kelene at eighteen rebelled against virtually everything her parents suggested. She was independent, willful, and stubborn. Athlone had seriously considered forcing her to marry or even sending her to another clan for a few years. But Gabria had bid him wait. She could see quite a few of Athlone's traits, without the strengthening of maturity and wisdom, in Kelene.

Lord Athlone grimaced at the lack of an answer to his question and added, "I guess she's out with that gelding of hers."

"That's not a difficult guess," Sayyed said. "She probably wants to check the competition for the Induran tomorrow."

"I forgot about that," Athlone admitted.

A hearty laugh burst from Sayyed, and he waved a hand toward the flats. "How could you have forgotten that? Your daughter has talked of nothing for the past year but her gelding and its chances to win that race. My son is probably over there too, goading her into another rage."

Athlone's mouth twisted in annoyance. "We should have known better than to expect Kelene's cooperation when the race is on." He stopped, his gaze lost in the distance. Some of the irritation eased from his face. "Since the accident," Athlone went on finally, "she hasn't even considered her talent."

"I thought she would turn against horses, not magic. It was not the fault of magic that that brute of a stallion rolled on her," Sayyed said.

"She had no business being on him," answered the chieftain, a father's frustration plain in his voice. "She was lucky that only her foot was crushed."

Gabria laid her hand on her husband's arm. "Give her time. She will learn in her own way."

"Perhaps," Athlone said. "But in the meantime we could certainly use her help!"

"I'll help, Papa!" Coren piped up with all the enthusiasm of a ten-year-old trying to outshine an older sister.

"You know, I think you could," Gabria replied, bending down to his level. "I want to visit a boy about your age. His name is Bennon. Would you like to come and talk to him?"

"Can he wield magic, too?"

"I think so."

"Good! I've got lots of spells I can show him!" Coren announced proudly.

Sayyed grinned, his teeth shining white against the black of his neatly trimmed beard. "Take Nara. She always impresses the children."

Coren matched his grin. "Could we, Mamma?"

As an answer, Gabria blew a sharp, piercing whistle that cut over the noises of the busy council grove. The men by the chieftains' tent looked up at the sound and turned their heads again when the call was answered by a distant neigh. From the far fields, where the clans' horses grazed, a black form cantered over the grassy valley floor—Nara, Gabria's Hunnuli mare.

Unlike the clan-bred Harachan horses, which were the pride and livelihood of the seminomadic clans, the Hunnuli were a breed of legend. Descended from a single stallion blessed by the clans' goddess, Amara, the Hunnuli had greater intelligence, strength, size, and longevity than any other horse. Originally bred to be the mounts of clan magic-wielders, they were endowed with the ability to communicate telepathically with the clanspeople who had the inherent talent to use magic. After the fall of Moy Tura, city of the sorcerers, and the slaughter of the magic-wielders that followed, the Hunnuli slipped into obscurity and almost died out. Then, two hundred years later, Gabria found a Hunnuli mare, Nara, trapped in a mudhole. She saved the horse's life, thus forging a friendship that had remained inviolable.

With that friendship came a renewed understanding of the Hunnuli horse and its purpose within the clans. It was partly because of the people's awe and respect for the Hunnuli that they learned to accept Gabria's power to use magic. Since that time, the numbers of magic-wielders and Hunnuli in the clans had slowly increased to about thirty each, and the admiration for the fabulous horses had continued unabated.

Even now, eyes were turning to watch Nara as she galloped past the Khulinin camp and swept into the shady council grove. Like every Hunnuli, the mare was ebony black with a white mark, in the shape of a jagged lightning bolt, on her right shoulder. Her thick mane and tail flew like black smoke as her long, powerful legs carried her easily over the ground. She stopped neatly in front of Gabria and nickered a greeting.

Gabria mounted and settled happily on the mare's warm back. She always felt safe and comforted in her old friend's presence. The prospect of a gallop to the Reidhar camp drove the confusing shadows of her vision to the back of her mind. She would probably learn soon enough what had caused that strange episode, but in the meantime she could do something she enjoyed—share her love of magic with children.

"Come on." She smiled to her son and held out her hand.

Coren whooped in delight and bounced up onto Nara's back in front of his mother. With a wave to the two men, Gabria and Coren rode off to visit the Reidhar clan.

1

For the third time in as many minutes, Kelene gritted her teeth and tightened her knees as her gelding vented his feelings in a bad-tempered hop and a buck. Head lowered, back arched, the horse barged around the starting line while the other riders cursed and kept out of his way. The gelding was feeling murderous—Kelene could sense it in every stiff jolt of his body.

Of course, that was nothing new for Ishtak. The gelding was a stone-gray Harachan, as hard, bleak, and difficult as a rock cliff. A more bad-tempered animal Kelene had never seen. She knew he tolerated her only when he felt like it, and she also knew he would dump her at the first opportunity. Yet she had chosen him, learned his moody ways, and put up with his ugly temper for one reason: the horse could race. When he channeled his anger into competition, he was as sure-footed as a goat and as fleet as the wind. Few Harachan horses could beat him.

The trick was to stay with him long enough to get him started. For Kelene that was sometimes tricky. Unlike the other riders, she had no saddle or stirrups, only a saddle pad strapped to Ishtak's back. She had learned the hard way that her crippled foot and ankle were too weak to bear her weight in a stirrup or remain in a bent position. The pain had finally forced her to ride bareback and to develop the balance, strength, and firm seat needed to help her control a recalcitrant horse.

She had learned too, that the usual women's skirts were a hazard on a cross-country race. Today she wore the special split-legged skirt her mother had made for her, a gold tunic, and soft boots. Her thick, dark hair was braided and coiled on the back of her head.

The girl cursed as the gelding crow-hopped out of line again, jarring her teeth. There was no way to cajole this foul-tempered beast with soothing words, encouraging pats, or treats. Nothing pleased him except getting the best of his rider or winning a race—whichever came first. Kelene pulled his head up and forced him back into the milling line of riders waiting for the start of the race. Just another moment or two and they would be away.

Twenty-five other horses waited with Ishtak, some of them prancing with excitement, some of them quiet and unimpressed by the crowds, the noise, and the mounting anticipation. There were no Hunnuli in line since the race was no contest to the big blacks, but some of the finest Harachan horses on the plains were there to represent the different clans. Dust billowed up under their stamping hooves, and the clan colors on the riders' tunics gleamed in the morning sun.

It was a perfect day for the Induran race: clear, warm, and dry—a typical summer morning. The sky arched over the river valley in a flawless dome of blue; a light breeze stirred the grass. The bazaar and the camps were quiet that morning and the council grove was empty. Everyone had gone to the flats to see the start of the most important race of the gathering.

The Induran was a cross-country endurance race that tested the stamina, skill, and courage of horses and riders alike. There were very few rules, and the race was open to anyone with the desire and the horse to ride. The fact that women rarely rode in the rough-and-tumble race was only an added challenge to Kelene. The year before she had entered and ridden well only to lose her favorite mare when the animal stepped in a hole and shattered its leg a league before the finish line. This year Kelene had Ishtak and was more determined than ever to win.

The girl glanced toward the starter on her right, but he had made no move to raise his horn. He was still waiting for last-minute entries. Someone several horses away caught her eye: a slim, young man on a chestnut horse. He grinned mockingly at her and waved. Rafnir, Sayyed and Tam's only son, was as fine a rider as the clans had ever produced and one of the few serious contenders who could beat Kelene in this race.

Rafnir was laughing at Ishtak's tantrums, but Kelene refused to give him the satisfaction of a response. Instead, she concentrated on the open stretch of land in front of them.

From the corner of her eye she saw the starter raise his horn. The twenty-six horses were abreast of one another and the riders were ready. The crowd roared with excitement.

Automatically Kelene wrapped her hands deep into Ishtak's mane and leaned forward over his neck. Ishtak had been known to bolt out from under her at the start of a race, and she did not want to end up ignominiously in the dust before the Induran really began.

The horn call came loud and sweet, and the horses sprang forward almost as one. Except for Ishtak. For once the gelding did not leap forward but threw up his head and dug in his heels. Kelene kicked him, which only made him buck and crab-step sideways. When he finally deigned to go forward, he was mulish, reluctant, and trailing by twelve lengths.

"You'll never get me off, you dung-headed sack of dog meat!" Kelene screamed at him.

He gave two more bronco kicks for good measure and swerved toward the spectators who were watching the show with mixed astonishment and amusement.

Kelene's feelings rose to a full fury. She wrenched on the rein to pull his head around and shouted at him. "Run, you stupid mule! Go, or I'll feed you to the buzzards!"

The gelding fought her hard. Then his head came around, and he saw the tails of his competition disappearing in the dust far ahead. He snorted angrily, all at once deciding to race. His stride smoothed out to a flowing run, his rage disappeared, and the fighting spirit that Kelene admired came surging back. He sped into a full gallop, his temper forgotten.

With a grin, Kelene settled down and let him have his head. There was a long way to go in this race, and much could happen. She was not bothered by the fact that they were dead-last.

For two leagues the horses cantered south, paralleling the Goldrine River along the flat grassy valley floor, running at an easy pace so as not to tire too soon. They stayed in a tight bunch for a while, then gradually spread out as the faster horses began to pull ahead. It was not long before Ishtak caught up with those at the rear. Stride by stride, the gelding pulled even with several runners and passed them.

Kelene kept her weight firmly planted on the saddle pad, her hands light on the reins, her legs just tight enough against her horse's sides to keep her balance. Ishtak didn't like fussy riders who interfered with his running with a lot of useless gesturing and urging. Like one creature, the girl and horse united in a common goal as they moved over the grass-covered flats: to win.

So far, the course had been open and fairly level, but as the racers neared the end of the two-league mark, the route turned east across the river and proceeded up into the more rugged hills that lined the valley.

Kelene squinted her eyes against the wind and flying dust to peer ahead. Already the front-runners were turning east toward the tree-lined bank of the Goldrine where she could see the sun glinting off the slow, broad river. A tenseness gripped her body as she turned Ishtak slowly left. She glanced back and saw several others cantering close behind. Using the gentlest pressure of her heels, she urged Ishtak forward until he was running in a clear space between several groups of racers.

They passed some scattered trees, jumped a fallen tree trunk, and raced for the river's edge. Then, before Kelene could draw another breath, the front-runners slowed and dropped from sight. Those behind the leaders pulled up just long enough to put some space between the horses, then they, too, rode their mounts over the edge.

When Ishtak reached the bank, he did not hesitate. Placing his hind feet perfectly, he lunged over the drop-off without a pause. Kelene caught a glimpse of a steep bank dropping ten feet down to the river, then she was holding on with all her strength and skill as the gelding fought to keep his balance and stride on the slope. He leaned so far back his tail scraped the muddy ground. Down he scrambled in a slide of dirt, gravel, and weeds.

One horse in front of Ishtak leaned too far forward, lost its balance, and careened into the path of two others. They fell into the river in a heap of flailing legs and yelling riders. Fortunately none of them were hurt, but the riders were unhorsed and automatically disqualified from the race.

In a jarring thud, Ishtak reached the narrow strip of mudbank at the bottom. He had to swerve to avoid another struggling, fallen horse, but he kept to his feet on the slippery mud and plowed into the river. Great fountains of silver spray splashed up from his feet.

The river was fairly shallow at either side, and it was only in the center, where the channel was deep, that Ishtak had to swim. By the time he and Kelene reached the far bank, they were both soaking wet and had passed three more horses. There were now only ten riders in front of them, including Rafnir. Four of the original twenty-six were out of the competition.

The race continued due east across the valley toward the rugged hills. The leaders picked up their pace on the level ground, hoping to put some distance between themselves and the rest of the pack before they reached the harder part of the trail.

Ishtak answered their challenge in a burst of speed that carried him past six more horses and brought him up near the leaders and Rafnir's chestnut.

Rafnir glanced over his shoulder, saw Kelene, and grinned. "What took you so long?" he yelled over the sound of the pounding hooves.

"I stopped for a walk," she retorted, feeling as if she had. The dust sticking to her wet clothes had turned to mud, and her face was streaked with river muck flung up by Ishtak's hooves.

Moments later the forerunners reached the faint trail leading up into the eroded, bleak hills that formed this section of the valley walls. The path abruptly narrowed and sloped upward, forcing the riders to go in ones and twos.

Kelene found herself directly behind Rafnir and one other rider. She tried to push Ishtak past them, but heavy rocks and brush lined the path on either side. As one group, Rafnir, a Dangari, Kelene, and a Wylfling cantered deeper into the hills. Gradually they pulled ahead and before long were out of sight of the rest of the riders.

The trail wound up steep, rocky slopes, down into deep gullies, and around outcroppings and rock walls that towered over their heads, until finally it dropped down into a high-walled, narrow canyon that twisted through the hills like a snake's path. The sun, directly overhead by that time, poured its heat onto the red and gray rocks of the hills, turning the canyon into an oven. Kelene's clothes were baked dry, and the dampness in Ishtak's gray coat turned to dark sweat on his neck, chest, and flanks. The four riders were forced to slacken their speed over the rocky floor of the ravine.

Suddenly the two leaders pulled their mounts to a stop. They had reached a place where several dry creek beds converged, forming a confusing three-way junction of rock walls and narrow passages. To the riders' dismay, this section of trail had been obliterated by a recent flash flood.

"Which way?" Rafnir shouted at the man beside him.

The rider, a young Dangari in a blue tunic, looked at all three in confusion. "That way!" he cried, pointing to the left.

"No," Kelene said as Ishtak snorted and fumed at the delay. "I think it's that way." She pointed to the right.

Rafnir shook his head. "That can't be, there's a rockfall in the way."

"Yes, but it's fresh, and I'm almost certain the path goes to the right," Kelene insisted.

Since she was the only one of the four who had raced the path before, Rafnir was inclined to follow her suggestion. But before anyone could decide, the fourth rider, a burly Wylfling on a red roan, kicked his horse past the group and turned down the left passage. Rafnir and the Dangari charged after him. Kelene hesitated long enough to look to the right, then Ishtak snatched the bit in his teeth and lunged after the other three horses.

The girl did not fight him. Perhaps this was the correct way. Yet it did not feel right; the deeper they rode into the canyon, the more convinced she became that they had taken the wrong path. The walls towered over their heads, and the passage grew so narrow Kelene could touch both sides with her outstretched fingers.

She was looking for a place to turn Ishtak around when she saw the riders in front of her increase their speed. The walls opened out into a wider space that was brilliant with sunshine and carpeted with grass, vines, and small shrubs. Strangely there was an oval-shaped mound sitting crossways in their path on the otherwise level canyon floor. Its grassy sides rose more than ten feet in the air and were twice that in length.

No one paid much attention to the mound as they rode around it, they were too intent on the path ahead. The Wylfling in the lead urged his horse into a canter again toward the far end of the canyon, and the other men followed suit. It was only a minute or two before they realized their mistake. The canyon was a dead end.

The blank stone wall rising in the distance barely registered on Kelene when she heard the Wylfling's shout of anger. She yanked Ishtak around and sent him galloping back the way they had come. Since Ishtak had been in the rear of the group before, now he was in the lead. Kelene wanted to take full advantage of it to help make up for the time they had lost coming down this box canyon.

Kelene was so intent on reaching the narrow defile first, she did not see the

Wylfling turn his horse and spur it up the slope of the strange mound in an effort to cut her off. She was aware only of the trail ahead and Rafnir's chestnut pounding close behind. She didn't know that just as the Wylfling's horse crested the mound, the animal suddenly pitched forward and crashed to the ground with bone-smashing force.

* * *

From a vantage point on a low hill near the finish line, Gabria snapped upright from her husband's side, her face as pale as ice.

Startled, Lord Athlone leaned forward, steadying her in his arms. "What is it?" he asked, deeply concerned.

She took a ragged breath, too stunned for a moment to speak. They were sitting on a rug in the grass, sharing a midday meal with Sayyed and Tam while they waited for the race to end. Gabria was still a little unsettled by her vision of the day before, but she had never felt anything like the powerful jolt of dread that had just shocked through her. "I don't know," she replied shakily. "It was as if something cold and repulsive touched my mind. It was horrible!"

Sayyed looked at her questioningly, and she shook her head. "No, it was not like yesterday," she told him.

"What happened yesterday?" Athlone demanded.

"I had another vision of the Corin massacre."

Athlone was shocked. "Why didn't you tell me?"

Gabria pulled away so she could turn and face him. "I wanted to think about it first. The vision was different this time. I felt as if Gabran were trying to warn me about something, but I don't know what or why."

Sayyed asked, "Do you think it had any connection to this strange feeling you just had?"

"I wish I knew!"

"Are the children all right?" Tam asked quietly.

Gabria looked startled at the question. "Yes, I think so. This wasn't a sense of disaster; it was something else. Something almost wicked."

"Wicked?" Sayyed and Athlone said together.

She nodded. "I know that's no help. I can't explain it any better."

"But I didn't feel anything," Athlone said.

"You don't have visions either," Sayyed pointed out. "That seems to be Gabria's special ability."

The sorceress smiled dryly. "I never thought of that. So what does it mean?"

Sayyed rolled his eyes heavenward. "Your gods only know."

"That's what I'm afraid of," Gabria murmured.

* * *

Unaware of the disaster behind her, Kelene slowed Ishtak to a trot and sent him clattering between the high stone walls of the narrow canyon trail. Rafnir missed the Wylfling's accident, too. He trotted his chestnut into the defile right behind the girl and her gray.

Only the young Dangari saw the horse thrashing in agony and the Wylfling rider lying unconscious on the grassy slope. Regretfully he reined his horse to a stop and dismounted to see what he could do to help.

Kelene meanwhile rode on, her eyes on the trail ahead and her ears listening to the ringing of hooves echoing between the rocky walls. When Ishtak reached the three-way fork in the canyon, the girl did not hesitate or bother to check for tracks but sent her horse clambering over the lowest section of the rockfall in the right fork. To her relief, Ishtak scrambled over the tumbled rocks without much difficulty. There on the other side, Kelene saw the hoofprints of at least six or seven horses. They were on the right trail.

Hard on her heels came Rafnir, joined by three other racers. Kelene risked one quick glance back and saw Rafnir and the horsemen coming up behind her. It never occurred to her that the Dangari and the Wylfling were no longer there. She leaned low over Ishtak's tossing mane and urged the gray down the dry creek bed.

The canyon continued for a short distance, then the trail led up again, out of the rocks and onto the slopes of the hills. Kelene felt Ishtak gather himself with a surge of his powerful muscles.

She moved forward on his shoulders and ran a hand down his wet coat. The gelding was drenched with sweat, but he did not seem to be tiring. He galloped forward furiously, passing two horses who were going at a slower pace, their riders saving their animals' strength for the last few leagues.

Kelene tried to ease Ishtak back a little. But the gelding only pulled at his bit and ran as he desired down the steep incline toward the smoother floor of the valley.

As soon as he left the last slope and reached the level ground, Ishtak extended his body and flew over the grass with long, even strides. Four horses were still in front of him, and Kelene could hear the drumming of many hooves behind. She smiled into the wind, her heart singing with the exhilaration of the race.

As the horses streaked toward the Isin River, Ishtak cut the lead of the front-runners. Nostrils flaring in exertion, he passed three horses until only one ran before him toward the finish. But Kelene knew Rafnir was very close. From the corner of her eye, she could see his red chestnut just to her left.

The racers reached the Isin River and made a broad turn to the south. Kelene, Rafnir, and another rider—an orange-clad Bahedin—were almost neck and neck as they swept along the bank toward the Tir Samod. On either side clansmen galloped, shouting and yelling encouragement, while the people lining the riverbank cheered on their favorites.

Like a hitched team, the three leading horses raced past the tents of Clan Murjik, past the nearly empty bazaar, and turned right toward the ford in the river. On the far bank crowds of clanspeople lined the raceway all the way to the finish.

"Come on, boy!" Kelene urged her gelding through clenched teeth. "Come on!" The gray gelding responded with a surge of speed that began to carry him past the two horses on either side.

Thundering, the three horses charged down the bank into the shallow river ford. Water exploded beneath their hooves, drenching them. Cheering erupted all around as the horses burst out on the western bank and entered the path to the finish line.

The Bahedin was still with Rafnir and Kelene, but his bay was tiring and falling behind. For a minute the two Khulinin were side by side, their horses matched in stride, then Ishtak began to pull ahead, and his nose stretched out past the chestnut's muzzle.

They were almost there—the finish line and the clan judges were just ahead.

Then Kelene saw something that made her blood turn to ice: Rafnir pulled a crop from his belt and raised it high to fan his horse.

Crops were not illegal in the race, and Kelene had nothing against them. But Ishtak did. He loathed crops and whips with a passion bordering on mania, and he was too close to Rafnir to miss that one. He saw the crop at the edge of his vision and went wild.

With a scream of fury, he whipped his head toward Rafnir in an attempt to attack the hated crop, jerking the reins from Kelene's hands. In that horrible instant, the gelding lost his balance, pitched into Rafnir's mount, and sent them both crashing to the ground in a pile of thrashing legs and bodies.

The two riders, thrown clear by the impetus of their speed, lay bruised and stunned in the dirt while the Bahedin jubilantly crossed the finish line. There was a shocked pause as the crowd stared in amazement, then the Bahedin wildly cheered their hero, and a few Khulinin ran forward to get the fallen horses and riders out of the way of the remaining racers.

Two men helped Ishtak and Kelene limp through the crowd to the shade of a tree. Two others brought Rafnir and his chestnut.

"Are you all right?" one man asked Kelene. At her nod the men left her alone to check on Rafnir's injuries. Kelene sank slowly to the ground by her gelding's front feet and stared in shocked disbelief at the dirt. She was filthy, disheveled, and she hurt in every bone in her body. But none of her aches and bruises could compare to the pain of defeat. For the second year in a row she had lost the Induran in an accident.

She looked up and saw Sayyed, Tam, and her parents hurrying toward her. Kelene pulled herself to her feet and faced her mother, but the ache in her heart proved too much for her self-control. Tears trickled down her cheeks. Gabria opened her arms, and Kelene did not turn away. She felt herself gathered into her mother's embrace and held close while she cried out her pain and disappointment.

"Is he hurt, Mother?" Kelene murmured after a while. "He fell so hard."

Gabria knew full well who Kelene meant. The girl wouldn't care a fig for Rafnir's well-being. She glanced inquiringly at Tam, who was talking in quiet tones to Ishtak.

Rafnir's mother understood the question, too, and gently squeezed Kelene's arm. "He is bruised and hurting and very, very tired. He is lucky nothing is broken," she said with a soft smile. "Rub his legs with liniment and rest him. He will be bucking again in a few days."

"Thank you," Kelene said to both women. She stiffened to her full height, threw back her head, and stepped away from Gabria. The tears were gone now. She had no more time for sadness; Ishtak needed her help. She forced her feelings back under control, unaware that as she did so, her face assumed a blank, almost cold expression. She went back to her horse and gathered his reins.

Behind Kelene, Gabria sighed to herself and let her arms drop. She knew that expression of Kelene's all too well. She had seen it more and more the past few years—a blank set of the face that was as frustrating and unyielding as a stone wall. Kelene had withdrawn again to her own thoughts, shutting out the moment of closeness with her mother.

Gabria almost reached out to stop her daughter and draw her back, but she didn't. She knew the gesture would not be appreciated and wondered sadly if it ever would. Once Kelene had been a loving, open, warm-hearted child who adored her parents and family. Now an eighteen-year-old, unmarried woman with a crippled foot, she was almost a stranger to them all.

Gabria bit her lip as she watched Kelene limp away, leading the gray gelding. She was not sure she could bear the thought of losing the Kelene she had known to this distant cool person. She wanted somehow to break through the blank mask and find the love and happiness that still remained inside. If only she knew how.

* * *

Later that evening when the cooking fires were burning in the Khulinin camp and the sun was sinking into an orange haze toward the horizon, Sayyed came to join Lord Athlone and his son Savaron under the awning of the chieftain's big tent. They sat on low stools, enjoying the peace of dusk and talking comfortably as old friends. Goblets of cool wine sat on a tray by their feet. Athlone's three dogs lay close by and chewed on the last scraps of the evening meal. The men could hear Gabria, Lymira, and Coren inside the tent laughing and talking as they got ready for the evening's dancing and music competitions to be held in the council grove. Kelene was nowhere to be seen.

The three men were almost finished with their wine when someone hailed them from the nearby path.

"Lord Athlone, good evening! I was hoping to find you still here." The speaker and a companion, both wearing light summer cloaks of indigo blue, came walking up the path to meet them. Two members of Athlone's hearthguard snapped a salute from their posts by the chief's tent.

Sayyed and Savaron rose peacefully to their feet. "Greetings, Lord Koshyn," Sayyed said.

Koshyn of Clan Dangari returned the greeting. "I didn't want to interrupt your time at home," he said to Athlone, "but I thought you ought to hear something interesting."

Stools and more wine were brought out, and the five men sat down under the awning. Lord Koshyn grinned broadly at his old friend. Only a year younger than Athlone, he had been a chieftain for a longer time, though the years had not been as kind. His fair hair was gray and thinning, and the faded pattern of blue dots tattooed on his forehead was almost lost in the weathered brown of his skin. His once athletic body was stockier, slowed by aching joints. But his smile was as infectious as ever. Although not a magic-wielder himself, he was one of sorcery's most influential supporters among the chiefs and one of Athlone's closest friends.

He sat thankfully on his stool, stretching his legs out before him, while Savaron poured some rich honey wine in a flagon and passed it to him. Koshyn sipped his drink and thought, for the thousandth time, how closely Savaron resembled his father. They were so much alike, not only in their tall physical build, their brown hair, eyes, and mustaches, but in their characters as well. Savaron even had his father's habit of cocking an eyebrow when he was questioning something. Like now.

Koshyn, noticing both men were looking at him the same way, couldn't help chuckling. "I'm sorry," he said between gusts of laughter. "Athlone, as a sire, you certainly have thrown true in your son. By Surgart's sword, you couldn't have done better." He wiped his face with his sleeve and grinned again a bit wistfully, thinking of his own sons, dead before they reached manhood. Athlone, he decided, was a very lucky man.

Lord Koshyn settled back on his stool and said, "So, I didn't come here to compare you two. I brought someone who has a tale to tell." He turned to the other Dangari beside him.

The young man, just out of boyhood, was staring at Lord Athlone with something close to awe. He had never met the sorcerer-chieftain face-to-face, but he had heard all the tales about his deeds. He bowed his head to the Khulinin lord and glanced at his own chief.

"Go on, lad," Koshyn prompted.

The young man tugged at his dirty blue tunic. "I rode in the Induran today, Lord," he said. "At least part of it. Unfortunately, I went with your daughter, Rafnir, and Moreg from Clan Wylfling down a box canyon."

Athlone nodded. He had already heard about that wrong turn.

"Well, while we were trying to turn around in the canyon, Moreg rode his horse over a big mound. I was the only one who saw the horse fall, so I stopped to help him." He leaned forward, his excitement overcoming his shyness. "Lord Athlone, I've never seen anything like it! His horse stepped through a crust of dirt onto what looks like a roof."

"A roof?" Sayyed exclaimed.

The Dangari demonstrated by slightly steepling his hands. "A timbered roof like we use in burial chambers. I think we found an old burial mound."

Athlone leaned forward, his elbows on his knees, his interest piqued. "A burial mound? In a hidden box canyon? How curious!" He paused, mulling over this news. "You said Moreg fell. Is he hurt?"

"He's got a bad headache, but his clan healer said he'll be fine." The Dangari's face saddened as he added, "The horse snapped its leg; we had to kill it."

Lord Athlone laced his fingers thoughtfully and said to Koshyn, "Are you thinking of riding out there tomorrow?"

The Dangari chief gave a slow smile. "Of course. Late afternoon, after the council meeting. I thought I might bring some strong men and shovels."

Athlone returned his smile. "I know some others who might be interested in a little digging."

"There you are, lad," Koshyn said, slapping his young companion on the shoulder. "Your wrong turn may be propitious after all."

Pleased, the rider sat a little straighter on his stool and grinned at his chief's approval.

The men were still discussing the mound and its strange location when the clan horns were blown a few minutes later. The call was to signal the sunset and the changing of the outriders who rode guard on the grazing herds.

Sayyed rose to his feet. "My lords, if you will excuse me," he said. "It's time to make my prayers."

Both chieftains nodded farewell, and Sayyed took his leave. He walked across the broad open space in front of the chieftain's home and passed in among the felt tents that comprised the large Khulinin encampment. Automatically his feet stepped down slightly onto the bare path that led from the center of the camp. Whistling, he wove his way past playing children, cooking fires, and a few tethered horses toward his own home.

Two large dogs and a smaller shaggy one lying beside his tent saw him coming and bounded to their feet to bark a vociferous greeting. A lamb and two goats bleated hungrily from a small pen by the entrance. In a wicker cage hanging on an awning pole, a small owl with a splinted wing blinked at the sudden noise and ducked its head down into its shoulders in annoyance.

Without even looking in the tent, Sayyed knew his wife Tam was not there. She would have been out in an instant at the sound of all of that barking and bleating. He shook his head and quieted the dogs before he pushed back the wolf-skin flap and stepped inside.

Sayyed glanced around. He was right, the tent was empty except for another large white dog nursing a litter of puppies on Tam's favorite rug. He found his prayer rug by his pallet and hurried out to find an open spot where he could recite his prayers in peace.

Although he had been with the Khulinin for many years and had adopted most of their customs, there were still a few habits from his youth in the Turic tribes that he had refused to give up. He still wore a burnoose under the traditional cloak of the clans. He still carried the long, curved blade he had earned on the eve of his manhood ceremony. And he still prayed twice a day to his god.

The clans worshipped four deities—Amara, mother of life and birth; her sister Krath, goddess of fate and the darker passions; Sorh, god of death; and Surgart, god of war—but they were not usually fanatical about it and had not tried to force Sayyed to give up his belief in a single god. It was a tolerance that Sayyed deeply appreciated.

Finding a quiet place in the meadow not far from the edge of camp, Sayyed spread out his small rug, knelt, and bowed low to the south where the tribes of his father believed the holy city of Sarghun Shahr was located. As the quiet words of the evening prayers flowed from his lips, the peace of the moment filled his mind and the familiarity of the ritual gave him comfort.

He hadn't quite finished though, when he suddenly felt disquieted. Something had changed. His peaceful solitude had been interrupted by something or someone. He rose to a kneeling position and turned his head to see Tam standing behind him. She was waiting for him to finish, but her foot was tapping the ground and her hands were tightly clasped as if trying to hold in her impatience. Sayyed closed his eyes to shut her out for a moment longer, shifted to ease the stiffness in his legs, and finished the final chants of his prayer. Then he slowly pushed himself to his feet.

I'm growing too old, he thought wryly as he stretched and worked the pain from his knees. He had barely time to roll up his rug before Tam grabbed his arm and hustled him back through the camp toward the Goldrine River and the bazaar on the other side.

Sayyed went along willingly, although he wondered what she was up to. In spite of her obvious hurry, Tam hadn't said a word to him. Of course, Tam rarely said anything to anyone. A difficult, sometimes cruel childhood had driven her behind walls of silence that even a loving marriage and maturity had not completely broken down. Sayyed looked across at her lovely, fine-lined features, at her enormous eyes outlined by black lashes and delicate eyebrows, at her mouth pulled to a firm line by determination, and he thought that she had the most expressive face he had ever seen in a woman. She did not need to talk; she could say almost anything she wanted with her face, her gestures, and her body.

Now she was radiating excitement. Her face glowed pink and her eyes sparkled. She rushed on past the camp and down to the temporary footbridge that spanned the river to reach the bazaar. Her long black hair braided with bright ribbons danced a jig on her back.

Sayyed was pushed to keep up with her as she fairly flew across the narrow bridge to the opposite bank. He chuckled to watch her. Knowing Tam, she had probably found another bird or animal held by one of the numerous merchants that came to the clan gathering. While most women shopped in the bazaar for fabrics, spices, jewelry, utensils, or pottery, Tam prowled the shops looking for animals being misused or abused by the traveling merchants. Whenever she found one, she would acquire the animal and either set it free or add it to her growing collection of four-legged charges.

This time she didn't seem to be angry, Sayyed noticed, so if it was an animal she wished to show him, it was probably in good health.

They hurried on into the marketplace of booths, stalls, and stands that sat on the east side of the Goldrine River. Every year merchants from the Five Kingdoms to the north and the Turic tribes to the south came to the gathering bringing goods from many lands in exchange for the clans' livestock, horses, saddles, rugs, woven work, jewelry, and handcrafts. The bazaar was a busy place and open from dawn to dusk.

Sayyed hadn't been to the bazaar yet this year, but Tam didn't give him a chance to look around. Without slackening her pace, she hustled him to a large, richly caparisoned booth on the far edge of the bazaar.

The booth was spacious by any standards, with a roof and walls of brightly painted canvas. One entire wall was rolled up, allowing the breeze and customers to enter. A banner identifying a merchant from Pra Desh hung above the entrance.

It was obvious the owner of the booth did not specialize in any one ware. There seemed to be a little of everything from all over the civilized world crammed into every available space. Bolts of fabric crowded clay pots and rare glass vessels on shelves; swords and dried herbs hung from the roof; children's toys, helmets, and rugs filled the countertops. There was barely room to turn around.

Sayyed's eyes narrowed. What in the world had Tam found here? He followed her into the interior and waited as she walked up to the proprietor and tapped his arm.

The merchant, a huge, pale-skinned Pra Deshian turned, saw her, and beamed. "So you came back for her! I knew you would."

Her? Sayyed thought. He watched while the merchant went to the back of his tent and came back bearing a large, well-made crate. The man set the box down on a counter in front of Tam and stood back, a smile of satisfaction on his broad face.

Very carefully she reached into the crate and drew out a small, furry animal.

Sayyed rolled his eyes. Of course. Nothing but animals ever got Tam that excited at the bazaar.

"She is a beautiful beast, yes?" the Pra Deshian said. "And very rare. I brought her mother, already pregnant, from the city of Macar far to the east. This little one is the last I have left. I sold the mother for a fine price to the Fon of Pra Desh himself."

"How fine?" Sayyed asked, trying to keep the sharpness out of his voice. He was not going to be beggared for the sake of an animal, no matter how much his wife liked it.

The merchant cast a speculative eye at Tam and then at Sayyed, as if weighing his opportunities. Tam had the little creature cradled in her arm and was gently scratching the base of its small, pointed ears. It was pushing its head against her hand and making a faint rattling noise.

"The lady is obviously pleased by my little pet." He paused and added with a broad gesture, "For her, I am willing to negotiate."

Before Sayyed could answer, Tam plopped the furry animal into his arms. He held it up in both hands, and it dangled there watching him with equal curiosity. The creature was a pure shade of white with fur as thick and soft as thistledown. Its legs and tail were long compared to its lean body, and its head was round with a short nose and round, golden eyes. Sayyed decided the animal reminded him of a tiny copy of a cave lion. "What is it?" he asked.

"A cat," the merchant answered proudly. "About half a year old. She is little trouble to keep. She hunts her own food, grooms herself, and walks on her own. All she asks is a warm bed and a loving hand. Both of which I believe your lady has. I do not sell my animals to just anyone, sir. I sell them at any price I choose to people I feel will appreciate them."

Sayyed regarded his wife mildly. "I don't really have a choice, do I?"

Tam shrugged, her eyes twinkling—which brought a smile to the merchant's face. Without a word, she took the cat from her husband and set it carefully on the counter before her. For a long minute, she and the little animal stared at one another eye to eye, as if reaching an agreement. Then Tam tensed, closed her eyes, and raised a finger.

Sayyed leaned against the counter. He knew what was coming next. It was too late to try to talk Tam out of the cat now, even if he wanted to. She would make it hers with one simple magic spell.

Gently she tapped the cat's head and spoke for the first time in a soft, singsong voice. There were no obvious sparks or bolts of light to mark the execution of her spell. The cat only blinked and sat down, its golden eyes staring intently at Tam. *Meow.*

A radiant smile lit Tam's face. "She said yes," she told Sayyed.

The merchant's mouth opened. "What? Who said yes?"

"The cat," Sayyed explained. "As you can see, my wife adores animals. She has perfected a spell that allows her to understand what an animal is communicating."

"And she just did that? Here? I didn't see anything!"

"There isn't much to see. The magic is very subtle and doesn't hurt the animal."

"But the cat only meowed. She said nothing that I could understand," said the merchant, still perplexed.

"Only other magic-wielders can understand animals that she has spelled." Sayyed reached out and patted the cat. "Unfortunately no one else has been able to copy her spell. Tam has a very strong empathy with animals, and I think that's why she can work this sorcery so successfully."

"Interesting," the Pra Deshian said, turning to look thoughtfully at Tam and the cat, who were both watching him intently. "So what did the cat agree to?"

"She is willing to stay with me," Tam replied. When she chose to talk, Tam's voice was neither weak nor hesitant. Her words came out with a quiet firmness that revealed the strength behind the silence.

The merchant leaned over and waggled a finger at her. "I am agreeable to that as well . . . for a certain compensation. You cannot use sorcery on my merchandise and expect me to give it away."

"Of course not," she said mildly, undaunted by his bulk looming over her.

Sayyed watched, his arms crossed, and wondered how she intended to pay for this cat. Gold was a rare commodity among the clans of the plains, more often being used for jewelry or decoration than money. The clanspeople relied on the barter system. And that was the problem to Sayyed. He could think of nothing they had that would interest this merchant for an exchange. The Pra Deshian seemed to have everything already!

Tam must have seen the question on his face, because she winked at him before turning back to the merchant. "I understand you have been having problems with some of your draft horses," she said.

The man was startled by the question. "Yes, but what has that to do with this?"

"Would you consider my services to your animals a fair trade for this one small cat?"

"What sort of services?" the merchant asked suspiciously.

"If I can talk to them, I can learn their problems. Find out who is ailing or hurts, what they need to make them happy. I can tend their sores and ease their fears."

The merchant was quiet for a very long moment. His gaze bored into Tam's, weighing her words and the possible benefits of her help against the value of a white cat. His fingers tapped the wooden counter. "I have eighteen horses," he said at last.

"For the cat I will speak to them all," said Tam.

The Pra Deshian hesitated again, until Sayyed began to think the merchant would not accept. Then the man shrugged heavily under his robes. "Dobs has a harness sore on his shoulder I can't seem to cure, and Ben has been favoring a leg. . . ."

Tam said nothing. She scratched the cat's ears and let the man think.

"How do I know you can really understand these animals?" he demanded at last.

"Come." Tam turned and strode from the tent. The merchant signaled to his helper to take over, then he hurried after her with Sayyed and the cat trailing behind. The group went around the back of the tent where five large wagons were parked and a string of big, short-legged, powerful draft horses was picketed in two lines under an awning.

Sayyed nodded with approval when he saw them. The horses were clean, well fed, and cared-for. He began to think Tam's offer just might be enough to sway the Pra Deshian, who obviously made an effort to see to his beasts' comfort.

Tam walked in among the picketed horses without hesitation, patting rumps and running her hands down soft noses. When she came to a large gray, she paused. "Ben?" The merchant nodded.

Once again, Tam drew on the magic energy around her, formed her spell in her mind, and with her soft words set the spell into motion. The gray bobbed his head once, then turned to look at her out of a dark, liquid eye. Nickering, he lifted his front left hoof off the ground. Silently Tam pulled her small dagger from the sheath at her belt. She cradled the horse's hoof on her skirt between her knees and carefully began to probe into the crevice by the frog, the triangular-shaped pad under the hoof. No one else moved.

After a time she smiled and slowly pulled out a sliver of rock that had become wedged out of sight and was bruising Ben's foot. The horse snorted in relief.

The merchant nodded once. "It's a deal."

Like a child with a treasured gift, Tam swooped up the cat and twirled with it among the horses, the delight shining on her slender face.

The Pra Deshian grinned. "That's quite a woman you have there, clansman."

Sayyed barely nodded, for his eyes were following his wife around in her dance of joy. The merchant was right. Tam was something special—but Sayyed had known that for twenty-three years.

2

"Lord Athlone, this is intolerable! We cannot have your wife kidnapping any child she sees fit to take!" Fiergan, chieftain of Clan Reidhar, slammed his palm on his knee and glared at the Khulinin from beneath his bristling eyebrows.

Sayyed could see Lord Athlone's jaw tighten as he tried to control his anger. The son of old Lord Caurus, Fiergan had inherited his father's ferocious temper, intolerance for things he did not understand, and ability to infuriate Athlone.

Lord Athlone was sitting on a cushion, idly twirling the contents of a horn cup in his hands. Sayyed as his hearthguard, Savaron, and the Khulinin Wer-tain Rejanir, were at his side. To anyone who was not familiar with the chief, Athlone appeared amazingly calm, but Sayyed knew his lord was seething by the deadly frost in his earth-brown eyes and the rock-hard lines of his jaw.

Lady Gabria often attended council meetings, but she had excused herself that day to introduce the Reidhar boy, Bennon, to some of the other children in her care. Lord Fiergan hated arguing with her, and Sayyed knew full well the Reidhar chief was taking advantage of Gabria's absence to expound on his complaint of 'kidnapping.'

It is a good thing, Sayyed thought to himself, that weapons are not allowed in the council tent during meetings. Half a day of arguing with Fiergan would drive any man to bloodlust.

"I will forgive you this time for accusing Lady Gabria of kidnapping," Athlone said with deceptive mildness. "All the children she has found with the talent to wield magic have been given the choice to remain with their families or foster with us. All have come to our clan willingly to learn under Gabria's tutelage *with* their parents' permission."

Lord Fiergan slapped his words aside with a jerk of his hand. "You cannot take a child—or any member of a clan—without the *chieftain's* permission!" he said in a loud, distinctive voice that reached every ear in the tent.

"We have had the chieftain's agreement in every case . . . but yours."

"Yet you still took Bennon!" Fiergan thundered.

Athlone set down his cup, his eyes never leaving Fiergan's face. The burly Reidhar chieftain was red-faced and sweating from the heat, yet he showed no sign of backing down.

Sayyed sighed. It was going to be a long, tense meeting if Lord Ryne didn't exercise his authority as council leader and step in to end this. He had hoped this first day of council meetings would be calm and short. The fifty-three people—chieftains, sons, wer-tains, elders, priests, and priestesses—from every clan had met in the tent early in the day when the air was cool and the day fresh. They had dealt with a few minor problems at first, such as the theft of some of Clan Dangari's valuable breeding stallions by a small band of Turic raiders, the settlement of a dispute over pasture rights between the Shadedron and Ferganan clans, and the final acceptance of the betrothal contract for young Lord Terod of the Amnok clan and the sister of Lord Hendric of Clan Geldring.

All had seemed well until Lord Fiergan brought up the subject of teaching young magic-wielders. It was afternoon by that time and even with the walls rolled up to allow a breeze, the big tent was uncomfortably hot and full of flies. The men were sweating and tempers were short.

"He is visiting us for only a few days to make up his mind," Athlone was saying. "Of course, if you insist, he will be returned immediately."

Fiergan glanced at the other men crowded around the tent. "I am only trying to protect my people. How can we be certain that the children you take away really are magic-wielders? We have only Lady Gabria's word for it."

"And the Hunnulis'. Do you call them and my wife deceitful liars?" Athlone asked, his voice cold.

Fiergan's red face paled slightly. An affirmative answer to a question like that could lead to a duel of honor, and Fiergan was not willing to face a warrior like Athlone over swords. "Perhaps not," he said sharply. "Yet we—"

Before he could go on, Lord Koshyn put up a hand to interrupt him. "Lord Fiergan does bring up a good point," he said in a conciliatory tone. "There have been several children who have shown no signs to us that they can wield magic, yet Lady Gabria says they have the power and that they must learn to control it. I suggest that we devise some sort of test or find a way to prove to everyone's satisfaction that a certain individual can use magic."

"And even if a person passes such a test, why is it necessary for that person to leave the clan and go to the Khulinin?" asked Lord Dormar of Clan Ferganan.

Athlone replied, "Eventually we hope it won't be. But there are too few magic-wielders in the clans. Right now, Gabria, Sayyed, Tam, and I are the only ones with enough experience to teach. You must remember, the stay is only temporary. We are teaching these young magic-wielders how to use their talent to the best of their abilities with the hope that they will return to their clans to help others whenever they can."

Lord Sha Tajan nodded. He was the youngest brother and heir of Athlone's old friend, Sha Umar, and he was pleased to help the magic-wielders whenever he could. "Two of my people have come back to us, and I don't know what we'd do without them."

"But why teach them at all? What if they don't want to leave their families or learn this sorcery?" Fiergan spat out the last word like a foul bit of gristle.

"If a person with the talent wants no part of it and fights any suggestion of learning how to use it, then of course we do not force them. But it is wiser and safer to train a magic-wielder to control his power. Magic can be inadvertently used at the wrong moment." Athlone half-smiled, unconsciously rubbing the scar on his shoulder where Gabria had once nearly killed him with an inadvertent bolt of magic. "Once someone is sure of his ability, he can always choose not to use it."

Fiergan snorted. "Sorcery is just like any other heresy against the gods. Once you're a heretic, you're always a heretic."

"I believe the law calling sorcery a heresy was dropped twenty-three years ago," Koshyn said sharply.

Fiergan subsided back into his seat, grumbling.

Ar that point, Lord Ryne of Clan Bahedin rose to his feet and said, "The afternoon grows too hot for sensible argument. Let us call a halt to this discussion until tomorrow when we can talk with cooler minds."

"I agree," Lord Koshyn put in, and he, too, stood. "But before we go, I want to let you know that several of us are riding up to the hills today to take a look at that mound in the canyon. If anyone wants to come, bring a shovel."

The mood in the tent immediately lightened. The news of the mysterious mound had spread through the camps overnight, and everyone was curious about its contents and its odd location. As soon as Lord Ryne officially ended the meeting, the people interested in the expedition hurried away to their camps to get horses and tools.

* * *

While their fathers helped organize the large party of clansmen preparing to leave, Savaron and Rafnir called their Hunnuli and went to look for Kelene to see if she wanted to go, too. They found her standing thigh-deep in the cool, silty Isin River with her gelding Ishtak. The horse's right front knee had swelled during the night, so she brought him to the river in the hope that the cool water would ease his injury.

The gelding was too tired and sore to be in his usual obnoxious mood, yet he still laid his ears back as the two men rode their Hunnuli into the water.

"We're going to look at that mound of yours in the canyon. Would you like to come?" Savaron called to his sister.

Kelene didn't answer immediately. She looked up at her big brother and his friend sitting so proudly on their powerful black horses, and she thought how handsome they both looked, so tall and strong and self-assured. She supposed she could excuse Rafnir for being so good-looking. The gods had given him the best of his parents' qualities—his father's slim, athletic build and his mother's expressive eyes and inner strength—without the burden of sharing with brothers or sisters.

But it wasn't fair that her brother had those brown eyes with the golden flecks that looked like amber in the sunlight while her eyes were so dark they were almost black, or that his hair was thick and curling while hers was straight, coarse, and black. Their father had told her she looked like their grandfather, Savaric, but right then she wished she had more of her brother's looks . . . or anyone else's instead of this swarthy, skinny appearance she disdained.

In that instant she loved her brother and hated him. She wished he would go away and take his friend with him. "It's not my mound. Take Moreg. He's the one who fell over it."

Savaron shrugged off her snappish reply. He had gotten used to his sister's uneasy temperament even if he didn't understand it. "As you wish."

Rafnir winked at her roguishly and patted the place behind him on his Hunnuli's back. "Sure you won't change your mind? You can ride with me."

"Your Hunnuli has enough trouble already carrying you and your arrogance," Kelene retorted.

Rafnir laughed. With a grin and a wave, he and Savaron turned their horses away and rode back to join the party of men already on their way toward the eastern hills.

Kelene rather wistfully watched them go. It would have been interesting to ride out with the men to get a closer look at that strange mound. But while she would never admit it to Savaron or Rafnir, the fact was that she doubted she could make it as far as that canyon today. Never had she felt so sore and bone-tired as she did that afternoon. The race, the hard fall, and the bitter disappointment had taken more out of her than she had imagined. Her leg ached from toe to knee, her head throbbed, and her thigh muscles felt like jelly. Ishtak, with a swollen knee and aching muscles, was in no better shape.

She could have ridden a Hunnuli, of course. None had tried to befriend her over the years, perhaps knowing in their wise way that she would not welcome their advances, but not one would have refused her request. It was simply that she felt very uncomfortable around the big horses. They were bred to be the companions and mounts of magic-wielders, and Kelene believed if she rode one, it would be a tacit acceptance of her talent—an acceptance she refused to make.

Without warning, Ishtak jerked his head away from her and began to wade toward the shore. He had obviously had enough of the river and wanted some shade and grass. Kelene didn't argue. The cool water was making her leg ache all the more, and the thought of sitting down was beginning to appeal to her. She hung on to the gelding's lead rope and hobbled as best she could through the water.

The idea of sitting down suddenly reminded her that Gabria had asked her to help with the fosterlings this afternoon. Kelene, feeling a little guilty for forgetting her promise to help two days ago, had agreed. Of course, her mother didn't really need any help. There were seven children, no, eight with the Reidhar boy, from ages eight to fourteen. They were fairly well behaved, and all had chosen to come to Gabria to learn to use their talent, so they were no trouble. The only reason, Kelene decided, that Gabria wanted her there was the hope that her daughter would listen to her teaching and storytelling and perhaps absorb some of the children's enthusiasm.

Kelene knew that was a vain wish. Nevertheless, Gabria was going to tell the children the tale of Valorian, the clans' hero-warrior, and a chance to listen to that was worth the time spent with the group. Kelene never grew tired of hearing the story of the man who had brought his people to the Ramtharin Plains nearly five hundred years ago.

The girl and the horse reached the bank where the ground rose up several feet to a grassy edge, and Ishtak lunged forward to leap up the steep incline. For a person with two healthy legs, the climb up the bank was not difficult. For Kelene it was usually a challenge that she could manage. But as Ishtak lunged upward, he yanked the lead rope in her hand. The sudden wrench pulled her weight onto her weak ankle. Pain shot up her leg like a fiery bolt, and her foot and ankle, unable to bear her full weight, collapsed beneath her. With a cry, Kelene fell face first into the muddy bank. Ishtak, tail high and ears forward, trotted stiffly away, trailing his lead rope behind him.

"Sorh take that horse!" Kelene shouted furiously, wiping mud off her face. She struggled painfully to her feet in time to see her gray head out toward the pastures on the far side of the valley.

Well, there's no catching him now, she decided. He would just have to wear that halter and rope until someone could chase him down.

Kelene sank down on the edge of the drop-off and rubbed her throbbing ankle. She could hardly bear to look at it any more. The thickened joint, the shorter shin, and the twisted, disfigured foot all sickened her. It was so unfair. Why did that accident happen to her? She was only trying to help her father. And why of all times did it happen right after her friend, the clan healer Piers Arganosta had died in his sleep? In a twist of had fortune, Piers's apprentice had been away, and there had been no healer to help set her bones.

Her parents and the horse healer had done their best, but the weight of the stallion falling on her ankle had crushed it beyond their simple skills to straighten. She was lucky, they told her time and again, that she could walk at all. Perhaps that was so, but she couldn't help feeling the resentment that rose like nausea every time she looked at her foot, tried to walk normally, or had to face the pitying looks of other clanswomen.

A noise behind her pulled her from her reverie, and she turned to see an eagle in a dead tree nearby. The bird gave a piercing cry and launched itself into the air. Its white and brown wings outstretched, it soared out over the meadows to catch the rising afternoon drafts.

Kelene threw her head back and wishfully watched it go. To be so free, she thought, to be swift and light and graceful as an eagle. It must be joyous to ride the sweeping wind currents wherever you want to go and feel the heat of the sun on your outstretched feathers. She wondered what the plains would look like from high above. What would it be like to leave the earth behind and soar among the clouds?

She smiled at her own fantasies. If the gods ever took it into their immortal minds to grant her a wish, she would be delighted if they would let her fly. She had always dreamed of sailing on the wind as fast as she could go or soaring out over the tall prairie grass like a falcon on the hunt. Just once, that's all she wanted, just one moment to feel as free and light as a bird.

For just the tick of her heart, she thought of her talent. Could magic help her achieve her dream? And just as quickly she rejected the idea. She laughed, a half-mocking, half-amused sound. Of course not. Magic was too dangerous, too uncontrollable, too unknown.

Long ago in the golden age of sorcery, it had been different. The clan magic-wielders gathered in Moy Tura, the city of the sorcerers, to study and learn. They had known how to use magic to the fullest human potential. Some of the more powerful sorcerers had learned how to alter their forms, heal the sick, or summon the gorthlings from the realm of the dead to do their bidding. Now, though, most of the ancient spells were lost or forgotten, and the few magic-wielders in the clans were trying to learn magic from one old book of spells and a lot of crude trial and error. No, magic could certainly not help her accomplish anything now. It was too unmanageable.

Painfully she climbed to her feet and hobbled back to the Khulinin camp. She saw her mother and Tam and the fosterlings already gathered under a tree, but she didn't join them until she had changed her muddy clothes and cleaned her hair and face. Then, with a cup of cooled goat's milk in hand, she went to join the group.

Her mother was sitting on a leather stool with her beloved Hunnuli mare, Nara, and Nara's filly, Demira, standing just behind her. The children, sitting in a semicircle around her, watched with rapt attention while the sorceress wove the tale of Valorian with magic, words, and images. She used dust from the ground and smoke from a cooking fire to form small pictures in the air before her of Valorian and his black horse, Hunnul. Just beneath the skin of her right wrist, a diamond splinter, the symbol of a full magic-wielder, glowed red with power and emotion.

"Valorian took Hunnul's soft muzzle in his hands and closed his eyes to begin the spell," Gabria was saying. She moved her images to replicate the words.

Kelene was pleased. She had come in time for her favorite part, where Valorian teaches his stallion to communicate. Gabria glanced up and smiled at her as she joined the group; Kelene smiled tentatively back. She sat down beside Tam and reached out to scratch the white cat loafing on Tam's lap.

Kelene soon became so engrossed in the story she did not notice Nara's filly, Demira, sidle up behind her. While the girl listened in wonder, Demira lowered her nose to a handspan away from Kelene's back, sighed contentedly, and went to sleep.

* * *

The sound of hooves ringing on stone echoed around the long line of clansmen as they rode in single file down the narrow defile. The sun had dropped low enough to leave the canyon in cool shade, which was a welcome relief after the heat of the valley, but no one seemed inclined to remark on it or on the beauty of the variegated colors of red and brown in the smooth stone around them. They were too busy looking ahead or nervously eyeing the high, enclosing walls over their heads.

Before long, the Dangari rider led them out into the wider end of the canyon where the sun slanted down on the eastern wall and a light breeze riffled the patches of weeds and grass. The mound sat in lonely solitude, its crown trampled and flattened from the accident the day before. Off to the right side, vultures were flocking over the carcass of the horse, and a small pack of wild dogs left their meal to dash off into the rocks. The smell of corruption filled the air.

The clansmen filed in and reined to a halt in a circle around the mound. Silently they studied it: the oblong shape, the weed-grown slopes, the summit that rose over their heads.

"Well?" Lord Athlone said to a priest in red robes. "What do you think of it?"

The man, a white-haired, fierce-eyed old whiplash of a Jehanan, dismounted without answering and stalked up to the top of the mound. He walked the length of the top from east to west, poked and prodded around the hole made by Moreg's horse, and pulled up some more clumps of grass to study what lay beneath. At last he straightened.

"It is a burial mound," he pronounced, and a babble of excited, wondering voices burst from the watching crowd.

"Whose is it?" several asked loudly.

"Why is it out here in this forsaken place?" another man shouted.

"May we open it?" others demanded.

Ordan, the priest, held up his hand to quiet them. He was the oldest man in the clans and well-respected for his wisdom and service to Sorh, god of the dead. The men quieted immediately. "I cannot answer all those questions at once," he snapped. "This mound appears to be very old. That's all I can tell you without further study."

"Will Lord Sorh be angry if we open it?" Koshyn asked.

"The god of the dead will not be angered if the proper prayers are said and the contents are not disturbed," Ordan informed them.

"It shall be done!" said Lord Athlone. And with that everyone dismounted and set to work. The horses were led away and picketed at the far end of the box canyon. The men who had brought spades set to work digging at both ends of the mound. Other men cleared away the weeds and grass on the slopes and on the top, looking for anything—a marker, a sign, a plaque—that would tell them who was buried in this grave.

By clan tradition that dated back hundreds of years, burial mounds of this size were usually built only for special purposes. Sometimes, as in the case of the massacred Corin clan, a mound would be built to bury a large number of people, or for a highly respected priest. Usually, though, the big mounds housed a dead chieftain and all the possessions he would need to maintain his honor and dignity in the realm of the dead. Clan lords had been known to be buried with their horses, dogs, weapons, clothes, household goods, gold, and other personal belongings. If there was a chief within this lone mound, there could be many things in the inner chamber and maybe an invaluable chance to learn more about the clans' past.

With a strength fueled by excitement and curiosity, the clansmen worked feverishly to clear the mound. Rafnir, still sore from his fall in the race, helped pull weeds and clumps of grass. He grinned at his father when Sayyed paused from shoveling to wipe the sweat from his forehead.

"We could have done this much faster with magic," Rafnir suggested.

Sayyed leaned on his shovel and said, "Yes, but we don't really know what's under there. We could damage it with a misplaced spell."

"And I suppose," Rafnir added, still grinning, "the others would resent being left out of the fun of all this hard work."

"You're learning," Sayyed said and went back to digging.

It wasn't long before the slopes were stripped to the dirt and the roof of the burial chamber was exposed.

"Look at this," Ordan said to Lord Athlone. He pointed to the wooden beams that still lay partially covered with dirt. "This is older than I thought. Maybe two hundred years. Whoever built this didn't cap the inner chamber with stone as we do now. This is only a timber-framed roof. It's a wonder that horse didn't crash all the way through."

The Khulinin chief squatted down to take a closer look. He saw immediately what Ordan meant. The thick, square beams had once supported a slightly angled roof of wooden planks, but time and the damp earth had rotted away the planks and the covering cap of soil had settled down on the supporting beams.

The beams themselves were soft and crumbling. The packed earth around them seemed to be the only thing holding the timbers together. "Maybe we should move most of the men off the top," he suggested.

Just then, a shout from one end of the mound drew everyone's attention, and Athlone and Ordan hurried down to see what had been found.

Sayyed, Rafnir, Koshyn, and several other men were clustered around a large hole they had dug into the slope of the eastern end. "I think we found the entrance," Sayyed shouted.

All the men dropped what they were doing and gathered close by to watch as the dirt was carefully removed from a large area around the initial hole. When they were finished, the workers stood back to show what they had discovered.

Three stone steps were laid into the ground down to a doorway into the burial chamber. The entrance was of stone with two carved stone pillars to either side of a narrow stone door. There were no handles, handholds, finger holes, or latches of any kind on the door and nothing to indicate who lay within. The stone on the door was perfectly blank.

"That's odd," remarked Ordan. The old priest leaned forward until his wispy white beard was inches away from a dirt-encrusted pillar. "Give me your dagger," he said to no one in particular and stuck out his hand. Lord Athlone obliged him by handing over his own polished blade.

Quickly and carefully Ordan began to scrape and scratch away the soil clinging to the stone. In just a few moments he had cleaned off several runic markings cut into both pillars and two small, intricately inscribed marble tiles inset on both sides of the doorframe. "Interesting," he muttered.

"What? What is it?" clamored the men around him.

The old priest ignored them and, with sharp blue eyes, studied the marks. At his request, several other priests joined him to examine the carvings, but finally they all shook their heads in frustration.

Ordan jabbed a finger at the markings. "These—here and here," he said to the crowded clansmen, "are too old for us to read. I believe they are Clan. They look similar to old runic signs once used for the gods. But we have lost the knowledge to understand them."

Lord Athlone, craning his neck to look over the priests' shoulders, saw the doorframe and felt a jab of recognition. "I know what those two tiles are," he exclaimed.

Ordan moved aside so the chieftain could step in and take a closer look.

Athlone pointed to the marble panels. "They're magic wards. This door has been sealed by magic."

"Heresy," one of the priests muttered under his breath.

In spire of his longevity as a holy man, Ordan was one of the few priests in the clans who had an open mind regarding magic. Unlike most of his counterparts, he was willing to consider the possibility that magic was a gift of the gods, not an evil mutation of their powers. Therefore, he did not flinch away from the doorway as did two of the other priests or cross his fingers in a sign against evil. Instead he put his fingertips along the almost invisible seam of the door and looked fascinated. "Is it possible to break the seal?" he asked Athlone.

The sorcerer-chieftain considered the tiles for a moment or two. "Probably. They've been weakened by age. But should we? I've never heard of a burial chamber sealed with magic wards."

"Neither have I. On the other hand, this appears to date back to the days before the downfall of the sorcerers. We know so little of that time. Perhaps it was accepted to seal some tombs with magic."

Athlone touched the cool, damp stone with a finger. "Well, I'm willing to try to open it if you are."

Ordan's thin lips pulled into a rare smile. "My curiosity has gotten the best of me. Break the seals, magic-wielder."

Hastily the men backed up several paces to give Lord Athlone more room. The chief stretched out both arms and placed his fingertips on the wards. He closed his eyes to concentrate on the magic around him. He knew the power permeated the natural world. Magic was in the rocks, the earth, the living plants, and it was in the souls of those born with the talent to wield its energy. As he drew magic from the earth at his feet, he felt the energy flow through him, as natural and comforting as his own blood.

He wished he had a diamond splinter such as Gabria's to help him intensify his spell, but the splinters were emblems of an older age and only one had been found since the destruction of Moy Tura. He would have to rely on his own strength. Visualizing exactly what he wanted to do, he focused his spell down through his fingertips and sent a powerful, explosive jolt of magic into the tiles. The wards were stronger than he expected. Old, worn, and eroded as they were, they had been constructed by a master sorcerer and their power was still potent. Athlone had to send a second, more powerful burst into them before the marble finally cracked and the tiles shattered to dust.

The chieftain leaned against the frame, breathing heavily. "Are you all right?" Koshyn asked at his side.

"Yes." He pushed himself upright. "But if they hadn't been so old and worn, I would never have broken through. Someone wanted to make sure this body was not disturbed."

"Well, let's go see what's in there," someone yelled eagerly, and the men shouted their agreement.

Still weary, Athlone stood aside and let Savaron step in to put his shoulder to the stone door. Together, Koshyn and Savaron heaved against the entrance until the stone groaned and creaked and a black crack appeared along the right-hand edge.

* * *

Under the tree in the Khulinin camp, Lady Gabria lunged to her feet and screamed a terrible cry of anguish.

"Mother!" Kelene shouted in horror, hobbling to her side as the sorceress buried her face in her hands. The children clustered around, clamoring with fear and confusion. The white cat took off like a streak, and Demira neighed a nervous challenge. White-faced, Tam tried to calm the young ones while Kelene and Nara gathered close to Gabria.

"What is it? What's wrong?" Tam cried over the uproar.

Gabria was sweating and lightheaded and shuddering uncontrollably. She clasped Kelene's arm with one hand and Nara's leg with the other, too upset to speak.

Kelene responded. "I don't know!" She stared at her mother's stricken face and felt her heart twist. Kelene knew she had pushed aside her love for Gabria many times in the past few years, but, behind the facade she showed to the world, that love had never waned. Now she was horrified by the pain she saw in Gabria's eyes. "Mother, please! What's the matter?" she cried.

Gabria could only shake her head. She gasped for breath and held tighter to Kelene's arm.

Frustrated, Kelene looked to Tam, but she was still distracted by the frightened children. The girl steadied her shaking legs. There was one way to get a partial answer, if she wanted to do it. Kelene had always been sensitive by touch to other people's emotions. She didn't know why she had the ability, and she had never told anyone about it. It was usually something she regarded as painful and a nuisance. This time, though, fear for her mother overcame her reluctance, and she laid her other hand over her mother's. Opening her mind to her mother's feelings, she concentrated on the touch of her skin against Gabria's. The results were immediate.

"She's not ill. She's terrified," Kelene cried to Tam.

"Terrified of what? Gabria, is this like yesterday? Or the day before?" Tam demanded.

Kelene was surprised. "What are you talking about?"

"Your mother had a vision two days ago, then a strange experience during the race yesterday. Was this the same thing, Gabria?"

The sorceress finally nodded. "Only worse. Much worse. For just a moment I felt a hatred so strong . . . so malevolent. . . . O Mother of All, what was it?" she moaned.

"I don't know, but I think you'd better lie down. The moment Athlone and Sayyed get back, we have to tell them Tam insisted. "You're not going to keep it to yourself for a day or two like you did the vision."

Gabria drew a long, ragged breath to steady her voice and let go of Kelene and Nara. "Yes, we'll tell them. But . . . I don't want to lie down. The feeling is passing." She smiled reassuringly at the children around her. "Why don't we go on with the story? It will take all our minds off this for a while."

Kelene and Tam eyed her with some disbelief, but Gabria composed herself. Although her face was pale and there was a tremor in her hands, she took up the tale of Valorian where she had left it. The children settled back down, looking relieved. Tam shook her head and went to search for her cat.

Only Kelene could not relax. She had never sensed a fear like her mother's before; its intensity had left her badly shaken. If it had touched her so deeply, how must it have affected Gabria? She hoped when her father returned they could discover the cause of these strange attacks. Her mother did not deserve such terror.

* * *

The men pushed harder, and the door slowly ground open to a shoulder's width.

"Stop there," Ordan ordered. "Let the air within freshen before we open the door fully."

When they all tried to peer into the interior, they could see nothing beyond the small patch of light in the entrance. The darkness beyond the portal was complete.

Overcome perhaps by the silence of the tomb and the closeness of death, the men fell quiet, their eyes riveted on the empty opening. For a long while no one moved. Then Ordan slowly raised his arms to the sky and began a chanted prayer to Sorh. The rest of the priests joined him until the canyon sang with their voices.

When their last words died into the early evening, the men stirred and muttered among themselves, feeling slightly better now that they had appeased Lord Sorh.

"Open it now," Ordan commanded.

Savaron and Koshyn obliged, and the stone door swung fully open. Several torches were passed around, then Ordan stepped into the burial chamber. The other priests and several chieftains slowly filed in after him until the narrow space within was full. By the flickering light of the torches, they stared around the room in surprise.

The chamber was built in the older clan tradition of stone walls, dirt floor, and a shallow timbered ceiling. The walls were dirty and stained with moisture, and a heavy smell of mold and rot permeated the air. Those who were expecting to find a large trove of objects were disappointed, for the room was virtually empty. There was only a single stone sarcophagus sitting on a platform in the center of the chamber and a pitifully small pile of personal items lying on the platform. There were no weapons, no bags of salt or dishes for food, no trappings befitting a chieftain—nothing to reveal who lay within the coffin. The clansmen looked in every deep shadow and dark corner and found only dust.

"What's in there?" one man shouted from outside. There were still quite a few waiting for their turn to come in.

"Not much," replied Lord Terod. Disappointed, he and several more men went out to make room for others. One by one, the men filed through to look at the results of their work. Some were interested in the chamber; others were disappointed at the lack of things to see.

"It's as if whoever buried this man didn't like him," remarked Savaron.

Ordan turned from studying the sarcophagus. "Why do you say that?" he asked, his voice sharp with interest.

The Khulinin warrior picked up a small comb from the pile on the platform. "There's so little here. A respected chieftain or priest is always buried with his belongings. It looks like this man was given only a few grudging tokens."

"An interesting observation, young man. Tell me what else you notice."

"The walls have been painted," Rafnir spoke up. He held a torch up close to one wall. "Most of it has flaked off, but you can still see bits of color through the dust and mildew. I think it's red."

"What do you make of all this?" Athlone asked Ordan.

"Precious little. I've never seen anything like this. The red paint on the walls indicates this was probably a priest of Sorh, but there are no items of his office, no staff, no prayer scrolls, no jars of incense. Your son is likely right—this man was thoroughly disliked." He peered around at the walls and went on. "What I want to know is why he was buried out here in this empty, forsaken canyon? Why is his grave unmarked and forgotten? Why has his identity been so carefully hidden?"

"We could open the sarcophagus," Rafnir suggested. "Maybe there is a name on the coffin or some writing that could help us."

Ordan nodded. "Do it. Carefully. I do not want to disturb the body."

Savaron, Rafnir, and two others stepped forward, lifted the heavy slab off the top of the stone box, and gently set it on the ground by the platform.

"Good gods!" exclaimed Athlone. "Why did they do that?"

Inside the sarcophagus lay a large, full-length wooden coffin. Its lid was nailed with heavy iron spikes and chained with thick bronze links at both ends. On top of the wood lid was carved a string of ten runic letters similar to the ones on the doorframe.

One of the young men tried to shove the chain off one end of the coffin. To his dismay, the chain was also nailed in place. He started to yank hard at the bronze links.

"No. stop!" Ordan commanded. But he was too late. The man pulled with such strength that the coffin slid toward him and slammed against the stone. The wooden lid, rotten and weakened by time and moisture, cracked at one end.

"There is no need to open the coffin," Ordan said harshly. "It is best left alone."

The young man looked guilty. "Why? Don't you want to know who's in it?"

The old priest shook his head. "No. Any man sealed in his tomb with magic and nailed in his coffin is best left undisturbed."

"I agree," Athlone said, staring at the chained box.

The men glanced at one another and saw the same uneasy look on all their faces.

"I want this mound sealed shut again. Rebury it. There is nothing here for us," said Ordan.

Savaron glanced outside. "That will take hours and it's almost dark. Could it wait until morning?"

Ordan nodded his assent and silently left the burial chamber. The rest of the men hurried after him into the open air. The meadow was filling with darkness by that time; a few stars twinkled in the evening sky. While the men brought their horses and mounted, Savaron and Rafnir closed the stone door.

"We'll send some men in the morning to rebury the mound," Athlone told the other chiefs. They quietly agreed. The mound lay black in the gathering night, cloaked in shadow and mystery. More than a few clansmen muttered a prayer to stifle the fear that chilled them. They rode away hurriedly without looking back, leaving the opened grave to the mercy of the night.

* * *

The canyon fell deathly still. Nothing moved. No living creature set foot within its boundaries. Night passed slowly into the deep, chilled hours before dawn.

Within the mound, darkness as black and thick as ink filled the chamber much as it had for over two hundred years. But something was different now. The seals that had shut out life, light, and air were broken; the heavy stone lid of the sarcophagus was lying on the ground; the wooden coffin itself, so carefully built and nailed shut, was cracked. For the first time since the coffin had been sealed, fresh air was leaking into the interior.

Outside the tomb a waning moon rose above the hills and cast its dim radiance into the canyon. A finger-thin beam of light eased through the small hole in the mound's roof to shine into the darkness of the chamber. As the moon rose higher, the pale shaft of light moved until it came to rest on the coffin directly below.

Something began to stir. A faintly luminous wisp of air curled from the crack in the coffin. It hung almost hesitantly between the stone and the wood before it wafted upward. More followed it like a thin, reddish smoke. The glowing air writhed and twisted about the moonbeam, slowly rising toward the ceiling. The mist began to pour out faster, as if encouraged by the fresh air and the light. Soon it filled the whole chamber with a ghastly phosphorescence.

The shaft of light faded and vanished as the moon sank toward the west, but the mist continued to glow with its own bloody radiance. It stopped writhing and hung in the chamber, motionless and still.

Another tendril of red mist began to creep out of the crack in the coffin. This one was darker and thicker; it spilled over the edge of the sarcophagus like a heavy stream of fog. Silently a shape took form from the dark mist. As tall as a man and as nebulous as smoke, it hovered by the platform drawing the last of its substance from the coffin. Then it deliberately moved toward the chamber's entrance. At the door the reddish form paused and extended a part of itself through the stone. When nothing happened, a strange sound like harsh laughter emanated from the figure. Eagerly the shape plunged through the stone into the dark night and was gone as quickly as it had formed.

The mist left in the tomb began to settle. By dawn it was gone, leaving only a barely discernible coating of red dust over everything in the chamber. The coffin rested in its stone housing, as still and enigmatic as death.

3

By late morning, the clansmen had returned to the canyon. A small party of ten, drawn from the Khulinin, Dangari, and Jehanan clans, came clattering into the box canyon with spades and orders to rebury the mound. There were no chieftains, priests, or elders among them since the council was meeting again to debate the difficult subject of magic and the training of magic-wielders. The young men had come willingly for the chance to see the mound and the opportunity to turn a hot, dirty job into a merry-making gathering. They started shoveling dirt back onto the sides and top of the mound while they talked and laughed and looked forward to the food and cooled wine they had brought in their saddlebags.

Four men went to the entrance. Priest Ordan had specifically asked them to replace the lid of the sarcophagus before they covered the door. They pushed the stone entrance open and entered the dark chamber.

"Krath's blood!" the Khulinin exclaimed. "What is that stench?" A foul putrescence filled the room as thick and gagging as smoke.

"It wasn't here yesterday," the young Dangari rider said. "Maybe the old man is rotting in the fresh air."

"He should be dust and bones by this time. Let's just get the lid on and get out of here," a third man replied.

In complete agreement, the four clansmen walked around the sarcophagus, not noticing the little puffs of dust kicked up by their feet. They heaved the lid up, moved it over the stone box, and were about to set it down when the Dangari lost his grip on the corner. The heavy stone slid from his fingers, knocking the entire lid off-balance. All four men yanked their hands out of the way as the lid crashed down on top of the sarcophagus. There was a loud crack; the lid split in half and fell with a cloud of dust into the box.

In dismay, the men stared at the lid then at each other. It was one thing to open a tomb and look inside; it was another thing entirely to deface the contents.

The Khulinin, a young warrior named Ritan, threw up his hands in disgust. "Now what do we do? Tell Ordan?"

"Not on your sword belt, we don't," the fourth man said. A thin-faced Jehanan who was already in his chieftain's bad graces, he was not going to aggravate anyone else in authority, especially a priest. "We'll just leave it. After all, we're going to rebury the mound. No one will see it."

"But the sarcophagus must have a new lid," the Dangari said worriedly.

"Why? That body isn't going anywhere," replied Torel the Jehanan.

One man gave a sharp, nervous laugh. "You're right. What the priests don't know won't hurt us. Let's just get out of here."

The Dangari nodded reluctantly. They arranged the broken pieces of the lid as best they could over the coffin, then filed out. Torel, the last one out, hesitated while the others went through the doorway. When he was sure no one was looking, he picked up a small jade box, a horn comb decorated with silver, and a slim flask embellished with garnets from the belongings on the platform and slipped them into the pouch hanging from his belt.

His eyes glittering with amusement, he went outside and helped close the door of the chamber. The four men immediately began to shovel dirt over the stone steps and doorway before anyone else asked to see the inside of the chamber. They were so busy, they didn't pay attention to the red-colored dust that clung to their pants, boots, and hands.

It was a happy group that rode back to the gathering late that afternoon. Laughing, boasting, handing the wineskins around, they rode toward the council grove just as the chieftains' council was finally ending for the day.

Torel saw his chief leaving the tent and turned his horse away before Lord Sha Tajan could see him. He hurried past Clan Murjik's camp and skirted the bazaar until he came to the painted booth of the Pra Deshian merchant. He waited until the booth was empty of customers, then slipped into the tent, pulled the jade box, the comb, and the flask out of his pouch and laid them on the counter in front of the proprietor.

The Pra Deshian, his broad face impassive, leaned over and examined the items carefully. He picked up the jade box, wiped the dust off with a cloth, and held it up to the light. It was only a simple box with a fitted lid and had any number of uses, but it was made of opaque, dark green Ramtharin jade and had the added bonus of being very old. There was a ready market in the Five Kingdoms for such an item. The comb and the flask were marketable as well.

"What did you have in mind?" the merchant asked casually.

Torel tried to keep his face expressionless. "These items belonged to my wife's father. They're very old and precious." He shrugged sadly. "But, there are things we need more."

The merchant studied the Jehanan's face, his dusty clothes, and dirty hands. He didn't believe the clansman's flimsy story for an instant. The Pra Deshian, though, kept up with the news of the clans and had an excellent idea where the man actually found them. Not that it was necessary to know. The important fact was that these three items had been brought to him and no other.

"Indeed," said the merchant. "Perhaps I have some of those items you need."

Torel's face lit up. The bartering began and ended fairly quickly to each man's satisfaction. When the Jehanan left bearing his goods, the proprietor quickly wrapped up his prizes and put them away. There was no point displaying them at the gathering and drawing needless questions.

He picked up the cloth he had used to wipe the jade box and was about to throw it aside when he noticed something odd. The dust on the cloth was a peculiar shade of red, almost like dried blood. There was dust on his hands as well. He studied the cloth momentarily, then dismissed it when Tam walked in to visit his horses. He tossed the cloth under the counter and went to greet her like an old friend.

* * *

Torel's companions were having such a good time, they did not notice he'd left. They were still laughing and talking as their horses splashed into the river for a well-deserved drink.

Just across the water, Lords Athlone and Koshyn came out of the council tent, feeling drained by the long, hot afternoon of negotiations and arguments. They saw the party of young men nearby, and Koshyn hailed his young rider. The Dangari broke off from the group and came trotting over. Although he saluted promptly, his eyes seemed to look everywhere but at his chief's face.

"Is it done, lad?" Koshyn asked.

"Yes, Lord. We finished it a while ago."

"Good work."

"Thank you, Lord," he said hastily, riding off before Koshyn could ask him anything else.

Athlone watched him go. "Did he seem a little nervous to you?"

"Like a dog caught with his nose in the dinner pot," Koshyn said. His eyes crinkled with amusement. "What do you suppose they were up to?"

"A lot of drinking by the looks of them," Athlone said.

"True. But that wouldn't set a burr up that boy. I just hope they finished the job before they started celebrating."

"We could send someone to check."

Lord Koshyn nodded. "Good idea."

Both chiefs picked up their weapons from the pile left guarded by the entrance and began to walk slowly toward the camps. Athlone stretched his arms and groaned, "Gods' truth, I'm tired. I thought Fiergan would never give up on that kidnapping accusation against Gabria."

Koshyn laughed. "The man could argue a gorthling to death. I suppose he'll come up with something equally as perverse tomorrow. Speaking of Gabria," he said, "how is she? I heard she's had a few strange turns lately."

"Very strange. Truth is, I'm worried. We talked for a long time last night and could find no real answer. She is certain her brother was trying to warn her of something in a vision she had three days ago. She thinks these sudden feelings of dread and fear she's had since are somehow connected. We just can't figure out how."

Koshyn whistled softly. "I didn't know she'd had another vision."

"Of the Corin massacre again," Athlone said grimly. They reached the edge of the grove and stopped at the last pool of shade.

Koshyn mulled over that news. "I can't believe that was really her brother. Spirits don't leave the realm of the dead. Maybe she had a premonition of some unknown danger that revealed itself as something familiar?"

The Khulinin chief shrugged in frustration. "The gods only know, and they seem to be tight-lipped right now."

"Have you talked to Ordan about it?"

"Ordan is tolerant of magic, but he makes no effort to understand it. I don't think he can help," said Athlone, his tone short.

Koshyn understood his friend's reluctance. After so many years of dealing with prejudice and hatred, especially among the priesthood, it was difficult for any of the magic-wielders to believe that a few of the clan priests were making an effort to accept them. "You may be underestimating him, Athlone. Talk to him. If nothing else, he may give you a different perspective on Gabria's vision."

"I'll think about it," Athlone said reluctantly. He clapped his friend on the back and suddenly grinned. "How about a shady seat and a cool drink?"

Koshyn's blue eyes lit with pleasure. "My thoughts exactly."

The two chiefs walked to the Khulinin camp and were soon taking their ease under the awning of Athlone's big tent.

Late afternoon slowly mellowed to evening, bringing with it a few scattered thunderstorms and an invigorating coolness that drew the clans from their heat-induced drowsiness. As the flies and the herds settled down to rest, the people came awake, excited and enthusiastic for the night's entertainment.

After the evening meal, men, women, and children of all ages swarmed to the council grove for the competitions between bards, both apprentice and master, from all eleven clans. It was always a long, exciting night, and it gave the clanspeople an opportunity to hear many of the tales known among the clans. Some were old, beloved stories of the clans' deities; some were more recent tales about Lady Gabria and her battle with the gorthling. The Khulinin bard, to the delight of his audience, told Gabria's tale of Valorian. When he was through, he rose to the sound of thunderous applause and bowed to Gabria in her seat among the chieftains.

All the bards had brought their musical instruments, and as soon as the story and poetry competitions were over, the singing and music began. The space in front of the musicians was filled by dancers of every age, who reveled in the wild whirling tunes from the pipes and the slower, throbbing beat of the drums. The dancing and music lasted far into the night, long after the prizes had been awarded and the children put to bed. When the final bard bowed to exhaustion, the light of dawn was streaming over the eastern hills.

The fifth full day of the gathering had begun.

The morning passed quietly since many of the clanspeople slept later than normal. By midday when the council reconvened, the day's heat wilted what little activity was stirring. The camps were almost lifeless as people dozed in their tents or splashed in the shallows of the rivers.

As soon as the council meeting was over, Sayyed hurried back to his tent. He tucked his hammock under his arm and went to a place he knew at the far edge of the Khulinin camp where two trees grew a perfect distance apart to hang a hammock. The hammock was a favorite of the Turic tribes, but it had become more popular among the clanspeople after Tam wove one for Sayyed. He liked to show off its comforts at every opportunity.

He had the opportunity now and planned to take full advantage of it. Tam was busy helping the Pra Deshian merchant with his horses, Rafnir was off somewhere with a friend, and Sayyed had just finished his duty as advisor and hearthguard to Lord Athlone during the long and wearying council meeting. He was ready for a well-deserved nap.

He tied the ends of the hammock to the two small cottonwoods and blissfully stretched out his length on the swinging bed. The trees overhead shaded him with dappled green; a tiny breeze cooled the sweat on his forehead.

He was just about to close his eyes when something small landed with a thump on the middle of his chest: Tam's cat. With a sound of contentment, she curled up on his tunic, her eyes half closed, her paws curled daintily under her chest.

Sayyed scratched her ears and let her stay. She was an odd animal, he thought, not at all obedient or willing to please like a dog. She walked on her own, as regal as a priestess, granting her affection to those few she deemed worthy. He, obviously, was acceptable. He had to admit he didn't mind. There was something very appealing about her soft white fur, her unperturbable gaze, and that strange, muted rumbling she made in her throat. The sound was peaceful, contented, like the gentle humming of insects and it affected his mood like the heat. In a matter of moments, he was asleep.

"Father!"

Sayyed heard his son's voice from far away and chose to ignore it. The arms of sleep were too comfortable.

"Father! Wake up."

The voice was closer now and insistent. Sayyed hoped Rafnir would see he was sleeping and go away.

"Father, please! I need help!"

The desperation in the words snapped the bonds of rest and brought Sayyed wide awake. He sat up in the hammock, still holding the cat, and saw Rafnir walking toward him from the meadows. His son was trying to carry someone over his shoulder.

"It's Ritan!" the young man shouted. The worry for his friend was plain in his face and voice. "He suddenly collapsed and I couldn't rouse him. I need help getting him to the healer."

Sayyed dropped the cat on the hammock, swung to his feet, and strode to help his son. They carried Ritan back to the camp, down the worn paths to the healer's tent.

The Khulinin clan healer, Gehlyn, was napping in his tent with his door flap wide open, so they brought the young man in and laid him down on an empty pallet. The healer woke immediately. He was an unexciting man in appearance, of medium height with an ordinary build, thinning brown hair, and a preference for dull colors. But what he lacked in visual appeal, he made up for in medicinal skill. He had been chosen and trained by Piers Arganosta, the finest healer in the clans, and his talent, persistence, and caring enhanced that training to a rare ability.

He rose from his own pallet, without bothering to put on his boots or tunic, and came over to look at his patient. "Tell me what happened," he urged the two men as he gently probed Ritan's throat for a pulse.

Rafnir answered hurriedly, "We were out in the meadows looking at a horse he wanted when he suddenly fell over. Just like this."

Gehlyn frowned. "Had he been feeling ill before? Did he cry out as if in pain? Or complain of anything?"

"Well, no . . . he didn't . . . I . . ."

Sayyed realized his son was badly shaken. Ritan was one of Rafnir's best friends, and it had to have been a shock to see him collapse for no apparent reason. He gripped Rafnir's arm with a steadying pressure and said, "Try to think. What has he been doing today?"

The hand on his arm was what Rafnir needed to settle his dismay. "He didn't do much today at all. He was too tired from yesterday. Remember, Father, he went out with the men who reburied that mound. They were gone most of the afternoon. Then he was up all night dancing."

"All night, huh?" the healer grunted. "Then walking around the fields in this heat? Could be exhaustion or heat-fever. He does seem to be very hot." He lifted Ritan's eyelids, checked the inside of the warrior's mouth and throat, and felt the glands under his jaw. "Hmm. I don't like this."

"What?" Rafnir demanded.

"There are small boils in his mouth and lumps here and there." He pointed to places under Ritan's jaw. Sitting back on his heels, he pursed his lips. "You'd better leave him here so I can watch him."

The worry deepened on Rafnir's face. "Will he be all right?"

"I don't know. I'm not certain what's wrong."

Sayyed rose to his feet, pulling his son with him. "Thank you, Gehlyn. We'll go tell his family."

The healer waved without answering. His plain features creased with concern, he began to wipe Ritan's flushed skin with a damp cloth. Sayyed and Rafnir hurried away.

For two days Ritan lay in Gehlyn's tent while the healer tried desperately to ease his symptoms and learn what was wrong. Little by little Ritan's fever grew hotter until he tossed and moaned in a delirious frenzy. The lumps in his neck enlarged, and others appeared in his armpits and groin, and developed into hard, poisonous swellings that caused him to thrash with pain whenever they were touched. The boils spread over his body from head to foot in reddish yellow pustules that burst and seeped a foul liquid. The only blessing Rafnir could see when he came to visit his friend was that Ritan never regained consciousness.

On the third day, Gehlyn went to the council tent and requested entrance to talk to Lord Athlone. The healer was welcomed, but the noisy conversations in the tent came to a stop when he bowed to the Khulinin lord and said sadly, "Ritan is dead, my lord."

Sayyed bowed his head not only for the loss of a fine young warrior but for the grief his son must be feeling. Then his head jerked up and his skin grew cold as Gehlyn went on to say, "I've been talking to some of the other healers, and we've discovered that there are three more men who have the same symptoms."

The attention in the tent sharpened to a tense wariness.

"Who?" demanded Lord Hendric.

"A Jehanan has been ill for two days with a high fever and boils over his upper body."

"And two in Clan Dangari," Koshyn added. The chieftain climbed to his feet, his face noticeably paler. "They have been bedridden since last night with fevers. One is unconscious."

Shahr above all! Sayyed said to himself. Rafnir had been with Ritan when he was stricken and visited him several times before the warrior died. Could his only child catch this strange illness? His fingers unconsciously clenched into fists.

"Do you have any idea what killed your man?" Lord Dormar of Clan Ferganan asked into the uneasy silence.

Gehlyn shook his head and began to pace back and forth. "It is definitely a disease, not heat-fever or a bodily injury as I first thought. Unfortunately, none of us have seen anything like it. None of our remedies have even eased the symptoms."

A subdued murmur rumbled through the crowd of men, growing louder as they realized the possible import of what Gehlyn was telling them.

"Is it contagious?" Sayyed asked for them all.

Gehlyn threw up his hands. "I don't know. I found out these four men entered the burial chamber when the grave mound was covered over. Perhaps that is significant. No one else has yet fallen ill."

The clansmen looked at one another worriedly, the same thought on all of their minds. Most of them had helped dig out the burial mound and had walked through the chamber. If this strange disease sprang from some foulness within the mound, then nearly everyone there was susceptible.

Lord Ryne banged his fist on a shield to draw the men's attention and said, "I suggest we end for the day and each chief return to his clan. Check your people. If anyone is ill, report it to the healers. The gods willing, the other three men will recover and that will be the end of it."

The chiefs quickly agreed. In little groups they hurried from the council grove and went their separate ways to the eleven different camps.

By that evening, Ritan's family had given him a quick burial, and Gehlyn learned that no one else but the three sick men had more than the normal aches or sniffles or monthly pains. He and every other healer prayed that might be the extent of their troubles.

For two more days the gathering continued as usual while the healers, priests, and chieftains anxiously waited. Then at noon on the third day, the two Dangari died. Torel, the thin-faced Jehanan, followed them to the realm of the dead that afternoon. All three men died as miserably and inevitably as the young Khulinin, and not one of them responded to any medicinal herb or poultice or powder.

At Gehlyn's insistence, the relatives of the dead men agreed to a funeral pyre rather than a grave. He hoped the flames would help destroy whatever evil had stricken them.

That night, the chiefs and clan members of the Dangari and Jehanan clans, along with Lord Athlone and Lady Gabria, gathered in the meadows around a large pyre where the three bodies lay with their personal belongings. Relatives brought bags of salt, loaves of bread, and small gifts to send with them to the realm of the dead, and Lords Sha Tajan and Koshyn laid weapons at their sides. Ordan and the priest of Sorh from Clan Dangari chanted the prayers of the dead.

Gabria closed her eyes when Ordan took a torch and lit the oil-soaked wood. She did not need to see the flames igniting or hear the sudden crackle and roar as the voracious fire consumed the pyre. She had seen it too many times before. Too many people dear to her heart had passed on to the realm of Sorh leaving behind only memories and an ache in her heart.

She felt Athlone's arm go around her waist, and she leaned into his protective warmth. At least she hadn't had any more of those hideous feelings of dread. Perhaps a premonition of the deaths of these four young men had been what had triggered those strange episodes. Perhaps now it would all be over, and things could return to normal.

With the softest sigh, Gabria turned her head away from the flames and opened her eyes to look past Athlone's shoulder to the dark beyond. Her sigh turned to a frightened gasp.

Athlone's arm tightened around her. "What's wrong?" he whispered urgently.

"I thought I . . . saw something. Out there in the darkness."

The hearthguard accompanying them took one look at her face and put his hand to his sword.

Athlone turned to look and saw only a few campfires and the dim, distant shapes of the camps faintly illuminated by the light of a dying half-moon. "What?" he asked.

Gabria squinted hard into the night, but whatever she had seen was gone. "It was there!" she insisted fearfully. "A shape like a man standing in the shadows." She shuddered. "It was glowing, Athlone, with a horrible reddish light. Like a dead-lamp in the Goldrine Marshes."

With an overwhelming rush of dread, Gabria suddenly knew that the vision of her brother, the feelings of dread she had experienced, and this sighting of a half-seen fearsome light were somehow connected. The fear and tension that had been churning inside of her since the day of her vision burst loose, and she hid her face in Athlone's shoulder. Her tears wet his tunic and leather vest; her shuddering sobs shook his whole body. He cradled her close and silently cursed whatever agent had brought her to such anguish.

"It's not over," she forced out between gasping breaths. "Something horrible is out there."

Some of her fear reached with icy claws into Athlone's mind. Gabria had been right too many times in the past to ignore her warnings as foolish imaginings. If she insisted some evil was lurking in the night, it was. But by all the gods, what was it? And what were they going to do about it?

He glanced at the guard by his side and saw the same apprehension in the man's wide gaze and tight jaw. "Come on," Athlone said sharply. "Let's go home." With a nod to Lord Koshyn, he steeled himself to leave the crowd of clanspeople and walk out into the darkness. His arm still around Gabria, he led her silently away from the pyre, the guard walking close by her other side.

The hearthguard drew his sword as they stepped out of the light. The rustling sound of leather and the rattle of his mail shirt drew Gabria's attention. She wiped her face with the sleeve of her blue tunic, took a long breath of the warm night air, and laid her hand on his arm. "You won't need that. Whatever hides in the night cannot be beaten by swords."

The hearthguard and Athlone both shivered at the cold, hollow tone of her voice. They shared a look over her head and walked a little faster through the darkness toward the fires and tents of the Khulinin camp.

Nothing bothered them on the way back, and Gabria did not see the strange form again that night. But she knew it was there, somewhere, waiting beyond sight for something she could not understand. She managed to hide her anxiety by the time they returned to their tent and was able to smile at Coren's antics when he tried to get out of bedtime. She talked to Lymira about her betrothed, helped Athlone feed the dogs, and settled her home for the night.

Only Kelene, sitting by a small lamp and mending Ishtak's halter, noticed the odd glitter in her mother's eyes and the tight lines of tension around her mouth. Gabria was still awake and standing by the open door flap, staring out into the darkness, when Kelene was ready to sleep. Kelene hesitated, then in a rare gesture, she quickly hugged her mother goodnight.

For just a moment, Gabria clung to her with a desperate strength that surprised her. Through their touch, Kelene sensed her mother's feelings as powerfully as her own, and the turmoil scared her. She wanted to ask what was wrong, but something in her mother's stiff expression told her that she would get no answer that night. Maybe Gabria would feel better in the morning when the sun shone and the black shadows of night were gone.

Kelene slipped into her blankets with a sigh and for a long while watched her mother standing motionless by the open flap.

* * *

"Lord Athlone!" Gehlyn's shout from outside startled everyone in the tent awake. Kelene sat up, wondering if they had slept only a few minutes. Her mother was still standing by the door, and the lamp on the clothes chest was still lit. Then she noticed the pale light of dawn glimmering outside and felt the coolness of early morning.

"Lady Gabria!" Gehlyn called again. "Is Lord Athlone awake?"

"I am," the chieftain called sleepily. He rose and stretched as Gabria and the hearthguard outside moved away from the entrance so the healer could enter. The three younger ones got up also and stared curiously when Gehlyn and Savaron dashed into the tent. One look at their faces told everyone there was bad news.

"The other six men who reburied the mound have come down with the sickness," the healer said without preamble. "All of them fell ill during the night."

Gabria's face turned deathly pale. As if preparing for battle, she silently tied up her hair and began to gather her small stock of herbs, medicines, and cloths for bandages.

"That's not the worst of it, Father," Savaron said. "I've heard one of the Pra Deshian merchants in the bazaar is sick with a high fever."

"O gods," Athlone groaned. He pulled on his boots and a clean shirt while he tried to muster his thoughts. "Savaron, ask the chiefs to come to the council tent. Gehlyn, take someone with you. Check the merchants and the whole bazaar."

"Do I tell them what is happening?" questioned the healer.

Athlone stifled a curse. If the merchants were told that a deadly and possibly virulent disease had shown up in the clans, they could panic and flee—at best leaving the gathering without a market, at worst running the risk of spreading the illness to other places. On the other hand, was it fair *not* to warn them? They would find out soon enough and probably blame the clans for negligence.

"Yes, tell them. But assure them there is no need to panic. And if you can, ask them if they know what this disease might be. Maybe it's something they're familiar with, or maybe they brought it in themselves unknowingly." With a speed bordering on fury, he buckled on his belt and hung the gold chieftain's torque around his neck.

Gehlyn nodded. He didn't think the foreign merchants had anything to do with the disease, but he understood the need to ask. "Yes, my lord."

"Thank you," said Athlone. "Report back to me as quickly as you can." Both men saluted and hurried out.

"Is there anything we can do, Father?" Lymira asked.

Lord Athlone looked at Gabria, at her bloodless lips, at the unyielding, upright slant of her jaw, and at the tenseness in her movements as she collected the supplies. "Help your mother," he ordered, and with a swirl of his golden cloak, he strode from the tent into the morning.

That day in the summer, which dawned like so many others before it, became a day the eleven clans would never forget. Before then, "plague" had always been a vague word used to describe something frightening that happened somewhere else. Plagues struck cities like Pra Desh or the heavily populated areas of the Five Kingdoms and the Turic regions. Not once in the long history of the clans had a devastating disease struck at the entire population. Each clan had its share of influenza, yellow fever, or the red rash Piers Arganosta had called measles. But the semi-nomadic clans were often widely scattered and on the move. An epidemic had never caught up with them—until this gathering.

That day, under a hot, dry, clear sky, the clans learned for the first time the terrible reality of a plague.

In the morning the situation did not appear to be out of hand. The six men who had fallen ill—two Jehanan, a Dangari, and three Khulinin—were brought to a spare tent set up away from the other camps. The healers hoped that putting them in quarantine would stop the spread of the disease. They were soon joined by the Pra Deshian merchant who had accepted the stolen grave-goods, as well as his young apprentice.

The news of the new victims swept through the camps and bazaar like a storm, and the chiefs spent a busy morning reassuring everyone, including the merchants, that there was no reason to expect the worst.

The lords were still gathered in the council tent at noon when several girls brought jugs of cooled water and wine and platters of food for the busy chiefs.

Lord Morbiar of Clan Wylfling was the first one to reach for the water. He grabbed a jug and drank almost frantically. "By the fires of Gormoth, it's hot in here," he complained. He stood in the center of the tent, his face flushed an angry red and sweat running down his face. All at once he swayed and staggered, then collapsed unconscious to the floor.

No one in the tent moved. Horrified, they stared at him, seeing clearly for the first time that the disease had gone beyond the bounds of the ten young men and was striking into the heart of the clans.

In that stricken moment, the healer from Clan Ferganan burst into the tent and cried frantically, "Lords, I have two women with the fever. What do I do with them?"

Before anyone could speak or react, Lord Athlone said, "Bring them here."

The other chiefs looked at him as if he had lost his mind. "What for?" demanded Lord Fiergan.

"This plague is spreading," Athlone answered as calmly as he could. The other men winced at the word "plague," for it was the first time anyone had spoken it aloud. "We need to contain it quickly and get the victims away from the healthy. The only tent large enough to hold the eleven people we have now is this one, and there will probably be more sick to come. Clean it out, set it up as a hospital, and keep everyone but the healers away."

"I think we should leave," Lord Terod said, his voice loud with nervousness. "There are none in my clan sick yet. I'm going to pack and get away from here."

Two or three other chiefs muttered in agreement.

"That would not be wise," Athlone stated flatly. "What if your clan is stricken? How would you deal with the sick while you're on the move? How could your healer take care of them by himself? What if you came in contact with a caravan or a band of Turics and spread the sickness to other people?"

"You're assuming my clan already has the disease!"

"How do you know they don't? Look at Morbiar. Did you know he was sick this morning?" Athlone pointed out.

Terod looked around wildly as if seeking support, but the other chiefs only watched in silence. "No!" he cried. "But I see no reason to stay here and risk dying!"

Athlone strode up to him, his expression as unyielding as a granite wall. "I see many reasons! We cannot split up. Not now. We have to fight this together. Join our minds and our healers and our prayers to find a cure. If you leave, where will you go? We are surrounded by leagues of emptiness! If your clan is out on the trail somewhere, dying for lack of help, and we find a way to stop this disease, we might not be able to reach you in time!"

From his position near Lord Athlone, Sayyed saw the war of indecision on young Terod's face—fear of the plague if he stayed, terror if it caught his clan alone out on the empty plains, and a flicker of hope that they just might find a cure. Sayyed understood how he felt. Anxiety for Rafnir had preyed relentlessly on his mind since Ritan had died. He wanted more than life itself to get his family out of the path of the deadly pestilence, but he knew Lord Athlone was right. Their only hope was to stay together and look for some means to stop the epidemic.

The other men seemed to accept that, too. They stirred and nodded among themselves, the immobility of shock wearing off as they realized there was a war to be fought. Terod backed away from Athlone and stamped to the entrance of the tent.

"Clan Amnok will stay," he said, his words harsh. "But I am posting guards around my camp. No one goes in or out without my permission." He turned on his heel and left.

"Actually that's not a bad idea," Koshyn said, moving to help the fallen Morbiar. "We should postpone the rest of the gathering activities and limit movement of our people until we see how far this disease is going to spread."

His suggestion was immediately accepted, and within the hour, the vast, busy gathering began to take on the appearance of a besieged encampment. The council tent had been cleared of the rugs, cushions, and trappings of a meeting place to make way for the sick. The race grounds, the shallows where the women gathered to chat and wash laundry, and the meadows where the children liked to play were all empty. Armed men guarded the camps' perimeters and patrolled the virtually empty bazaar. Only the outriders who rode guard on the herds grazing in scattered pastures along the valley were allowed to leave the area. The women and children stayed close to their tents. The priests of Surgart and Sorh and the priestesses of Amara gathered on the sacred island of the Tir Samod to pray for aid from the deities. That day, and through the coming days, their fires burned within the temple of standing stones, and their voices were heard in an unending chant of supplication.

By nightfall, eight more people had been brought to the council tent.

Sayyed was helping several other men haul water to a large barrel for use by the healers when he heard a small, feminine voice calling his name. He hesitated, peering into the thick twilight. The unfamiliar voice spoke in his mind in the manner of the Hunnuli.

Then he heard a yowling noise. *Sayyed!* He saw a flash of white, and a small creature charged from the grass to his boots. It meowed sharply. *Come! Come!* the voice cried in his thoughts. *She needs you.*

In a flash of dread he recognized Tam's cat. His bucket dropped to the ground, and he raced after the dimly seen form running ahead of him. Rafnir! his heart cried. Not his son, please! They reached the Khulinin camp, charged past the guards without stopping, and ran for his tent.

The dogs were cowering by the entrance when he arrived; even the goats were quiet, huddled in a wide-eyed group. Sayyed was so upset, he paid little attention to them or to the two Hunnuli standing by the tent. Tam's black horse was perfectly still, his head held high in distress. Afer, Sayyed's stallion, neighed urgently for him to hurry.

Sayyed dashed after the cat into the tent, expecting to see his son, and stopped dead in his tracks. His soul was struck with a numbing despair. All the time he had worried about Rafnir, he had never imagined his wife could get sick.

Yet there she lay on their pallet, her face scarlet with the heat of her body, tears welling from her eyes. When she saw Sayyed, she tried to rise in a vain attempt to keep away from him. "No, no, my love," she whispered hoarsely when he knelt by her side. "Do not come near me."

He ignored her pleas and gently pushed her back onto their bed. Using a handy cloth, he began to wipe the perspiration from her face. The little white cat crouched by Tam's head, her golden eyes enormous. She was purring frantically as if trying to reassure her mistress.

"Maybe it's something else," Sayyed said desperately. "A cold, bad food, or an insect bite. Spider bites always make you sick."

"It's not spiders and you know it," she replied with a flash of her old spirit.

Sayyed did know it. He could see the track of the disease in the heat of her skin and in the swellings under her jaw. "Then you know what I have to do," he said, his voice breaking.

Her chin trembled. "What you must."

Never in his life had Sayyed had to do anything so difficult as pick up Tam's slight form and carry her in his arms from their tent. She clung to him while he walked slowly down the path, the two Hunnuli close behind. Neither one could find the words they wanted to say. The Khulinin guards at the edge of camp took one look at his burden and stepped sadly out of his way. Sayyed didn't even see them through the dark fog that was descending on his mind. Almost blindly he bore his wife down to the council tent and into the dimly lit interior. Three rows of pallets had been laid down for the sick, and a fire was burning in the central hearth. The four healers on duty were so busy caring for their patients they did not notice Sayyed come in.

With shaking hands he laid Tam on a pallet beside the tent wall. He knew he had only a moment to say something to her before one of the healers saw him and forced him to leave, but how could he put twenty-three years of friendship and love into a few meager words? This woman had saved his life, loved him, borne his son, and given him a world of laughter and joy. How could he leave her here alone to die? Tears clogged his throat, and he groped for her hand.

Something soft brushed past his arm. The white cat had followed him down from the camp and was nestling into the blanket by Tam's shoulder. Just outside the canvas walls the two Hunnuli nickered to her.

Tam tried to smile. "I am not alone now. Go my husband. Care for our son. Remember our love," she whispered.

Sayyed's head dropped. "I'll be back when I can." He brushed a finger over her cheek, then stumbled to his feet and fled from the tent.

4

Kelene woke in the middle of the night feeling uncomfortably hot. Her eyes opened blearily to an unfamiliar glow, and she saw her mother hunched over the *Book of Matrah,* trying to read the pages of the old tome of sorcery by the light of a single hand lamp. She blinked her eyes and dazedly wondered why she was so hot. Her blanket was soaked with sweat, and something heavy lay pressed against her left side.

All at once she sat up, her heart pounding. Coren had crawled onto the pallets beside her that evening and fallen asleep. At some time he had rolled over almost on top of her. He looked strangely flushed in the dim light of the lamp, so Kelene laid her hand on his damp forehead. It was the first time she had ever tried her empathic touch on a sick person. The results shocked her. She could sense the symptoms of Coren's illness as clearly as his fear and confusion.

"Mother!" she cried.

Her voice woke everyone in the tent. Gabria rushed to her feet and hurried to kneel by Kelene's side. Coren was half awake and breathing rapidly. "My throat hurts, Mamma," he mumbled.

Kelene eased out from under him and gently stretched him out on the pallet. "His temperature is rising," she said to her mother, trying to keep the fear from her voice for Coren's sake. "His throat is starting to swell, and he's losing consciousness fast. You've got to do something!"

Gabria took a cloth and wiped Coren's skin. Her hands were shaking. "I've read the *Book of Matrah* from cover to cover and I can't find a single healing spell," she cried softly. "I don't know what I *can* do."

"There's got to be something we can try," Kelene insisted. "Maybe we could wrap him in damp blankets to lower his temperature."

Athlone and Lymira came to kneel by Coren's side, their faces deeply worried. "Perhaps we could transfer some of our strength to Coren to help his body fight the disease," Athlone offered.

Gabria considered that. Magic-wielders used a combination of mental and physical strength to control the power of magic. They often joined their strength together to maintain difficult spells, but Gabria had never tried giving her energy to a much smaller, weaker person who was unable to control his own power. She didn't know what to expect. She could only hope that the combination of the added strength and lower body temperature would give Coren the help he needed to beat the disease invading his body.

She nodded at last, without lifting her eyes from her son's face. "It's worth a try."

Kelene and Lymira grabbed two blankets from the pallets and together dashed from the tent to the river. They were back in a few minutes, lugging the wet blankets between them, and they wrapped the cool fabric over and around their little brother. He moaned once before lapsing into a restless sleep.

Ever so carefully Gabria laid her fingers on Coren's head and trickled some of her own considerable strength through her fingertips into the boy's body. Athlone and Lymira watched and waited, while Kelene kept her hands pressed flat to Coren's arm, her eyes closed as if concentrating on something only she could hear.

The spell seemed to work at first. Coren's breathing slowed and the fiery red in his cheeks faded to a dull flush. Kelene opened her eyes, looked up at Gabria, and smiled. Then her smile slipped. "His heart is beating faster," Kelene whispered.

Gabria, leaning closer, saw it was true. Coren's pulse pounded in his neck; he began to struggle to breathe.

"Mother, stop!" Kelene cried at once. "Stop! He can't take it."

Gabria yanked her fingers away and stared in dismay at her son. His pulse slowed down to normal, but the deadly red flush crept back into his face. When she touched him again, his skin was fiery hot.

"I'm sorry," Kelene said, on the verge of tears. "His body couldn't tolerate the added strength. It was making his heart work too hard."

Lymira looked at her older sister with some surprise. "How did you know that?" she asked quietly, but Kelene only glanced at her distracted parents and shook her head.

A bitter silence filled the chief's tent. The family stared at one another in a confusion of anxiety and dismay. No one knew what to say in the face of their disappointment. They understood what had to be done next—no matter how desperately they wanted to avoid it—but no one was ready to make the first move.

Gabria's own mind felt paralyzed. "I won't take him down there," she whispered finally.

"We have to," said Athlone. The hard truth trembled on the edge of his voice.

Gabria shuddered as if shaking off his words. "No!"

"Gabria, there is no choice. We tried, but we can't stop his fever. Now we have to keep the disease from spreading."

"It already has!" she hissed as she grasped Coren's hand in her own.

The chieftain blinked hard and nodded toward their daughters. "Do you want it to go farther?"

Gabria said nothing while she grappled with her fears. She knew Athlone was right, but she also knew that, so far, not one person had recovered from this disease. Every instinct in her screamed not to abandon her little boy to the council tent.

Her chin lifted. "Then I will take him," she said quietly, "and I will stay with him."

Lymira gasped with dismay. Kelene looked wildly at their father to stop Gabria. But he only looked from Coren's feverish face to Gabria's set expression.

"It has been two days since you set up the hospital. There are over forty sick people by now and more coming every day. The healers are being overwhelmed," she said, her voice soft and full of resignation. "They need help. If I go, I can give Coren and Tam the attention they need and do what I can to aid the healers."

"You won't be able to come back here right away," Athlone reminded her.

"Mother, you can't go!" Lymira cried. Tears trickled down her fair face, and her eyes were enormous in the dim light.

Gabria touched her cheek. "I'll be all right. Just pray to Amara to watch over Coren." She scooped the boy into her arms and stood up, her features fixed with a grim determination. The chieftain picked off her golden cloak from a loop on the tent pole, draped it over her shoulders, and pushed aside the flap.

Gabria gave her daughters a smile of love and encouragement and, with Athlone at her side, walked out into the darkness. Nara and Eurus left their customary places by the tent to come with them. Silently Athlone and Gabria made their way down the empty paths toward the council grove. The night was muggy and warm, and lightning flickered on the northern horizon. Coren lay still, his eyes closed and his fingers wrapped around the folds of Gabria's rumpled tunic.

At the edge of camp, Athlone stopped to say a few words to the guards. Gabria waited quietly while they talked, treasuring these last few moments alone with her son. She was staring at Coren's face when, without warning, the two Hunnuli neighed a furious challenge.

Gabria's head snapped up. Just beyond, in the dense black shadows of the night, hovered a form. Tall as a man, nebulous as smoke, it glowed with a lurid red light that repulsed her. She curved her body protectively over her son, her mouth twisted in a snarl of rage. "No! Stay away from me," she screamed. "You will not get this child!"

In one motion, Athlone and the guards drew their swords and lunged toward the form. At the same time, the Hunnuli charged forward. But Gabria was faster. Shifting Coren's weight to one arm, she raised her free hand and sent a brilliant blue bolt of magical energy searing past the horses toward the phantom figure. The bolt lit up the grass with its radiance as it streaked toward its target.

It struck the form dead-center, only to pass through and explode harmlessly on the ground behind it.

The ghastly form emanated a sound like harsh laughter and vanished, leaving behind a putrid smell of rotten carrion. The men came to a stop by Gabria.

"Gods above!" one of the guards exclaimed. "What was that thing?"

Gabria didn't answer. She had never seen a thing like that before. "Did you recognize that form?" she asked the Hunnuli.

Both horses were very agitated and upset. *No,* snorted Nara. *Hunnuli have never known anything like that.*

It smelled foul, Eurus added, the disgust heavy in his thought.

Whatever the form was, Gabria knew without a trace of doubt that it was evil. She had sensed a powerful cognizance in that brief moment of visibility and had felt an almost palpable aura of hate and obsession that sent her senses reeling. She clasped Coren tighter to her chest. The being wanted something, of that she was certain, something that seemed to be connected to this gathering and the clanspeople. There had to be more than just coincidence that the form and the epidemic had appeared at the same time.

She glanced at Athlone as he slid his sword back into its sheepskin scabbard and saw the angry, thoughtful lines on his face. He must have reached a similar conclusion, for he said, "I'm going to talk to Ordan."

He took her arm, and they continued warily across the open space toward the grove of trees by the river. The big tent in the center was lit from within by lamps and torches. They could see vague shadows moving across the canvas walls and the black shape of Tam's Hunnuli where he stood patiently by the tent, as close to his rider as he could be.

Even at that late hour there were people moving about the grove, some bringing in more supplies or more sick, some merely waiting for news of their loved ones. A sad, wrenching undertone of moans, cries of pain, and soft wailing filled the night air.

At the open entrance to the tent, Athlone stopped his wife and, cupping her chin in his hands, he looked down into the deep green jewels of her eyes to the love and courage he always found there. "I will do what I can," he said simply.

She leaned into his hand. "So will I."

He kissed her and Coren, then trudged away before his own courage faltered.

Gabria did not wait to see him go. She was afraid if she did, she would go running after him. Instead she forced herself to walk into the hot, noisy, reeking tent. Even then she almost fled.

Too much had changed for the worse since the tent had been transformed into a hospital. Forty-seven people of all ages now lay on pallets in several long rows. The clan healers had been working in shifts nonstop, but they were too few to keep up with the endless task of helping so many seriously ill people. The tent was a mess of discarded rags, bandages, dirty blankets, old poultices, and buckets brimming with indescribable contents. The combined heavy smells of blood, vomit, torch smoke, and burning incense struck Gabria's nose in a raw stench. A few of the sick were crying, many were unconscious, and judging from the still, covered forms lying at one end of the tent, some were already dead. Worse, Gabria saw two of the healers, one Jehanan and the other a Wylfling, lying among the sick.

She was looking for a place to put Coren when Gehlyn came hurrying past the pallets. "Lady Gabria, please. Give me your son and leave. I will do what I can for him."

She took a close look at the healer's face and was deeply concerned by what she saw. "You can barely take care of yourself, Gehlyn. Have you had any sleep or food?"

He grimaced. "I'm not hungry."

"You're not well, either!"

"I can still care for the sick," he said forcefully, even though he looked like he could barely stand.

"So can I," Gabria returned mildly. "I am not leaving my son alone here."

"But, Lady . . ."

She shook her head. "Victims are coming faster than the healers can handle. You need help." Before he could argue further. she found an open place in the row near Tam and laid Coren down on a blanket. A gasp of dismay slipped out at the sight of her friend. The poisonous boils had spread over Tam's body, and even as Gabria stood immobile, the woman suddenly retched and vomited blood over her chest and neck. The white cat meowed piteously.

Gehlyn picked up a scrap of cloth and moved to clean up the blood, but Gabria plucked the rag from his fingers. Kneeling by Tam's side, she swallowed hard to force down her tears and gently wiped away the blood and vomit.

Tam's eyes flickered open once, and a ghostly smile crossed her lips. Then she sighed and slipped again into unconsciousness.

Gabria looked up, stricken. "Have you found anything that will help these people?"

Gehlyn bowed his head, his gray gaze nearly lost in the shadows around his eyes. "We've tried everything," he groaned. "Every powder, poultice, infusion, herb, or mixture we could find. We interrogated the merchants and searched through their foreign medicines. All in vain. There is nothing in our experiences or our tales that gives us any help. The only thing that has given the sick some slight relief is a plant from the north called angelica. A merchant from Pra Desh had it. He said it was used in his city to ward off the plague. We tried making a strong tea of cottonwood buds and angelica, and it seems to ease the fever for a short while, but we are almost out of our supply."

"Show me where it is," Gabria said tersely.

The healer hesitated while he tried to think of some way to get her to leave, then, with a weary shrug, he decided it was too late. The healers did need help badly, and besides, it was very difficult to win an argument against Lady Gabria. He picked a way through the mess of debris, belongings, and pallets and led Gabria to the fire pit in the center of the tent. A small cauldron was simmering over a low bed of coals tended by a sleepy young apprentice.

Gehlyn picked up a pitifully small handful of dried leaves and small white flowers. "This is all there is."

Without a reply, Gabria took them from his hand and went outside the tent. Gehlyn followed curiously. He watched while she pulled several handfuls of grass and put them in a pile by the entrance.

When she was satisfied, Gabria came to kneel by the pile. She laid the angelica down beside it and stayed there studying the small white flowers, the thick stalks, and the leaves. The flowers had a faint, honeylike fragrance, and the stalk had a sweet, hardy flavor that reminded Gabria of anise.

As soon as she was certain that she knew the plant well enough, she closed her eyes and began to pull in the forces of magic around her. Her words formed a spell that shaped the magic to her bidding; her strength of will put the spell into motion. She raised her hand over the pile of grass, and before Gehlyn could ask what she was doing, she transformed the grass into a heap of angelica.

"It's not much," she said apologetically as she handed the stalks to the healer, "but I've never tried that spell with an unfamiliar plant. I will make more later if this is effective."

He gazed down at her handiwork and a weary smile warmed his face. "That's why you needed the grass," he remarked.

Gabria touched the stalks in his hand. "Magic-wielders cannot create things out of thin air." She sighed a breath of frustration. "There are a great many things we cannot do."

"Well, thank you for the herbs," he said gratefully. "I don't suppose you can use magic to heal these people."

She bit her lip. "I've thought of nothing else. But I don't know how. We have lost all the old skills."

"Didn't the sorcerers at Moy Tura have healing records?"

At the mention of Moy Tura, something shifted in Gabria's memory. There had been a reference to an old healing guild in a book she had read in the library at the Citadel of Krath. A guild could explain why there were no healing spells in the *Book of Matrah* and the lack of oral history about healing spells. "How do you know?" she asked.

Gehlyn said, "Piers told me when he gave me the healing stone."

Ah, yes, the red healing stone—a priceless link to an ancient art, made solely to remove traces of harmful magic from a victim. Piers Arganosta had had it for years before passing it on to his apprentice. Gabria's face grew very thoughtful.

She was about to reply when a voice called to her from the night. Sayyed came hurrying toward her. Gehlyn ordered him back, but Gabria laid a hand on the healer's sleeve and shook her head. "I'll talk to him," she insisted softly.

The healer nodded once to her request and slipped back into the tent with the angelica.

"Gabria!" Sayyed called. "I saw you come out. I know she's still alive. Is she getting better? May I see her?"

Gabria tried to find the words to answer, but her expression told him everything he needed to know. His handsome face seemed to age before her eyes.

"For two days I've hoped," he murmured. Abruptly he strode forward and seized her arms. "Please! Let me see her! I don't care if I get sick. I have to see Tam!"

"I care!" Gabria snapped. Her hands clenched his arms in turn, and she shook him. "She wouldn't want you to see her like she is, or to catch this plague. If you go into that tent, you will have to stay there under quarantine. Then who will be with Rafnir? Who will take care of Tam's animals?" She spat out anything she could think of to change his mind, but she might as well have argued with a wall.

He pulled her hands off and ran into the tent before she could stop him. By the time she reached him, he was squatting by Tam's pallet, carefully mopping her face with one hand and scratching her white cat with the other. Sadly Gabria left him alone. Sayyed had made his own decision and could be as implacable as she.

She spent the rest of that long, long night caring for her son, organizing the apprentices to clear up the mess in the tent, and feeding cupful after cupful of warm tea to every victim who could still swallow. Four more people died, including Lord Morbiar, in the cool hours before dawn. Fifteen new victims were left by terrified relatives at the entrance to the tent.

At sunrise the healers decided that they would need more tents for the sick and more help. They sent a message to arrange a meeting with the clan chieftains, then bitterly carried the bodies of the dead out to the meadow where the previous funeral pyre had left a black, smoldering ring. There, grieving families identified their dead and another pyre was built. Gabria had a dread feeling that it would not be the last.

The clans struggled as best they could that day to adjust to the panic and fear that was spreading through the camps faster than the plague. Not a clan had been left untouched by the disease; not an age, rank, or sex was immune.

The worst of it was that no one could say for sure where this epidemic had sprung from. It had come from nowhere like a lightning bolt that strikes dry tinder and sets off a fire storm. Priest Ordan, Lord Athlone, and Lady Gabria were forming their own vague opinions about what had bred the deadly pestilence. But the vast majority of the clanspeople had only their superstitions and imaginations. Speculation ran rife and, despite the patrolling guards and the strictly enforced curfews, rumors and unrest spread through the camps like locusts as the people tried to find something or someone to blame.

Some believed the opening of the sealed mound had brought the wrath of Sorh down on the clans; some thought the rivers had been poisoned; and others blamed the foreign merchants. A few, especially among the priests and the Reidhar clan, blamed magic, and even they couldn't agree. Several priests decided the gods were punishing the clans for not rooting out the heresy of magic at their first opportunity, while the Reidhar speculated that magic, an evil corrupting power, was itself out of control and destroying all who stood in its way.

Whatever their reasoning, the people of Valorian did everything they could think of to defend themselves and their families against the silent killer. They drank bitter draughts of bayberry and wine vinegar to keep up their resistance to disease. On the advice of foreign merchants familiar with plagues, the clanspeople hung bundles of rue and feverfew in their tents, burned incense, and wore amulets of amber to ward off the disease. All to no avail. People fell ill in every corner of the gathering with no apparent cause or reason.

To the clans the world around them became disjointed and terrifying. The people didn't know who or what to trust or where to turn for help. Nothing seemed to be safe. Families were torn apart by the disease. Fights broke out among clan members over minor things, and discipline became increasingly difficult. A party of Turic merchants had to be tracked down and forcibly returned to the gathering after they tried to sneak away.

The chieftains did their best to calm their people and maintain some semblance of order, but they were hardpressed by the overwhelming demands of their responsibilities. The death of Lord Morbiar hit them hard, reminding them of their own vulnerability.

The chiefs spent most of that day supervising efforts in their own clans, so it was late afternoon before the healers had the chance to talk to them in a group. Across an open space of fifteen paces, Gehlyn and his companions faced Lord Athlone and seven other chiefs. Lord Terod was nowhere to be seen, and Lord Dormar was already within the tent in a fever-induced delirium.

"We need more tents, more blankets, clothes, buckets, and water. We also need more food," Gehlyn told them.

Athlone turned to the other chiefs, who wearily nodded. Healers and chieftains alike were exhausted from lack of sleep and overwork. Lord Koshyn especially was looking haggard under his tan. "Done," Athlone replied.

Gehlyn went on grimly. "It would also be a good idea to send crews to cut more wood and to dig a large pit in the meadow."

The significance of his words was not lost on any of the chiefs. They stirred uneasily. "Is that necessary?" demanded Lord Fiergan, his eyebrows drawn together in a fierce anger.

Gehlyn made a convulsive gesture of frustrated anger. "The dead must be burned. Do you want to make matters worse by leaving them to rot? Do we dishonor our kinsmen by throwing their bodies in the river? Do *you* want to be left for the dogs and the carrion birds?"

Fiergan's scowl deepened. "All right, all right. We'll find woodcutters. Is that all?"

"Yes," Gehlyn sighed. "For now."

The healers nodded their thanks and walked back toward the tent. The chiefs, looking grim, prepared to leave to make the arrangements for the badly needed supplies.

Lord Athlone was talking to Koshyn when he saw Gabria come out of the tent. Relieved to see her, he lifted his hand to wave. She was raising her hand to return the greeting when all at once she stiffened. Athlone saw her head jerk toward Tam's Hunnuli; he yanked his attention to the stallion just in time to see the horse suddenly shudder from nose to heel. At the same instant, Athlone and every magic-wielder in the vicinity were assaulted by a mental scream of grief that brought them to their knees.

The black stallion reared, his hooves slashing at the canvas tent, his head thrown so far back the stunned people thought he would crash over backward. A long, heartrending cry tore from his throat. The terrible sound echoed through the camps and brought everyone to a shocked standstill.

Everyone but the other Hunnuli. They came galloping to the grove from every direction until all thirty-three Hunnuli in the clans were gathered by Tam's stallion. He reared again, and this time the other horses neighed to him a message that sounded as mournful as a dirge. The moment his feet touched the ground, he spun on his heels and galloped from the grove toward the west. Transfixed, the clanspeople watched him until he vanished somewhere into the hills.

Movement came back to the people in fits and starts as they tried to understand what had just happened.

"By all that's holy," exploded Fiergan. "What was that all about?"

Athlone knelt on the ground, his body shaking. With Koshyn's help, he managed to climb to his feet and straighten under a crushing weight of sorrow. "A magic-wielder has died," he told them. "Tam, the wife of my friend, Sayyed. That was her Hunnuli." He closed his eyes, wishing more than anything he could break quarantine and go to his wife.

Gabria was kneeling by the tent entrance, her head buried in her hands. "Nara!" she cried in misery. She felt the Hunnuli mare close by, and she reached out to grab the horse's knee. Using Nara's foreleg for support, Gabria pulled herself to her feet. She buried her face in the mare's thick, black mane. "What happened? Where did he go?" she cried.

He is gone. Nara told her.

"Gone! Gone where?"

The mare's thoughts were almost more than Gabria could bear. *He and Tam were as one. Without her he cannot be whole again. He will go where he can join her.*

Grief rolled over Gabria. She clung to her horse, sobbing for the double loss of her dear friend and the Hunnuli that was Nara's second-born. It was all Gabria could do to leave the mare and stumble into the tent. She made her way to Tam's pallet where Sayyed was sitting, staring down at his wife's still body. Her face was peaceful in spite of the ravages of the plague, but the vibrant expression and the lively light of her eyes was gone.

Sayyed did not move when Gabria sat down beside him. He said nothing as she leaned against his shoulder, tears still streaming down her face. His entire body was rigid and straight as a lance. His face was drained of all humor, feeling, and warmth. He sat oblivious to everything: to Gabria, the activity in the tent, to the Hunnuli still gathered outside, and to the white cat huddled miserably by his knee. He simply stared at Tam's white face as if he could not believe what he was seeing.

Gabria watched him and felt her heart break. When he made no move to cover Tam's face, Gabria gently wrapped a blanket over the woman's body and left Sayyed alone. Cold and aching, she went to sit by her son and wondered how much longer Coren would be able to fight for his life.

The rest of the afternoon passed quietly enough. The clanspeople, deeply shocked by the disappearance of Tam's Hunnuli, were subdued and pensive. A magic-wielder and Hunnuli had not died in the years since Gabria befriended Nara, and no one, not even the magic-wielders, had realized how permanent the friendship between horse and rider could be. The people wondered what was going to happen if another magic-wielder died. Had Tam and her horse been unique, or would other Hunnuli leave to join their riders in the realm of the dead?

No one felt inclined to ask the Hunnuli themselves. The horses remained outside the council tent, keeping vigil with Sayyed in his grief. Silent and still, they waited while the long, difficult day waned to a close.

It was late evening before Sayyed stirred. From outside the tent, the loved voice of his Hunnuli, Afer, spoke soundlessly into his thoughts. *Rafnir is here, Sayyed. He wishes to come in.*

A jolt of dread brought him out of his stupor. "No!" he rasped. "Keep him out." With an effort he climbed to his feet, his knees stiff as old wood, and lifted Tam into his arms. Her slight body was lighter than the last time he had carried her, but the weight of his grief was almost more than he could bear. Oblivious to those around him, he staggered outside and came face-to-face with the Hunnuli herd waiting for him. Their large, luminous eyes glimmered with pale stars in the deep twilight; their shapes were ebony shadows.

Behind them, he saw Rafnir pacing, sadness, anger, and frustration clouding his lean face. The young man stopped when he saw his father and the wrapped body in his arms. Lord Athlone, Kelene, Lymira, and Savaron came to stand beside Rafnir. Gabria emerged from the tent and joined the Hunnuli.

In silence, Afer stepped up to Sayyed. The warrior placed his wife's body on the stallion's broad back, and they walked together toward the meadows where the other bodies of the dead had gone to the funeral pyres. Nara, Demira, Eurus, the rest of the black horses, the six Khulinin, and one little white cat followed behind.

The funeral fires from that day had burned down to hot embers that glowed yellow and orange in the dusk. A priest of Sorh stood guard over the place and two more bodies that had been brought that afternoon. He made no protest when Sayyed and Gabria began to pile more wood onto the coals. In minutes the fire was blazing again in long, dancing flames that leaped toward the stars.

While the priest chanted the prayers of the dead and the Hunnuli watched, Sayyed carried Tam's body to the pyre. He paid no attention to the smoke that stung his eyes or the heat that singed his hands and sleeves; he didn't hear the roar of the hungry flames. All he could see was Tam's long, brown braid that dropped out of the blanket wrappings as he pushed his wife into the fire. He stared, hollow-eyed, while the brown hair and its bright ribbons smoked and burst into orange flame. Gabria had to pull him back before his own clothes caught fire.

The priest, the mourners, and the Hunnuli watched the fire burn long into the night. So intent were the people on the pyre, they did not see Sayyed mount Afer and disappear into the night.

* * *

The sun was hot and high in the sky before Rafnir found his father sitting on Afer at the top of a ridge several leagues from the Tir Samod. The warrior was staring out over the bluffs of the Goldrine River toward the south. His expression was hopelessly bleak; his body sagged in the filthy, smoky clothes he had worn for four days.

Rafnir's Hunnuli came quietly to stand by Afer, who turned his head in greeting. The young man sat on his horse without saying a word and waited for his father to notice him.

Sayyed stirred after a while. "I almost left," he said, his gaze still far to the south. "I was going to go back to the desert."

Rafnir shifted on his horse's back. He wasn't surprised. There was still a lot of Turic left in Sayyed's heart. "I hope you won't," he murmured.

With an effort, the warrior shook his head. "Even with her gone, there is still more for me here." His voice nearly choked off, then he pushed on. "It seems so senseless. I can't believe she's gone."

There was little Rafnir could say to that. He couldn't believe it either. The fact of his mother's death was too enormous for him to face so soon. He swallowed hard and said, "Lady Gabria asked me to find you. She wants your help."

Sayyed bowed his head and turned Afer back toward the gathering. He didn't ask what Gabria wanted. He was too numb to care. All that mattered in the haze of his pain was that she needed him.

The council grove was in an uproar when Sayyed and Rafnir returned. Seven new tents, borrowed from several different clans, had been erected in the grove near the council tent. A surprising number of people were moving back and forth between them.

"At last count over eighty people are sick," Rafnir explained. "The healers gave up trying to handle it alone. They've decided to allow anyone who dares attend to the sick—as long as they stay quarantined."

Sayyed accepted this news with a dull nod. Then his attention was drawn to two widely separated knots of people that had gathered on the point of land between the rivers near the shore of the sacred island. It was obvious from the distant noise and angry gestures on all sides that several arguments were in full cry.

The two Hunnuli lengthened their stride to a trot that carried them across the river's ford and up the bank into the grove. Sayyed saw Gabria, Gehlyn, and several healers standing in one isolated group while Lords Athlone and Koshyn, in the forefront of another group, were standing nearly in the water of the river's confluence. Athlone had finally urged Ordan to leave the temple long enough to talk to him, and he was speaking animatedly with the priest as several clan chieftains, a party of bazaar merchants, and a handful of other people quarreled and jostled around them.

"Lord Athlone, this situation is intolerable!" a merchant from the south was hollering. "We will not be held here against our will."

Lord Fiergan, his eyebrows bristling, was berating Gabria and the healers across the space that divided them. "Why aren't you doing more to find a cure? What good are all of your powders and teas if you can't even stop a fever?"

"We're running low on fresh meat. If we don't send hunters out soon, we'll have to start butchering some of the stock," a second chieftain was saying.

And Lord Terod, a jagged edge in his voice, was telling anyone who would listen, "I think we should leave this place. The gods have put a curse on us here. Let's go back to our own holdings where the plague can't reach us."

In the midst of all the racket, Athlone ignored the merchants and his fellow chiefs and continued to talk urgently to Ordan. His hands made short, pointed gestures as he spoke.

Sayyed watched it all as if from a long distance. He had no real interest in what was being said, for it was taking all of his concentration and strength to keep the fierce grief in his heart from tearing him apart. He sat on Afer near the healers' group and waited for Gabria to acknowledge him.

He might have sat there all day if a frantic yowl hadn't suddenly pierced through the noise around him. Sayyed's back snapped straight, his hands clenched into fists, and a roar of fury burst from his lips.

A priest in red robes was striding through the grove toward the river, carrying Tam's cat by the scruff of the neck. He held the struggling animal up high, and over the voices of the people he shouted, "Here is the cause of our affliction! This foreign vermin beast! Look at it. It is white, the color of sorcery, the color of evil. I say drown it! Sacrifice this creature to appease the gods!"

Before he could think about what he was doing, Sayyed raised his hand and sent a blast of blue energy exploding into the ground at the priest's feet. The man stopped as if he had walked into a tree. The whole council grove was stunned into silence.

"Put that cat down!" bellowed Sayyed. "She is nothing more than an animal, a pet. She is no more evil than a dog or a horse, and if you harm one hair on her, I'll sear you where you stand!"

"Blasphemy!" screeched the outraged priest.

"Put it down, Serit," Ordan demanded in a voice that brooked no argument. "The cat is not the cause of our calamity."

The younger priest's arm dropped reluctantly. Red-faced and fuming, he flung the cat away and watched in disgust as she streaked through a forest of human legs and leaped frantically up Sayyed's boot to land in his lap. Once there, she crouched, ears flat, and hissed at the priest.

"And you, Sayyed, owe these people an apology," Ordan said fiercely. "I know you are distraught, but it is against clan law to use the Trymian force in the council grove."

Apologizing was the last thing Sayyed wanted to do. His fury was aroused and any emotion felt better than the grief that filled his heart. Unfortunately, Ordan was correct. Sayyed knew he could not make matters right by venting his rage with magic. He dismounted and, holding the cat tightly, bowed before Ordan. "Forgive me," he said, forcing the words past his anger. "This cat has become very precious to me."

Ordan's eyebrows eased out of their frown. "That is no excuse for breaking the council's laws," he said a little less angrily.

"So punish him!" shouted Serit. The priest came stamping up to Ordan. He was a Murjik, short-legged, stocky, and flat-faced. His disgust for magic was a fact he voiced at every opportunity. "If it is not that beast, then what *is* the reason for this plague that kills us? I say it is the flagrant use of magic that has angered our gods." Athlone made a warning noise in his throat that Serit ignored. "Fulfill the laws, Ordan! Perhaps the death of this heretical heathen will appease the gods' wrath against us."

Sayyed clenched his jaw and ground out, "There have been too many deaths already, priest. Your gods should be delighted by now!" He felt a warning hand on his sleeve and looked to see Gabria by his side, her grimy, tired face full of concern.

"Magic has nothing to do with this," Lord Koshyn argued.

Fiergan snorted. "How do you know? How can we be certain that sorcery has not angered the gods?"

"Why would Sorh wait twenty-three years to punish us for allowing sorcery to return to the clans?" demanded Koshyn irritably.

The Reidhar chief glared. "Why not? Who is to say why the immortals do anything?"

"Your priests!" Sayyed snapped. "Don't they study the stars and the omens? Don't they pray and sing day and night? Why don't they have an answer?"

"Sometimes there is no answer," Ordan replied heavily.

At that, the uproar broke out again on all sides. Serit shouted at Ordan, and Lord Koshyn exchanged heated comments with Fiergan. Gehlyn was trying to say, "It's just a disease, like smallpox or the sleeping fever. Does there have to be an excuse?"

"I still think we should take our clans away from here," Terod insisted.

Voices rose higher and louder until finally a piercing whistle split the noise. All eyes turned in astonishment to Gabria. Her husband smiled gratefully.

"Thank you," she said into the silence. "Ordan, my husband has told you of my vision and the strange apparition I have seen. Do you know what to make of that?"

Ordan looked troubled. "Others have reported to me of seeing this glowing figure, Lady. It is apparently growing stronger and becoming more visible. But nothing in our traditions can tell me what this portends."

"What are you talking about?" demanded Fiergan.

Lord Athlone answered, "An unearthly form like a man that walks at night and glows with an eerie light. Several of us have seen it."

"Could that be the cause of our plague?" Koshyn asked the priest.

"Possibly. The coincidence of its appearance at this time is very provoking," said Ordan.

Gehlyn threw up his hands. "Apparition, poisoned water, magic, or curses. The results are the same. People are dying! We must find a way to cure this disease!"

"There is one possibility," said Gabria. She deliberately looked at Ordan, Sayyed, and Gehlyn in turn before she finished, "The city of the sorcerers: Moy Tura."

Fiergan sneered. "Of all the dung-headed ideas. How is that cursed old ruin going to help us now?"

But Gehlyn understood. "The healers," he breathed.

Gabria nodded. "Before the downfall of sorcery and the massacre of the sorcerers, the art of healing was more advanced. Maybe these healers who lived in

Moy Tura knew of plagues like this; maybe they found a way to fight them and left a description of that cure in their records. If we could find those—"

"And if horses had wings they could fly!" Fiergan interrupted scornfully. "Are you sure you're not feverish, Lady? Those sound like the ravings of an over-heated head."

"I haven't heard you offer any suggestion, feverish or otherwise," the sorceress retorted. "It's a chance only. A slim one at best. But what do we have to lose? Send a small party of magic-wielders—their Hunnuli are the only horses that could get there in time—and have them search the ruins."

"What about the Korg, the stone lion that guards the city?" asked Rafnir.

"That is a danger they will have to face," admitted Gabria.

Gehlyn said, "What if they get sick?"

"That, too, is a chance they must be prepared for."

Fiergan was still not convinced. "This sounds like a fool's mission to me."

Gabria rounded on him, fire in her eyes. "Yes, but with the survival of our people at stake, shouldn't we try every possibility . . . no matter how foolish?"

Sayyed had been silent during this exchange while he stared at the white cat in his arms. He knew now why Gabria had summoned him. This plan of hers was not an inspiration that had popped into her mind at that moment. She had been thinking about it for some time. That was as obvious as the look of inquiry that she was giving him, as clear as the dark smudges of grief that darkened her jewel-green eyes. She didn't want to ask him, he knew, but he was the oldest, most experienced magic-wielder after Athlone and herself, and he had been to Moy Tura once already.

Sharp and biting, his anger flared again. Something he could not feel or see or sense had killed his wife, some invisible enemy he could not burn with magic or hack with a sword. If there was a chance, no matter how risky or foolish, to fight this cruel killer, he would find it for the sake of Tam, for the sake of those people he loved poised on the brink of death.

He held the white cat close and said to everyone, "I'll go."

Ordan's wrinkled face creased into a half smile. "Your crime of using sorcery in the council grove is absolved, magic-wielder. The journey to Moy Tura should be punishment enough."

5

Kelene stood flabbergasted when her father told her she was to go with Sayyed's party to Moy Tura.

Her first reaction was "No!" Her response did not spring from fear. Part of it came from simple habit—her father informed her she had to do something, she automatically said "no."

The rest of it was simply confusion.

"Why?" she demanded. "Why do *I* have to go? What possible good will I do?"

Lord Athlone had no real answer for that because he wasn't sure *why* Gabria had insisted that Kelene go. "Because we want you to," he said flatly.

"That's ridiculous!" Kelene limped around the tent, flinging newly washed clothes around in a flurry of agitation. She and Lymira had taken over the duties of keeping the family tent and preparing meals, but Kelene was so upset she gave no thought to the laundry she had just finished. She turned to her father again, her dark eyes as hard and piercing as her grandfather Savaric's used to be when he was in his worst temper. "Father, you know I can't ride Ishtak that far, and I have no Hunnuli to ride. I would be better off here where I can help you than traipsing off across the plains after some moldy old records that probably don't even exist. Send Savaron or Lymira if you have to send someone."

Athlone crossed his arms, his expression implacable. "Savaron is going. Lymira is too young. We will find a mount for you to ride. Now you will pack some clothes and whatever belongings you need and you will be in the council grove before the sun moves another handspan."

Kelene was about to argue further when the tight note in her father's voice made her stop pacing and take a good look at him. She was immediately struck by how the past days had taken their toll on the powerful chieftain. His tanned face was gray, and lines of worry and grief cut deep around his features. His eyes were sunken into dark circles of fatigue.

For the first time, Kelene was forced to face the fact that her strong, loving father and mother were not invulnerable. They could become victims of this hideous sickness as readily as Coren. What if they fell ill and there was no help for them? Kelene could not bear the thought of losing her parents. So, what if her mother was right and there really was an answer in Moy Tura?

Kelene's stubborn resistance crumbled, and she squared her shoulders in a gesture that was totally hers. "All right! If you think it will do any good to send me, I'll go," she announced.

Athlone made a mock half bow. "Thank you." He turned on his heel and left the tent without another word.

Kelene stared after him, torn by resentment, anger, love, and fear. Then she snatched up her saddle pack and began to stuff clothes into it without thought or heed. Her sister's favorite gauze veil, her father's leather gloves, and Coren's torn pants found their way into her pack before she realized what she was doing. Irritably she pulled everything out, bit her lip in thought, and started over.

She was about to toss Coren's pants aside when an idea occurred to her. Why not? the young woman thought. If her mother had done it, so could she. She dug around in a bundle of old clothes—things too old to fit their former wearers but too useful yet to throw away—and found a pair of Savaron's drawstring pants cast aside when he moved to his own tent. Woven of undyed heavy cotton, they would be tough enough for a long journey but not too heavy for summer heat.

Kelene pulled them on, and with the judicious use of her small dagger, she altered them enough to fit her shorter legs. She tied the waist strings tight around her slender waist and nodded. The pants were baggy, but they would do. A bright red tunic laced down the front and her soft leather boots finished her outfit.

After that, she packed more carefully, taking only a thick blanket to sleep on, a few clean short-tunics, the split-legged skirt her mother had made for her, and some basic necessities. Last of all she tucked in the leather medicine bag the healer Piers had given her many years ago. She usually used the contents only on her horses, but the bag might be useful on a trip like this.

Just before she left the tent, Kelene coiled her hair behind her head to get it out of the way and grabbed her golden clan cloak and her packs. Backward glances were for weaklings, she decided on her way out. Yet she paused at the tent flap and glanced around at the empty home. So many frightening thoughts crowded into her mind of what she could find here when she returned—if she returned—that she wanted to dash back inside and tie the tent flap tight against the future.

Unfortunately that would be useless, she thought, giving her head a rueful shake. They would only send Savaron to drag her out. She shouldered her pack and limped slowly down the path toward the council grove beside the sparkling rivers.

By the time she arrived at the edge of the grove, a group of clanspeople and the rest of the party were already waiting for her. Savaron was there and Sayyed, whom Kelene had expected, as well as three other magic-wielders she knew from when they studied with her mother. They all greeted her, and she was about to return their greeting when she saw Rafnir mounted, packed, and obviously ready to go. Her heart sank. She was going to be stuck on a long, dangerous journey with her arch rival? The obnoxious, crop-toting rogue who took malicious delight in annoying her at every opportunity?

Already he was giving her clothes an appreciative grin, albeit a tired one. "Want to ride with me?" he called.

"I'd rather walk," Kelene snapped and wondered if she could change her mind about going. She would be useless on this journey, a cripple who wouldn't wield magic. What had her mother been thinking?

As if reading her daughter's thoughts, Gabria came up behind Kelene and said quietly, "I won't hug you because I am unclean, but I wanted to tell you that I am proud of you for going."

"I didn't have much choice," Kelene pointed out irritably, turning to face her mother.

Gabria nodded sadly. "Yes, you did. You have never done anything in your life that you did not agree to."

"But why do you want me to go? If you're trying to get me out of the plague, it won't work. Savaron, Sayyed, and I have all been close to sick people."

"No, I'm not trying to send you to safety. If I wanted that, I wouldn't have suggested that you go over two hundred leagues away to a ruin guarded by a crazy stone lion." Gabria lifted her hand as if to reach out to her daughter. "You have reached a difficult place in your life, Kelene, where you must choose a place for yourself in the clans. There is more to your womanhood than racing horses. I hope perhaps this journey will help you decide what you want to do."

Kelene made a sound like a half-laugh, half-snort of disbelief, and Gabria smiled a weary grimace. "You'll understand someday. Just say I sent you to take care of your brother. He can't boil water to feed himself." She paused and brought out a wrapped bundle. "I brought some angelica for you. I want you to take it, just in case. Now I have only one more thing to add." She took two brooches from the pouch on her belt and held them up to the sun. Two dazzling, scintillating lights flashed in her hands. "This is the Fallen Star given to your grandfather by Lord Medb, and this is the Watcher that we found after Medb's death. Do you remember?"

Kelene nodded. The magnificent gems were a part of the stories she had grown up with. They were ensorceled with a spell that enabled the bearer of the Watcher to see through the two gems to the wearer of the Fallen Star. Amazement warmed her when Gabria tucked the Watcher into the bundle of angelica and tossed it into Kelene's hands.

"Don't worry," Gabria said lightly. "You do not need to use magic to make this work. Simply concentrate on its center, and it will show you what the Star sees." She fastened the other brooch to her own dress and tapped its brilliant surface. "We won't be able to talk to one another, but as long as the Star's light is bright, I will know you are alive. Any time you want to check on us, you have only to look."

Kelene pinned the brooch to her tunic, trying hard to keep the tears from her eyes. "Thank you, Mother," she said. She surreptitiously wiped her face and added, "But I still don't have a mount."

Gabria chuckled. "I wondered about that, too. Savaron's Hunnuli could carry you, but it would be hard on him to carry a double load on such a long journey."

"So?" Kelene nudged.

"So. We found a volunteer."

"Who?" There were only a few young Hunnuli in the clans who had not already befriended a magic-wielder, and the others would never willingly leave their riders for any length of time.

"Demira," answered her mother.

"Demira! She's only a two-year-old."

But I'm a strong two-year-old, a light, distinctly feminine voice spoke in Kelene's mind. *And don't forget, my dam's second-born went all the way to Pra Desh when he was only a baby.* The black filly came up beside Kelene and shook her head in greeting, her mane rippling like ebony water.

The young woman looked full into the Hunnuli's large, lustrous eyes. "You wish to bear me all the way to Moy Tura?"

Yes.

"I cannot promise you anything more than good care and companionship. I am not a magic-wielder."

A wise light, almost like a glint of humor, shifted in Demira's eyes. *I know.*

"Walk with Amara, my daughter," Gabria said to Kelene, then she backed away so Athlone and Lymira could come to say good-bye. Quietly the chieftain helped cinch the saddle pad to Demira's back. Hunnuli usually did not tolerate a bridle or saddle, but on long journeys they accepted a blanket or saddle pad for their riders' comfort and their own. Demira, though, had never worn any kind of tack before, and she snorted as Athlone pulled the cinch tight around her barrel. Kelene's pack and two saddlebags of supplies were added to the load.

Kelene patted Demira's neck. "Are you sure about this?"

Just get on! was the filly's tart reply.

Kelene looked up at the Hunnuli's broad back and grimaced. Although only two, Demira's withers were already level with Kelene's eyes. This horse was quite a bit taller than Ishtak, and that could pose a problem. When Athlone offered her a leg up, however, she declined. "I have to learn to do this eventually," she said.

Grabbing the filly's mane in one hand and the saddle pad in the other, she hopped high on her good foot, then hauled herself up with her arms until she could hook her crippled foot over the Hunnuli's other side. It wasn't graceful, but it worked. She settled down onto Demira's back.

Relax, the filly told her. *You're as stiff as a tent pole.*

"It's just odd not to have reins in my hands," Kelene said uneasily. To give her hands something to do, she reached down and rubbed Demira's neck, missing the look of satisfaction that passed between her parents.

After that, the good-byes went quickly, and Kelene rode over to join the others who had just finished dividing the rest of the supplies. Sayyed, with a glazed, distant look in his eyes, sat motionless on Afer, waiting patiently to leave. The white cat sat on the blanket in front of him. As soon as Kelene joined the group, Sayyed raised his fist to salute Lord Athlone.

"Farewell on your journey, clansmen!" Athlone responded, returning the salute.

Other well-wishers shouted their blessings and good-byes as the little group began to trot from the grove toward the north. No one said a word about the dread feelings in their hearts that perhaps this was the last time they would see one another.

Gabria watched her children go—like two arrows that she and Athlone had smoothed and shaped and at last let fly. Would their flights be straight and true or wobbly and torn by the winds of fate? Where would they land, those two precious arrows? She found herself crying soundless tears. She watched the black Hunnuli through her blurry, sparkling tears until they were mere dots against the golden hills far away. Then she drew a long breath and tried to bury her anxiety within. There were many troubles close at hand that required attention; she should not waste her strength fretting about something over which she had no control.

Gabria was about to return to her littlest child when something made her pause. She stopped, her head high, her attention searching inward to seek for the odd sensation that disturbed her mind.

Athlone noticed the strange look in her face and came as close as he dared. As chieftain, he had decided to keep himself separate from those tending the sick so he could continue to help the other chiefs and maintain order in his clan. But that didn't mean he liked the distance he was forced to keep from his wife and son. At that moment, he wanted desperately to take Gabria in his arms. "What is it?" he called to her.

"Something has changed," Gabria answered, her voice puzzled.

"What do you mean?"

Her shoulders shifted slightly. "I'm not sure. It's as if some feeling has left me."

"That's odd. Are you sure it isn't just the relief of sending someone out to do something that might be helpful?"

"There is that, but this is different . . . like the ease of an apprehension or fear I'd grown used to."

Athlone sent her a tired grin. "Maybe that's a good sign."

The sorceress took one last look to the north where the travelers had disappeared. "I hope," she said aloud. But even from fifteen paces away, Athlone heard the doubt in her voice.

* * *

As soon as they left the gathering, the seven Hunnuli found the faint trail that pointed north, and they stretched out into a smooth canter. League after league through the hot summer afternoon the horses ran, as tireless as the endless winds that chased the dust of their passing. They soon left the valley of the Tir Samod behind and came up onto the long, rolling grasslands that stretched unbroken to the horizon and beyond. To their left flowed the Isin River in a silvery trail of shallow white rapids, dark green pools, and mud bars where otters and muskrats played. Overhead was the great blue bowl of the sky.

Many people who traveled the scattered trails and caravan routes that crisscrossed the high plains found the Ramtharin grasslands desolate and empty beyond tolerance. Hot in the summer, cold in the winter, and often dangerous, the plains did not attract large numbers of settlers. Yet the nomadic clanspeople who had lived with this land for five hundred years could not imagine living anywhere else. The land had become their bones, the rivers and streams their blood, and the vast, wind-sung spaces had become their souls. As tough and enduring as the plains they loved, the people of Valorian had made this realm of wind and grass an inseparable part of themselves. They had survived drought, floods, storms, blizzards, war, and rebellion to spread to the far corners of the plains and build a society that was strong in kinship and tradition.

But, Kelene wondered to herself while she rode beside the Isin River, would those strengths be enough to save the clanspeople in their present disaster? Would the ties of blood and custom hold the clans together in the face of such a devastating plague long enough for help to be found?

She had never given much thought to the clans' past or future. Her people had always just been there, the unheralded backbone of her life. But now they were facing possible extinction. The notion of all eleven clans disappearing from the Ramtharin Plains frightened her more than she imagined. That couldn't happen! Some people had to be saved to carry on the blood and traditions and history that went back beyond Moy Tura, beyond Valorian and the Tarn Empire, back to a long-forgotten time when the first clanspeople befriended a horse and began to move east. That ancient society was worth preserving.

All at once Kelene chuckled at herself. This was a change. It had been a long time since her introspection had moved beyond horses, racing, and her foot. In fact, this afternoon was full of changes: leaving her parents and her clan for the first time and riding on a mission with a company of magic-wielders. It was enough to turn anyone's mind to unfamiliar musings.

It was very different, too, to be sitting on a horse that did not try to throw her into a patch of prickly pear or jar her spine to jelly. She had never ridden a horse whose gait was so smooth or whose back fit her seat so comfortably. After Ishtak, Demira seemed to float effortlessly over the ground like a black cloud scudding before the wind.

The filly seemed to sense her thoughts, for she asked with a hint of wistfulness, *Do you like to run?*

Kelene threw her dark musings to the wind. "Yes!"

Then hold on.

Demira lunged forward into a full gallop over the treeless ground. Her neck stretched out; her nostrils flared to catch the air; her stride lengthened until her legs were a blur and only their shadows kept pace.

Kelene's breath was snatched away by the speed of the Hunnuli's run. She felt Demira's mane whip her face and the wind burn her eyes, but she paid no attention. She had never experienced anything like this! This incredible, exhilarating, delirious speed. Ishtak was fast, but Demira was an arrow. On the filly's back the young woman knew grace and speed and freedom like an eagle in the sun. Kelene flung out her arms, threw back her head, and laughed as she had not laughed for years.

Far behind them, Sayyed watched the girl and the Hunnuli go and made no move to bring them back. He knew the filly was too sensible to get lost. Although he wasn't sure why Gabria had insisted that Kelene come with him, he thought he began to understand when she and Demira finally came back, panting, sweating, and thoroughly pleased with themselves. As the filly slowed to a more sedate canter and fell in beside Afer, Sayyed glanced at the young woman on the Hunnuli's back. He had never seen her look so beautiful. The wind and excitement had turned her cheeks to a glowing pink, loose strands of hair floated in a halo around her face, and her eyes were shimmering like sunlight through black glass. His pain receded a little in the face of her joy, and he smiled at her, as pleased as her own father.

"I never knew it could be like that," she said, scratching Demira's neck.

Sayyed agreed. "I often think that riding a Hunnuli is as close to flying as we can get."

Kelene started at his words and stared at him in surprise. A look of speculation slowly spread over her face, and she fell quiet as if deep in thought.

Behind her, astride his Hunnuli, Rafnir was also staring. It had not occurred to him before how pretty Kelene could be. He had always annoyed her, competed with her, or simply ignored her because she had never shown the slightest interest in anyone but her horses. Now he was seeing a new side of her, and the intent look of reflection in her face intrigued him. What had piqued her interest so deeply? He started to wonder if there was more to this girl than the ability to win races. His own curiosity sparked, Rafnir kept his eye on her the rest of the afternoon.

The small party stopped briefly at sunset to rest the Hunnuli and have a quick meal. While the others unpacked fruit, trail bread, and dried meat, Sayyed took his prayer rug to the bank of the river to say his evening prayers. As the western sky kindled to gold, then red, then purple, and the deep star-bright night poured over him, the warrior stayed on his knees, his head pressed to the ground and his heart full of tears he had not yet shed for Tam. The white cat crouched beside him like a ghostly sentinel.

Kelene watched for a time, then turned away, her heart sad. Sayyed's grief was a personal matter; she did not want to intrude with needless words or unwanted pity. She sat down by Demira to eat her meager meal. Around her, the Hunnuli were grazing and the other clanspeople were talking, eating, and stretching their stiff legs.

Rafnir and Savaron were sitting together, their heads bent over a broken pack they were trying to fix.

Niela, a Jehanan woman well into her thirtieth year, was brushing the dried sweat from her Hunnuli's coat. Niela had always known she had a talent for magic but had not learned to use her power until her husband died, leaving her alone and free to seek her own way. Kelene had liked Niela from the first day she rode into the Khulinin winter camp to find Gabria eight years before. Square-jawed and unpretentious, Niela kept her unruly red hair tied behind her head with a leather thong and wore an old split-skirt and brown tunic.

Morad was different. A young, cocksure Geldring, he had charged into magic like a bull and frequently got himself in trouble with spells he could not control. His physical build reminded Kelene of a bull, too. Muscular and brash from his training as a warrior, the stocky Geldring was a dangerous opponent when aroused.

His younger brother, Tomian, was quieter and more careful with a power he was just beginning to understand. Although he was smaller than his brother and not as proficient with weapons, he had an excellent eye for detail and was a superb tracker and hunter.

Both brothers, though still under Gabria's tutelage, planned to return to their clan in a year or two. They, like Savaron and Rafnir, had volunteered to come with Sayyed. Niela, Kelene suspected, had been asked to come as a chaperon for her.

Kelene finished her meal and brushed the crumbs from her lap. In the process she noticed the Watcher on her tunic sparkling with countless points of new starlight. Curious, she pulled it off and held it in her cupped hands. The Watcher tingled under her touch with a faint pulse of magic power. The gem was round, faceted on the sides to enhance its beauty, and flat across the top. It was set in a cloak brooch of finely woven gold.

Her mother had said she had only to concentrate to see into its heart, so she focused her attention down into the scintillating interior. Nothing happened for a while. The stone remained cold and lifeless in her hands. Kelene was trying harder to shut out the distractions around her when all of a sudden, she heard it—the low, faint sobbing of someone in despair. The sound seemed to be emanating from the jewel, for it was very soft and distant, yet its grief cut Kelene to the heart.

Gradually an image began to form in the stone's center. The scene was shaking slightly from her mother's movement, but it was there in full detail. Tiny at first, the picture grew larger in Kelene's sight until she could clearly make out the dim interior of the council tent. There were the rows of sick, the fire in the central hearth, and the busy healers. Then the scene moved down as Gabria apparently bent over, and Kelene saw her little brother's face for the first time since Gabria had carried him out of their tent to go into quarantine.

A sob jerked out of her, and the Watcher fell to her feet. She wrapped her arms around her knees and began to cry.

"Kelene! What's wrong?" someone said worriedly.

She looked up in surprise to see Rafnir bending down beside her. Savaron and the others were crowding around.

"Coren is dead," she told Savaron through her tears. Her older brother went visibly pale and stood hunched in the darkening night as if someone had punched him. Niela and Rafnir squatted down beside Kelene.

"I'm sorry," Rafnir said so quietly Kelene almost didn't hear him.

His sympathy and unexpected solicitude jabbed a raw nerve. She moaned, "Your mother is dead and I didn't say anything to you. Not an 'I'm sorry,' or 'I'll miss her horribly,' or 'Sorh treat her well,' or anything. I loved Tam! I loved Coren! Why did they have to die?"

Kelene paused, and her voice died away. She tilted her head to listen to a faint sound she could barely hear. The noise came again, low and cruel in the darkness. Someone was laughing.

Beside Kelene, Rafnir and Niela slowly straightened and stared into the night. Sayyed left his rug and joined them.

"What is that?" Morad demanded. "Who's out there?"

The laughter sounded again from somewhere close by. It was so harsh and gloating, it sent chills down Kelene's back. Everyone moved closer together, and the men drew their swords.

"Who are you?" Sayyed yelled. He received no answer. The laughter only changed from a low note of derision to a crueler ring of triumph.

Shaken, the clanspeople peered out into the dark, trying to find the intruder, but they could not see anything. All they could hear was the disembodied laughter cutting through the night. The Hunnuli snorted angrily and gathered around their riders. Even they could not see or smell any stranger beyond the circle of the clanspeople.

The noise reached a final shriek and slowly faded as if its maker were moving away. When the night was quiet again, the seven people looked at one another in frightened confusion.

"What in Sorh's name was *that?*" Tomian gasped.

"Mount up," Sayyed said in reply. "We're going on."

No one needed a second urging. As fast as they could move, they grabbed their saddlebags and sprang to their horses' backs. The Hunnuli leaped forward into the darkness. Before long their resting place and the source of the fearful noise were left behind. Or so they hoped.

The party rode late into the night, following the trail by the river. They lit no lights to guide their way, but trusted to the surefootedness and clear vision of the Hunnuli to find the path over the uneven ground. Although the riders were tired, they were too nervous to doze or relax their vigil for a moment. Everyone rode with their thoughts dwelling on the strange, cruel laughter.

They stopped at last near dawn and made a cold camp in a small depression between two hills. The riders threw themselves down to sleep while the Hunnuli stood protectively around them. Yet in spite of their fatigue and the late hour, not a single person slept well. They tossed and thrashed on their blankets in a welter of emotions and worry. When they did sleep, their rest was bedeviled with vivid dreams and images of fear.

Kelene dozed just as the first light gilded the horizon. Her eyes were barely closed before a dream overtook her and carried her back to the gathering. She saw her family's tent, warm in the afternoon sun, with the dogs sleeping by the entrance and her father's gold banner hanging above the awning. It looked so peaceful and normal, she cried gladly and dashed inside through the open tent flap. At the scene that met her gaze, her joy turned to horror.

Her family was all there, even Savaron, lying or sitting about the tent in varying degrees of decay. Her father was a skeleton sprawled on his bed, her mother a maggot-ridden corpse sitting on her favorite stool. But the worst was her little brother. Even as she watched, choking on her terror, the boy's corpse, ravaged by plague sores, rose slowly to its feet and held out a hand to welcome her inside. Then he began to laugh, the same cruel, derisive laughter she had heard in the darkness by the river.

Kelene woke to her own screaming and found someone was shaking her. Shuddering and gasping for air, she clutched at the person beside her and struggled to sit up.

"It's all right," soothed Rafnir. "You had a nightmare, too. It's over now."

For once Kelene didn't care or wonder why Rafnir was there. All that mattered to her was that he was solid, comforting, and real. She hung onto his arm until she could bring her fear under control.

Kelene, are you well? she heard Demira say worriedly in her mind. The filly was standing close by, her muzzle lowered to Kelene's head.

The young woman rubbed her gritty eyes. "I'm awake at least." She shivered and regarded Rafnir gratefully. She was pleasantly surprised that he seemed to be more caring and friendly than she believed possible. "Did you have a dream, too?" she asked, letting go of his sleeve.

His mouth tightened at the memory, and he sat back on his heels. "I saw my mother come out of the funeral pyre."

"I dreamed of a man," Niela told them from her sleeping place. "At least I think it was a man. He glowed with a hideous red light. It was horrible!"

The other three men were awake, too, and sitting, bleary-eyed, on their blankets in the pale light of dawn.

"Gods," muttered Savaron, running his hand through his tousled hair. "If we have many nights like that, we'll be too tired to reach Moy Tura."

Sayyed groaned and climbed to his feet. He hadn't had any nightmares since he had not slept. His body complained painfully about yesterday's long ride and resting on the damp ground; his head ached with a dull, persistent pain. He looked at his small party and said simply, "Let's go."

Wordlessly they gathered their gear and struck out again on the trail north. The day was warm and dry, and the sky was bright blue scattered with fluffy clouds. The plains, already turning gold in the midsummer heat, stretched away for league after league in all directions.

By afternoon the travelers reached the fertile uplands leading to the Himachal Mountains, a narrow, rugged line of peaks that ran north and south. At the southern tip of the Himachals was Dangari Treld, the winter camp of Lord Koshyn's people.

The Dangari were more sedentary than most of the clans, and a few of their people stayed at the treld year round to raise crops and care for the clan's treasured studs and brood mares. Even though the Dangari would have gladly welcomed them, the magic-wielders pressed on, reluctant to risk spreading the plague and determined to cover as much ground as possible in the daylight. They cantered past the foothills and followed the Isin north along the flanks of the Himachal Mountains.

During the long, tedious hours of riding, Kelene had ample time to think. To keep her mind off fear and plagues and death, she turned her thoughts to speed, Hunnuli, and Sayyed's words from the day before. How incredible it would be, she kept thinking.

When the mountains loomed on the left and the hot sun was drifting toward their cooling peaks, she touched the white lightning mark on Demira's shoulder. "Have you ever thought about flying?" she asked the filly, trying to sound casual.

Demira frisked a few steps, then bounded after a meadowlark that swooped over the grass ahead of them. *Flying? I fly when I run.*

"No, I mean really flying. Like a bird."

Demira's ears flicked with interest. *No, I have not thought of that. Hunnuli do not have wings.*

"Valorian helped his horse fly with magic when they tried to cross the cavern in Gormoth," Kelene said.

That is true. The filly was silent for a while as she watched the meadowlark again. *I think I would like it.* And to prove her enthusiasm, she kicked up her heels in a playful buck and leaped forward into a spirited gallop.

Kelene threw her arms wide to embrace the wind and laughed in delight. For a short time she was able to forget her fear and worry in the glorious speed of Demira's run.

When the filly had tired and was trotting back to join the other travelers, Kelene lifted her eyes to the sky. If only she could . . .

6

That night there was no moon; the darkness grew as dense and deep as the bottom of an empty pit. Stars sparkled in glittering swathes and patterns across the sky, but in the small lightless camp by the Isin River the night crowded in on the clanspeople like an oppressive fog. They could see nothing beyond their own camp. Even the Hunnuli standing in a protective circle around their riders could only be seen by the faint glimmer of the lightning marks on their shoulders and the occasional reflection of starlight in their eyes.

The travelers lay close together on their bedrolls, trying to sleep, but even though they were bone-tired they could not close their eyes. Each of them felt a cold, shivering dread that settled in their bellies with a clammy grip. No one knew what caused the apprehension. Perhaps they feared to sleep and face their nightmares again. Perhaps they dreaded hearing that hideous laughter. Whatever kept them awake, the clanspeople tossed on their blankets for hours and heard nothing beyond the rush of the river.

Their suspense was broken at last, not by laughter or dreams but by a ruddy glow that appeared out of the night. The Hunnuli saw it first on the crest of a hill above the camp, and they neighed a warning to their riders. The people scrambled to their feet. They stared, appalled, as the red glow brightened, its phosphorescent light burning with a sickening hue that swallowed the light of the stars. Swiftly the radiance took shape, and its outline became distinct against the black sky.

The form appeared to be a man wearing robes and a cowled hood that covered the head. The apparition carried no weapons or items of any kind that the travelers could see, and it made no obvious move to attack them. It merely loomed above the camp, tall and ethereal, and watched the people with a cold malice.

"Is that the thing Gabria saw?" Niela asked, her voice shaking.

"Yes," Savaron snarled.

Slowly the form raised its head and laughed in the same remorseless voice that had frightened the travelers the night before. The inhuman sound struck them all with dread.

Morad suddenly yelled an oath and flung his hand forward. A bright blue bolt of what Kelene recognized was the Trymian force shot from his palm and rocketed toward the figure on the hill. The apparition did not move when the bolt passed through its shape; it only laughed again with malicious pleasure. The form then turned and walked out of sight over the crest of the slope, leaving the hilltop empty and dark once more.

No one moved.

"What *is* that thing?" Kelene said hoarsely, voicing the question in all their minds.

"I don't know, but it seems to be resistant to magic," Sayyed replied. "That's not encouraging."

A mild understatement, Kelene thought. The travelers continued to peer into the darkness until their eyes ached.

"What are we going to do?" asked Niela, the nervousness shaking her voice.

Sayyed slowly sheathed his sword. "Try to sleep. Savaron was right. If we don't get some rest, we'll be too exhausted to reach Moy Tura and too tired to control our magic."

"Shouldn't we set up a protective shield?" Morad asked.

"I don't think so," Sayyed replied. "A shield takes too much strength and concentration, and we need the rest. The Hunnuli should be able to warn us in time if that form reappears." He turned to Afer, who was standing by his elbow. "Do you agree?"

The stallion swished his tail, a sign of his agitation. *Yes. Now that we know its smell, we will be ready.*

"Do you know what that thing is?" Sayyed asked him.

It is dead. Afer's short reply was sent on a broad thought to all of the magic-wielders.

Sayyed's mouth dropped open. "It's what?"

It reeks of death. Demira added with a snort.

"But it looks human," Niela protested. "If it was the soul of a man, the Harbingers would have taken him to the realm of the dead."

We know that. We do not understand it either. We only know that its smell is death and that it is very dangerous.

"Can you still smell it?" Kelene asked.

Yes. But it is not near, Afer told them. *Rest, and we will watch.*

Reluctantly the clanspeople took his advice and crawled back into their blankets. But they were no sooner asleep than the nightmares began. Dredged from each person's deepest fears, the dreams were vivid, terrifying visions of death, loss, and tragedy. This time Niela wasn't the only one who dreamed of a man in glowing red robes. Interspersed through all their nightmares walked a tall, gaunt figure who watched their terrors with the cold interest of a predator.

When the sun's gleam finally edged the eastern horizon, the seven travelers, groggy and heavy-headed from the remnants of their dreams, staggered from their beds.

Rubbing his temples, Savaron threw himself onto the riverbank and plunged his head into the cool water. "I feel lousy," he groaned, his face and hair dripping.

"I never want to go through another night like that again," Niela muttered fiercely to her blankets as she rolled them up.

Even the white cat looked disgruntled until Sayyed picked her up and cradled her in his arm. Almost desperately he rubbed her ears and ran his fingers through her fur. He had slept for the first time in several nights and wished fervently he hadn't. All of his sleep had been riddled with dreams of Tam, until the emptiness in his soul left by her death had grown to a mind-numbing misery. He could never remember having dreams so shattering. He'd had so little rest, his fatigue dragged on him like chains until he could barely move or think.

This is hardly the best condition for the leader of an important journey, he thought to himself, wondering if there was more to his state of mind than grief and weariness. It was true he had never lost someone so important to him as his wife, but he'd always considered himself to be a strong, self-controlled man who could face his god-given fate with some semblance of fortitude. At the moment he felt like a man standing on the crumbling edge of despair.

Strangely, the one thing holding him together was this small cat his wife had loved so well. The cat's warmth drove back the chill creeping into his heart, her purr soothed him, and her ties to Tam seemed to comfort his desperate loneliness. Without her, he wondered if he would have been able to continue.

It isn't like me to be so weak, Sayyed pondered. Perhaps there were other things affecting him—such as the red wraith. Sayyed believed the apparition was somehow affecting everyone's dreams, and if that was the reason for the nightmares, then the question was why? What was this being that followed them, and why was it here? He had no answers to that yet, only hope that it would leave them alone so they could continue their journey in peace. Unfortunately, he doubted his hopes would be answered.

The cat meowed, breaking into his thoughts. *I'm hungry.*

He gently set her down and forced himself to move. It took all of his willpower to feed the cat, choke down some food himself, and repack his gear. He was so involved in his struggle to function that he did not remember his morning prayers or notice the way Afer stayed close to him. Neither did he see the worried looks that passed between his companions. When they mounted and left their camp, Rafnir rode by his father's side.

The sun slowly climbed high into the cloudless sky. The heat rose, too, and the Hunnuli were forced to slow down and stop often for small drinks of water. They continued to canter north along the Isin River until shortly before noon, when the river abruptly veered west into the Himachal Mountains and the Defile of Tor Wrath. Out of respect, and a little curiosity, the party paused on the point of a hill and looked upstream to the bluffs at the mouth of the defile.

High on a ridge of rock that thrust from the southern cliffs sat the ancient fortress of Ab-Chakan. Built before the time of Valorian when the Tarn empire ruled the Ramtharin plains, Ab-Chakan was a huge fortification of black towers and massive walls. Although it had been abandoned for five hundred years, most of its well-built structures were still intact.

Twenty-four years ago, the Khulinin, Dangari, Jehanan, and Bahedin clans had taken refuge within those stone walls from the advancing army of the sorcerer, Lord Medb. Little had changed in that valley since then. The old fortress still remained empty, full of shadows and ruin, inhabited only by birds and lizards. At its feet in the broad valley meadow were the two burial mounds, one for the dead of the clans that fell in the battle for Ab-Chakan and one for Athlone's father, Lord Savaric.

Wordlessly Kelene looked down on the grave of her grandfather, who had died by a murderer's hand at the moment of his victory, and she wondered what he had been like. She knew the tales her father and mother told of a man with her dark looks who loved hawks, his family, and his freedom; of a man who had taken in the sole survivor of a massacred clan and was the only chief who had defied Lord Medb face-to-face.

But who was the man behind the tales? What had he been like as a real person? Had his blood carried the talent to wield magic? She wondered what he would have done about it if he had known. Her eyes fell lower to the glittering Watcher on her tunic, and she remembered that its companion, the Fallen Star, had been Savaric's. He had not been loath to use that magic power to his advantage! Her fingers strayed to the stone's smooth surface with the thought that if Savaric had known he had the ability to wield magic, he probably would not have let it go to waste.

"Sorh grant him peace," she whispered when the party turned away. As soon as they were moving again, Kelene pulled the brooch off her tunic and cupped it in her hands. It had been too long since she had made use of the stone's spell to check on her mother.

She stared into the gem's center and soon an image appeared. The scenes were brighter this time since they were happening in the daylight. She saw the face of the healer from Clan Ferganan, who was talking to her mother. His voice and Gabria's came clearly through the stone, aided by the power of the Watcher's spell.

Kelene listened for quite a while before she returned the brooch to its place. She dropped her hands in her lap and stared stonily into the hazy afternoon.

"Are they well?" Savaron asked, riding up beside her.

His voice startled her from her reverie, and she jerked her head around to stare at him. He pointed to her brooch, repeating his question.

"Yes, for now," Kelene responded, but her voice was stricken. "It's getting worse, Savaron. Mother is still in the council grove helping the healers. But there must have been hundreds of sick people there. The healers were frantic! Gehlyn died yesterday." She threw her hands out in a helpless gesture. "Now Lord Koshyn is sick, and Wer-tain Rejanir. And they've lost four more magic-wielders."

Savaron winced. "Did their Hunnuli leave like Tam's?"

"I think some did. Mother could hardly bear to talk about them to the healer she was with." Kelene paused, drew a hard breath, and went on. "That's not the worst of it. Lymira is sick, too."

"Since when?"

Kelene looked into the distance. "Last night."

"Gods," he said miserably. "Even if we find something in Moy Tura we couldn't make it back in time to save her."

Kelene's reply was a whisper of sadness. "I know."

Neither of them spoke again after that, yet they rode side by side for the rest of the afternoon, drawing comfort from each other's company.

The Hunnuli continued to canter north along the skirts of the pine-clad foothills where small streams tumbled out of the mountains and high bluffs formed a barrier wall into the rugged interior. At dusk a stiff wind swept from the northwest, and storm clouds began to build on the horizon.

By then the travelers were drawing near to the northern end of the Himachal range. They were not far from Geldring Treld or the notorious Citadel of Krath, but by unspoken consent the clanspeople avoided both places and made a rough camp in a copse of tall pine. Geldring Treld was too far out of their way, and even another night of wraiths and nightmares was preferable to walking into the stronghold of the cult of the goddess Krath. Too many people had tried it and never walked out.

While the Hunnuli cropped the thick grass, Sayyed took his prayer rug to make his evening oblation, and the others had a quick meal. Afterward, while Kelene watched, Savaron, Rafnir, and Tomian gathered several spare blankets and stretched the fabric out on the ground. Each man laid his fingers on a blanket, drew in the magic around him, and initiated a spell taken from the *Book of Matrah*. The spell was simple: it enlarged the blankets, waterproofed them, and finally transformed them into three small traveling tents. Kelene had to admit the spells were neatly done and the results were very welcome.

Nevertheless, the confident use of sorcery only served to depress Kelene further. She shook her head. There was so much power in the world around them—stones, trees, earth, grass, water, everything carried vestiges of the mighty forces that had created the mortal world. That remnant of ancient power was known to humans as magic, and for those few, rare magic-wielders who could shape the power to their will, it was a limitless source of energy.

But endless power had its drawbacks, too. Magic was dangerous for those who did not have the strength or the determination to master it. If a magic-wielder did not know exactly what he or she was doing or lost control of a spell, the unleashed power could destroy anything in its path. Using magic also took its toll on the wielder, draining both mental and physical strength. Those who used the magic used it carefully and learned quickly how far they could go before exhaustion endangered their spells.

That was what frustrated Kelene. There was all the power of the gods at their fingertips—power to heal their families and save their clans—yet human magic-wielders were too weak and unskilled to use magic to its full potential. They could not snap their fingers and wish away the plague or speak a word and transport themselves instantly to Moy Tura. They could only work within their own knowledge, abilities, and mortal frailty.

Kelene kicked a clump of grass in disgust and limped from the pines to a broad swath of grass where the tired Hunnuli were grazing and resting. Irritably she pulled her golden cloak tighter across her shoulders, leaned against a tree trunk, and watched the black horses in the twilight.

Demira was there, too, looking small and slender against the bigger, more powerful bodies of the full-grown Hunnuli. She was shorter than most two-year-olds, probably because she was the last foal of an aging mare, but her shape was well proportioned, graceful, and no less strong than others her age. And she was so fast. . . .

"You're far away," someone said close by. "What are you thinking about?"

Kelene cocked her head and saw Rafnir standing beside her, his arms crossed and his face curious. She thought with a flash of surprise that he seemed somewhat different. His usual cocky casualness was nowhere to be seen. Instead he seemed vulnerable. His smile was hesitant, his eyes were genuinely friendly.

"Speed," she answered glumly. "There isn't enough of it. By the time we reach Moy Tura and go back to the gathering, they'll all be dead."

"If any of us make it back, there will be some still alive," he said, sounding more hopeful than certain.

"But not Gehlyn, or Lord Koshyn, or Lymira!"

Rafnir blanched. "Lymira is sick?"

"She's going to die, too. Just like Tam and Coren." Kelene pounded her fist into the tree, her helplessness burning. "What good is all of this magic if we can't save them? Why didn't the gods just keep their power?"

At the sound of her rider's voice, Demira raised her head to listen. Silently she came over to stand at Kelene's side.

Rafnir grunted. "You're a fine one to be talking about magic. You won't use it!" he said, uncrossing his arms. "You have a talent that could be used for so much good, and you waste it! You won't even try."

Stung, Kelene turned on him, her face reddened by anger and shame. "I've tried to use magic! I just can't control it," she snapped before she realized what she was saying.

Rafnir pounced on Kelene's words. "When did you *ever* try to use magic?" He pushed his face closer to hers to see her better in the fading light and was astonished to see tears trickling down her cheeks. Her eyes were enormous dark pools, and her jaw was clenched hard as rock.

In a voice that was very quiet she replied, "About five summers ago."

He studied her, trying to remember what had happened when they were thirteen, then his gaze dropped to her crippled foot.

"That's right," she answered before he could ask. "I wanted to help Father gentle that wild stallion he had caught. I thought I could do it, but he said no."

Rafnir shook his head at the memory of that horse. "So you did it anyway."

She nodded. She couldn't believe she was telling this to Rafnir of all people! She had never told anyone the truth. Without realizing she was doing it, she wrapped her hand into Demira's mane and held on for comfort and support. "I thought if I could use a spell to help calm the horse, I could train him faster and impress Father. But I couldn't do it. I lost control of the spell when I was on his back, and he panicked. He reared and fell over backward on me, just because I couldn't handle a little magic."

"And you've been afraid to try it again ever since," he finished.

She made a swipe at her face with her sleeve and said, "What's the use? You know as well as I do that the talent is strong in some, weaker in others. Savaron and Coren have the best ability in my family. Let them use it."

"Coren is dead," Rafnir reminded her softly.

"Yes," Kelene said into the darkness. Overhead, the pine trees swayed in the growing wind, and a faint flicker of lightning flashed to the north.

"You know, I heard Coren tell Father once that he thought *you* had the stronger talent."

Startled, Kelene asked, "Coren said that? Why?"

"I don't know. Children can be perceptive sometimes." He reached out and scratched Demira's shoulder. "You could try again, you know. Just because you failed once doesn't mean your talent is worthless."

The young woman shook her head. "Next time I could kill myself—or hurt someone else."

"Not if you start slowly. When you used that spell on the stallion you were too young and inexperienced."

"Now I'm too old and inexperienced."

He scratched his chin, exasperated. "If you'd just decide to channel some of that stubbornness into action, you would be unstoppable."

"Ha!"

"Try it. Think of one thing that you want to do and work toward that goal."

The girl hesitated while she debated the wisdom of revealing her dream to Rafnir. Would he laugh or would he see the depth of desire in her words? "I want to make Demira fly," she said at last.

"I'll help you," he responded immediately.

She was startled by his serious and quick response. "You don't think that's ridiculous?"

"If it works, she'll be able to travel faster. Maybe she could save a few lives."

"But what if I can't?" Kelene asked.

"You won't know until you try."

Kelene thought quietly for a moment then lifted her chin and said, "You won't pull out any more crops?"

Rafnir laughed. That was the first time she had said anything about their accident in the Induran. It seemed like a year since then, not fifteen days. "No crops." He was going to add something else when all seven Hunnuli raised their heads in alarm.

Someone is coming. Demira told Kelene.

"The wraith?"

No. This is human. But not clan.

In one group, the other six Hunnuli left their grazing and hurried to join their riders. Kelene and Rafnir quickly followed, and the whole party gathered in the clearing by their tents. The night was almost complete by that time, broken only by distant flashes of lightning. The sky was overcast, and the wind roared through the pines. Thunder grumbled in the distance.

"Where are our visitors?" Sayyed softly asked Afer.

"Here, Clansman!" came a voice from the darkness.

The travelers drew closer, their eyes searching the night for the source of the voice. They saw nothing but the shapes of trees until a figure moved cautiously out from behind a pine only ten paces away from where they stood. More forms eased from the shadows all around them, and the clanspeople realized they were surrounded. The Hunnuli snorted menacingly. Savaron immediately shaped a spell to form a glowing sphere of light high above their heads that cast the entire clearing into stark relief.

No one tried to move, for they all recognized the black-clad figures illuminated by the silver light—men with whips at their belts instead of swords. They were the Oathbreakers, the men of the Cult of Krath who worshiped their dark goddess with secrecy and blood. The clanspeople knew that if the cultists had wanted to kill them, they would be dead by now, murdered in silence and without mercy.

"To what do we owe the honor of a visit from the Men of the Lash?" Sayyed called over the wind. The white cat crouched at his feet and growled.

The strangers made no move to come closer. They simply watched from within their black hoods, their faces completely obscured in shadow.

"We came to seek the truth," the first man said.

The clanspeople shivered at the dry, harsh pitch of his voice. "What truth is that?" demanded Sayyed.

"We have seen many strange and evil visions. Is it true there is a contagion in the clans of Valorian?"

Sayyed answered wearily, "Yes. We have been struck by a plague that seems to have no cure. Many have died and more are dying." There was no point hiding that truth. The men who joined the Cult of Krath forswore any oaths, loyalties, or kinship from their pasts. They lived only for their bloodthirsty goddess. What was happening to the clans would not matter to them.

But the speaker surprised him by inquiring, "Is Lord Athlone still well?"

Kelene moved a step forward. "He was this afternoon, High Priest Seth." Her companions murmured in surprise. All of the Oathbreakers were identical in their plain black robes and hoods, and no one had seen the high priest face-to-face for many years.

"How do you know?" whispered Savaron.

Kelene hissed back, "I guessed."

Almost arrogantly, the Oathbreaker pushed back his hood to reveal the face of an old man. Yet even aged by years and the rigors of his life as a cultist, there was still an incredible strength in his dark, lean features, a toughness like that of an oak root grown gnarled and enduring with time. Although none of the clanspeople there had known Lord Savaric, they felt certain they were facing his brother, Seth.

"Who are you?" The priest spoke, his voice deadpan and his eyes hooded above his hawk nose and iron-gray beard.

"I am Kelene, daughter of Lady Gabria and Lord Athlone. Granddaughter of Savaric, your brother. I have the Watcher, so I can see what is happening to my parents."

Seth did not reply right away. He stared down at Kelene, surveying her from head to boot. It was said the followers of Krath could look into men's hearts and reveal the deepest fears and evils hidden there. They pried into secrets and opened guarded hatreds that were buried behind facades. Because of this, few men dared to look an Oathbreaker in the eye for fear of having their souls laid bare.

But Kelene was too used to challenging authority. The dark visage of her great-uncle brought a chill to her skin, yet she stiffened her neck and assumed the empty, indifferent expression that always irritated her mother.

To her surprise, Seth gave a short, dry chuckle. "You are indeed the child of Gabria and the blood of Savaric." He turned his basilisk stare from her to Sayyed again. "Tell me why you are here."

Sayyed did not look away either. "We're going to Moy Tura."

Seth showed no reaction other than a short nod of understanding. "The healers' records. That is a possibility."

"Is there anything in your library that could help us?" Savaron asked.

"No," the high priest said with a voice like granite.

Savaron curled his lip. "Would you have offered it if there were?"

"I will tell you this: beware of the spirit that follows you. It is stealing your life-force as you sleep. Especially yours." He pointed to Sayyed. "Your soul is dangerously weak. If it can, the wraith will kill you to gain your strength."

"What life-force? Who is this wraith?" Rafnir demanded.

"We do not know who it is. Somehow it has evaded the realm of the dead and remains here to poison this world with its evil. This spirit must be sent to Lord Sorh soon, before it finds a way to stay in this world permanently."

Rafnir threw up his arms with the frustration they all felt. "How do we do that?" he asked angrily.

"Look for your answers in Moy Tura," Seth replied. Then, with an almost imperceptible nod to his men, the high priest glided back into the darkness and vanished. The clanspeople gaped in surprise at where the other cultists, too, had disappeared without a sound. Lightning cracked overhead, banishing the shadows and brightening the entire area. The copse was empty.

Niela's Hunnuli snorted and flattened her ears. "I agree!" Niela said. "Those men give me the creeps."

Rafnir put his hand on his father's shoulder. "Why don't we set a watch tonight? Maybe if some of us are on guard, the wraith will not be as likely to approach us."

"Is it still following us?" Tomian wanted to know.

It is. Afer told them all. He lifted his muzzle to the wind. *It is waiting not far away. In truth, we would like the company of other watchers. We are very weary tonight.*

"Then set a watch of two," Sayyed ordered. "Tomian, you and I will be first. Then Savaron and Kelene, and Rafnir and Morad. Niela, you'll get your turn tomorrow night."

Rafnir shook his head. "Father, you sleep tonight. I will take the first watch."

Sayyed wanted to argue, but in truth he knew his son was right. He was so weary he was lightheaded and numb; he barely had the strength to stand upright. He would be a worthless guard if he could not keep his eyes open. With a nod of acceptance, he scooped up the white cat and made his way to the nearest tent. He crawled in and was asleep before the cat had time to stretch out by his arm.

Outside, Savaron evaporated his ball of light while the others made ready for the night. Kelene and Niela took one tent, Savaron and Morad the other. Tomian stayed with Rafnir to keep watch in the black, storm-tossed darkness.

As soon as the others were settled, Rafnir went to his father's tent. Quickly he spoke the words of a spell, raised his hands in a small arch, and formed the magic into an opaque dome of red energy that surrounded the small tent. The dome was a protective shield that allowed only air to enter; it would remain in place as long as one of the magic-wielders maintained the spell.

"Do you think that will keep the wraith away from him?" Tomian asked dubiously.

Rafnir studied the red shield. "I hope so! Priest Seth said Father was in the worst danger. I have to try something to help him."

The young Geldring nodded his approval. While Rafnir held the shield in place, Tomian rigged a small shelter close to the tents. The two men settled under the roof just as the first drops of rain heralded the downpour to come.

There was a tremendous crack of lightning, and the rain began to fall in windblown sheets. The Hunnuli huddled together, their heads turned away from the pelting rain.

Under the shelter, Rafnir peered into the darkness so hard it made his head hurt. Keeping the magic shield intact was taking more energy than he'd imagined. He was getting very tired. His eyelids were heavy weights; his body felt leaden. He shook his head to clear the sleep from his mind, but that didn't help. Slowly he leaned back against the shelter wall.

Beside him, Tomian was already dozing, his face slack with fatigue. The wind eased a little, and the rainfall steadied to a heavy drone on the tents and trees.

Rafnir's eyes slid closed. As his consciousness slipped into sleep, his concentration on the magic shield around Sayyed's tent wavered. The spell weakened, allowing the magic to dissipate. By the time Rafnir was fully asleep, the shield was gone. Sayyed's tent lay open to the night.

7

"Sayyed."

He heard Tam's voice, soft and enticing in the darkness, and his heart leaped with joy. He knew her death had been a dreadful mistake. Now she was somewhere close by, calling for him. He was still weak and groggy, but he managed to stagger to his feet and look around. The tent and the camp and his companions had vanished, leaving him alone in a dank, enveloping fog. He was not sure where he was, for even the trees and sky were hidden by the dreary pall of mist. The silence was so absolute he could almost listen to it.

"Sayyed," the voice called again from somewhere closer.

He turned on his heel, looking frantically for her. "I'm here!" he cried. She had to be there!

He turned again, and there she was, coming out of the mist as alive and lovely as always. Her face was alight with love; bright ribbons gleamed in her dark hair. She smiled at him with that heart-melting dimple in her cheek and merriment in her eyes, and held out her hands to him.

Sayyed felt himself growing weaker. He could barely stand, yet at the same time his vision of Tam was growing clearer and brighter. Summoning the last of his strength, he took a step and reached his right hand toward her.

"My husband," she murmured, welcoming him.

He took another step and another, until he was only two paces away.

Sayyed!

This time a different voice was calling him. It sounded familiar somehow— light and feminine and oddly imperious. He had no idea where it was coming from and had no desire to find it. Tam was with him again, so close all he had to do was reach out and touch her. He lifted his fingers to grasp her hand when sudden pain ripped down his arm.

Astounded, he stared at his bare forearm. Five long scratches marked his skin, and blood welled from the wound. He jerked his head up, ready to ask Tam what had hurt him, but she was gone. In her place stood a man dressed in long red robes. His dark eyes glared at Sayyed with such hatred that the warrior stumbled backward. Before he could recover, the man was gone. Sayyed was alone again in the fog. A dread, chill loneliness struck him, and he cried, "Tam!" with all the tears in his heart.

Sayyed! the strange voice called again.

The warrior paid no attention. Tam was gone again; he had to find her. He staggered into the mist.

Still the voice kept after him persistently, until at last he grudgingly answered, "What? What do you want?"

Pain suddenly shot through his arm again, and he looked down and saw five more scratches crossing the first. "Stop it!" he shouted into the mist.

Then wake up, the voice cried back. *They need your help.*

Sayyed shook his head to clear it. Whose was this voice? Who needed help? He saw the mist darken to black, and he found himself at the bottom of a deep tunnel. Somewhere up ahead the voice urged him to come, its insistence like a lifeline in the dark emptiness. It took all of his will to respond. He forced himself to move up through the thick, clinging blackness.

Hurry, Sayyed. Please, wake up, another, more masculine voice pleaded in his head. That voice, he knew, was Afer's. There was real desperation in the stallion's thoughts, and the plea gave Sayyed the strength he needed to reach consciousness. His eyes dragged open to look into a pair of blurry golden moons.

Something behind the moons growled and grumbled, and the female voice in his head fairly shouted, *We almost lost you!*

Outside Sayyed's shelter, a faint flash of lightning flared, lighting the interior of the small tent. Sayyed's vision cleared enough so he could see Tam's cat crouched by his scratched arm, her fur on end, her ears flat on her skull. "You," he mumbled.

Yes, now get up! she yowled.

Her sense of urgency was beginning to transfer to his fuzzy thoughts. Something was happening; he was needed. He heaved himself to his hands and knees. A wave of dizziness and nausea nearly knocked him flat again, and he had to take several deep breaths before he could move another muscle.

At the same time, sounds began to penetrate his groggy mind. He could hear his companions shouting at one another and the Hunnuli neighing in rage. Then Sayyed heard something else over the uproar: the cruel laughter of the wraith.

Sayyed threw himself headlong through the tent's flap and somehow scrambled to his feet. The scene before him was in utter chaos. The dark, wet clearing seemed to be filled with wild animals fighting five clanspeople and the Hunnuli.

Sayyed gaped in confusion, then gathered his wooly thoughts and very carefully formed a sphere of light over the combatants' heads. The light was red so as not to interfere with the humans' night vision, and it threw the fighting below into a strange, blood-colored relief. Sayyed saw Afer close by, trading blows with a wild stallion; Kelene and Niela were back-to-back, fighting off five wolves with a dagger, a tree limb, and the help of their Hunnuli. Rafnir was trying desperately to reach the women, but several large stags were keeping him pinned against a tree. Savaron and Morad were struggling to get out of their tent while a bear mauled the fabric in an effort to reach them.

Sayyed barely had time to register on the chaos around him when something growled behind him. He whirled and came face-to-face with a crouching, feral dog. The dog was a massive male of the breed often used by the clans to hunt cave lions. It snarled again, then leaped for Sayyed's chest.

Tired as he was, the warrior reacted instantly. He drew his sword in a wide backhanded arc that sliced the blade into the springing dog's neck. The dog's head flopped sideways. The force of the blow knocked the animal to the ground, but to Sayyed's dismay it gathered itself and sprang at him again, its head still hanging at a crazy angle. Sayyed slashed at the dog's neck again. This time the head came off completely, and the head and body flopped at his feet. He stared down in amazement at the head, still snarling and trying to snap at his boots. He took a closer look at the animal. There was something peculiar about it that he hadn't seen in the rush of its attack. The dog's hide was rough and full of holes. As Sayyed bent nearer, the thick stench of decay filled his nostrils. The dog was already dead.

Horrified, he looked around at the other wild animals. They did not appear to be whole either. Some had hideous wounds or injuries, as if they had been attacked, some were skin and bones, and none of the animals moved with the usual grace and alertness of living creatures. Every one of them was dead.

Sayyed didn't pause to reflect further on that gruesome reality, but raised his hand and sent a fistful of magic exploding into the bear attacking Savaron and Morad. Although Sayyed was weak and the bolt was not as powerful as usual, it was enough to blast the dead bear to fragments. At the same moment, Niela managed to put up a protective shield of magic around herself and Kelene. The wolves drew back snarling, only to be pounded to bloody bones under the hooves of the enraged Hunnuli.

Sayyed turned next to help his son, but as he drew back his hand he saw something else that turned his blood to ice. Young Tomian lay on his back in the grass at the edge of the camp. Crouched over his body was a huge cave lion, the largest Sayyed had ever seen. Its mane was matted and filthy. Its pelt was rotting off its carcass. The lion's eyes were only ant-riddled sockets, and one of its ears was missing. But its teeth and claws were terribly intact and its jaws dripped with fresh blood.

The lion raised its decaying head and stared straight at Sayyed. The warrior stumbled toward Tomian. Just as he raised his fist to fire another bolt of magic, the reddish form of the wraith materialized beside the big cat. With a wave of its hand, the form stopped the wild beasts in their places. The wraith turned slowly toward Sayyed, its visage uncovered for the first time.

The warrior stopped so fast he nearly fell. There before him was the man from his dream. He recognized every detail from the man's robes, his hawk-nose, and long dark hair to the almost maniacal look of hatred in his face.

"You will not escape again, magic-wielder," the apparition hissed. "I know where you are going and what you seek. You will not succeed. I plan to finish what I began two hundred years ago." With that he vanished into the night.

At his leaving, the driving force behind the dead animals disappeared. Their corpses sank into the grass, no more than lifeless, harmless carrion.

Shocked and disbelieving, the five young people slowly gathered around Sayyed. Kelene and Niela were unhurt, but Savaron had a laceration in his shoulder from the bear's claws, and Rafnir's arm had been torn by a stag's antler. Morad was white-faced as he knelt beside his brother. No one had to ask if Tomian was dead, for his throat had been torn to bloody shreds. Nearby, in the shadows of the bushes, lay Tomian's Hunnuli, its black coat ripped by claws and fangs, its neck bent at an unnatural angle.

Rafnir was the first to speak. "We fell asleep. I don't know how, but we fell asleep." His words were hoarse with disbelief. Morad looked up at him, tears streaming down his face, and Rafnir forced himself to go on. "The first thing I knew, that lion was attacking Tomian's Hunnuli. Tomian tried to save him, but the cat was too fast. Then all those animals came. Gods above, what were they?" he implored.

"The Oathbreakers said the wraith was trying to kill us. It seems to have found a way to do it," Kelene said, her arms wrapped tightly around her stomach.

Savaron kicked angrily at the dead lion. "But how did it move these beasts? And why did it take Tomian?"

The others fell quiet and stared around at the wreck of their camp and at the carcasses of the animals strewn about like the trophies of a grotesque hunt.

"The wraith will be back," Niela whispered. Her hands twisted the hem of her tunic into a knot.

"Without a doubt," replied Sayyed. He rubbed a hand over his face. He was so tired he could hardly focus and so weak he could barely hold his sword. But the despair that had eaten at him for days was gone. Deep in the pit of his soul, a small seed of determination germinated. Tam was dead. He accepted that now in every part of his heart. The dreams could not deceive him again. He had seen the face of his enemy, and although he did not know exactly what it was yet, he vowed silently to his god that he would do everything in his power to see it destroyed. "We're going to leave, now," he said abruptly.

All eyes snapped to him at the sharpness of his voice.

"But what about Tomian?" Morad demanded angrily.

"And Savaron's shoulder must be tended before infection sets in," Kelene insisted.

Sayyed held up a hand and took a deep breath of the damp night air to still his trembling legs. "I know," he reassured them. "Tomian died with honor, and we will bury him with his Hunnuli. Kelene, you will see to your brother and Rafnir. Then we must leave. We will move at night and rest in the daylight. The wraith hasn't tried to attack us during the day. Perhaps it's weaker then."

Savaron sat down heavily on a log. "Is it weaker in the day? Or do we just not see it through the sunlight?"

"I guess we'll find out," Sayyed muttered. Letting his head fall back, he stared up at the red ball of light still hanging over the clearing. The thunderstorm had moved to the south with its wind and rain. Except for the thunder that rumbled on the horizon, the copse of pine was quiet. He felt Rafnir's hands on his shoulders pushing him down to sit on the fallen tree trunk by Savaron.

"Stay there," Rafnir ordered. "Niela, Morad, and I will tend to Tomian."

The warrior decided not to argue. Given time his strength would return. In the meanwhile the younger ones were capable of handling the tasks waiting to be done. Afer came to stand behind him, and he leaned back against the Hunnuli's strong legs. The black's head loomed protectively over him. He was about to close his eyes when Tam's cat came stepping through the wet grass and hopped onto his lap.

Sayyed felt her soft fur under his fingertips. "Thank you," he whispered. "I was not ready to die."

Of course not, she meowed, settling down on his knee. *Tam told me to watch out for you.*

He chuckled softly and let his eyelids slide closed.

While Sayyed rested, the other travelers set to work. Niela and Morad took the sad task of preparing Tomian for the grave. They moved aside the dead lion, cleaned Tomian's body as best they could, and wrapped him in his cloak. Morad chose a wide spot between four pines, and, together, he and Niela used their magic to move enough dirt to open a deep pit. As they worked, Niela's voice joined the rustle of leaves and the faraway thunder to sing an ancient song of death. Her words trembled on the darkness with the power of grief and filled the copse with a sadness as old as the clans.

On her seat on the tree trunk, Kelene paused from stitching Savaron's wounded shoulder. She listened to the ancient words and felt the song shiver in her blood. She would miss Tomian, and she grieved for Morad, but it so easily could have been Savaron who fell, or Sayyed . . . or Rafnir. The thought sat like a hard lump in her throat, and her fingers tightened convulsively on Savaron's shoulder.

"Are you all right?" her brother asked softly.

She snapped out of her reverie, accidentally jerking her needle in the middle of a stitch. The unexpected pain made Savaron nearly leap off his seat. With a yelp, he swiveled his head and glared at her.

"So sit still! I can't sew a squirming snake!" she growled at him.

Gritting his teeth, he straightened so she could continue to stitch the two ragged claw marks on his back.

"Curse it all," Kelene said irritably. "I can't sew in this red glow. Rafnir, give me some real light."

Rafnir held a rag to his torn arm and said evenly, "Do it yourself." Both Savaron and Kelene looked at him in such astonishment, he added, "You're a magic-wielder. You know the spell. You do it."

The young woman frowned. He was challenging her, she knew that, and there was no way to get out of it with her self-respect intact without actually trying the spell. Her chin lifted, she closed her eyes, concentrated on the unseen power of magic around her, and repeated the spell her mother had tried to teach her so many times. She felt the magic stream into her like a comforting heat. Through her closed eyelids she saw a dim gleam of light. When she opened her eyes, it was there: a whitish sphere the size of her fist bobbing near her head. The light was small, and it flickered, but the results were hers!

Rafnir winked at her, and Savaron nodded in approval.

"Your shoulder has a nasty tear," Kelene observed as if nothing had happened. She went back to work, missing the grin that passed between Rafnir and Savaron. "Bear claws are filthy even when they're on living bears. I've cleaned the wound, but I will make a poultice for you when we have time." She pushed the small bone needle through his skin again and gently drew the horsehair through to tie a knot. Savaron's Hunnuli had donated the hair from his tail, and Kelene had the needle and a pot of wound salve in her medicine bag. She was glad now she had brought it.

Savaron nodded once, his jaw clenched too tightly to answer. When Kelene was finished, she dabbed the salve onto the wound and wrapped strips from one of Tomian's tunics around her brother's shoulder. "Try not to move it too much," she warned him. "I don't want to have to sew you up again."

Pale and cold, but relieved, he turned around again and asked, "Where did you learn how to do that?"

She smiled then, a twinkle of merriment in her black eyes. "I used to watch Piers. He taught me a lot. And," she chuckled as she helped him put his tunic back on, "I practiced on my horses."

Savaron grinned back at her. "Well, they must have been good patients, because you are very quick and gentle."

Kelene warmed at his praise and was still smiling when he moved to make a place for Rafnir.

"You ought to smile more often," the young sorcerer said, holding his injured arm out for her inspection.

Her smile faded, and she dropped her eyes to the torn skin on his arm. A strange nervousness crept into her, an embarrassment that startled and dismayed her. Her hands hovered in midair, hesitant to touch Rafnir. She did not mind touching her brother, for the feelings she sensed in him were familiar. The closeness they shared as brother and sister was something she had always accepted—even when she thought she could ignore it.

But Rafnir was different. He was, really, a stranger. Kelene did not know what he truly thought or felt. It frightened her when she realized suddenly that she cared very much what he was feeling. She wanted to think he was becoming her friend, but what if she touched him and sensed only dislike, dismay, or revulsion?

He regarded her quizzically, his face grubby with dirt and a two-day stubble, his eyebrow slightly arched.

To Kelene's consternation, she felt a warm flush rise up her face. "Blasted hands," she muttered to herself. It was probably her magic talent that gave her the empathic touch, but she had never used the strange ability enough to know what it really was or how to control it. Thank the gods, her empathy did not extend to understanding people's thoughts—their feelings were sometimes more than she wanted! She was glad Sayyed's red light overhead helped mask the blush in her cheeks.

To cover her nervousness, she tore off another piece of Tomian's tunic and used some clean water to rinse the blood and dirt off Rafnir's upper arm. Just looking at it in the light of her little sphere, she could see the tears were mostly superficial. The muscle of his arm had not been damaged, and the bone was intact.

Forcing her mind to concentrate only on keeping her magic light glowing, she leaned forward and grasped the edges of the wound with her thumb and forefinger to pull it together. Rafnir stirred, whether from pain or something else she didn't know, because at that moment the full force of his emotions battered at her concentration. She tried to block him out, but his feelings were so strong they shot through her mental defenses like a flight of arrows. Confusion, nervousness, surprise, pleasure, and fear were all there in a jumbled swarm that made her gasp. He was as unsettled as she was!

Calm down! It's all right! she told herself over and over until she could stop the trembling in her fingers. To her surprise, he seemed to absorb some of her reassurances. The overwhelming force of his emotions relaxed to a steadier, more accepting calm. Ever so gently she started stitching, refusing to look up into his face or acknowledge any of what she felt.

When she was finished, Kelene wrapped a torn strip of cloth around his arm and busied herself putting away the salve, the precious needles, and the remains of fabric. She looked everywhere but at Rafnir.

The young sorcerer did not move for a long moment. "I think Coren was right," Rafnir said slowly. "You have more ability than you think you do." He stood up. "Thank you," he said and hurried away to help with Tomian's grave.

Kelene watched him go, uncertain whether she felt surprised or pleased.

Thoughtfully, she took her medicine bag and went to check the Hunnuli for any injuries that might need tending.

A short time later, the gear and tents were packed, and the bodies of Tomian and his beloved horse were placed in the grave. The magic-wielders laid his weapons beside him and piled the earth into a mound, while the Hunnuli watched with star-filled eyes and Niela sang the prayers of the dead. It was late by the time they finished. The night was still and black; the sky was overcast with thick, rolling clouds. A wind promising more rain stirred the tops of the pines.

With Sayyed in the lead, the small party rode from the copse and headed north by northeast, away from the mountains, for the final leg of their journey. If all went well and the weary Hunnuli could maintain their pace, Sayyed estimated that, even if they rode straight through, they would reach the high plateau of Moy Tura only by sunset the next day. He hoped, perhaps, the ruins of the city would offer them some protection from the wraith. If not, he doubted they could stay in Moy Tura long enough to search for anything. The deadly spirit *and* the Korg, the ferocious guardian of the city, were more than his little band could handle at one time. He had already lost one of his companions; he did not want to lose any more.

The Hunnuli moved out at a jog trot, a steady, ground-eating pace that soon left the tree-clad slopes of the Himachals behind. The rolling grasslands opened out before them in a vast black emptiness. Only an occasional flash of lightning broke up the immense dark spaces that surrounded the travelers. Fortunately the ground was good and fairly level, so the Hunnuli had no trouble finding their way.

Rain began to fall again in scattered showers that came and went with annoying frequency. The clanspeople and horses were soaked, miserable, and tired to the point of exhaustion. The riders dozed intermittently, but the bad dreams clung to their minds, and fear rode by their side when they awoke. Everyone kept an anxious eye on the trail behind them, yet they saw no sign of the apparition in the heavy darkness.

When dawn came, the light was slow and grudging. The storm clouds hung tenaciously overhead, blocking the radiance of Amara's sun behind a low, threatening roof. The magic-wielders studied the sky and felt their spirits drop as low as the clouds. The Hunnuli were miserable, too. The horses had been traveling at a hard pace for three days with little sleep or food, and even their iron endurance was beginning to flag.

Then the wind veered to the east and strengthened to a strong gusting force. In what seemed only a few minutes, the winds ripped the clouds to shreds and opened the sky for the glorious morning light. The grasslands came to life under the warming sun. Insects shook off the wet and began to rustle in the tall grass. Birds soared on the wind, and the small wild antelope came out of sheltered gullies to feed.

Shortly Sayyed began to look for a place to stop. He wanted a place sheltered from the wind and the view of any passersby, but the grasslands were virtually treeless, gently rolling, and wide open. There wasn't any real cover as far as he could see. He settled at last for a depression at the bottom of three hills and led his small party down. The Hunnuli came to a grateful stop. The riders sighed and slumped on their horses' backs. No one tried to move.

Sayyed was about to dismount when he saw the birds. There were two of them, long, lanky, bald-headed death birds that were soaring in lazy circles overhead. Disquieted, Sayyed glanced around and saw nothing obvious that would attract carrion eaters. The other clanspeople didn't remark on anything strange. They were still sitting on the Hunnuli, too weary to move.

Are you well? Afer inquired quizzically.

"Yes, but look at those birds! What are the ugly things searching for?"

Afer lifted his muzzle. *What birds?*

Sayyed jabbed a finger at the sky. "Those birds. Can't you see them?" he demanded in disbelief.

No.

Sayyed's eyes narrowed. He could see the birds clearly, yet the Hunnuli did not, and now that he noticed, the other clanspeople did not seem to see the birds, either. In fact, his companions were looking rather strange. They were stiff and glassy-eyed and motionless on their horses. Kelene had drawn her dagger and was staring at her leg, Niela seemed asleep, and the three young men were gazing toward a far horizon as if an enemy troop were about to appear. What was going on? Sayyed glanced back at the sky.

The birds were still there. Three more joined the circle, then another five. The sky seemed filled with the black, silent birds slowly spiraling down, closer and closer. Sayyed ducked as one bird swooped by his shoulder, so close he could smell the odor of rotten meat clinging to its feathers. He slid off Afer and pressed his back close to the big stallion's side.

What is wrong? Afer snorted. Alarmed, he tossed his head in agitation.

"Birds," hissed Sayyed. "Everywhere." He looked up to see the carrion birds still floating above. "They're waiting for us to die." His voice grew louder and his hand crept toward his sword hilt.

There was a sudden bloodcurdling war cry behind him, and Sayyed whirled to see Savaron and Rafnir fling themselves from their startled mounts and come charging toward him, brandishing their swords.

The two young warriors were fast as lightning, and their murderous blades slashed toward Sayyed before he had time to react. Savaron's sword would have taken his head off if Afer hadn't plunged into the young man's path. Savaron rammed into the Hunnuli's bulk and fell flat on his back. At the same time, the white cat leaped from the stallion's shoulder to Rafnir's head and clung like a spitting, scratching cap. The young man was thrown off balance. The cat made an agile jump from his head and landed in the grass as Rafnir swerved, made a wild swing at Sayyed, tripped, and fell. Only Sayyed's quick parry kept the blade from slashing deep into his thigh.

All at once the six Hunnuli trumpeted a furious warning. The sound seemed to shatter the morning. To Sayyed, the scene shifted slightly out of focus, then snapped back into startling clarity. The birds were gone, his party was huddled in a sunny dale, and his son was looking up at him, white-faced and appalled.

"Father! I thought you were a Turic raider! I was going to kill you," Rafnir choked out.

Savaron, too, was stunned. "We both thought you were. I saw a mask, a black burnoose, and a Tulwark blade!"

"And I saw death birds." Sayyed leaned over and pulled his son to his feet. "Thank Afer that I did not become carrion for real birds."

"But what caused us to see these strange things?" Kelene cried. "They seemed so real. I thought a viper was on my leg. I was about to stab it when the Hunnuli neighed."

"I think our old friend is back, trying a new way to kill us," Sayyed said, slamming his blade back into its scabbard.

"But it's daylight," Kelene pointed out worriedly. "The wraith has never bothered us in the day before."

There was a muffled, choking cry, and everyone turned toward Niela. "Look," she said, pointing toward the brow of the nearest hill.

This time even the light of the sun could not hide the glowing outline of the apparition's shape. It stood above them, its face gloating and its robes perfectly still even in the strong wind. It lifted its head and howled in glee.

"It's getting stronger," Sayyed noted with apprehension.

"I don't think I want to wait around to see what he's going to throw at us next," said Savaron, jumping for his stallion's back. Rafnir and Sayyed followed his example. Weary as they were, the Hunnuli hastily abandoned the hill and broke into a canter away from the glowing wraith.

"Why doesn't it attack us directly?" Rafnir asked his father when they had returned to their northern heading.

Sayyed looked back. They seemed to be outdistancing the apparition, but how could he trust his eyes anymore? "I guess it's not strong enough yet. Maybe with each life it takes, it becomes more powerful. Besides," he growled, "why should it bother? It's defeating us now."

Conversation died out after that, and the little party continued on in silence, full of misgivings and fear. They rode fast across the sunlit grasslands with the wind at their backs and the wraith at their heels. The strange spirit did not try to waylay them again with more hallucinations. Instead it seemed content to simply follow them and bide its time.

By noon the cool dampness of morning had burned off to a dry, crackling heat. The wind blew away any extra moisture left from the rain. It tossed the long grass and kicked up the dust in stinging clouds.

Niela suddenly broke the long stretch of quiet. "Why doesn't the wraith attack us again?" she cried.

The others jumped at the sound of her voice. Sayyed answered, "It's probably waiting for us to stop. We're easier to reach then."

"We're going to have to stop sometime. The Hunnuli can't keep going without water," Kelene said worriedly. She had her hand pressed to Demira's sweaty neck; it was obvious that the smaller filly was tiring.

Rafnir thought about the magic shield he had used to guard his father the night before. That one had failed because he had fallen asleep. Perhaps a shield was still a useful idea. "What if we find a water hole and put up a defense shield around us while the horses rest? Between the six of us we should be able to hold the spell long enough for a break," he proposed.

"That wraith didn't react to my magic bolt," Morad grumbled. "What makes you think it will respect a shield?"

"Maybe it won't, but we have to try something!" Rafnir shot back.

Sayyed rubbed his gritty eyes. They were all getting short-tempered from fatigue and the heat, and most of the water in the water bags was gone. Kelene was right, they had to stop, if only long enough to water the horses. "Can you find a water hole, Afer?"

The big stallion slung his head in answer and veered off toward the right with the others close behind. They cantered along the slope of a long hill, over another wide, treeless swell, and down into a shallow valley. A dry creek bed meandered along the valley floor, its gravel bars still damp from the night's rain. A few sparse willows and cottonwoods lined the banks.

In the shadow of a rock outcropping beneath a trailing willow, the Hunnuli found water in a low, muddy pool that barely reached their hocks. They plunged in happily and dropped their heads to drink the warm water.

Rafnir wasted no time forming a spell that surrounded the travelers, the horses, and the water hole with a red, shimmering dome of magic impenetrable to everything but the outside air. Whether it would be proof against the wraith's strange ability to influence their minds, no one knew. Neither did they know how long they could hold their dome. Shields of magic power were difficult to maintain for a long period of time because they required a great deal of strength to keep them intact. No one in that little group would be able to hold a shield for long. They were all weary and feeling the strain of their difficult ride.

One by one the people dismounted, stretched, and began to open their packs for some food. The Hunnuli took their time drinking their fill, then fell to grazing on the thin grass growing along the banks.

The travelers had barely begun to eat when Kelene tugged Sayyed's sleeve and jerked her head toward their trail. He followed her frightened stare and saw the wraith coming slowly toward them. The clanspeople froze in place. The figure was moving steadily through the grass with a long, deliberate stride, its eyes fixed menacingly on the dome before it.

Alarmed, Sayyed realized the form was no longer nebulous. It had solidity, depth, and detail. Beneath the glowing outline of phosphorescence, its robes were the same dark red of a priest of Sorh, its feet wore woven sandals, its hands were long and supple, and in the depths of its dark blue eyes burned a loathing that drove a chill down Sayyed's back. The emotion was so intense on the wraith's face, its features were twisted askew in a mask of rage and abhorrence.

The figure walked to within two paces of the magic shield and stopped. It ran its fierce gaze over the dome, then studied the magic-wielders one by one. Every eye was locked on it; no one dared move. Very deliberately the wraith stepped forward and began to force its way through the magic wall. The shield wavered and dimmed under the assault.

"I can't hold it!" Rafnir shouted, and Sayyed, Savaron, Niela, and Morad came to his aid. Together they clasped hands and joined their power to his to strengthen the dome.

Kelene hesitated, because she had never tried to form or hold a shield. But when she took Rafnir's hand and joined the circle, she discovered the task was easier than she thought. Magic poured through her body from hand to hand; it sizzled in her blood, roared in her ears, and brought her mind brilliantly alive. She knew what she had to do and threw her entire will into the union of magic-wielders.

The shield suddenly burst into a blindingly bright scarlet hue, and the wraith, its form caught in the surge of power, was thrown backward. The wraith shrieked with fury and threw itself at the red barrier only to be forced back by the intense energy. Finally it spat a curse and stood back, its luminous outline glowing with its rage. "Sorcerers!" It hissed the name like a malediction. "Together you are strong, but you cannot endure against me for long. I will have my revenge."

"Who are you?" Sayyed demanded.

The apparition gave a sharp, bitter laugh. "Your destruction," it swore ferociously, and in the flick of a finger, it vanished.

The clanspeople stared at the place where the wraith had been standing, half expecting it to return and try again to break their shield. When nothing happened, they began to breathe easier. One after another, they withdrew from the union until only Rafnir was holding the shield together.

"At least we know it is not completely impervious to magic," Rafnir commented as he sat down on the outcropping.

"Yes," Savaron said, "except look how much power we used just to keep that thing away. How are we going to get rid of it?"

"One thing at a time," Sayyed suggested. He sank down to rest in the grass by Afer's feet. "We know we can keep him at bay for a short while, so relax while you can. We must reach Moy Tura by nightfall."

Morad paced around between the walls of the shield. "What good will that do us? What if it follows us in?"

"I'm hoping it won't want to invade a sorcerers' domain," said Sayyed.

"'Sorcerers' domain,' my mother's stew pot! That place is nothing more than an empty pile of rocks," Morad snapped.

"Do you have another suggestion?" Sayyed asked mildly, to which Morad only muttered something to himself and subsided into his own thoughts.

The others wasted no time following Sayyed's advice to rest. Savaron ate some food, then took over the shield from Rafnir so he could eat, too. Tam's cat sat by Afer's hooves and meticulously cleaned her fur. The Hunnuli drank and grazed while Niela brushed their sweaty coats, and Kelene checked Savaron's and Rafnir's wounds. Morad sat on the outcropping and stared morosely at the hills.

It was he who caught the first ill omen on the wind. He straightened and sniffed the air worriedly. Their magic shield was not impervious to smells, so when another breeze wafted around the dome, Morad rose like a startled hound. "Do you smell smoke?" he asked.

8

"Smoke?" exclaimed Sayyed, sitting upright fast. The clanspeople were all too familiar with the dangers of grass fires. They came to their feet in alarm. Savaron dissolved the shield, and the Hunnuli lifted their muzzles to test the air.

He is right, Afer confirmed. *There is smoke to the east. It smells of grass, not dung or wood.*

"You don't suppose the wraith had something to do with this?" Kelene suggested.

Niela, looking pale, added, "What if this is just another delusion?"

Sayyed shook his head. "The wraith's dreams and illusions have never affected the Hunnuli, and Afer confirms the smoke. I think this is real." He picked up his saddle pad. "Mount up," he ordered.

A short time later, the small party rode up the slope of the valley. The wind was stronger now, full of dust and sharp pieces of brittle grass. It snarled their cloaks, pulled at Sayyed's burnoose, and set the horses' tails flying. The riders paused at the top and looked back to the east.

The women drew a sharp breath at what they saw. Sayyed's palms broke into a cold sweat. The entire eastern skyline was ablaze with orange and yellow and smudged with rising black. As he shielded his eyes against the stinging wind, Sayyed discovered his clothes were covered with little black flecks. There were cinders in the air.

"North!" shouted Sayyed. "We'll cut across the fire's path and try to reach the plateau."

Strengthened by their rest and by growing fear, the six Hunnuli galloped north. They knew as well as their riders that they could outrun almost anything on the ground—except a firestorm. The wind swept across their trail, picking up dirt and debris and bringing the acrid smell of smoke. The Hunnuli pushed until their legs were blurs and their hooves thundered over the dry earth.

Far ahead, the travelers could see where the land began to change. The level grasslands grew hillier and more uneven. Small hills evolved to flat-topped buttes and rounded mounds; larger hills rose to ridges and eroded bluffs.

Sayyed knew that about three or four leagues beyond the first butte was a huge plateau and a trail leading up its steep side to the ruins of Moy Tura. If the travelers could reach that trail to the top of the plateau, they would be safe. Otherwise, Sayyed did not want to give much thought to their chances.

Gritting his teeth against the flying dust, he straightened over Afer's rising and falling neck and risked a glance to the east. The wall of fire was moving incredibly fast. Already it had halved the distance between its towering flames and the desperately running Hunnuli. The smoke was thickening, too, making the air hard to breathe.

Terrified animals began to cross their path. Antelope and deer went racing by without a glance; a wild dog, rabbits, and foxes darted side by side through the long grass. Birds flew frantically from the increasing gloom.

Sayyed looked ahead and saw the first butte just off to the right. The plateau was not far, but the warrior had a sick feeling in the pit of his stomach that it was too far. Already he could hear the fierce roar of the fire over the thunder of the Hunnuli's hooves. "Can you run any faster?" he yelled to Afer.

The stallion's reply was short and full of regret. *No.*

Sayyed understood. The Hunnuli had traveled an incredible distance in four days and were weary to the bone. Already Afer was having trouble breathing the hot, smoke-laden air, and his usually effortless pace was becoming labored. If Afer was having trouble, the others would be too, especially the smaller Demira. Sayyed looked back over his shoulder and saw her far behind the other horses. He took one more glance at the raging fire and made his decision. They weren't going to beat the flames, and there was no point breaking the horses in the vain effort of trying. They would have to stop and stand their ground.

"Pull up!" Sayyed bellowed. He brought Afer to a halt on the top of a low hill where a weathered outcropping of rock formed a cap over the hill's summit. As soon as the other Hunnuli gathered around in a huddled group, the warrior spoke rapidly to his companions. "Stay close together. I'm going to make an airtight shield around us, but I'll need your help to hold it."

"Will that work against such a fire?" Savaron yelled over the increasing roar of the flames.

"I don't know," Sayyed shouted back.

They all looked apprehensively at the approaching fire. From their position on the low hill they could see the towering wall of flames sweeping toward them. Tufts of tall prairie grass were exploding into flames, adding more and more smoke to the great cloud that billowed into the air to obliterate the sun. The noise was deafening, like an endless, rolling thunder.

Sayyed waited no longer. He had learned the spell from Gabria many years before, and the words came clearly to his mind. He envisioned exactly what he wanted—an airtight, impervious dome of magic—gathered in enough power to form it, then began the spell. Gabria had used this spell to contain a fire; Sayyed hoped it would work to keep one out.

At his command, five red pillars of energy rose from the stony ground around the horses and their riders. The pillars grew until they reached above the tallest man's head, then they curved over and united in the center. A clear red curtain spread out from each pillar and joined to form a dome surrounding the travelers. The roar of the fire was immediately silenced.

The clanspeople watched as the fire rushed toward them. The trapped air in the dome was hot and smoky, but it was certainly better than the stifling atmosphere outside.

Sayyed felt perspiration trickling down his face and shoulders, and his limbs began to tremble. He closed his mind to everything but holding the dome. Beneath him, Afer's sides were heaving, his black coat slick with sweat. Yet the stallion stayed as still as possible, so as not to distract the sorcerer. Hunnuli could not wield magic themselves, but they could lend their strength to their riders when such help was necessary. Afer gave Sayyed some of his power now, sending it pulsing through the mental link they had forged through years of friendship and devotion. Sparked from the white-hot lightning that gave the Hunnuli their power, Afer's might surged into his rider and bolstered Sayyed's flagging spell.

A moment later, Sayyed felt Rafnir join his power to the spell, then Kelene, Savaron, Morad, and Niela. The red dome flared to a brilliant ruby red.

And just in time. The wind blew burning pieces of grass around them and whipped the flames to a frenzy high over their heads. Smoke from the blaze rolled around them, almost smothering the lurid glow of the fire outside the red walls.

The great sea of flames was almost upon them when Morad yelled in alarm. His sudden cry startled them, and they looked up, horrified, to see the wraith standing by the dome's wall, the firestorm directly behind it. In that critical instant, their concentration slipped, and the spell wavered. An incredible heat and raging noise burst through the thinning walls and knocked the people reeling on their mounts.

"Enjoying my fire?" the wraith shouted. "All it took was an ember and a wave of the hand. Too bad it won't be so easy for you to survive." He laughed in anticipation.

But he laughed too soon. With the last of his energy, Sayyed threw all of his fury into the spell. The walls intensified again, just long enough for the others to recover and jump to his aid. The noise died down as the horribly bright wildfire engulfed them. The young people closed their eyes to the light and to the sight of the wraith waiting in the flames. They poured all of their abilities into holding the shield against the conflagration.

The seconds seemed to turn so slowly that the six riders thought the ordeal would never end. In truth, though, the firestorm passed as quickly as it came. Pushed by the high winds, it roared over the magical dome like a stampede, then thundered on to the northwest. The flames' glowing light died down, and the clanspeople opened their eyes. Outside the dome the smoke was still thick. A few small fires lingered behind in tufts of grass and shrubs, and the blackened earth smoldered. The wraith was nowhere to be seen.

The magic-wielders waited until the air in the dome was too old to use before they dissolved their life-saving shield. The hot wind struck them the moment the dome disappeared. The wind was still laden with ash and dust and acrid with the smell of burned grass, but it was blowing the worst of the smoke away.

The Hunnuli stepped gingerly off the unburned rock outcropping onto the charred, hot ground. As they walked, the scorched grass crackled under their hooves.

"Now I know what a loaf of bread feels like," Rafnir said into the quiet.

The riders broke into laughter that was made richer by the joy of their escape. The unspoken tension among them eased when they realized they were safe from the fire and only a few leagues away from the trail that led up to the top of the plateau and their destination. The fire was still raging to the east and north; however, it posed no threat to the plateau or to themselves as long as they stayed behind it.

"Can anyone see the wraith?" Sayyed asked his group.

There was a pause while the others studied their surroundings. "I think he's gone again," Savaron answered for them all.

"Where does he go?" Rafnir wondered aloud. "And how in Sorh's name does he keep up with us?"

The travelers remained silent. They had no answers about the wraith's baffling powers, only fears that the next time he took their party by surprise he would be more successful. The light mood of their escape dwindled away to trepidation. There were still a few leagues to go to Moy Tura and no guarantee that the apparition would not follow them inside the city.

The company hurried on and soon saw the high plateau rising like a fortress from the plains. They reached the trail without incident and without seeing the apparition again. The tired Hunnuli gratefully trotted off the burned-out path of the fire onto the stone-paved road that wended its way up the sides of the huge tableland.

The road was an old one, a remnant of the golden days when the clan sorcerers lived in the isolated splendor of Moy Tura on the crown of the highland. In those days, nearly three hundred years ago, men had revered magic-wielders, and a steady stream of visitors and supplicants had beaten trails to the city gates. But something had happened to erode the clans' trust in their sorcerers. In the short span of one generation, they turned completely against magic.

Sadly, no living clansperson knew the full truth of the tragedy, for when the clans betrayed Moy Tura, they destroyed everything touched by magic, thereby losing forever an important part of their heritage and tradition. Only a few scars remained to remind their descendants of the past. The old road was one of those.

Despite its age, the road was in fairly good condition. Its paving stones were still intact and only partially overgrown by grass and weeds that had crept between the seams. The going was easy enough that the Hunnuli completed the climb to the top of the plateau by early evening.

The younger people looked around curiously and were disappointed that there was not much to see. The high, bald-topped plateau stretched away as far as the eye could see without feature or landmark to break up the empty expanse. There was nothing but the arched sky, the setting sun, and the golden grass.

"Where is it?" demanded Morad, his flat face hard with irritation. He had expected to see the city's ruins rising in front of him like a giant pile of rubble.

"It's ahead. Not far," Sayyed answered wearily. At least he hoped it wasn't far. He was so exhausted he wasn't sure he could trust even his memory.

The rest of the party didn't seem much better. They were all black with soot and reeking of smoke. Kelene was dazedly patting her drooping filly while Niela sat on her horse, her shoulders sagging and her eyes half-closed. The three young men were looking more alert, but Morad's temper was showing and Savaron and Rafnir were grim-faced.

They were about to ride on when they heard the clop of hooves on the trail behind them. Sayyed warily straightened; the others looked back nervously. They were certainly not expecting anyone to be following them, so who else would be riding up that particular trail?

The sound of hooves drew closer.

The wind had died to a steady breeze and was blowing away from them, so the Hunnuli could not scent who was coming. Neither could they see the trail beyond the point where it dropped over the side of the plateau. Their only clue was the steady thud of hooves on the road.

Kelene felt the hairs on the back of her neck begin to rise. There wasn't supposed to be anyone on the trail behind them. Not on this plateau. She was at the end of the line of riders and had the clearest view of the road, so she pushed herself higher on Demira's shoulders and craned to see who was coming.

She was the first to spot the rider as he topped the slope. Her heart sank in recognition—it was the wraith. But it was his mount that clogged the breath in her throat and transfixed her with horror.

The glowing form was astride a Hunnuli, or what had once been a Hunnuli. The left side of the horse's head was crushed as if from a terrible fall; its neck was broken behind the ears forcing the head to hang at an unnatural angle. The once shining black coat was filthy with dirt and loose patches of decaying skin. The Hunnuli was obviously dead, yet by the wraith's uncanny power its corpse was making its way toward the travelers.

Kelene stared at the horse, her eyes bulging until she heard a choked gasp behind her.

"It's Tam's Hunnuli," Sayyed cried in a voice taut with rage and grief.

"That's how it followed us!" Morad yelled. "On a Hunnuli!" Outraged, he raised his palm to blast the animal.

Kelene saw Sayyed flinch as if he wanted to stop the Geldring, but the warrior clenched his hands into fists and watched wordlessly as Morad fired a bolt of the Trymian Force at the dead Hunnuli.

The bolt seared by Kelene and Demira, its blue energy crackling in the evening air. The blast struck the horse on the chest and sank harmlessly into the rotting hide. Somehow, Kelene was not surprised. Hunnuli were impervious to magic, and apparently that protective ability lasted beyond death.

The wraith lifted his head in a shout of derision. Kicking his mount into a gallop, he headed straight for Kelene and Demira.

Before Kelene could react, Demira wheeled away and bolted. The other Hunnuli took one stricken look at their dead former companion and fled with her. They galloped across the flat highland as fast as their tired legs could move, while behind them came the hollow rattle of the dead horse's hooves pursuing them into the gathering twilight.

Kelene ducked her head low over Demira's neck and dug her fingers into the filly's mane. She didn't need telepathic communication to know that the little Hunnuli was exhausted. She could feel it in every swing of Demira's legs, in the frantic cast of those lovely deep eyes, and in the red-cupped nostrils that could not suck in the air fast enough. Demira's coat was soaked with sweat and spume flew from her mouth.

Kelene wanted to cry for her. Even though she was falling farther and farther behind, the filly was struggling on with every muscle and sinew to keep going.

The girl stole a quick glance over her shoulder and saw the wraith was drawing close. His menacing form was bent forward; his hand was reaching out toward her. She felt a powerful urge to scream. She had no clear idea what would happen if the wraith touched her, but she had no wish to find out. She pushed forward over Demira's neck, her eyes squinted against the wind, and felt her fury kindling.

Kelene was sick to death of this hideous being! She hated his power over their minds and the terror that clung to his presence. She deeply resented his merciless pursuit, which was forcing this Hunnuli she liked and respected to run beyond the edge of endurance. All she wanted to do was get away from him. But how? She couldn't just turn her back and hope he would go away, nor could she use her clumsy, unskilled magic against him. Somehow she had to help Demira go faster.

The girl glanced back to see the wraith only a few paces behind. Now would be a good time to learn to fly, Kelene thought, trying to force down her growing panic. She desperately scanned her mind for any idea that could help her, but all she could think about was flying. If Demira could fly, she could escape, Kelene was certain of that. There had to be something she could try.

She searched her mind again, and this time she remembered the story of Valorian's escape from the chasm in Gormoth. Even though he had been untrained in his new power, Valorian had created a magic spell that used the wind to lift his horse. Perhaps she could do the same thing—if she could lift Demira out of the wraith's reach and relieve some of the strain on the young horse's legs.

Her problem was she had never tried to use a spell that complicated. Gods, she hadn't used *any* spell in five years—until last night. What if something went wrong again? What if she hurt Demira or killed them both? A cold pit of fear settled in her stomach, but she knew she couldn't let it stop her. The wraith was almost alongside. She could smell the stink of the dead horse and hear the apparition's throaty chuckle.

"You are mine, you broken-footed excuse for a magic-wielder," he hissed at her.

Clenching her teeth in fury, Kelene ducked away from him until she was almost hanging on Demira's right side. "Watch your feet," she warned the filly. "I'm going to try something."

Hurry! Demira responded. Beneath the entreaty there was an undertone of faith and trust that gave Kelene the last boost of confidence she needed. With all the will she could muster, she pulled magic from the earth and forced its power into her control. She pictured in her mind a moving platform of wind, large and strong enough to hold a horse's weight, yet swift enough to carry them away from the wraith. Using her magic, she caught the evening breeze, bound it to her spell, and shaped the wind to her purpose. Because she had created the spell herself, she had no formal incantation, so she set the spell into motion by using her own words to describe exactly what she wanted.

The words were barely out of her mouth when Demira stumbled. If Kelene hadn't had the skill and strength of an Induran rider, she would have been pitched off. As it was, she was knocked even farther off Demira's right side, and her concentration on the magic began to falter.

Strengthen the spell! Demira sent to her frantically. *I am falling through it.*

Hanging on to the filly's mane with both hands, Kelene fought to keep her leg hooked over the Hunnuli's back while she closed her eyes and forced her will into her spell. She felt the magic pour through her, a wild primitive power that made her blood sing with its energy. Fiercely she sent it downward to reinforce the support under Demira's body.

Almost at once, the little Hunnuli stopped galloping. At the same time Kelene felt a strange rising sensation in the pit of her stomach.

"Kelene!" the girl heard Rafnir yell, but she ignored his voice and ignored the increasing wind that tugged at her. All she heard was the wraith's howl of rage. Her eyes flew open to see the ground moving by nearly eight feet below. Demira was airborne!

Shaking with relief and pleasure, she scrambled back up onto Demira's back. The filly, relieved of the weight on her legs and the hard resistance of the ground, bobbed her head in thanks. Although Kelene's wind was carrying her, Demira instinctively moved her legs back into a canter. Her hooves dug into the wind, and she soared forward, skimming the ground like a falcon. The wraith and dead mount fell behind.

Faster than Kelene imagined, they came up beside the others. Morad and Niela watched her, openmouthed. Rafnir looked up, grinned, and clenched his fist in salute.

She lifted her hand to wave back, then changed her move to a warning gesture. The wraith, furious at his loss of one victim, had increased his mount's speed and was closing in on the other Hunnuli. The five black horses put all their strength into that desperate run, but they were worn and hungry, and their speed was badly diminished. The dead Hunnuli was catching up.

Kelene saw their danger all too clearly. She wanted to help, except she could barely keep Demira going. She had not realized she would need so much strength to keep her spell intact. The girl knew her friends' only hope was to reach the ruins before the wraith. Perhaps if they knew where to go . . .

She directed the wind carrying Demira to lift the filly higher above the racing horses. From that vantage point Kelene scanned the darkening horizon. A little to her right she saw something large and dark rising from the plain ahead. It was difficult to distinguish its character in the twilight, yet the irregular outline could be only one thing on this flat plateau.

"Moy Tura!" she shouted to Sayyed. A wave of his hand sent her to the forefront, and she led the frantic rush toward the old ruins. Stride by stride the horses drew closer to Moy Tura. Soon everyone could see the high, crumbling walls, the broken parapets, and the empty towers.

"There lies your city of the sorcerers," the wraith suddenly shouted. He was close behind Morad, and his harsh voice made the Geldring cringe. "Its walls are shattered! Its corrupt and evil towers have been ground into dust. Its heretics lie dead in their own blood. That is the fate of all magic-wielders who defile the powers of the almighty gods! You can flee, profaners, but you will still perish!"

Kelene shut her ears to the wraith's cruel words and guided her companions toward the only entrance she could find in the high city walls. She saw two broken towers to either side of a wide, rounded archway, and caught a glimpse of the gates that had once hung there, now lying in pieces in the dirt. A moment later, she and Demira were through the gateway and into the shadowed streets of the city. She lowered Demira to the ground before gratefully dissolving her spell. Rafnir, Niela, and Savaron came thundering in just behind her.

The four of them gathered close together just inside the gates and waited for Sayyed and Morad. They knew there was nowhere to run in the ruins if the wraith came in after them, so they prepared to stand and fight.

Just outside, Sayyed and Afer slowed until Morad and the wraith were nearly alongside. The apparition's mount was bumping Morad's Hunnuli, and the young man was hanging onto his stallion's neck for dear life.

With a shriek, the wraith reached out for Morad. His long, grasping fingers were almost on the young sorcerer's tunic when Sayyed shouted angrily, "Priest!"

His sharp voice drew the apparition's attention away from Morad. Afer, trying to forget that the dead Hunnuli had been his friend and companion for twenty-three years, veered sideways and slammed into the horse's side. The broken stallion staggered, giving Morad's horse the chance to shoot ahead through the gateway and join the others.

Snarling a malediction, the wraith turned on Sayyed. "Profaner," he cursed. "You think to escape me, but I spent my life hunting your kind." It wrenched the dead horse toward Afer.

The big black made one last valiant plunge into the ruined gateway and wheeled to a stop within the stone walls. There Afer paused, and he and Sayyed faced the apparition on the other side of the entrance. The white cat, who was clinging to the saddle pad and packs behind Sayyed, poked her head around his side and spat at the dead priest.

The warrior raised his hand. "Come no farther, priest," he commanded. "You do not belong here!"

The wraith hesitated, his glowing eyes staring at the high gateway. A flash of doubt crossed his enraged face as if he had seen those gates before. But the doubt was gone in a flash of arrogance and scorn, and he laughed out loud. "Neither do you, sorcerer. Your ways are dead." He kicked his mount forward.

The clanspeople tensed, ready to come to Sayyed's aid. Sayyed did not move. He was too weary to run any longer and too angry to try. If the wraith wanted to enter Moy Tura to fight the magic-wielders, he would have to get past him. He watched coolly as the grotesque horse came closer and closer. The wraith's phosphorescent outline gleamed with a sickening hue in the dark twilight; the stench of death saturated the air. Sayyed felt his guts twist as the wraith came within two paces of the gate. His warrior's instincts brought his hand to the hilt of his sword. Although he doubted the blade would help him against this fearsome apparition, the familiar grip of the leather-bound hilt felt comforting in his hand. He was about to unsheathe it when the dead Hunnuli stopped.

It was almost nose to nose with Afer, but it could not seem to come any closer. The wraith shouted furiously and leaped off the Hunnuli, letting the dead horse collapse back to the ground in a heap. On foot, the apparition lunged at Sayyed and was brought up short by some unseen power.

Sayyed raised his head to the thick stone roof of the gateway and silently breathed a prayer of thanks to Amara and to the ancient builders of Moy Tura. Some of the old wards of the city were still intact.

Screeching with rage, the wraith tried again and again to force his way into the entrance, only to be thrown back every time. The old wards were as powerful as the wards that had guarded his tomb; he could not overwhelm them.

Finally he stood back and glared balefully at Sayyed. "So. Not all of the magic was destroyed. No matter. You are trapped." His expression shifted to one of gloating contempt. "I have been watching you, magic-wielder. I know you are here to seek help for your dying people. But you won't find it in this dead shell! Soon you will have to leave . . . and I will be waiting." He turned on his heel and strode into the night.

The clanspeople stayed still until the red phosphorescence of the wraith's robes disappeared in the dark. Then Sayyed's hand fell from his sword. That slight movement was like a signal that broke the tension. The younger people gathered around the warrior and Afer, talking all at once in loud, excited voices until their leader held up his hand. For the first time in days, he gave them a weary smile. "Let's find a place to rest," he suggested.

They were very willing to do that and were just turning back into the city when a deep roar echoed in the distance, the voice of a hunting lion.

"The Korg," Niela whispered.

Rafnir looked around at his companions' sooty faces and at the sweating, drooping Hunnuli. "I think we just jumped out of the fire into the cooking pot," he said.

9

The clanspeople went no farther that night. They found shelter in the ground-floor room of a tumbled-down tower beside the old city wall and made camp as best they could. No fire was lit and no one spoke above a whisper for fear of attracting the guardian lion of Moy Tura.

Sayyed was the only one of the group, and one of only three people still alive in the clans, who had ever seen the Korg. Nevertheless, he did not need to impress a sense of caution and danger on his companions. They had all heard the legends of the Korg and listened to the tales of Gabria's journey through Moy Tura over twenty years before. They knew the huge stone lion defended the ruins against any intruders and would kill as mercilessly as any real lion.

With the wraith outside the walls and the Korg prowling somewhere in the ruins, the travelers felt like rabbits trapped between a hawk and a fox. Still, they were grateful for the shelter and the chance to rest. Each Hunnuli and rider took a turn at standing watch while the others slept. For the first time in three nights they were able to sleep long and well without terrors stalking their dreams.

Daylight was streaming through broken timbers in the roof when Sayyed came slowly awake to find a warm, rough tongue licking his cheek. He felt a soft weight standing on his chest, and paws that gently kneaded his neck.

Get up, the white cat insisted noisily. *You are awake, and I am hungry.*

He cracked an eye and saw her golden orbs staring at him intently. "Did you ever have a name?" he whispered, speaking more to himself than the cat. Tam had always felt an animal should name itself, but she had not had enough time to learn her cat's name, and Sayyed had not thought about it until that moment.

The cat tilted her head and meowed. *Name? No name yet. I am she who walks with the moon. I am Tam's friend. I am Sayyed's friend.* Afer stuck his nose close and gently nudged her. She swatted at the big horse, knocking herself down and rolling over on Sayyed's face. *I am Afer's friend, too,* she growled playfully.

Sayyed plucked the cat off his head and sat up. "Do you want a name? You have certainly earned one."

Like a weasel, she slipped from his grasp and sat down on the ground, her regal eyes unblinking. *I will think about it.*

"Good. Meanwhile, we must get to work." The warrior climbed to his feet and roused the others. Savaron was already outside, keeping a watch for unwelcome intruders. The rest of the party stretched and yawned their way to their feet. As quietly as possible, they ate some trail bread, cheese, and dried fruit, then readied themselves to begin the search for the healers' records.

When they were set to go, Sayyed picked up a broken stick and began to sketch in the dust. "This is just a rough map of the city, since the last time I was here I was only trying to get out. From what I remember, the city was built like a twelve-sided geometric shape with four gateways, one here in the south and three more to the west, north, and east." He pointed his stick at each place and drew lines from the gates to the middle of his map. "These broad streets go straight from the entrances to the center of the city. We know this area must have been the heart of Moy Tura, since the Sorcerers' Hall and a large temple are there. That's a good place to begin."

Niela asked, "What exactly are we looking for?"

"Anything that could be connected to healing. Look for places where the healers might have stored records, for libraries, houses of healing, shops that sold herbs, or even burial places. Use your eyes and your imaginations. Don't disregard anything that catches your attention." Sayyed ran his fingers over his bearded chin and looked at each face in turn. "We'll start at the center and work our way out. I don't need to tell you the Korg is dangerous. Just be alert. If we get separated, meet back here," he finished.

The others nodded, their expressions a blend of nervousness, apprehension, and excitement. They tied strips of cloth around the horses' hooves to muffle the sound of their movements on the stone streets and removed any metal objects on their persons that could jingle or rattle. When everyone was finished, they rode from the tower room in single file.

The sun was well up as they gathered by the shattered gate. The light gleamed on the stones and filled the ruins with bright heat. A flawless sky soared overhead, and the wind was breathlessly still. Other than the dead Hunnuli still lying by the gate, there was no sign of the wraith, and no evidence of the Korg, either. The city was eerily silent.

The Hunnuli left the shadow of the city wall and walked out onto the wide, rubble-strewn road that led into the heart of the city. For once the white cat did not ride with Sayyed but trotted ahead of the horses, her tail held high.

For a long while it was a very quiet group that rode through the ruins, their eyes wide with awe and curiosity. They stared at the remnants of what had once been the most beautiful city on the Ramtharin Plains.

Built by the clan sorcerers over three hundred years ago, Moy Tura had been the epitome of their skill and love of beauty. Within its walls had lived the finest of the clan magic-wielders: the teachers and apprentices, the healers, the shapeshifters, craftsmen, and the all-powerful Council of Twelve. They had loved their city so well, they had introverted themselves in its isolated beauty. They never recognized their own clans' distrust, envy, and hate until it was too late.

Through treachery and betrayal, an army of clansmen broached the city's defenses and took Moy Tura by storm. The army slaughtered almost all of the inhabitants, plundered the city, and razed the buildings so Moy Tura would never be used again. After that, they marched on the summer gathering and massacred every known magic-wielder in the clans.

What became known as the Purge proved horribly effective. Only a few magic-wielders escaped death by fleeing the Ramtharin Plains or going into hiding. Magic became reviled and despised, sorcery was forbidden on pain of death, and Moy Tura, the once glorious jewel of the plains, crumbled into dust and faded into legend. For two hundred years it had lain abandoned, shrouded in mystery and guarded only by a lonely stone lion.

Gabria and her companions had been there once, years before, on the trail of Lord Branth. Sayyed remembered that journey well. It was on that expedition that he had met Tam, learned to use his power, and found Afer. Moy Tura had been only a brief and terrifying stop on a long journey, but the memories of the place were burned indelibly into his mind.

He thought he would not be bothered by the emptiness and desolation, yet the old ruins touched him more poignantly than they had that morning so long ago. He stared as hard as his young companions at the piles of rubble covered in dust and clambering vines, at the weed-choked streets, the roofless towers, and the empty gaping windows. He saw piles of broken statuary blotched with lichen, shattered fountains, and gardens long overgrown and filled with debris. The city looked so bleak and forlorn in the morning sun it made him heartsick, and he cursed the terrible waste of life, talent, and wisdom.

Behind him, the other magic-wielders were studying the ruins with mixed emotions. Morad saw only heaps of rocks and places where enemies could hide. Niela was ready to leave at her first chance. She had a cold, sick feeling about this place, and although she wouldn't speak of it, she was badly frightened. Savaron and Rafnir were curious, but they were too busy checking their surroundings to see beyond the narrow streets and the ruined buildings that crowded around them.

Only Kelene looked into her imagination and tried to see the city as it might have been—whole, clean, alive with people, crackling with the magical energy of hundreds of magic-wielders. It must have been lovely, she mused, before the gray and white granite buildings were torn down and covered with dust, before the flowers and gardens were trampled, before the streets ran with blood and became barren stream beds wending their way to extinction.

Sorrow tightened Kelene's throat with unshed tears. The images in her mind were so vivid, she stared around at the destruction, half expecting to see a face in one of the dark doorways or hear footsteps in an alley. But there was no life to see beyond a lizard that scuttled into a crevice and the flies that followed the Hunnuli. The emptiness hit her like a sharp ache.

Tears filled her eyes. Her feelings were startling in their intensity, for until this journey, she had never been deeply moved by the history of her people, especially the magic-wielders. Now she found herself mourning the murdered sorcerers and their families almost as deeply as she grieved for her brother. Blind and thoughtless to their clans though they might have been, they had not deserved their fate.

Kelene shook her head. This is ridiculous, she chided herself. Why should I weep for people whose bones have turned to dust, when my own family is dying two hundred leagues away? Her fingers clutched the gem on her tunic, and she remembered that in all the haste to reach Moy Tura, she had not checked on her mother in two days. Anything could have happened in that length of time. She promised herself to do it that night when she could concentrate on the stone in the peace and relative safety of their shelter.

The little party rode deeper into the vast ruins. They said nothing to each other since it seemed better to ride in quiet haste and start their search as soon as possible. The silence around them was oppressive, the emptiness thoroughly depressing. Clanspeople were accustomed to busy camps and open spaces; this dead city was almost intolerable.

They were all relieved when the Hunnuli came to a high stone wall with four arches opening into the spacious courtyard of a large temple. The temple, once a magnificent, multi-columned edifice, was now only a heap of old stone.

"I recognize this," Sayyed murmured. "We almost caught Branth here. The Sorcerers' Hall should be just beyond."

The Hunnuli picked their way around several piles of rubble, went past the stone wall, and walked into a wide, sunny square where the four main roads converged.

Two hundred years ago the square had probably been an open-air market and gathering place for the entire city. Its wide expanse had been skillfully paved with slabs of granite that had withstood years of trampling feet, wagon wheels, and horses' hooves, only to be stained with blood and left to the mercy of sun and weather. The stones were pitted, cracked, and worn, but they were mute evidence to the love and labor of the artisans who had laid them.

"Look over there," Rafnir said softly, pointing to the center of the square. The others followed his gaze and saw a black obelisk topped by a golden, rayed sun. The sun design was easily recognizable since it had been used by the clans for generations to honor Amara, the mother goddess. The clanspeople gathered around the pillar and stared up at the sun shape towering nearly twenty feet over their heads. It was lovely even through its cloak of grime and bird droppings. Its gold gleamed in the clear sunlight, and its rays were straight and intact.

"I wonder why the warriors didn't tear that down, too," Rafnir commented. He waved at the remnants of the buildings around the square. "They didn't miss anything else."

Savaron tore his eyes away from the gold sun and glared around at the ruins. "They probably didn't want to anger the goddess," he said, then added with real bitterness, "though why they should worry about that when they were destroying her city and washing themselves in their own clan blood, I don't know!"

Kelene looked toward her brother in admiration. So he felt it too—the grief and anger and sense of loss. She wondered if the reason she and Savaron felt the disaster of this place so keenly was because of their parents. Not just because Gabria and Athlone had come through here and brought their own impressions of Moy Tura to the clans, but because the chieftain and the Corin woman were the first clanspeople since the Purge to be allowed to live and practice sorcery. Gabria and Athlone could have so easily become victims of the same hatred that razed this city. The realization made Kelene shudder.

"There's the Sorcerers' Hall," said Sayyed, interrupting her thoughts.

At the north end of the square sat a broad flight of steps that led up to the skeleton of what had once been a large building. It seemed to the onlookers that the building had suffered the worst of the victors' savagery. Not only were its outer walls torn down to its foundation, but the broken pillars and heaps of rubble within showed the unmistakable scorch marks and heat fractures of a large fire.

"Not much left of it," Morad said sourly. "How do you know that's what it was?"

"By its height," Savaron answered before Sayyed could reply. "Look at those steps. The Sorcerers' Hall was said to be the tallest building in the city. The Council of Twelve had their chambers in the very top, so they could look down on their whole domain. Sorcerers came to study here and to teach those who followed. Matrah wrote his tome in one of those vanished rooms."

Morad grimaced. "Yeah, I know all that. So tell me something I don't know. Where are the healers' records?"

"And where is the Korg?" Niela added. She had to clear her throat to steady her voice.

Sayyed slid off Afer and patted the black's neck. "Two excellent questions. Let's see if we can find the answer to just the first." He studied the buildings around the square before he continued. "We'll split up into two groups and start at the Sorcerers' Hall. Rafnir, Kelene, and Savaron, work your way along the eastern side. Niela and Morad will come with me to the western side."

The travelers quickly dismounted, broke into their groups, and hurried toward the Sorcerers' Hall, the Hunnuli and the cat following along. At the steps of the great hall, they realized there was no point wasting time searching that ruin. Everything above the foundation was destroyed. They went on to the next set of buildings at either side.

Sayyed and his companions disappeared into the remains of what could have been a barracks or dormitory. Kelene and the two warriors found themselves in a structure comprised of numerous spacious rooms. The roof had collapsed onto the second floor above and most of the walls were crumbling. Fortunately, a few support beams held up enough of the first-floor ceiling to give the three people spaces to search.

Carefully they worked their way into the dim interior. The first room was lit only by beams of light gleaming through cracks in the ceiling. Nevertheless, there was enough illumination to show the clanspeople that the place had been deliberately wrecked. The floor was a shambles of broken furniture, smashed glass and crockery, and tools, all buried under two centuries of dirt, cobwebs, and windblown debris.

"This must have been a house of artisans," Rafnir speculated. "Wood-working tools," he said, holding up several old chisels, their wooden handles rotted away.

"You may be right," Kelene called from another room. "There are stone-carving tools and slabs of marble in here."

For the next few hours they searched, room to room, house by house, one building at a time around the square, and found nothing. Early in the afternoon they entered what looked like a large apothecary shop where they spent the better part of an hour searching through shelves, bins, and broken jars. After a while Rafnir went outside through an overgrown garden to check some outbuildings. Kelene and Savaron continued their investigation into the next set of rooms facing the square.

Kelene's ankle and foot were throbbing when she finally dropped down on a fallen timber and pushed her hair back from her face.

"You made a smudge," said Rafnir from the doorway. He walked into the room, carrying something small under his arm. With a smile, he wiped the dirt off her forehead and sat down beside her.

Savaron, just behind them, grinned to himself and slipped out of sight into another part of the building.

Kelene felt her heart begin a slow pound. If anyone had asked her on the afternoon of the Induran race if she would want to sit beside Rafnir, she would have spat in the speaker's face. Now, after all that had happened since that momentous race, she not only wanted him to sit there, but she felt safe, exhilarated, warm, and lightheaded all in one rush of emotion. It was a reaction she had not anticipated. Kelene sat close to him, so breathless and confused she didn't know what to say. She prayed he would not make any mention of her ankle at that moment. His pity she didn't need.

Happily, he didn't. Instead he tilted his head and looked at her. "How did you do that spell yesterday?"

Kelene was so startled by his question that she couldn't remember for a moment. "What spell?"

"Valorian's spell to form a platform of wind. It was brilliant."

She blushed at his compliment and looked down at the rocks by her feet. "It was desperation."

He laughed, a deep, pleasant sound. "Well, it worked. Demira flew like the wind."

"No," Kelene said, raising her head again. Her confusion was forgotten in the remembrance of the day before. "She didn't fly. Not like I want her to fly. She was only carried by air and magic, and I couldn't have kept her up much longer. The spell took too much strength to sustain. If Demira is going to truly fly, she must do it on her own."

Rafnir grinned broadly, his eyes boring into hers. With deliberate casualness, he uncovered the object under his arm and handed her a flat chunk of weathered marble. "I found this for you. It was part of a frieze over a door in the garden back there."

The marble felt cold to Kelene's hands. The top was featureless, but the bottom was knobby and uneven to the touch. The girl turned it over and stared at the delicate relief carving on the stone. The subject was fanciful; the workmanship was exquisite and detailed. It was so perfect it brought tears to Kelene's eyes.

"A winged horse," she breathed. She ran her fingers over the raised figure, tracing its prancing legs and the wide, outstretched wings that curved gracefully from powerful shoulders.

She turned her shining eyes to Rafnir, and he felt a quiver tingle through him. "I, uh, broke it off . . . I didn't think the owner would mind," he managed to say.

"This is it," Kelene said, jabbing a finger at the carving. "This is what we have to do!" She subsided into silence while her imagination sprang free of the earth and went wheeling among the clouds. "A winged horse," she sang to herself, and the words glittered in her mind. She hugged the old stone carving to her chest. She had the image now; the end result was clear in her mind. Somehow they had to devise a workable spell that would create that result without injury to Demira.

Was it possible? Kelene tucked the marble tile inside her tunic. She hoped so. By the gods, she hoped so!

"Thank you," she began to say to Rafnir when she heard Niela call somewhere outside.

"Kelene! Rafnir!" Niela shouted nervously. "Savaron! Where are you?"

Kelene rushed to her feet in alarm. "She shouldn't be yelling like that." Before she could limp to the nearest opening, Rafnir was past her and running out the doorway.

Just as he left the building, the quiet was abruptly shattered by a tremendous roar that reverberated through the square. Kelene heard all six Hunnuli neigh a wild challenge as Niela screamed in terror.

"Niela! Run!" Kelene beard Rafnir yell. Kelene lunged frantically for the doorway. Under the sudden pressure of her weight, her weak ankle gave way, and she stumbled into the wall. She would have fallen if Savaron hadn't come up behind her and caught her arm.

"What's happening?" he cried, steadying her against the broken doorframe. They both looked out in time to see the Korg bounding across the square toward the running figure of Niela. Kelene's fingers clenched the wood, and her voice rose in a scream. "No!"

Half again as large as a Hunnuli, the Korg was shaped of gray stone in the form of the maned cave lions that roamed the Darkhorn Mountains. Long, powerful legs drove its massive body with incredible speed after the fleeing clanswoman. Kelene felt herself go numb as she watched Niela desperately trying to reach the cover of the nearest building. Sayyed and Morad raced after her from their side of the square, and Rafnir closed in from the opposite direction, but Kelene realized they had little hope of reaching the Jehanan woman. The Korg was gaining too rapidly.

Only Niela's Hunnuli moved faster than the stone lion. Like a black streak, the mare galloped across the paving stones to defend her rider. The Korg was a leap away from catching Niela when the Hunnuli charged between them and reared, pounding her hooves in the face of the huge lion. The Korg barely paused. It towered over the furious horse, its round eyes glowing with an uncanny gold light, its stone teeth bared. In one swipe of a large front paw it smashed the black mare to the ground.

Niela stumbled in horror. She clamped her hands to her head, and wailed a long, rending scream of anguish.

The remaining Hunnuli neighed again, their voices high in anger and grief.

"Stay here," Savaron snarled to Kelene. He threw himself on his stallion and galloped after the other men. From several different directions, the four men raised their hands and fired a barrage of the deadly blue Trymian force at the Korg. The lion roared in anger. It was knocked back a pace by the powerful energy, but the bolts bounced harmlessly off its body. Before the men could fire a second time, the Korg pounced forward.

Kelene screamed again as the fearsome beast crushed her friend under its stone paws. Through her tears she saw the lion trample Niela and toss her like a bloody rag onto a heap of rubble.

Her face hot with fury, Kelene limped out the doorway ready to find Demira and join the battle against the Korg in spite of her brother's order. She had no more than set foot out the door when the Korg turned and, as quick as lightning, went after Sayyed. The warrior sprang for Afer's back.

Sayyed bellowed, "Scatter! All of you!" and Kelene threw herself back inside the shadowed building.

The young men obeyed, too. Vaulting astride their Hunnulis, Morad and Rafnir fled from the square in two different directions. Savaron disappeared past a broken archway down a side street. Sayyed took one last look after his companions, then fired another bolt of magic at the Korg to draw him on. Afer, the Korg close on his heels, galloped down the northern road and vanished into the ruins.

The square, empty now except for the bodies of Niela and her Hunnuli, fell silent. From the dark doorway, Kelene peered out and spotted Demira close by, pressed into a narrow space between the broken walls of two buildings. The little Hunnuli was visibly trembling. Thankfully, the girl eased out the door and joined the horse in her hiding place. They stood for a long time pressed together while Kelene's tears wet Demira's dusty coat.

When the silence and solitude of the square became too much to bear, Kelene and the filly slipped from their shelter and moved warily toward Niela. There was no question that the woman and the mare were dead. Their broken, torn bodies were already swarming with flies.

Kelene swallowed hard and looked around the square. There was no sign of anyone to help her with the task she wanted to do, but she was not going to leave Niela to the carrion eaters. While Demira kept watch, Kelene dragged the woman's body close to the mare and laid them out together. There was no time to build a pyre or dig a real grave, so Kelene used a levitation spell to move chunks of rock around and over the bodies until they were completely covered.

The magic worked so well for her she was able to complete the task before the sun had moved perceptibly in the sky. All the spells and lessons her mother had tried to reach her must have soaked in after all, she mused when she placed the final stone on the cairn. She was growing more confident with her talent and more comfortable with the feel of magic coursing through her. Niela would have been proud of her.

Sudden anger made Kelene kick a rock across the paving. She raised her fist to the sky. "What do you want us to prove?" she shouted to the gods in their firmament. "First the plague, then the wraith, now the Korg. Can't you give us a little help?" There was no answer from the bright sky—not that Kelene expected one from gods who remained so mysterious and aloof.

But Demira tossed her head nervously. *Kelene, I do not think yelling is a good idea.*

The young woman clenched her teeth to keep her anger from boiling out any more. The filly was right—shouting could bring trouble. Kelene bent down instead and twisted a piece of flowering vine around the top stone of the cairn.

She felt a soft muzzle nudge her elbow, and she wrapped her arms around Demira's neck. The sweet, familiar smell of horse filled her nostrils; the black hairs tickled her cheek. To her, though, the most soothing sensation was the warm trust and comfort she felt in the Hunnuli's presence. Gone was her old reluctance to ride the black horses. Now she felt only pride and honor as she pulled herself up onto the filly's back. She wasn't certain how Demira felt about their new friendship, but Kelene had a notion that her gelding, Ishtak, would have to find a new master.

The filly cautiously trotted across the square toward the southern road, her muffled hooves making dull thuds on the stone, her nostrils flaring to catch the slightest scent. They were almost to the walled temple when they heard a yowl behind them. They looked back to see the white cat streaking across the rubble.

Wait for me! she cried. With a powerful leap, she sprang onto a pile of stone and up into Kelene's lap.

Kelene pulled the cat close. "You're trembling," she said. "Are you all right? Where is Sayyed?"

The cat meowed, *I am not hurt. Scared! That was big cat! I have not seen Sayyed since lion chased him away.*

"The Korg is not a real cat, you know," Kelene told her in an uneasy whisper. She was glad for the small animal's company. Talking to her helped take her mind off her own fear. "My mother told me the Korg was once a powerful sorcerer, a shapeshifter who changed his form to hide from the warriors who destroyed this city. She thinks he has been overwhelmed by loneliness and grief and can't change back into human form."

Tam's cat hunkered down into the warmth of Kelene's lap. *Ha! that explains it. He hunts as human, not as cat.*

"What do you mean?"

He did not stalk. He did not hunt. He saw Niela and killed with paw. Cats kill with teeth and claw.

Kelene patted the cat nervously. "Is the Korg anywhere nearby?" she asked Demira.

I cannot smell him, the filly replied.

Kelene was grateful for that. But though the Korg was too far away for the horse to scent, it was close enough for them to hear. Roars of anger echoed through the ruined city, sometimes coming from far away, other times sounding too near for comfort. Demira hurried toward the tower by the gate, where they hoped to find the remaining travelers.

They had just passed an intersection when they heard another voice call, "Kelene!" Kelene's heart stopped, then skipped with joy and relief.

It was Rafnir, dusty and pale under his tan. He was so glad to see her he kicked his Hunnuli, Tibor, into a canter. The stallion snorted at the crude assault to his ribs but went dutifully, his eyes glowing warm at the pleasure of seeing Demira and Kelene safe.

"Thank the gods, you're alive," Rafnir exclaimed in a rush of breath. "That

Korg chased Tibor and me all over the city before we lost him. I had no idea where you were."

"What about your father?" Kelene wanted to know.

"I don't know. I haven't seen anyone else since we left the square." Deeply worried, he stared out over the ruins.

Words of reassurance came to Kelene's mind, but she rejected them. As strong and intelligent as all three magic-wielders and their Hunnuli were, the Korg was cunning, powerful, and unpredictable. Too many things could go wrong.

Together the man and woman rode silently back to the south gate, their fears for their kinsmen heavy in their thoughts.

10

A shaken Morad was the only one waiting in the shadowy tower room when Kelene and Rafnir arrived back at the southern gate late in the afternoon. The young Geldring was so glad to see them, he hugged them both before asking about the others. "Is Niela truly . . . ?"

Kelene nodded. To still the trembling of her chin, she told the men how she had built the cairn over the bodies.

Morad jerked his hands in a frustrated motion of grief and slumped to the floor to sit by his Hunnuli's feet. "Why did she have to shout? She was just supposed to find you, not announce her presence to the city."

"She was scared," Kelene replied sadly. "She probably didn't think beyond that."

The three clanspeople subsided into silence, mulling over their own thoughts as they waited for Sayyed and Savaron to return. Kelene remembered her decision to use the Watcher, so she sat down, her back against the cool stone wall, and unpinned the brooch from her tunic. Morad and Rafnir watched while she stared into the brilliant depths. When she was finished, without a word Kelene fastened the brooch back in its place.

"Tell us," Rafnir prompted.

The slender girl sighed, a sound as soft as a whisper. "There isn't much. I think Mother was resting under a tree in the Council Grove. I saw the grove full of tents. It's a mess! They're burning some sort of incense around the edges. There was so much thick yellow smoke it was hard to see details." Her voice began to tremble, and she had to clear her throat a time or two before she could continue. "What I could see was awful: there was a stack of bodies by the council tent."

"Did you see Lord Athlone or Lymira?" asked Rafnir.

"No. Some of the priestesses were there helping, and I saw Lord Fiergan, but there was no sign of Father."

"We're running out of time," Morad said gloomily. "We could spend days poking around this blasted ruin while the Korg picks us off one by one and still come no closer to finding anything that will stop the plague." He sprang to his feet and paced back and forth in the crowded space between several fallen timbers. "What good is all of this if the clans are dead before we can get back?"

"None whatsoever," Sayyed's voice said from the entrance. The warrior strode into the room with the intensity of a man about to fight a duel to the death. His swarthy skin was flushed and swearing from exertion and his face was haggard, but his dark eyes were hard with angry resolve.

The three young people crowded around, clasping his arms and grinning with relief. Kelene hugged him fiercely. Then, to her intense relief, Savaron appeared in the doorway, also safe and unharmed. He was swiftly pulled into her arms.

"By Surgart's sword, I didn't think I'd ever give that beast the slip," Savaron swore. "He's not only big, he's cunning."

A small smile rugged at Kelene's lips. "But he doesn't hunt like a cat." The men looked blank and she added, "Tam's cat said that. I told her the legend of the Korg, that he is really a sorcerer, and she said that's why he doesn't hunt like a cat. He hunts like a human."

Rafnir scratched his jaw. "I wonder if that's true."

His father slapped his shoulder and said, "Tomorrow we're going to find out. We're going to set a trap."

Startled, the others exchanged quizzical glances. Savaron was the first one to comprehend what Sayyed was saying. "You want to *capture* him?" he burst out, horrified and intrigued at the same time.

"He seems to be our only hope," Sayyed explained. "Morad is right, we wasted a whole day and lost Niela. I can't see the sense of keeping up this blind search when our people are dying."

"So what are you going to do with the Korg? Keep him out of the way?" asked Morad.

"We're going to see if the legend is right. If the Korg is a shapeshifter, maybe we can convince him to change back and help us find the records."

The four magic-wielders were shocked into wide-eyed consternation. "How?" cried Kelene.

Sayyed's body seemed to sag a little, and he leaned back against the wall. "I don't know that part. I'm hoping something will present itself. Any suggestions?"

They talked quietly late into the evening, discussing every course of action, farfetched or otherwise, that they could think of. Long after the stars began to shine, they decided on a plan of sorts. Sayyed told them, "We'll set watches like last night so everyone can get some rest. You'll need your strength in the morning."

After a quick meal they bedded down, Rafnir taking the first watch. The men were quickly asleep, but Kelene could not find rest so easily. Her thoughts kept turning on a treadmill of images—the council grove with its pall of yellow smoke, the look on Niela's face when her Hunnuli died, the Korg's ferocious gold eyes—and underneath it all was a gnawing sense of urgency. Even if they found the records tomorrow, there was still a three- or four-day ride back to the Tir Samod. And what if the wraith was still out there beyond the walls waiting for them to step foot outside the city wards? How could they escape him again?

Kelene stewed until her restlessness propelled her from bed. Without consciously intending to, she wandered outside and found Rafnir sitting on a fallen pile of rubble at the foot of the old tower. The Hunnuli stood close by, black shapes against the stone wall.

Rafnir smiled, his teeth a pale blur in the darkness, and he shifted over to make room for her on his perch. Conscious of her weak ankle, she picked her way up the stones and eased down beside him.

They sat for a while in companionable silence, each glad for the other's presence. The ruins lay around them in a black, silent mass full of dense shadows and whispers on the wind. To the west a new moon was sinking from a sky bejeweled with countless stars.

Kelene drew a deep breath of the warm night air. She was about to expel it when she saw something from the corner of her eye that made her gasp. Her hand grabbed Rafnir's arm.

"I know," he whispered. "I saw it, too."

Beyond the portals of the broken gate, past the rotting corpse of the dead horse, was a reddish phosphorescent glow standing near the remains of the lion statue that had once guarded the entrance. The figure did not move, but waited with malicious patience for the prey he knew would have to leave soon.

"That thing makes my skin crawl," Rafnir admitted.

Kelene shivered. "What does it want? Why is it trying to kill us?"

"It hasn't been very talkative," he said dryly. "But it certainly has an aversion to magic." His gaze left the wraith and settled on the corpse of his mother's Hunnuli. "I've been thinking," he said, struggling to keep the sadness from his voice. "Finding the healers' records is only part of our problem. We still have to get them back to the gathering. We know we can't outrun the wraith, and so far, we haven't been able to outfight him, either. Demira seems to be our only hope. If she had wings, maybe she could outfly him."

Kelene dropped her eyes to Tam's Hunnuli. She remembered the frantic run across the plateau the day before and Morad's vain attempt to destroy the wraith's horse. "Yes, you're right," she murmured. "But we have a problem. Hunnuli are impervious to magic. How are we going to work a spell on Demira if the magic won't affect her?"

"That's what I've been thinking about," Rafnir answered. "We've always been told Hunnuli are impervious to magic, but none of us have ever tested that belief."

Kelene peered at him through the darkness as if he had lost his sanity. "Of course they have. Mother and Nara proved it when they fought the gorthling before we were born!"

"They proved that a Hunnuli is protected from destructive magic, but what about other kinds of spells? Maybe their resistance to beneficial magic is not so strong."

"That's crazy," snapped Kelene, and yet maybe it wasn't. It was true no one had tested the full strength of the Hunnulis' defenses. What if there were weaknesses? The possibilities popped in her thoughts like fireflies. "How do we find out?" she said in the next breath.

Rafnir squeezed her fingers. "Why don't we ask the Hunnuli?"

That seemed such a sensible idea Kelene scrambled down the rubble pile, pulling Rafnir with her. They went to the sheltered corner of the wall where the five Hunnuli were resting. None of the horses was asleep, for they were on guard against the Korg, and the close proximity of the wraith made them nervous. They welcomed Kelene and Rafnir into their midst with soft nickers. The pale blur of Tam's cat meowed sleepily at the two people from a warm perch on Afer's back.

Rafnir patted his stallion, Tibor, then got right to the point. "We were wondering if any of you know how strong your resistance to magic really is," he said to all five Hunnuli.

"Are you protected against *all* magic?" Kelene added. "Or just dangerous magic?"

The Hunnuli lifted their heads, surprised by such a question. They looked at one another, but none of them had a ready answer.

Tibor finally responded, *Certainly we are protected against any destructive spells, but beneficial ones? I do not know.* He turned to Afer. *What do you think?*

Afer did not answer at first. He was one of the oldest Hunnuli in the clans and one of the few who had once run wild in the Darkhorn Mountains before the return of sorcery. The younger Hunnuli deeply respected his wisdom, but even he seemed taken aback by the question. He stood for a long while, his deep liquid eyes lost in thought. When at last he stirred, he shook his mane. *Many years ago, I broke my leg and would have been destroyed if Sayyed hadn't stepped in to fight for my life. At the time, the King Stallion told us that no magic would help Hunnuli. Yet after spending all these years with magic-wielders, I believe the King Stallion was wrong.*

The old stallion looked straight at Rafnir and Kelene. *I am not certain, but I think a trusted rider could break through his or her Hunnuli's defense with magic, as long as the spell is not harmful.* He broke off his words, stretched out his neck, and pointed his muzzle at Rafnir's chest. *Why do you want to know?*

Kelene and Rafnir exchanged glances. "We want to give Demira something," Kelene said nervously. She hadn't thought until this conversation that the other Hunnuli might not approve of her idea.

Like what? asked Savaron's stallion.

After a moment's hesitation, the girl pulled out her marble tile. "That," she said, jabbing a finger at the carving. "This is what we want to do."

The Hunnuli's excellent night vision needed no extra illumination to see the figure of the winged horse. The black horses crowded around in incredulous silence. Even the white cat interrupted her nap to peer over Afer's shoulder.

Demira was the first one to respond. *Wings? I could have wings?* she asked, delighted.

Tibor, though, snorted in disbelief and stamped a hoof at the filly. *This is ridiculous. Insects fly. Birds fly. Why should a Hunnuli fly?*

And what law said we have to remain earthbound? Demira retorted.

Afer snorted at them both. *Why do you want to do this?* he asked the humans.

Kelene explained as best she could the reasons why she and Rafnir wanted to attempt such a feat. When she was finished, she looked from one horse to another, waiting for their response.

Is this something you are willing to do? Afer addressed Demira.

Yes! the filly's reply was adamant.

It is an astounding plan, Afer commented. He nudged Demira's shoulder. *Well, I see no reason why you cannot try it.* The big stallion returned his wise regard to Rafnir and Kelene. *But what are you going to use for wings?*

Kelene's hand tightened on Rafnir's sleeve. She had to get a tight rein on her excitement before she could answer. "We really don't know. Since we can't create living flesh or make anything as complicated as a wing, we're not certain what we should use. Do you have any ideas?" she asked the Hunnuli.

Don't be silly, meowed the cat from Afer's back. *Ask horses about wings? You want wings, ask bird.*

"What bird?" asked Rafnir dryly.

The white cat stood up; her tail began to twitch. *You want bird? I will find bird.* She jumped lightly to the ground.

Kelene's face grew very thoughtful. "A bird could be useful," she murmured.

Then I hunt, the cat growled. *Do you want a big bird or a little bird?*

"Whatever you find would be a help," Rafnir told her. His imagination was beginning to follow the same path as Kelene's thoughts. A bird just might be the key to the success of their plan.

Her tail twitching in earnest, the cat meowed a farewell and slipped into the ruins. Her departure seemed to signal the end of the talking, for the Hunnuli drifted back to their previous positions and relaxed once more. Pleased by what the horses had told them, the two magic-wielders returned to their post by the tower.

"I wonder why no one ever asked the Hunnuli about their invulnerability," Rafnir said.

Kelene chuckled her soft, rich laugh and said, "No one thought of it, I guess. Don't forget, the Hunnuli had no riders for over two hundred years."

Rafnir nodded once and eased a little nearer to the girl. With their heads bent close together, they whispered long into the night about magic, wings, and flying. They sat through Rafnir's watch, then Kelene's and Savaron's. The moon had long set when they finally yawned and woke Morad for his turn at guard. They bid each other a quiet goodnight and retired to their beds, contented.

* * *

The men were up and eating breakfast when Kelene awoke. She cracked open an eye, realized that it was morning and that she had slept late, and opened both eyes—to find her brother grinning at her.

"Thank you and Rafnir both for taking my watch last night," he said, a teasing note in his voice.

His grin widened, making Kelene wonder just how much he knew or guessed about what she and Rafnir were doing. Their plans for Demira weren't exactly a blood-sworn secret, but she was hoping to keep it quiet until after they had failed or succeeded. She didn't want to listen to any ridicule or build up anyone's false hopes. It would be better to surprise everyone. She climbed out of her blankets and shrugged. "We didn't mind. We couldn't sleep last night."

"Fine," Savaron said, transferring his grin to Rafnir. "You can have my watch tonight, too."

"Perhaps we'll take it. Your sister is certainly prettier than you in the moonlight," Rafnir retorted.

At Savaron's delighted guffaw, Kelene's face turned a fiery red, and she turned her back on the men to hide her embarrassment. Pretty in the moonlight! Of all the insolent remarks! She put her hands to her hot cheeks. Was Rafnir teasing, or did he really mean what he said? They'd had such a pleasant time last night, she hoped he wasn't just ribbing her for her brother's entertainment. Kelene liked Rafnir more than she expected, but her feelings for him were still too new. She didn't know how he felt about her or what she should do with her own growing attraction to him. Time will work it out, she told herself firmly. But she put away her gear, plaited her hair, and ate her breakfast in a very pensive silence.

The party was ready to go when Sayyed called, "Mount up!" from the gap in the wall they used for a doorway. He glanced around at the shadowy room and frowned. "Has anyone seen Tam's cat?"

"She went hunting last night," was Kelene's truthful reply. As far as it went.

The warrior looked worried, but all he could do was shrug. "I suppose she'll be all right. Now," he said to his four companions, "you know what we have to do. Be wise. Do not try to prove your boasts today. We need the lion, not more cairns. Kelene," he went on heavily, "I'm sorry to do this to you, but you and

Demira must be the bait since she is smaller and faster through those debris-choked streets than our horses. Can you do that?"

Kelene's eyes involuntarily slid to Rafnir's face. She was rather startled to see he had gone very pale. She nodded once, unwilling to trust her voice, and pulled her gaze down to her boots.

They went over their plan one more time, then silently went outside to mount their Hunnuli.

Demira greeted Kelene with a warm muzzle to her cheek. Her breath fanned the woman's face. *You are frightened,* the filly sent worriedly.

Kelene didn't say anything more than, "We're about to bait the Korg," as she pulled herself up onto the filly's broad back.

As soon as they were ready, the searchers made their way through the ruins as circumspectly as possible. In due time they all arrived safely at a building Sayyed had spotted the day before in the northern quadrant of the city, not far from the central square.

What was left of the building was perfectly round, about twenty paces in diameter, and built of stone. At one time there had been two substantial timber-framed stories built over the massive stone foundation that formed the walls and ceiling of the ground floor. The upper stories had been partially burned during the attack on the city and left to rot, but the stone walls of the lower floor were still standing as thick and stout as the day they were built.

The clanspeople dismounted and walked inside through a double-width doorway large enough for a wagon to enter. The heavy ceiling towered nearly fifteen feet over their heads and was still intact, keeping the space below in damp gloom. The remains of what could have been a huge grinding stone lay in several pieces in the center of the round room. A second large entrance lay directly across from the first, the rotten remains of its wooden doors hanging lopsidedly on the hinges.

"Must have been an old warehouse or mill," Sayyed surmised. He studied the heavy stone walls like a commander planning an attack. "It should be strong enough. Are you ready?" He turned to Kelene.

Her face had assumed the blank, withdrawn expression they all knew well, and for the sake of her own resolve, she made no effort to change it or look at anyone. She bowed her head once and, without a word, made her way from the gloomy interior.

Her task was to find the lion and lure it to this building where the men would trap it within. The plan was fairly simple, but their prey was dangerous and unpredictable. Kelene did not relish the beast's chasing her and Demira through the treacherous ruins. She had to take several deep breaths before she could pull herself onto the filly's back.

The other Hunnuli nickered to them as Demira trotted down a road toward the central square. Fortunately, the warehouse was not far from the main road and would be easy to reach. Sayyed had suggested that she go to the square and let the Korg find her rather than search through the maze of shattered buildings, clogged alleys, and cluttered roads to find him. Less chance of getting lost.

Kelene's stomach was roiling by the time Demira stepped into the square near the ruins of the old Sorcerers' Hall. The open, sunlit space looked much the same as it had yesterday: dirty, desolate, and very empty. Kelene looked toward Niela's cairn and was relieved to see it was untouched.

Demira slowly clopped toward the obelisk in the middle of the square. The filly's head was up, and her nostrils were flared like cups. Her ears swiveled at every sound.

The horse and rider waited by the obelisk for a long, breathless time in the hot sun and the silence. Then, from out of nowhere, Kelene laughed out loud. The unexpected, slightly hysterical noise startled Demira so badly she skittered sideways, banged her rump into the obelisk, and squealed in pain and irritation. A flock of crows burst from a nearby building to the right, their raucous voices protesting the intruders' presence.

"Well, those birds ought to get his attention," Kelene said nervously.

You could have warned me, Demira complained as she stepped away from the stone pillar.

Kelene apologized. "I'm sorry. That laugh just came out. Here we are, standing around waiting for a stone lion to chase us, and he's not coming! Let's get him here, the sooner the better. I don't think I can stand much more of this. Do you smell him anywhere?"

No, and why are you talking so loudly?

Kelene didn't reply but burst into a bellowed and slightly off-key version of her favorite ballad:

> "Riddle me a riddle, love
> Of a buttercup that bore a sword
> Of a horse of darkest ebony
> And the fall of a renegade lord.
> Of grief withheld and rage sustained,
> The scarlet cloak reborn,
> And the love of the Golden Belt
> For an Exile girl forlorn."

"Trot around," she ordered Demira. "Make noise." As she plunged into the next verse, the filly trotted in circles around the square, her hooves ringing to Kelene's song.

They had made their seventh circuit around when Demira's ears snapped forward. Kelene felt the hairs rise on the back of her neck. Her skin suddenly began to tingle, her hands went cold, and she knew without a doubt that they were being watched.

The filly tilted her head toward the Sorcerers' Hall and eased to a walk. Kelene peered toward the piles of masonry, debris, and stone. "Do you see him?" Her fingers twisted into the Hunnuli's mane.

No. I smell him. Over there behind that broken wall with the arches.

"Gods' blood! He's too close to our road. If we break for it now, he'll cut us off."

What do we do?

"Go past him. We'll try to get him to chase us, then circle back."

Demira stepped forward, her tail twitching and her legs so stiff she was almost walking on the tips of her hooves. Both of them stared wide-eyed at the gray wall for the first sign of the Korg.

When the lion's attack came, it happened so fast he almost took them by surprise. One moment the old wall was empty and the next the huge beast was bounding over it, glistening teeth bared and yellow eyes burning with anger. A tremendous roar shook the buildings.

"Go! Go!" screamed Kelene.

With a squeal, the Hunnuli spun on her hind feet and fled the Korg's crushing paws. The lion roared again and charged after them.

Kelene glanced back to see its hulking form so close she could feel the tremor of its heavy paws. Frantically, she raised her hand and fired a blast of the Trymian force at the Korg's chest. Although the blue bolt was powered by desperation, it was weakened by lack of skill. It only stung the old lion into a greater rage.

"Run!" Kelene yelled to Demira. She ducked low over the filly's neck and hung on with every ounce of strength as the horse veered in a circle around the open square. Lightning-swift, Demira shot by the obelisk and headed for the northern road that led to the warehouse. Behind came the crashing thuds of the stone paws on the paved road and a growl like a rumbling avalanche.

Kelene's eyes were screwed almost shut against the wind and the filly's whipping mane. She refused to look back again, expecting any moment to feel the heavy paws smashing into her back or sweeping Demira's hindquarters out from under her. All she could do was hang on while Demira swerved past heaps of rubble and galloped frantically two steps ahead of the Korg.

Then they saw the side street where the warehouse lay and the men waited. Demira turned so fast around the corner that her hooves skidded on the worn paving stones. Kelene shifted her weight to help steady the filly, and they bolted like an arrow down the narrower passage. The Korg roared again, shaking the tumbled buildings. It followed only a few leaps behind Demira's flying tail.

Lifting her head a little, Kelene saw the warehouse ahead, with its gaping black doorway leading to safety. There was no sign of anyone around the decaying building, but Kelene knew they were there. Demira stretched out her neck and fairly flew over the rough ground.

They were only two strides from the opening when Kelene felt Demira's hind leg slide out from under her on a slick stone. The girl had only that flash of realization before the filly lost her balance and fell toward the ground.

Kelene had just enough time to pull her leg up and over Demira's back before the horse crashed to her side on the rocky earth, but she couldn't stop herself from being thrown to the stone paving. A roaring agony exploded in her head and burst into her shoulder and arm. Shock rocked her. She heard rather than saw a heavy form come toward her. Terrified, she tried to struggle upright, only to fall back under a wave of pain and nausea.

She and Demira lay still, panting and wild-eyed as the Korg loomed over them. Kelene stifled a shriek when the cold weight of its paw fell on her hip. She reached out with her fist, the only weapon she had, and pounded on the huge foot. "Get off me!" she screamed.

To her astonishment, the old lion lowered its head and peered at her through its yellow jeweled eyes. A deep, grinding sound issued from its mouth, not a growl but a word forced from a stone throat unaccustomed to speech. "Kelyra?" The tone of surprise and hope was unmistakable.

Kelene was so startled by the voice, her fist uncurled on the lion's leg. She did not think about what she did next; she only reacted instinctively to the intelligence she heard in the Korg's voice. Her mind opened, and her empathic talent reached out to it.

In a heartbeat, Kelene's hand on the Korg started to shake under a torrent of very real human emotion that swept into her mind with breathtaking force: grief, unutterable loneliness, sadness, confusion, and above all the other jumbled emotions, surprise and a flare of recognition. Her brain reeled under the onslaught of the strange emotions.

She was just coherent enough to hear Rafnir bellow, "Kelene!" and see a powerful blast of blue energy strike the Korg's chest.

No! her thoughts protested, *don't hurt him. He doesn't understand.* Then her world collapsed into a dizzying, nauseating whirl.

From what seemed a long distance away, she felt the weight of the Korg's paw leave her leg, and she heard a tremendous roar. Through bleary eyes she saw the Korg charge away from her into the open doorway of the warehouse. There was a loud burst of noise as a bright red shield of magic erupted into place across the doorway, trapping the Korg within. Things went a little blurry after that. Kelene must have passed out for a few moments, for the next thing she knew, someone was urgently calling her name.

Kelene groaned, stirred, and opened her eyes to see Rafnir's face hovering over hers. "I'd smile, but it hurts," she whispered, suddenly very glad that he was there.

His answering grin was so full of relief, she did smile and promptly yelped at the pain on the whole left side of her face. Kelene blinked and decided to stay still for a few more minutes. Her head was cradled on Rafnir's lap, and her body was stretched out on the ground. If she did not move, she was not too uncomfortable. She gently tested a few muscles and decided nothing was broken—just battered and scraped.

"Demira?" she asked.

I ruined my coat, the filly grumbled nearby. Her mental tone was tinged with red flashes of pain and aggravation, yet it was strong. *I have several bad scrapes on my shoulder, which will leave scars, and I twisted my hind fetlock!*

"Thank the gods, you'll both live!" Rafnir exclaimed. "I thought the Harbingers would be coming for you when I saw the Korg pounce on you."

As if the lion had heard its name, it began to roar again in horrible, angry bellows that made the thick stone walls tremble. Rafnir jerked his head toward the doorway to their right, where Kelene could see Sayyed holding the magic shield across the opening.

"He may be impervious to the Trymian force, but he hasn't broken through the shields yet," Sayyed observed.

Wordlessly Kelene struggled upright. Her head reeled with dizziness, then settled back to a throbbing ache that allowed her to carefully climb to her feet. Rafnir gave her his arm to steady herself as she limped to the doorway and looked inside through the glowing red shield. Across the round expanse she could barely make out Savaron in the opposite door holding another shield.

"Savaron and Morad are over there," Rafnir replied to her questioning look. "Morad is filling in the entrance with stone blocks so we don't have to maintain two shields."

"There's the Korg," Sayyed said and pointed to the darkest clump of shadows on the left side of the room where a black form was pacing furiously in tight circles.

Kelene and the Korg saw each other at the same time. Abruptly the roaring ceased. The old lion began to pace toward her until it reached the magic shield blocking the door. It made no attempt to test the shield, but simply stared at Kelene's face with bright gold eyes.

She did not move or look away, only held her hand out in a gesture of peace. Sayyed and Rafnir watched, amazed at the strange encounter.

"Sayyed," Kelene said without moving her eyes from the Korg's ferocious face. "I think I know how to reach him."

11

"No!" Rafnir's refusal was absolute. "You're not going to do it!"

"Who asked for your permission?" Kelene shot back. "We have to break through to the Korg to get him to tell us about the healers, and what better way to do it?"

"Many ways. Ways that don't include your getting anywhere near that big cat," he yelled.

"Like what?" she challenged.

In the twilight of a warm evening, Sayyed crossed his arms and watched the confrontation between his son and Kelene. The clanspeople had moved their camp to a shelter in a wrecked building near the warehouse, which made it easier for someone to maintain a constant vigil on the shield guarding the Korg.

But ever since Kelene described her incredible plan for the Korg a short while ago, Rafnir had been like a buck deer defending his harem. Sayyed had to hide his smile. Rafnir might not realize it yet, but it was as obvious as his aquiline nose that he was in love with Gabria's daughter. The realization surprised and pleased his father. Sayyed had always been fond of Kelene, and he had seen her mature a great deal in these past six days. However, he wasn't sure how Kelene felt about Rafnir. He could only hope his son would not drive her away with his sudden overprotectiveness and that slight hint of jealousy. Kelene was a proud and stubborn woman who would not take kindly to his overbearing solicitude. She had been very patient with him. Until now.

"Name one way to reach through to the Korg that does not include me!" She was shouting at Rafnir from barely a foot away. Her dark hair was tossing like a mare's tail in her agitation, and her eyes were crackling. "I am a part of this group just like you, facing the same responsibilities and dangers, and if I have a plan to help hurry things along, you'll just have to accept it!"

"But a mind-meld with the Korg? That's a stone lion you're talking about, who may or may not be a crazed sorcerer," Rafnir retorted in a voice just as loud and determined as hers. "You might as well place yourself under his paw and say 'crush me.' He'll never let you get close."

Kelene's temper flared, then slowly subsided. She said in a much more patient tone, "Yes, he will. He thinks I'm someone he knows. He didn't kill me by the warehouse, and I think he'll be willing to talk to me now." She paused, and her anger cooled completely in the memory of the Korg's emotions. "He is . . . *was* a man. I felt his loneliness, Rafnir. I think his mind is trapped in the past by his grief. If I can meld with his mind and bring him into the present, wouldn't it be worth the risk?"

Rafnir snorted. "And what if he realizes you're not this person he knows and turns on you? You'll be on foot. You won't have Demira to carry you away! Shall we bury you beside Niela?"

"That's a chance we have to take. Do you really want to keep the Korg trapped for days on end while you think of a better plan?" she replied evenly.

Oblivious to Sayyed and Morad, who were watching the argument with silent interest, Rafnir gently cupped his hand along her jaw. The left side of her face was already turning black and blue from her earlier fall. He winced when he thought about how close he had come to losing her. "All I want is for you to be safe."

For once Kelene was speechless. Her mouth opened and closed, and her fingers tightened into fists. She didn't know whether to be thrilled that he seemed to care so much or outraged that he was being so selfish and presumptuous to assume that her safety was his sole duty.

Sayyed chose that moment to step into the conversation. "Rafnir, I don't like the plan any more than you do." He held up a hand to still Kelene's outburst. "But she's right. We don't have time to hope the Korg will come around on his own. Kelene, if you feel well enough in the morning, you can talk to the lion."

Kelene stepped back from Rafnir and bowed to his father, pleased that one person at least saw some merit in her plan. Rafnir bowed his head to Sayyed, too, and stamped away without another word.

It was fully dark by that time, so Kelene found her bedroll among the packs and lay down in a corner of the shelter where she could see the stars through the remains of the ceiling. She was weary and sore; her entire left side ached every time she moved. Morad and Sayyed came in and were soon asleep, but once again, no matter how still Kelene lay, how many stars she counted, or how often she closed her eyes, she could not find rest. Her thoughts were full of Rafnir and the look of hurt on his face when he left, and of the Korg and the anguish that still cried in his stone body.

She was so embroiled in her own musings she didn't see Tam's cat jump through a hole in the shattered wall and come trotting to her bed. Kelene nearly leaped from her blanket when a soft paw touched her cheek.

I found one, the cat meowed.

Kelene subsided back into her bed. "Found one what?" she gasped in a half laugh, half whisper.

The cat sat down, obviously pleased with herself. *Bird,* she growled. *It is dead, so you can look at wings.*

The young woman jumped up, her mind suddenly clear of worries and her aches forgotten. "Where?"

In answer the cat padded softly past Morad and Sayyed asleep on their blankets and slipped silently from the building. Kelene jerked on her boots and followed her out into the dark ruins. Light from a quarter moon delicately outlined humps and piles and broken walls with a pale dappled white and deepened the shadows to an impenetrable gloom. The old city was unnaturally quiet at night, a fact Kelene had not noticed before. There were no sounds from insects, owls, or wild dogs. There was only the muffled rumbling from the Korg pacing in his prison and the mournful whisper of the wind through the dead city.

Kelene glanced toward the warehouse and saw Savaron keeping watch on the shield. She ducked down a side street after the cat before her brother saw her. They turned through a wide alley between the foundations of several houses and were walking down an open street when Rafnir suddenly called out her name in the darkness.

Surprised, Kelene stopped and saw him sitting on a fallen column in the moonlight. He didn't have a chance to say more before she ran to him, held out her palm, and said, "Truce?"

Rafnir narrowed his eyes at her change of attitude. "What is it?" he insisted.

She gave him a smile. "Tam's cat found a bird."

That was all he needed to hear. His palm met hers in a clasp of peace, and they hurried off side by side behind the pale blur of the little cat.

They had walked only several minutes when they saw the cat slide through a hole in a high wall. There was a much larger hole farther down where part of the wall had collapsed, and the two people were able to climb over with ease. They found themselves in a courtyard garden between several buildings. From the size of the foundations and heaps of rubble, the building on their left had once been an imposing structure. The second building, on their right, was quite a bit smaller and in slightly better condition. It had been left alone by the marauding clansmen. Only time and neglect had brought its roof and two of its walls down and erased the bright paint that had once adorned its columned front.

In the moonlight, Rafnir and Kelene saw the white cat trot across the courtyard. She came to a stop near the partial remains of an old arcade in the shadow of the smaller building. It was only when they followed the cat to the arcade that they recognized the sun designs on the arches and on the portico of the ruined edifice. The smaller building was a temple to Amara, the mother goddess.

Kelene bowed her head and whispered, "Bless us this night, O Mother.

Grant us the strength to do your bidding and the wisdom to follow your will."

They found the cat waiting for them by a column. There, in the shadows at the cat's feet, they saw a large bird lying on its back, its long wings partially outstretched, its eyes glazed in death.

Rafnir drew his breath in a gasp as he ran his finger reverently over the velvety black feathers. "An eagle. By Amara's grace, it's a black-headed eagle from the Himachal Mountains!" Clanspeople revered the great eagles, the sacred birds of Amara, and were strictly forbidden by law to harm one.

"What happened to it?" whispered Kelene.

The cat regarded the eagle indifferently. *It was hurt by storm and by fire. I waited. It died.* She was promptly rewarded by a scratch behind the ears.

"Thank you then, you marvelous cat," Kelene said with total sincerity. "You are the Lady of Hunters."

The white cat curled against Kelene's hand, her golden eyes glowing. *Of course,* she purred.

"The wings are in perfect shape," Rafnir noted. "We could use them in our spell, if we enlarge them. But do we dare remove them from an eagle's body?" The bird was, after all, the beloved of Amara. It did not seem right to Rafnir to mutilate its body and run the risk of angering the goddess.

With gentle hands Kelene tucked in the powerful wings and cradled the bird in her arms. It was still warm and pliable. "I think it is a gift," she said softly. "This is her city, her temple. If she had not meant for us to use this bird, we would not have found it. Besides, what better wings to give a Hunnuli?"

Rafnir had no argument for that. The goddess Amara had given the Hunnuli the gifts of speed, endurance, and strength. Could she not also grant to one small filly the gift of flight?

There was only one way to find out. Rafnir's and Kelene's eyes met in understanding.

"Tonight," Kelene murmured. "If we wait too long, the wings will decay." Rafnir agreed.

Kelene turned to Tam's cat. "Will you bring Demira and Rafnir's Hunnuli, Tibor, here? We will try our spell on the grounds of Amara's temple."

"You aren't too tired for this?" Rafnir asked Kelene as the cat melted into the night on her errand.

Kelene bit back a snappish retort. Just because she was still irritated about Rafnir's earlier attempts to protect her didn't mean he wasn't asking a valid question. If she was too tired to wield magic, the spell could fail.

"I am tired," she admitted, "but I will take the easy part. I'll help Demira relax, and you can try to attach the wings."

For a moment they both simply stared at the elegantly streamlined wings. Long and broad with the notched primaries of a glider, the wings were black at the shoulders fading to a delicate gray on the tips of each feather. The inner wing feathers were a white that gleamed like milk in the moonlight.

"They're beautiful," said Rafnir in a hushed, almost awed voice. He lifted his eyes to her face and voiced the last hesitation he could think of. "Should we do this to a Hunnuli? I feel like we're trying to change a legend."

Kelene touched the eagle's black head and closed its eyelids before she answered him. She understood what he was saying because she had had the same thought. But now a certainty surfaced in her mind that stilled the trembling in her fingers and added strength to her voice. "We're not changing a legend, we're making history. We've been making history since we took that wrong turn in the canyon and found the mound. The plague, the wraith, the Korg, Moy Tura, and now Demira have all become a part of this history. Who is to say, except the gods, that this is not the way it is supposed to be?"

Rafnir's only answer was a firm nod of approval. He took the eagle out of her hands, laid it on the ground, and stretched the wings out to their full span. Kelene pulled out her dagger and knelt by the dead bird. Her hands were steady when she laid her fingers by the bird's right shoulder. She barely nodded her satisfaction. As carefully as she could in the darkness, she cut through the eagle's skin and detached the wing from the bird's shoulder. She laid the wing aside, then began the delicate operation on the next.

As soon as both wings were off, Kelene and Rafnir carried the remains of the eagle's body up the broken steps into the ruined temple of Amara. On a small pyre of rocks by the front entrance, they laid the eagle down and stood back.

Kelene raised her arms to the sky and cried, "Great bird, beloved of Amara, you have given us a treasured gift. We shall always remember your generosity in our hearts and our prayers. May your spirit fly to Amara, and your strength and grace live always in these wings."

When her last words faded away into the night, Rafnir lifted his hand. From his palm came a pale yellow magic sphere that landed on the bird's body and burst into flame. The eagle was consumed in moments, her spirit sent with honor to the realm of the dead.

Two sets of hoofbeats thudded in the darkness, and Demira and Tibor came into the moonlit courtyard with the white cat riding on the filly's back. Kelene saw her Hunnuli, and she ran down the temple steps to throw her arms around the filly's neck. She hesitated to speak, suddenly afraid of what they wanted to do. In spite of her brave speech about history, so many things could go wrong. Kelene knew she wouldn't be able to bear it if she caused anything to hurt or kill this horse.

"We have wings for you. Are you still willing to try this?" she asked hesitantly.

Demira's excitement nearly knocked her back a step. *Wings? For me? Where?* and she neighed a high cry of happiness.

Slowly Kelene picked up an eagle's wing and held it out for Demira's inspection. The filly sniffed once and her whole head sagged. *It's so small. How can a little wing like that lift me?*

Her disappointment was so obvious that even though Rafnir didn't hear the question, he realized her dismay.

"These wings will serve you well by the time we're through," he promised her, at which Demira said emphatically to them both, *Let's do it.*

From that moment, Kelene knew they could not turn back. The tools of the spell had been placed in their hands. It was up to them to weave the magic, the wings, and the Hunnuli into a unique whole. Fiercely she forced her fear and self-doubt down into the deepest, most obscured part of her mind. If she showed even a taint of doubt during her joining with Demira the filly might not relax, and her innate defenses would resist the magic Rafnir needed to use.

Rafnir, meanwhile, was explaining to Tibor what they were going to do. The powerful stallion snorted. *I still think this is foolish. Hunnuli belong on the ground!*

Demira tossed her head. *If you won't help your rider, then leave! I'm sure he can do as well without you!*

Rafnir nearly choked at her audacity, but Tibor only nickered a laugh. *Little one, it is your body. If you wish to fly, I will try to help. But remember, once done, it will be very difficult to undo. Be certain this is what you want.*

It is, Demira replied instantly.

With that settled, Kelene and Rafnir went to work formulating the spells they would use. They decided first to attach the wings to Demira's shoulders, then gradually enlarge them to fit her bulk. They had Demira lie down, her legs curled under her. Kelene sat beside the filly with her head resting on Demira's chest.

In that position, Kelene opened her mind to the waiting magic. The wondrous power poured into her and filled her mind, body, and soul with its invigorating energy. In the past, when she had used her ability to sense other people's emotions, she had not deliberately used magic to enhance her empathy. This time she tried it. The result was like suddenly opening a door into a bright and busy room. One moment she was lying beside her Hunnuli, and the next she was feeling Demira's every emotion and living her every sense.

As one, they lay immobile, united by touch, thought, and the power of magic. In that gentle union a bond was established between Hunnuli and magic-wielder that would protect and sustain them both in the years ahead.

Kelene, lavished by Demira's trust and love, relaxed the Hunnuli, comforted her, and soothed her into sleep. Every muscle, bone, and nerve of the black horse fell into complete relaxation. Her breathing and heart rate slowed; her mind drifted into a tranquility where she would feel no pain.

Lulled by her rider's presence, Demira's defense against magic dwindled to a mere protest as Rafnir gingerly laid his knife to her shoulder, cut a small slit into her skin, and carefully inserted the end of the wing bone through her muscle to her shoulder. Little by little, the magic-wielder joined bone to bone, muscle to muscle, and blood to blood, using magic to seal the union and make the parts compatible. Tibor stood close behind him, his muzzle resting against Rafnir's back. Through their mental rapport, the stallion added his fiery strength to Rafnir's to increase the efficacy of the spell.

To Rafnir's surprise, the procedure went very easily. The injury healed almost as soon as he finished the spell. That benefit, he decided, came from Kelene's presence in Demira's mind. He suspected the woman's talent and her empathic ability were helping the filly's body heal faster than normal.

As soon as one wing was joined, they attached the second. This operation went faster since Rafnir was a little more sure of what he was doing. When he finished, he sat back on his heels and rubbed a hand over his forehead. He was very tired, soaked with sweat, and stiff, but when he looked at the two wings lying gracefully furled along the horse's shoulders, he felt a hot burst of jubilation. He looked across at Kelene, wishing he could share his victory, and he could only smile. She was deeply asleep, as calm and serene as her Hunnuli.

Gods, he thought to himself, she is so beautiful.

Before he could let his mind get too distracted, he began the next part of the spell: enlarging the wings to fit the horse. The difficulty was he didn't know exactly how large to make eagle wings to fit a Hunnuli. He knew from years of training and hunting the Khulinin clan's hawks that bird wings were perfectly designed to fit their bodies. If he made Demira's wings too long or too bulky, they would be too heavy to work. If he made them too light or too short they would break from the stress of Demira's weight, or they wouldn't give her enough lift to get airborne.

He finally decided to keep the proportion of width to length the same, and he settled on a wing length equal to her height at her withers—a little over five feet—giving her a total wing span from wing tip to wing tip of about twelve feet. Rafnir hoped that size wouldn't be too cumbersome.

Once again he drew on Tibor's massive strength to supplement his own while he poured the magic energy into Demira's sleeping form. The wings gradually grew, their bones, feathers, and muscles stretching and lengthening.

By the time the wings reached their full length, Rafnir and Tibor were exhausted. The young magic-wielder carefully folded them neatly along the filly's side and ended his spell. He felt the horse's blood warm the wing muscles under his hand, and he was content. He had done the best he could for Demira and Kelene. The results were spectacular, but the question of whether or not Demira could actually fly would have to be settled later. The filly needed healing sleep.

Rafnir sighed, too weary to stand up. He sank down on the cool ground and stretched out by Tibor's front hooves. He was asleep before the stallion could bid him goodnight.

* * *

Kelene woke the next morning to find the sun well on its way to midday. She sat up with a stretch and a yawn and grinned at the sun. By Amara's crown, she felt good! She hadn't slept so well in days. Her face was a little stiff and swollen and her shoulder ached, but it was hardly noticeable. She looked around curiously, wondering where everyone was. Then the memory came flooding back, and she sprang to her feet.

"Demira!" she shouted.

She couldn't wait, a deep voice informed her. *She rushed off a little while ago to practice.*

Kelene whirled to see Tibor standing peacefully in the shadow of the broken arcade. "Practice?" she echoed in surprise.

Of course. You gave her wings, but you didn't give her the knowledge to use them.

Kelene's eyes grew round. "You mean it worked?"

Yes, Tibor snorted. *Rafnir has some of his mother's rapport with animals. The combination of his talents with yours was very successful. But*—Tibor stuck his big muzzle against Kelene's chest—*do not try that foolishness with me! I am perfectly content to keep my hooves on the ground.*

She laughed happily, not the least put out by his threatening tone. "Never," she promised.

The big stallion tossed his head. *Probably would not work anyway. You were lucky with Demira. She is small for a Hunnuli. Her size will be to her advantage since she will have a Hunnuli's strength without the full weight. I doubt any wings would get me off the ground.*

"Thank you for your help last night," Kelene said, scratching Tibor's favorite spot to placate his mood.

Tibor leaned into her fingers and replied, *You are welcome. Rafnir told me to tell you they need you to take your turn guarding the Korg. Everyone else has stood their watch.*

The girl nodded. Although she wanted to dash off to find Demira, she knew it was her duty to relieve the men. On the way out of the courtyard, though, Kelene asked the stallion, "Does anyone else know what we did last night?"

Only the Hunnuli.

"Well, please don't tell the men yet. Let Demira show them when she is ready. I don't think they'll believe me otherwise."

Tibor whinnied a short burst of laughter. *You are probably right.*

The girl and the horse walked together back through the ruins to the old warehouse and found Rafnir and Savaron eating some trail bread and cheese outside the shelter where the party had made camp. Rafnir was sitting on a stone, his eyes ringed with fatigue. He had found time to shave the old stubble off his jaw, but his face still looked haggard.

Savaron eyed his sister in Tibor's company and gave Rafnir a grin. "You two must have been busy last night."

Kelene winked at Rafnir and said in a very innocent voice, "Yes . . . very."

Savaron chuckled. "Well, Morad and I will expect you two to stand guard on the Korg tonight."

The mention of the Korg reminded Kelene and Rafnir at the same time what Sayyed had said the day before.

"I can't let you do it," Rafnir jumped in before Kelene could say a word.

"You can't let me. Who gave you authority over me?" she yelled back. "It's my decision who I talk to."

"What if his mind is too far gone to understand?"

"I don't believe it is! I sensed his feelings. He is confused, but he is not insane."

They were so busy glaring at each other, they did not see Sayyed stagger from the shelter.

"That's enough," he said hoarsely into a brief lull in the shouting. The two young people shot aggrieved looks at the older warrior and suddenly their argument was forgotten. Sayyed was barely standing upright, his face drawn and his skin flushed with fever. His cat was meowing piteously around his ankles.

"Father!" Rafnir cried. He leaped forward and caught Sayyed just as he sagged to the ground. Savaron, Kelene, and Rafnir carried the warrior inside and laid him on his blanket.

"It's the plague, isn't it?" said Rafnir, his voice laden with dread.

Kelene nodded as her fingers gently probed Sayyed's neck. The swellings were there, hard and hot under her fingers. "It's only a matter of time," she answered sadly. "If the disease runs its course, he'll die in two to four days." Her expression hardening, she said to Rafnir, "Now do you want to take the time to tame the Korg, or shall I go talk to him?"

Rafnir didn't answer at once, for the indecision was rearing him up inside. What should he do, risk his father's life or the life of the woman he loved? He knew it now—he loved Kelene as he had never imagined he would love anyone. How could he let her take such a risk? Then again, now his father was sick with the same disease that had killed his mother. His only hope was an old sorcerer in the shape of a stone lion. The bitter truth that their time was running out had been brought painfully home.

Rafnir sighed once and pulled his gaze up into Kelene's eyes. Those dark orbs were bright and steady, forged with determination, and they made him realize, belatedly, that the decision was not really his to make.

Kelene had changed so much in the past days that he had forgotten she was no longer Savaron's little sister with the crippled foot and the self-pitying attitude. She was a proud, courageous woman who was willing to risk her life for her people. That was why he loved her, for Amara's sake! He could not deny her the right to decide for herself.

"By the living god and the gods of the clans," he prayed. "Keep her safe." Then he put his hand in Kelene's and said, "If this is what you want to do, I'll go with you."

Sayyed's hand came down on their two, and he clasped them both. "Be careful," he said in a strained croak. "Talk to him first, gauge his mood before you enter that cage."

Kelene squeezed the warrior's fingers in agreement. She brought out the small packet of angelica Gabria had sent and brewed a warm tea of the herb for Sayyed. After she helped him drink it, she covered him with his light cloak. She left him to sleep with the cat by his side and followed Rafnir and Savaron silently outside to the entrance of the warehouse.

Morad, standing guard by the shield, looked at her questioningly. At her gesture he stepped, with the other two men, to the side of the doorway, out of the Korg's sight.

Kelene stood before the doorway just a step away from the glowing energy field. She didn't have to call the Korg, he was already standing in the same position he had been in yesterday. His jewel eyes gleamed gold in the dim light of the warehouse; his mane tumbled over his pricked ears. He was so tall she had to look up to see his stone face. He did not snarl or show his teeth, he only stared at her as if waiting for something.

From his throat rumbled a low grinding noise that sounded something like a question. "What did you say?" Kelene asked, leaning closer.

The Korg growled again. This time Kelene heard the words more clearly. "Kelyra, where have you been?" The pain in the query was so plain it tore her heart.

"Far away," Kelene answered. "But I am back now. Will you talk to me?"
"Yes."

She studied him, from the huge paws to the curving mouth that hid the rows of wicked teeth. He was a dangerous beast, she knew that, but she couldn't shake the belief that he was not going to hurt her. "If I take down this shield, what guarantee do I have that you will not attack me or try to escape?" She waved sharply to stifle Rafnir's protest.

The Korg deliberately lay down on his belly, his paws crossed in front of his chest and his hind legs stretched out to the side. Kelene had seen Tam's cat in that pose often enough to know it was a relaxed position. The Korg was trying to show her he was not going to make any sudden moves. "Before Amara, Sorh, Krath, and Surgart, I give you my word," the old lion stated.

That was enough for Kelene. If the Korg was sane enough to swear before the gods, Kelene had to accept that he understood the consequences of the gods' wrath if he broke his oath.

The names of the deities seemed to ease Rafnir's reluctance, too, for he glanced at Savaron and nodded once to Morad. All three men eased closer to the doorway as the Geldring dissolved the shield.

Kelene stepped through into the cool interior. Standing, she was just able to look the reclining Korg in the face. However, she decided to assume his relaxed posture and sat down cross-legged just inside the doorway—where Rafnir could yank her out if there was trouble. She held out her hands in peace.

The Korg lowered his head so he could see her. "It has been so long, Kelyra. . . . I missed you," he said in his harsh voice.

"And I you," Kelene responded. She had to swallow hard to force down the nervousness in her stomach. She reached out warily and put her hand on the lion's paw. It felt hard, yet surprisingly warm under her fingers. "What has happened to you?" She cautiously probed with her touch into his mind as she had done with Demira.

But the Korg was no Hunnuli with a psyche receptive to human contact. His was the mind of a sorcerer, highly trained and very powerful. The moment he felt her touch he deliberately snatched control of her mind and drew her thoughts helplessly into the vivid pageant of his memories.

She flashed through thousands of images going back in time past his entrapment, Niela's death, through years of solitude and despair. She saw her parents and Sayyed, looking so young, face the Korg in a walled courtyard; she watched a ragged exile poke through the ruins and flee in terror with an old tome under his arm. The brief glimpses flashed by and moved on into an endless cycle of seasons and unutterable loneliness. The images were brilliantly colored and bitter, and they flashed by so fast Kelene could barely comprehend them. At some time, she sensed the Korg's perception change into a man's view and soon thereafter, he slowed the visions and brought them to a stop when Moy Tura was whole and alive with people.

"Ah, there you are," she heard him say, and the image came into sharp focus. She stared out of the Korg's eyes and saw herself coming toward him.

12

So alike and yet unalike. The resemblance was uncanny, Kelene thought, watching the woman draw closer. She was tall, slender, and dark-haired with the same narrow eyebrows and stubborn tilt to her chin. But this woman walked with a graceful, fluid stride. Her eyes were light brown, not black, and she greeted the Korg with the happy smile of a woman greeting her lover.

Kelene felt the Korg's onrush of love like a hot intoxication—a new, wondrous, unbelievable emotion that the man had never felt before this woman had entered his heart. Kelene had never felt anything like it either, and its painful, joyous intensity rocked her soul.

"Kelyra," he murmured.

From that point he shifted his memory forward. Kelene suddenly found herself looking around at a semicircle of eleven other men and women seated in high-backed chairs. She knew from the Korg's memory that this was the audience chamber of the Council of Twelve in the Sorcerers' Hall. The council was the head of the clan magic-wielders and the ruling body of Moy Tura.

A man stood before them, a chieftain by his golden torque and rich clothing. His furious face and forceful arguments reminded Kelene of Lord Fiergan. The man had the burning intensity of a zealot and a streak of violence that was barely under control. Lord Gordak of Clan Reidhar. The name came to Kelene's mind, and she knew the Korg didn't like or trust this man.

"This tribute you demand is absolutely intolerable!" the chief was ranting. "The clans will not support this pack of heretics any longer."

"Heretics!" a sorceress cried in anger. "How dare you!"

Gordak cut her off. "No, Lady, you are the ones who dare! You take our children away from us on the slightest pretext of magic. You demand that we feed you and clothe you and pay tribute from our hard work; you treat us like dogs when we try to talk to you. And what do we get in return? Grieving mothers, empty bellies, and the scorn of the very people who are sworn to serve the clans." Lord Gordak was pacing now, his hands swinging in furious gestures.

What startled Kelene the most, though, was the blank, almost bored expres-

sions on the faces of most of the council members. They seemed to be paying
no attention at all to Lord Gordak's grievances—grievances that Kelene
thought were very valid. Only the lady sorceress was looking irritated, and a
second sorcerer was watching the chieftain with some worry. But the rest did
not appear to care at all.

The odd thing was Lord Gordak seemed aware that his audience wasn't listening. Yet he carried on anyway, haranguing them with a long list of minor
complaints against the council and other magic-wielders. He doesn't care either, Kelene decided. He has already planned something else; this verbal tirade
is nothing more than a prelude.

The vision suddenly stopped. *You're right,* the Korg's voice spoke in her
mind. Kelene gave a mental start of alarm. She hadn't realized he could understand her thoughts.

*Do not fear. I know now you are not my Kelyra. I should have realized ear-
lier, but I was blinded by wishful hope and memories I thought I had forgotten.*

His mental voice rumbled in her mind. The presence was very strong, yet
Kelene sensed an aura of incredible age and abiding sadness. *Then why do you
show me this?* she replied in both respect and curiosity.

His reply was rather hesitant. *You do not have the splinter in your wrist, but
I know you are a magic-wielder. All these years I thought the magic-wielders
were dead. You are the first who has spoken to me since this city fell.*

Well, why didn't you stop to talk to Niela? She was a magic-wielder! the accusation flared in Kelene's mind.

Your friend? I am deeply sorry for my error. Remorse colored his thoughts. *I
did not recognize the Hunnuli. I saw only intruders in my home, and I reacted
as I have for two hundred years. The time in this prison has forced me to think
and remember, to see in you the blood of Valorian.*

Kelene held back her resentment for Niela's death and allowed herself a tiny
feeling of victory. The Korg, at least, was communicating. He was not as crazy
as Rafnir feared, and his memories were clear. She could not permit anger or
any misplaced sense of revenge to jeopardize a possible rapport with him. The
old sorcerer within the stone lion was the only one who could help them find
records of the healers' work.

I understand, she told the Korg. *But why do you show me these visions of
Moy Tura?*

*I want you to see who I was and why I became what I am. Showing you helps
me to remember myself too. It has been long since I thought of Kelyra or Lord
Gordak.*

Kelene smiled tentatively and asked, *Had Lord Gordak planned something
else?*

May his soul rot in Gormoth, yes! the Korg answered, fiercely hostile.

Was he right to call the council heretics? Kelene queried. The last days of

Moy Tura had been a subject that had been hotly debated by priests and clans-people alike, and everybody had their own opinions on the causes and the actions of all the known participants. But now Kelene had an eyewitness, and she found herself growing more fascinated by the minute.

Some of them. That was one reason why our people turned against us. The Council of Twelve was supposed to be comprised of the most talented and incorruptible magic-wielders in the clans. Unfortunately, it didn't always work out that way. Some of our number stirred up a great resentment and hatred among the priesthood when they tried to take away the holy ones' power and authority and assume it themselves.

Kelene was aghast. Magic-wielders stole the sacred rights of the gods' chosen? No wonder the priests were some of her parents' bitterest opponents. The reasons for the schism may have been lost in time, but the hatred for magic had been rigorously passed on.

It was the priests, the Korg went on, *and Lord Gordak who incited the hatred and prejudice against us. It was our own folly that encouraged it. There was one man I remember vividly, a priest of Sorb. He vowed to destroy every magic-wielder living, to wipe our filth from the plains. Filth. Quite an insult coming from a man who sacrificed children and slaughtered helpless captives.*

Kelene quelled a shiver. *Did he betray Moy Tura?*

Not in person. He plotted with Lord Gordak to bring down the Council of Twelve and helped plan the attack on the city. But he was too obvious even for our unseeing eyes to ignore. He became so dangerous we dealt with him ourselves. Sadly, that backfired, too. After his disappearance, he was made into a martyr for Lord Gordak's cause.

Well, what happened to the city? How did the clans get through your defenses?

The Korg's memory abruptly returned to the council room and zoomed in on the sorcerer with the worried expression. *That man. Cirys, one of our own! He brought Moy Tura to her grave.*

Kelene was rocked back by the fierceness of his reply. She could feel his anger shooting through his mind from the incredibly intense memory. She studied the image of the rather ordinary, sandy-haired man huddled in a yellow cloak. He was a Reidhar, too, she noticed. Lord Gordak's clan.

The memory images began again, clear and poignant with the knowledge of what was coming. It was summer. The plateau was still green from the spring rains; the herds of horses and Hunnuli grazed on the high pastures, and the clanspeople were trekking to the Tir Samod for the summer gathering. All except the inhabitants of Moy Tura. A few had left, but most were content to remain at home.

No one was surprised when Clan Geldring stopped by the city on their way south. Clans often camped near Moy Tura in the summers. Clan Amnok soon joined them, and still no one was concerned. Not even the unusually large numbers of armed men in the camps worried anyone. When Clan Reidhar appeared, however, and deliberately camped across the main southern road into the city, the council grew alarmed.

I have had years to think about that summer, the Korg told Kelene. *I still can't believe how blind and arrogant we were. We had three large, heavily armed werods at our door, and we did nothing about it. We never strengthened the wards, set a watch, or armed our citizens. We just assumed the warriors would never dare attack magic-wielders of their own blood.*

But they did, Kelene thought.

Gods, yes. They did. There was a long pause before the Korg went on. *I don't know everything that happened that night or why Cirys chose to trust Lord Gordak. I think perhaps he was trying to make amends for something. The gods only know! Late one night he shut down some of the wards on the southern gate and let Lord Gordak into the city. I saw Cirys later, brought bound and gagged to Gordak's feet. Gordak bragged about what was happening and reviled him for being a traitor. They slit Cirys's throat for his reward.*

After that, the warriors of all three clans poured into the city and slaughtered every magic-wielder they could find. Without guards to warn us, we had no chance.

Kelene shifted unhappily. *How did you escape?*

Once again she saw Kelyra, this time leaning dreamily against the frame of an open bedroom window in the moonlight. Kelene watched the woman try to turn with a warning on her lips and suddenly clutch at her side where an arrow protruded beneath her left breast. Her dying agony sent grief and rage crashing through the Korg. He leaped from the bed and caught her as she fell to the floor. Through the Korg's eyes, Kelene saw the blood on his hands and the dead face of his beloved.

A warrior sprang through the window with a strung bow in one hand and a battle club in the other. As silent as an assassin, he swung the heavy club at the Korg's head. The weapon would have smashed the sorcerer's skull if the Korg hadn't frantically lunged sideways to avoid it. The club caught him with a glancing blow that was enough to knock him senseless and splatter blood on the club's head. The warrior ran out, thinking he had killed both the man and the woman.

The image faded, and the Korg was very still, his thoughts lost to Kelene. She was content to let him be until he was ready to continue.

When I awoke I was crazy with pain and fear. The room around me was brightly lit, but the light came from a fire across the square. They were burning the Sorcerers' Hall. Somehow I staggered to my feet. . . . The Korg opened his memories again, and Kelene reeled under the sharp impact of his pain, dizziness, and confusion. The blow to the head had disoriented the man, she realized. Even his memories at this point were blurred and unsteady.

The old sorcerer gave a groan and added, *I made it to the window and looked outside.*

Kelene gave a mental gasp. The vision she saw was worse than anything she had imagined in the ruins. The magnificent Sorcerers' Hall was a conflagration of towering flames that lit the square with a lurid glow and illuminated the ghastly piles of bodies heaped around the burning building. There were hundreds of them—men, women, and children of all ages—lying in bloody stacks. The scene reminded Kelene too much of the bodies of the plague victims and the pyres at the gathering. It was all she could do to force herself to keep watching the images unfold.

Warriors by the dozen hauled in more bodies from around the city and casually tossed them into the gigantic fire. A few pitiful people were herded into the square, still alive, but Kelene saw Lord Gordak himself draw his sword and behead them all.

The Korg fell back away from the window. He had to hide. They would find him and kill him. He had to hide. The thought became a chant in his mind.

They were coming to search, he told Kelene. *I could see them with their swords in their hands and their clothes stained with blood. I stumbled from my room and into my workshop. I didn't know what to do or where to go. I could hardly remember who I was or what was happening to me. All I knew was I had to hide. Warriors came into my house. I heard them find Kelyra's body and throw her outside as I ran out into my garden. There were men out there, too, beyond the walls. I could go no farther without being seen, so I did the only thing I could think of at that moment, the only thing I remembered how to do. I changed my shape.* He showed Kelene a scene of his garden, bordered by a low stone wall and filled with flowers. Then his vision moved down, and she saw the bare feet of the man had been transformed to the stone paws of a lion. The paws remained fixed in place, one raised in a posture of defiance. The sorcerer had become a statue in his own garden.

I had to stand there and listen, he thought miserably, *while they slaughtered the rest of the people. They killed everyone in Moy Tura, even those who could not wield magic. Then they looted and burned and plundered until there was nothing left but bloody stone.* The lion was trembling in mind and in body. *I watched the warriors leave, but I did not move. Not for many years. I think my mind was in such shock, it could not accept what had happened. When I finally came to, I was alone and frightened. There was nothing here but these ruins. I wanted to leave, but I thought if I stayed here in this shape, I would be safe. I knew Lord Gordak would not stop with Moy Tura. He would kill every magic-wielder on the plains.*

He almost did, Kelene told him, *but a few escaped.*

The Korg surprised her with a faint, dry chuckle. *So I finally realized when you trapped me in this warehouse. It was a revelation.*

She felt the effort he was making to bring his feelings back under control. The grief and misery that preyed on his mind were forced back away from her, and the trembling of his body eased. At last the lion rose and stretched. He shook his great head, breaking the mental link, sending Kelene tumbling back into her own mind. She blinked in surprise.

"We will talk again later, young one." His gravelly voice spoke wearily. "I need rest from my thoughts."

The clanswoman pulled herself stiffly to her feet and hobbled out of the doorway. Rafnir caught her as her weak ankle gave way under her weight, and she tumbled toward the ground. Morad quickly snapped a command and the shield popped back into place.

With Rafnir's arm to help her, Kelene sank down on a chunk of masonry. Her breath came out in a ragged sigh.

"What happened?" Savaron blurted, kneeling down beside her. "You've been sitting there with him for most of the morning!"

"He can use his mind like the Hunnuli," Kelene said in a voice so soft they could hardly hear her. "He showed me his memories of the city and the slaughter." The images of the bloodbath were still so vivid she shuddered, and Rafnir gathered her close in his arms. There was a pause before she went on. "He went half crazy from pain, grief, fear, and the solitude of this place," she tried to explain. "But he knows now that he is not alone. I think he'll help us."

"Did you ask him about healers?" Rafnir wanted to know.

"I didn't have a chance. I will try when he is willing to talk to me again."

Morad said in a voice hard as stone, "If he is so friendly, why did he attack Niela?"

Kelene frowned. "Habit, I think. He's been protecting himself and this city for two hundred years, and he thought all the magic-wielders were dead. He has seen so few people in Moy Tura, he forgot about Hunnuli. Even Mother's journey through here was too brief to jolt him from his nightmare." She shifted her weight and leaned closer to Rafnir. "I think that's why he was showing me his past, so I would understand why he killed Niela, and so he could recall himself."

"What next?" asked Savaron.

"Rest. I'm tired," Kelene admitted. She made her way to her feet and waved off Rafnir's offer to help. "I'm all right. I just want to find Demira." After one last look at the Korg still lying by the blocked doorway, she limped away to look for her Hunnuli.

She is in the courtyard, Tibor called to her.

Kelene bobbed her head in acknowledgment and felt the rising pang of a headache in her temples. By Amara's crown, she was drained, weary to the last bone and muscle. She could hardly keep her eyes open as she made her way through the ruins to the old court where they had found the eagle.

The images of the Korg's memory weighed heavily in her mind like a bad dream that would not fade. The details she remembered gave the old city around her a new dimension of reality. She could picture now what it had really looked like and how its people had lived. Moy Tura had been a grand idea: a place separate from the individual clans where magic-wielders could study and teach. There was much she and the present day magic-wielders could learn from this city.

Sluggish with fatigue and her own thoughts, Kelene hobbled into the sun-drenched courtyard and stopped in her tracks. Her mouth dropped open and a cry of delight escaped her lips at the sight of Demira standing in the sunlight. She had tried to picture what the filly would look like with wings, but the truth was much more spectacular than she had imagined. Demira had already been a magnificent horse, tall, well muscled, and graceful. Her new wings only enhanced her beauty.

The wings were larger than Kelene had expected, with primary feathers almost as long as her arm, yet they fit the horse's sleek proportions perfectly, tucking neatly against her sides. The black feathers gleamed in the noon sun and matched her dark coat like a shadow on shining ebony.

It was only when Kelene walked closer that she noticed the droop in Demira's head and the sweat lathering the filly's chest and neck. Demira lifted her muzzle, dejection in her deep eyes. *They will not work! I cannot fly,* she groaned in Kelene's mind. *They feel so strange, I do not know what to do with them.* She raised the offending wings, then pulled them disgustedly back to her sides.

The young woman hid her own dismay in an encouraging smile and pressed her cheek against the filly's neck. "They're too new, Demira," she tried to explain. "You're not used to them yet." She ran a hand along the long, powerful inner wing to the velvety soft pinions. "They're so beautiful."

They may be pretty, but I cannot get them to lift me up! Demira complained.

Something in the word "lift" triggered a thought in Kelene's imagination. "How have you been trying?" she asked.

The Hunnuli backed up a few paces until she was clear of her rider and the piles of rubble. Then she fanned out the long, broad wings and began to flap them as hard as she could. The force of her effort set up a breeze that blew dust and leaves in all directions, but it only lifted her forequarters off the ground a mere foot or two. She sank slowly back to earth, weary and disappointed.

Kelene studied her closely before she inquired, "Have you ever watched a goose take off?"

I have seen geese on the river.

"Do you remember how they leave the water?"

The filly's ears perked forward and her head came up a little. *They have to run as they fly to get airborne.*

"Exactly, and whenever possible they run into the wind to give themselves extra lift. With your speed on the ground, that might give you enough momentum to overcome your weight."

Demira shook herself and carefully folded her wings into place. *I will try that,* she told Kelene in a tone lighter with new hope.

"Rest first," Kelene suggested. "We both need it." They found a pool of shade by a section of the wall, and while Demira relaxed, Kelene began to rub the filly's tired legs and wing muscles.

* * *

Kelene left the temple courtyard shortly after midafternoon. She and Demira had napped long enough to regain their strength, then Demira left, determined to test her new idea for takeoff. Kelene was hot, thirsty, and ravenously hungry. It had been a long time since her last meal. She walked back to the shelter, stretching her arms and legs as she went until she felt more energetic.

Sayyed was still on his blankets when she stepped into the shadowy room. Although he seemed to be sleeping, he flinched when she knelt beside him. Rafnir was sitting close by, his demeanor tense and worried.

Kelene picked up a cloth from a bowl of cool water and wiped the perspiration off Sayyed's flushed face. The man shuddered at her touch and tossed on his bed in the delirium of a high fever. Without deliberate forethought, Kelene laid her hand on his forehead and began to hum so softly that Rafnir could barely hear her. Sayyed's eyes flickered open for a second, and a weak smile flitted over his face. Then he eased back into a quieter, more restful sleep.

"How do you do that?" Rafnir asked wonderingly.

Kelene looked up in surprise. "I didn't do anything but try to calm him a little."

The young clansman came around to her side, took her hands in his, and turned them over, palms up. "Long, gentle fingers, strong palms, a wide space between thumb and forefinger." He looked into her face. "You have the hands of a healer."

Kelene snorted, suddenly self-conscious in the face of Rafnir's intensity. People had always been so aware of her foot, they had never paid attention to her hands. She pulled her fingers from his grasp. "A healer," she said lightly. "Don't be ridiculous. Piers was a healer. Gehlyn was a healer. I have no training and no interest!"

"No interest?" he retorted, his brown eyes glowing. "Look how well you treated Savaron and me." He held up his arm to show her the tear in his muscle was healing nicely. "Look at what you just did for Father. You have an incredible touch that eases people's emotions. Think how invaluable that would be to a healer."

Kelene made no reply. She was so taken aback by his observations that she didn't know what to say. She had never thought about being a healer—that profession was usually reserved for men in the clans. Except for midwives, women were not encouraged to pursue the training.

She folded her arms thoughtfully. Despite what she said aloud, Rafnir was right about her interest. The healer Piers had seen that before anyone else. Why else would he have talked to a small girl like an equal and allowed her to follow him everywhere? Perhaps if he hadn't died so soon, he would have encouraged her further. But Piers was gone. The Khulinin healer Gehlyn was dead, too, and the gods only knew how many more healers had succumbed to the plague. The clans would need new people to practice the arts of healing. Why not a sorceress?

Kelene looked down into the face of her parents' dying friend and felt her hope begin to rise. The more she considered Rafnir's suggestion, the more convinced she became that he was right. She jumped to her feet. If she was going to live to be a healer, she and her companions had to find a weapon against the plague, and the only one who might know where that weapon could be lay within the old warehouse.

"I'm going to talk to the Korg," she declared.

Before she knew where she was going, her feet carried her to the doorway of the warehouse. Her brother gave her a quizzical glance as she stopped before the shield.

Inside, the Korg was startled awake. He lifted his head, saw her standing against the bright light, and squinted. "Kelyra?" he growled in sleepy confusion.

The clanswoman jutted out her chin. "No! I am Kelene, daughter of Lady Gabria and Lord Athlone of Clan Khulinin." She said it forcefully and in a proud voice as much to steady her resolve as to inform the lion. Pointing to her brother, she added, "This is Savaron, my brother. Our mother and father broke the gorthling's curse against Valorian's heirs."

The old lion turned his head from one to the other and his golden eyes began to gleam. "Tell me about them," his deep voice commanded.

"I will gladly tell you when there is more time. But now I have to talk to you," Kelene countered. "My mother and father and Sayyed, that man lying sick in our shelter, defeated a gorthling twenty-three years ago. Since then they have struggled to learn sorcery from Matrah's book and their own intuition. They have been gathering other people with the ability to wield magic and trying to undo years of prejudice. It has taken a long time. Too much knowledge from Moy Tura was lost." She broke off and pointed toward the building where Sayyed lay. "Now we have a calamity we cannot stop, and we desperately need help."

The Korg stirred and said, "So you came all this way to find me. Why?"

"The clans have been stricken by a deadly plague. Ever since we opened this old burial mound . . ."

She got no further. Without warning the Korg roared to his feet. "Burial mound! Plague!" he shouted in a voice that shook the warehouse. "What burial mound?"

Kelene was so startled by his sudden ferocity she could only stand wide-eyed in the doorway.

"Speak!" he bellowed. "Whose mound did you desecrate?" He pushed up against the shield, glaring furiously at her from beneath his stone mane.

"I didn't—I mean, we—it was an old one in a box canyon," Kelene stammered, growing pale. She stepped back against her brother. She heard Rafnir, Morad, and the four Hunnuli come running up behind her, but she couldn't take her eyes off the Korg's face. His lips were curled back over teeth like stone daggers; his heavy tail was lashing in vicious arcs.

"In a box canyon," he repeated with a hideous growl. "In the hills near the Tir Samod? A large oval mound sealed with wards and bearing no marks?" He spoke with such vehemence, both Kelene and Savaron could only nod. Another roar rattled the old rafters. "You fools! You released the undead. We sealed him in his tomb forever! Didn't you read the warnings? Didn't you feel the wards? That tomb was not to be touched!"

"We didn't know that," Rafnir tried to say, only to be cut off by a snarl from the Korg.

"Where is he? Where is the man you released? Is he still at the gathering?"

"No," Kelene answered hesitantly, and Savaron filled in for her. "He was just outside the southern gate yesterday."

The words had no sooner been spoken than the Korg plunged forward, battering himself against Savaron's shielding. The magic energy flared at the impact, then faded to a dull pink. The Korg lunged again into the shield. Before anyone could move to help Savaron strengthen it, the energy field exploded. The force of its disruption flung Savaron and Kelene to the ground.

With a thundering bellow, the Korg launched his huge body from the warehouse and charged down the street toward the main road. "Bitorn!" the clanspeople heard him rage.

Stunned, they watched him until he disappeared between some broken walls, then they ran to their horses. Rafnir gave Kelene a hand onto Tibor's back, and she held tight to Rafnir's waist as the big stallion leaped forward. The other Hunnuli were quick to follow, until only Afer was left behind to guard Sayyed.

The Hunnuli galloped down the southern road, their hooves making staccato thunder on the flagstones. Ahead everyone could hear the Korg still roaring like a raging bull.

"What in all the gods' names is he doing?" Kelene cried. Craning to see over Rafnir's shoulder, she looked down the straight road toward the city gates. In the distance she could make out the broken towers of the city wall. "There he is!" she shouted to Rafnir. She saw the lion reach the gateway and go barging through.

All at once there was a flare of reddish light just outside the walls. The Hunnuli sped faster.

The red light was still blazing when the horses came to the high-arched entrance and slid to a stop just inside the gate. Peering out, everyone gaped at the stone lion hunched on his back legs, his front paw raised to strike, and his ears flat on his head. "Be gone, you blood-drinker," the Korg was snarling to the wraith.

The spirit had grown in height to stand eye-to-eye with the lion, and his form was glowing like a fiery pillar. "Heretic!" he screamed. "You cannot hide your human shape in that guise. Your perverted evil reeks through that moldy, lichen-eaten stone. Why are you still here? Was death not good enough for you? Show yourself! Reveal your face before I send you to the depths of Gormoth!"

The Korg laughed, a scornful rumble that echoed off the walls. "Why not? This shell served me well. But I have learned it is no longer needed." He spoke a string of sharp, unfamiliar words. There was a loud boom, and to the watchers' astonishment, the stone lion began to crack apart. Fine lines and fissures spread over his body from muzzle to tail; chunks of stone fell from his mane. In one loud crash, the lion's shape collapsed into a pile of rubble. Standing in its place was a man wearing only a loose wrap around his waist.

Kelene gasped. After the massive, murderous stone lion, the thin, grayhaired man was a surprise. In spite of his tall height, he had to crane his neck to look up at the towering apparition. He was so pale, his white skin looked incongruous against the wraith's blazing red light.

The dead priest cackled in glee and loomed over the old man as if to consume him in the red phosphorescence.

The sorcerer just smiled scornfully before he lifted his hand. A ruby light blazed from the splinter in his wrist, a magic-wielder's splinter identical to Gabria's, and a blast of energy flew from his hand, sending the wraith back several paces.

The clanspeople stared even harder. None of their attacks had had any effect on the apparition.

"Stay back, Bitorn," the Korg was saying. "Your power has little effect on me. Now you know me, now you see that one of the council is still alive!" Without the deep rumbling growls of the lion, his voice sounded very different to the clanspeople, more moderate and precise.

The undead priest hissed his laughter. "Little good it will do you, old man. It took seven of the council to confine me to my tomb, and all the others are dead. There are no more magic-wielders who can control me now! Those that live in this time are weak and untrained. I will soon wipe them all out, and my vengeance will be complete."

"Vengeance! The appalling excuse of a warped and evil mind. Spare us your vengeance, Bitorn. You earned every single verdict and punishment levied against you with your murderous cruelty and acts of hatred. There was no bloodier or more merciless criminal on the Ramtharin Plains than you!"

"Criminal!" the priest howled. "Only the council named me criminal. The chieftains called me ally, the clans called me savior. The gods themselves ordained me to purify the plains of the perversion called magic! You and your sordid little cult did nothing more than delay the inevitable. I *will* destroy every magic-wielder in the clans!"

"By wiping out the entire population?" Kelene shouted. Furious, she threw her leg over Tibor, slid to the ground, and limped forward a few paces. She moved around the dead Hunnuli lying in the dirt, unaware that as she did so, she inadvertently stepped from the protection of the wards in the archway.

The wraith turned his blazing eyes to her, but Kelene was too angry to feel fear. "You caused the plague, didn't you? You gave our entire people this vile illness just to kill a few magic-wielders?"

A slow smile slid over the priest's face as he saw where she was standing. "Yes, child, I did. For more reasons than you imagine."

"Oh, I can imagine a great deal," Kelene snapped to the wraith. "But you won't succeed. Magic-wielders have survived for over five hundred years since Valorian crossed Wolfeared Pass. We will fight you to the last flicker of magic in our veins to preserve our blood-right! Sorcery was a gift from the gods, not a curse. It is jealous, close-minded, vicious fools like you that keep us from fulfilling our destiny in the clans. Go back to your grave, priest. You failed in life, and you will fail again."

Bitorn flicked a finger at her, and Kelene's clothes burst into flame. Pain and terror seared her mind as she tried frantically to beat out the fire on her arms and legs. A scream tore from her throat. She felt Rafnir grab her and yell something, but the agony of the burning was too blinding for her to understand.

Then, just as quickly, the Korg spoke a command; the pain and fire vanished. Kelene was left hunched over, staring stupidly at her untouched tunic and pants. There was no sign of smoke or scorch marks or burns on her skin. It had just been another of the wraith's visions.

Trembling, she slowly straightened. Rafnir was beside her, his hands steadying her shaking body. She raised her head to thank the Korg and saw him turn slightly away from the wraith long enough to check on her. In that split second of inattention, the dead priest lunged at the sorcerer.

"Behind you!" Kelene yelled.

The Korg whirled back too late, for the wraith's hand clamped down on his shoulder. The old man screamed in pain as the red phosphorescent light flared around him.

In almost the same movement, Rafnir and Kelene raised their hands and fired twin bolts of blistering energy at the wraith. Savaron and Morad ran to their companions. They joined their power to the attack, too, forming a four-way barrage against the glowing spirit.

The wraith howled in rage. He tried to hold on to his victim, but the intense power of four magic-wielders forced him back. His hand slipped off the Korg's shoulder.

The old man staggered a step and fell to his knees. Ducking low under the men's continued barrage, Kelene ran forward and half supported, half dragged the Korg back to the safety of the city gate. The three clansmen ceased their attack.

Bitorn snarled an oath and sprang after them, but the men ducked in past the wards. The wraith beat his fist futilely against the invisible power that prevented him from entering the city.

At last he stood back, his chiseled face pinched with rage. He turned his fiery eyes on Kelene. "You have spirit, child. When I catch you, your death shall be interesting. And you," he snapped to the Korg, *"you* are an ineffectual old man. You can hide behind your walls, but you will die with those people with you. Already my disease has struck in their midst. They have to find a cure, but I promise you, any false hope they find in Moy Tura will never reach the clans. My plan will *not* be stopped! So, Councilor, you can stay in your fallen city and die a hideously painful death, or you can leave and die a quicker death of my choice somewhere on the plains." He sneered, his expression triumphant. "It matters not to me."

There was a flash of red light, and the wraith disappeared from sight, leaving behind a strong putrid smell and a faint swirl of dust that settled slowly to earth.

13

There was silence at the southern gate. The four clanspeople exchanged glances before they turned all eyes to the man leaning wearily against the stone wall of the archway. He had his back to them, his shoulders hunched and his head drooping. He pushed himself away from the wall, tightened the wrap around his waist, and slowly turned to face Kelene, Rafnir, Savaron, and Morad. They stared back at him without speaking, wariness, curiosity, and suspicion on all their young faces.

"How do you know him?" Savaron asked abruptly.

The Korg flinched at the harsh tone in the warrior's voice. "His name was Bitorn," he replied wearily. "He was a priest of Sorh."

"So we gathered," said Rafnir. "What was he to you?"

"A bitter enemy. A foe I thought long gone."

Kelene tilted her head thoughtfully. "Was he the priest who was punished by the council?"

The Korg nodded, and for a moment Kelene thought the man was going to cry. The lines on his forehead deepened, and his mouth tightened to a narrow slit. He stared up at the ruined towers, the tumbled piles of rubble, and the rotting pieces of the massive gates as if seeing them clearly for the first time. His eyes, once ablaze with a golden light, were dulled to an ordinary yellowish brown.

Whatever he had been before, whatever he had done, Kelene knew now he was only a weary old man full of sadness and remorse. After years of isolation and emptiness, he had been thrust into a confusing new existence made bitter by old memories and perilous by new dangers he did not know how to face.

Kelene took the Korg's arm and led him back into the city. Savaron offered his hand to help him mount one of the stallions, but the Korg shook his head. "It has been a long time since I rode a Hunnuli. I think I will just walk." With Rafnir and Kelene walking beside the sorcerer, the small group made their way back through the city.

"How did you do it?" Morad asked after a time of silence. "How did you seal his soul in a tomb?"

The Korg took so long to answer, the four clanspeople wondered if he was going to. His deep-set eyes were questing over the ruins around them with a grim intensity that allowed no interruption.

The four young people cast speculative glances at him while they waited, studied his features, and marveled at his appearance. He was not quite as old as they had first thought. Although his skin was pale and lined, his facial muscles were still firm, and his hair had as much blond as gray in its color. Kelene wondered if his outward appearance had changed at all after two hundred years in a stone body. Was this the way he had looked to Kelyra?

Just when they had decided he was not going to answer, the old sorcerer shook his head. "We used Bitorn against himself. That was the irony of our plan." His long fingers gestured toward the blue sky. "Magic is not the only ancient power in the mortal world. The gods have left traces of their divinity in many places that men do not yet understand. Bitorn was a brilliant man with an indefatigable desire to learn and an obsession to avoid death."

"Then why did he become a priest of Sorh?" questioned Savaron, surprised.

"Two reasons, I think. If he could serve Lord Sorh as a devoted servant, perhaps the god of death would look favorably on his service and allow him to live longer. Then, he could learn all there was to know about death and find a way to avoid it entirely."

"Immortality?" Kelene exclaimed. "Did he succeed?"

"Partially. He discovered that every mortal soul has a trace of the gods' ancient power. When a person dies, this power that chains the soul to the body leaks away, allowing the soul to escape its mortal shell. By learning how to steal that energy and absorb it into himself, Bitorn made his soul virtually invulnerable." The Korg's hands clenched into fists. "He also slaughtered dozens of people before we realized what he was doing."

"The Oathbreakers told us he was stealing our life-force. Is that what you mean?" queried Rafnir.

"Yes," said the Korg. "His spirit became so strong, we could not kill him. The power of his soul preserved his body from fatal injury. All we could do was imprison him in a tomb and hope that he would eventually weaken and truly die."

Savaron grunted. "But we got there first."

"Unfortunately." The Korg continued to walk beside the Hunnuli, his expression grim. "His body must have died shortly before you found him, but he had enough energy left in his soul to avoid Soth's Harbingers and eventually escape the opened tomb. Is his body still intact?"

"We don't know," replied Rafnir. "We didn't open the coffin."

"If the coffin is undamaged, chances are his body is still complete," mused the old sorcerer.

"So?" prompted Kelene.

The Korg sighed. "That's why he wants the life-force so badly. If he can gain enough strength, he can rejuvenate his body and live again."

"Is that so bad? It might be easier to kill him if he is in a mortal body," Morad said, patting his sword hilt.

"You don't understand. Bitorn was right. It took seven of us to imprison him in the mound. His soul is so powerful he can manipulate the hidden centers of our thoughts, lend his force to dead bodies and animate them, and resist all but the most powerful spells. As a wraith, he is more vulnerable because he must use a great deal of energy to stay in the mortal realm.

Once he is joined to his body, though, the strength of his soul will protect him from mortality. He will be virtually indestructible."

"I don't understand," complained Savaron. "This life-force and magic seem very similar. What's the difference? And why does Bitorn use this other power when he is so opposed to magic?"

"A few other magic-wielders and I wondered the same thing," the old Korg replied. "We never had a chance to understand Bitorn's work, because he destroyed all of his papers and manuscripts before we caught him. But we did learn that magic is a much older power, springing from creation itself. It is more complex and can only be used by mortals with Valorian's blood. But the life-force is not as ancient. It seems to originate from Lord Sorh. It is Amara who breathes life into our bodies, but it is Lord Sorh who claims the soul at death."

"So anyone could use this power?" Rafnir asked.

"Anyone with the knowledge and desire. It is not an easy energy to command."

"Is Bitorn serious about destroying all the magic-wielders?" Kelene asked quietly.

"Completely." The Korg was emphatic. "Even before we brought him to trial for murder, Bitorn's mind had become affected by the power he had already absorbed. He was completely obsessed by what he called his 'holy duty.'"

They had reached their shelter in the crumbling building, and the Hunnuli came to a stop by Afer.

Rafnir turned his gaze to the shadowed interior where his father lay, and he said morosely, "Bitorn has already made a good start." He thought of his mother so slim and alive, of his friend Ritan, of laughing Coren, and so many others he would never see again. His voice went deadly cold. "How do we destroy the wraith?"

"I don't know. From what you tell me, there are not enough skilled magic-wielders left to stop him."

"There aren't going to be any," Kelene said sharply, "if we don't find the healers' records."

The Korg's eyebrows rose. "What healers' records?"

"That's why we came here, to look for any records left behind by your healers that might help us fight this plague."

"Is it that bad?"

For an answer, Rafnir pulled the Korg into the shelter and pointed to Sayyed. "See for yourself!"

Kelene brushed past them both to kneel by the warrior's side. Cup in hand, she lifted his head and let a trickle of angelica tea flow into his mouth. "It begins like this: a high fever and these painful swellings in the neck." Her fingers gently touched the lumps under Sayyed's jaw. He moaned at her feather-light pressure, and the white cat growled protectively. "The pestilence kills within several days," she added, "and we have nothing to stop it."

The Korg stared, horrified, at Sayyed, understanding for the first time the calamity that had driven these clanspeople to his city. He stirred, and rubbed a hand over his chin. "I don't know if you will find what you need in this city. I don't remember anything like your plague striking our people. There was some pestilence in Pra Desh at that time. Maybe Bitorn found a way to store it and take it with him. Maybe it is a disease of his own corruption."

"Well, we can look can't we?" Rafnir flared, his patience suddenly at an end. "Bitorn must think there is something here we can use. Why else would he leave the gathering to follow a few magic-wielders all the way to Moy Tura? Did the healers have any kind of books or manuscripts or *anything* that described their healing spells?"

"I don't know." The sorcerer was trying to think, but Rafnir's outburst had flustered him.

"You don't know a lot, old man! Think! I've lost my mother and half my clan to this disease. I will not let it take any more." Wearing a scowl, Rafnir strode back outside before his anger and raised voice disturbed his father. The men followed, leaving Sayyed in the more peaceful company of his cat.

Kelene checked the warrior one more time. She sighed with pity at the handsome, powerful man lying helplessly in a sweat-soaked coma while an unseen foe ravaged his body. Her heart ached at the thought of losing his vibrant humor and charming smile.

Quietly she left him and dug through the packs to find some of Tomian's clothes that they had saved. The young Geldring had been bigger than the Korg, but his brown tunic, lightweight pants, and soft leather boots ought to fit the Korg well enough for now.

Outside, she found the men morosely studying the ruins around them and saying very little to each other. The tension was so thick she could almost see it. She handed the clothes to the Korg, who accepted them with a wan smile, and she waited while he dressed. As she feared, the pants were too wide and the boots too big. She was about to suggest the use of a dagger and a needle and thread when he spoke an easy spell and altered them to fit his smaller frame.

"I haven't had to do that in a while," he said to Kelene. His eyes shifted apologetically to the men standing about. "I'm sorry I'm not much help. I was not a healer, and they kept their secrets within their guild."

Kelene, arms crossed, regarded him steadily. "We knew it was a slim chance. Is there anything you can suggest? Some place we could just look?"

He pondered her question and finally suggested, "You could try their hall."

Rafnir snapped alert. "What hall?"

The Korg looked at the warehouse and down the streets. "It has been so long since I tried to remember what these ruined buildings used to be. The Healers' Hall was a big, two-floored building not far from here . . . with a garden courtyard, if I remember."

"Beside a temple to Amara?" Kelene asked excitedly. At the Korg's nod, she smiled. "We know where that is."

Rafnir's expression brightened with recognition, and the two of them led the others through the alleys and streets to the courtyard where they had found the eagle.

Kelene took a quick glance around and was relieved to see Demira was off somewhere, probably foraging for grass or strengthening her new wings. She winked at Rafnir, glad she did not have to explain her horse's radical new appearance at that particular moment.

The Korg was looking quizzically at the broken columns around the courtyard and at the heaps of weathered and crumbled masonry on the foundation of the building he had indicated. "This must be it," he muttered as if to himself.

The clanspeople needed no more encouragement than that. They fanned out and searched every crack, nook, hole, and cranny they could find in the ruined Healers' Hall. They pulled down the remains of walls, tore apart piles of rubble, and dug through layers of packed ash and dirt.

Unfortunately there wasn't much left to examine. The attackers had been thorough when they ransacked and destroyed the building, and the years had taken anything perishable that was left. By the time the sun touched the horizon, the clanspeople had examined everything in the old foundations and found nothing. They were dispirited and unhappy when Savaron finally called a halt.

"Are you sure this is the only hall they kept?" Rafnir asked the Korg. "Didn't the healers have some other place they might have stored records?"

The sorcerer bowed his head. "None that I know of."

Morad made an aggravated grunt and threw up his hands. "Well, now what do we do? Go home?"

"We can't," Rafnir rapped out. "We'll have to keep looking."

"For what? More rocks? More lizards? Another dead end? Face it, Rafnir, this whole journey has been a waste of time. There isn't anything here but old stones." Morad picked up one and threw it as hard as he could into the twilight. "At first light, I'm leaving. I'm going back to Geidring Treld."

"By yourself? Past the wraith?" Kelene exclaimed.

"I'll slip out the northern gate and find my own way. That stinking priest will be too busy keeping a watch for *him*." He jabbed a finger at the Korg.

"You won't go alone," Rafnir noted in a voice both quiet and forceful. "You'll take the plague with you. If you don't die alone somewhere on the plains, you'll make it to your treld and spread the disease to those who stayed behind."

Morad reddened, angry at himself for showing fear and angry at Rafnir for trapping him with the obvious. He was about to make a retort when an exclamation from Savaron startled everyone.

"Good gods!" he burst out. "What was that?"

The others whirled to see him staring toward the western sky. The landscape of Moy Tura was flat, so it was possible to see a long distance in areas of the ruins where the building walls were leveled. But when his companions followed Savaron's gaze, they saw nothing out of the ordinary.

"Did you see it?" Savaron said excitedly. "Over there by that far tower. It was either the biggest eagle I've ever seen or—" Frowning, he broke off and asked the Korg, "There aren't any other large beasts around here, are there?"

The old man looked anxious. "Of course not. This is my home."

"An eagle? Do you mean it was flying?" Kelene inquired in a very controlled and innocent voice. She avoided looking at anyone for fear they would see the sudden shining in her eyes. Demira, it must have been Demira!

Her brother squinted. "I think so. I only saw it briefly against the setting sun. It was huge!"

At that, Morad shook his head in disgust. "Wonderful. Stone lions, dead priests, giant eagles. What next? I'm going to find something to eat. At least I know where the food is!" He stomped from the courtyard, his back hunched with anger.

Savaron took one last look toward the western sky, then shrugged and followed a little more slowly. The Korg trailed close behind. Kelene hesitated. She wanted to wait in the courtyard for Demira to return to find out if the filly had truly learned to fly, but the memory of Sayyed's worsening condition convinced her to return to the shelter. The warrior might need her during the night; she did not want to leave him unattended just to satisfy her own curiosity. Maybe Tibor could find out for her.

That night, while a cool wind muttered around the dingy walls, Kelene and Rafnir took turns sitting with Sayyed, keeping him as comfortable as they could while his fever climbed and the boils began to break out on his neck and arms. The little white cat never budged from his side. She lay by his head and purred frantically, as if she were trying to encourage him to fight the thing that was slowly burning up his body.

Savaron and Morad traded off guard duty again, this time just keeping a watch on the shelter. The Korg had accepted a proffered blanket and gone to sleep outdoors with the Hunnuli. Although he craved the company of people, so much of it so quickly was making him uneasy.

No one slept well. The darkness seemed interminable to them all, for it blanketed the world around them and offered nothing to distract their minds from the simple, terrible fact that they were almost out of time and no closer to a solution than they had been two days ago.

A pale pink light was painting the eastern sky when Kelene stepped from the shelter to stretch her aching back.

"Bad night," Savaron commented from his seat on a rock wall nearby. He climbed stiffly down and came to stand beside her. "Is he any better?"

She had to blink hard to stop the sudden tears. "No. I've tried everything I could think of to lower his fever; he just gets worse. If something doesn't help him soon, I don't think he'll live through another night."

The young warrior smacked his hand on his sword hilt. "There has to be something else we haven't tried. I can't believe we came all this way for nothing."

"We knew that was a possibility," Kelene sighed.

"I know, but I kept hoping for some twist of luck, a little nudge from the gods." He grimaced, the hope nearly gone from his heart. "Perhaps the priests were right. Maybe the gods have turned their backs on us at last."

A long, thin hand was laid on Kelene's sleeve, and she looked around to see the Korg. For the first time in two hundred years the sorcerer had a day-old stubble of blondish-gray beard on his cheeks, giving him a tired, slightly scruffy appearance. His eyes were red-rimmed from lack of sleep, and the lines around his mouth and nose seemed deeper. "The gods do not forsake their children," he told them, his voice quavering with emotion. "Never think that."

Morad, who had been listening to the conversation, came over. "What else are we supposed to think? Our prayers go unanswered. We have no hope. No help."

"Maybe they have found an answer at the gathering," the Korg said softly. "With the wraith gone from their midst, perhaps the plague has died down."

Savaron snatched at that hope and turned to his sister urgently. "Kelene, have you looked in the Watcher lately?"

Her fingers went to the stone reluctantly. "Not for a day or two," she said, "but I don't think—"

"Try it anyway," interrupted Morad. "See what is happening."

It was all she could do to unpin the brooch and cup it in her hand. Kelene didn't believe the disease had eased off or that the healers had found a cure. She had seen no sign of it the last time she had looked in the Watcher, and on that day her mother—and her father as much as she knew—were still healthy. She wasn't certain she wanted to know if their condition had changed.

The Korg sensed her reluctance, for his slender hands covered hers. He gave her a pale smile. "Strength to endure comes from within," he whispered.

Bowing her head, Kelene emptied her mind of everything else and concentrated on the brilliant center of the stone. The images were slow to develop; they came reluctantly through a hazy curtain of light as if slowed by her own unwilling participation. When at last the tiny picture came into focus, Kelene realized part of the problem: her mother was facing the east. The rising sun's golden light filled the Fallen Star on her tunic.

Kelene sighed. At least that meant Gabria was still well enough to be outside and on her feet. Kelene realized her mother was praying to Amara, for she saw a pair of hands held up in supplication. Before she could delve deeper into the stone to hear the words, the scene swung around, and her mother entered a tent.

Kelene felt her mouth go dry. It was their family tent; she recognized the red-and-white hanging on the wall and the folding clothes rack her father had made. What was Gabria doing back in the Khulinin camp? Why wasn't she with the healers at the Council Grove?

The tiny image was difficult to see now because of the tent's dim interior and because her mother was moving around. She appeared to be preparing something with a pot of hot water and a handful of dried flowers. Kelene watched, wondering what she was doing.

Gabria moved again toward the back of the tent where the sleeping curtain hung. She pulled aside the curtain and knelt down by someone lying on the pallet.

Several hundred leagues away Kelene saw the face of the prostrate figure in the depths of the gem. She gave a strangled cry and dropped the Watcher on the ground. She raised hollow eyes to Savaron. "It's Father."

Her brother's knees lost their strength, and he sagged back onto his stone seat. "Dead?" he managed to ask.

The girl felt her body grow numb with despair. "No. I think it just happened. He was tossing with fever, but there were no boils yet."

"Not that it matters. He will be dead before we get back." Savaron dropped his head in his hands.

The Korg looked from one to the other, his eyes troubled by their grief. "Your father? This is Lord Athlone?" At Kelene's nod, he bent over, picked up the Watcher, and pressed it back into her cold fingers. "I was awake most of the night, trying to remember Moy Tura as it was," he went on hesitantly in his dry, raspy voice. "Talking to you yesterday stirred things I have not thought about in years, and last night a memory came to me. It's probably just as useless as the hall, but there do not seem to be many choices left."

"What is it?" Rafnir called from the entrance to the shelter. He was leaning against the wall of the opening, his arms crossed and his face wary.

"The tunnels," replied the old sorcerer. When the others gave him unknowing stares, he elaborated: "We built a series of underground tunnels from the Sorcerers' Hall to four or five of the main city buildings for use by students and magic-wielders. I know there was one to the Healers' Hall. It occurred to me that maybe some of their important works were in storage rooms underneath the main hall."

"Tunnels," Morad repeated, his tone dripping with disbelief. "Beneath the city. We've never heard of that!"

"Very few people outside of Moy Tura knew they were there. If Lord Gordak knew of them, he would have destroyed them, too. But the doors were enhanced with magic to seal automatically when they were shut. Gordak could have missed them when he razed the city."

"I didn't see any sign of an entrance, sealed or otherwise, to a lower level at the hall," Savaron declared.

The Korg rubbed his hands thoughtfully and said, "I didn't either, or I would have remembered it sooner. It must have been destroyed when the walls were torn down."

Kelene carefully pinned her brooch back into place while she listened to the men. A tiny seed of hope stirred in her mind, pushing aside a little of the despair that had settled over her when she saw her father lying sick and helpless. If it was just wishful thinking, she didn't care, so long as some small possibility offered another chance. "Is there another building with an entrance close to the Healers' Hall?" she suggested.

The old sorcerer hesitated. Then his face brightened a little. "The closest one was the Temple of Ealgoden. That building is still partially intact." A grimace slid over his face. "The clan warriors didn't dare tear down a holy place."

Savaron, Morad, and Kelene traded glances and without saying a word, agreed to try. Only Rafnir hesitated, torn between staying with his father or searching the temple.

The stallion, Afer, understood his indecision. *Go,* the Hunnuli reassured him. *I can tell you if he needs help.*

The people were about to leave when the white cat came trotting from the shelter, grumbling irritably. *Afer told me to go with you. He says I can hunt for cracks and little holes that your human eyes might miss.*

The Korg watched in amusement as she set off without waiting for anyone, her tail held high, her whiskers twitching. "For one so small, she has the bearing of a lioness," he commented, smiling. "Where did she learn to communicate like that?"

"My mother," Rafnir said curtly, gesturing for the Korg to take the lead.

Following the old man, the searchers walked south past the square to the southern road. A few minutes later they entered an archway through a high wall into the spacious courtyard of the huge temple they had seen before. The Korg had been right: the temple had suffered little damage from the marauding clan warriors. At least it had not been burned and razed to the ground like the Sorcerers' Hall.

But time, neglect, and weather had inflicted their own grievous damage. The roof had fallen into the interior, most of the walls had collapsed, and the facade of marble columns and frieze-work was cracked and broken. Debris was scattered across the paved courtyard. Grass and weeds grew between the cracked flagstones, and a small wild cedar struggled to live in what had once been a garden. Not even the morning sun could drive away the dingy, forlorn look of the temple and its faded grandeur.

The young clanspeople looked at the huge pile in dismay, wondering where to begin.

The Korg walked slowly across the courtyard and up the broad stone steps that stretched across the face of the temple. He raised his arms to the ruined building.

"It was named the Temple of Ealgoden after the sacred peak in the realm of the immortals. We wished it to be a place where we could venerate all the deities together under one roof." Then he cried loudly, "Mighty Surgart and his Sword of War; the Judge and Executioner Lord Sorh; the capricious, dark Krath; and the Mother of All, Amara! If the Sorcerers' Hall was the brain of Moy Tura, this was the heart! Enter with me to seek the answers to your prayers."

Across the courtyard, Morad blew his nose rudely. "That old man has lost more than a couple pounds of stone," he hissed. "He's a few threads short of a full warp."

Kelene glared at the Geldring. Perhaps the Korg was being a little dramatic, but there was nothing wrong with his mind. And if he could find a tunnel that led to the Healers' Hall, she wouldn't care if he began orating from the city walls. She hurried after the sorcerer, not bothering to see if Morad was coming. Rafnir and Savaron followed. Finally Morad, muttering to himself, brought up the rear. They made their way up the worn and pitted steps in time to see the Korg and Tam's cat pick a path through the broken main doors.

The doors were double-hung, bronze goliaths that perched precariously on the remains of the front wall and doorframe. The clanspeople edged past, being very careful not to jar the doors' fragile balance. Once inside, it was almost impossible to discern the layout of the building. Whatever had been within had been crushed and buried under the massive weight of the roof. Overhead, the blue firmament of the sky was the only ceiling the temple would ever have.

"Where was the entrance to the tunnels?" Rafnir inquired dubiously, poking around a heap of broken stone.

The Korg pointed. "To the left. The door came out in an anteroom just off the far aisle." He led the way toward a tumbled mass of masonry, roofing material, and windblown trash that covered several partially collapsed walls.

"In there?" Rafnir groaned when he saw the mess. "It will take all day to get through that."

He wasn't totally correct. The task only took them half a day. Under the Korg's direction, they used magic to lift the stones aside and very carefully dig out the remains of what had once been several priests' chambers and ante-rooms. The work was delicate because they did not want to weaken the remaining walls or bring down any more debris.

When they were finished, it was past noon, and they were all tired from the exacting spells they had had to control. The rooms were still filthy with heaps of debris and trash, but now there was space to move within the walls.

"This is the place," the Korg told his companions. He pointed to a small chamber. Tam's cat was the first one into the ruined room. Behind her, the clanspeople crowded into the entrance to look around.

Rafnir crossed his arms and leaned against the doorjamb of the room the Korg had indicated. He was hot, sweating, had a lousy headache, and he didn't see anything that looked like another door or entrance out of that room. It was barely ten paces across, windowless, and unadorned. Any furniture or decoration within had rotted long ago. There was nothing but dirty stone and the heavy smell of rot and mold.

He watched the white cat delicately pad around the room, looking here and there, prodding with a paw, or sniffing fastidiously at the stones. Her ears were pricked and her nose was busy, but she did not seem particularly excited about anything. After a few minutes, she sat down near the back wall and began to wash her paws.

Rafnir gave a snarl of disgust, made harsher by his growing frustration and fear for Sayyed. "Another dead end. So where is your entrance, old man?"

The Korg did not take offense. He was very familiar with feelings of fear and disappointment. He eased past Rafnir's larger, more powerful bulk and went to squat beside the cat. "I believe she's sitting on it," he replied mildly. "I told you the doors were sealed."

The cat meowed. *I cannot see door. I can only smell what is beneath the floor.*

She stepped aside, and the Korg picked up a scrap of wood and scraped away a layer of grime on the floor. An octagonal stone no wider than a man's hand was uncovered beneath the dirt. The stone, a polished tile of black marble, had a small depression in its center. The Korg set his thumb into the depression, spoke a strange word, and pushed.

The four young people looked on in amazement when the stone gave way beneath his hand. An entire section of the floor and part of the wall came loose and slid haltingly out of sight. The Korg winced at the rough grinding noise it emitted in its efforts to overcome so many years of disuse and layered grime. Underneath was revealed a narrow stone stairway leading down into a black pit. A strong smell of dank rock filled the air, and a heavy chill leeched from the blackness. There was no sound, no sign of life; there was nothing but the first three steps and the unknown darkness.

Silence gathered around the clanspeople. Faces grim, they stared down into the black well. No one wanted to take the first step down, not even the Korg.

Kelene felt her stomach grow queasy from the sight of that stair. It was like looking into a bottomless chasm. She remembered the story of Valorian and wondered if he had felt this scared when he stood on the lightless threshold of Gormoth. "Well, at least there are no gorthlings down there," she said in a hearty voice she had to force.

The men were startled by her words. Then Rafnir began to grin, and Savaron chuckled. Morad unbent enough to shrug and take the first step down the stairs.

"How about some light?" the Geldring suggested.

The magic-wielders quickly obliged by shaping magic into small, floating spheres of light to take below. In single file the men and Kelene followed Morad down the steps into the blackness.

Last to go, Rafnir glanced at the white cat, who was watching them with her unwinking solemn eyes. "Coming?" he invited. Her tail went up, and regal as a priestess, she padded down the stairs ahead of him.

Rafnir gave one last look at the sunlit ruins, took a deep breath, and went down into the depths of Moy Tura.

14

The narrow passage plunged down into the bedrock beneath the temple without a curve or deviation. Its walls were so close together, the people had to stay in single file. Fortunately, the steps themselves were fairly wide, and a stone railing had been placed on the right side about waist-height. The walk down wasn't too bad—except for the air that chilled the searchers to the skin and the darkness that pressed in around the edges of their little lights.

The clanspeople hadn't gone down more than ten steps when a single feeble light began to glow on the ceiling just ahead. Morad started so badly he nearly tripped on a step.

The Korg put his hand on the Geidring's shoulder. "No need to be alarmed," he said sadly. "There used to be a string of lights along the ceiling that were spelled to shine whenever a magic-wielder came near. I'm surprised one still works."

There was something rather comforting about the light and its reminder that other magic-wielders had walked underneath it every day. Its pale illumination couldn't compete with the spheres the travelers had made themselves, but its presence helped to diminish some of the fearsomeness of the tunnel as the men, the woman, and the cat passed below and continued their descent.

A few minutes later they reached the bottom and gathered together in a tight group. By the light of the magic globes, they could see that they were standing in an intersection of several tunnels. The passages were much like the stairs, smooth-walled and obviously man-made, but here the way ran wide enough for two people to walk abreast. One tunnel continued straight ahead. Others led away to the left and right.

"Which way?" Savaron's voice boomed in the quiet.

Kelene started and bumped into Rafnir. She felt his hand, warm and strong by hers, and she clasped it to help settle the tendrils of fear that were curling in her head. His fingers tightened around hers, inadvertently opening his emotions to her touch. She sensed an uncomfortable mix of nervousness, worry, apprehension, and a warm pleasure at her closeness, before she forced herself to close off her mind. At the same time she was aware of Rafnir mentally drawing away from her, too, and the flow of feelings was cut off. Kelene was relieved. She knew now it was possible to control her talent around Rafnir and allow him some privacy of feeling. That ability might be important later on if their new-found friendship continued to flourish.

Without speaking, the Korg turned to the left-hand tunnel and led his companions cautiously along the passage. Because the tunnels had been sealed for so long, there wasn't much dust or litter along the way, and very little moisture had accumulated. Other faint lights glowed like ghostly candles on the ceiling overhead.

They hadn't been walking very long when the Korg stopped so quickly Morad and Savaron slammed into him and sent him stumbling forward. Muttering and apologizing, they reached out to help him and saw what had shocked him so badly. There, just a step away from the Korg's boots, was the skeleton of a man. It lay sprawled at the foot of another set of stairs, its flesh long gone and its bone gleaming palely through the scraps of a long yellow tunic. An arrow protruded from its back.

"Sentran," murmured the Korg.

Kelene saw his cheeks were wet. "You knew him?"

"A friend. He always wore that awful shade of yellow." He stared up the black hole of the stairway. "Sentran liked to work late. He must have been shot and made it this far before he died. . . ." His voice trailed away.

Morad leaned over and fingered the fletching on the arrow. "If the colors were the same then as now, it's Geldring." His face turned a ghastly hue in the greenish white lights of the spheres. He let go of the arrow as if it had stung him.

They hurried on, leaving the body of Sentran in undisturbed peace, and pushed a little faster through the tunnels.

At last the Korg reached a place where the tunnel widened and came to an end in a very solid-looking door. The door had a stone lintel and was covered with hammered sheets of bronze. A strange emblem of a golden hand with a red jeweled eye in its palm adorned the center of the door.

"This is it; I recognize the Healers' symbol," the Korg told the small group. Then his expression grew puzzled. "But I didn't know there was a door here." He pushed it to no avail.

Savaron and Morad added their shoulders with his against the door and pushed, but the door did not budge. There wasn't enough room for anyone else to help them, so they gave up and looked for another way. They were disheartened to find no visible latches, hinges, or locks.

"The door must be magically locked," the Korg decided.

Morad glared at it. "I don't suppose you know how to break the spell," he said to the old man.

The sorcerer exhaled with an irritated rush. "I told you, the healers were very protective of their secrets."

"Could we blast it open with magic?" Rafnir suggested.

"Probably not. The door is protected. It would take so much power to break the spell, the backlash of the magic would kill us in the confined space of this tunnel."

The men fell to thinking about alternatives while Kelene watched frustration darken their faces. To come so far and be thwarted on the doorstep of their destination by the very people they were hoping could help them seemed unfair.

And yet it struck her odd that healers would take such pains to lock a door in what was essentially a public tunnel. The spell on the entrance in the temple above had not been very complicated, perhaps this one wasn't either.

"Maybe you're making too much of this," suggested Kelene. There was no octagonal stone with a thumb depression on the door, so she tried the next best thing. She laid her palm and fingers on the emblem and pressed hard on the golden hand.

A faint stir of magic tingled against her skin, so Kelene knew she had the right idea. But the door remained firmly closed. There had to be something more. Her next thought was to try magic. This was a magic-wielders' door, after all, and maybe sorcery was needed to open it. Kelene gathered the ancient energy around her and directed it through her hand into the emblem. "Open," she commanded.

Instantly the jewel in the palm flared with a brilliant red light so bright it shone in a beam of scarlet through her hand. The power of the door's spell flashed through her arm to her head and all the way to her feet, prickling on her skin and making the hairs rise on her arms and neck. The reaction of the magic barely registered in her mind when the light went out and the door cracked open. Kelene blinked in pleased surprise.

Impressed, the clansmen grinned at her. But the Korg scratched the back of his neck and studied her thoughtfully. Kelene stepped out of the way while Savaron pushed the heavy door open. Over the groan of the hinges, the people heard a strange, hollow, rattling noise that made everyone jump.

"What was that?" Morad exclaimed. He mentally shoved his sphere of light through the doorway into the darkness beyond. The green-white light shone on the floor, illuminating a scattered collection of human bones.

Kelene made a small sound somewhere between a gasp and a cry. "They're only children." She limped through the door into the corridor beyond and knelt on the cold floor by a huddled group of three small skeletons lying along the wall. Two more sets of bones had been knocked aside by the opening door. She picked up a skull no bigger than her little brother's head and turned tear-filled eyes to the men who were standing pale and silent in the doorway. "What were they doing here?" she whispered.

The Korg clasped his hands behind his back to hide their trembling. "Someone must have hidden them down here. Most children weren't allowed in the tunnels until they had passed their first rites." He paused to clear his throat. "They wouldn't have known how to open the doors."

"Put them down here to keep them safe, not knowing it would be their tomb. Poor babies. They must have been so frightened!" Ever so gently, Kelene laid the skull beside the others and wiped her face. She was cold and miserable down in these tunnels and the sight of those small bones depressed her even more. The dark, chilled air and the enclosed spaces affected her more than she had thought and teased her imagination with violent images of that night so long ago. She wanted nothing more than to get out of there before they found another gruesome reminder of her people's folly and cruelty. Instead she forced herself to rise and step away from the skeletons.

Tam's cat padded carefully around the bones into the corridor. Kelene, with the men close behind, followed the small animal toward the several doors that stood open on both sides of the hall. The first door on the right led into a large room well furnished with long tables, benches, and two tattered rugs. Dusty, faded tapestries hung on the walls, and a few lamps were suspended from the ceiling.

"That was probably a study room or gathering place," observed the Korg.

Kelene, Savaron, Morad, and Rafnir looked around the room and were impressed. The only rooms those four clanspeople knew well were in the chieftains' halls in their clans' winter camps. This large, comfortable-looking study fascinated them. "There must have been many healers here at one time," said Rafnir.

The Korg frowned. "Not really. The Healers' guild was the smallest in Moy Tura. It was learned long ago that not every magic-wielder can heal." His glance shifted to Kelene, but she had already moved back into the hall to continue the search.

There were three more doors in the hall, each one made of ironbound hardwood fastened with simple latches. Behind the doors were rooms much smaller than the first that led nowhere. One had a worktable and some benches sitting along the walls. The second seemed to be a storage room half full of everyday items: cast-aside clothing, pots, earthen dishes, a few empty storage jars, a broken stool, several mouse-eaten cloaks, and a wooden box full of small clay jars similar to the ones the healer Piers had used for his medicines. Some of the things had been broken and strewn around the floor, probably by the children in their search for food to eat.

Kelene shuddered and moved to the last room. She stuck her head in the doorway and felt a sour pang of disappointment. The chamber was the last one she could see, and it was barren—no shelves, no alcoves, no doorways leading to other rooms, no cupboards or closets. Nothing but dust and aching silence.

Frustrated, she withdrew to the hallway. The men obviously hadn't found anything either, since there were no excited voices or calls for assistance. They were wandering from room to room, too, their globes of light following along obediently above their heads.

Kelene turned her attention to the only place at the end of the hall where she had not explored. There she found the stairway leading to the upper floors. It was very obvious why they had not found the stair when they explored the hall. In the process of razing the building, the victors had pulled down a wall over the hidden staircase and the door had collapsed under the weight of the crashing stone. The entire stairwell was blocked with chunks of masonry and broken stone. The children trapped down there never had a chance to escape.

Kelene kicked a stone aside with the toe of her boot. The hall ended by the stairs in a blank wall. There was nowhere else to look.

She was about to go back when she noticed Tam's cat by her feet. The little cat's white fur was bedraggled and dirty, and her whiskers were dusty, but the animal was too distracted to notice. Something fascinated her along the blank stone wall directly across from the stairs. She sniffed the stone and poked at it with her paws, all the while pacing back and forth with her tail swishing.

"What is it?" Kelene inquired.

The cat made a puzzled sound. *The rock has no smell. It is cold and gray like other. Just no smell.*

How odd, Kelene thought, putting her hands on the wall. It did feel like the rest of the walls—cold, damp, dirty—and yet there was something slightly strange about it. It didn't seem as dense? As textured? The difference was so subtle she couldn't even describe it, and she certainly wouldn't have noticed it without the cat.

Fascinated now, she began to examine the wall from ceiling to floor while the cat wound around her legs and sniffed at different sections of stone. There was certainly nothing as obvious as the outline of a door, a symbol on the wall, a latch, or a lock. The only thing Kelene found were two small, faint depressions in the stones about shoulder height and perhaps an arm's length apart.

Kelene put a thumb in one of the depressions, spoke the Korg's spell word, and pushed. Nothing happened. She tried the other, and still nothing happened. The stone remained immovable and enigmatic. Finally Kelene tried placing a thumb in each indentation and pushing at the same time. Once again nothing seemed to change.

Then she happened to glance down and saw Tam's cat walk between her legs into the wall and disappear. Kelene was so startled, she reached out to grab the cat, lost her balance, and fell headlong through the stone into total darkness.

She tumbled onto what felt like another floor. The stone beneath her hands was as cold and dirty as the hallway, but she couldn't see it well enough to be sure. To her eyes, accustomed to the light of her sphere, the space around her seemed densely black. She froze in the darkness under a cold wash of fear.

What are you doing? meowed the cat from some place close by.

Kelene stifled a yelp of surprise and unclenched her hands from the floor. Warily she pushed herself up to a sitting position. "What is this place?" she whispered.

Room. Like others. The cat's tone sounded surprised at Kelene's reaction. *Turn around and there is doorway.*

Kelene turned her head, and sure enough, just behind her was a rectangular opening outlined by the faint light of her sphere that dangled just beyond the entrance. The odd thing was there was no physical door, only an open space looking out on the stairs and the hallway.

The girl quickly pulled her light into the room and increased its bright glow to shine on the room from corner to corner. The chamber she had found was not a particularly large one, perhaps fifteen paces deep and twenty long, but Kelene realized instantly that it had been an important place.

Floor-to-ceiling shelves, tall wooden cupboards, and detailed murals covered all four walls. A wide worktable sat in the center of the floor. Everywhere Kelene looked, she saw bottles, vials, small boxes, mortars and pestles, bowls, utensils, many odd tools, and things she could not identify. There had to be something here they could use!

"Come here!" she called excitedly. "I found another storeroom."

The men came hurrying at the sound of her voice, but she was surprised when they stopped at the end of the hallway and milled around, looking perplexed.

"Kelene, where are you?" Rafnir called.

She hobbled to the door, a mere step or two away from him, and said, "I'm right here!" He started like a spooked horse. She stuck her head out the door, and to her amusement, all four men leaped backward. "The entrance is right here," she informed them.

Morad stared at her, his eyes bugged out. "What entrance? All I can see is your head in a stone wall!"

"Well, I can see the way from this side!" Kelene insisted. "Just put your thumbs in those little depressions and push. You can walk right through."

However, the spell would not work for them. One by one they tried it, but no one could go through the entrance. It was the Korg who finally understood. "It's keyed to healers," he said half aloud. "I didn't know they used that, too."

Rafnir smacked his hand against the wall. "Used what, too?" he asked irritably.

"Use spells that could only be triggered by magic-wielders with specific talents. Like healing. Obviously Kelene has that talent, so the doorway opened for her."

Kelene felt a strange flush of excitement warm her face. The truth was confirmed. Her empathic touch and her interest in healing were not coincidences but part of a greater talent to heal with magic. "Oh, Amara! Thank you," she whispered. Smiling now, she said to the men, "Tam's cat is in here with me. How did she come through?"

"She must have stepped in as you tripped the entry spell," the Korg replied.

Kelene abruptly stepped through the stone. "Then let's try it with all of you," she said in a brusque tone. Putting her thumbs in the depressions, she repeated the old spell. One after another the men ducked under her arms and stepped into the storeroom.

The Korg made a grunt of satisfaction as Kelene followed the last man in. "No wonder they used a door keyed to healers. This was probably their pharmacy," the old sorcerer explained. "The healers prepared all the medicines used in Moy Tura."

"So there might be something here that could help us," Savaron said. He and the others spread out, opening drawers and poking around shelves.

"Maybe," the Korg responded hesitantly. "But most of those powders, herbs, and oils will be worthless by now."

"Why would they need medicines?" Kelene asked from a corner where she was looking into a row of large jugs. "Couldn't your healers heal everything with magic?"

The Korg sighed and leaned against the table. "Of course not. The human body is too complicated, too fragile to assail with heavy doses of magic. All a healer can do is influence the natural healing processes of the body. Look at those murals." He pointed to one on the wall near Kelene's head.

Kelene twisted around to look up at a life-size painting of a human male. At least she guessed it was a male. Although the mural was faded and dusty, she recognized it as a detailed representation of the bones and major muscles of the body. Her mouth dropped open.

"Healers studied anatomy and physiology for years, as well as medicines and magic." He chuckled dryly. "You have to know what is broken before you try to fix it."

A sharp and poignant memory surfaced in Kelene's mind of her mother and the Khulinin horse healer looking helplessly at her smashed ankle as they tried to work the broken pieces back together. Even though they had tried to be gentle, the pain had been agonizing. Yes, Kelene decided, it would be very useful to know what to do. She nodded mutely and went back to her search, her expression thoughtful.

It wasn't long before Rafnir made the first discovery. Behind the closed doors of a tall wooden case he found a collection of rolled scrolls, tied with silk cords, and two small leather-bound manuscripts. Bursting with hope, he carried the fragile writings to the worktable and began to gently undo them. The Korg and Kelene joined him, and the white cat hopped up on the table to play with the cords.

"Look at this," said Kelene. She was scanning the yellowed pages of one of the small books. "Recipes! I know this one. It's a cough syrup from wild cherry bark. Here's an astringent made from something called marigolds."

"What's an astringent?" Rafnir asked from behind an unrolled scroll.

"A skin wash to help heal small wounds," she replied. "And here's a restorative that looks very interesting. I wish I knew more about herbs and medicines. I'll have to show this one to Mother." She continued to turn the pages, yet her face slowly clouded over. "There is some valuable information here and many things I don't recognize, but I don't see anything that specifically mentions a plague or any illness with the effects we have seen."

Rafnir turned to the Korg. In spite of the chill in the room, the young warrior's face was sweating. He had to wipe his forehead before he asked, "Did the healers have any other books or manuscripts?"

The sorcerer's reply was discouraging. "I remember they had a large collection that they kept in a room . . . upstairs. I doubt the clan warriors made an effort to save them."

Just then, Savaron gave a yell of delight. "Hey! Didn't Piers have one of these?" He held up a smooth red stone about the size of an eagle's egg.

Kelene nearly bowled him over in her rush to see what he had found. He carefully laid the stone in her hand and stood aside to reveal the place where he had found it. Kelene's fingers curled around the precious stone. There, in a long, shallow drawer Savaron had pulled from a cupboard, lay a wooden tray neatly divided into seven sections. In each compartment lay a variety of polished stones of different sizes and colors. Kelene pulled the tray out of its drawer and reverently laid it on the table by the scrolls.

She put the red stone back in its place and asked the Korg, "Do you know what all of these are for?"

The sorcerer's brow wrinkled even more as he studied the collection. "I know they're healing stones. The healers used them to help treat specific problems. That red one you had was made to remove traces of magic from a body. The healers made several of those at the request of the clan chieftains in case of accidents or malicious attacks. Anyone could use those, but I think the rest of the stones could only be used by healers."

"Piers did have one of those red stones, but he never told me about any others. What do they do?" Kelene asked, almost breathless with hope.

"Well," he said, pointing to some green stones, "those have a sleeping spell. These yellow ones are topaz used to help heal broken bones. Now these might be interesting." He picked out several opaque golden stones that gleamed with dark translucent streaks. They were about the size of a baby's fist and polished to a brilliant sheen. The Korg held one up to his eye. "Lion's Eye," he chuckled lightly. "The healers had to use this one to help Kelyra after a miscarriage. It breaks fevers."

Kelene's chin came up, and her dark eyes bore into his yellow-brown ones. "Fevers. Are you sure?"

"Certain. It saved her life."

"Could it help Sayyed?"

The flicker of humor died from his eyes, and his face became heavy and set. "That I cannot answer, Kelene. It is for you to find out."

She plucked the golden stone from his hand and juggled it in her fingers. She was suddenly frightened—afraid of the immense job of learning the healing craft and of the awesome responsibility of trying to save lives. "I know so little about healing," she murmured as if to herself. "Will I be able to do any good?"

Savaron, Morad, and Rafnir were silent, watching her, but the old sorcerer drew himself straight and stood before her like the councilor he had once been. "You were born with a rare talent to heal, Kelene. It is a talent that requires compassion, desire, and courage. You have all of those in full measure, clanswoman. Don't let a little self-doubt stand in your way."

Her gaze snapped up to his face, to those yellowish eyes that had seen so much, and she felt her fear recede enough so she could banish it to the back of her mind. Trained or not, she had the potential to be a healer and the talent to use the healing stones. It was the best hope her party had found to fight the wraith's deadly plague.

There was only one way to find out if she and the stones could be effective. She held the Lion's Eye up to the light. "How do I use this?" she asked the Korg.

A slow, satisfied smile creased his face. "Before you try anything, perhaps you should have one of these." He reached into the tray, drew out a small package wrapped in soft leather, and laid it on the table beside her.

Kelene untied the cord holding the package together. Her breath came out in a gasp of surprise as the contents rolled glittering onto the tabletop. Savaron, Morad, and Rafnir crowded around her to see the crystal slivers that sparkled like diamonds under the white light of the magic spheres.

Savaron was the first to recognize them and his strong hands reached out to touch them. "Splinters! Why are they here?" The others shifted and smiled at one another. The diamond splinters were the traditional emblem of a true magic-wielder.

"A healer was always present to insert them during the rites of completion," the Korg informed them. "But I am surprised you know of splinters since none of you have one."

"My mother received one," Kelene said.

"Then you know what a splinter does."

Rafnir replied, "It enhances a person's ability to control magic."

"Can you insert them?" Savaron asked the Korg.

The sorcerer tipped his head toward the door. "Outside."

Kelene felt her hands begin to tremble. Hurriedly, she returned the stones to their tray, piled the manuscripts and scrolls on top, and covered the whole thing with a cloth. Tray in hand, she led the way from the room and down the hall, the men and the cat close behind. They filed silently past the children's bones and out the door into the tunnels.

Rafnir, at the end of the line, paused to rub his aching temples before he softly closed the door behind him. Gods of all, he felt lousy. Sweat was running down his forehead and chest, and his strength was draining away. He had to draw several deep breaths before he could walk after the others up the passage toward the exit.

The sun hit them with its blinding light when the searchers climbed from the stairwell into the ruined temple. The day was well advanced, and the ruins sweltered in the afternoon's indolent heat.

The Korg took Kelene's hand and led her to the steps of the temple, where he turned her to face the sun in the western sky. He stretched out her arm, palm up. "There is usually more formality than this," he apologized, "but I don't think your friend, Sayyed, has the time." While the clanspeople watched, he retrieved a splinter from Kelene's tray and began to speak the words of the ancient rite.

Kelene's trembling eased. A warm, still peace infused her soul. Her nervousness and fear fluttered once more and disappeared as the words of the rite filled her mind and the significance of their meaning finally put to rest the last of her reluctance. Her anger from the past rose in her mind and was cast away along with her indecision and insecurity about herself. She had taken the first step with Demira when she accepted at last her power to wield magic. Now she faced the Korg and embraced the full range of her power with her entire heart and soul. She would be a healer, the best she could be, and the knowledge sang in her mind like a litany of joy.

Her face was radiant when the Korg finished the last prayer of the rite and lifted the diamond splinter to the sun to absorb the heat and light of Amara's grace. The sliver glowed between his fingers with a pure white light. Then, the Korg pierced Kelene's right wrist and slid the splinter under the skin. There was not a drop of blood spilled.

Pain shot through her arm and the heat from the diamond burned under her skin. The splinter immediately began to pulse a reddish light to the pounding of her heart. Kelene stared down at it, entranced. She could feel an invigorating sensation spread up her arm, to her head, and down into every part of her body. It sang in her blood and filled her with an incredible sense of completeness. She lifted her eyes to the Korg and smiled her understanding.

All at once, a huge dark shadow swept over them. The Korg ducked, and, with yells of surprise, Savaron and Morad drew their swords. Rafnir's hand went to his hilt, too, but he was so weak by that time that he simply gave up and sat down on the stone steps. Only Kelene looked up at the sky and grinned in triumphant delight.

A joyous neigh echoed in the temple ruins. *I can fly!* Demira trumpeted to the skies. She curved around and swept overhead again, the wind thrumming through her magnificent, outstretched wings.

The men stared up at her, their eyes bulging, their jaws slack. "Good gods!" Morad cried. "Look at her!"

The filly glided down toward Kelene, drew in her wings, and tried to land by the steps. Unfortunately, she had not learned yet to coordinate two wings, four legs, and a heavy body. She came in too fast, tripped over her legs, and nearly fell on her nose.

Rustling her wings, Demira righted herself and shook off the dust. She snorted at Kelene.

Savaron's eyes went from the filly to Kelene and back again. Sometime in between he found his voice. "So this is what you and Rafnir have been up to."

15

Kelene took several minutes to explain to her brother, Morad, and the Korg exactly how Demira had been transformed. The men marveled at the filly's wings and ran their hands incredulously over the satin-smooth feathers.

"You did this?" the Korg exclaimed. "Bitorn may be wrong. You are more resourceful than even I thought."

Savaron was obviously impressed, too. "She's fantastic!" he said to his sister. "You and Rafnir make an unbeatable pair." He looked around Demira's neck toward his friend. "Why didn't you tell . . ." he began. His voice broke off when he saw the Khulinin's face. "Rafnir!" he cried sharply. "What's wrong?"

Savaron's tone brought Kelene up short. She whirled, her heart in her throat, and saw Rafnir slumped on the steps. His face was as red as his tunic, and he was shivering in spite of the heat.

A cry of fear sprang from her lips. She hurried to his side and was horrified to feel the incredible fire in his skin. "Why didn't you say something?" she admonished, wiping his damp hair off his face.

He tried to grin at her and failed miserably. "I wanted to help. Besides . . . it did come over me rather faster than I expected."

Savaron, his face full of worry, knelt beside her. "Is it the plague?" When she nodded, he groaned. "Are you sure it's not a wound fever from his arm or a heat fever?"

"It's the plague," Rafnir answered for her. "My head feels like a forge and my neck hurts."

"Carry him to the shade," Kelene ordered. "I'll need the Lion's Eye."

But Rafnir's hand clamped over her wrist. "No. See to my father first. He is nearer to death and will need your strength to survive."

"I don't want to leave you like this," she protested, even though she knew his argument made sense.

Rafnir pulled himself up to look her right in the face. "You can and you will. Sayyed needs you more!" He gasped, then fell back into her arms, too weak to even sit upright.

Kelene hesitated for a long moment, torn by her love for Rafnir and her sense of duty to Sayyed. Her love for Rafnir, by the gods, how hard it hit her! The possibility of losing him brought the truth out like a shining star. She did love him with an incredible yearning that burned her heart. How could she leave him now, knowing she might be able to ease his suffering?

But as she looked at his anxious face, she knew through the midst of her turmoil what she had to do. "Savaron, please bring him to the shelter as quickly as you can. I will see what I can do for Sayyed."

Rafnir's fingers tightened gratefully around her arm before falling limp at his side. She rose hesitantly to her feet. For all of her brave talk and the new diamond splinter that glowed beneath her skin, Kelene was very uncertain of her ability to work a cure for the deadly plague. She did not really know how to use the healing stones or whether they would still be effective. A few of the spells set in Moy Tura were working, but Kelene had no assurances that the healing spells would work, or if they would be enough to break the course of the disease. All she could do was try the stones and hope their magic would be sufficient.

Her jaw set, Kelene fetched the tray of stones and the manuscripts. With the Korg's help, she scrambled up onto Demira's back between the furled wings. She tucked her legs around the upper wings and held on as Demira broke into a trot toward their shelter by the warehouse.

"Thank you for coming now," Kelene said. Then she added wistfully, "You looked so beautiful up in the sky."

It is incredible! The filly's thought was a song of delight. *It took a long time to learn how to do it right, but I remembered what you said about the geese, and it worked! I am getting stronger and stronger.*

Kelene patted the filly's shoulder. "If this healing stone works, do you think you will be strong enough to fly to the Tir Samod?"

The Hunnuli did not answer at once. Her hooves were clattering loudly on the road, and her ears were swiveled back to hear Kelene. She was almost to the shelter before she replied, *I do not know. I have only made a few flights around the plateau.* Then she rustled her feathers and neighed. *I would like to try, though.*

Her call brought the other Hunnuli from the shade of the old building where Sayyed lay. Kelene sent Tibor, as well as Savaron's and Morad's stallions, to help the men bring Rafnir back. Afer and Demira followed her into the shelter.

They found the white cat had already returned to her position by Sayyed's head. She was curled close to his neck, purring her reassurances softly in his ear.

Kelene kneeled beside Sayyed and laid the tray of stones on the ground before she could bring herself to look at his face. The sight of his once-handsome features made her blanch. The warrior was unconscious, sprawled on his back on his rumpled golden cloak. Although he had not suffered from the devastating vomiting and diarrhea that had afflicted many plague victims, his hot skin was taut and yellow as old parchment, his face and upper body were a mass of open sores, and his neck was thickened with the swellings under his jaw, making the breath rasp in his throat.

Methodically Kelene unwrapped the stones and picked out the golden Lion's Eye that was spelled to fight fevers. She decided to attack this illness from several directions: first the stone to ease Sayyed's fever, then poultices for his sores, and a warm tea to fight dehydration and improve his strength. If that didn't work . . . she would try every stone and medicinal recipe in her tray until *something* brought Sayyed back from his trail to the grave. Then she would help Rafnir.

Did you find something? Afer's deep, masculine voice spoke in her mind. His mental voice was so full of worry and sadness that a tremor shook Kelene's body.

O Amara! In all the hurry to find something to help the people, she had not thought of the Hunnuli. If Sayyed died, would Afer leave to join him like Tam's horse? Would big, stolid Boreas follow her father to the realm of the dead? And Tibor and Nara and Demira and every Hunnuli in the clans that was attached to a human rider? Kelene realized she wasn't just trying to save her friends and family, but their beloved Hunnuli as well.

Instead of making her nervous, the thought strengthened her determination. Her hands steady, she wiped Sayyed's forehead with a cloth. Since she did not know the proper way to use the Lion's Eye, she decided to try Piers's method of placing the stone on the victim's head. The old healer had shown her his red healing stone many years ago, and she still remembered the awe she had felt when he used it to help a young girl hurt by a spell gone out of control.

Kelene laid the golden stone on Sayyed's forehead. She was about to withdraw her hand when a thought occurred to her. The red stones were meant to work by themselves so anyone could use them, but the Korg had told her the other stones could only be used by healers. Maybe she was supposed to stay in contact with it. She just hoped the stone did not require a specific verbal command to start the spell.

With a pounding heart, Kelene placed her fingers on the stone and closed her eyes to concentrate. Almost at once she felt a heat radiating from the diamond splinter in her wrist, as the power flowed down her hand into the Lion's Eye. But she noticed right away that the magic wasn't complete. Something was missing from the spell.

Keeping the magic under control, Kelene tried to think what else she could do. There was obviously another step in the process that triggered the spell, but what was it? She started to shift closer to Sayyed's body and bumped into his bare forearm, which lay on the cloak in the way of her knees. Absently she grasped his hand to move his limb out of the way, and the magic in the stone flared under her touch.

That's it, Kelene nodded. The healer not only had to be in direct contact with the stone, but the patient as well. She clasped his hand tighter. Instantly she felt as if a circle had become complete—she and Sayyed and the stone had become united in the power of magic. She tried to sense his emotions, but his mind was so deep in the pit of his illness that she could only feel the most basic sensations of pain and confusion and somewhere buried in the recesses of his innermost being, a hard kernel of resistance to death.

A smile flitted over her lips. Sayyed hadn't given up yet. Even in his desperate state, he was still trying to struggle for life. That would make her job a little bit easier.

Kelene turned her attention back to the Lion's Eye and the power in its core. She was pleased and relieved when the character of the spell became clear in her mind. It was a strong, well-formed work of sorcery that was still potent after all those years. Best of all, the spell was easily initiated by the force of the healer's willpower.

The clanswoman opened her eyes a slit and saw the splinter gleaming ruby-red under her skin and the gold stone glowing under her fingers like a coal waiting for tinder. She took a deep breath, said a silent prayer to Amara, and sent the power of her will deep into the Lion's Eye.

The dark gold stone reacted instantly. It burst from a dim coal to a tiny brilliant star resting on Sayyed's head. Its light bathed his face with a golden glow and illuminated the entire shelter. The white cat sat motionless in its brilliance, her fur a shining yellow and her eyes a pair of fiery jewels.

Kelene shut her eyes tightly against the stone's blaze, while she sat very still, keeping her fingers in place. Although she did not see the golden light sink into Sayyed's skin, she felt the spell penetrate his head, its power radiating into every cranny of his skull. The stone worked for a long time before revealing its effectiveness. It was so slow in fact, that Kelene took several minutes to notice Sayyed's fever was declining.

Little by little the deadly heat dropped until it reached a more normal temperature that dried the sweat on Sayyed's face and returned his skin to a healthier pink. At last the light in the golden stone faded and went out. Kelene sensed Sayyed's return to consciousness and used her empathetic touch to ease him into a more restful sleep. He was still a very sick man, but his fever was under control and his body's own healing abilities could now work on destroying the rest of the disease.

There was a warm flash of relief from the warrior's mind, then he drifted away into contentment. The white cat meowed softly and curled up to doze, her tail over her paws.

Thank you, Afer told Kelene. *Sayyed sleeps. He will be well.*

Kelene picked up the stone between her thumb and forefinger. In the low light of the shelter, the Lion's Eye sat dull and shadowed on her palm, as ordinary as any polished pebble. There was nothing to indicate the priceless gift that lay within the stone's core. Slowly Kelene's fingers curled over the stone. When Savaron, Morad, and the Korg carried Rafnir in a few minutes later, the radiant expression on her face was all they needed to see to know the spell had worked.

Savaron and Morad laid Rafnir next to his father on a pad of blankets. The Korg, at Kelene's instructions, lit a small fire to boil water for tea and poultices.

Kelene brought the Lion's Eye to Rafnir. "Your father's fever broke. I think he is out of danger now," she told him, knowing the good news would strengthen his own fight against the disease.

His flashing smile came back, and his hand groped for hers. Their fingers interlocked in a tight clasp.

"I love you," he whispered. The depth and truth of his words were confirmed by such an enveloping aura of delight, passion, and need that Kelene gasped at the wondrousness of it. It was the same incredible emotion she had felt in the Korg's memories of Kelyra, only this time it was for her. She blinked, turned bright red, and began to grin—probably like an idiot, she thought, but she didn't care. He loved her! And by the gods, she was not going to let him die!

She placed the golden stone on his forehead before he could say anything else, then used her will to begin the spell. The stone once again ignited to its incandescent glow, completing the circle of power between itself, the healer, and the patient. As the magic flooded Rafnir's body, Kelene projected her own feelings for him into his mind. She felt his welcoming delight like the life-giving warmth of the sun.

Since Rafnir was not as sick as Sayyed, this time the healing went faster. In just a short time the yellow light faded back into the stone and the spell was complete.

Rafnir sighed once; his dark eyes sparkled with a glint of his old humor. "Not bad for a beginner," he said huskily. He tried to sit up, but Kelene pushed him back to his blankets.

"Don't even try it. You're not well yet. You need rest!" She picked up the Lion's Eye from where it had fallen, put it back with the other stones, and started to stand.

Grabbing her arm, Rafnir pulled her down almost on top of him, and kissed her long and deep with all the love he felt in his heart. When he let her go, he was astonished to see tears in her eyes.

"You're going, aren't you?" he asked.

She nodded, saying, "I have to. This is why we came, why we gave Demira wings. If I don't go now, *my* father will die." She removed four splinters from the tray and laid them in his hand. Then, unpinning the Watcher, she fastened it to his tunic. "Keep it and you will know when I reach the gathering."

He lifted his hand to cup her chin. "Be safe," he said forcefully. "You and I have just started." He wiped the wetness from her cheeks.

The men watched silently while Kelene packed the healing stones and the scrolls in an empty leather bag and gathered a small pack of food for herself and Demira. They made no comment when she brewed tea from angelica and comfrey, made the poultice, and told them how to care for Sayyed and Rafnir.

"Don't let either of them ride until they're strong enough," she warned Savaron and Morad. "They could suffer a relapse if they try too soon."

Savaron looked proudly down at his little sister and saw that her difficult years of girlhood had come to an end. Kelene had matured at last to a selfless, confident, capable woman who was about to, literally, spread her wings and fly. "Will Demira be able to carry you so far?" he asked quietly.

"I don't know. If not—" Kelene patted the filly standing beside her "—she still has four legs."

"I wish you weren't going by yourself."

"There's no other way."

"I know, but Bitorn is still out there, and it's a long way to the gathering," Savaron said.

Kelene understood his concern and loved him for it. Big brothers were supposed to worry about their sisters. "If we can slip out of the city without the wraith seeing us, we should be able to keep ahead of him," she replied. Then another thought occurred to her, and she frowned. "But what about all of you? How will you get out?"

"I will help with that," the Korg spoke. The old sorcerer was leaning against a far wall, his face lost in shadow. "I should be able to distract Bitorn long enough for all of you to get off the plateau."

Kelene turned in surprise. "What do you mean? Aren't you coming to the Tir Samod?"

"No." His sad reply surprised them all.

Kelene stepped toward him to better see his face. "But why not?" she demanded, her voice rising. "We need you. We need your power. There is so much you could do to help, so many things you could tell us. How can the magic-wielders fight the wraith without you?"

"You have survived this long without me. You and your mother and your father will find a way to destroy Bitorn."

"But this is ridiculous!" Kelene cried. "You have been alone for so long. How can you bear to be left alone again?"

The Korg closed his eyes, and his body trembled with a long sigh. He came slowly forward from the shadows, his face worn and very tired. He put his hands on Kelene's arms. "You don't see me as I really am, do you—you who are so strong and full of determination? You think of me as the ferocious lion I pretended to be. Well, you're wrong, Kelene. I am a very old man. I doubt I could tolerate the long ride back to the Tir Samod."

"You're not old. You look barely forty years," she insisted, her eyes huge against her pale face as she watched the Korg.

"I may seem to be forty-one, which was my age when Moy Tura fell, but that's only because my body's physical appearance was preserved within the stone of my shapechanging spell. In reality I am two hundred sixty-five." His mouth twitched with a dry chuckle. "I feel every year of it. Without my stone form to protect me, I will age and die, probably within a year or two."

"Well, why don't you change back into a stone lion?" Savaron suggested.

"No!" the Korg responded. "I have finished with that! I want to live out what's left of my life and die as I should have two centuries ago."

"But you don't need to be alone," Kelene interrupted sadly. "There are people out there who would welcome you and venerate the wisdom you can bring."

The Korg shook his head almost desperately. "Kelene, I cannot leave here. Moy Tura is my home. It sustains me."

"You would rather stay here among these old ruins than come back to the clans?"

The sorcerer stopped in front of her again and said quietly, "See Moy Tura through my eyes. Whatever else these ruins are, they are the foundations of a beautiful city. I still have my power, and now, thanks to all of you, I have my memories and my perspective back. The stone lion is dead, but this city needn't be. Perhaps I will try to rebuild part of it in the time I have left."

Kelene took a deep breath and let her anger drain away. She didn't understand his refusal to leave, but the old man had chosen his path the night Moy Tura died, and he had a right to follow his choice. "Maybe I will come back, if I can," she said, unhappily resigned. "I would like to see the healers' herb room again."

He bowed his head gratefully. "It will be there for you."

Kelene stepped away from him, picked up the leather bag with the stones, and looked around at the men watching her: her big, handsome brother; Morad still suffering from Tomian's death; Sayyed asleep on his blankets; the old Korg; and last of all Rafnir, who had stolen her heart without even trying. At that moment she loved them all and could not accept the thought that she might not see them again. Her throat tightened; her eyes sparkled with unshed tears.

"Be careful," Savaron said. "Without you there is little hope."

She nodded. "Come as soon as you can. Even if I can stop the plague, there is still Bitorn."

"We'll be there," Morad promised.

Kelene gripped her bag and hurried out before she lost control of the tears that threatened again to spill down her cheeks. Demira, Savaron, Morad, and the Korg followed her outside.

The early evening sky was warm with the yellow-orange light of the fading day, and a gentle breeze blew from the west. The three Hunnuli waiting by the entrance bowed their heads to Kelene as she came outdoors.

Tibor extended his head. *Sayyed and Rafnir live,* he snorted, his breath warming her face. *We cannot thank you enough.*

"Bring them safely back to the gathering, and that will be my thanks," Kelene told the stallions. Then she turned and faced her filly.

Demira nuzzled her arm. *I am ready to go.*

Kelene rubbed her hand down the filly's neck and was about to mount when Savaron took the bag from her hand and offered his knee to help her up. Thankfully she accepted and settled herself on the horse's back between the great black and gray wings. "Can you lift off from the square? Is there enough room there?" she asked the filly.

Demira's tone was apologetic. *My wings are not strong enough yet. I need to get a good running start.*

"So we have to get out onto the plateau to give you enough room?"

That would be helpful. I slipped out of the city's northern gate several times to practice where the wraith could not see me. There is a good place to take off on the western side of the plateau.

"Then we'll find the wraith and distract him at the southern gate to give you a head start," Savaron told Kelene. "Wait for our signal." He handed her the bag, and his hand gripped her knee in farewell. Neither of them could say anything else, though their hearts were full.

Kelene forced a smile, ruffled her brother's hair—which she knew he hated—and urged Demira into a walk away from the shelter and toward the old road. They left without a backward glance, hearing only the clatter of the Hunnuli's hooves as Savaron, Morad, and the Korg rode south to find Bitorn.

The young woman clenched her teeth. She lifted her chin to its stubbornest tilt and turned her thoughts to the job at hand: getting Demira airborne.

The filly broke into a trot that took them onto the main road, toward the gate in the northern wall of the city. Kelene hadn't been in this section of Moy Tura, and she watched warily as they passed by alleys, streets, and buildings in no better condition than the rest of the ruined city. Gordak's warriors and the elements had left nothing unscathed.

When they neared the high city walls, Demira slowed to a walk and stopped in the shadow of a roofless tower. The northern gate was identical in workmanship to the southern gate, with a high arched entrance through the thick walls and two towers to either side. Unlike the other entrance, though, this one still had one of its heavy doors hanging on one side of the archway.

Since they had not seen the wraith inside the city, some of the old wards must still be working at all the gates, Kelene decided. She wondered if he had tried to enter any of the others.

Demira cautiously stepped up to the entrance, and she and Kelene peered around the gate. The old road stretched out before them like a spear into the blue-gold haze of dusk. There was no sign of anyone or anything, just the two crouching stone lions that stood guard at the roadside. The filly rolled her eyes at the statues and pulled back behind the door. She and Kelene looked to the southern skyline for Savaron's signal.

They didn't have long to wait. Before the sun dropped noticeably lower, a blue fireball rose on the distant horizon and exploded in a blast of blue sparks. Demira charged out the gate onto the road. Her pace quickened to a fast canter over the hard, level ground. She left the road and angled to the west toward the nearest edge of the highland.

Kelene glanced back toward Moy Tura, surprised by the regret she felt at leaving. She had once thought the old city was nothing more than mournful, useless rock, but she had seen it come to life in the Korg's memory, she had found some of its treasures, and she had left a good friend behind. Her mention to the Korg that she might one day come back solidified in her mind as a vow. There was still much the old city had to offer to anyone with the desire to explore its ruins.

She turned her thoughts back to the present and looked ahead. She saw they were running directly toward the fiery orange sun that was settling like a brand on the horizon. The light was so bright she could not see the edge of the tableland, though she knew it had to be close.

"Where is the road on this side of the plateau?" Kelene queried, squinting into the sun.

Not here exactly. But this is the best place for me, Demira responded. There was a twinge of humor in her thought that should have alerted Kelene, but at that moment the filly sped into a gallop.

Kelene automatically leaned forward and adjusted her seat to the change in Demira's pace. As the horse's neck rose and fell in rhythm with her galloping legs, her head blocked the sun from Kelene's eyes. All at once Kelene saw the rim of the plateau not more than ten paces ahead. There was no road there, no slope, and no gradual drop to the grasslands below. To Kelene's horror, the plateau came to an abrupt end in a sheer cliff that fell suddenly down hundreds of feet to the highland's rocky lap.

The clanswoman sat up in a panic; her mouth dropped open. "Wait! You can't go over that!"

Hang on! Demira warned.

Kelene stared at the edge rushing toward them. She ducked down, hanging on with steel fingers to the filly's mane. The sorceress felt the Hunnuli gather herself. The long wings lifted slightly, and the horse's powerful hind legs bunched underneath her weight. Kelene looked down in time to see Demira tuck up her front legs, and with a mighty leap, launch herself over the rim of the plateau.

Kelene's stomach lurched upward. She took one look at the empty air and the ground far below and screwed her eyes shut. Her cry of fright was torn away by the wind.

Suddenly she felt Demira's muscles move beneath her legs and heard a loud rustling sound and a soft thump. One eye peeked open to see the long, black wings stretched out beside her and the hard, stony earth flowing beneath them in a brown and green patterned sea.

Kelene's eyes flew open wide. Delighted and still a little frightened, she leaned sideways and peered over the edge of Demira's wings.

The filly faltered. *Sit still, please!* Demira begged. *I am not very good at this yet, and your weight will throw me off balance.*

Kelene hastily obeyed, clamping her backside firmly to the center of Demira's back. She contented herself with watching the gentle rise and fall of the Hunnuli's wings, how they tilted to meet the flow of the air, and how the feathers adjusted to each gusty breeze. The filly was using her wings to glide on the last of the day's rising air currents, and Kelene realized that Demira was copying the graceful, efficient flight of an eagle.

Joy whispered in Kelene's heart. She watched wordlessly as Demira curved southward along the edge of the towering plateau. The sun dropped below the brim of the plains, casting long shadows on the world below. Kelene saw the old road curving like a dry snakeskin up the southern side of the plateau. Far away at the farthest edge of visibility, almost lost in the coming night, she saw the dark hump of Moy Tura.

Kelene lifted her hand and threw a fistful of dazzling blue energy into the twilight sky.

Outside the crumbling wall of Moy Tura's southern gate, Savaron saw the flare of blue on the horizon and recognized it for what it was. He breathed a silent prayer of thanks. Their ruse had worked—Kelene was gone. With the help of Demira's wings, Kelene and the filly should get enough of a head start so even if the wraith realized they were gone, he would not be able to catch up with them.

Now all Savaron and his companions had to do was break off the Korg's confrontation with Bitorn and make a convincing retreat back within the safety of the walls.

"Let us pass!" the Korg was bellowing to Bitorn. The old sorcerer had seen Kelene's signal, too, and to make sure the wraith did not turn around and notice it, he fired a blast of energy at the priest's glowing form.

Bitorn laughed as he sidestepped the scorching power. "You're weak, old man. What's the trouble? Mortality catching you at last? Die soon so I can take every spark of your life-force and make it my own!"

"You'll never have the pleasure, Bitorn," the Korg responded fiercely.

The apparition rose in height to tower over the old sorcerer. Behind the ruddy figure, a huge, semicircular wall of flames appeared.

Savaron instinctively flinched. The fire was so realistic, he couldn't tell if it was real or illusion. But it didn't matter—they were not going to stay to find out. The Khulinin chopped his hand downward in a prearranged signal. Together, he and Morad charged their horses forward to the Korg's side and surrounded themselves with a magic defense shield.

"Come on!" Savaron yelled. "We can't get out this way!" Ignoring the Korg's loud, and assumed, protests, both men grabbed his arms and dragged him back toward the gate.

Bitorn roared with derisive laughter. He strode after the retreating magic-wielders, but though he tried to force apart their shield, he could not break through the magic.

The three men and the two Hunnuli scrambled past the corpse of the dead horse and into the safety of the archway two steps ahead of Bitorn.

The wraith raised his fist. He was about to curse the sorcerers when he hesitated in midmotion. The imprecations died on his lips. He paused, silhouetted against the lurid flames, his head turned to the south. An odd look crossed his harsh features, then he snapped his attention back to the men in the dim archway. His fierce gaze seemed to probe into each, as if seeking an answer to some silent question. Without another word, the wraith banished his fire. He stepped back into the gathering darkness and strode out of the men's sight.

Morad let out a gusty sigh of relief. He was breathing heavily and drenched in sweat. "Thank the gods, that's over."

Savaron scratched his jaw, his face worried. "Bitorn certainly left in a hurry. Do you suppose he suspects something?"

"We'll know soon enough," the Korg answered dryly. "Bitorn is so full of hate and pride, he'll let us know if he finds out what we've done."

16

The first light of Amara's sun had barely lit the eastern horizon when Savaron and the other men awoke. A long sleep had worked wonders for Sayyed, and he lay on his bed alert, hungry, and full of questions. While Morad fixed a meal for everyone and Rafnir told his father what had been happening, Savaron decided to go to the south gate and check on the wraith. Bitorn's strange behavior the evening before still bothered the young warrior. He wanted to be certain the dead priest was still outside the walls.

The Korg offered to go with him, so the two men mounted Savaron's Hunnuli for the ride to the southern gate. They had gone no more than halfway through the city when they heard a bellowed summons that shook the old ruins.

"Sorcerers!" Bitorn's voice blasted the air. "Come forth, heretics! Show me your craven faces."

Savaron's stallion needed no urging. He bounded forward at a canter along the road. Savaron and the Korg felt their apprehension rise as Bitorn continued to call. He was still shouting outside the walls when the stallion slid to a stop in the gateway.

The wraith was standing near Tam's dead Hunnuli, his form brilliant with red rage, his face livid. "One of your number is gone!" he roared at the two magic-wielders. "I sense her presence is missing, and I saw tracks at the north gate. Where is she?"

"She was afraid of the plague," Savaron growled in return. "She fled on her own instead of following us."

"Not that one! She is strong. She would give her life for you pitiful people. I believe she is returning to the gathering." Bitorn stooped and laid his hand on the dead Hunnuli. At his command the corpse lifted its head. The horse had been lying in the sun for several days. Flies swarmed around it, and the stench of its rotting flesh gagged the two men, but it slowly staggered to its feet. It stood by the wraith, its head hanging from its long, sunken neck.

"I am leaving you for now," the wraith hissed at the men. "You are free to stay here and die or come to the gathering to meet your doom. One way or another, I will find you when I am ready." He mounted the decaying Hunnuli and turned it south. It broke into a gallop down the old road.

"No, wait!" Savaron yelled. He leaned forward to send his Hunnuli chasing after the wraith, but the Korg's hand closed over his shoulder and pulled him back.

"Let him go. You can't fight him alone."

"But Kelene—"

"Is leagues away. Bitorn will not catch her now," the Korg said.

"Then why is he leaving us? What did he mean 'when I am ready'?" Savaron asked worriedly.

"It is what I feared: he is returning to the gathering and his tomb. He wants to rejuvenate his body before Kelene finds a way to stop the dying."

"Why didn't he do that before?"

"I think he took a chance," the Korg replied. "Remember, Bitorn has to be in the vicinity of a dying person in order to steal the life-force at death. When your party left the gathering, he hadn't stored enough energy to return to his body. He was forced to decide: should he stay at the gathering among the dying and regain his strength at the risk of allowing you to succeed in your mission, or should he follow you and destroy your party alone somewhere on the plains. Knowing Bitorn, the fact that you were all magic-wielders certainly swayed his mind. He could have killed you and your friends, sustained himself on your life-force, and returned to the gathering to accomplish his ultimate goal." The Korg paused and smiled ironically. "However, together you proved too strong for him. Now he has realized he made a mistake. He will certainly waste no more time returning to the gathering."

Savaron shrugged, half in frustration, half in anger. "Then what can we do?" he demanded.

"Nurse your friends back to health and go back to the Tir Samod as fast as you can. Kelene will need your help."

* * *

Far to the south of Moy Tura's highland, Kelene and Demira were continuing their flight across the Ramtharin Plains. They had traveled for hours the night before until Demira was too tired to safely continue. After a brief rest in the lee of a tall hill, they had gone aloft again at sunrise.

On Demira's back, Kelene watched the filly slowly flap her wings to lift higher to another air current. The horse tilted her long, black feathers ever so slightly, then glided on the warm, rising air. Kelene studied the filly's movements with delight. Demira had learned a great deal about the characteristics of her unusual wings and about her newfound relationship with the air. She flew now with an increasing grace and confidence.

Kelene relaxed on Demira's back and patted the filly's neck. She and Rafnir had been right about the advantages of flying above the terrain instead of struggling over it. Flying was considerably easier, and the land more beautiful. Kelene had tried to imagine what her world would look like from a bird's view, but she hadn't even come close to the truth. The plains spread beneath her in an endlessly changing panorama of patterns, colors, and shapes. Ordinary objects took on new reality when seen from high in the air. Trees became green spheres; eroded creek beds became serpentine trails; wildflowers, shrubs, and grasses became delicate patches of color that blended and swirled. Best of all were the dappled cloud shadows that soared across the land with silent, gentle grace.

Kelene was so entranced by the world below she did not notice the passage of time or Demira's increasingly labored breathing. They had reached the eastern slopes of the Himachals and had turned south when Demira finally called for a rest. She spiraled down to the ground, landing heavily, and stood wearily while Kelene dismounted.

I am sorry. I just cannot fly very well yet, Demira apologized.

The woman laughed softly and took the Hunnuli's muzzle in her hands. "Don't apologize for that! Do you know how far we've come? We have already passed Tomian's mound and the Citadel of Krath. We're somewhere near the Defile of Tot Wrath and the Isin River. My beautiful horse, be proud of yourself!"

Demira nickered, a sound of gratitude and pleasure, and after a drink from a small creek, she and Kelene walked until her wings were rested. They traveled the rest of the day, flying as long as Demira could safely stay in the air, walking or trotting when she was tired, and stopping only for water. They passed Ab-Chakan and followed the Isin River south toward Dangari Treld.

When night came Demira and Kelene both were exhausted. Neither of them had traveled so hard in their lives and the effort had expended almost everything they had. They ate some food and slept where they were on the bank of the Isin River.

They rose before the sun, cantering south in the early dawn light until the plains were bright with day and a fair breeze was blowing. Demira turned into the wind, increased her gait to a gallop, spread her huge wings, and soared into the morning. She was stiff from her exertion the day before, but sleep had refreshed her and the cool wind from the north helped lift her weight into the sky.

Kelene was quiet and subdued. She tilted her face to the sun and prayed. Two days had passed since Lord Athlone had fallen ill. If his sickness ran the normal course of other plague victims, he had perhaps one or two days left. Kelene knew she and Demira had one more full day of travel before they could reach the Tir Samod. Any mishaps or bad weather could be disastrous. They had to arrive at the gathering in one day, or they could be too late to save the Khulinin chieftain.

Late in the afternoon when the hot air currents were rising from the plains and the clouds were beginning to billow into the sky, Kelene spotted something in the distance near the river. She pointed it out to the Hunnuli, and Demira slowly glided down for a closer look.

"Oh, no," Kelene breathed. The dark blobs on the ground became more distinct and recognizable: five clan summer tents set up in a haphazard cluster under the thin shade of some cottonwood trees. Strangely, there seemed to be no animals and no people. There were only the tents sitting alone.

Kelene hesitated. She was badly torn by the choice that had suddenly been thrust at her. Should she ignore this group and push on to the gathering and her father, or stop to check for any plague victims and use up valuable time?

Her healer's instincts guided her decision, and she told Demira to land. Ever so carefully the filly dropped down, trotted a few steps, and came to a stop by the edge of the little camp. Several death birds flapped heavily out from between the tents and settled into the trees to wait.

Kelene reluctantly slid off Demira, her bag in her hand. "Hello, camp!" she yelled, but no one answered. The tents remained ominously silent while their felt walls twitched in the wind.

Kelene studied the place before she moved. There was no outward sign of trouble—no tracks of marauders, no arrow-riddled bodies or burned tents. There was only a blackened fire pit, an empty bucket, two carts, some saddles on the ground, and a broken halter hanging from one of the tent poles. But there were no animals and no people in sight.

It took all of Kelene's willpower to step away from Demira and walk to the nearest tent. The heavy reek of decay surrounded her the moment she reached the entrance. Covering her nose and mouth with the hem of her tunic, she peered through the open tent flap and saw two bodies lying on the pallets. The people had been dead for days and were so disfigured by decomposition and the teeth of scavengers that Kelene could not tell what they had looked like. Only a blue cloak hanging on a tent pole identified them as Dangari.

Kelene blinked her eyes and ducked out of the tent. Her skin was clammy in spite of the heat, and her head felt dizzy. She made herself go to the next tent and the next, in the hope of finding someone still alive. But she was too late. She counted ten adults and three children dead in the hot, dusty tents. She almost tripped over one man lying sprawled in the dirt between one tent and the river, an empty waterskin in his outflung hand. He had died very recently, for his skin was still intact enough for Kelene to see the open red marks of plague boils on his arms and face.

When she was through examining the camp, she leaned against Demira and buried her face in the filly's mane. She inhaled the warm smell of horse to try to rid her nose of the stench of death.

"They're all dead," she murmured into Demira's neck. "They must have tried to flee the gathering and brought the plague with them." There was nothing more she dared take the time or strength to do—their clan would have to come later and bury them. She mounted Demira, and the Hunnuli galloped away from the little camp.

The carrion birds waited only until the horse and rider were out of sight before settling back to their meal.

Through the long hours that followed, Kelene hung on to Demira and prayed for strength. She knew from her previous glimpses in the Watcher that the Dangari tents were probably a forewarning of what she would find at the gathering. The memory of the bodies by the council tent and the fact that her parents were in their own tent, rather than in the grove, were indications that the clans could no longer deal with the number of victims.

The thought of the dead and dying led her into another probability that she hadn't considered yet: the numbers of sick and living. She had the first real hope of a cure in her bag, but she was the only one at that moment who could use it, and the idea that she would have to treat hundreds of sick people alone was enough to start her shaking. There *had* to be a few healers still alive and a few more magic-wielders with the talent to heal. Maybe even Gabria.

Kelene rubbed Demira's sweaty neck, as much to encourage the filly as to comfort herself. All she had to worry about now was carrying the stones to the gathering. Once she was there, Gabria would know what to do. With her mother's help, Kelene knew she could handle whatever she had to face.

But only if Lord Athlone were alive. Kelene knew her parents well enough to know that they lived for each other. If her father died . . . Kelene did not want to imagine beyond that possibility.

The afternoon wore on, hot, dusty, and breezy as Kelene and Demira worked their way south toward the Tir Samod. They were so tired that each step became harder than the next and each flight became shorter. By the time early evening crept onto the plains, the little filly was exhausted.

"We're almost there," Kelene reassured her. "I see the hills that border the river valley."

Demira didn't answer. She pushed into a trot to the crest of a tall hill overlooking the valley of the Isin and Goldrine rivers and paused at the top. She and her rider looked down into the broad, green valley stretching away into a blue haze.

Kelene saw the smoke before she saw the gathering place downriver. Dark columns rose in thick, curling strands through the trees before the light winds bent the plumes over and sent them drifting south. The fumes were too dense and yellowish to be wood smoke and too concentrated to be a grass fire or an attack on the camps. The priests must still be burning incense to drive away the plague. Kelene took that as a positive sign.

Demira pricked up her ears. Her head lifted a little, and she snorted as if gathering herself for the last challenge. *We have a good wind behind us. I think I can fly the rest of the way.*

The clanswoman scratched the filly's shoulder where the white lightning mark gleamed gold in the light of the setting sun. "Your dam and sire will be proud of you," she whispered in Demira's black ear.

The Hunnuli turned back to face the wind and cantered down the slope of the hill. Without the wind and the aid of the smooth incline, Kelene doubted the struggling filly would have made it into the air. As it was, she was barely able to stay above the height of the trees when she winged slowly down the length of the valley.

Before long the land beneath them began to look more and more familiar. Kelene saw scattered herds of stock animals and horses peacefully grazing, apparently undisturbed by the devastation of their human masters. She saw the faint trail of the Induran race winding from the eastern hills and across the valley to the river. Then, Demira flew over the old empty Corin ground and the first of the clan camps.

Her heart in her throat, Kelene looked for signs of life. Among the crowded tents of the Murjik clan, she saw a few people moving. Some cooking fires were burning and, thank the gods, she even saw the glittering helmet of a mounted guard on duty. The Murjik, at least, were managing their plight.

She heard a shout from the camp, and dogs started to bark, but she ignored the noise to watch Demira swing away from the river and begin a slow descent toward the edge of the Khulinin camp. The evening light had dwindled into twilight, and Kelene could make out some scattered torches and cooking fires twinkling in the camp. She chose not to look toward the council grove and its sick tents, concentrating instead on finding the big chieftain's tent near the center of her clan. The council tent and its sick would have to wait until she had found Gabria and Athlone.

She was so busy peering through the gathering dusk for the gold banner on her father's lodging that she didn't see the danger that came running out from between the tents.

But Demira did. She neighed frantically and veered sideways as a spear flew by her legs. The sudden movement threw the filly off balance, and she struggled to right herself before her aching wings lost all control. Kelene fought to hold her place and stay as still as possible so she wouldn't throw Demira off even further.

From the corner of her eye, she saw a clan warrior on the ground below running after the winged horse. He stopped, raised a bow, and took aim. "No!" she screamed. "It's me, Kelene! Don't shoot!"

She was reaching into her mind for the words to a shielding spell when a large, black horse came hurtling past the dark tents and deliberately slammed into the warrior, knocking him to the dirt. His bow flew wildly out of his hands. Demira neighed again and to Kelene's everlasting delight, the filly was answered by her dam, Nara.

Slowly, painfully, Demira brought her bulk down from the sky to an open space not far from the prostrate warrior. She landed heavily, then staggered from exhaustion. It took the last of her strength to pull herself upright, but she forced her legs back under control and tucked her wings into place. For just a moment Demira and Kelene were still, too relieved and grateful for their safe arrival to stir. Kelene put her arms around the horse's neck and hugged her fiercely.

Nara came up then, nickering, and snorting. *Demira. what have you done?* the old mare demanded.

"She has come all the way from Moy Tura in just over two days," Kelene said proudly, sliding off Demira's back.

Just then a hand grabbed Kelene's arm and she was yanked around to face a frowning gray-bearded warrior and the polished edge of his unsheathed sword. The clanswoman grinned wearily at him, and his eyes widened.

"Kelene! By Surgart's shield, I thought you were one of Krath's minions, or another wraith coming to finish us off," the warrior cried. "What are you doing here? Where are the others? And—" he waved a wild hand at the filly "what is that?"

Kelene was so glad to be back, to hear another living voice and to see a friendly, if shocked, face she hugged him, too. "Secen, you remember Demira, Nara's foal. Rafnir and I and the mother goddess gave her the gift of flight so we could bring help back to the clans."

The warrior, a retired member of Lord Athlone's hearth-guard, was used to the miraculous workings of sorcery, but a winged horse stole his breath away. He could only gape in awe at the horse who had traveled over two hundred leagues in two days. It took a minute for the rest of Kelene's words to sink in. When he realized what she had said, he sucked in his breath. "You found a cure in the ruins!" Without waiting for details, he hustled her into the camp.

Kelene waved to Demira, knowing she would be cared for by Nara, and hurried to keep up with Secen.

"I've been keeping watch and doing two turns a day as outrider because so many of the warriors are sick or dead," Secen told her as he strode along. "Lord Athlone has worked like a slave holding the clans together, calming those who wanted to flee, organizing food and water, keeping everybody busy. I don't think we'd have made it this long without him. But he wore himself out and took sick three nights ago. I hope to all the gods that you can save him!"

The warrior was hurrying so fast he broke into a jog along the worn trail. A few guards and some people out by their cooking fires heard the jangle of his weapons and looked over to see why Secen was hurrying. They recognized Kelene, and immediately the news began to spread through the Khulinin that the chieftain's daughter was back from Moy Tura.

Kelene hung on to her leather bag and hobbled as fast as she could after Secen. The thing that struck her the most while she walked was the pall of silence hanging over the camp. Usually the clan would be bustling by this time of the evening when the outriders changed duties, the women cooked around their fires, the families ate under their awnings, and the children played before nightfall. But that evening Kelene saw no more than twenty or thirty people among the tents, and those few were haggard and grim. There was no singing or music, laughter or loud talk. The only sound Kelene heard was the wailing of a grieving woman.

Smoke and the smell of death lingered in the air. Everywhere Kelene looked, she noticed amulets and dried herbs hanging from tent poles to drive away the plague. Just ahead of Secen, Kelene saw two men carrying a wrapped body from a tent and fasten the tent flap behind them with red cords—the sign that an entire family had died. She was shocked to see at least ten more dwellings tied with red just on the way to the chieftain's home. She didn't want to imagine how many more red cords there were in the Khulinin.

Her tired legs were aching by the time Secen led her into the wide space before her parents' tent. The warrior stopped and pointed to the unlighted tent, where the gold banner flapped sadly in the dusky light.

"No one but Lady Gabria has been able to get past Eurus for two days now. The only way we know our lord is still alive is by that big black yonder."

Kelene peered into the shadows where her father's Hunnuli was standing under the awning and breathed a prayer of thanks. She heard Secen say, "My blessings on you, lass. I'll go see to your filly." With that the warrior stamped away.

She limped toward the tent, her mouth dry. Suddenly Eurus was beside her, offering his strong shoulder to help support her weight. Kelene was startled by the change in the big Hunnuli. His coat was rough under her hands and she felt the hard outline of his bones. He said nothing to her as he escorted her to the tent, but she sensed his relief and hope like an embrace.

The tent flap was open, so she patted the stallion and stepped inside. It took her eyes some time to adjust to the gloom so she could see the interior. Her father must still be alive because she could hear his hoarse, wheezing struggle to breathe, yet there was no sign of her mother.

Kelene found a small lamp on her mother's table, lit it with a coal from the hot brazier, and looked toward the sleeping area. Her hand went to her mouth. Lord Athlone was lying on his pallet, loosely covered with a thin blanket. Even though Kelene had known what to expect, her father's condition was a shock. He was unconscious, drenched with sweat, and almost unrecognizable under the poultices wrapped around his swollen neck.

Then she saw her mother. Gabria was lying beside her husband, her eyes closed and her hand resting on his chest. Eurus's thin condition had surprised Kelene, but Gabria's appearance wrenched a cry from her. Her mother was pale and haggard. Her fair face had sunk into deep shadowed hollows, and her normally lithe form was as thin as a tent pole. Kelene stumbled forward, afraid that Gabria was sick, too.

Her mother raised her head and blinked sleepily in the unexpected light.

"Kelene!" The glad cry was the sweetest sound the young clanswoman ever heard. She fell to her knees and felt her mother's arms go around her in a very healthy embrace.

"I *knew* you were coming!" Gabria cried joyfully. "I saw you in a dream on a great black bird."

Between laughter and tears, Kelene hugged her tightly and told her about Demira.

Gabria was too astonished to do more than shake her head at Kelene's description of the winged filly. "You have had adventures to fill a tale," the sorceress said. Then the light died from her face and she brushed a finger over Lord Athlone's still face. "But did you find what we hoped for?"

Kelene replied by pulling the tray of stones and manuscripts from her bag and unwrapping them before Gabria's wide eyes. Gabria recognized the red healing stone immediately, and she grew very still when she saw the small bundle of sparkling splinters. Silently she turned over Kelene's wrist and saw the faint ruby glow of the crystal under the skin, exactly like her own. Her chin trembling, she looked into her daughter's face and saw everything she hoped to see.

Kelene picked out one of the three Lion's Eye stones. "These have been spelled to fight fevers," she explained. Taking her father's hand in her own, she gently laid the stone on his head. The brilliant golden light burst from the stone at her touch.

Gabria watched, hardly daring to breathe. When the light died out and the angry flush faded from Athlone's skin, she dried his face and covered him with a dry, warm blanket before she would allow the first real ray of hope to gleam in her mind.

Kelene tucked the stone back into the tray. "We had to test these on Sayyed and Rafnir," she said quietly. "They were still alive when I left. I told Savaron to treat their swelling with poultices and their weakness and dehydration with tea."

Gabria barely nodded, her words overcome by bittersweet feelings of sadness, relief, and happiness. She examined the stones in their compartments and picked up the manuscripts to look through the pages.

"There is one recipe near the end for a restorative that might be good. I thought you should see it," Kelene said.

Gabria thoughtfully read the list of ingredients. Interested, she set about preparing the infusion in a pot of hot water on her brazier. The aroma of mint and other herbs filled the tent like a breath of spring air. As soon as the liquid was ready, Gabria mixed in honey and wine, poured the results into three cups, and handed one to Kelene.

"This looks like an excellent combination. Try it." She swallowed hers in several gulps and went to feed the contents of the third cup to Athlone.

Kelene gratefully drank hers to the dregs. The tart liquid warmed her all the way down to her stomach and spread invigorating energy to all parts of her body. The soreness in her legs and ankle disappeared, her strength returned, and her weariness was gone.

By the time she had finished, her father, with fresh poultices on his plague sores, was sleeping, and her mother was donning a clean tunic and gathering more herbs. "Tell me how the stones work," Gabria urged.

Kelene smiled. She could see Gabria was returning to her old self now that her husband was better and her daughter was home. The daunting task of healing every sick person in the clans did not seem to worry her. Hope had given her a full measure of determination and new energy which, Kelene knew, she was very capable of putting to good use.

Kelene explained about the Lion's Eye stones while Gabria listened intently. The older sorceress frowned, deep in thought. "I doubt I can help you with the stones. I do not believe I have a talent like yours. My skill in healing is limited to herbs and bandages." She gathered her bundles. "Come. We'll start in the council tent."

Kelene picked up her tray of stones and followed her mother outside, where the night had settled to full darkness. Gabria paused long enough to reassure Eurus and leave him a huge armload of fodder, then she led Kelene down the paths toward the council grove.

"Perhaps I ought to warn you," Gabria said over her shoulder, "this pestilence has devastated our people. We could not keep up with it, let alone try to flee it. It has taken all of our strength and resources just to survive. The council grove has . . . changed."

"I saw a little of that in the Watcher." Kelene paused before she asked the question that had been preying on her mind since she had arrived at the camp. "Is Lymira gone?"

Gabria nodded without looking around. "And Coren and Gehlyn and Wertain Rejanir and Lord Koshyn and—" Her voice caught and she barely finished. "Too many to name."

The two women said nothing more, only walked a little faster to the edge of the camp, not noticing the scattered Khulinin people among the tents who saw them and called out. At the border of the camp, a heavily armed warrior stepped into their path and held out his hand.

"Lady Gabria, we haven't seen you or Lord Athlone in—" Then he saw Kelene and his eyes widened.

Gabria touched his arm. "Lord Athlone is still sick, but we think he will live, if he is allowed to rest." The smile that spread across the man's face was so brilliant Gabria responded with a smile of her own. "Now we all have work to do. I need you to find the Priestess Camra. Go with her, search the clan, and make a list of all the sick here in the camp. Kelene and I will be in the council grove, but we'll be back as soon as we can to treat the plague victims."

With a whoop the warrior dashed away to seek out the clan's priestess of Amara, and Gabria and Kelene continued to the grove.

The grove of trees by the river was not hard to see in the darkness, for it was surrounded by a chain of fires that stretched in a great half circle from one river-bank to the other. Priests in red and black robes were tending the fires and pour-ing jars of incense on the flames to keep the pungent yellow smoke rising to the sky. In the night, the fires cast a ghastly glow on the rows and rows of tents that filled the grove and on the few people who moved slowly through the dancing shadows.

Kelene couldn't stifle a shudder. The scene looked like something from a hideous nightmare or Valorian's tale of Gormoth. And worse than the view was the stench. The breeze had died to a mere breath; the smoke, the odors of sick-ness, and the stink of death lay over the area like a noxious fog.

Gabria entered the grove and strode to the big council tent without a side-ways glance, but Kelene slowed down to stare at the area in dismay. The grove was a shambles of trash, fouled clothes, and filthy blankets. Debris from trees cut down to feed the fires littered the trampled grass. Tents, large and small, had been pitched everywhere with no thought to organization. Worst of all was the pitiful pile of bodies heaped near the council tent. This was far worse than she'd expected from the tiny images in the Watcher. She gritted her teeth and forced herself to keep moving through the wreckage of the plague.

She saw her mother disappear into the council tent and hurried to catch up. The tent's interior was much the same as Kelene remembered from the jewel. It was still crowded with the sick and dying and with people trying to help—only the faces of the patients and the caretakers had changed.

There was one caretaker in particular that caught Kelene's attention. She had to stare at him for a long minute before she recognized the Reidhar chief, Lord Fiergan. He, too, had changed in the past days, having lost weight and much of his bluster. He was bent over a pallet, carefully helping a woman drink some water, when he glanced up and saw Kelene. To his credit, he did not startle or drop the cup or shout in surprise. He laid the woman's head down, patted her arm, and came to meet the young sorceress.

Gabria was talking to three very tired-looking healers, so Kelene held on to her leather bag and bowed politely to Lord Fiergan.

He did not dither, but went straight to the point. "You found something in Moy Tura?"

Kelene indicated her bag, not sure what to expect from the burly chief, who hated sorcery and had been against the journey to Moy Tura. "We found some healing stones. They are not an instant cure, but there are some that break fevers."

Fiergan shot a glance at the woman he had left and back to Kelene. She was startled by the look of hope and relief in his dark, heavy-browed eyes. "I know there are others you must help first, but when you have time, will you see to my wife?"

Kelene nodded, too surprised to speak. Lord Fiergan had *asked* her—a woman, a magic-wielder, and a Khulinin—to help? She noticed her mother was still talking to the healers, and she made a quick decision. She had to start somewhere and Lord Fiergan's wife was as good a patient as any. Besides, if the lady was recovering, Lord Fiergan might be more inclined to turn some of his energy and authority to helping organize the shambles in the council grove.

"Come on," she said, leading Fiergan back to the pallet. His wife been sick for only a day and was still coherent enough to understand Kelene when she took the stones from the bag and carefully described what would happen. She stared hopefully up at her husband who indicated to Kelene to proceed.

By the time the golden light of the Lion's Eye had faded back into the stone, there was a crowd of people standing around the pallet watching Kelene; the entire tent was silent. The sorceress picked up her stone. "She can rest now, Lord Fiergan."

"Thank you," said the Reidhar chief with genuine gratitude.

"Lord Fiergan," said Gabria, who had seen the whole incident and understood her daughter's reason. "There is a young man in your camp named Alanar. Is he still alive?"

Fiergan hesitated while he tried to think. "Yes," he finally growled. "He was yesterday."

"Good. Then please bring him here."

The chief bristled at Gabria's tone. Alanar, a magic-wielder, had left his clan against the chieftain's orders and studied sorcery with Gabria. When he returned to Reidhar Treld to try to talk some sense into Lord Fiergan, the chief had all but exiled him from the clan. "Why?" demanded Fiergan.

"I believe he might have a talent to heal like Kelene. With so few magic-wielders and healers left, we shall need all the help we can get," Gabria replied evenly.

Fiergan felt his wife's fingers slip into his hand, and his old resentments retreated a step. He realized this was no time to renew his animosity toward sorcery. "I'll get him myself," he agreed and stalked from the tent.

By the time Fiergan returned with Alanar, Kelene was taking her stones from one plague victim to the next, starting with two sick healers and working her way around the tent. As soon as Alanar arrived, she handed him a second Lion's Eye.

The young Reidhar gripped the stone in his long hands like a lifeline, but Kelene was pleased to see there was no fear or hesitation in his eyes. He knelt down with her beside a tall Ferganan girl barely out of childhood. Sweat matted the girl's long hair, and plague sores disfigured her fair face.

Kelene gently mopped the girl's skin. "Place the stone on her forehead," she told Alanar. He followed her directions exactly as she explained the rest of the spell. To Kelene's relief, the stone flared under his touch. As soon as the golden light faded and the girl was resting more comfortably, Alanar's round, serious face broke into a grin of delight.

They set to work in earnest then. With Gabria beside them working tirelessly to organize help and make tea and medicines, Kelene and Alanar moved methodically from tent to tent in the council grove, treating anyone who was sick.

As Kelene had hoped, Lord Fiergan marched himself into the effort. He found every chieftain who still lived and alerted them to what was happening. In just a few short hours, the rest of the surviving magic-wielders had come to help, and one older woman from the Wylfling clan surprised everyone by revealing a talent to heal. She joined Kelene and Alanar with the last Lion's Eye and calmly settled into the routine as if she had known all along she would be a healer.

Before long, the word that help had arrived spread; people came clamoring to the magic-wielders to come to their camps first. The situation could have gotten out of hand, but Lord Fiergan found warriors to escort the small party of healers and organized the healthy clanspeople into groups to find the most seriously ill victims for faster treatment.

Midnight came and went with few noticing it was late night. There was too much to do, too many sick to treat, too many living who felt the first stirrings of hope in days. The camps came alive with activity as people came from every corner and cranny. Some passed on information, some started cooking fires and heated food, and some furnished wine and honey for Gabria's tonic. Many others just watched in a welter of emotions while the clans crawled slowly back to life.

17

Rafnir looked up at the three men watching him and grinned triumphantly. "Kelene and Demira made it," he said, pinning the Watcher to his tunic. "They're at the gathering."

Sayyed slapped his knee. "That's it, then. We're leaving. Kelene is at the Tir Samod, and the wraith is right behind her. We can't wait any longer."

Rafnir opened his mouth to protest, then shut it again. He and Savaron had been arguing with Sayyed for two days to keep him in bed and resting. Their insistence had worked for a while, but no longer. Although Sayyed was still weak, he was able to ride. Nothing was going to keep him from returning to the gathering. Rafnir glanced at Savaron and shrugged. Sayyed was already on his feet, dressing and packing his gear. The white cat sat patiently by his bedroll. There was nothing Rafnir could do but get ready for the journey.

While the Korg packed food for them, the three men collected their belongings and ate a quick breakfast. When they were prepared to leave, Sayyed clasped the Korg's hand in thanks and climbed slowly onto Afer's back.

"Are you sure you won't come with us?" Rafnir asked the old sorcerer one last time.

The Korg bowed his head. "There is little I could do to help. I will be here if you decide to come back."

"Come back?" Morad snorted. "I never want to see this pile of rocks again!"

The men waved good-bye and rode rapidly through the ruins toward the southern gate. Morning sun from a perfect summer sky streamed on their backs, but the men paid no attention to the beauty of the day. All they saw was the road ahead and the open archway leading from the city. The four horsemen charged out the gate and galloped away from Moy Tura as if all the fury of Gormoth were at their heels.

* * *

Kelene, Alanar, and the Wylfling woman, Pena, finished with the patients in the council grove shortly after sunrise. They were about to move into the camps when there was a stir on the sacred island in the rivers and a group of priests came wading through the rapids to the grove.

A worn, thin, and weary priest came slowly up to Kelene and Gabria and bowed before them, leaning on his staff for support. The priests behind him were silent, but the clanspeople watching murmured in surprise. Ordan, the holy one, had never before accorded obvious respect to magic-wielders.

Kelene and Gabria were taken aback and quickly returned his bow.

"I won't keep you for long," Priest Ordan said in his dry voice. "There is much to do and we have come to share in the work. But I must ask you something." He spoke to Kelene. "We have seen strange visions in the smoke and felt the wrath of our god. Lord Sorh is angry, and we do not know why. Did you learn of something that could have caused this plague?"

Kelene arched an eyebrow in a gesture so like her father's that Gabria had to smother a smile. "Do you know the name Bitorn?" she countered.

Ordan visibly paled. His eyelids lifted, and he straightened slowly. "We are aware of the name," he said warily.

"It was he who lay in the mound we opened. It was he who followed us all the way to Moy Tura to stop us from finding the help we so desperately needed. He is growing stronger, Priest Ordan, and I'm afraid he's coming back."

Ordan couldn't have known all the details about Bitorn's imprisonment and his powers as a wraith, but he obviously knew enough to understand their danger for he asked, "How long do we have?"

"A day, seven days, I'm not sure. The Korg said he would keep him there for as long as he could."

Gabria nearly choked. "The Korg?"

Kelene smiled. "The legends were right, Mother. He was a shapeshifter and a very sad, old man. He and Bitorn were sworn enemies."

"Gods above!" Gabria exclaimed.

Ordan made no further comment about the wraith. He only said, "We shall have to talk of this later." Then he and the remaining priests and priestesses rolled up the sleeves of their robes and joined the work.

By late afternoon Kelene and her two companions had attended to the worst cases in the eleven camps. Bone-tired, they stopped long enough to sleep and eat, and by nightfall they were again visiting the clans to treat the remaining sick. Although some of the sicker patients died before they could be helped, and some succumbed in spite of the stones' magic, the old spells proved to be reliably effectual. A few new cases of the plague appeared around the camps, but not in the previous uncontrollable numbers. Slowly and surely the plague was losing its grip on the clans.

Activity in the clan camps began to reflect the new hope. Everywhere people were taking stock of the devastation and working hard to bring the clans back to order. One of the first and most distressing problems the living had to face was the vast numbers of the dead.

"We gave up burning and burying the bodies when we ran out of people to do the work," Lord Sha Tajan told Kelene that afternoon while she aided the sick in the Jehanan camp. "Sorh knows how many people have actually died. We've burned them and buried them and piled them in the meadow and left them in their tents. Some crawled away to die, and a few even threw themselves in the river."

Kelene looked alarmed. She hadn't had time to think about anything other than the sick, and now she realized the clans had to get busy on something else very important. "The bodies should be removed immediately!" Kelene told the chief. "Piers told me a long time ago that bodies left to rot can cause more diseases."

That threat so horrified the Jehanan chief he wasted no time forming grave parties to find, identify, and remove every corpse in the gathering. The leaders of the clans went from tent to tent, taking names and counting those who had died. When night came most of the camps were cleared, and the meadow where the funeral pyres had burned was filled with wrapped bodies. While most of the people went to their beds for the first good night's sleep in days, the priests began the dismal task of compiling the sobering tallies.

At noon the next day the surviving clanspeople gathered in the meadow to make their final farewells to the dead. Overhead, the sun beat down on the meadow and on the heads of the mourners. It glinted on the spears and polished mail of the honor guard from each clan and gleamed on the colored banners. Its bright beams streamed into the huge pit that lay at the clans' feet, filling it with warmth and light for the very last time.

The pit had been a joint effort of every clan. Excavated with magic and dug with shovels, knives, and even bare hands, it represented the last effort made for all the fathers, mothers, sons, and daughters that had died. In its cavity were the ashes from previous funeral pyres and on top of that lay the dead, wrapped in their blankets or cloaks like so many colorful cords of wood.

All that remained was to bless the mass grave and fill it in. Before the priests began their chants, however, Ordan climbed to the top of the big pile of excavated earth and raised his hands to the crowd. "We have finished counting the grievous toll of our losses," he said in a voice that filled the meadow. "Of our clan chieftains, Lords Morbiar, Koshyn, Maxin, Dormar, and Gerrand have died. The healers and the magic-wielders who worked so hard to help our people lost half of their numbers—ten healers and fifteen magic-wielders."

A sad, angry silence filled the meadow as the dreadful list went on. Ordan read the numbers of visiting merchants who had died, of the clanspeople who had secretly fled and were missing, and of the members of each clan that had succumbed to the dreadful pestilence. When he was through, the total rang like a clap of thunder in their ears. Over three thousand warriors, sorcerers, mid-wives, healers, mothers, children, priests, herdsmen, weavers, elders, people of every age and rank were gone.

And for what reason?

That question pounded in the mind of every person who watched Priest Ordan lift his arms high and begin the songs for the dead. The daily give-and-take of life and death, the constant competition between Amara and Sorh, was something every clansperson accepted. Life on the plains was never easy, but its risks had a certain familiarity. Wars, weather, accidents, age, and common illness were all faced and taken for granted.

But this plague was an unknown, unseen adversary that had struck three thousand people while the clans had stood by and helplessly watched.

Three thousand! Almost as many as killed in the Corin massacre, the war with Lord Medb, and the last twenty years combined. Not since the fall of Moy Tura had so many people died all at once, and even in that horrible slaughter there had been a visible enemy wielding very real swords.

A slow rage began to kindle in the grieving survivors. The dying had stopped, thanks to the magic-wielders, and life was returning to some semblance of normality. But the anger ran deep, and the clanspeople wanted to strike out at someone, or something, for all the pain and loss and despair they had suffered.

Lord Athlone understood that reaction well. He had lost his youngest son, his daughter, two very dear friends, and more kin and clansfolk than he cared to think about. Still weak and barely upright, he climbed the mound to stand beside Priest Ordan.

The white-haired priest bowed low in respect to the Khulinin lord. "Between the two of us, we unleashed a great wrong on our people," Ordan said very quietly.

Athlone, his face and neck stiff with healing sores, returned the bow and replied, "Then together we must put it right."

They stood side by side, the priest and the sorcerer, and faced their people. Loudly, and hiding nothing, Athlone and Ordan gave the clanspeople an enemy to blame. They told the gathered clans everything about the sealed burial mound and its undead occupant, how he had been released, and how the plague had sprung from his cruelty.

Just as they were finishing their speech, Athlone saw a large shadow pass over the heads of the people, and he smiled. She was right on time.

Someone shouted and everyone looked up to see a black Hunnuli wing gracefully over the meadow. Voices burst out in surprised cries and fingers pointed. No one had seen Demira since her arrival two days before. Rumors of her altered appearance had run rife through the gathering, but this was the first time everyone had been able to observe her.

Shouting and pushing for a better look, the people stared as Demira glided down and made an easy landing at the foot of the dirt mound. Only then did the crowd notice Kelene on the filly's back.

Two nights and days of rest had worked wonders on the filly. Her coat was shining, and her wings gleamed in the sunlight. Well aware of the effect she was having on the crowd, she arched her ebony neck proudly and lifted her wings in a gentle curve for all to see.

Kelene sat quietly. As soon as the crowd had calmed a little, she urged the Hunnuli to climb halfway up the mound of dirt. From that vantage point, Kelene took up where her father had left off. She described the journey to Moy Tura and the attacks of the wraith. She spoke of the Korg, the healing stones, and Demira's wings. And last of all she warned of the dead priest's history, his power, and his terrible danger.

The telling was long, but the clanspeople were so enraptured by the story they did not seem to mind the heat, the flies, or the passage of time. As Athlone had hoped, the presence of Demira gave added credence to Kelene's story, and his daughter's firm, serious voice, a voice so many people had heard and come to trust lately, brought the truth home more effectively than anything he could have said or done.

"I wanted to tell you all of this today," Kelene finished, "so you would know the full story of this disaster that stole so many lives. It is my belief that the wraith will be returning to finish what he began. He is obsessed with destroying every magic-wielder in the clans; he does not care who has to die to achieve that end. His pestilence killed magic-wielders, yes, but it struck mercilessly into our people, destroying everyone it touched. This is not just a problem for magic-wielders to solve, it is a crisis for all of us."

Lord Athlone looked out over the crowd and saw by the darkening expressions that the warning had not been lost. Satisfied, he, Ordan, Kelene, and Demira withdrew from their places and began the final burial.

The clanspeople were pensive while they piled the earth back over the grave and shaped it into an oblong mound. The Plague Mound, as it was always called thereafter, was crowned with a ring of spears and seeded with wildflowers to make a fitting tribute to the dead. Afterward the clanspeople returned to their many tasks, but what they had heard at the burial stuck in their thoughts and stoked their anger like a hot wind. Everywhere, in all eleven clans, people were talking of little but the wraith and his return. There was no mention of leaving the gathering, only of vengeance.

Later that evening, while the clans settled down for the night, Gabria and Kelene slowly walked through the council grove on their way back to the Khulinin camp. Kelene was so weary her crippled foot would barely hold her weight, and she had to lean on her mother's arm. Never had Kelene worked so hard for such a long time and never had she expended so much strength wielding magic. The days of struggling to save the clanspeople had paid off, but the effort had left her totally drained. When Gabria finally insisted that she go home to sleep, Kelene had to agree.

Gratefully, she leaned on her mother's support and drew a long breath of the evening air. The fires and the smoke of the burning incense were gone, the stench of the council grove had virtually dissipated, and a fresh breeze blew from the west. The air smelled of familiar things again: dust, animals, dry grass, the rivers. It was a combination Kelene savored as never before.

She was still enjoying the breeze when she felt her mother stiffen. Kelene stopped. "What is it?" she asked.

Gabria was frowning. "I don't know. I felt something odd."

"Like what?"

"I'm not sure. This happened when you and the others left for Moy Tura. I felt a lightening, as if a dread had left me. But this time . . . a feeling of dread has come back. It's very vague, but," she said, shivering, "I feel so cold."

"Could it be the presence of the wraith?"

"Maybe." Gabria looked around at the gathering shadows. "No one has reported seeing him, but that doesn't mean he hasn't returned."

Kelene groaned. "I hope your feeling is something else."

"I know. The clans are hardly ready to fight him. Perhaps I am only tired from today's burial. I finally had a chance to say good-bye to Coren and Lymira."

Kelene's grip tightened around her mother's arm. The day had been traumatic for both her parents and herself. Maybe tomorrow—after a good night's sleep—they would all feel stronger. Then, Kelene decided, she would take Demira on a few flights to see if she could find any sign of the wraith or Sayyed's party. She had a sense that Gabria's feeling of dread was more than exhausted grief.

* * *

"Father!" Kelene's excited voice floated over the council grove, catching everyone's attention. Lord Athlone and the men with him watched in wonder while Demira and her rider circled over the grove and dropped down for a landing outside the trees.

Lord Athlone still could not quite believe what his daughter had wrought, or the new cloak of maturity she wore with such aplomb. He watched in illconcealed pride as she slid off her horse and came limping into the grove.

"I found them," she called eagerly even before she acknowledged the priests and chieftains with her father. "They're about a day's ride away!" Only then did she remember her manners and properly greet Lord Athlone's companions.

They were a worn, tired-looking group, yet the changes in the grove about them were evidence of the changes that had been taking place all over the gathering. It had only been one day since the mass burial, but in that time the tents, trash, and debris had been cleared away and burned, and the remaining sick were recuperating in their camps or in the council tent.

Kelene barely finished her greetings to the chieftains and turned back to her father. "Sayyed and Rafnir are almost recovered. They left Moy Tura two days ago." She was smiling, still warm from the pleasure of seeing Rafnir and the others. She and Demira had been making reconnaissance flights all day to look for the wraith, missing clanspeople, or Sayyed's party. She had found the men late that afternoon cantering south along the Isin River.

"There is some bad news, though," she continued. "Savaron told me Bitorn left the city six days ago. He may be here already."

Lord Terod paled. The young chief of Clan Amnok was still weak from his bout of the plague and he wanted no part of any more trouble. "Well, we haven't seen him," he declared. "And we have beaten his plague. He's not coming back here."

Kelene shook her head forcefully. "Bitorn followed us all the way to Moy Tura just because we were magic-wielders and were looking for ways to stop his plague. His hatred is fanatical. He will be back if only to reclaim his body." She snapped her fingers. "That was something Sayyed suggested, Father. Take Bitorn's body out of the mound and find a way to destroy it. A few people are still dying, so the wraith may be able to steal enough life-force to return to his body."

"Remove the corpse?" Terod interrupted again. "What if we go in there and bring out the disease all over again?"

"There is a chance of that," Athlone agreed, "but this time we have the healers' stones to fight it. Killing Bitorn is worth any risk."

Lord Fiergan shook his head in disgust, whether at Terod or at the prospect of entering the mound again Kelene didn't know. "I'll go with you," he said. "I want to see the end of that gorthling spawn once and for all."

Kelene turned her head so the Reidhar chief would not see her grin. She didn't know of any time in her life that Lord Fiergan had willingly volunteered to help her father with anything.

"I will go, too," said Priest Ordan. The venerable priest glanced at Lord Athlone, then transferred his gaze out past the trees to the far meadow where the burial mound lay. His eyes were transfixed on some image only he could see; his voice was low and angry. "It took a plague to prove to me that we need each other, and now I see that we will have to use that cooperation in fighting the wraith, or *we* are the ones who will be destroyed."

Even Lord Fiergan did not argue with that statement.

Although Lord Athlone was ready to go that afternoon, the day was too advanced to warrant a journey to the box canyon. It would have been night by the time the party entered the mound, and no one was willing to risk facing the wraith in the black confines of his burial chamber. Athlone didn't mind putting off the trip until the next day. He was not completely recovered from the debilitating fever, and he wanted to be rested and strong when he began his offensive against the killer of his children and his clan.

As it turned out, it was just after noon by the time the party of chieftains, priests, and warriors were able to leave. Athlone, Fiergan, and Sha Tajan brought several hearthguard warriors each, and Ordan came with two assistants, an incense burner, and a jar of quicklime.

Kelene decided to ride with them, since she had not gone the last time. They rode from the gathering heading due east, found the faint Induran trail, and followed it into the hills where they soon rode between the towering walls of the narrow defile.

Demira had to tuck her wings very close to her sides to pass through the tighter sections of the rock faces. Looking ahead, Kelene recognized the widening passage into the end of the blind canyon where the mound lay, and an involuntary shudder ran down her back. She wished Rafnir were beside her with his humor and his steady courage to keep her company. She half-expected to see Bitorn standing by his grave ready to welcome them, but the mound and the box canyon were empty.

The party of riders halted in a tight cluster by the mound and sat staring at it, half afraid to dismount. The grave looked much the same as it had that day so long ago when the young clansmen came to restore the dirt. Its earthen walls looked innocuous; there was nothing in the shape or composition of the mound to warn against its deadly contents.

The men reluctantly dismounted, bracing themselves to face an unpleasant task. Kelene stayed on her horse. She was very cold in spite of the sun's warmth, and the hairs began to rise on the back of her neck. There was nothing that she could see to cause her fear, and yet she suddenly wished she had not come. Trembling, she watched Lord Athlone and the others walk around to the other end of the mound to the entrance.

"I thought they were going to close and rebury the door," she heard Sha Tajan say. Nervousness made his voice loud enough for Kelene to hear him clearly.

"They said they did," Athlone replied.

Kelene could not see the men or the entrance from where she was sitting on Demira; she could only hear their voices grow muffled and some thuds and a grinding noise from the doorway. There was the sound of footsteps, a crash, and silence.

Kelene strained upward on the filly's back, every sense taut with tension. "Father?" she called worriedly.

Almost at once Lord Athlone came bolting around the side of the mound, the other men fast on his heels. His face was white under the healing sores, and his expression was a twist of fear and fury.

"The body's gone!" he shouted to Kelene. "The wraith was already here. Go back to the gathering. Warn your mother."

Demira turned on her heels at his last words and galloped out of the canyon into the defile. Kelene clung tightly to her back, letting the filly find her own way over the rocky, uneven ground. She didn't hear the pounding of Demira's hooves echoing around her or see the high rock walls and the strip of blue overhead. All Kelene heard over and over in her mind was Athlone's warning, "The wraith was already here!" All she could see in her mind was an image of Bitorn gloating over her mother's dead body.

The thudding echo of hoofbeats died away, the light increased, and Kelene looked up to see the mouth of the canyon. Demira sped forward along the trail and up onto the nearest open hill. At the crest she spread her wings and plunged into space. Like a black storm cloud she flew across the valley toward the Tir Samod.

18

The camps were in plain view when Kelene saw columns of smoke rising from the edge of the Khulinin camp. It was not the yellowish smoke of incense this time, but the blacker, more scattered plumes of smoke from burning tents. The wraith was already there. The outlying camps hadn't noticed the trouble yet, for the people she could see in the Amnok camp below were going unhurriedly about their business.

But that changed an instant later.

The special blaring call chosen by the chiefs in case of the wraith's return soared out over the camps, echoed a second later by another frantic horn blast for help from the Khulinin guards across the rivers.

The gathering burst into action. From her vantage point above the valley, Kelene saw people from all the other camps swarm toward the Khulinin tents. Sunlight glinted on weapons of every description, and an angry rumble rose on the air from hundreds of voices. The enemy had come at last, and the rage and grief that had been festering in the clan survivors came to a boiling head.

Kelene's heart was thudding, and her stomach lurched into her throat as Demira dropped again toward her clan's camp. Where were Gabria and the other magic-wielders?

She saw the wraith first—or what had been the wraith. Now the spirit was returned to his body, and the power of the life-force he had stolen from dying clanspeople had rejuvenated his physical form to its previous health and vitality. His body was solid and muscular; his dark red robes swirled about his legs. He looked like any mortal man walking through the camp.

But Kelene would have recognized Bitorn anywhere. His upper body leaned into his furious stride, and his long, black hair tossed like a stallion's mane around his cruel, arrogant face. Only the red phosphorescent light was gone, replaced by the light of a flaming torch he held in one hand. He thrust the torch at every tent he passed, leaving a path of flames, smoke, and screaming people in his wake. In his other hand was a long, black staff of Sorh's priests, which he wielded against the warriors who were trying to stop him.

So far, there had been no organized effort to attack Bitorn. Kelene could see many of the Khulinin warriors were being distracted by the fires, and the other clans had not yet reached the priest. He was moving directly toward the center of the camp, where the chieftain's tent stood in its large open circle.

Did Bitorn know about her mother and father, Kelene wondered, or had his choice of camps been random? Somehow she doubted the attack on the heart of the Khulinin camp was coincidence. It was too determined, too deliberate.

Just then, she saw her mother ride Nara out from behind the big tent and canter the mare forward to meet the priest. They came together at the edge of the open space and stopped, the undead priest facing the sorceress. Kelene couldn't hear what they said to each other. It hardly mattered, though, for the conversation abruptly ended in an explosion of blue energy. Gabria had lost no time launching her own attack.

The priest threw back his head and laughed at blast after blast of magic that exploded against his body.

Many other clanspeople had arrived by that time, and they gathered in ever increasing numbers around the center of the camp, staring at the priest in horrified awe. Two more magic-wielders, Alanar and another young man, ran to Gabria and joined their attack to hers. And still the priest did nothing but laugh his scorn.

So far Bitorn had not seen Kelene, and she took advantage of his distraction to unsheathe her small dagger. Forcing her mind to relax, she formed a transformation spell and used the magic to change her dagger into a spear. Just as she was about to throw it, though, Bitorn dropped his staff and began to grow taller.

Kelene felt her mouth drop open. She had seen him increase his size when he was a wraith, but she didn't expect him to be able to do that when he was encased in his body. In less time than it had taken her to work her spell, he doubled in size. A few moments later, he doubled his size again and loomed over Gabria, his huge hands reaching for her.

Kelene yelled an oath and launched the spear at Bitorn's back. To the giant man, the wooden shaft was no more than an arrow thrown by a puny hand, but to Kelene's surprise the spear point pierced his back and stuck there.

He roared in fury, turned, and saw her. "You!" he bellowed, and his great hand swung out toward Demira. The filly swerved toward him and swooped under his swinging arm, away from his bunched fist. Frantically, Demira darted behind him and soared out of his sight behind the column of smoke from the burning tents.

Breathing a sigh of relief, Kelene risked a glance to the east and saw a party of riders galloping across the valley. Lord Athlone was on the way.

Two more magic-wielders mounted on their Hunnuli had joined Gabria by then, and the small group had retreated to the highest point of the clearing, right beside the chieftain's tent. Bitorn turned his attention back to them.

He wrapped his hand around a young tree, snapped it off at the ground, and ripped off its foliage. The huge priest's shadow darkened the ground as he raised his new staff and brought it up over his head. But instead of swinging it at Gabria, he suddenly whirled and sent it crashing down on a young man who was riding a Hunnuli past the tents to reach the sorceress.

The tree trunk smashed the magic-wielder against his horse and crushed them both to the ground, killing them instantly. "That's one!" he shouted to Gabria.

Nara screamed her rage, and her cry was taken up by all the Hunnuli in the gathering. Every magic-wielder left in the camps mounted their horses and came in response to Nara's challenge.

Some of the Khulinin warriors led by Secen formed a line, raised their bows, and fired a swarm of arrows at Bitorn. He swatted the shafts away like gnats, then reached behind his back and pulled out Kelene's spear. Already the blood was dry and the wound was healing.

"Puling mortals!" the priest bellowed in a voice that shook the camp. "Down on your knees before me and give thanks that I have come to release you from the evil of sorcery."

"You're not our master," Secen shouted back. "We don't want you here!"

Bitorn took several menacing steps toward the Khulinin warriors, but the men and clanspeople behind them scrambled out of the way. Bitorn did not press his attack. He sneered and said, "Run while you can. I will deal with you later. Now I must fulfill my sacred vow to the gods." He bent toward the cluster of magic-wielders, his face gloating. "I have waited long, but the gods at last have called me to my duty."

It was Gabria who laughed then. "You're not a servant of the gods, Bitorn, you're only a vicious, selfish brute who should have died in your own time."

"Profaner!" he screamed. His staff crashed down, only to ricochet off a dome of shimmering red energy. Gabria and the magic-wielders with her stood together beneath the shield and held it with all of their combined power.

The priest, yelling in rage, tried again and again to smash the dome with his staff. He stamped and roared around the shield, flattening tents and scattering people in all directions, and still the little group beneath the dome withstood his efforts.

Kelene, though, knew how much strength it took to hold a shield like that, and she realized her mother's group would not be able to endure much longer. She was about to try distracting Bitorn again when a different voice boomed across the trampled space.

"In the name of Sorh, Lord of the Realm of the Dead, Commander of the Harbingers, Ruler of Gormoth, and Reaper of Souls, I command you to hold!"

Bitorn hesitated out of sheer surprise. The force of old habits stirred in his mind, and he slowly lowered his staff. "Who dares speak to me of Lord Sorh?"

"I do!" Priest Ordan stepped from the crowd in a position that forced Bitorn to turn around. Unseen by the grim giant, Athlone and Eurus slipped into the clearing and joined Gabria.

"Fool!" Bitorn hissed to Ordan. "How can a doddering old bootlicker know more of Lord Sorh than I?"

Ordan glared ferociously, his white eyebrows lowered in annoyance. "I know he is angry! You have betrayed his trust, priest! You slaughtered innocent people to feed your own greed for life. You have flung your arrogance in the god's face by refusing your own death. You must die, Bitorn, before the god wreaks his awful vengeance on your eternal soul!" The old priest marched up to the towering man, snatched Bitorn's priestly staff from the ground, and broke it at the man's feet.

There was not even a flicker of fear or hesitation on Bitorn's face. His booming laugh flung away Ordan's warning, and the contemptuous wave of his hand knocked the old priest to the ground. "I do not fear the gods. The only vengeance here will be mine! The evil of magic will be destroyed once and for all!"

"Not this time!" Lord Fiergan's voice roared out. The big chieftain kicked his horse forward and rode between the fallen priest and Bitorn. "We don't want your hatred any more. We've had enough of it! Go back to your mound and rot!"

"Magic lovers!" Bitorn spat out the words like a curse. He raised his hands to the mass of people crowded among the tents and said, "Are there none left among you who despise the evil of magic? Have you all fallen into the pits of deceit and wickedness?"

An eloquent silence met his question. Then, suddenly Fiergan raised his sword and bellowed the Reidhar war cry. It was answered by over a thousand voices from every clan in a tremendous roar that shattered the afternoon and swept down the valley on the wind. A mass of mounted men and warriors on foot surged forward to attack the giant.

At the same moment, Gabria, Athlone, and the eight magic-wielders with them dissolved their shield and loosed a furious barrage of magic at the priest's chest. Demira glided out of the smoke, and her rider added her own bolts to the intense assault.

Bitorn staggered under the combined blows, and Fiergan and the clan warriors leaped in with spears, swords, and battle-axes. They slashed at the backs of the priest's knees and ankles in an effort to cut his tendons and bring him down. His blood spattered the ground and the warriors.

The pain and the magic enraged Bitorn into a frenzy. Screaming incoherent oaths, he swung his staff right and left at the warriors swarming around him. He crushed three Khulinin warriors underfoot and trampled more until the men were forced away. Bitorn stood back and looked wildly around for the next target.

His eyes caught sight of Demira flying overhead. Before Kelene could understand what was happening, Bitorn's energy-hungry soul drained the life-force from the dead men under his feet and used it to double his body size once again. All at once he was as tall as a cottonwood tree, and his hand shot out and grabbed the filly in midair.

Kelene screamed as she felt the merciless fingers close around them. A thick, heavy pressure surrounded her and pressed her down onto Demira's neck. The filly, neighing in fright, struggled desperately to escape the cruel grip.

Kelene knew she had to do something fast before Bitorn crushed them like he would a fly, but before she could initiate a spell, something odd began to happen. Without conscious direction, her empathic talent began to sense the priest's emotions. The sensations were faint at first, then as the mental channel strengthened, the full force of his feelings hit her like a storm. Rage was the strongest, a tempestuous, uncontrollable rage that buffeted her with maniacal strength. Underneath that was hatred and contempt like two poisonous twins, and somewhere, buried in the maelstrom, was a little thread of fear.

The last one surprised Kelene. What did Bitorn have to be afraid of from a bunch of weak, half-sick, overworked magic-wielders and a mob of people one-eighth his size? She sent her mind probing swiftly after that tendril of fear, deeper into the priest's turbulent emotions.

The answer that she found stunned her with its simple truth. She knew from the Korg that the life-force energy was similar to magic, but she hadn't realized that Bitorn, like a magic-wielder, could only use as much power as his own strength would allow. Since the dying had all but stopped at the gathering, the wraith had been unable to go to his burial mound and rejoin his body until just a short while ago. The union had taken a great deal of his strength. He was still comparatively weak to handle the vast amounts of energy he needed to attack the magic-wielders *and* all eleven clans. That was why he was taking action that was more defensive than offensive. He didn't have enough strength to deal with such a large number of people. Maybe he hadn't expected so many to come after him, or perhaps his blind anger simply wouldn't let him wait until he was stronger. Whatever his reasons, Kelene knew he was overextending his power.

She only had a moment or two to sift through the jumbled impressions of his mind before he changed his grip on Demira and began to squeeze tighter. But those precious moments were just enough for her new knowledge to spark an idea. All she had to do was survive long enough to tell her parents.

Desperately Kelene shaped a spell to form a shield around herself and Demira. At her command the red energy coalesced into a skintight shell between the horse and rider and the giant's hand.

Bitorn swore furiously. He brought both hands around his prey and tried to crush them in his fingers. Kelene closed her eyes, gritted her teeth, and held on to her spell with all her might. She and Demira could hardly breathe beneath the shell and the heavy weight of the giant's hand. Kelene gasped for air. She grew dizzy and feared she might black out and lose control of her spell.

Then all at once Bitorn let go of her with one hand and began to swing his staff again. Kelene opened her eyes and saw on the ground below that the clan warriors led by Lord Fiergan and Sha Tajan had renewed their attack on the priest. Kelene breathed a prayer of thanks for the distraction.

Bitorn still had one hand wrapped around Demira, but he was too busy defending himself to turn his attention back to his prisoners. Kelene rapidly formed another spell. In a flash of motion, she dissolved her shield and sent a white-hot bolt of fire into Bitorn's palm.

The priest yelled in pain. Shocked and furious, he flung the winged horse toward the earth.

Demira never had a chance to right herself. The force of Bitorn's throw tumbled her over upside down. Her shrill neigh and Kelene's scream blended into one cry of terror.

The young sorceress thought she heard a familiar voice call her name, but it was lost in the sickening, tumbling fall toward the earth. She saw the ground below spinning up to crush her, and her heart cried out to the one she loved and would never see again. "Rafnir!"

Incredibly, her plea was answered with a platform of air that formed beneath and caught Demira just before she and Kelene smashed into the ground. She bounced once on the invisible cushion and settled slowly on her side to the earth just a few steps away from the group of magic-wielders.

Demira scrambled to her feet, shaken and ruffled but unhurt, and a hand was thrust out to Kelene to help her stand. It took a heartbeat before she realized the hand was Rafnir's. She was on her feet and in his arms before her heart had a chance to beat again. Savaron was there, too, on his exhausted Hunnuli, and Sayyed, looking wan but alive with his white cat on his shoulder, and Morad, dusty and tired. They had to have ridden like Turic raiders to get there so soon. Kelene hugged them all, happier than she had ever been.

"I learned that spell from you," Rafnir whispered in her ear, and he showed her the diamond splinter under his wrist.

Kelene kissed him delightedly. Still holding his hand, she glanced at Bitorn. The priest was surrounded by archers and warriors who were sending a merciless barrage of arrows, spears, and lances at his lower body. Kelene hoped she had a minute or two to talk before he turned his attention back to the magic-wielders. "I have an idea," she told her parents, explaining about her probe into Bitorn's mind. "The Korg said the life-force is similar to magic. As long as people die, there is all the life-force Bitorn needs. But he can only use so much energy before he starts to tire."

"He's not showing much sign of that," Rafnir said dryly.

"So let's help him along," Kelene cried. "If the life-force is similar enough to magic, maybe we could try drawing his strength *out* of him. Perhaps we could weaken him enough for the warriors to kill his body."

Gabria and Athlone looked at one another, their faces bright with understanding.

"Secen!" Athlone called to his old hearthguard nearby. "Tell Priest Ordan we need a distraction that will keep Bitorn's attention for a short time, and have Lord Fiergan pull his men back."

Secen obeyed with alacrity, working his way through the milling clanspeople to the priest of Sorh. The old man listened and nodded once across the space to Lord Athlone. A moment later a horn blew, signaling the warriors attacking Bitorn to fall back. A wide circle opened up around the huge man, and for the space of several moments the gathering fell quiet.

Bitorn stood in the center of the space. He was panting and bleeding from several gashes on his legs. He stared at the surrounding people with utter contempt.

Then, along the edge of the crowd, came the priests of Sorh from every clan. Robed in dark red and grim in visage, they formed a ring around the giant man. Ordan stood before Bitorn and raised his black staff to the sky. Softly at first and then louder, the priests began to chant a litany no one had heard in years.

Kelene heard Gabria gasp, "They're stripping him of his priesthood!"

"They can do that?" Kelene asked, startled. A person's holy calling was granted by the gods and was not usually taken away by men.

"Sometimes," her mother replied. "In extreme cases."

Bitorn recognized the ancient chant, too, and he stood still, scarcely believing what he was hearing. "No!" he bellowed. "You won't do this to me!"

Athlone nodded to his family. Around them, the magic-wielders were all together at last. There were only sixteen left, and half of them were not fully trained. But they all knew how to attract power, and their determination made up for their lack of skill. As one, they focused their inherent talents on the priest and began to pull out his energy.

Bitorn did not recognize their ploy at first; he was too intent on the ring of priests and their inexorable chant. He raised his staff like a club and took a step toward Ordan. Suddenly he staggered. Only then did he realize what the magic-wielders were doing. Furiously he struggled to fight the drain on his power before he lost all control. He was successful at first and was able to back away from the group of magic-wielders. But he hadn't gone more than a few steps when he put his hands to his head and swayed. He bellowed his fury, his angular face red and ugly with twisted hate.

Still the magic-wielders pulled at him, stripping him of the energy he had stolen from their own dying people. His gigantic body started to shrink.

Lord Fiergan, Lord Sha Tajan, and the other chiefs and warriors saw his growing weakness. They edged into the circle and sprang in to attack. A handful of Khulinin men feinted to the priest's right. As he swung around to drive them off, Fiergan charged under his shadow. There was a bright flash of a sword, and Bitorn's left knee collapsed under his weight.

The priest screamed, almost desperately, and struggled away from the Reid-har chief only to be blocked by Dangari spearmen. Archers crowded on his right, more swordwielding warriors charged in behind him, and a solid mass of incensed clanspeople cut off any hope of escape.

Bitorn was almost back to his normal height when he turned to see Priest Ordan. Their eyes met, and the mask of hate and arrogance fell away from Bitorn's face, leaving only terror behind. He stared in appeal at Ordan's implacable expression, but the old Priest of Sorb only lifted a hand to his priests. The circle of men shouted in unison and pointed their staffs to the sky.

"Your priesthood is finished, Bitorn!" Ordan shouted. "You are no longer a servant of Lord Sorh. Prepare to meet your master."

A wail rose from Bitorn's lips, and from the group of magic-wielders, Lord Athlone shouted, "Now!"

The clanspeople struck with a terrible vengeance. The warriors within striking distance swarmed over Bitorn's body, hacking, slashing, and stabbing the priest to bloody shreds. He screamed once before his voice was cut off to a gagging wheeze and then to silence. His body sagged to the ground.

Satisfied, the men drew back from the corpse, but they had barely lowered their weapons when a red phosphorescence began to glow just above the priest's remains.

Kelene's fingers tightened over Rafnir's arm, and the clanspeople stopped in midmotion. It was as the Korg had warned—they had killed Bitorn's physical body, but they still had to control his soul. The wraith coalesced before their eyes, his tall form glowing with the sickly red light.

"You cannot be rid of me that easily," he hissed.

At that moment the Hunnuli horses raised their heads, their ears pricked forward. *Riders come!* Eurus neighed.

The magie-wieldlers were startled. Riders?

A tremor shook the wraith, and he wavered as if blasted by a powerful gust of wind.

The young clanspeople heard it next—a muted pounding of hoofbeats from some far distance. The sound grew louder and more distinct, and soon everyone heard it. Heads turned, eyes searched, yet the noise had no direction or obvious source.

Ordan saw them first, five riders on pale horses coming out of a curtain of mist in the blue afternoon sky. "They come! They come!" he cried and flung himself prostrate to the ground.

The wraith screeched in terror.

Every face turned to the sky, and even though no living mortal had ever seen their forms, every single person there recognized the five riders. They had been described once by Valorian, who had ridden in their midst and returned to life.

They were the Harbingers, the messengers of Sorb who came to escort souls to the realm of the dead.

The clanspeople froze in their places. There was no sound in the camp except for a dull clang when Fiergan's sword fell from his nerveless fingers.

Shining white in the sun, the Harbingers rode their shimmering steeds down the sky and came to a stop on the mortal earth just in front of Bitorn. They were huge, clothed like warriors in polished mail and armor. Brilliant helms covered their faces.

Bitorn quailed before the riders' silent scrutiny.

"Know this!" one Harbinger spoke in a masculine voice that was rich and powerful. "The days of enmity are over. The gorthling's curse that brought down Valorian's children is finished!"

"No!" shrieked Bitorn in one last attempt to have his way. "They are evil. They are a profanity. They must not be allowed to live!"

The Harbinger lifted a finger. "Come. This time you cannot escape Lord Sorh."

"No!" Bitorn screamed. He rose up to flee, but the white rider raised his hand. A bolt of shining energy flew from his palm and caught the wraith. The power wrapped around him like a rope and trapped his sickly red glow within a bond of white light. The five riders swiftly surrounded him. They cantered their steeds up into the sky, dragging the soul in their midst.

The clanspeople watched them go until the last flicker of light faded from sight and the Harbingers vanished into the curtain of mist that bordered the mortal realm and the realm of the dead. Only then did the clans know the ordeal was over.

Out of the group of magic-wielders Lord Athlone made his way across the shambles of the clearing to help Priest Ordan to his feet. "That was incredible," Athlone said. "Did you know the Harbingers were coming?"

Ordan's mouth jerked up in an odd smile. "I hoped they would, but I never expected to see them." He was about to add more when Fiergan and Sha Tajan hurried over to meet them.

"What happened?" Sha Tajan cried. "I thought Bitorn was too strong to submit to the Harbingers."

"He had no choice this time," Ordan told him. "When the priests, the magic-wielders, and the clanspeople turned against him, he lost everything."

Fiergan shook his head, his big, irascible face full of wonder. "Those Harbingers were magnificent! But why did we see them?"

"Did you hear what the one rider said?" Ordan said quietly. "The days of enmity are over." He looked pointedly at the three chiefs. "The gods have spoken that all may hear."

Lord Fiergan slowly turned. He looked at the dead bodies, the trampled and burning clan tents, and the bloody remains of Bitorn. He watched Kelene hug

Sayyed and Savaron and return to Rafnir's embrace; he saw Gabria and the surviving magic-wielders bending over the crushed bodies of the Hunnuli and his rider; and last of all he studied Lord Athlone from head to boot and everything in between that he had once loathed.

Deliberately the Reidhar chief stuck out his fist to Lord Athlone in the salute of one chieftain to another. "Looks like we have a lot of work to do," he said to the sorcerer lord.

EPILOGUE

A cool, windy day in the ninth month of the clan calendar brought a party of riders to the ruins of Moy Tura. A gold banner flew at their head, signifying that the Khulinin lord was in their midst. Overhead soared a black Hunnuli on long, broad wings who glided ahead of the party and came down to land just outside the city's southern gate.

The Korg walked out to greet her and to welcome her rider with a glad cry. They waited for the other riders, and in a few minutes Kelene was introducing her parents to the sorcerer who had once chased them from his domain.

Eyes twinkling, he bowed low to them. "It is an honor, Lord Athlone and Lady Gabria, to welcome you to Moy Tura." He took his visitors on a tour of the ruins, including his house that he was rebuilding and the beautiful grave mound he had made for Niela and her Hunnuli. They talked for hours of magic and the city and life before the Purge.

When they were settled in his garden, sipping wine and relaxing in the late-day peace, the Korg smiled at Rafnir and Kelene. "I do not need to ask if you two have made your betrothal vows. It is written all over you."

Kelene's face warmed with pleasure. "We will be joined during the Birthright next spring." She paused and put her hand in Rafnir's. "If it is all right, we'd like to come back here for a while. I want to study the healers' room and learn all I can."

"Of course, you are welcome! Anyone is welcome."

The young sorceress glanced at her betrothed, and he nodded. "Do you mean that?" she asked the Korg.

Gabria sensed something was coming up. "Why do you ask?"

"Mother," Kelene said, both excited and a little wary. "What do you think about rebuilding the city?"

Gabria could only stare, and Athlone's mouth went slack. "Rebuild Moy Tura? Why?" the chief demanded.

"I think we have learned enough from our mistakes to try it again. We could tear down the city walls, reconstruct the buildings, begin teaching magic-wielders here again. But this time we will make the city open and accessible to anyone."

Lord Athlone shook his head at his daughter's unexpected enthusiasm. "Rafnir, did you know about this?"

The young sorcerer nodded, grinning. "We've talked about this for days. I would like to give it a try."

"You may be on your own here for a long time," Gabria warned. "Sixteen magic-wielders hardly make a city, and those few we have left want to spend some time with their clans."

Kelene's and Rafnir's eyes met. "We know," she said. "It is only a beginning."

By the gods, Gabria thought to herself, how true that was, and if Kelene wanted to take her place in that grand beginning, let no one stand in her way!

Gabria pulled her daughter to her feet and gently touched the splinter glowing under Kelene's wrist. "By Amara and her gift to her chosen people, I give you my blessing, daughter. Live and prosper in this city and bring it to new life." Then she took Kelene into her arms and sealed her words with a proud embrace.

And so in the ancient city of Moy Tura, what was ended began again.

Winged Magic

To Mary Helene
Because every writer should have
a fan as wonderful as you.
Love, Mom

PROLOGUE

The meara raised his head, his shapely ears pricked forward, and he turned his nose into the night wind. His nostrils flared wide at the chilled smells on the breeze. The winter camp of the clan lay close by in its sheltering basin between two tall, easy hills. Its heavy odors of leather, smoke, dogs, and humans were clear in every detail to the sensitive nose of the stallion. The humans peacefully slept, except for the outriders who rode guard duty around the scattered herds and the large cluster of tents, pens, small outbuildings, and the chieftain's timbered hall that marked the treld, or winter camp. The outrider near the meara's herd seemed to be dozing, too, for his head drooped over his chest and his horse stood relaxed.

The big stallion snorted irritably, his sides rippling like molten bronze from a tension he could not identify. He had been chosen to be the meara, or king stallion, not only for his conformation, beauty, and speed, but also because of his fierce desire to protect his mares. Some unidentified sense in his mind whispered something was wrong. He could not understand what it was yet, and that disturbed him enough to set him trotting up a gentle slope and away from the treld to a spot from which he could survey the meadows.

Up on a rise, he lifted his head to the cold wind. Spring had come in name only, and the frost hung thick in the air. On the eastern horizon, a pale gold band of light heralded the coming day. The breeze stirred again, riffling the meara's heavy mane.

He breathed deeply of the biting cold and caught a taste of something new on the edge of the wind. There was a hint of softness, a faint wisp of warmth that hadn't been there before. The wind had swung around from the south, and its swirling tide bore the spicy scent of the Turic deserts far beyond the Altai River and the Ruad el Brashir grasslands. The stallion felt the coming change in the weather as surely as the cold that tingled in his nostrils.

But he realized the wind was not the object of his unease. Wind was a natural part of his existence; something else out there in the night was not. He inhaled again, and this time he caught another scent. It was faint and south of the treld, but it was unmistakable now: horses, many of them, and all strangers. A low sound rumbled deep in his chest.

His neck arched like a strung bow, he pranced along the edge of the meadow where his herd grazed to another hilltop south of the camp. He stopped there, for the scent was stronger and coming closer. He could smell other things, too: leather, metal, and the heavy scent of humans. Not clanspeople. These men smelled different, spicy like the desert.

The meara could hear them now. The strange horses' pace abruptly broke into a gallop, and their hoofbeats pounded closer. In the dawning light, the stallion saw the horses rise over a distant slope in a long line and charge down the incline toward the sleeping treld. The soft light gleamed on the blades of many swords and on the polished tips of spears.

Wheeling, the meara bellowed a warning to his mares. He galloped back toward his herd while the strange horses thundered over the frozen grass. Somewhere in the camp, a guard shouted. Then another. A horn blew a frantic high note. More cries rang in the chilled dawn air, and men began to appear among the tents.

All the horses in the meadows were alert now, their heads raised to watch the unknown horsemen approach. The newcomers gave a great shout as their mounts reached the first tents on the southern end of the camp. Suddenly there were screams, and the wind became tainted with the smell of blood. The horses grew frightened. The meara alone paid no heed. His only thought was for his herd. Like a tornado he roared across the pasture, bellowing and snapping at the mares to get them moving.

They needed little urging. Neighing with fear, they cantered ahead of their king, away from the blood and the panic and toward the open grassland. No outrider tried to stop them, for the guards were galloping frantically back toward the treld.

Another horn blast cut across the gathering din of shouts, screams, and the clash of weapons. The meara hesitated, stirred by a faint memory from his younger years when he had been trained for battle. The song of the chieftain's horn had once been an important signal to his mind. His steps slowed, and he turned once to look back. In the brightening day he saw the treld consumed in chaos. The strangers were everywhere, their swords rising and falling among the struggling clanspeople. Women and children scattered everywhere, and the people fought fiercely to defend their homes. Already smoke and flames rose from the chieftain's hall.

The stallion trumpeted a challenge. He waited for the chieftain's horn to call again, unaware that the horn lay broken in the bleeding hand of the dying chief. The wait became unbearable, the fear for his mares too great. The stallion turned away from the killing and galloped after the fleeing horses, driving them toward safety on the open sweeps of the Ramtharin Plains.

1

The wind blew from the south for three days. roaring with the first fanfare of spring across the frozen plains. It was a tossing, tumbling, tumultuous wind, a great warm ocean of air that tossed the trees, swirled the winter-cured grass, and swept in an irresistible current over the far-flung hills. Its warmth erased the last of the snow and filled the valleys with the rippling sheen of water.

In the winter trelds of the eleven clans of Valorian, the clanspeople shook out their rugs and bedding, aired their tents, and rejoiced in the change of the seasons. The clans' horses lifted their muzzles to the rushing wind and filled their nostrils with the warm, dry breath of the deserts far to the south. The mares waited patiently, knowing the Birthing was coming soon, but the youngsters kicked up their heels to race the wild wind.

In the brilliant blue sky above the high plateau of Moy Tura, one horse did more than lift her heels to the wind. A Hunnuli mare, as black as obsidian, raced to the abrupt edge of the highland and launched herself into the skirts of the wind. For a moment she tucked her front legs and dropped toward the rocky base several hundred feet below. Her rider, a young woman with hair as black as her Hunnuli's tail, gave a sharp cry of elation; then the horse spread her wings and rose high into the currents.

Wheeling, soaring, hearts high with release, horse and rider flew with the spring wind in the bright, clear light of the morning sun. They headed south on the tides of the air for several hours, until the mare was drenched in sweat and the rugged Himachal Mountains rose like a fortress wall to their right. Southward, where the wind continued to roar, the rolling grasslands faded away into the gray-blue horizon.

The young woman Kelene, realized it was time to return home, but for a while longer she stared south into the wind. To the south lay Dangari Treld and the Isin River, and farther still lay the winter treld of the Khulinin Clan, the home of her parents, Lord Athlone and Lady Gabria.

Kelene shrugged her shoulders somewhat irritably. She had never imagined three or four years ago that she would move so far from home and miss her parents so deeply. As a girl she had avoided her parents' love and concern, much as a stubborn child would refuse a sour draught. It wasn't until she married and moved two hundred leagues away to Moy Tura that she realized how much of her mother and father's time and wisdom she missed.

"It would be nice," she said, unaware that she had spoken her wistful thought aloud.

The Hunnuli mare, a horse descended from an ancient and revered breed, cocked her ears back. *What would be nice?* she asked in the silent, telepathic communication that linked all Hunnuli to their riders.

Kelene started out of her reverie and laughed at her own musings. "To see my parents again. It has been so long; I was just thinking how nice it would be to keep flying south and surprise them with a visit."

The mare, Demira, snorted. *That would be a surprise. Especially to Rafnir. He's expecting you to help with the wells this afternoon.*

The reminder brought a grimace to Kelene's tanned face. Unexpectedly the delight in the morning dwindled, and she muttered between her teeth, "I am getting just a little tired of that ruin."

As if the words had opened a dam, her frustrations welled up uncontrollably, like gall in her throat. Kelene shook her head fiercely, trying to deny them. What did she have to be angry about? She had the most wonderful horse in the world, a winged mare who could fly her to any place she chose to go. She had a husband who adored her, parents who loved her, and a rare and gifted talent to heal that made her one of the most respected women in the clans. The weather was glorious, spring was on the way, and this flying ride was everything she had ever dreamed. So why, Kelene asked herself, why do I feel so dissatisfied?

She pondered that question while Demira winged her way home on the northern track of the wind. Truth to tell, Kelene decided, her frustration hadn't been a sudden thing brought on by the thought of her parents or the reminder of unpleasant work. It had been building, layer by thin, brittle layer, for quite some time, and that bothered her.

After all, she knew frustration and setbacks all too well. As a girl she had been crippled and willful, afraid of her own power and too stubborn to ask for help. Then three years ago during the clans' annual summer gathering, an old evil escaped and a virulent plague struck the clanspeople. In a desperate attempt to help, Kelene, her brother Savaron, his friend Rafnir, and several other magic-wielders journeyed with the sorcerer, Sayyed, to the forbidden ruins of Moy Tura to look for old healing records that could help save the clans.

Through the midst of the monumental tragedy, Kelene grew to become a competent, caring woman. She learned to accept her strengths and weaknesses and to use her gift of empathy and magic to her utmost. With Rafnir's help, she gave wings to Demira; she befriended the Korg, the sorcerer in the shape of a

stone lion who guarded Moy Tura; and she learned to use the healing stones
that helped cure her dying people.

When the dead were buried and clan life began to return to some semblance
of normal, Kelene and Rafnir took her parents to Moy Tura and made a startling
proposal: they wanted to rebuild the city. Kelene still remembered the exhilarating excitement and anticipation of their hopes and dreams. It would be a
monumental task, but they had been empowered by their own optimism and
newfound maturity.

That had been three years ago.

Demira's light thought teasingly interrupted her reverie. *Do you mean that
ruin?*

Kelene glanced down and saw they had already reached the huge plateau
that bore the ruins of Moy Tura on its flat crown. "Don't land yet," she said.

Obligingly the mare stretched out her wings to catch a rising draft and lazily
circled the city.

Kelene sighed. From this bird's-eye view there certainly wasn't much to see.
There wasn't much to see from the ground, either, even after three years of unending work. Moy Tura had proved to be a tougher problem to crack than either
she or Rafnir had imagined.

At one time Moy Tura had been the jewel of the clans' realm and the center
of wisdom and learning. Magic-wielders, those people descended from the
hero-warrior Valorian and born with the talent to wield the unseen, gods-given
power of magic, built the city.

But over the years the clans grew fearful and suspicious of the sorcerers'
powers. In one bloody, violent summer, the clanspeople turned against their
magic-wielders and slaughtered every one they could find. A few fled into hiding, but Moy Tura was razed to the ground and magic was forbidden on pain of
death. So it had remained for over two hundred years.

Until Mother came along, Kelene thought with a sudden grin. She still wasn't
certain how Lady Gabria had done it. Gabria had faced incredible odds, including the massacre of her entire clan and the opposition of a clan chieftain turned
sorcerer, and somehow returned magic to clan acceptance. It was her determination, strength, and courage that made it possible for Kelene to be where she was.

"But where am I now?" Kelene asked the sky above.

I believe you are with me above Moy Tura, Demira answered for the cloudless sky. When Kelene didn't respond to her teasing humor, the mare cast a
quick look back. *You are certainly pensive today.*

Kelene's hands tightened on the leather flying harness Rafnir had made for
her. It was the only tack the Hunnuli wore. "This morning was fun, Demira. I
needed it."

But it has not helped.

Kelene snorted in disgust. "Moy Tura is still nothing more than a heap of rubble. For every building we clear out or rebuild, there are a hundred more to do. We can't get enough help. No one wants to leave their comfortable clan to come live in some cold, drafty, haunted pile of rock and, since the plague, there aren't even enough magic-wielders to go around the clans, let alone resettle Moy Tura. The clan chiefs won't support us. And where in Amara's name are the city wells? The Korg told us there were cisterns, but he couldn't remember where. Why can't we find them?"

Kelene stumbled to a startled silence. She hadn't meant to explode with such an outburst; it just came pouring out, probably loosened by the first taste of spring after a long winter's drudgery.

Actually you have accomplished a great deal, Demira reminded her in a cool, matter-of-fact manner. *You learned the craft of healing, you are an accomplished sorceress, and you are the only clanswoman to do an inside loop.*

Kelene laughed at that. The "inside loop" was a trick she and Demira had accomplished—once. It had scared the wits out of them and sent Rafnir into fits of rage at their foolhardiness. He had promptly constructed the flying harness to hold Kelene on Demira's back and forbade them from flying without it. Kelene had to admit it proved very useful.

"Looking at it that way, you're right," Kelene conceded.

But Demira knew her rider's every nuance of speech and character. *It is not just the city that bothers you, is it? You have been there only three years. You knew it would not grow overnight.*

"No," said Kelene, her voice flat. "It is not just the city." She couldn't go on. There was one fear left she could not put voice to, one emptiness inside her that ached with a cold dread and made every other setback more difficult to face. After all, what good was building a home if there were no children to fill it? She had not said anything to Rafnir about her inability to bear babes, nor he to her, but she felt his disappointment and concern as poignantly as her own.

Perhaps that was why she was struck with such a desire to see Lady Gabria again. Her mother would provide a loving, sympathetic ear for her worries, and maybe she could suggest something Kelene had overlooked. Unfortunately, there was too much to do at Moy Tura to even consider a journey to Khulinin Treld.

The young woman sighed again. The clans would be gathering at the Tir Samod in three months' time. Maybe Rafnir would agree to go this year. They needed various tools, herbs, and foodstuffs even magic couldn't supply, and they could use the time to talk to other magic-wielders. Surely there were a few who would be willing to give Moy Tura a helping hand. Kelene could then talk to her mother and share her anxieties. Until that time she would have to be patient. As Demira pointed out, neither cities nor babies grew overnight.

Kelene was about to ask Demira to land when the Hunnuli turned her head to the south. *Someone is coming,* she announced.

Kelene's spirits rose a little. It was always pleasant to see someone new. "Who?" she asked.

In reply the mare veered away from the ruins and followed the pale track of the old southern road where it cut across the top of the plateau. At the edge of the highland the trail dropped over to wend its way down to the lower grasslands. *He is there, on the lower trail. Coming fast.*

Kelene saw him then, a rider on a black horse cantering up to the foot of the plateau. Her heart caught a beat when she recognized the color of his clan cloak. Every clan had its own individual color to identify its members, a color that was always dyed into the comfortable, versatile cloaks the people wore. This rider, who was obviously heading for Moy Tura, wore the golden yellow of the Khulinin.

At Kelene's request, Demira landed at the top of the trail and waited for the rider to climb the plateau. Kelene tried not to fidget, yet she couldn't help straining to look over the edge. Her parents did not send messengers often, only when the news was important. She mused, too, over the coincidence of her wish to visit her parents and the arrival of their messenger on the same morning.

The rider came at last, his Hunnuli winded and sweating. He raised his head at Kelene's greeting and grinned a very tired and dusty reply. The stallion climbed the last few feet of the incline, topped the trail, and came to a grateful halt beside Demira.

"Kelene! I thought I saw a big black vulture hovering over that dead ruin." The rider's weathered face crinkled around his green eyes.

Demira snorted indignantly.

"Veneg," Kelene addressed the Hunnuli stallion. "How do you put up with him?"

He is rude only to people he likes. Everyone else he ignores, Veneg replied with tired good nature.

The young woman laughed. "Gaalney, he knows you too well." She paused, taking in for the first time the man's exhausted pallor, his dirty clothes, and the nearly empty travel packs on the Hunnuli's back. These two had traveled long and hard. "Are my—" she began to say.

Gaalney rushed to assure her. "Lord Athlone and Lady Gabria are fine and send their greetings. My message is ill news, but it is for Sayyed and Rafnir, as well as for you."

"Then save your words and tell them once before us all." She gestured north toward the city. "Come. There is food and drink in Moy Tura and a proper welcome."

Side by side the two Hunnuli cantered slowly along the old road to the city. The pace gave Kelene a little time to study the man beside her. Gaalney was a distant cousin to her father. He was a young man, rash at times, but with a dauntless courage that helped him excel in his studies of magic. He had stiff yellow hair cut much shorter than she remembered, full green eyes, and a thin mouth that always seemed to lift in a quirk of a smile. She also noticed he had a newly healed wound on his neck just below his ear.

They rode in silence until they reached the tumbled walls of the once-great city of the sorcerers. As they approached, Kelene glanced at Gaalney to see what his reaction would be. She was used to the massive entrance by now, but newcomers were always impressed. Gaalney was no exception.

The horses slowed to a walk, and Gaalney ran his eyes over the repaired stonework, whistling in appreciation. Kelene smiled. She, Rafnir, and the Korg had worked very hard to restore the old gateway. Although it was one of four entrances into Moy Tura, it was the only one they had repaired so far. Most visitors came on the southern road to this gate, and Rafnir wanted to give them a good first impression. The gate was a huge, arched opening between two powerful towers. Both towers had been rebuilt down to the decorative stonework around the defensive crenellations. The road was repaired and repaved with new stone slabs, the archway was cleaned of several hundred years' worth of grime and old debris, and a golden banner hung above the arch.

The best touch of all, to Kelene's mind, was the restoration of the two stone lions that had once guarded the gateway. Crouched in perpetual attention, the beasts stood to either side of the road and fixed their red-jeweled eyes on travelers who approached the city.

Gaalney looked at both lions and shook his head. "They're magnificent." The horses walked together through the gateway, and the young man waved a hand at the stone arch. "Is this any indication of your progress in the city?"

Kelene reached out to run her fingers along the cold, smooth stone. The old wards in the gates were still intact—they had saved her life once—and she felt their ancient potency tingle on the tips of her fingers. She drew strength from their presence, a power that had endured for generations, and she drove her own frustrations and worries back into the dark recesses of her mind from where the wind had shaken them loose. Smiling now, she rode Demira out from the shadow of the stone into the sunlight and pointed to the city walls that still lay in tumbled ruins.

"Well, no," she acknowledged. "That is more like the rest of the city. We've had some problems the past few years. Clanspeople have lost the art of working stone."

She did not elaborate further, allowing Gaalney to see for himself. The outlying areas of the city along the walls were as yet untouched. The buildings lay in crumbled heaps where the attackers and the elements had left them. In this part of Moy Tura only the main road was cleared and repaired. The rest of the wind-haunted ruins remained as they had since the Purge.

Gaalney was quiet as they rode. His eyes tracked back and forth over the devastation and slowly filled with wonder. "How can you live here?" he questioned. "All this would depress me too much."

His choice of words startled Kelene, and she freely admitted, "It depresses me, too, sometimes."

"Then why do you stay here? Why don't you come home?" Gaalney asked, voicing a question Kelene was certain a number of people had wondered.

Before she would form a sensible reply—if there was one—Gaalney's face transformed into a picture of delight. They had been riding along one of the major roads that led to the inner heart of the city where the primary public buildings had once stood. One such edifice sat to the left of the road in grand, shining eminence among the destroyed bones of its neighbors.

It was a temple, built three hundred years before to the glory of the holy quartet of gods worshiped by the clans. The Korg, before he died, had restored the temple as his gift to Kelene and Rafnir. With the last of his strength, before his worn and aged body had faded, he used his knowledge and magic to return the large temple to its previous magnificence. Now, shining in the sun, the white marble building sat as a fitting monument to the Korg and his wish to protect and restore his city. When he died, Kelene and Rafnir buried him at the foot of the large altar that graced the central sanctuary.

"And I thought all you had fixed was the gate," Gaalney laughed, obviously impressed.

Kelene, observing her cousin's delight, looked at the temple anew for the first time in a long while. She had been so used to working on other ruined buildings, she had momentarily forgotten how lovely this one was. She nodded and thought of her friend, the Korg. Two years after his death she still missed him deeply. "That is the Temple of the Gods," she explained. "The Korg hoped they would bless our efforts here in the city if we restored their sacred temple."

"And have they?"

"More or less," Kelene replied dryly. "Come on, Rafnir should be back at our house by now."

Gaalney made no reply but followed Kelene and Demira along the road, past a stone wall and several piles of rubble, to the wide central square of the city. The huge open space in the very heart of Moy Tura had once been a market and gathering place for the entire community. Its broad expanse was paved with slabs of granite, and at its center, where the four main roads of the city converged, a tall, black obelisk towered nearly twenty feet into the air. Atop the obelisk hung a golden rayed sun, the emblem of the goddess Amara.

Kelene watched the Khulinin sorcerer gaze around at the city of his ancestors, and she saw the subtle shift of expression on his face, from awe to anger. It was a change she had witnessed on many magic-wielders' faces. It would have been very difficult not to feel anything. The rage that had massacred an entire population still lay mutely evident in the shattered wreckage of the old square, where skeletons of walls and hollow foundations lined the open space.

The grand Sorcerers' Hall showed the worst of the attackers' fury, for its desecrated remains still had unmistakable signs of heat fractures and scorch marks from a large fire. It was known from the Korg's tale that the attackers had thrown hundreds of bodies into the burning Sorcerers' Hall—and Kelene believed it. Two hundred years had not been enough time in this semi-arid land to totally erase the bits of ash, remnants of bone, and the black stains of soot that still lay in the cracks and crevices of the ruined stones of the hall. She and Rafnir had made no attempt to restore any part of the old foundation.

But if the square had been the scene of tragedy, it was also the center of returning life—little to be sure, but life nonetheless. Turning away from the dead hall, Kelene pointed Gaalney toward a side street where he could see several restored buildings just off the square. At the corner of the street and facing the square was a house of some dignity, completely rebuilt, and gleaming in the sun like a pearl among dross. It was the house Kelene and Rafnir had chosen when they moved to Moy Tura. Broad, open, and airy, it was a comfortable abode for people used to living in cramped, movable tents. It had taken Kelene some time to adjust to the differences in housekeeping, but now she loved the house and called it home.

Gaalney's tired face lightened when he saw it.

"There is a guest hall down that street," Kelene told him. "You may leave your things there and clean up if you wish while I find Sayyed. Rafnir should be at our house for his midday meal. Join us there. If Veneg would like to rest, there is a stable by the guest hall or he can join the other horses out in the fields."

Gaalney's mouth lifted in his quirky smile. "Guest hall, huh? How many people do you have here?"

"Not enough," Kelene replied honestly. "We built the guest hall for the people who visit but don't want to stay. At the moment we have three historians from the Five Kingdoms, an architect from Pra Desh who is helping us learn to build, two bards, two healers, several exiles who are trying to earn their way back into the clans, and a priest from Clan Dangari. The rest of our residents, the permanent ones, equal all of eighteen."

Gaalney grimaced at the cold numbers. Even he as a newcomer could see eighteen permanent residents—no matter how many guests they might have—were not nearly enough to make a viable colony. He spoke his thanks for her information and turned his stallion down the road to the guest hall.

Demira trotted across the square toward the Sorcerers' Hall. Kelene did not need to tell her where to find Rafnir's father. Sayyed had been going to the same area almost every free moment since he'd arrived nearly two years ago. The mare bypassed the old foundations, walked up the main road, and turned left into the ruinous streets west of the hall.

Before the Purge the area had been one of the finer residential neighborhoods in the city. While a few of the houses had been destroyed in the fire that consumed the hall, many other homes had simply been plundered and left to rot.

One day, out of curiosity, Sayyed decided to see what he could find in the crumbled ruins. Beneath the decay and rubble, he was fascinated to discover a wealth of artifacts from the golden age of Moy Tura, and most important of all, a few precious relics and scrolls left by the magic-wielders themselves. He had been excavating ever since.

While some visitors thought Sayyed's work was rather frivolous compared to the rebuilding and everyday chores, Rafnir and Kelene found his self-appointed task invaluable. Useful items were kept by the colony, the magic relics were sent to Gabria, and the jewelry and rare items unearthed in good condition were readily traded by numerous clanspeople interested in their past or sold to merchants from Pra Desh who detoured from the main caravan routes to pay a visit to the city that had once been forbidden. The coin Sayyed raised went in turn to buy livestock and needed supplies for the tiny colony.

Magic-wielders though some of them were, the inhabitants of Moy Tura could not use magic to provide everything they needed. Living creatures like wool-bearing sheep or work horses could not be created, and unfamiliar things, such as carpentry tools or masonry equipment, could not be duplicated until they had some in hand to study. They also knew they could not function effectively if they used magic all the time. The gift of the gods was infinite, but mortals' ability to use it was not. Wielding magic was exhausting and sometimes dangerous, and the sorcerers had long ago learned that physical labor combined with a judicious use of magic was the safest and most effective way to get a job done.

That morning Sayyed was relying on simple muscle to accomplish his task. Kelene and Demira found him in the roofless room of a once-luxurious house. Sunlight poured into the ruin, washing the fallen rock and rotting floor timbers with a warm, golden light. The young woman slid off her horse and poked her head through a large gap in the wall. She saw Sayyed carefully lifting chunks of stone one by one from a pile by the far wall. Hot from his labor, Sayyed had removed his tunic and wore only his leggings and leather boots.

Kelene grinned at his bronzed back. Still slim, erect and vigorous at forty-four, Sayyed was handsome enough to attract most women. Just below middle height, he had a short, neatly trimmed beard and sharp, piercing black eyes.

Once his face and eyes had been filled with gaiety and mischievous good humor, until the plague struck the clans and claimed his beloved wife, Tam. Unable to bear the memories and sadness of her passing, he had left the Khulinin to live with his son and Kelene in Moy Tura. He had brought only Tam's animals, his Hunnuli, and a fierce desire to bury his grief in hard manual labor. He had found plenty to do in the ruins of the city.

Several dogs and one white cat lounged around Sayyed, patiently waiting for his attention. The dogs wagged their tails in greeting to Kelene; the white cat lifted her head with its jewel-green eyes and meowed softly.

The sorcerer turned his head to welcome Kelene. They had grown close since she saved his life three years before, but Kelene sensed a deep, aching loneliness in her father-in-law that nothing yet had filled.

"Kelene, you're back!" he exclaimed in a voice rich with excitement. "Come see what I found."

The woman held on to her message a moment more and hurried to see what he had discovered.

"There's an old chest under this pile," Sayyed explained. "A good one from what I can see. It's still intact." He smiled, a flash of white beneath the dust and the black beard. The value of the objects did not interest him. He enjoyed uncovering the mysteries, learning the secrets of the past, discovering new items that might be useful. He had no idea what was in the chest he'd found, and he could not wait to find out.

Kelene hated to disappoint him, but the exhaustion and urgency in Gaalney's demeanor forced her to say, "I'm sorry, but Gaalney is here with a message from Father to you and Rafnir."

Sayyed slowly straightened, the anticipation fading from his face. Without further question, he reached for his tunic. The dogs jumped to their feet. He scooped up the cat, then quickly followed Kelene and Demira back to the square, the dogs close at his heels.

When they reached the house, they found Gaalney, looking somewhat cleaner, and Rafnir standing in the garden behind the house. Nothing was blooming in the garden this early in the season, but on this warm, windy day, it was a pleasant place to sit, eat, and talk.

Rafnir, Kelene was pleased to see, had already provided bread, cheese, a bowl of fruit, and a pitcher of ale. Gaalney helped himself with a gusto.

Abruptly the young man broke off his meal and stared in astonishment at Kelene. "You're not limping!" he sputtered through a mouthful of bread.

"Of course, I'm not—" Kelene broke off and beamed. She hadn't seen Gaalney in three years. How could he have known what she had done to her crippled foot? "I used a spell similar to the one Lord Medb used and straightened the bones in my ankle and foot. It's not perfect, but I can walk now without pain."

Gaalney's surprise turned to delight, and he made her walk back and forth so he could admire her graceful stride. "Why didn't someone try that spell sooner?" he asked.

"No one had the skill to work on such complex bones until we found the healers' records here in the city, and Mother didn't want to risk experimenting on her own daughter." She stopped by Rafnir's side to give him a quick hug. His arm went around her waist and stayed there, strong and comforting against her back. "Rafnir gave me the strength to try," she went on, and her tone turned teasing. "He needed someone whole to climb those high towers since he's afraid of heights."

Rafnir chuckled and handed Kelene a mug of ale. The four made themselves comfortable on low seats, and while the others ate their meal, Gaalney gave them his message.

"How much news from the south have you heard up here?" he asked first.

"Little enough," Rafnir replied. "Most of our visitors have either been here for a while or are from northern clans."

"Then you haven't heard the rumors of war with the Turics."

Sayyed straightened in his seat, his dark eyes sharp as dagger points. He was a half-breed, raised by his Turic father until the father rejected him because of his inborn talent to wield magic. Although he had lived with his mother's clans for over twenty-five years, he was still Turic in the far corners of his heart.

"The trouble started along the border last autumn," Gaalney went on. He leaned forward to rest his elbows on his knees, and all humor fled his face. "It was mild at first—a few horses stolen, travelers robbed—nothing out of the ordinary and no one was hurt. We thought it was just a few brigands, but the raids did not stop in the winter as they usually do. They got worse and more deadly. Wylfling Treld, Ferganan Treld, and Shadedron Treld have all suffered serious depredations from a large and well-organized band. Just last month a caravan returning north over the Altai River was ambushed. Everyone in the party was killed. The raiders have even reached as far north as the Khulinin grazing lands."

Kelene stirred. "Is that how you were wounded?"

Gaalney automatically touched the new scar on his neck. "I was in a group of outriders taking a yearling herd to the Blue Mountain meadows when we were attacked. An arrow pierced my neck. Veneg saved me, but we could not save the other men or the horses." His eyes burned darkly as he said, "Lord Athlone is furious. He has called for an emergency gathering of the council and has petitioned the Shar-Ja to meet with the clan leaders at Council Rock to settle these border clashes before emotions get out of control."

"Have the other chiefs been called?" Rafnir asked.

"I have already been to the Bahedin, Amnok, and Geldring. They are coming. You are my last stop."

Rafnir and Sayyed exchanged glances. The Shar-Ja was the ruling head of the Turic tribes. If Athlone felt it necessary to meet with him, the situation in the south was grim.

"Has the Shar-Ja agreed?" Sayyed inquired. The present Shar-Ja had held the throne of the Turics for nineteen years, and in all that time there had never been any serious trouble between tribe and clan. Sayyed found it rather odd that trouble was brewing now.

Gaalney answered, "We had not yet received a message when I left, but the Shar-Ja has always been steadfast in his friendship to the clans. The chiefs think he will come. That is why Lord Athlone requests that you three join him for the council. He wants your expertise and, as he said, 'the presence of three more powerful magic-wielders won't hurt.'"

Kelene remained silent and pondered the emotions that flew through her mind on the wind of Gaalney's news. Most of all she felt outrage at the Turics' greed and audacity. Peace with the Turics had always been tricky, but it was generations old and to risk it for the sake of livestock and plunder was folly. What was the point? The Turics were a numerous and thriving people. Their realm stretched for hundreds of leagues, from the Absarotan Mountains across the flat Ruad el Brashir grasslands to the Sea of Tannis, from the Altai River to the Kumkara Desert far, far to the south. The clans had very little the Turics did not have. So why would the tribesmen want to antagonize their neighbors? Were the raiders from a few disgruntled tribes along the border, or was the entire Turic nation preparing to sweep over the Ramtharin Plains?

Kelene's eyes turned to Rafnir. Even with a husband who was part Turic and a father-in-law who was half Turic, she knew very little about the southern tribes. The emotions on Rafnir's open face were clear enough though. There was still too much to do here: the cisterns had to be found, the few broodmares they had would foal soon, the herb and vegetable gardens Kelene had planned needed to be tilled and planted, and the new forge was about to be put into operation. How could all this be left for a journey that would take at least several months?

Kelene felt his frustration, too, but deep within her heart, in a small space reserved for herself, she found a pleased relief that she might be able to see Lady Gabria after all. Then her thoughts paused, and she asked Gaalney, "Why does Father want me to come? I do not speak Turic as Rafnir or Sayyed do, nor am I really needed at a council."

"Your reputation as a sorceress healer has spread beyond our borders," Gaalney replied. "It is rumored the Shar-Ja is ill from an unknown malady. His ambassador, who received our message, hinted the Shar-Ja might come to a meeting if you are there to examine him."

Kelene's dark eyes widened. "The tribes do not have skilled healers of their own?"

"Dozens of them," Sayyed said, suddenly rising to his feet. "But none like you." He offered his hand to her. "Will you come with me? You and Rafnir? Come see my father's people."

She gazed up at him and recognized a flicker of bright interest in his face that she had not seen in years. Rafnir must have noticed it too, for he stood and clasped his father's arm.

Kelene had no premonition of the coming events, no vision of disaster or pricking of the thumbs to warn her. She felt only the need to serve and the anticipation of a journey to the Khulinin. She took Sayyed's proffered hand and said to Gaalney, "We will come."

2

It took two days for Kelene, Rafnir and Sayyed to pack and settle their immediate duties in Moy Tura. The residents and some of the guests were dismayed by their departure and the reasons for it, but the three vowed to return as soon as possible and left leadership of the tiny community in the capable hands of Bann, a middle-aged widower, sorcerer, and the builder of the new forge. Sayyed also very reluctantly left his dogs and Tam's cat in the care of Bann's delighted son.

With Gaalney accompanying them, the three magic-wielders mounted their Hunnuli in the dim light of a chilly dawn and left Moy Tura for the journey to the Goldrine River, where they would meet Lord Athlone and the Khulinin delegation.

The warm, tumbling wind from the south had ended the day before, leaving the way open for a change of weather. The air had turned damp and cool; the great arch of open sky became a leaden ceiling of low-hanging clouds. There was no rain yet, but the horses smelled it, heavy and close in the morning air.

The riders pulled their golden cloaks close as the Hunnuli cantered across the plateau toward the road that led down to the plains. At the edge of the tableland, the other three horses slowed for the descent on the steep trail, while Demira sped forward alone. Like a huge black eagle, she launched herself over the sharp edge and soared into the air. She could not canter hour after hour with the endless ease of the other Hunnuli, for her lighter legs and body and her large wings made long runs too difficult. Yet, borne on the air's invisible hand, she sped far swifter than any land creature over the rolling plains.

Casually she wheeled overhead, waiting for the others to reach the lower trail. When the three stallions broke into a gallop on level ground, the winged mare turned south and led the way with the north wind at her tail.

* * *

They reached the Goldrine River three days later, after an uneventful though wet journey. Under a clearing sky, twilight deepened into night and a full moon sailed into the east.

Although the moon was full, Demira did not like to fly at night, so as soon as she spotted the fires of the Khulinin camp on the southern bank of the river and located a passable ford nearby, she joined the others on the ground.

Warm weather had begun melting snows in the Darkhorn Mountains, but the high waters and the swelling rains of late spring had not yet affected the Goldrine. Its waters ran shallow in the ford, making it easy for the four Hunnuli to cross. They trotted up the southern bank, swung left, and broke into a trot along the grassy, rolling valley toward the horseshoe-shaped bend in the river where the Khulinin camped.

They had not gone far when all four Hunnuli perked their ears forward. Soon, everyone could see the glow of the cooking fires and the solid shapes of the clan's small traveling tents.

Kelene tensed and leaned forward. Even from this distance out in the night, she could see the camp was in an uproar. Men ran back and forth, dark shapes darting through the dancing firelight. Horses neighed, and the harsh sound of raised voices mingled with the quieter noises of the river and the night insects.

Kelene heard a pounding of heavy hooves, and two more Hunnuli galloped out of the darkness to meet them. Nara, Gabria's beloved mare, and Eurus, Lord Athlone's proud stallion, neighed a strident call of both welcome and urgency then turned on their heels and escorted the newcomers rapidly into camp. Activity, light, and noise surrounded them as they rode in among the tents.

Kelene noticed the unexpected haste was not confused chaos, but alarmed organization as people moved rapidly to tear down the camp. Tents collapsed around her, packhorses were loaded, and supplies were repacked as quickly as possible.

In the midst of the frantic labor stood Lord Athlone, rigid with fury, a rolled scroll in one hand, a tattered scrap of fabric in the other. His dark hair was grizzled now, and deep lines etched his weathered face. Tall, strong of body and mind, he wore the authority of a clan chieftain with ease and passionate ability. Although forty-nine years of life and a close brush with the plague had slowed his endurance and stiffened his joints, his strength of command was unabated, and his eyes still studied the world like those of a vigilant hawk. He spotted Kelene and her companions, and his anger receded before his pleasure when he came to greet them.

Sayyed dismounted and, as senior clansman, saluted the chieftain. "Hail, Lord Athlone, we of Moy Tura answer your summons."

A smile broke over Athlone's face, warming his eyes from stone to brown earth. He returned the salutation and embraced his friend, his son-in-law, and last of all his only surviving daughter. Kelene returned his hug fiercely and let it linger for a moment longer before she let him go.

Like most magic-wielders, Kelene had certain abilities that were more developed than others. Her talent for healing came not only from a natural desire to ease pain, but also from a unique ability to sense other people's feelings. While she could not understand their thoughts, she could feel their emotions through the touch of her skin on theirs. During the past few years she had learned to control this gift until she could use it at will.

In the grip of her father's embrace, she opened her mind to his emotions for just one beat of her heart and felt his fury and sense of injustice. To her silent relief, there was no personal grief or the stunned shock of loss. "What happened, Father?" she asked worriedly.

Athlone stepped back, his hands clenched around the objects he carried. He lifted the scrap of fabric in one fist. In the firelight, they could all see the cloth was a piece of a light blue cloak splattered with darker smears and spots.

"This was brought to me just before you arrived," he said, darkly smoldering. "A large force of Turics attacked Ferganan Treld five days ago. Lord Tirek was killed, along with twenty-eight of his hearthguard and warriors, when he tried to protect the fleeing women and children. The raiders devastated the treld."

Kelene, Rafnir, Sayyed, and Gaalney stood shocked by the ghastly news. The Hunnuli gathered around them, still and silent. Ferganan Treld, the winter camp of Clan Ferganan, sat in the fertile valley of the Altai River just north of the Turic realm. Of all the eleven clans, the Ferganan had the most amiable relationship with their Turic neighbors—in part because the Raid tribe that lived in the vicinity was ruled by Sayyed's father, the man who had married a Ferganan woman. That the raiders had turned so viciously on Lord Tirek's people was a betrayal of the worst sort to the generous, proud clanspeople. The rage on Lord Athlone's face was mirrored in the expressions of every chieftain in the clans when they heard the news.

At that moment Gabria and Savaron hurried through the fevered activity to the small group by the fire. The sorceress's face was troubled, yet she welcomed her friends with genuine delight and gathered her daughter close.

Kelene smiled, silently pleased to see how little her mother had changed the past few years. Gabria was still lithe and straight-backed, with clear green eyes and the hands of a young woman. True, the lines were etched deeper on her forehead and around her mouth, and her braided hair was more gray than gold, but what did that matter when the spirit was still resilient and the heart still sang with gratitude to Amara, the mother of all and the source of all bounty?

"What about me?" chided Kelene's brother.

Savaron, wearing the gold belt of a wer-tain, hugged her too. Tall, muscular, dark-haired and, to Kelene's eyes, handsome, her older brother had been leader of the clan warriors, the werod, since the plague when Wer-tain Rajanir had died. Savaron was married now, with two little boys and a wife he adored. Kelene marveled how much he had come to resemble their father as the years passed.

He held her out at arm's length. "Mother told me you had healed your ankle, but she failed to mention how beautiful you've become." He let her go and playfully punched his friend, Rafnir, on the arm. "You two had better quit play-ing in your ruins and get to work on a family."

Kelene bit her lower lip to stifle a retort that she knew in her heart to be un-necessary. Savaron was always teasing her, but he would never deliberately hurt her if he knew the extent of her concern.

She was relieved when the levity in Savaron's eyes died, and he returned to the subject at hand. "The riders are ready to return to the treld," he informed the chieftain. "We leave at your command." He spoke reluctantly, plainly showing he was not happy with the decision.

Lord Athlone nodded once and turned to Sayyed. "You gave up your place in my hearthguard, but will you accept it again for as long as I need you? After this raid, I have decided to send Savaron back to reinforce the guard on the clan and the treld. I still need a strong arm by my side and a translator I can trust. We heard this morning the Shar-Ja has accepted our invitation to meet at Council Rock in ten days' time."

Sayyed's eyes glittered. His grim expression was yellow-lined in the fire-light. Half Turic though he was, the Ferganan were his mother's kin, and many of them had become his friends over the years. His hand tightened on the hilt of his curved tulwar, a prize won during his rites of manhood in the Turic tribes. He bowed before the Khulinin. "I accept with honor," he said.

Rafnir, too, grasped his sword. "Lord Athlone, I have never taken the rites of the hearthguard, but I ask to be allowed to join your guard while you attend the council."

His request pleased the chieftain. "Granted," said Athlone with the hint of a smile. "And you may start tonight. We ride to meet the Dangari. Lord Bendinor passed us yesterday, but he is waiting for us so we may ride to Council Rock to-gether. I intend to be there before the Turics, so they cannot have any nasty sur-prises ready for us."

The last of the tents had been packed already, and the warriors doused and buried the fires. In moments Savaron and half the troop of mounted warriors— eighty in all—cantered west toward Khulinin Treld, their pack animals and sup-plies close behind. In the darkness the magic-wielders mounted their Hunnuli and joined the remaining guard of clan warriors. At Athlone's quiet command, the Khulinin delegation set out, riding south and east to meet the contingent from Clan Dangari.

The Dangari chief, a middle-aged warrior of courage and sense, had sent the messenger bearing the news of the Ferganan attack to Lord Athlone. He had also suggested they travel together to Council Rock. Athlone readily agreed under the premise that no Turic, no matter how greedy, well armed, and vicious, would dare attack a large troop of clan warriors containing several trained magic-wielders. The addition of Lord Bendinor's men gave him the excuse he needed to send Savaron and half the werod guard back to the clan despite his son's arguments. The safety of the Khulinin was more important than a show of strength at the peace council.

The Khulinin met Lord Bendinor near dawn after a long, chilly, damp night. He led them to his temporary camp, fed them well, provided a tent for Lord Athlone, Gabria, and Kelene, and patiently waited while the Khulinin rested and cared for their horses.

Bendinor was a quiet man, capable, efficient, and well liked by his people. He had little of the charm and charisma of his predecessor, Lord Koshyn, but he and Lord Athlone respected each other, and even if friendship had not come yet, they had a useful working relationship. With unspoken consent, they had their clans ready to leave shortly after noon. Beneath their blue and gold banners, the two chiefs led their warriors south toward the Altai River and the meeting with the Turic tribes.

* * *

Council Rock had earned its name nearly two hundred years before when the chieftains of the Dark Horse Clans and the tribesmen of the Turics met to establish the Altai River as the formal boundary between the two nations. Since then it had been used occasionally as a meeting place between clan and tribe to solve minor disputes, trade negotiations, and border clashes.

Although its name was simple and obvious to the casual observer, the landmark was not so much a rock as an island in the middle of the river. Clanspeople who were curious about such things sometimes wondered where such an enormous chunk of rock had come from, but no one really knew. It had always been there, as far as anyone remembered, a tall, rounded boulder surrounded by water. Over the years a gravel bar had formed around the base of the rock. The gravel had caught more debris through seasons of flood and drought until a long, low island built up like a skirt around the massive rock. Local tales called it Altari's Throne, after the beautiful water maiden who was believed to be the soul and spirit of the stately Altai River.

The maiden's namesake, the Altai, was an old watercourse, running deep and staid through gently rolling hills. Over time it had formed a wide, fertile valley where groves of trees, lush meadows, and broad sweeps of marsh grew like a wide green ribbon across an otherwise semi-arid plain.

While early spring barely touched the northern grasslands. it spread its warm breath over the Altai valley. A pale green glowed along the riverbanks and meadows where the grass was sprouting in thick layers; the damp curves of abandoned river bends sparkled with the delicate whites, pinks, and blues of early wildflowers; and a haze of misty green buds spread through the scattered groves of trees.

Kelene drew a pleased breath when she saw the tranquil river from the air.

She had not been this far south and had never learned to appreciate the beauty or the importance of the Altai valley. She turned her gaze farther south to the Turic lands that rolled away beyond her view. The landscape appeared much like the plains on the northern side of the river, but farther away the green faded to tan and eventually vanished in a brown-gold haze.

The sorceress and her Hunnuli completed their duty as scouts, and when Kelene reported to her father that the valley and the Council Rock were empty, Lord Athlone said with satisfaction, "We're first."

He and Lord Bendinor established their camp on a level rise across from the island, far enough removed to be out of arrow range from the ford, yet close enough that they could easily survey the island as well as the opposite bank. Guard posts were organized, and outriders were sent on patrols to watch for the approach of the other chieftains.

With Sayyed and Rafnir's help, and under the fascinated gaze of the Dangari men, Lord Athlone drew on the magic power steeped in the world around him and enlarged a traveling tent to resemble the large council tent that was used every year at the summer clan gathering. Willing hands raised the huge shelter on Council Rock and made it comfortable in preparation for the Shar-Ja's arrival.

Two days after their arrival at Council Rock, the Khulinin and Dangari welcomed three more clans. Lord Jamas brought a small contingent of brown-cloaked Wylfling. His treld to the west was the other clan whose lands bordered the Altai River. He had left most of his werod with the clan and brought only his hearthguard and an unabated anger at the depredations suffered by his clan during the winter. Lord Wendern of Clan Shadedron arrived next with a young, shattered-looking man barely out of boyhood, who looked as if he had aged years in the past few days. One Ferganan warrior stood with him.

Carrying his light blue cloak and weaponless, the young man bowed before the chieftains. "Hail, lords," he saluted them. Bruises discolored his face, and his arm hung in a crude sling. But the surface pain of his wounds was nothing to the grief that burned in his face. "I am Peoren, youngest son of Lord Tirek. I come to represent the Ferganan and to demand the weir-geld that is due us."

Lord Bendinor looked dubiously at Peoren and his lone guard. The boy looked barely sixteen or seventeen. "Are there no others to come with you, lad?"

Peoren drew himself up. "My father, an older brother, and the wer-tain were killed. Almost all of the hearthguard are either dead or wounded, my lord, except for Dos here, who vowed to attend me. I am the only male left in my family, and I felt it was my duty to attend this council even though I have not been accepted as chief. I decided the rest of the warriors were needed to guard the clan and help the women care for the wounded."

Kelene, who had been studying Peoren's bandaged arm, asked worriedly, "Where is your healer? He should have seen to your arm before you left camp."

The young man winced. "He was killed in the first surprise attack. We've been doing what we can."

"Are you certain you want to do this?" asked Athlone.

Lord Wendern, his long features masked with concern, stood beside Peoren. "I saw what was left of the treld. Peoren has done a man's job of organizing the clan and caring for his people. I feel he's earned the right to stand in his father's stead."

The sorcerer lord accepted his word, and the other chiefs made no further comment. Nor did the remaining chiefs when they joined the council. They came by twos and threes, traveling together with their mounted guards for convenience and safety. Another sorcerer, Kelene and Rafnir's friend Morad, came riding in with Lord Hendric of Clan Geldring.

Last to arrive were clans Amnok and Murjik, the two northernmost clans. The chiefs and their men came late in the night, weary from days of relentless travel to reach the council before the appointed day. They had only one day left before the Shar-Ja was due to arrive, and there was still much to do to prepare to meet the Turics.

The tribesmen, however, followed their own schedule. The following morning, only a few hours after the clan horns had blown to welcome Amara's sun, the horns blew again in warning. As the horn blasts died away, they were echoed by a blast of deeper horns that sounded from somewhere across the river beyond a long, low ridge.

The clansmen paused at their tasks for a brief moment, and in that space of silence they heard a distant murmur of sound: the dull thunder of hooves, the rumble of wagons, and the din of many voices. Over the gently rising hills they saw a wavering cloud of dust that rolled closer, spreading wider as it approached. The murmur of sound grew to a constant clamor.

"To your horses!" bellowed Lord Athlone in a voice that cracked like thunder.

Every man grabbed his weapons and ran to mount his horse. The standard bearers brought the chieftains' banners and took their places by the lords in a line along the northern riverbank. By the time the Turic vanguard rode into sight. the clans were ready, sitting in rank after rank behind their chiefs. The bright colors of their cloaks glowed in the morning light; their mail and weapons glinted like scattered pieces of silver. As the Turics came into view, the clansmen raised a forest of spears above their heads in salute.

At the forefront of the clan contingent sat Lord Athlone on his towering Hunnuli, Eurus. Beside him rode Gabria, Sayyed, Gaalney, Rafnir and Morad, representing the clan magic-wielders. Their black Hunnuli stood as an impregnable bulwark across the path to the river's ford.

From where he sat on Afer, Sayyed felt his heart twist at the sight of his father's people. He should have worn away the Turic in his mind by this time, but the blood of his fathers still clamored for recognition. The sight of the tribesmen, dressed in traditional burnooses and long, flowing robes and pants, and riding their sleek desert horses was enough to jolt more memories than he had believed still remained.

Although he deplored the viciousness of the attack that destroyed his mother's people at Ferganan Treld, he couldn't help but be pleased as the standards of the fifteen tribes came over the crest of the hill and lined up on the banks opposite the clans. There among the colored banners he saw the lion rampant on red, the emblem of the tribe of Raid. In twenty-six years of contentment and happiness among the clans, Sayyed had learned to forgive his father, the Raid-Ja, for rejecting him so many years ago, and he wondered now if any of his family still lived.

"By Amara's crown," he heard someone breathe in awe. "How many are there?"

Sayyed glanced at his son and saw interest and amazement play across his face. Although Rafnir could speak fluent Turic and understood Sayyed's devotion to the Turic god of ages, he was clan from boot to plaited hair. He did not really understand the strict and honor-bound codes of the Turic.

"The Turic believe it is necessary to show an opponent their power and strength before negotiations of any peace treaty," Sayyed explained. "Because the Shar-Ja is with them, they have probably brought his entire retinue to prove to infidel clansmen that the Turic hold the upper hand."

Rafnir jerked his head around at the word "infidel" but the quick retort died on his lips when Sayyed winked at him. They both turned back to watch the vast procession. Even after his talk of retinues and shows of strength, Sayyed had to admit his words paled in comparison to the overwhelming numbers of horsemen, wagons, and chariots that gathered across the river.

The Turic had always outnumbered the people of Valorian, but Sayyed had not realized until now just how wide the discrepancy had become since the plague killed over three thousand clanspeople a few years before. This was not going to make negotiating a settlement for damages and peace any easier.

At that moment a ringing fanfare of trumpeters announced the arrival of the Shar-Ja. An enormous wooden wagon rumbled over the hill, drawn by a team of eight matched yellow horses, the sun-gold mounts of the desert monarch. A peaked roof covered the top, and the windows at the sides were hung with silk hangings of silver and blue. Elaborate carvings decorated the wagon from wheel to roof.

If the Shar-Ja rode inside the wagon, Sayyed couldn't tell, for the ruler did not reveal his presence. But flanking the vehicle rode the heavily armed troops of his royal guard, followed by a group of nobles and attendants.

The wagon creaked down the easy slope to the rows of Turic warriors and stopped nearly opposite Lord Athlone. A strange, wary silence fell over the valley as the two forces stared at each other across the water.

A clan horn suddenly sounded, pure and sweet, and Sayyed nudged Afer forward into the rushing water. The big Hunnuli splashed as far as the edge of the island, where he stopped and neighed a ringing welcome. Sayyed raised his hand palm outward in a gesture of peace. He felt a twinge of humor at his position. He had left his usual burnoose and tulwar in his tent and wore instead the clan cloak, tunic, leather-and-mail shirt, and the short sword favored by the clans. The Turics would take him for nothing more than a bilingual clan sorcerer.

"Hail Rassidar al Festith, Shar-Ja of the Fifteen Tribes, Ruler of the Two Rivers, Overlord of the Kumkara Desert, and High Priest of the Sacred Rule," Sayyed bellowed in perfect Turic. Then he proceeded in impeccable tribal decorum to greet the representatives of the fifteen tribes. "The Eleven Clans of Valorian, Masters of the Ramtharin Plains, welcome you to Council Rock. May wisdom walk among our people and peace shine upon us," he concluded.

The words had no sooner left his lips than a winged shadow flitted over the gathered clansmen. A babble of excitement rose from the watching Turics when Demira, Kelene on her back, soared effortlessly overhead on a fresh spring breeze. Full of grace and beauty, she circled over the Turic ranks, then made a gentle landing on the island, beside Afer.

Sayyed grinned at them both. Kelene loved to make an entrance, and while the Turics had certainly heard of the winged Hunnuli, few had seen her until now. Her altered appearance was a peaceful reminder of the power of the clan magic-wielders.

The crowd near the Shar-Ja's wagon parted for a solitary rider who cantered his horse to the river's edge. Obviously a tall man, he sat his mount with practiced ease and total command. When he swept aside his burnoose he showed a face of middle years, swarthy, grim, and forged with resolution. His hair was knotted behind his head in the manner of the Turic people, and a trim beard etched his jaw with black. His deep-set eyes seemed sunk in shadow, and there was little sign of humor in his graven features.

"I am Zukhara, Emissary of the Shar-Ja and First High Counselor to the Throne of Shar. I bring greetings from His Highness." The man spoke, in polished Turic, from the far bank. It seemed he would not deign to yell, yet he made no effort to cross his half of the river to meet Sayyed and Kelene. The two of them could make out his words, but the clan chiefs could not hear him at all over the splashing flow of the river.

"Sadly, our monarch is weary from his hard journey. We ask to postpone any meeting until midday tomorrow. Then we will meet on the Council Rock."

"We?" Sayyed murmured. "Who is this man?"

The Shar-Ja's son? Afer suggested.

"No. The Shar-Yon is younger. And more personable, they say. This is a new counselor. I wonder where he came from?" Sayyed had tried to keep informed of Turic news and politics, until Tam died and he moved north to Moy Tura where he had lost interest in the world of his father. Now he regretted his ignorance. He bowed over Afer's neck to the Turic and replied, "We are willing to wait. Until tomorrow. May the Shar-Ja find rest and comfort." As soon as they received a reply, Sayyed and Kelene trotted their Hunnuli back to the clan lines.

"I'm not surprised," Lord Athlone responded when they told him the emissary's words. "In fact, I will be surprised if the Turics do not keep us kicking our heels for several more days."

"But we will wait," Peoren ground out. "I will wait for as long as it takes."

* * *

To everyone's annoyance, Lord Athlone's words proved correct. The Turics set up their camp in a wide meadow across the river and forced the clan chiefs to wait for four days before announcing the Shar-Ja was ready to hear their grievances. By that time even Lord Terod, the most complacent and timorous of the eleven chiefs, was swearing under his breath at the delay.

The time, though, gave the lords an opportunity to hear the full accounts of the raids on the southern clans, to plan their strategy, and to agree on their objectives. They kept a careful eye on the big camp across the river and made certain their own defenses were fully prepared.

Kelene, to her amusement, had discovered she and Gabria were the only two women in the entire camp of nearly two hundred men. The absence of other women was not a deliberate exclusion, for by rights established by Gabria many years before, the priestesses of Amara and the wives of clan chieftains were permitted to attend important clan meetings. But the ancient ritual of the Birthright, the women's festival of fertility and thanksgiving was about to be celebrated by every clan, and the other women had chosen to remain at the trelds for the very important sacred ceremony.

Kelene and Gabria, therefore, assumed the role of hostesses for the whole camp. They treated minor injuries, supervised the cooking, took water and ale to those too busy to stop their work, and settled a number of brief disputes among the proud and free-tongued clansmen. Kelene was so busy she had no time to talk privately with her mother. She contented herself with staying close to Gabria and sharing the older sorceress's companionship.

The day of the council came cool and windy with a cloudy sky and veiled sun. Soon after the morning meal, horns blew on both sides of the river, calling the start of the meeting.

The island was too small for every man to attend the council, so the ten chiefs and Peoren, with one guard apiece, represented the clans. Rafnir asked if he could represent Moy Tura at the council, and the chiefs, anxious to have as many sorcerers as possible with them, agreed. Kelene quickly offered to serve as wine bearer, for work at negotiating was always thirsty business. She stated boldly that she had been asked to come because of the Shar-Ja's poor health, and she wished to see for herself how the man fared. Lord Athlone had no objections, and Rafnir, who knew his wife well, merely shrugged his shoulders. Gabria stayed behind with Gaalney and Morad to keep watch from the river's bank.

In the Turic camp, a similar number of men—priests, counselors, and several tribal leaders—accompanied the Shar-Ja down to the river. The monarch rode in a little chair slung between two horses. He made no move and gave no smile as the entire group rode across their half of the ford.

The two forces met and dismounted on the island without exchanging a word. The clansmen watched as the Shar-Ja was helped from his litter by a solicitous young man and escorted into the big clan tent. Everyone else quickly followed, leaving their weapons at the entrance.

Although the Turics did not generally permit their women to attend councils, no one objected to Kelene's presence. They knew who she was, the healer, the sorceress, the rider of the winged mare, and Kelene realized their silence was a mark of their respect.

She stood mute beside Rafnir and curiously watched the Turics stride into the tent, their faces dark and taciturn. Everyone wore long robes in subdued colors and burnooses so white they seemed to gleam against the duller blues, browns, and grays of the robes. Only the Shar-Ja wore the pelt of a desert lion over his shoulder as a symbol of his authority, but many of the others wore silver-linked belts, brooches of gold, armbands, and chains of gold or silver. They were handsome men overall, dark-eyed, golden-skinned, with full, even features. They often wore their black hair in intricate knots and plaited their long beards.

Kelene recognized immediately the emissary who had spoken four days before. He stood a head over the tallest Turic in the tent, and his hooded eyes watched everything with a cold, avid gaze. He made no move to help the Shar-Ja but waited with ill-concealed impatience behind the others while the young man settled the Shar-Ja in a heavy wooden chair provided for that purpose and propped him comfortably with rugs and pillows.

Kelene craned around Lord Wendern's big head to see the Shar-Ja. She frowned when she finally got a close look at the man. Rumors of his ill-health were obviously true.

The Shar-Ja was barely fifty, yet he looked as old as seventy. A gray pallor clung to his face, and his skin hung loose over his shrunken frame. His hands shook as he pulled off his burnoose and revealed a ring of grayish hair that clung to the back of his balding head. Until recently he had been a powerful man, strong, athletic, and known for his just and firm government. In a society ruled by a strict code of conduct, the Shar-Ja was known as an honorable man.

So what, wondered Kelene, had brought on this rapid decline? She glanced at Sayyed, who stood beside her father, and saw that he, too, was frowning. He did not like the appearance of the Shar-Ja either. It seemed odd to Kelene that she had not been invited to attend to the monarch. She had understood that the Turic messenger had specifically asked for her to come to the council, yet sick as the Shar-Ja appeared to be, no one had bothered to request her assistance.

Kelene suddenly realized the tent was very quiet. Every man had taken his seat and was waiting for someone else to make the next move. Her father glanced at her and nodded once. Clan hospitality dictated that guests were sacrosanct and that any gathering, small or large, was always made more pleasant with food and drink. Because the clans had initiated the council, they considered the Turics their guests, even on an island that was essentially a no-man's-land. A fire had been laid in a central hearth to chase away the morning chill; rugs, stools, and pillows were provided for comfort; and trays of food, pottery cups, and wineskins had been left in the tent for refreshment.

Kelene stepped into the watchful silence and bowed politely to the Shar-Ja. She held herself tall and proud as she walked to the cache of food and wine. She had braided her long black hair in a matron's braid that hung to her waist and danced with its ties of jaunty green ribbons. Keeping her hands steady, she knelt, laid out the cups and trays, and poured a single measure of the heavy red wine. She paused only when a strong, sour smell reached her nose.

Her eyes narrowed as she tasted the wine and calmly swallowed it. Fools, she thought fiercely to herself. Someone had brought wine without bothering to check if it had spoiled on the journey.

Smoothly she took the cup to Lord Athlone to confirm her findings. His expression did not change at the bitter taste. He only glanced at his daughter and inclined his head as he handed the cup back to her. He had confidence that she would rectify the problem.

Kelene knew every eye was on her by that time. Clansmen and Turic alike were awaiting refreshments. There was really only one thing she could do. Serving the spoiled wine would insult the Turics and cast dishonor on the chiefs. Running back to the camp for more wine would take too long and could irritate the Shar-Ja and his counselors. She would have to use magic.

She knew the Turics did not approve of sorcery. They did not despise it with the fervent zeal of past generations of clanspeople, but like anything not understood, sorcery was condemned in Turic society. In order not to infuriate the already defensive tribesmen, she would have to work surreptitiously and pray no one noticed her spell.

She smoothed all expression off her face and looked about for a useful vessel. Fortunately someone had left a large pitcher with the wineskins, and Kelene carefully filled it to the brim with soured wine. With her hand over the pitcher's mouth, she thought of the finest beverage she could remember: a mead, a cool, light honey wine, delicately sweet as spring flowers, as golden as morning light, fermented from honey harvested from a bee colony she and Demira had found in the southern cliff face on Moy Tura's plateau. No one outside of Moy Tura had tasted that wine yet, but if she could duplicate it with magic, she was sure her father would approve.

Kelene concentrated on what she wanted. She felt the magic around her in the earth, the grass, the stone of Council Rock, and with her mind she pulled the magic into her will, shaped it to her design, and silently whispered her spell to clarify exactly what she wanted. When she pulled her hand away, the red wine was gone, replaced by a crystal yellow liquid that smelled of honey and spices.

Kelene tasted a little from her father's cup. The resulting mead was not as full-bodied and rich as the original, but it was delicious enough to be served to the clan chiefs and the Turic nobles.

She served her father first, to reassure the Turics that the wine and the food were not poisoned; then she swiftly and efficiently served the Shar-Ja, his men, the chieftains, and the clan warriors. That her mead was appreciated quickly became apparent by the low hum of conversation, the occasional quiet laughter, and a more relaxed atmosphere.

Besides Sayyed and Rafnir, a few clansmen from Clan Shadedron and Clan Wylfling could also speak Turic, and several Turics could converse in Clannish. Before long the two groups were passing plates of dried fruit and sweetcakes and exchanging wary compliments.

Kelene looked on with satisfaction. She quickly converted all the spoiled wine to mead, placed filled pitchers within reach of the men, and wordlessly sat beside Rafnir. Her husband took her hand and gave her a wink.

Finally the Shar-Ja raised his hand for quiet, and one by one the men fell silent. The clanspeople leaned forward, waiting for the Shar-Ja to speak and open the negotiations.

Instead he inclined his head to the young man beside him, relinquishing his authority. The man approached the stand, a square of space between the two groups where a person had the right to speak. In his midtwenties, he was a good-looking man with strong cheekbones and a thick cap of black hair tied in a single plait. He bowed to the clan chiefs. "I am Bashan al Rassidar, the Shar-Yon, eldest son of my father. In the name of Shar-Ja Rassidar, I welcome the Lords of the Eleven Clans," he began. His voice, firm and assured, spoke in credible Clannish and went on to greet each chief and apologize for the delay.

While she listened, Kelene stared intently at the Shar-Ja, who was watching his son with obvious pride—the father grooming his heir to assume the throne. Sooner than later, Kelene judged. There was too much gray shadow in the old man's face, too much lassitude in his body. If only she knew what was wrong.

A quiver of awareness ran up her backbone, a cold, trickling feeling that lifted the hairs on the back of her neck. She tensed, her eyes wide and her nostrils flared, her senses as alert as a wary deer's. She felt something odd, a surge of intensity in the air around her. Normally she could sense emotions only if she was in physical contact with a person, but she had honed her empathic talent until once in a while she could sense strong feelings from someone close by.

She concentrated all her ability on the strange tingling, and like a form taking shape in the mist, the emotions clarified in her mind: greed that shook her with its need and hatred as cold and implacable as a glacier. The focus of those feelings was not clear, only their intensity. Heat and ice raged unseen in a man's heart, and no one but she was the wiser.

Slowly she lifted her eyes and found herself drawn into the bitter, dark gaze of the man named Zukhara. He stared full into her face, devouring every detail of her features. Then he deliberately lifted his cup to salute her, and his thin mouth lifted in a smile that pulled his lips back from yellowish teeth, like the snarl of a waiting wolf.

Kelene's eyes flashed a bright and steely challenge.

Still smiling, Zukhara turned his gaze away from her, dismissing her as obviously as a master sends away a slave. Almost immediately the powerful sense of emotions faded from Kelene's mind.

She sat, feeling cold and oddly disturbed. The strength of the counselor's mind, the intensity of his emotions, and the unshakable presence of his arrogance were all enough to cast a gloomy shadow over her thoughts. None of the clansmen seemed to know who Zukhara was or where he came from, and Kelene began to seriously wonder why he had come to the council. Whom did he hate with such intensity?

She slowly sipped her drink and decided to forget her worries for now. She determined to keep an eye on Zukhara in the future, but at that moment the Shar-Yon was talking favorably of peace and the council was off to an auspicious beginning. Better to help the peacemakers build their bridges than fret over one individual.

3

There is a storm coming.

"What?" Kelene muttered from somewhere under Demira's belly. She gave the mare's front leg one last swipe with the brush and moved to the hind leg where reddish mud had caked into the ebony hair.

There is a storm coming, Demira repeated patiently. *From the north.*

Kelene did not doubt her. The Hunnuli's weather-sense was as infallible as their ability to judge human character. The sorceress continued brushing and asked, "Can you tell what it is?" A thunderstorm would be a pleasant change. The turbulent lightning storms provided a phenomenon for magic-wielders by enhancing the magic already present in the natural world. The increased power energized the magic-wielders by strengthening their spells and increasing their endurance to wield magic. She was disappointed, though, and a little alarmed when Demira answered, *Snow. It is already snowing beyond the Goldrine River. It will be here in a day or two.*

Kelene straightened and stared up at the huge arch of the sky. A solid, featureless sheet of cloud moved overhead, pushed by a steady wind from the north. The afternoon air was still mild, almost balmy, but Kelene knew that could change very quickly. This time of year, when winter and spring vied for rule of the plains, storms could be tricky and often treacherous.

"That's just what we need," she said irritably, stretching back under the mare to reach her inner hind leg.

"What's what we need?" asked a different voice.

Kelene glanced around Demira's leg and saw a familiar pair of boots and a red split-skirt, a red the same scarlet as that of the long-dead Corin clan. "A storm," she called out to Gabria, then popped up and flashed a grimace at her mother over the mare's folded wings. "Demira tells me a storm is moving this way."

Picking up another horse brush, Gabria began to polish Demira's other side. "Nara said the same thing. It will probably turn to sleet or freezing rain by the time it reaches us . . . which will make things only slightly more chilly and uncomfortable around here than it already is."

Kelene grunted in agreement. "I don't understand what's the matter with the Turics. There's a strong undercurrent of tension in their midst that has nothing to do with us. We've had two days of meetings and have accomplished nothing. It's almost as if the Turics are afraid of saying much for fear of spooking someone."

"Who?"

"I don't know," Kelene replied. "It isn't the Shar-Ja. He almost never reacts. He sits in his chair and dozes half the time. Bashan, the Shar-Yon, is doing his best to push a settlement through, but the others keep blocking him with petty gripes and details." She paused. She had not mentioned her misgivings about Zukhara to anyone, but perhaps her mother could give her a different perspective on the counselor. "There is one man . . . even the Shar-Yon treads carefully around him."

"The emissary Zukhara?" Gabria guessed.

"You know of him?"

"Sayyed and Rafnir told me about him," Gabria hesitated, then added, "Sayyed said this man stares at you during the meetings."

To that Kelene shrugged. She hadn't realized anyone else had noticed. "He stares, but he says nothing. Perhaps he is only curious—and ill mannered."

He is not just curious, Demira put in. *There is a taint about him I do not like. He will not come near the Hunnuli when we wait on the island for the council to end. The other Turics have spoken to us; the Shar-Ja has patted my neck. But this Zukhara stays away from us.*

Kelene's brows lowered. "I didn't notice that. I wonder why?"

Gabria leaned against Demira's warm wing and turned a concerned eye on her daughter. "Have you heard the Turics speak of the Fel Azureth?"

It seemed a simple question, but Kelene caught a distinct note of worry in her mother's voice. She shook her head, the horse brush forgotten in her hands.

"The Azureth have surfaced only recently. It is a fanatical religious group sworn to the overthrow of the Shar-Ja's throne and a return to the ancient practices of the Prophet Sargun."

"Why hasn't the Shar-Ja done anything about them?"

"I don't think he can," Gabria said sadly. "He's too sick. His son has been handling many of his responsibilities, but he is too inexperienced to deal with such organized fanatics. The Azureth are very secretive. Even their leader, whom they call Fel Karak, is unknown to all but a few of the most trusted members. They are well organized, well supplied, heavily armed, and very dangerous."

Kelene was both fascinated and alarmed. "But I thought the Shar-Ja was respected by his people. Have the tribes done anything to stop these rebels?"

"Our sources tell us the tribes are too busy trying to survive themselves."

"Our sources?" Kelene chuckled. "Sounds so mysterious."

Gabria's fair face lit with a gleam of humor. "It's amazing what you can learn from caravan drovers, traveling bards, merchants, and traders. They love to talk when you bring them in off the cold plains and give them a hot meal and a dry bed. We learned much this winter about the Fel Azureth and the tribes' troubles." She shook her head, and the humor faded from her green eyes. "They haven't had good rain in two years. The land is dry, and the rivers are low. The Shar-Ja has done little to help. The tribes grow so desperate, even this extremist group looks promising to some."

"And you and Father think this Fel Azureth may have something to do with the attacks on our people?" Kelene suggested shrewdly.

Gabria nodded. "That was one reason why he asked for this council, to spur the Shar-Ja into some sort of action against these fanatics before their raids lead us into war."

"Then perhaps we'll see some reaction today at council," Kelene said. "Peoren is going to have his say about the attack on his clan. He has been very patient so far, but I think he's about to explode."

"Just be careful of Zukhara," said Gabria with motherly fervor.

Kelene's eyes narrowed as a new thought occurred to her. "Do you think he has some connection with the Fel Azureth?"

"No one knows. But as Demira pointed out, there is a taint about him."

Across the river a horn blew a sonorous note to call the clans and the tribes to council. Another meeting was about to begin. Demira's ears swept forward as Eurus, Tibor, and Afer cantered by to meet Lord Athlone, Rafnir, and Sayyed. The little Hunnuli nickered impatiently while Kelene gathered her combs and brushes, restored them to the carry bag, and handed them to Gabria.

Kelene took leave of her mother and trotted Demira down to the river to join the clan chiefs. This time she paid close attention to Counselor Zukhara when he arrived with the Turic delegation. Just as Demira described, while other Turics admired the magnificent Hunnuli, Zukhara held well back, keeping the Shar-Ja and Bashan between himself and the black horses.

Interesting, thought Kelene. Was he afraid of them? Or was he just not interested? Did he know of the Hunnuli's intuitive ability to read human character?

Keenly aware of Zukhara, Kelene followed the men into the council tent. She noted that he seemed to avoid the Shar-Ja and his son, as if he did not want to associate with them. He refused to sit but stood aloof, his hands clasped behind his back, his long legs apart and braced for a lengthy wait. The other tribal leaders were deferential to him, yet Kelene saw many of them eye him with subtle wariness or shift their gaze away from him completely.

The sorceress pursed her lips in thought while she poured and served refreshments as usual. The wine was good this time, a light crisp fermentation from the Khulinin's own reserves, and the Turics appreciated it.

Only Zukhara turned it down. When she came to him, he grasped her tray in both hands, forcing her to stop in front of him. He was so tall she had to lift her eyes to see his face, and when she did so, with a bold, angry glare, he curled his lips in that condescending smile that so rankled her.

"What, no mead today, my lady?" he said softly. "Not even for me?" His long fingers suddenly grasped her right wrist and twisted it upward to expose the diamond splinter that lay beneath the skin of her forearm. He studied it, tracing his finger along its glowing length.

The splinter was a slender sliver of diamond, embedded in the wrist of a magic-wielder when he or she completed training. It was a powerful emblem, and to Kelene, a personal one that should not be revealed and examined without her consent. Her face flamed red at the man's audacity, but she controlled her famous temper for the sanctity of the council and deftly twisted her arm out of his grasp. "Not today, Counselor Zukhara," she replied with frosty calm and turned away before her father or her husband came forward to protest the man's rudeness. It wasn't until she finished serving the refreshments and sat down that she realized Zukhara had spoken to her in perfect Clannish.

She was still inwardly seething when Peoren took the stand before the council to describe the surprise attack on his treld. Eight days of rest, Kelene's gentle ministrations, and his own youthful energy had worked wonders on the boy's battered countenance and his sense of maturity. Although only sixteen, he had left his boyhood behind on the bloodied fields of Ferganan Treld, and he stood before the gathered chiefs and tribesmen with the determination and authority of an adult. Knowing he had the support of the ten chieftains, he launched into a passionate and detailed description of the tragedy. Sayyed translated for him and did not change or leave out a single word.

At first there was little reaction from the Shar-Ja or his nobles—which little surprised the clansmen. The Turics had shown almost no emotions to any of the previous complaints. But as Peoren continued with the account of his father's last stand and the bravery and sacrifice of his hearthguard, the Turics began to grow restive and visibly upset. Their impassive faces darkened in anger; their heads turned toward one another to exchange agitated whispers.

Kelene, her attention still centered on the tall counselor, noticed Zukhara was the only one who remained unmoved. In fact, his expression had the look of a man who had heard the tale before and lost all interest.

"Your Highness," Peoren was saying to the Shar-Ja, "to my knowledge, our two peoples have not declared war upon one another, nor has there been a state of animosity between us. My father died not understanding why his neighbors and those he called friends were killing his people." The young man took a step forward and held out the bloodied scrap of blue cloak sent to Lord Athlone. His pale gray eyes flashed like steel. "There was no reason for your people to attack mine, Highness. Therefore I demand weir-geld, blood money to be paid for the deaths in our clan. Thirty-six people were dead when I left and several more were badly wounded. If we are not recompensed as stated by our clan laws, we the Ferganan will wage a blood feud until every Turic in that raiding party is dead."

The Turics were silent now, their faces grim and intent. They knew Peoren was deadly serious. Blood feuds were sacred to clan society; revenge was a survivor's right and honor.

Kelene held her breath while she waited for the Turics' response. How they dealt with Peoren's demands would tell a great deal about who was truly responsible for the raids across the border. If the tribal leaders were softening the clans for war, they would brush over the Ferganan's claims as unimportant. But if Lady Gabria was right and the rebel extremists were attacking the southern clans, then the Turics would respond with honor and, Kelene hoped, with action.

The Shar-Yon started to stand, but his father gestured to him to remain seated. Slowly the Turic overlord pushed himself to his feet and drew up to his full height. Some measure of his old vigor and spirit still remained in his beleaguered body, and he drew on that now to address Peoren and the clan chiefs.

"Young man, it is my deepest grief that this tragedy has come to pass," the Shar-Ja spoke. Although his hands trembled with the effort of standing upright, his glance was clear and his voice was still steady and powerful.

While Sayyed translated, the clansmen and Kelene gave the overlord their full attention, for this was the first time the Shar-Ja had spoken at the council.

"I did not know of the disaster," said the Shar-Ja, "and judging from the expressions of my advisors, I believe it is the first time many of them have heard of it, too. We knew a band of malcontents and rebels was marauding along the border, and men were sent to end these raids. But, to my disgrace, I did not follow through to be certain the raiders had been stopped. Obviously, my troops failed me." He paused there and cast a cold look of disapproval at Counselor Zukhara before turning back to the chiefs. "You must understand, difficulties have arisen from the two-year drought that has stricken our realm. My people grow desperate as we face another year of crop failure and dry wells. But it was never my intention that our problems would spill over onto you. My lord chieftains, I shall pay your weir-geld out of my own coffers, and any damages resulting from earlier raids will be paid by the marauders themselves or by the northern tribes who have harbored these thieves."

Several Turic nobles looked shocked, but the others inclined their heads in agreement. Whatever had held them back before had apparently been put aside for the moment, because most seemed to agree that a settlement was necessary.

As Sayyed finished translating the Shar-Ja's speech, a murmur of approval ran through the ranks of clansmen, and a feeling of relief, too. Now they finally knew they were dealing with outlaws, not the entire Turic nation. Perhaps the Turic tribesmen, in spite of their overwhelming numbers, knew they had enough problems in their own land without incurring the wrath of the Dark Horse Clans and their magic-wielding sorcerers.

Peoren threw the scrap of cloak into the fire and bowed slightly to the Turic in acceptance. Lord Athlone and Lord Fiergan, the fiery, red-haired chief of Clan Reidhar, joined the youth. Sayyed accompanied them, as well, and as Lord

Athlone made his reply he translated the fluid, rolling tongue of the clans into the more abrupt and literal speech of the Turics.

The lord of the Khulinin formally thanked the Shar-Ja for his generosity and presented the Turic scribe with a complete list of damages, stolen property, and lives lost among the four clans hit by the rebel marauders.

"Shar-Ja," Athlone continued civilly, "we did not come to this council just to make demands. We offer a renewal of peace, a treaty of cooperation between our peoples. Let us offer vows of alliance, if not friendship, to you and your nation. We are not rich in goods or many in numbers, but what we have we share with our neighbors."

Kelene lifted her chin, her senses suddenly attuned to those around her. She felt that strange tingling in her spine again, the furious hot and cold emotions of a man with a powerful mind. Immediately her eyes sought Zukhara, and although he had not moved or changed expression. she knew the rage came from him as surely as heat emanated from a fire.

"What in Sorh's name is he so angry about?" she murmured to herself.

Whatever infuriated the tall man, he did not make any indication or show any obvious sign of his fury to the rest of the council. Like a statue he stood aside from the proceedings and merely watched. Only Kelene had an inkling of the volcano behind his deep-set eyes.

Kelene studied him worriedly and wondered if she should warn Rafnir or her father. But what could she tell them? That the counselor was rude to her and angry about something? That was less than useful. Not every Turic was as diplomatic as the Shar-Ja or likely to be happy about a peace treaty. A few of the tribal leaders were sure to be disgruntled about the Shar-Ja's decision to make the northern tribes responsible for the damages to the clans. Perhaps Zukhara was one of those. Whatever his problem, he did not seem inclined to make trouble at this meeting, and because of that, Kelene decided to keep her peace—at least until she had a clearer cause to speak up. The Shar-Ja was speaking to her father again, so Kelene set her unproductive thoughts aside and turned her attention back to him.

"The present Treaty of Council Rock is thirty years old. It was signed, in fact, by your father, Lord Savaric, and by the lord of the dead Corin clan, Lord Dathlar." A ghost of a smile flitted over the old man's face. "Much has changed in thirty years, Lord Athlone. Your powers have become accepted above the Altai River and your magic-wielders work wonders. Perhaps it is time we craft a new treaty of peace. Magic such as yours would be a better ally than enemy."

The tremor in the Shar-Ja's hands became more pronounced, and his face faded to a bloodless pallor. He sank back into his chair, his strength gone.

Kelene jumped to her feet, deeply concerned by his appearance, but before she could get close to the Shar-Ja, Counselor Zukhara moved to block her path to the chair. He paid no attention to her, only gestured to the litter-bearers, who came instantly to the monarch's side.

"Forgive me if I do not stay to finish this," the Shar-Ja managed to say. "My son will speak for me, and you may write the treaty with him."

The chiefs bowed as the Shar-Ja was carried from the tent. Kelene did not know whether to feel annoyed that Zukhara went with him, preventing her from slipping out and trying to visit the overlord alone, or relieved that the counselor had gone. Without his imposing, negative presence, the whole tent seemed lighter, as if a dark cloud had moved from the face of the sun.

Maybe the other delegates felt it too, or maybe they were simply anxious to end the council. Whatever the reason, the afternoon flowed productively until dusk, when the clan chiefs and the Turic tribesmen called a halt to the meeting. Both sides had a copy of the rough draft of their treaty, hastily written by scribes and witnessed by all there. A final draft was to be completed and signed the next day.

As the chiefs left the tent, Lord Fiergan slapped Peoren on the back. "Good job, boy," he said gruffly. "Your father will rest at ease."

"Do you really think the Shar-Ja will pay?" Peoren asked anxiously, retrieving his short sword from the weapon rack by the front entrance.

"The overlord is a man of his word," Lord Athlone assured him.

"If he's allowed to keep his word," Kelene interjected.

The Amnok, Lord Terod, hoisted his eyebrows toward his thinning hair. "What do you mean by that? Who would prevent the Shar-Ja from fulfilling his promise?" he asked sharply.

Lord Bendinor, walking beside Athlone, jerked his head toward the Turic camp across the water. "If I had to make a guess, I'd say that rock-faced counselor, Zukhara. He hasn't done much talking during these meetings, but everyone walks on nails when he's around. He would bear watching."

Kelene hid a smile. She was beginning to like this shrewd and sensible Dangari.

The clansmen reached their horses and mounted for the return ride to camp.

Rafnir looked up at the sky that had darkened to a deep blue-gray. "Here it comes," he said and wiped off several wet splatters from his face.

More raindrops pattered on the rocks and speckled the water. The north wind freshened and roared among the trees, tossing their branches and making the trunks creak and groan. It pulled at the riders' cloaks and chilled man and horse with its sudden damp cold. Across the river, only a few small fires fought bravely against the wind and coming rain. The riders said no more but hurried back to the shelter of their tents and the hot meals awaiting them.

* * *

The rain fell through the night in steady sheets that swayed and danced in the wind. Lightning crackled a few times, and the magic-wielders felt their blood stir and the energy sing in their heads. But the storm cell moved in harness with the wind and was gone as quickly as it had arrived, leaving behind the steady rain and slowly dropping temperatures.

The thunder had faded and the lightning passed to the south when Gabria rose from her blankets beside Athlone and quietly stirred the embers in her small brazier back to life.

Kelene, wakeful beside Rafnir, saw the dim light beyond the sleeping curtain in the tent they shared with her parents, and she slipped out to join Gabria. The older sorceress silently brought out a second glazed mug, poured water for two into her pan, and spooned several heaps of her favorite tea into a teapot.

They huddled together around the small warmth of the brazier while the tent around them heaved in the blustery wind and the rain beat on the waterproofed fabric. They said nothing until the water boiled and Gabria poured it into the pot to steep.

Kelene saw with alarm that her mother's hands were trembling. "What's wrong?" she whispered, conscious of the men sleeping behind the curtains.

Gabria's eyes were huge in the dim light and rimmed with shadows. She shakily set her pot down and pulled her arms tight about her. She nodded gratefully when Kelene brought her gold cloak and wrapped it around her shoulders.

"Something has happened," she said in a soft tone that was terribly certain.

"What?"

"I don't know. I had a dream as dark and foreboding as this night, but nothing was clear."

A dream, Kelene thought, feeling the first stirrings of dread. Gabria's talent for magic sometimes manifested itself in prophetic dreams and visions. The problem was the dreams were not always clear enough to understand until it was too late. She thought about her mother's words and asked, "You said *has* happened. It cannot be stopped?"

"I fear not. I sense the Harbingers are near," Gabria replied in a hollow voice.

Kelene's heart turned cold. The Harbingers were the messengers of Lord Sorh, god and ruler of the Realm of the Dead. If the Harbingers had entered the mortal world, someone or several someones had died.

Already forewarned, neither she nor Gabria were surprised when a distant horn suddenly sang in the storm-wracked night. Somehow they had been expecting it.

It blared again, insistent and furious, until it was joined by others that blasted their warnings into the dark.

Gabria heaved a deep sigh and stood, ready to face what would come. The horns were Turic, and in her deepest sense of the unseen world she knew the Harbingers had arrived.

Behind her, Athlone and Rafnir sprang from their pallets, pulled on their boots, and reached for their swords. There was some advantage to sleeping in one's clothes, for the two men were racing for the tent flap before the horn blasts had ended.

"Wait," Gabria called. She and Kelene hurried into their boots and joined their husbands, cloaked and ready to go. Just outside under a canopy their four Hunnuli stood ready. The horses tossed their heads in agitation, and their star-bright eyes rolled in anger. Their breath steamed in the cold air.

Someone has used magic across the river, Eurus's deep masculine thoughts reached the four people.

"Oh, gods," groaned Athlone.

The Hunnuli carried their riders at a canter through the rain-soaked darkness to the river. Activity already stirred the clan camp, but Lord Athlone refused to wait. He urged Eurus on across the Altai. Water fountained beneath the Hunnuli's hooves as they charged through the ford to the opposite bank. Abruptly they came face-to-face with a solid phalanx of Turic guardsmen.

The guards lowered their spears to face the magic-wielders, forming a deadly barrier across the road. Their actions were swift and angry, and their faces were cast in rage. Behind them, the Turic camp was an uproar of shouting voices and running men. Torches flickered everywhere in the rain, and armed guards rushed to defend the perimeters.

"Stop there, infidels!" a commander bellowed in credible Clannish.

Eurus slid to a halt, his hooves sliding in the muddy earth. Lord Athlone carefully unbuckled his sword and held it out to show he came in peace. "I am Athlone, Lord of the Khulinin. I came only to learn of your trouble and offer our help."

"I know you," the officer snapped. "You are one of those sorcerers, so you already know what disaster has overtaken us. Begone from here before I have your horses brought down."

Kelene felt her fury rise. Hunnuli were impervious to magic, but not to normal weapons. To her the Turic's threat was underhanded and unwarranted. She opened her mouth to say so when another figure appeared on the path behind the guards. The tall form stopped when he saw the clanspeople and shook his fist at them.

"You!" he bellowed over the sounds of the storm. "Curse you for your deeds! What you have done this night will plunge our people into war!"

It took the magic-wielders a moment to recognize Zukhara in the wild night; then Athlone raised his voice. "Whatever has happened, Counselor, we have had no part in it. We came only to give our aid to the Shar-Ja."

"He will not see you," Zukhara answered wrathfully. "He lies crushed in grief. His eldest son, the Shar-Yon, is dead."

A small, heartsick moan escaped Gabria's lips, and she leaned over Nara's neck. Her dream had been right.

At that moment Sayyed galloped up on Afer, his head bare to the pouring rain. He had heard the counselor's last words, and his hand clenched tight on his stallion's mane. Like most clansmen, he was unafraid to speak his mind before his chief or any other figure of authority. Immediately he shouted back, "Prove it, Counselor! Show us the Shar-Yon's body that we may see you do not lie for your own devices!"

A roar of dissension burst from the guards, but Zukhara raised his hand to silence them. "I grant the Khulinin that right. Lord Athlone, you and your guard may enter if the others remain here. I want your word that you will keep your people under control. No weapons, no magic while you are in this camp."

Although the clanspeople could not see it, Zukhara's mouth twisted into a smile of satisfaction while Lord Athlone gave his bond. "I must attend the Shar-Ja," Zukhara called. "Officer, take the infidels to the Shar-Yon, then escort them off our land." He turned on his heel and strode out of sight, his cloak snapping in the wind.

The commander of the guards looked as if he would burst with outrage, but the Turics were more reserved and strict in their ranks, and he managed to stifle his objections to trusting a clansman. Grudgingly the guards parted before the Hunnuli.

Athlone glanced apologetically at Gabria before jerking his head to Sayyed. The two men slid off their Hunnuli and followed the fuming commander. Five guards fell in behind them and followed them into the heart of the camp to the Shar-Yon's large tent.

On the riverbank, Gabria, Kelene, and Rafnir waited in growing impatience. The rain soaked them quickly in a cold, drenching downpour, and the Turic guards made no move to offer them shelter. The guardsmen simply stared balefully at them and kept their spears lowered. A long time passed before Athlone and Sayyed came trudging down the slope to rejoin them.

Both men were speechless with anger and frustration. Curtly they took leave of the Turics, remounted their Hunnuli, and trotted down to the ford. Kelene, Gabria, and Rafnir traded glances, but they would not ask any questions until Athlone was ready to talk. They fell in behind and thankfully recrossed the river.

As soon as they reached the opposite bank, Gaalney, Morad, and several chiefs came running to meet them. Athlone spoke a vehement curse and slid off Eurus. His anger smoldered in his movements and in his words. "The Shar-Yon is dead," he told the listening people.

"How did it happen?" Rafnir demanded.

The reply came hard and dagger-sharp. "The Turics think we did it."

"That's ridiculous!" Fiergan snarled. "They can't think we're that stupid. That boy's the best thing they have."

Rafnir looked searchingly at his father-in-law. "Something made them think it was us. What was it?"

Athlone clenched his fists as if he were trying to crush his impotent wrath. "Oh, there was something all right. Something only seven of us here can use. Sorcery. The Shar-Yon was killed by the Trymmian force."

4

"Bad news comes in threes," the clanspeople often said, and the second piece of ill-tidings came at dawn on a frigid wind from the north. The temperatures, which had been falling steadily throughout the night, took a plunge, and the rain gradually slowed to a heavy drizzle and began to freeze. The sunrise came reluctantly, lightening the darkness to a gloomy morning heavily cloaked in cloud and mist that showed no signs of thawing the building ice.

The clansmen cursed and struggled against the freezing sleet to reinforce their tents, bring the horses into shelters hurriedly erected in the lee of the tents, and gather up any firewood that was not already encrusted in sheets of ice. Ice storms were rare on the northern plains, which made them that much more dangerous, and the clanspeople hated them almost more than the blinding blizzards that often swept the grasslands.

Across the river there seemed to be a furious swarm of activity in the Turic camp. Tents were coming down, wagons were being loaded, and horses were being saddled in spite of the weather. A constant, heavy guard patrolled the banks, and no one would answer Lord Athlone's frequent requests to meet with the Shar-Ja or any of his counselors.

The chiefs, meanwhile, tried to solve the mystery of the young Shar-Yon's death. He had been, Athlone reported, burned almost beyond recognition by a blast of the Trymmian Force, a power used only by magic-wielders.

"But that's impossible," Rafnir said for the third time. "We were all in our tents. Gaalney and Morad have witnesses to their whereabouts, Father was on watch, and the four of us were asleep."

The other chiefs, who had crowded into Athlone's spacious tent for a quick council, looked at one another in grim confusion. There were only seven known magic-wielders in their midst. Three of them had excellent alibis and the other four, while not necessarily witnessed by other clan members to be in their tents, were too well-known to be conceivable murderers.

"That leaves two possibilities," said Athlone. "There is either a clansman with the talent to wield magic whom we have not yet detected, or there is one we do know who is hiding close by."

Sayyed glanced up, his eyes unreadable in the dim light. "There is one other possibility, my lord." He paused and held up his own hands. "Another Turic half-breed with clan blood."

"Now how could any untrained Turic use the Trymmian force to kill?" Lord Terod wanted to know. Terod, chief of Clan Amnok, had no magic-wielders in his clan and little practical knowledge of magic.

Lord Sha Tajan of Clan Jehanan, on the other hand, knew sorcery well. "The Trymmian force is easy to use, especially during a thunderstorm. It wouldn't take much skill to blast the unprotected Shar-Yon."

"There certainly wasn't much skill involved," Athlone growled. He remembered the seared corpse vividly. "Bashan was struck by an uncontrolled blow."

"Then, too, there is the question of why," said Bendinor the Dangari. Like most of his clan, he had a blue-dotted design tattooed along his forehead and down his left cheek. Unconsciously he rubbed at the dots as he deliberated aloud.

"We have no real motive to dispose of the most capable son the Shar-Ja has; that would be harmful to our own cause. But what if Sayyed is right? What if there is a Turic with enough talent to wield the Trymmian force and enough ambition to use it? Why kill the heir? Why make it look as if we did it? Perhaps someone wants to interrupt succession to the high throne, cause further trouble with the clans, or open the way for a new leader."

"The Fel Azureth have been threatening to do that for almost a year," Lord Athlone pointed out. "Maybe they found a way."

"So what do we do?" Rafnir grumbled. "We're in the middle of an ice storm, the Turics are preparing to leave without the treaty, the Shar-Ja won't speak with us, and the Turic nobles think we killed their heir."

"Short of attacking their camp and forcing our way in to the Shar-Ja's presence, the only thing we can do is keep trying to talk to someone in authority and make them see reason," suggested Bendinor reluctantly.

Cursing at the sleet, the ten chieftains, Sayyed, and Peoren mounted their horses, called the hearthguard warriors, and rode to the river ford. The Altai ran fast and turgid, swollen by the earlier rains. The ford was still serviceable, but the clansmen rode warily across, watchful of the current that now reached their legs.

On the southern bank, the tribal guards eyed the riders suspiciously and stood in ranks across the road with their hands on their sword hilts. A row of archers stood in the line of trees by the bank and held their crossbows ready to fire at a second's notice. The Turics waited silently while the clansmen drew to a halt at the water's edge.

This time the Lords Fiergan and Sha Tajan approached the guard together. The big red-headed Reidhar and the tall, cool-eyed Jehanan presented an attitude of determined commitment as they spoke to the guards' commander.

This man was a different officer from the belligerent one of the night before, and though he gave no orders to move his ranks, he sent a man to deliver the chieftains' message.

With nowhere else to go, the clansmen sat on their restive horses and waited impatiently in the steady, freezing drizzle. They drew their hoods low over their faces, but it did not seem to do much good. The wet sleet soaked through their cloaks to their clothes, trickled down their boots, and spattered on their hands and faces until all but the sorcerers were chilled and miserable. Athlone, Sayyed, and Rafnir were slightly drier and warmer from the vibrant, glowing warmth exuded by their big Hunnuli.

Finally a lone figure followed by a large and shaggy brown dog wandered down the path to the guard post. The person looked like a boy of twelve or thirteen, well dressed and fine-featured, with thick black hair and an irrepressible grin. He greeted the commander of the guards with cheery enthusiasm. The officer saluted him peremptorily and promptly ignored him.

Undaunted, the boy patted his dog and studied the uncomfortable chieftains for a moment; then he called, "Hello!" in a merry voice.

Sayyed lifted his head, surprised that the boy spoke Clannish. He glanced at Athlone, who gave a nod, and returned the greeting in Turic.

"Oh, please, speak in your tongue," the boy insisted. "I'm trying to learn it." He had a pleased, open expression that paid no heed to the weather or the tension around him.

Sayyed grinned. "What is your name?" he called back, raising his voice to be heard over the ranks of soldiers.

"Tassilio. Are you a chieftain?"

The sorcerer's grin grew wider. "No. They won't let me." Several guffaws came from the men around him, and Sayyed pushed himself a little higher on Afer's neck to see the boy better. "These men," he explained, pointing to the lords beside him, "are chieftains. They're waiting to see the Shar-Ja."

The light abruptly faded from the boy's face. He tilted his head as if listening to something beside him and shook it fiercely. "Tell them? Of course I can't tell them!" he shrilled.

The officer of the guard rolled his eyes.

"I can't take them to see him either, you know that!" Tassilio said forcefully to the empty air. "He's very sad. He won't talk to anyone. Why? I don't know why! No one ever tells me anything!" He suddenly turned on his heel and stamped back the way he had come, the dog close to his heels.

The clansmen watched him go in surprise, the boy's unhappiness obvious even from a distance. The Turics paid no attention.

When Sayyed asked the officer about the boy, the man shrugged and answered indifferently, "The Shar-Ja's son by a concubine. But he's a sandrat and a simple one at that."

Most of the northern chiefs looked blank when Sayyed translated that bit of news, so he explained. "A sandrat is another name for a bastard." He chuckled mirthlessly. "The concubine was probably not his own, but the Shar-Ja was honorable enough to accept the child."

"Too bad he's a simpleton," growled Fiergan.

To everyone's relief, a small contingent of counselors arrived at that moment led—to no one's surprise—by Zukhara. The elegant counselor tried to look apologetic for the first time since they'd met him. He marched his companions just to the first rank of guards and there stopped, once again keeping his distance and forcing everyone to shout.

"My lords," he called, "we have received your message. Unfortunately, the Shar-Ja is unable to accept visitors. His grief has taken a serious toll on his stamina and has forced him into seclusion."

"I'd like to bet on that one," muttered Fiergan.

"Then perhaps we can talk to you, Counselor," Sha Tajan shouted back. "The treaty we worked so hard to bring about is at risk. Grant us, we ask, time to work through this tragedy. We can prove to you that none of our magic-wielders is responsible for the murder of the Shar-Yon."

Zukhara replied, his words crisp and forceful. "I'm afraid that is impossible. The Shar-Ja is leaving tonight to return to Cangora for the burial of his son. His only words to me were that he would not sign the treaty until the murderer of his son was found and brought to justice."

The chiefs slumped in their saddles, discouraged and cold. They were at an impasse, and no one knew yet how to get around it.

"Counselor," Athlone tried again, "I give you my word that the magic-wielders in our camp had nothing to do with—"

"So you say, Lord Athlone," Zukhara interrupted through a thin veneer of civility. "But only clan blood carries the talent to wield magic, and magic killed Bashan. If you wish to make peace with us, *you* must find the killer! So the Shar-Ja has spoken." He sketched a bow to the clansmen, turned his back on them, and led his followers away.

Fiergan made a disgusted noise somewhere between a grunt and a snort. "So that's that."

A blood-red look of fury crept over young Peoren's face, and the Ferganan reached for his sword. Shaking with emotion, he kicked his horse past the chieftains and wheeled it around in front of the officer of the guard. The archers in the trees raised their bows, but Peoren, if he saw them, paid no attention. He flung his sword to the earth point-first, where it stuck upright in the mud, an emphatic confirmation of his outrage.

"The Ferganan called the Turics 'friend.' We have given your people our hospitality; we traded on good terms. We dealt with them honorably, and they slaughtered my family!" he shouted with all his despairing fervor. "Until the

Shar-Ja fulfills his vow to pay the weir-geld, our clan will seek our revenge in Turic blood!"

The tribal guards surged forward to unhorse the boy, but their officer roared. "Stand off!" and thrust himself between Peoren and the angry men. "Be off, boy," he snarled to the Ferganan, "before your blood is spilled."

Not the least bit daunted, Peoren reined his horse around and galloped it back to the Ramtharin shore. The older men, subdued and grim, followed close behind.

* * *

The coals were hot, the herbs had steeped, and Gabria and Kelene settled down at last in the empty peace of their tent for the long-awaited cup of tea. The hot drink was a special mixture of Gabria's made with lemon balm, tea leaves from Pra Desh, a hint of wild mint, and a sweetening of honey. On this chilled, wet day the tea reminded the drinkers of summer and wildflowers and simmering afternoons.

Kelene sipped carefully and sighed her pleasure. She made a mental note to ask her mother for some cuttings of lemon balm to grow in her garden at Moy Tura. A smile crept across her face at the thought of her garden. At Khulinin Treld, Gabria's herbs grew wild in the sun-warmed glades beside the Goldrine River. At Moy Turn, the plants, like the stone, the wood, and the earth, were shaped to men's will—an accomplishment clanspeople were still learning to perfect.

Kelene's thoughts were interrupted by Gabria's gentle laugh. "You and I have been together for days now, and this is the first quiet moment we've had alone. Tell me about Moy Tura."

So, over the tea, Kelene talked about their lives in the ruins. She told her mother about the temple, their house and garden, the guests who came and went so frequently, the numerous underground passages they had found under the city, Sayyed's excavations, and all the many problems they had had. She talked for a long time while the sleet pattered on the canvas over their heads and the brazier softly glowed.

Gabria listened and asked a few questions and watched her daughter's face. When Kelene's words finally dwindled to silence, the older sorceress squeezed her hand and said lightly, "What a tale to tell your children. You should have a bard there to record your adventures."

Kelene stilled. She had not said a word about her failure to have children or her hope that Gabria could advise her. She looked around at her mother almost apologetically and said, "What if we have no children?"

Gabria's fingers tightened over Kelene's. "I was wondering when you were going to talk to me about that. As much as you and Rafnir love each other, your city should be full of babies."

"I have tried everything I know," Kelene murmured sadly. "Prayers and gifts to Amara, herbal remedies. I even went to Wylfling Treld last spring for the Birthright to be blessed by a priestess of Amara."

"You found no help in the healers' records?"

A few tantalizing records, medicinal recipes, murals, and healing stones had been found under the old Healer's Hall at Moy Tura, but they had been sadly lacking in pregnancy information.

Kelene wrinkled her nose at her remembered disappointment. "No. Nor have the healers who come to study the old records." She broke off, feeling a sudden prickle of tears behind her eyes. "Oh, Mother, to be a healer and not know how to heal yourself! I don't know what's wrong with me. Why can't I have children? Rafnir and I wanted a big family to fill that shell of a city with life! But I feel as empty as the ruin."

She fell quiet while her own words echoed in her head. Empty. It sounded so final! So pitiful. She shook herself and drove away the threatening tears. Self-pity would get her nowhere; that lesson she had already learned. But as she sipped the last of her tea and smiled wearily into Gabria's loving face, she had to admit she felt a little better for having poured out her worries to her mother.

Gabria, meanwhile, listened patiently to the silence, knowing for the moment there were no platitudes Kelene would want to hear. Now that the pain was in the open, they could ponder and study and maybe work out a solution. Gabria fervently hoped so. Besides the delight of having grandchildren, she cherished the practical hope for an increase in the number of magic-wielders to carry on the traditions of Valorian's blood. Kelene and Rafnir were an excellent match, and should they produce children, their offspring would be powerful indeed.

Their companionable silence lasted for a few precious minutes more before the two women heard the sound of running feet. A head hooded in a gold cloak abruptly thrust itself through the tent flap, and a male voice cried, "Come quickly! There's been an accident by the river." The speaker vanished just as hastily, and his footsteps pounded away before the sorceresses recognized him or could ask any questions.

"That was helpful," Kelene grumbled, gathering her healer's bag and her cloak. "He could've stayed long enough to say who or what."

"He did look very flustered," chuckled Gabria. She swept on her own gold cloak over her warm split-skirts, leather tunic, and boots. She gathered an extra blanket from the bed and hurried outside behind Kelene. The messenger was nowhere to be seen.

Nara and Demira stood side by side under the slanted roof of their shelter.

"Did you see which way that man went?" Kelene asked, squinting through the cold gloom.

Toward the grove of trees by the river, Nara responded. *He was in a hurry.*

Without complaint the two Hunnuli left their dry shelter and bore their riders along the faint trail left by the messenger's footprints down toward the Altai.

There was no sign of the chiefs, but neither Gabria nor Kelene worried overly much. They half expected their husbands to be at the scene of the accident.

Both women peered ahead through the gathering twilight and saw little more than dark shapes and shadows. The temperature had dropped further during the afternoon, and now snow mixed with the sleet to form a slushy white coverlet over the freezing mud.

The Hunnuli bore left along the bank and trotted into a grove of cottonwood, wild olive, and shrub oak. The trees, barely budded, clustered thickly along an old bow of the river and formed a dense screen beside the bank.

Gabria glanced around. She could not see very much in the flying snow, and the clan camp was lost from view. "Are you sure he went this way?" she asked her mare.

"Over here!" a voice shouted. "Quickly!"

The two mares thrust their way through the thick undergrowth toward the sound of the voice until they reached the edge of the trees by the water. In the dull light they saw a body lying prostrate on the stony shore, and four or five men in clan cloaks bending over it.

The Hunnuli's ears suddenly swept forward in a single motion. Their nostrils flared red, and both mares dug in their hooves and slid to a stop. *Danger!* flared their minds.

Kelene caught a glimpse of two men whirling around and throwing what looked like dark balls at the horses. In the space of a heartbeat, she saw the balls burst into a dense yellowish powder directly in the faces of the mares. Nara trumpeted in rage, but the powder, whatever it was, filled her lungs. She staggered sideways and crashed against a tall tree trunk before Gabria could stop her. Two men immediately dropped from the trees and pulled the sorceress to the freezing mud. Another man roped Nara's head and neck.

Kelene had no time to react. Desperate to save her rider, Demira flung herself forward to free her wings from the crowded trees. Then the powder took effect, and she lurched and fell to her knees at the edge of the water, her eyes rolling. Kelene fell hard. Pain shot through her right arm and down her back. Fury and fear flamed her blood, but a hand clamped a damp cloth over her nose and mouth. Unable to speak, unable to use her magic, Kelene inhaled foul, metallic fumes from the cloth and felt her body go numb. The dim light faded to gray before it blinked out and was lost.

The men quickly flung their clan cloaks and the dead outrider into the river. Swiftly they blindfolded the dazed mares and roped them side by side. They flung the women's bodies over the Hunnuli's backs. Several more men and horses worked their way across the river. With the strength of the additional horses to steady them, Nara and Demira were forced forward across the rising Altai into the darkness on the opposite bank. In less than a moment the river was empty, and Kelene and Gabria were gone.

* * *

Across the clan camp, Eurus lifted his great head. He stood in a huddle with Afer, Tibor, and the smaller Harachan horses of the other chiefs, trying to keep warm while the men conferred one last time in Sha Tajan's tent before the darkness became complete. The stallion stirred irritably and blew a gout of steam, like smoke from a dragon's mouth.

Something was wrong. Eurus could feel it like an ache in his belly. He slammed a hoof into the slush and snow. The Harachan, though handsome, graceful animals, had little of the Hunnuli's intelligence, endurance, or power. They rolled their eyes at the restless giant in their midst and shifted nervously away from him.

Afer nickered to reassure them, and they settled warily back into their group. Only the Hunnuli could not calm down again. Afer and Tibor both grew restive, and after only a few minutes, the three Hunnuli sidled away and trotted back to the Khulinin tents.

At first glance, everything looked normal to the Hunnuli. The tents were holding their own against the gathering ice, a few sheltered campfires were burning, the guards were at their distant posts, and the camp was quiet.

When the stallions came to the chieftain's tent, though, their anxiety blew up into alarm. The two mares and the women were gone, and their tracks, already filling with snow, pointed down toward the dark river.

Afer neighed a long, demanding clarion call that rattled the camp and brought men alert, but there was no response from either Nara or Demira. Like black thunder the three stallions galloped along the mares' trail to the grove of trees. There they slowed to a walk and let their keen eyes and sharp sense of smell lead them through the dense undergrowth to the river's edge.

They caught the scent of Nara and Demira in the crushed grass and of Hunnuli blood mingled in the slush and mire of the shore. There, too, they detected traces of many men: churned footprints, a pool of human blood, and the scent of sweat and fear.

Another smell teased Eurus's nose, a scent that was pungent, powdery, and metallic. It made him dizzy, and he quickly snorted it out. He scented Gabria's faint scent in the brush by the trees and Kelene's on the rocks by the Altai. And that was all.

The riverbank was empty. The women and the mares had vanished.

Tibor and Afer wheeled and charged back the way they had come, while Eurus searched up and down the bank for some sign of his mate and her rider. At his side, the Altai tumbled and rolled in a muddy, heaving current that reached higher and higher up the shore, washing away the scent and sign of the attackers and their victims.

Troubled shouts and running feet crashed through the quiet of the grove, and hooded lamps bobbed their light in the deep twilight. The old stallion returned to meet Athlone, Sayyed, and Rafnir, who were out of breath and wild-eyed. Afer and Tibor came with them.

"Tell me," gasped Athlone. Other men, Gaalney and Morad among them, joined their chief on the bank, and Eurus told the five sorcerers what had been discovered.

Lord Athlone breathed long and deeply before he roared, "Sayyed, I want the entire camp checked tent by tent to be certain they are not there. Rafnir, take squads of men up and down the river to search the banks. The rest of you come with me!"

Without hesitation everyone leaped to obey. They searched for hours, as the darkness closed in and the sleet completed its change to driving snow, and yet they found nothing more of Gabria, Kelene, or the two Hunnuli mares.

In all the furor of the search, no one on the northern bank of the Altai saw the Shar-Ja's great wagon leave the camp, nor the long line of supply wagons and baggage vans that followed in its wake.

At last the men gathered in the center of the camp by a huge fire built as a signal on the slim possibility the two women were lost in the storm.

Rafnir's face was blanched when he reported to Athlone the dismal results of the searches. "Only one guard noticed them leave the tents, but they seemed fine to him and he thought nothing more about it. No one knows why they rode down to the river. We have found no more traces of them anywhere close by." He bit off his words fiercely as if to contain the worry and fear that ate at him. "Downstream, they found the body of one of our outriders washed up on a snag. His throat had been cut, and his cloak was gone."

Athlone, Sayyed, and Rafnir looked at one another, their minds coursing along the same track. Other chiefs and clansmen clustered around the roaring fire, but to the three men they seemed only a distant, murmuring part of the background. For the sorcerers there was only their common anger and burning anxiety for their wives and kinswomen.

Sayyed spoke first, his dark eyes glittering in the shifting light of the fire. "The Turics had some hand in this."

There was no firm evidence to back him up, and yet Athlone nodded in agreement. "None of the clans could profit by their capture."

"What about exiles or even strangers on our land?" Rafnir ventured.

Athlone pondered those possibilities, then shook his head. "It would have taken a fair number of men to capture and hide two Hunnuli, Gabria, and Kelene. They must have been taken by surprise. I don't think a large group could have slipped past all our outriders without leaving some trail. Whoever it was struck fast from close by and fled where we can't follow."

"What if they weren't captured? What if they're dead?" Rafnir said miserably.

The stallion Tibor laid his muzzle gently against the young man's chest. *I do not believe they are dead. I would surely know if Demira had left this world.*

And Eurus, who had run with Nara for twenty-six years, nickered his agreement. Hunnuli had the capacity to make powerful mental and emotional connections with their riders, so powerful that many Hunnuli sought death on their own if their rider died before them. This deep mental attachment was often extended to each other as well. Hunnuli such as Eurus and Nara, Tibor and Demira, whose riders were passionately in love, mated for life.

If Tibor said Demira was still alive, then Kelene must be, too, and Rafnir accepted his word wholeheartedly. He rested his brow on the stallion's wide forehead. "We will go after them," he declared.

"The council is over," Athlone said, sweeping his hand in a sharp gesture. "Pack your gear. We'll leave—"

Lord Fiergan bullied his way into their midst, and his commanding voice rang over the snap and crackle of the fire. "Don't be a fool, Athlone. You can't just ride into Turic territory and demand your women back. They'd either laugh at you or kill you. You don't even know who took them. Could have been the Shar-Ja, those crazy fanatics, or even that cold fish, Zukhara. Maybe the women were taken to lure you over the Altai and into a trap."

"Lord, he's right," Gaalney put in fervently. "And if you crossed the river and tried to pass yourself off as a Turic, you wouldn't get far! You don't look enough like one. Please listen! You're too important to us to lose. You can't leave the clan for a venture this dangerous."

"Venture!" exploded Athlone. For once his temper got the best of him, and he turned on both men with fury raw on his face. But before he could vent his anger, another sound reached the ears of the clansmen, a sound that froze them where they stood and turned every eye to the east. Beyond the edge of the fire, in the swirling darkness, the dull drumming of hoofbeats pounded closer and closer.

"Lord Wendern!" wailed a frantic voice.

The Shadedron chief lunged forward several paces. "Here! I'm here. Is that you, Hazeth?"

"Lord Wendern!" the voice cried again, and out of the night, guided by the bright beacon of the fire, came a dark horse carrying an apparition of ice and snow and blood. The exhausted horse staggered into the firelight, its sides heaving and its nostrils red as flame. Steam poured from its drenched hide, and its legs shook from its effort.

The figure on its back, swathed in a snow-blanketed black cloak, slid sideways and fell into the arms of his chief. Blood from a head wound had frozen in rivulets down the young rider's face, and another wound on his shoulder had left a hard, icy crust on his cloak. Even so, in spite of his injuries and exhaustion, the boy struggled to remain on his feet.

"The treld has been attacked, my lord," he panted. "By Turic raiders!"

This time, the bad news had come in a set of four.

5

"Lord Athlone, please!" Wendern pleaded. "Please see reason. Hazeth says the raiders attacked yesterday before the weather turned foul. They could not have made it to the river yet. In this snow they'll be holed up somewhere, ready to bolt as soon as the sky clears. If we leave now, we can cut them off. We have a chance to put an end to this raiding for good!"

"Your logic is persuasive, Wendern, but you don't need me. I have to go seek my wife!" responded Athlone adamantly, and he squared his shoulders as if to fend off further argument. He turned his back on the Shadedron chief and continued to pack his gear with an urgency bordering on frenzy. The other chiefs had returned to their own parts of the camp to organize their men and prepare to leave at first light, but Wendern had followed Athlone to his own tent and stood shifting from foot to foot, the blood of his youngest warrior still staining his hands.

Wendern was one of the new chiefs, a robust, middle-aged man who had won his torque three years ago when the previous chief died in the plague. He was a strong, capable leader, but he had no experience in warfare and little idea how his clan had fared in the attack. He truly did need help, Athlone acknowledged, help that would have to come from someone else. Gabria and Kelene were more important.

Athlone slammed a waterskin onto his pile of gear and had just reached for the bag containing his flint and firestone when a sound at his tent flap interrupted him.

"What is it?" he growled, barely pausing in his activity.

A choked gasp from Wendern brought Athlone around, hand on dagger hilt, to see two Turics standing in the entrance. Their long-sleeved brown robes were starred with snow, and their burnooses gleamed white as the moon. They appeared to be unarmed. The first man stepped quietly into the tent, the second close on his heels. Because the ends of their burnooses were wrapped across the lower halves of their faces to protect them from the stinging wind, only the Turics' dark eyes could be seen. The first Turic's eyes seemed to crinkle in some sort of amusement.

He touched his fingers to his forehead and his chest in the Turic form of salute and greeted Athlone in the tribal language.

Athlone's hand dropped. If the garb wasn't familiar, the voice was. "Sayyed," he said, exasperated, "don't you think that's rather dangerous at the moment? Someone could take offense and put an arrow through you."

Sayyed chuckled as he pulled the cloth away from his face. "It proves my point though."

"Which is?"

"That I should seek Gabria and Kelene beyond the Altai, while you go after the marauders with Lord Wendern."

"No. I am going to find Gabria."

"Athlone, listen!"

The chieftain hesitated, his attention caught by the intensity of his friend's voice.

Sayyed crossed his arms and said, "Gaalney had a point. You do not look like a Turic, nor act like a Turic, nor have any hope of ever speaking like a Turic. If you go over the river, you will be an invader, and no one will help you. Fiergan was right, too. We have no proof who took Gabria and Kelene. We need someone on this side of the border to eliminate other possibilities."

Athlone was still, his face unreadable, his big body held with such tight control that the knuckles of his hands were white. Wendern stayed wisely silent, leaving the arguments to a stronger voice than his. The second Turic, too, was quiet and watchful.

"I propose you go with Wendern and cut off the escape of the raiders. There are not enough warriors close enough to help. The Ferganan have their own troubles; the Wylflings and the Khulinin are too far away. There are only the chiefs and their men. They need a sorcerer to help."

"Gaalney and Morad can go," Athlone said forcefully.

"Gaalney and Morad are not leaders! They are not even wer-tains. They've never fought in battle. They are not Lord Athlone! If Lord Athlone, the renowned sorcerer lord of the Clans of Valorian, moves against the invaders of the Ramtharin Plains it will send a message to others who consider our people too weak to fight." He raised a finger and shook it at the chief. "And don't forget the Shar-Yon. Other Turics may want revenge against us for killing Bashan. If you are here defending the borders, the Turics may think twice about attacking us in force."

Athlone grunted. "You give me too much credit."

"That's dung and you know it. Wendern needs *you*. Not Morad or Gaalney. Of course, if you capture those raiders, you might have a bargaining chip to ransom in exchange for Gabria and Kelene. Whoever took them took pains to remove even the Hunnuli. They wanted the women alive."

Athlone's expression lost a little of its ferociousness as Sayyed's words sank in. His friend's arguments made sense to Athlone's mind; it was just his heart that had to be convinced. "And what are you going to do if I go haring off after brigands and thieves?"

Sayyed bowed slightly. "My companion and I intend to infiltrate the Shar-Ja's caravan, learn of the women's whereabouts, and free them at our earliest opportunity."

"Your companion?" Athlone asked dryly.

The second Turic tugged his burnoose free and smiled wanly at his father-in-law. "Father thought it was time I learned more about the other side of the family," replied Rafnir.

Athlone's knees seemed to collapse, for he sat down abruptly on the cushions in the center of the tent. Gabria's teapot and the two cups were still on the low table where she had left them, and the coals in the brazier were still warm. The chief's gaze went from one man to another in a long, pondering stare, while his mind struggled to choose the best path.

"Eurus!" he suddenly bellowed. When the Hunnuli poked his head in the flap, Athlone jabbed a finger at Sayyed. "Did you hear what he said?"

The stallion's head bobbed yes.

"We must also consider Nara and Demira, so I ask you, what do you suggest?"

Eurus, one of the oldest Hunnuli in the clans and one of the few horses to have run wild with the King Hunnuli, had grown wise during his years with humans. He replied simply, *Sayyed has a better chance to find Gabria and Kelene. You would have a stronger hand against the Turics if the raiders are stopped.*

"And you're willing to let Afer and Tibor go without you?"

I would hardly tell you to go somewhere if I were not willing to follow.

"But," Wendern offered almost apologetically, "they can't take the Hunnuli into the Turic realm. The horses would be recognized immediately."

Rafnir gestured outside. "Come see. We've already taken care of it."

The men trooped out into the night. The wind had slowed a little, and the snowfall was lighter. With the help of the gods, Athlone thought, the storm would blow over by the next day. He patted Eurus and glanced around, expecting to see Afer and Tibor. All he saw were two large horses bridled, saddled with deep-seated Turic saddles, and tethered to the tent peg.

The horses seemed to be black, although in the darkness it was hard to tell. One had a small star on his forehead, and the other had two white socks on his forelegs. There was no sign of the Hunnuli's usual white lightning mark on their shoulders or any of the breed's power and grace. The two stood, noses down against the wind, looking anything but regal.

"Nice animals," Wendern commented. "Where did you find mounts so big?" Then to his amazement, one of the horses lifted its head and nickered at him. His jaw dropped.

"You can't be serious," Athlone chuckled. "How did you get Hunnuli to wear tack?"

It was Afer's idea, Tibor complained, shaking the saddle on his back. *Only for Gabria and Kelene would I do this.*

Sayyed laughed. "They even suggested the dye to hide their shoulder marks and the white paint to decorate their coats. If no one looks too carefully, and they keep their wits, they'll pass."

Athlone decided he could hardly fight such a united front. He embraced his friend and his son-in-law in gratitude. "You have my permission to go," he said, too overcome with sudden emotion to say all that he felt he should tell them. But he did add one more admonition. "If I don't receive a message from you in the next fifteen days, I will gather the clans and march south after you!"

* * *

A pale glow softly tinted the eastern horizon by the time the clansmen discovered the Shar-Ja's entourage had already left. A heavy guard still patrolled the southern bank, but only a small camp remained where the day before the entire meadow was filled with the rounded Turic tents. Most of the wagons were gone, too, including the Shar-Ja's elaborate, covered vehicle.

Sayyed shrugged when he heard the news. "They can't have gone far in this weather. We'll find them."

The clan camp quickly disappeared as well, the traveling tents and supplies loaded in wagons or on pack animals. The snow still fell in fitful showers through air damp and cold, but it was the last gasp of a storm already dying. That morning the sky looked dove gray instead of the steely blue of the day before, and the wind had left to blow its mischief elsewhere.

As soon as it was light enough to distinguish detail and color, Sayyed brought his prayer rug out of his pack and laid it carefully on the bare patch of ground left by Gabria's tent. He knelt in the time-honored tradition of the Turic to pay homage to his god at sunrise. Twice a day he prayed, bowing to the south where his fathers believed the sacred city of Sargun Shahr was located. Although he had lived with the clans for twenty-six years and participated in some of their festivals, Sayyed still practiced the religious beliefs of the Turics and still carried the love of his god deep in his heart. He was grateful the clanspeople were not fanatical about their religion and had not tried to convert him. In respect to clan ways, he had allowed Rafnir to be raised in the traditions of Amara, Lord Sorh, Surgart, and Krath, telling his son only the meanings behind the different beliefs.

That morning, though, as he knelt in the cold light, he slanted a glance over his shoulder and saw Rafnir watching him. "Get a rug," he ordered. "You don't have to believe, but if you're going to be a Turic for a while, you need to pretend."

Rafnir gladly obliged. He spread out a horse blanket, knelt beside his father, and bowed his head. Wordless and attentive, he listened to the lines of his father's prayers. The words were ones he had heard as far back as he could remember. They were songs really, songs of praise and gratitude and hope for a new day, and they rolled off Sayyed's tongue with salutary humbleness and joy. There was comfort to be found in the phrases, and Rafnir found himself repeating them after his father. The deities addressed may have been different, but the heartfelt sentiments of each man's prayers were the same.

By the time they were finished, the chiefs had gathered their men to leave. Sayyed and Rafnir rolled their rugs, loaded their bags behind their saddles, and threw clan cloaks over their Turic garb. They joined the mounted warriors and rode with them toward the rising sun. On Council Rock, the huge tent sat empty and abandoned, its task unfulfilled. Across the Altai, the Turic rearguard watched the clans ride away.

The chiefs were forced to set a slow pace for the morning because of the drifted snow and the snow-encrusted ice beneath the horses' hooves. The warriors rode carefully, paralleling the Altai River toward the ruins of Ferganan Treld. If all went well, they would reach the sand hills south of Shadedron Treld in time to cut off the Turic raiders' retreat over the border river.

Sayyed and Rafnir rode with the clans for nearly an hour until they reached the next passable ford on the swollen river. On a small knoll overlooking the Altai, they stopped with Lords Athlone, Wendern, and Bendinor.

Sayyed pulled off his cloak. He felt a genuine sadness when he passed it over to Athlone, a tug of regret he had not expected. True, he was secretly excited about returning to the Turic lands, but he had lived with the clans longer than the tribes, and he realized the Ramtharin Plains were now and forever his home. He grinned at Athlone, lively mischief suddenly glinting in his eyes, and he saluted his lord as a clansman. "Until we ride together again, Athlone." He waved, then urged Afer into a canter down the slope to the river. His voice, lifted in the wild, high-pitched ululation of the Turics, sounded eerily on the still morning air.

Rafnir tossed his cloak to Bendinor, sketched a salute to Athlone, and turned Tibor after Afer. The lords watched as the two black horses plowed across the river and emerged dripping on the other side. In a moment the two were gone, lost to sight beyond a belt of trees.

For a while Athlone sat rigid on his stallion, his gaze lost on the southern horizon. It took all of his strength to sit still and not send Eurus galloping after Afer and Tibor. Fear for Gabria clung to the Khulin Lord like a wet cloak, and he wanted to challenge it directly, not delegate such vital responsibility to someone else. But Athlone was shrewd enough to accept the truth: he would be more effective north of the border in his own territory.

Silently he breathed a prayer, to Amara rather than Surgart, that the gods keep watch over his wife, his daughter, and the two men who risked so much to find them. At last he nodded to his companions and turned Eurus east, his thoughts already ranging ahead to Shadedron Treld and the hunt for the killers of his people.

* * *

It was midafternoon by the time Sayyed and Rafnir caught up with the Shar-Ja's caravan. Sayyed had been right; it had not moved far in the snowy night, only going a few leagues deeper into tribal territory before stopping again. The huge cavalcade had been underway since early morning, traveling slowly along a beaten caravan road toward Cangora, apparently in no hurry to reach its destination.

A large covered wagon, draped in black and royal blue, carried the coffin of the dead Shar-Yon at the head of the caravan, and a procession of priests and royal guards surrounded it. Word of the death had already passed ahead, for the road was lined with mourners and spectators who came from nearby settlements to pay their respects to the royal dead.

The weather seemed to reflect the sad occasion with a low roof of clouds and a faint mist that teared everything in drops of glistening dew. As so often happened in spring storms, this one lost its ferocity on the northern plains. By the time it crossed the Altai and hit the arid, warm winds of the desert realm, its teeth were gone. The icy snow lasted barely five leagues into the Turic lands before it turned to mud and melted away. Only the clouds and the mist remained of the storm that had swept the Ramtharin Plains.

On the crest of a low hill, Sayyed and Rafnir sat side by side, watching the caravan pass by on the road below. They carefully studied the long ranks of warriors representing the fifteen tribes, the disciplined rows of royal guards, the mounted counselors and nobles who had stayed so reticent at the council meeting, the dozens of war chariots, the Shar-Ja's enormous personal retinue, and the innumerable wagons, carts, and baggage vans that followed in the rear.

"I don't see anything that even resembles a Hunnuli," Rafnir said glumly.

"Did you expect to?" Sayyed replied in a thoughtful murmur. His eyes were still on the caravan below, his brows drawn in concentration.

"Well, no," admitted the young man. "That would be too easy. If they're with this caravan at all, they'd have to be out of sight."

Sayyed scratched his beard. "Hmm. Maybe we're looking at this from the wrong direction. We've assumed Gabria and Kelene were taken to trap Lord Athlone or to incite the clans to war, but what if they were kidnapped for a more personal reason?"

Rafnir looked startled. "Why do you say that?"

"Just a guess, really. I was counting heads," Sayyed answered. "There are more men among the tribal ranks now than there were at Council Rock."

"Are you sure?"

The older man nodded. "Law requires each tribe to send a specific number of men to escort the Shar-Ja on official journeys. I counted forty men for the Raid tribe at Council Rock. The other tribes should have sent equal numbers, but some of the units have gained more men."

"That seems odd. I wonder who they are and why are they coming now?" said Rafnir.

"Two excellent questions."

"So you think someone in the caravan is expecting trouble and may have taken the women to protect himself?"

"It's possible. Two sorceresses are a powerful shield—or weapon." Sayyed grimaced as he pushed himself to his feet. The cold, damp weather had played havoc with his knees, and unbending them was a slow process. "We'll stay out of the way until dark, then join the caravan when it camps for the night."

His son sprang upright with the suppleness of youth. "What if they're not here?"

"We'll give it four days," advised Sayyed. "If we can't find any sign of them here, we'll ride north to find the Fel Azureth and start again."

Quickly the men returned to the Hunnuli at the base of the hill. They withdrew from the road into open country among the folded hills and scrub to follow the caravan at a safe distance. The afternoon wore away slowly. The mist ended before evening, and a brisk breeze sprang up to tear away the roof of clouds.

Shortly before sunset the royal caravan stopped in a broad, flat basin near the first of a series of big oases that lay like jewels along the golden string of the caravan route the Turics called the Spice Road.

The road was an old trail that passed on a long diagonal from the merchant city of Pra Desh in the Five Kingdoms southwest across the Ramtharin Plains and the Ruad el Brashir to Cangora, the seat of the Turic overlords tucked in the foothills of the Absarotan Mountains. The Absarotan, or Blue Sky Mountains, were a southern extension of the Darkhorns and rose like a giant's fortress above the Kumkara Desert.

The first stop along the Spice Road in Turic territory was the Tarzul Oasis. The staging settlement of mud-brick houses, inns, shops, and suppliers had grown up beside the wells of the oasis and served not only the locals but pilgrims, travelers, nomadic shepherds, and caravans as well. When the Shar-Ja's officers stopped the caravan for the night, a flock of people, excited children, and barking dogs rushed to the camp to help, watch, or just get in the way.

Sayyed and Rafnir watched the oasis from a vantage point on a nearby rise. The caravan's setup was quick and organized in spite of the confusion from the additional oasis people, but the two clansmen were pleased to see the Turics set few guards around the perimeter of the camp. Only the Shar-Ja's tent was under a very tight and heavily armed guard.

Just as the sun touched the tops of the distant range of mountains, the clouds opened a window in the west, and slanting rays of golden light swept across the basin and gilded the trees of the oasis. At that instant a horn sounded a long, sonorous call to prayer.

To Rafnir's astonishment, the entire bustling population of the Shar-Ja's camp, the oasis, and the village fell silent, turned to the south, and stood motionless, their heads bowed in prayer. Some kneeled, and a few lay prostrate on the ground. The young sorcerer stared, awed at the scene. He felt his father kneel beside him and heard him murmur the evening prayer. Slowly Rafnir sank down beside him and turned his thoughts to the gods in a wordless supplication for strength and wisdom.

The sun dipped lower; the golden light faded. A moment later the horn blew again, and the Turics bustled back into activity. Rafnir rose, feeling strangely comforted.

"Let's go," Sayyed said softly. They turned to the Hunnuli and removed their saddles and bridles. "I don't want to take the chance of leaving you two in the picket lines tonight. You'll be safer with the herds or on your own." he informed the stallions.

Thank you, Afer sent, grunting with relief as the tight cinch was unbuckled.

"But," Sayyed said, pulling two leather halters from his saddle pack, "you'd better wear these."

Why! snorted Tibor. *Those are humiliating.*

"Exactly. Even the Turic know Hunnuli will not wear tack. If you are seen, no one will suspect you are Hunnuli if you are wearing a halter."

Afer sighed gustily. *He is right, Tibor. Be grateful he did not suggest hobbles.*

Chuckling, Sayyed buckled the halters on their heads and sent them out to graze with the caravan herds; then he and Rafnir shouldered their saddles and gear. They decided to make their way down the back side of the hill and work their way around the base to the outskirts of the camp through a shallow gully lined with shrubs and high weeds.

They had covered barely half the distance through the gully when the first small sounds reached them through the quiet backdrop of evening noises. The two men halted and stood listening intently. One sound came again, a single metallic clink, like a blade hitting a rock, then a rustle of bushes, and the unmistakable mutter of subdued voices from somewhere in front of them.

Sayyed nodded to Rafnir and eased his load to the ground. They padded forward as quietly as possible through the undergrowth to the edge of an open space between several tall clumps of brush. Sayyed froze, his hand raised to warn Rafnir.

Dusk pooled in the shadows of the gully, but there was still enough daylight left in the clearing to see five men hunched together, speaking softly among themselves. They were dressed in the dark robes, high boots, and warm wool knee-length coats the tribesmen preferred for travel, and they were heavily armed with tulwars, knives, and hand axes. One man was busy sewing something to the front of his coat.

Sayyed jerked his hand back, and he and Rafnir retreated up the hillside where they could watch the clearing undetected.

"Now why were five tribesmen lurking in the bushes?" Rafnir whispered.

"Look!" Sayyed hissed in reply, and he pointed to the gully they had just left. One by one, the five men slipped out of their hiding place and split off in five different directions. In just a few minutes, all five had nonchalantly disappeared into the crowded camp.

"Who were they?" wondered Rafnir.

"Of that I'm not certain, but did you see the man sewing? He was tacking a tribal patch on his robe." Sayyed pointed to the embroidered lion of the Raid on his own chest. "Every tribesman wears his emblem on his clothes, so why was that man adding one at the last minute?"

Neither man had an answer to that puzzle, so they put it aside for the time being and proceeded back down the hill to the borders of the camp. Following the lead of the others, the two men casually walked out of the deepening twilight and into the Shar-Ja's camp. They left their gear beside a pile of other saddles near the picket lines where some of the horses were kept close by for quick use. The smell of roasting meat led them to a cook tent, where they got a meal of bread, cheese, meat, and dates.

When they were finished, they meandered around the enormous camp to see what they could find. They stopped to chat now and then with other tribesmen, shared a cup of wine beside a fire with some villagers from the settlement, and exchanged pleasantries with them. They stopped to admire the Shar-Ja's elaborate wagon, and they paid their respects to the dead Shar-Yon in his draped coffin. When they tried to get close to the Shar-Ja's tent, however, several guards blocked their path and suggested forcefully they go elsewhere. They caught a brief glimpse of the Shar-Ja's son, Tassilio, playing with his dog, and once they saw Zukhara striding purposefully through the camp.

They had heard the counselor had taken charge of the caravan in place of the Shar-Ja and that no one had seen the Turic overlord since the debacle at Council Rock. A few rumors circulating the camp whispered the Shar-Ja was dead, but nothing had happened to confirm that.

Sayyed observed how people fell back from Zukhara and how all but the royal guards warily saluted him. To Rafnir's shock, Sayyed called out a greeting and saluted, but the counselor barely acknowledged him and continued on his way, his tall form lance-straight, his face dark and resolute.

By dawn the clansmen were weary and disappointed. They had found nothing to indicate Kelene and Gabria were in the caravan, nor had they heard anything even remotely connected to sorcery or the kidnapped women. All the talk in the camp had been about the religious zealots in the north, the Shar-Ja's ill-health, and the growing unrest in various areas of the realm.

At sunrise, after the morning prayers to the Living God, the Turics broke camp to continue the journey to Cangora. Sayyed and Rafnir retrieved their saddles and whistled in the Hunnuli. Afer and Tibor reported they had been unable to scent or even sense the presence of the mares. Unhappily the sorcerers and the Hunnuli joined the groups of tribesmen riding in the caravan. No one commented on their presence or questioned their right to be there. A few eyebrows were raised at the size of the black stallions, but Sayyed explained they were crossbreeds from a certain breed of plowhorse. He suppressed a laugh when Afer whipped his head around to snap at a "fly" on Sayyed's leg.

The caravan wound onward at the slow pace of the funeral cortege toward the next oasis on the trail. The Spice Road ran due south for a few leagues, then curved southwest toward the high foothills of the Absarotan Mountains.

Although Rafnir was not familiar with this territory, Sayyed had traveled this road several times in his youth with his father, the Raid-Ja, and he saw with deep misgivings that the tales he'd heard of the drought were painfully true. The area they rode through was still open range and usually rich enough to support sheep, cattle, goats, and the Turics' tough desert horses. In most years, spring rains refreshed this land, replenishing the stock ponds, bringing wildflowers to bloom, and enriching the tall, thin grass that would cure to a golden brown by summer.

But this year the green that should have carpeted the broad hills had already faded to a dull, wilted tan. The grass was sparse, and the stock ponds, man-made ponds dug to catch the spring rains, were mere mud holes. The herds Sayyed spotted were thin and far between.

When he mentioned this to a man riding beside him, the man's expression turned mournful. "Aye, we've had to sell or eat almost everything. My family has only our breeding stock left. If we don't get rain soon, we will have famine by the Feast of the Prophets."

Sayyed glanced at the man's emblem and recognized him as a member of the Mira tribe that had its hereditary demesne to the northeast. He frowned in sympathy. The Feast of the Prophets was in nine months, in the cool season of winter. Not much time to save a population from starvation. "Haven't the priests stockpiled grain in settlements as they are supposed to do?" he asked curiously.

At that his companion turned red with ill-concealed irritation. "Perhaps the Raid have honest officials and no dealings with the Fel Azureth. But the priests of our lands have had to pay grain for taxes to the Shar-Ja's collectors, and what is left has been *claimed* by the Gryphon to feed his army of zealots."

Sayyed slouched in his saddle and tried not to look too interested. He had heard that name from Athlone as the title of the unknown leader of the Fel Azureth. Gryphon seemed an appropriate title for such a man, Sayyed mused. Real gryphons had once existed in the Absarotan Mountains and were known to be cunning, secretive, and fiercely loyal to their mates. "Have you seen the Gryphon?" he asked casually.

"Not face-to-face," the tribesman said glumly. "He sends his commanders to tithe the settlements and towns in the name of the Living God and the Prophet Sargun." The man suddenly realized his voice was growing louder with his anger, and he bit off his words with a harsh laugh. "Shahr keep the Gryphon in the palm of his hand, and," he tacked on in an undertone, "keep him away from my family." He clucked to his horse and rode forward, away from the curious strangers.

"That was interesting," Rafnir said. "Not all tribesmen are happy with the Fel Azureth either."

Sayyed stared thoughtfully ahead, far beyond the caravan, beyond the horizon, to things only his mind's eye could see. There was so much to consider, so many facts he did not yet have, so many nuances he could not put into place. He needed to talk to someone who knew the current news around the entire realm, someone who would not inquire in turn about his big horse or his lack of knowledge or his curiosity. But there was not one person he could think of, or anyone he could trust. He and Rafnir would have to continue their blind search without drawing the attention of those who might have Kelene and Gabria in their control. One slip could prove deadly for them all.

The sorcerer stifled a yawn. Time was precious, but he and Rafnir could not function much longer without sleep. They had spent three anxious days and two nights with virtually no rest, and the effects were wearing them down. Sayyed yawned again. His head felt heavy and ached behind his eyes.

He glanced at Rafnir and saw the same weariness dragging on his son's features. There was more there, too, a brittleness of worry and a tight-jawed self-control. Rafnir had said little of his fear for Kelene, but it was there to read in the banked fires of his dark brown eyes.

* * *

That night at the second oasis, called the Tears of Al Masra, the evening was much the same. The caravan halted in a level field and set up camp beside the string of shallow pools that formed the oasis. After prayers, food was prepared, the horses were herded out to graze under the watchful eye of mounted herders, and the travelers relaxed. Sayyed and Rafnir walked about, observing the activity and looking for something that would lead them to the missing women.

They saw little to help them. The Shar-Ja remained in seclusion. The counselors kept to themselves, and the tribesmen ate and rested. Tassilio seemed to be the only one in camp with a light heart. He ran with his dog, laughing and barking and chasing imaginary prey.

As night settled on the oasis, Sayyed saw seven more men slip out of the darkness and mingle in with the camp's inhabitants. They were like the first group, totally unremarkable except for their full complement of weapons. When Sayyed tried to approach one, a lean wolf of a man with a mole on his cheek, the tribesman glared at him and hurried away.

At last, exhausted, Sayyed and Rafnir sought shelter in a quiet place under the tall, slim trunk of an oasis willow. They slept undisturbed until morning, when they woke to horns calling the faithful to prayer.

That day followed much like the last. Three days were gone, and there was still no word or clue as to the whereabouts of Kelene and Gabria. That evening the caravan traveled late into dusk to reach the next oasis on the Spice Road, one unimaginatively called Oasis Three.

"There's one place we haven't tried yet," Sayyed told his son as they ate their meal. "The baggage train. We'll take a look in some of the bigger vans and wagons."

They waited until the night was late and the camp had settled into subdued nocturnal peace. The enormous dome of the sky arched over their heads, clear and afire with countless stars. In the pale starlight, the sorcerers crept to the supply wagons and began a slow, methodical search of the interiors of each one, large or small. Soft-stepping, they checked the first row then moved to the next.

Sayyed put his foot on the wheel of a large covered vehicle and was about to lift himself up to see inside when he heard the faint crunch of soft boots on sandy soil. He turned to warn Rafnir and glimpsed several shadows spring around the corner of the wagon. Balanced on one foot and with his hands on the wagon sides, he could not react fast enough to defend himself. He fell sideways, hoping to throw off the attackers long enough to form a defensive spell. Something flashed in the starlight, and a brilliant pain exploded in his head. He heard a muffled thud beside him, and as he collapsed he felt the body of his son fall silently on top of him.

6

Sayyed hung suspended in a black pitiless limbo somewhere between consciousness and oblivion. He could not see or move or speak; he could only dwell in the pain that racked his body. He thought at first the pain was only in his head, in a blinding crack behind his ear that threatened to split open his entire skull. But as he concentrated on that agonizing sensation, more of his senses became aware, and other parts of his body began to complain. His neck, shoulders, and arms ached for some reason he did not yet understand, and his shins and ankles felt battered. Confused at this unknown assault, Sayyed's mind scrambled farther out of the black fog to seek a way to end the pain.

He became aware of several things at once. First, although he knew his eyes were open, he could not see. Fabric had been wrapped around his head, effectively blinding and gagging him. Second, he realized his arms and shoulders hurt because someone had roped his arms up over his head and was dragging him, facedown, over ground rough with short shrubs, rocks, and small prickly cactus.

Groggily he struggled against the tight bonds on his arms, but his efforts brought only a vicious kick that landed on his ribs. He groaned and stayed still while he forced his mind to full alertness.

He briefly considered summoning magic to break his ropes; then he set that idea aside for the moment. He was still too groggy and could neither speak nor use his hands. Without those guides and the strength to control the powerful energy, he could cause more trouble for himself than he was in now. The magic could burst out of control and destroy all who were in the vicinity.

Instead, he let his body hang limply in his captors' hands and listened to the sounds around him, hoping to learn more about the men who held him and what had happened to Rafnir. As he concentrated, he discerned more footsteps, perhaps five or six pairs, and what could be the sound of another body being dragged close by.

The attackers moved swiftly and silently up an easy slope, then down a long, gentle incline to a hollow lined with gravel and short spindly plants that crackled under Sayyed's weight. There the unseen men stopped and dropped their captives on the ground.

"By the Path of Sargun, these brigands are heavy!" one voice complained. "Why did we have to drag them out here?"

A second, harsher voice answered, "He said no more killing in the camp. It'll start to be noticed."

Sayyed bit his lip to stifle a moan of pain. His arms were still up over his head and felt as if they had been racked from his shoulders. He felt the other body rolled over beside him, and to his relief, he heard a third voice say, "This one's still alive."

"Anyone know these two?" demanded the second voice, probably the leader.

Sayyed felt himself pushed onto his back, and the fabric was yanked away from his face, jarring his aching head. The groan he tried to stifle slipped out of his clenched teeth.

Six faces peered down at him, smirking and merciless. "He's Raid tribe, that's all I know," one dark face said. "He was probably looking for things to steal."

"Raid," another sneered. "Nothing but thieves and brigands. No wonder they do not follow the Path of Light and Truth."

"Kill them," ordered the leader.

Sayyed frantically tried to lick his lips, to swallow past a dry and bitter mouth. He had to take action now before the assassins slit his throat. Using all his will, he drew on the magic in the earth beneath him. He felt it surge into his body, a furious, energizing power that flowed through bone and muscle as easily as his own blood. He formed the magic into the only weapon he could use instinctively without forming a specific spell: the Trymmian force.

He saw the thugs draw their knives, the long, fat-bladed weapons the Turics often used, and he pulled his arms down to his chest. His muscles tensed; his heart beat hard against his ribs. One man stepped close to grab Sayyed's hair.

"Oh! Excuse me," a boyish voice called cheerfully.

Every man whirled and looked up to see a short figure standing halfway down the hill.

"Excuse me," the voice cried again. "I was just looking for my dog. He is big and brown and looks as ugly as you!" Swift as a hunter, the figure drew back his arm and fired a rock from a slingshot at the man closest to Sayyed. The missile struck the man's temple with such a crack, he fell sprawling, dead before he knew what hit him.

The leader yelled a curse and sprang up the slope after the boy.

"Tassilio!" a new voice bellowed and, to the astonishment of everyone, a black-clad warrior lunged down the hill, his tulwar drawn and ready. He charged past the boy into the midst of the surprised men and swung his curved sword with both hands into the belly of the leader. The assassins hesitated only a heartbeat; then the four still on their feet drew their own blades, circled around their lone attacker, and rushed in like wolves.

Sayyed struggled desperately to sit up and free his hands. A pale blue aura formed around his fists from the power of the Trymmian force, and he made use of a fraction of its searing energy to burn through the ropes on his arms.

In that instant he heard the boy cry out and a dog bark. Looking around, he saw the boy run furiously down the hill toward the warrior with the sword. The black-clad man had injured a second thug, but the others had pressed him so closely he tripped over an outcropping and lay sprawled on his back. The assassin's swords rose over his head.

Sayyed had lifted his hand to fire a blast of magic when suddenly horses' hooves pounded on the hillside, and the enraged scream of a stallion interrupted the thugs' intent. Two huge horses blacker than night, their eyes like moons of green fire, rushed into the three remaining attackers. The men screamed in fear and flung themselves away, but only one escaped the horses' trampling hooves. That man tried to break past Sayyed to escape to the relative safety of the distant camp.

A blast of the Trymmian force shot from the sorcerer's hand, flared a fiery blue path through the darkness, and scorched into the chest of the last assassin. The thug crashed on his back, his robe smoking.

A strange stillness sank over the hollow. The dead lay motionless in the settling dust. The warrior leaned on the hilt of his sword and gasped for breath. His small companion stood just above him on the hill, his mouth open and his eyes bulging. His dog pressed close to his knees. The two black horses sniffed the dead men lying at their feet, then swung their great heads to look at Sayyed, who bent over his son.

"By all that's holy," a wondering voice said softly. "Sayyed. It is you."

The sorcerer lifted his head. The voice, once familiar and remembered with pleasure, put a name to the unknown warrior. In the pale light of the icy stars, he saw a face he had not seen in twenty-six years: his brother Hajira, one year older than himself, the sixth son of the Raid-Ja and his wife, the clanswoman from Clan Ferganan.

They built a small fire in the hollow out of the way of the cool night wind. While Sayyed tended Rafnir, Hajira dragged the bodies out of sight into a thicket. Tassilio raced off to the distant camp and soon returned carrying a wedge of cheese, a box of sweet oatcakes, and a jug of *firza,* a drink made from fermented grain and dates. Rafnir was conscious by that time and nursing his pounding head by the fire. The two brothers sat on either side, unsure yet of what to say.

Grinning like a conspirator, Tassilio laid out his offerings with several plates and a pair of matching flagons.

Hajira rolled his eyes when he saw the things. "Tassilio may be son of the

Shar-Ja, but he steals like a street urchin," he said as the boy sat close beside him.

The boy grinned and winked at Sayyed with such intelligent mischief that the sorcerer began to seriously doubt the general belief that Tassilio was "simple." Up close, the Shar-Ja's son was rangy, athletic, and the image of his father, with a straight nose, strong jaw, and two huge, wary eyes that stared unwaveringly at the two sorcerers.

"You're clansmen, aren't you?" the boy said to Sayyed in Clannish. "Yet you speak Turic, ride with the caravan, and look like Hajira."

"You don't miss much, do you?" Rafnir said, offering him a weak smile.

To the clansmen's surprise, the boy slouched forward, letting his hair fall over his eyes. His mouth slackened into a loose-lipped grin, and the bright glint of awareness in his eyes dulled to a blank stare. He looked so much like the simpleton people thought him to be, Sayyed simply stared.

"It's amazing what you can hear when people pretend you don't exist," Tassilio laughed. He straightened and as quickly snapped back into his alert, cheerful self.

Hajira stirred for the first time. "Tassilio was the one who saw the thugs jump you at the baggage wagons. He came to get me."

Sayyed sipped his wine, letting the tart liquid soothe his dry and aching throat. He wondered where to go with this conversation. How far could he trust even a brother he had not seen in so long? Hajira knew him for what he was, and when they were boys Hajira would have died before betraying his brother. But what would this man do? Who was he now?

"How did you know I was here?" he asked Hajira after a short pause.

"I recognized you from that day on the riverbank," Tassilio answered for his companion. "So I told Hajira you were in the caravan, and he told me to keep an eye on you."

The Turic warrior lifted an eyebrow at this enthusiastic speech. He seemed to be as quiet and taciturn as the boy was voluble. "We've heard many tales about a half-breed sorcerer who rode with the Lady Gabria," he said finally. "But Father would never allow your name to be spoken after you left. I did not realize it was you until tonight. We always thought you were dead."

Sayyed shook his head at the memory of his father. A stern, unrelenting man, the Raid-Ja believed that as leader of the Raid tribe he had to follow the exact letter of the law. When his youngest son revealed the unexpected and forbidden talent to wield magic, Dultar sadly but mercilessly disinherited him and exiled him from the tribe. The hurt of that rejection had dulled over the years, and after a time Sayyed accepted the results of that exile with gratitude. If he had not fled to the Clans, he would not have met Gabria and Athlone, nor his beloved Tam, nor would he have his handsome, if rather battered-looking son. In gratitude to the Living God who had watched over him so well, he leaned over and affectionately squeezed Rafnir's shoulder.

"Your son?" Hajira asked, eyeing his new nephew.

"Yes," Sayyed said. He leaned forward to study this brother he had known so long ago. Hajira did not look very different. He had matured, of course, but he still wore his mustache long to help elongate his broad face. His wide-set eyes were deep and large above a hawk-nose and a strong jaw, and when he stood, he still topped Sayyed by several inches.

What had changed, and what disturbed Sayyed, was the cut of Hajira's hair. His brother's long, thick hair and the intricate knot of a tribesman had been shaved off close to his skull—a cut that was usually reserved as a punishment for some crime of dishonor.

Sayyed took another sip of the wine and said, "And what of you? If you have heard tales of me then half of them are probably true and you know my life. How is yours? Tell me of the family."

Hajira laughed a short, sharp bark of amusement. "The family goes on as always. Alset is Raid-Ja now, and he is as unforgiving as Father ever was."

"Father is dead?"

"Four years ago. He died in his sleep."

"And Mother?"

"Well and happy and rejoicing in her grandchildren. She will be overjoyed to know you live." He paused and glanced at the two Hunnuli standing protectively behind Sayyed and Rafnir before adding, "As for me, I chose to join the Shar-Ja's guard, and there I have been for twenty years."

Sayyed was impressed. The Shar-Ja's personal guards were the elite warriors from every tribe. Initiates went through several years of rigorous training and conditioning and had to swear undying loyalty to the overlord. All would give their lives for the Shar-Ja. Almost unwillingly his gaze lifted to Hajira's head, and his brow furrowed.

His brother recognized his unspoken question. He cocked a half-smile. "Things have been changing in Cangora the past two years. I made the mistake of voicing my opinion of Counselor Zukhara rather forcefully. He could not dismiss me, but he had me reprimanded and transferred to guard Tassilio—a huge step-down in honor, he thought, sentenced to 'babysit the idiot.'" He chuckled as he repeated the counselor's words in a good imitation of Zukhara's sonorous voice.

A glow of humor lit like a lamp in Tassilio's face. "Smartest thing Zukhara ever did, and he doesn't even know it," Hajira went on. "This imp's mother sent him to court a year ago. He took one look at the political situation and has been acting the fool ever since to save his hide. He is the accepted, right-born second son of the Shar-Ja, and his heir after Bashan. You saw what happened to the Shar-Yon."

"The Fel Azureth have sworn to kill the Shar-Ja and all his offspring," Tassilio said in a flat voice. "When Father got sick, I pretended to go crazy. The law protects lepers and fools."

Sayyed blinked, both amazed at the boy's wit and dismayed by the circumstances that drove him to such desperate measures. "What does your father think of your subterfuge?"

The boy looked away quickly, but not before Sayyed saw the glitter of unshed tears in his eyes. "I doubt Father has even noticed. He saw only Bashan."

Sayyed sat straighter to draw the boy's attention back to himself. 'Who do you think killed the Shar-Yon?" he asked Hajira and Tassilio with deliberate emphasis. His brother and the boy, young as he was, would make good allies in the caravan, and Sayyed wanted to put to rest any suspicions they might have.

"Perhaps we did. Do you think we are here to assassinate the Shar-Ja as well?" Rafnir put in. "As Zukhara said, only clan blood carries the talent to wield magic."

Tassilio squirmed and looked as if he would say something, but this time he waited and deferred to the warrior sitting beside him.

It was Hajira who spoke first. He put more fuel on the fire, poured more *firza,* and thought carefully before he made his answer. "I didn't know what to think when I heard a clan magic-wielder was in the caravan. The thought that this sorcerer was here to harm the Shar-Ja crossed my mind. But I know you. Twenty-six years would not be enough time to turn my brother into an assassin."

Tassilio's head shook vigorously. "Not the half-breed who turned sorcerer, fought gorthlings and plagues and stone lions, who tames the black Hunnuli and rides with the Lady of the Dead Clan," he blurted out. "Do you really have a diamond splinter in your wrist?"

Sayyed's lips twitched at the boy's outburst. He was amazed that Tassilio knew so much about his past and viewed it with such enthusiasm. Sorcery was supposed to be outlawed, but obviously the stories of the clans had traveled over the borders. Obligingly he pulled back the long sleeve of his robes and revealed a tooled leather wristband on his right arm. As soon as he loosened the lacings, the band slid off, revealing the pale glow of the splinter just beneath his skin. About two inches long, the slender diamond gleamed dusky red through the blood that flowed around it.

Tassilio's eyes grew wide. "So you are not here to kill Father. Why are you here?" he asked directly.

"To find Bashan's murderer?" Hajira suggested.

Sayyed pulled the armband back on. "If we can, and to find the Lady of the Dead Clan and the healer with the winged horse," he told them in a terse voice.

Both guard and boy sat up with a jerk and shared a bewildered look. "Lady Gabria and—"

"Kelene," Rafnir finished for them. "My wife. She and Lady Gabria disappeared the night your caravan left Council Rock. We are trying to find them."

Hajira did not ask why they had come to search the caravan. The fact that they had risked doing so gave enough credence to their news. "I can promise you they are not with the Shar-Ja or any of his immediate servants. Tassilio or I would know if they were there. Where else have you looked?"

Sayyed told him everything they had seen and examined so far. "We were checking wagons in the baggage train when we were jumped."

"Odd place for an ambush," Hajira said, scratching his neck thoughtfully. "I wonder if someone has something to hide and has set guards. They obviously didn't know you were sorcerers, or they would have killed you instantly."

"There are several big covered vans that could carry two Hunnuli," Tassilio pointed out. "We could check them tomorrow night." His sadness put aside, he turned his youthful enthusiasm to the thrill of the mystery.

His dark-clad guard turned on him. "What is this *we*? *You* will stay in your tent where you belong."

Tassilio drew a long, quivering sigh, but one eyelid drooped in a quick wink to Sayyed.

They doused the fire and thoroughly erased every sign of their presence in the hollow. With Tassilio and his dog leading the way, the two brothers walked side by side back to the sprawling camp. Tibor carried Rafnir, who still suffered the ill-effects of the vicious blow to his head. Sick and weak, Rafnir decided to find his blankets and sleep in a sheltered nook where Tibor could watch over him. Sayyed helped him find a place and settled him comfortably.

Tassilio dubiously eyed the big black horse standing over Rafnir. "Is that your Hunnuli? Where is its lightning?"

Tibor obliged his curiosity by turning his right shoulder to Tassilio. The boy dug his fingers into the stallion's hair and crowed with delight when he found white skin beneath the black dye. To the brothers' amusement, Tassilio asked if he could join Rafnir, saying he'd rest better if a Hunnuli guarded his bed.

Hajira acquiesced, and Tibor gently sniffed the boy all over and nickered his acceptance. Tassilio quickly bedded down next to Rafnir, his dog cuddled beside him, before Hajira could change his mind.

Although his head pounded and his muscles felt sore and weak, Sayyed did not want to sleep yet. Under Afer's close watch, he and Hajira walked around the outer perimeter of the camp, talking for hours about everything that came to mind. Their companionship pleased Sayyed, for the years seemed to fall away, and he and his brother moved back into the easy, confident relationship they had enjoyed before their father tore them apart and sent Sayyed into exile.

For the first time since the plague, Sayyed found himself talking at length about Tam. While Hajira strode silently at his side, he told him of their life together, how Tam saved his life while still a girl, how he waited five years for her to reach maturity, of her love for her animals, her courage and strength, and at last, in a voice that still trembled after three years, he told his brother of her death in the plague tent and of the fatal grief of her Hunnuli.

When he was through, he drew a long breath and slowly exhaled, feeling better somehow for opening his thoughts to Hajira. He had kept his memories of Tam buried deep in his mind, out of sight where they would not hurt so badly, but now that he had brought them out fresh and shining for his brother, he realized he had been missing an important part of his healing. He needed to talk about Tam, to remember their love and joy together. To fail to do so diminished the life she had left behind.

When Sayyed's words trailed away and he lapsed into his own thoughts, Hajira laughed softly, his black, brilliant eyes filled a new measure of respect. "For years I have hated Father for sending you away. Now I see that, knowing or unknowing, he did you the greatest of favors."

They walked on peacefully for a while until they passed the cluster of luxurious tents set aside for the counselors and the tribal leaders who attended the Shar-Ja. As they approached the Shar-Ja's huge tent, several loyal guards on duty snapped to attention and saluted Hajira. The warrior did not return the salutes but nodded at the men's mark of respect.

The sorcerer noted the strange exchange and said, "You were more than a guardsman, weren't you?"

Hajira hesitated an instant, then drew himself up with a warrior's pride. "I was Commander of the Tenth Horse, the oldest and most honored cavalry unit in the Shar-Ja's guard. We were called the Panthers for our silence, our cunning, and our speed in the attack. Now I am a foot soldier in the lowliest ranks, whose only duty is obligatory guard on a simpleton of a sandrat." Bitterness shook the timbre of his deep voice, and his hands curled as if gripping an invisible weapon.

"But that's some sandrat," Sayyed remarked, hoping to ease Hajira's tension.

His words helped a little, for the warrior's hands relaxed, and he laughed ruefully. "That boy was a real surprise."

"What happened?" Sayyed asked. They had passed the Shar-Ja's tent and were walking by a large area of tents and crude shelters. The escorts from all fifteen tribes camped together, drinking, gaming, talking, and bickering half the night. Girls from the oasis settlement came to entertain them for coins, and enterprising tradesmen brought trays of food and kegs of drink to sell. Even at that late hour, a few fires still burned, and occasional laughter and song could be heard mixed with the mournful howls of wild dogs sniffing for food about the edges of the great camp.

Sayyed remembered the six dead assassins and wished the dogs a good meal. He glanced at his brother. There was just enough distant firelight for him to recognize the stony set of Hajira's broad face, and he wondered if the warrior was going to ignore his question.

But Hajira had brought his anger under control and fully regained his trust in the younger brother he had once thought dead. "You know the Shar-Ja has been ill almost a year," he began. "It was about that time that the Gryphon and his extremists captured the holy shrine of the Prophet Sargun and declared their intention to destroy the Shar-Ja's corrupt court and return the leadership of the tribes to a high priest. No one paid much attention to them at first because the priests and the tribal councils were too busy dealing with the effects of the drought and the Shar-Ja's declining health. No one was able to find the cause of his malady or a cure, so he turned over many of his responsibilities to his son.

"For a while, Bashan did a good job. But then things started to go wrong. Grain shipments to the cities disappeared; the tribal chiefs grew resentful; counselors were murdered; violence on the roads increased dramatically. Then news came that the Fel Azureth was spreading across the realm and causing problems over the Altai. The remaining counselors lost confidence in the Shar-Ja and his son. Finally someone suggested Counselor Zukhara replace the Shar-Yon and take control of the royal council until the Shar-Ja returned to health."

Here Hajira paused, and a wry smile crossed his lips. "Royal guards, even Panthers, are not permitted to draw weapons in the council chambers, but when that weasel-eyed, honey-tongued Zukhara agreed and ordered the Shar-Yon to leave the council, I objected." He drew his long, curved tulwar and held it out at arm's length. "With this. If Bashan had not ordered me to stand down, I probably would have killed the counselor and paid for it with dishonor and disemboweling. Zukhara has hated me ever since." His arm fell, and the gleaming blade whispered back into its sheath. "Bashan saved my life that day, but I was not there to save his. For the honor I owe his father, I will protect his brother and I *will* find Bashan's killer."

Sayyed stopped. "Then we hunt the same trail, for the Turics will not give the clans peace until the Shar-Yon is avenged." He raised his right hand, palm upward, and extended it toward his brother.

Hajira's hand met his, clasped it tightly, and lifted both into a joined fist that wordlessly sealed their vow of mutual trust and commitment.

Together they turned and began to walk back toward the place where they had left Rafnir and Tassilio. Afer dutifully followed, looking for all the world like a simple horse on a lead line. Only Sayyed and Hajira, who had seen both the killing fury and the loving devotion in the glittering dark eyes, knew the stallion for what he was.

The two men found the younger ones wrapped in their blankets, contentedly asleep under the attentive watch of the Hunnuli and the dog. Exhausted at last, Sayyed threw himself down by his son and fell into a rightfully earned sleep. Hajira prowled around the perimeter of their sleeping area for several more minutes, the ingrained caution of years urging him to check the dark shadows one last time before he slept. At last, cocking an eye at the two black stallions, he stretched out near Tassilio and allowed himself to rest.

* * *

Just before sunrise and the morning horns, Hajira woke Sayyed. Without speaking, they left the Hunnuli and the other sleepers and strode purposefully in the direction of the baggage wagons. They climbed a short rise where they could see the wagons and vans parked row by row in the early light. Talking and gesturing to hide their true intent, they took turns studying the wheeled vehicles.

After several minutes of this, Hajira's expression turned thoughtful, and he said in a low tone, "Take a look at the large, covered van. Last row, near the end. There are several men lounging nearby."

Sayyed made a casual turn as if he wanted to look at something on the paling horizon. "I haven't noticed that one before. The brown one, wood roof, and some sort of red emblem on the side?" He felt a surge of hope. The van looked big enough to hold both the mares and the women.

"That's the one. It looks worn. It's probably a merchant wagon that was rented or borrowed. But those men down there do not look much like drivers."

"Hmm, no. They are dressed like the men who attacked us. More guards perhaps?" Sayyed suddenly stiffened, and he had to force himself to look naturally away from the men below. "I know one of those men. The lean one. He has gray in his hair and a mole on his cheek. I saw him slip into the caravan two days ago."

Hajira's face lost its friendliness, and his eyes turned hot and frustrated. "Have you seen others coming into the caravan?"

"Several groups," the sorcerer confirmed. "They were heavily armed and arrived at dusk."

The warrior frowned. "I was right!" he said fiercely. "Someone is fattening the tribal levies with mercenaries and fanatics. I have tried to warn the counselors, but no one will listen to me. I am dishonored!" he spat. "And other men are too afraid to talk. The Gryphon has sworn to call a holy war, and no one wants to get in his way."

Sayyed sucked in his breath. A holy war was a call to battle in the name of the Living God, a call that few Turics would ignore. Usually the holy war was used in times of invasion or war with other nations. Never had a holy war been called to incite rebellion within the Turic nation itself. "The God forbid," he murmured.

"Indeed. The Gryphon may be planning a coup before we reach Cangora in nine days." He turned on his heel and strode down the rise away from the wagons. Sayyed followed. "We'd better find your women and get them out. We certainly do not need two magic-wielders caught in the middle of a civil war."

Sayyed couldn't agree more.

They split up after that, Hajira taking his charge to the front of the caravan near the funeral wagon and Sayyed and Rafnir riding in the midst of the tribal escorts. For fear of attracting attention, they all kept their distance from the wagon train that brought up the rear.

The ride that day was long and hard, over a rolling, twisting road that reached to the rising Absarotan foothills. It was dark by the time the caravan stopped at the next oasis, the Impala Springs. The people were too tired to set up a full camp, so they put out crude shelters, ate cold food, and went thankfully to bed. Only the Shar-Ja and his counselors had their tents erected for the night.

Hajira waited only until the camp was settled before he sought out the clansmen. Ignoring Tassilio's protests, he left the boy with the Hunnuli and led Rafnir and Sayyed back to the parked wagons and vans. They did not have to search long before they made an alarming discovery.

The large wooden van with the red emblem on its side was gone.

7

Almost frantically the three men checked the baggage wagons again, from one end of the field of parked vehicles to the other. There was no brown van and no guards, only a few drivers tending to their wagons. Sayyed asked several about the van, but no one had paid much attention to one brown vehicle among so many, and no one had noticed it leave. The men then looked everywhere in the oasis village, around the stone-walled springs, in other areas of the camp, even in some outlying gullies, hollows, and dry valleys. All to no avail. The unremarkable brown wagon had vanished from the caravan.

Frustrated and upset, Sayyed and Rafnir returned with Hajira to the Hunnuli. The night was well advanced, but the men were too agitated to sleep. The allotted four days were gone, and their only possible lead had disappeared somewhere along the leagues of the Spice Road.

"We have several choices," declared Sayyed, his arms crossed and his face grim. "We can go back to the Altai and find the Fel Azureth, to learn if they have Gabria and Kelene. We can continue to search the caravan, or we can abandon both ideas and go in search of an unknown wagon that may or may not be holding the women."

"The road forks three ways," Hajira said softly. "Which way does the heart go?"

Tassilio put his hand on Sayyed's sleeve. "The Fel Azureth would not take them. They believe too firmly in their own righteousness. They would not stoop to coercing a power they believe to be heretical."

All three men gazed at Tassilio, astonished at the boy's astute observation. His earnest, eager face brightened under their stare, and he pushed a foot forward, crossed his arms, and lifted an imperious chin in such an excellent imitation of his father, Hajira nearly choked.

"He's right," the guardsman conceded. "The core of the Fel Azureth are extreme fanatics who despise any religion or power not their own. Of course, that doesn't mean someone else didn't kidnap the sorceresses to make trouble for

the fanatics." He lapsed into silence and brooded over their lack of tangible results, his fingers drumming on the hilt of his sword.

Rafnir, too young and intense to bear his patience stoically, began to pace
step after angry step between the men and the Hunnuli. "So where does that
leave us, Father?" he demanded. "There's nowhere to go forward and too many
places to go back!"

The older sorcerer rubbed his neck against the throbbing pain in his head. It
had been a very long day and night, and he was still suffering from the after-
effects of the blow to his head. He closed his eyes and drew a long, filling
breath. "I wish to sleep on this decision," he said. "I will decide in the morning
which fork in the road we'll take."

The other men did not argue. There was little point wasting more time or effort on discussion when there was nothing they could do about it until daylight
anyway. With Tassilio between them and the Hunnuli keeping guard, they rolled
themselves in their blankets to wait for morning.

Deep in the night, Sayyed's dreams fled to the Ramtharin Plains. He rode
frantically on a desert horse after a golden cloaked woman on a cantering
Hunnuli. He chased her, shouting, until she slowed and waited for him. He
expected to see Tam, but when he neared and the woman turned around, she
pulled off her hood and revealed Gabria's face as she had been twenty-six
years ago when he first saw her that spring day and fell instantly in love with
her. Sayyed's heart ached at her loveliness. She smiled at him with all the
warmth and love he remembered, and without a word she lifted her arm to
point to a range of mountains. Abruptly she disappeared, and Sayyed found
himself in a stifling darkness. He cried out, more at her loss than at the
blackness that covered him, and he tried to lunge away from the constricting
dark. He discovered he could not move his arms or legs. Something pinioned
him from head to foot, something that groaned and creaked close to his
head. Then he heard her voice, no more than a faint whisper in his head,
"Sayyed."

"Gabria!" he shouted, and his own voice jolted him awake. He jumped to his
feet and saw morning had already lit the skies with apricot and gold. Afer
nudged him with his muzzle, and Sayyed leaned gratefully into the stallion's
powerful shoulder.

Rafnir, with five days' growth of beard on his face, yawned and clambered
out of his blankets. His eyes met his father's, and they locked in a long, consid-
ering stare.

"I think we should look for the wagon," Rafnir said quietly. "I don't believe
they are here."

Sayyed said nothing, for he had looked over Rafnir's shoulder to the mountains northwest of the oasis. He had seen the peaks in the days before as the caravan slowly traveled closer. Last night, though, when they reached the springs,

it had been too dark to see details of the great, gray-green chain of mountains that still lay perhaps ten or twenty leagues away. Now he saw them clearly, bathed in the morning light, and he recognized their rugged crowns as surely as he had known Gabria. She had pointed west to those same mountains in his dream. He pondered, too, the other elements: the meaning of the darkness, the creaking noise, and Gabria's voice.

Was a dream any more of a clue than a hunch or a guess or an idea? Was it a sign sent by Amara or just his tired mind furnishing a solution to his dilemma? Perhaps Gabria's talent was reaching out to him. Whatever its meaning or its source, he decided to follow its lead, for lack of any other evidence. "The wagon it is," he said.

Hajira, who had awakened with Tassilio, drew a small knife from a sheath hidden in his boot. Thin and slender as a reed, the blade fit easily into his palm. The handle was a tiny gryphon's head carved from a flat slice of opal so the beast's face shone with rainbow colors in the sun. Hajira handed the blade to Sayyed. "Keep this when you go. If you need me for anything, send the knife with your message and I will come." He put his arm around Tassilio's shoulders, a fatherly gesture the boy accepted gladly. "We will keep our ears alert. If anyone has the women close by, we will learn of it."

Sayyed ran a finger along the hilt. Although gryphons were extinct, they were still powerful symbols of loyalty and courage in the Turic faith. "A beautiful knife," he said.

"A gift from the Shar-Ja," Hajira replied, unable to completely disguise the ironic bitterness in his voice.

The sorcerer tucked away the knife and took something from his saddlebag. It was a rope as thick as his little finger. "Many years ago magic wards were made of ivory or wood, carved into balls of great beauty," he explained to Hajira and Tassilio. As he talked he deftly cut a length of the rope and began tying an intricate knot in the middle of the section. "Unfortunately, I do not have time to carve. This will have to do for now." He laid the knot on the ground and before Tassilio's fascinated gaze, he touched the knot and spoke the words to a spell he had memorized from the *Book of Matrah*.

The magic glowed red on the rope knot for just a minute before it sank into the twisted fibers. Sayyed picked it up, tied it into a loop, and gave it to Tassilio. "This is not as strong as the old ones, but this magic ward will help protect you against all but the most powerful of spells."

Tassilio marveled at the gift. He accepted the knot without his usual blithe smile and hung it gratefully around his neck.

After morning prayers, the four ate a quick breakfast together, saddled the Hunnuli, and made their farewells.

"Watch your back," Sayyed told his brother. The two men embraced, both thankful for this unexpected meeting after so many years. The clansmen mounted and waved to the lone guardsman and his royal charge. Hajira lifted his arm in salute.

The Hunnuli unhurriedly trotted through the outskirts of the caravan camp toward the settlement. The camp bustled with preparations to leave, and everyone was too busy to pay attention to two tribesmen minding their own business.

Before long the camp and the oasis with its slow bubbling springs were left behind. As soon as they were out of sight of the camp, Rafnir and Sayyed split up, each taking a side of the beaten caravan road. The chances of finding the tracks of one wagon, particularly the right wagon, were very small. On the other hand, the men knew the conveyance had left the caravan somewhere between the Impala Springs and Oasis Three, and they planned to search every square inch of territory along the road until they found some trace of the missing van.

With the help of their stallions' keen sense of smell and their own knowledge of tracking, the men examined the Spice Road for leagues. It wasn't easy. The Shar-Ja's vast caravan had left a huge trail of hoofprints, wheel tracks, boot marks, trash, and dung piles, while subsequent traffic had added its own signs. Well-traveled side roads joined the trail here and there, and the route passed through two tribal settlements, each with its own collection of carts and wagons.

The clansmen asked for information at the tiny villages, and they questioned other travelers, but no one remembered seeing a wagon of that description. They fought a constant struggle between their desire to hurry in case the wagon was somewhere ahead of them on the road and the need for slow, careful scrutiny for tracks in case the wagon had been driven off the road to some remote destination. Through most of the day, the men forced their frustration aside and worked their way slowly northeastward.

The afternoon sun slanted toward evening when Sayyed and Rafnir returned to the road and walked their horses side by side. The caravan route passed through a hump of tall hills, forcing travelers to go through a narrow cut walled with steep slopes and shaded with fragrant cedar and pine. Father and son rode quietly, each occupied with his own thoughts, until they rode out of the hills and came to a long, rolling stretch of road.

There is another track to the left, Afer told Sayyed. The stallion was right. It was faint and overgrown, but a two-wheeled track split off from the main road and wended its way into the barren, brown range. The horses followed the track a short distance and stopped to allow Sayyed and Rafnir to dismount.

"Something heavy has traveled this way very recently," Sayyed observed. He pointed to wheel marks in the dirt and crushed clumps of grass.

Rafnir bent to look. "But is it our missing wagon?" He looked back the way they had come toward the hump of hills. "If you were planning to leave a caravan with little notice, this would be a good place to do it."

Sayyed studied the hills and saw what Rafnir meant. A wagon lagging behind could easily veer off the road when the rest of the baggage train turned out of sight into the tree-lined cut. "So, do we continue along the road or try this track?"

"Try the track," Rafnir suggested. He shaded his eyes with a hand and looked down the course of the trail as far as he could see. If the track continued its apparent direction, it would eventually reach the mountains.

The men mounted again, and the Hunnuli stretched out into a slow, easy canter. There were few places a wagon could leave that track, and the trail wound on, clear and obvious even through the dry vegetation. They had ridden for almost half an hour, one in front of the other, when Tibor veered off the path so abruptly, Rafnir was unseated. Reacting quickly, the sorcerer grabbed the stallion's mane and hauled himself back into the saddle.

Look! Tibor sent excitedly before Rafnir could voice any of the words that came to his lips, and the stallion nosed something on the ground.

Rafnir could not see the object over Tibor's big head, so he slid off and pushed the stallion's nose aside. All he saw was a thin strip of red dangling from the long, sharp leaves of a dagger plant. His eyes suddenly popped wide, and he whooped with delight. "It's Kelene's hair ribbon," he yelled, waving the trophy in the air.

"Are you sure?" Sayyed's brow rose dubiously.

I am. Tibor neighed. *It has her smell.*

"They're just ahead of us!" Rafnir crowed. "She must have left this as a sign."

The two men grinned at each other. For the first time in five days they had a definite lead, and they did not want to waste it. Rafnir quickly tied the ribbon around his arm and leaped into the saddle. The Hunnuli sprang away.

The wagon had a day's lead on them, but no living creature could outrun or outlast a Hunnuli. The horses ran for the rest of the daylight hours, until the sun slid behind the mountains and night fell. They saw no more signs of the women, only the wagon track drawing nearer and nearer to the mountains.

As soon as the sun set, the Hunnuli were forced to stop. Although they could have run all night, a high veil of clouds covered the sky and hid the light of the moon and stars. The men were afraid to proceed for fear of missing another sign or losing the faint trail in the darkness. Reluctantly they made a cold camp and bedded down for some much-needed sleep.

Just before dawn the men roused, ate a quick meal, and made their prayers on bended knee. Rafnir felt comfortable now with this morning oblation, and he silently sent his plea to the mother goddess to watch over his wife and her mother. By the time the light was strong enough to see the trail, the men and the Hunnuli were on their way. The path went on before them, like two pale parallel ribbons that led ever westward into the foothills of the Absarotan Mountains.

Swiftly the land rose into bleak, rumpled uplands whose brown slopes lay bare to the arching sky. Dry creekbeds and gullies ran like cracks down the slopes, and rough outcroppings of weathered stone poked up like ancient ruins through the grass. Not far ahead the mountains reared their towering peaks above the parched plains and sat like brooding giants over their deep, unseen valleys.

A warm wind from the east blew steadily during the day and slowly piled clouds up against the mountains' lofty heads. By midafternoon, towering thunderheads began to form, and the elemental forces of a storm were spawned in the battle between air, stone, and fire.

On the ground the men and Hunnuli sensed the coming storm in the magical energies around them. In a phenomenon little understood by the magic-wielders themselves, thunderstorms strengthened the forces of magic and enhanced the sorcerers' ability to wield it. Even before the sky turned to steel and the first bolt of lightning streaked to earth, the two sorcerers could feel the tingle in their blood and the building exhilaration as the storm brewed along the mountain's face.

Worriedly they hurried on, but there was still no sign of the elusive wagon except for its tracks winding ever higher into the inhospitable flanks of the mountains. In the late afternoon they rode up a rocky ridge, crested the top, and stopped to look around. Although the van was nowhere in sight, they saw two shepherds hurrying a flock of goats down a valley below. Afer and Tibor quickly caught up with the shepherds, and the clansmen cordially greeted the two Turics.

The shepherds eyed them and the big horses suspiciously until they recognized the Raid crests on the riders' robes.

"The True God go with you, travelers," the younger shepherd said over the bleating goats. "We thought you might be taxers or collectors for the Fel Azureth."

Sayyed chuckled. "The Raid ride only for honor, which is why we're so poor."

The shepherds relaxed a little, but they shifted their feet, anxious to be away. Their goats, the long-legged, rangy mountain breed, crowded around them, noisy and impatient. Sayyed quickly asked about the wagon.

"Haven't seen it today," the older shepherd replied. "We've had the herd in the meadows up there." He pointed toward one mountain rather isolated from the rest, a savage, lonely peak with its crown buried in the clouds. "Had to bring 'em down early, though. The Storm King grows angry."

"The who?" Rafnir asked.

"You are strangers here." The shepherd grimaced. "Yonder lies the Storm King," he pointed to the same peak. "The old man can force ferocious storms when his anger is up."

"Well, do you know where that road goes?"

The shepherds looked at one another as if trying to jog each other's memories. "Doesn't it go to that old fortress?" the young one offered.

The other shrugged. "Could be. The main trail to the place is south of here, but I've heard there was a back road going up there. I just never followed this one. Won't go up there myself."

Something in his tone caused Rafnir to ask, "Why not?"

Both men were startled when the shepherds crossed their wrists to ward off evil. "There's something dark far back in those mountains. Some old evil that won't die away. Something I wouldn't risk for all the gold on Storm King," the old shepherd said.

"If you're going on that road," suggested the young one forcefully, "don't stray off it. Find your wagon and get out as fast as you can." Without waiting for an answer, the shepherds rounded up their herd and turned away.

The Hunnuli returned to the track and resumed a canter. The men saw now that the trail headed toward the peak the shepherds had called the Storm King. True to its name, the mountain sat under a roiling gray-and-white mantle of cloud that obscured its upper slopes. Lightning crackled around its crown.

"We'd better find shelter soon," Sayyed called.

Faster now, the stallions galloped along the open path on the rising slopes of hills and ridges, but all too soon they reached the treeline and were forced to slow to a trot through the scattered groves of trees and heavy brush.

The hunters pushed on and on into the higher reaches, while the sky darkened and the wind began to roar through the trees. Dust and leaves whirled, and the warm, sultry air suddenly turned cold. Thunder rumbled in a continuous drumroll that echoed from peak to peak. The daylight died to a ghostly twilight.

Sayyed was scanning the trail ahead when a bolt of lightning snaked down from the clouds and exploded a tree close by. The thunderous shock wave nearly blew him from the saddle. Afer and Tibor neighed in pain from the horrendous sound. With that fanfare, the fury of the Storm King broke loose in a wind that came screaming down from the peak, snapping off branches and flattening grass.

Half-blinded by flying dust and grit, the men clung to the horses as the wind howled by them. The Hunnuli struggled on as best they could. In seconds, they had lost the trail in a whirlwind of dirt, debris, and leaves.

"Go on," Sayyed cried to Afer. "Find shelter!"

Obediently the old stallion plowed ahead, using his wits and his senses to locate any kind of shelter out of this terrible wind. Tibor struggled to stay close on his tail. Neither could see where they were going. All they could discern were darker shapes through the flying wind and the direction of the slopes under their feet. Lightning continued to explode, with shattering crescendos of thunder around them.

They had not yet found a safe place to stop when the hail came pelting down in curtains of stinging pellets. Mumbling an oath, Sayyed tied his burnoose tightly across his face and stopped Afer. He hunched down, his back to the wind, and waited for Tibor to come close.

"We don't have much choice. We'll stay here until the storm passes," he shouted to Rafnir. "Let's make a shield."

Rafnir nodded a reply. They started the spell to form a storm-proof dome against the wind and hail.

Afer lifted his head. *I smell something! I cannot tell what it is, but it smells man-made,* the Hunnuli told both men.

Sayyed grimaced. "Do we look for it?"

"Let's try. There's no knowing how long this storm will last, and shelter would be welcome."

Excitedly now, Afer plunged ahead into the wind and whipping ice. Using the magic they had already summoned, the men formed small shields of power and used the energy to ward off the worst of the weather. Tibor hurried after Afer along a saddleback ridge and down into a steep, narrow valley.

Dusk came and went too quickly, and an impenetrable night blanketed the mountains. The hail finally dwindled to a stop only to be replaced by a heavy torrent of rain. In moments Sayyed and Rafnir were soaked by the cold downpour in spite of their shields. Still Afer went on after the elusive scent, leading them farther up the valley along the banks of a small, tumbling stream. In the dense darkness and pouring rain, they were unaware that the valley walls were rising steeper and higher the deeper into the mountains they went.

Then, without warning, a towering shape loomed out of the darkness. Twice as tall as a man, thick and ungainly, it sat in the middle of the canyon floor like a misshapen row of large human heads set one on top of the other. The topmost head, its gruesome face nearly lost in the gloom, glowered down the valley at any who approached it.

It is stone, snorted Tibor.

"Yes, but what is it?" Rafnir exclaimed, not really expecting an answer. The huge statue was unlike anything he had ever seen.

"It is an ancestor pole, an ancient device used to warn evil spirits," Sayyed replied wearily.

Rafnir shivered in the icy blast of the wind. "I don't think it's working. Is this what you smelled?" he asked Afer.

Some of it. But now I sense other things, Afer answered.

So do I. Man smells on wood, stone, and smoke. Horses, too, added Tibor.

"Then let's go," Sayyed sighed. The need for shelter outweighed his caution and curiosity. They circled past the strange statue and pushed ahead up the canyon.

In the dark and the storm they did not see the top head turn slowly around to watch them ride up the valley.

Although they found a faint animal track that followed the course of the stream, the going proved very difficult. The path wound through heaps of boulders, rock outcroppings, marshy pools, and heavy brush. Sayyed and Rafnir had to dissolve their power shields because they could not concentrate on maintaining the magic and finding the path at the same time. Sayyed settled on a small globe of light instead. Once set alight, the magic sphere would glow without much attention, and its light was a welcome help in the storm-wracked night.

Barely an hour had gone by after they left the unknown statue when the canyon ended abruptly in a sheer wall of striated stone. At the foot of the wall, the stream bubbled up out of a deep, clear pool that steamed and frothed in the pouring rain. Instead of stopping, Afer turned left into a cleft in the walls that was so narrow the men would have missed it. The passage within was deep and dark and cut off nearly all the force of the wind and rain. The Hunnuli continued up the crevice without pause, ignoring the walls that closed in on both sides and towered nearly forty feet above their heads.

The men and horses walked in single file along the passage for several minutes, grateful for the respite from the weather. The Hunnuli's noses lifted high, and their ears strained forward to catch more sign of the humans they knew were close. They were so attuned to what lay ahead, they did not notice anything behind until they heard something akin to thunder followed by a rumbling, crashing noise from the mouth of the crevice.

Tibor neighed stridently, but in the flash of a moment, two ropes that glowed a pale silver in the darkness snaked down from above. The ropes looped around both men's necks and hauled them off their saddles. Jerking and twisting, they were pulled upward so swiftly the Hunnuli could only scream their rage and paw the empty air.

Hands grabbed at Sayyed just as he passed out, and for the second time he and Rafnir were taken prisoner by an enemy they could not see.

In the crevice below, the magic sphere died out, and the Hunnuli were left in darkness.

8

The gag bit deep into Kelene's mouth, drying her tongue and forcing her mouth open to such an impossible angle she could barely work her jaw. Her lips were dry and swollen, and her entire head ached with a pounding throb that brought tears to her eyes. Ignoring the pain in her right arm, she struggled again to reach the gag, but her hands had been tied tightly to her sides and the knots would not budge. Already her hands were swelling, and she could feel blood trickling down her wrists.

She had tried several times to break the ropes with magic, to no avail. Whoever had tied them knew magic-wielders well and had crafted bonds woven from the hairs of a Hunnuli's tail. Like the horse itself, the hair was impervious to magic. Briefly, Kelene wondered what horse the hairs had come from.

She subsided onto the pallet and thought of several vile curses she could heap on the head of the person who did this as soon as she worked her hands and mouth free. Close beside her she felt the heat and closeness of Gabria's body trussed in the same painful manner. She wasn't sure if her mother was asleep, unconscious, or simply biding her time. The older sorceress had awakened some time earlier, struggled against her bonds, and then slipped into a stillness without motion or sound.

Kelene sighed a short breath of frustration and looked through the dim light at her surroundings. She already knew by heart the few things she could see, yet she continued to hope she would notice something new that could help her. She and Gabria were in a wagon—that much she had realized the moment she regained consciousness hours ago. It was not a clan wagon, since the box was too big and enclosed with wooden sides and a slightly peaked wooden roof. One door at the rear allowed access into the wagon, and a tiny window opened under the roof for ventilation. The vehicle reminded Kelene of the merchant wagons she sometimes saw at the clans' summer gatherings, the kind that had room for sale goods and a small living space for the merchant.

She and Gabria were lying on a fold-down bed rather than on the floor, and from her place she could just make out a small table folded up against the wall and a short bench. The interior of the wagon was dark, except for a few pale glimmers of light that leaked in through a crack by the door frame and around the roof.

Just beyond their pallet, in the darker end of the van, stood Nara and Demira, side by side in a wooden stall Kelene guessed had been specially built for them. The wall separating them from the women was built from thick, heavy timbers that looked strong enough to contain even a Hunnuli. Neither mare had responded to Kelene's noises, and she wondered if they had been sedated. If she lifted her head as high as her bonds allowed, she could barely make out the two horses standing with their heads facing the front of the wagon. Each mare wore a halter and Demira's wings appeared to be fastened to her sides by a wide strip of fabric. Someone had gone to a great deal of trouble.

Angrily Kelene struggled upright until she was sitting on the edge of the bed board. Knowing they were in a wagon was useful, but she still did not know who had taken them or why, or where they were going. She tried to think back to that night they were attacked by the river. Was it last night or two nights ago? She couldn't be certain. Everything that had happened since she and her mother rode to the riverbank was a blank. She remembered seeing several dark men coming at her, and she recalled the pain and fear when Demira fell. Her arm had been hurt when she struck the ground, and then everything had gone black. She did not know how she, Gabria, and the horses had been moved to the wagon, nor did she see who had done it. Her memory was blank until this morning, when she woke with a crushing headache and a desire to see the perpetrator drawn and quartered by teams of slow horses.

Outside the wagon she could hear the crack of whips, the thudding of many hooves, and the creak of other wagons. Dust from the road filtered between the old wall boards and swirled in the tiny, pale beams of light that shone through the cracks in the roof. Kelene guessed their wagon was part of a caravan, but without further clues she had no clear idea which way they were going.

The wagon gave a sudden lurch, and Kelene lost her precarious perch on the bed. Unable to catch herself, she crashed to the floor on her injured arm. The pain almost knocked her out again. She lay on her back and gritted her teeth on the gag while tears trickled along her temples. Her stomach felt nauseated.

On the pallet above her, Gabria rolled over to the edge and looked down. Her green eyes were shadowed and sunken in her thin face, but they gleamed with awareness and concern.

The creak of the door alerted both women, and they lifted their heads just as daylight flooded the interior. A dark silhouette stood balanced in the open doorway in a block of light so strong neither sorceress could see who it was.

"Good. You're awake," a flat voice said. The speaker ignored the fact that Kelene lay on the floor and went on in a cold, deadpan tone. "We will be arriving at an oasis soon. I will bring you food and water then. If you cause any trouble, try to raise attention, or cast any spell I will kill your Hunnuli." The figure stepped down and slammed the door shut without further speech.

The women's eyes met in a silent exchange of confusion, worry, and anger. Kelene lay back on the floor. It seemed better to stay where she was than to struggle painfully back to the raised bed. At least her arm had quit pounding with such intensity.

She closed her eyes and turned her mind inward to the spells she had used the winter before to repair her crippled ankle. She wished she had the healing stones from Moy Tura, for one was spelled to help set broken bones. Some medicinal herbs like comfrey or boneset would be nice, too, but those and the stones were in her healer's bag and the gods alone knew what had happened to that. Her bag, their cloaks, boots, and jewelry were gone, probably stolen or thrown away.

She concentrated instead on the magic, turning it inward to seek the damage to her upper right arm. At least that part of the arm had only one bone to work with, unlike an ankle and foot that were a puzzle of small bones and tendons. She knew the bone was not shattered, but it felt badly bruised and probably fractured. Using only a small pulse of magic in her spell, she smoothed over the crack in the bone and gently increased her body's natural defense against pain.

The throbbing eased to a dull ache and, as the spell ended, Kelene became drowsy. In spite of the dust and the hard floor, she bowed to her own medicine and soon fell asleep.

* * *

Zukhara.

Kelene's eyes flew open in surprise at the name that appeared so clearly in her mind. She stared up through the darkness and wondered why she should think of the Turic counselor now. He was an unpleasant person who had little regard for the Shar-Ja or the peace council. He was well out of her life. Here, Kelene's thoughts faltered. Something had brought him to mind. Some memory or clue had jogged her overworked thoughts and brought him clearly and vividly to her attention.

She glanced around and saw night had come. The wagon had stopped swaying, and the world had fallen quiet beyond the wagon walls. The words of their visitor came back to her—he would be coming with food and water when the caravan halted at an oasis.

Kelene stiffened in her bonds. The words and the man's voice echoed in her head. The voice had meant nothing to her when she was distracted by her own pain and discomfort, but it struck a note of recognition now. Of course, she growled to herself. The silhouette now had a face: Zukhara's.

Soft footsteps crunched on gravel outside. The door opened, and the same lean figure climbed into the wagon and closed the door behind him. He was so tall he had to stoop under the wagon roof. He carried a small lamp, a waterskin, and several plates of food which he laid on the fold-down table.

Saying nothing, he bent over Kelene, picked her up. and set her effortlessly on the bench on the wall. Gabria, too, was shifted off the pallet and placed beside Kelene. Both women glared in unspeakable hatred at the man who had taken them prisoner.

Zukhara ignored their silent anger and set the food and water in front of them. He sat on the edge of the bed and let them stare for a long while at the refreshments set so tantalizingly close.

"Listen to me," he said finally. The tiny lamp flickered, sending harsh shadows shifting over the sharp angles of his face. "You are in the middle of the Turic realm. There is no escape. Your Hunnuli are safely sedated and will remain that way until we reach our destination. I know you will not leave them, but if you foolishly try to escape or cause any trouble while we travel with this caravan, I will not hesitate to kill them. Do you understand?"

Both women nodded, their eyes wide.

Zukhara continued, his words forceful and precise. "As long as you obey me, I will bring food and water twice a day. Defy me and one of you will die." He paused and pulled something out of the front of his robe. "I also have this." He showed them a small ball on a golden chain.

Kelene looked blank, but Gabria jerked in recognition. The ball was a beautiful piece of handcarved ivory, cut in a delicate tracery of interlocking knots. Within the ball were two more, one within the other, equally as intricate. Gabria had had a similar ball once, given to her by the high priest of the Cult of Krath. The balls, creations of an older age, were magic wards that protected their wearers from spells. There was no guessing how a Turic had found one or if he knew how to use it.

Zukhara acknowledged Gabria's recognition with a nod. "Now, if we understand each other, you may eat." With surprising gentleness, he untied the horsehair ropes around their arms and carefully eased the gags from their mouths. He left their feet tied.

Kelene and Gabria could do nothing more for a while than work some feeling back into their hands and arms. Their jaws ached miserably from the release of the tight gags, and their mouths were so dry they could barely swallow.

Zukhara poured water in mugs for them and watched impassively as each woman painstakingly sipped the liquid.

The first question Kelene thought to ask as soon as she could voice a word was, "Why?"

The counselor stroked his long, elegant chin while he considered how much he wanted them to know. "Let's just say I have need of you and your abilities." He would not elucidate further, and the clanswomen were too desperately thirsty and hungry to force the question. They ate and drank as best they could. The food was stew, surprisingly soft and tasty, and the water had been drawn from the fresh, clean springs of the oasis. It tasted marvelous to their parched mouths.

As soon as they finished, Zukhara swept away the dishes and faced them both over the empty board. "I brought you here," he said without preamble, "because I need your help."

A look of surprise slipped over Kelene's face at the change in the counselor's attitude and tone. The belligerent aggression had been tempered by politeness; the cold harshness in his voice was gone, and the rigidity of his shoulders and limbs had relaxed into an almost neighborly slouch.

He leaned forward, his elbows on the table, and went on. "You must understand, it was not an easy decision to kidnap two sorceresses."

"Why?" Kelene said sarcastically and gestured at the wagon's walls. "You had plenty of room."

The counselor shrugged off the question as he might a fly. "I did not wish to disrupt the peace council, but after Bashan's death, I thought I had no choice. When the Shar-Ja left Council Rock last night, I brought you with us."

"We didn't kill Bashan," Gabria spoke for the first time.

"I know, Lady Gabria, but I'm afraid I do know who did and, because of that, I had to move fast." He smiled then, and Kelene drew a sharp breath at the amazing transformation. The predatory anger that lined his face was wiped away by a pleasant, disarming smile of friendliness and good humor. If Kelene had not felt his rage and seen the hate in his eyes at the council, if she had not spent the last twenty-four hours in misery and been threatened by this same man, she would have liked him for this smile alone. She knew then that Zukhara was even more dangerous than she imagined, for he was not only influential, powerful, merciless, and ambitious, he could wear charm like a beautifully crafted veneer.

"What do you want?" Gabria replied warily.

"You have in your clan a man who is half Turic and half clan. His parents had twelve children, yet only he inherited enough clan blood to be a magic-wielder." The man steepled his fingers and met Gabria eye to eye. "There have been other half-breed children along the border; this aberration could turn up again."

Gabria's expression tightened into a frown. "Of course that could happen again. But such a child has not yet been brought to my attention."

His mouth widened to what most people would have seen as an expression of delight. To Kelene and Gabria, his broad grin resembled more the victorious leer of a wolf about to eat its kill.

"Perhaps now, then," said Zukhara, and he opened out his palm, spread his fingers, and formed a small sphere of greenish light directly over his hand. The implications struck both women at the same time, and they shrank away from the harmless little light.

"How can you do that?" gasped Kelene.

"My mother was raped by a Wylfling while she was on a journey. She was so terrified of her husband's jealousy she told him the baby was his. It wasn't until he died a few years ago that she found the courage to tell me." He gave them another friendly smile. "It explained some questions that had been bothering me."

Gabria and Kelene said nothing to his revelation. The same suspicion was brewing in both their minds that the counselor knew more about magic than how to form a simple sorcerer's light, and they watched him quietly and waited for him to explain more.

Zukhara bounced the little light gently in his palm; then with a snap his fingers closed over the sphere and crushed it out. "I had thought to visit you these past few years to study sorcery with your clan students, but other matters kept me busy. Now there is little time left. I must control this power now, and for that I have brought you with me." The charm cracked from his voice, turning his words hard and bare. He turned suddenly and pointed a finger at Kelene. "I want you to teach me how to use my power, how to control it, and how to turn it to my will."

Kelene was so startled by his choice, she exclaimed without thinking, "Me? I'm no teacher. I'm a healer!"

"You know sorcery. It is enough to begin. Lady Gabria may watch and contribute if she wishes. We will start tomorrow." He stood then and pulled Kelene to her feet. With deliberate care he slipped the gag back into her mouth and tied her wrists tightly together. His eyes glittered in the lamplight as he stared down at her angry face. His hands lingered on her arms for a moment longer than she thought utterly necessary before he lifted her back onto the bed. Kelene did not even try to sense his emotions but shut her mind and turned her head away for fear of what she might find.

Gabria was gagged and tied again and returned to her place beside Kelene. This time Zukhara did not bother to fasten their arms to their sides. He picked up the lamp and dishes. "Until morning," he said pleasantly and climbed out, locking the door behind him.

His footsteps had barely passed away before Kelene pulled her bound wrists up and used her fingers to wrench the gag out of her mouth. "That—!" she spat furiously, too angry to think of a worthy epithet.

Gabria removed her gag, grateful for the small relief. "That man is crazier than a mad dog in the summer heat," she observed dryly.

"Half-clan!" Kelene hissed. "Gods' truth!" She lay beside her mother, trembling with rage. Although she could not bring herself to say anything to Gabria, she realized she was fuming not just because of Zukhara's audacious kidnapping or his demand that they teach him sorcery, but also because of the brilliant look in his eyes when he pulled her up and the slow touch of his hands on her skin. It was enough to make her flesh crawl.

Gabria tilted her head toward Kelene. "You know," she said slowly, "I would wager Nara that Zukhara was the one who killed the Shar-Yon."

"I won't take that wager," Kelene answered. "Mother, we *can't* teach that viper sorcery. He is already a menace to the Turics and the clans!"

"No, we must not if we can help it." She paused and thought of Athlone's description of Bashan's seared body. "But perhaps we should teach him the rudiments of control. Wild magic, in his hands, is more dangerous than a controlled spell."

"What if he pushes me to teach him more?"

Gabria's thin smile was lost in the darkness. "Then perhaps we should convince him that his abilities are not as strong as he hopes. If his spells were to go awry . . ."

Kelene gave a dry chuckle. "You're not suggesting disrupting his spells."

"Nothing blatant. Just a nudge here and there to sour the effect."

They fell silent, their thoughts heavy with their dangerous predicament. After a long, unhappy pause, Kelene whispered, "Should we try to escape him?"

"Would you leave Demira in his hands?" Gabria asked heavily, although they both knew the answer.

"No. So we deal with Zukhara until we can leave with the Hunnuli."

"Or someone reaches us."

Lying there in the darkness, tied hand and foot, far from home and desperately worried, Kelene felt very much the daughter in need of her mother's reassurance. "Do you really think they would dare search for us here?"

In the darkness Gabria felt for her daughter's bound hands and clasped them tightly in her own. "Athlone, Rafnir, or Sayyed will find a way. I know it."

The certainty in those words was enough to satisfy Kelene and reinforce her own belief in her kin. Calmer now, she set her mind on her immediate problems of teaching sorcery to Zukhara and dealing with captivity.

Suddenly she gave a rueful laugh at herself. "Just before Gaalney came to Moy Tura," she explained to her puzzled mother, "I was riding Demira above the city and feeling sorry for myself because things weren't going my way." She chuckled again and felt better for it. "Right now I would happily trade all of this to be back in that mere muddle. I promise, if we make it back to Moy Tura, I won't feel sorry for myself again . . . for at least another three or four years."

Gabria laughed softly with her, and their tension eased enough to let them rest. They slept fitfully through the night, until Zukhara returned at dawn. The Turic brought food to his prisoners, allowed them to attend to their needs, and waited while they ate their morning meal. Gabria and Kelene watched him like a pair of hawks, but the man remained mute and did nothing to give the women any hope of escape. His movements were brusque yet meticulous, and his eyes burned unabated with their fierce zeal.

As soon as the captives finished eating, their hands were retied, and they were returned to the pallet. Instead of leaving right away, Zukhara stepped to the barrier and glanced over at the Hunnuli. Kelene craned her head around to see what he was doing, and her heart jumped in hope when Demira tossed her head. A hoof crashed against the wooden gate, but the two mares were so crowded, Kelene could not tell which one had kicked.

Zukhara did not flinch at the impact. He drew a glass flask from a pocket in his dark blue robe and uncorked it. A pungent, medicinal odor filled the interior of the wagon, alerting Kelene's curiosity. She strained her neck to watch Zukhara pour some thick greenish liquid onto a cloth and rub it on Demira's haunch. Nara was treated with the same liquid, and shortly after, the mares' stall was silent again.

Kelene cursed under her breath. Whatever drug he was using to sedate the mares must be very potent to affect the big horses so quickly. The door slammed and locked behind the counselor, leaving the clanswomen in darkness again. Shortly thereafter they heard whips crack, voices shout, and animals call. There was a great deal of noise and some jerky starts as the baggage train sorted itself out; then the wagon bounced forward, once more under way.

The weather that day seemed sunnier, for the light shining through the chinks in the wagon's walls was bright and full. Kelene watched one whip-thin beam move slowly across the wall and down to the floor in a course that indicated they were moving south, deeper into Turic territory.

In spite of their thirst and discomfort, evening came all too soon for Kelene and Gabria. The light dimmed and disappeared into twilight; the caravan reached its next stop along the Spice Road. Unbeknownst to them, Rafnir and Sayyed were eating their meal and talking to Turics not more than several hundred paces away.

No one came near the wagon for a long while, and the sounds of the camp dwindled to sleepy tranquility. They heard several sets of footsteps pacing past their prison, but not one person stopped to look in their wagon or check on their condition.

Kelene squirmed against the Hunnuli-hair ropes that held her fast. Her hands were swollen, red, and painful; her body ached from lying on a jolting board all day. She dreaded seeing Zukhara again, yet she reviled him with every scrap of her fury for not coming and getting this ordeal over. Her tongue had dried to thick leather, and her throat burned with thirst. "Where is he?" she ground out between clenched teeth.

She felt her emotions kindle the power of the Trymmian force in her bones and blood. It burned like a spark on touchwood, ready to ignite at her will.

Without any warning, the door swung open, and a tall figure loomed in the entrance. In that split second Kelene's thoughts exploded with her pent-up fear and rage and, before she could control herself, a wild burst of the Trymmian force flamed from her hands. Kelene gasped in horror.

Gabria reared up and tried to evaporate the blast, but it flew too fast and struck Zukhara full on the chest, where it exploded in a cloud of blue sparks. The counselor staggered backward from the force of the blow. Only the ivory ward around his neck absorbed the searing power and saved his life.

Kelene's eyes grew enormous, and her heart beat painfully as Zukhara climbed to his feet. The tall Turic stepped back into the wagon, placed the tray he took from a servant on the table, and deliberately closed and locked the door behind him. Swift as a striking cobra, his hand shot out and clamped around Gabria's throat. His fingers found her jugular and her windpipe and began to crush her neck within his ferocious grip.

"No!" screamed Kelene. "It was me!" She tried to grab his wrists, to pull him away from her mother, but she might as well have tried to uproot a tree. Zukhara ignored her and sunk his thumbs deeper into Gabria's throat. The clanswoman's eyes bulged above her gasping mouth. She struggled and thrashed in vain to escape his iron hands.

"I warned you," Zukhara hissed in sharp, fierce anger. "You did not heed me."

"I didn't mean to! I was angry and scared," Kelene raged at him. "Get off her." She abruptly pulled up her tied feet and kicked at him with all her might.

Her feet landed on his ribs and slammed him sideways against the wagon wall, jarring his hands loose from around Gabria's throat. Kelene swiftly rolled over the older sorceress, knocking Zukhara's hands off completely, and she managed to use her body to shove her mother off the pallet to the floor.

Gabria was too weak to stand. Sobbing, she lay supine on the dusty boards and tried to draw deep, rasping breaths through her bruised throat.

The counselor angrily pushed himself upright until he was kneeling over Kelene. His long, lean shape loomed above her like a black, forbidding shadow.

"It was an accident!" Kelene insisted. "If you kill her, you lose your best lever against me, and I'll see you in Gormoth before I teach you even one spell."

Zukhara leaned so close his trim beard brushed her chin. His hands rose and fell over her neck but instead of choking her, his long fingers caressed her skin from her earlobes down the soft length of her throat. "Then I guess we are at an impasse, my lady," he said huskily in her ear. "If you do not obey. I will kill, and yet if I kill, you will not obey. A fine challenge."

Kelene quivered at his touch. His warm breath by her ear made the hairs rise on the back of her neck, and his weight on her shoulder and chest frightened her. She lay rigid and cold, her heart beating rapidly. "Then it would be best if we struck a bargain," she made herself say.

Zukhara settled more comfortably on top of her, his hands still resting on her bare neck, one thumb caressing the frantic pulse in the base of her throat.

"I will train you in sorcery—as much as you need to control your power—and when I am finished, you will let my mother, me, and our Hunnuli go home unharmed."

The man chuckled, warm and throaty. "A bargain struck in haste is oft regretted. I will think about it. Perhaps in time we will devise a better arrangement." He pushed away from her and untied her hands. "In the meantime, eat. Then show me what you have to offer."

Kelene gritted her teeth. There was nothing else to do but agree—for now. She helped her mother to the bench by the table where Zukhara had placed their meal and a small lamp. Kelene drew on her skills as a healer and tenderly eased the pain in Gabria's bruised throat. She wrapped a cool, damp cloth around her mother's neck and helped her sip a cup of wine.

From his stool, Zukhara observed them impassively.

After a while, Kelene coaxed Gabria to eat some soup and was pleased to see a little color return to the older woman's waxen cheeks. With the flush came a reawakening of Gabria's steel spirit. She covered her forehead with a limp hand, sagged back against the wooden wall, and surreptitiously winked at Kelene. The young woman smothered a smile and ate her own food gratefully.

The moment she was finished, Zukhara cleared off the table and, in a lightning-swift change of mood, flashed his friendly, disarming smile. He pulled a small book out of his robes and laid it in front of Kelene. "Now, my lady. Where do we begin?"

Gabria and Kelene bent forward to look at the little volume in the light of the oil lamp. Although books were not common among the seminomadic clanspeople, both women had learned to read the old Clannish script from books preserved in the Citadel of Krath by the Cult of the Lash and from a few precious manuscripts unearthed at Moy Tura. To their astonishment, this book, no bigger than a man's hand, appeared to be a relic of clan history. It was made of white vellum stretched and scraped to thin, supple sheets and bound between a heavier cover of leather that, once dyed a rich red, had since faded to the color of old wine.

Kelene gingerly turned the front cover to the first page and heard her mother gasp. In a spidery, delicate script was written: Jeneve, Daughter of Lord Magar of Clan Corin.

Gabria's hands flew to the book, and she drew it closer to pore over the writing and illustrations on the following pages. "This is a spellbook," she breathed in surprise. "A personal collection compiled by Lady Jeneve! How did you get your hands on it?" she snapped at Zukhara.

He smiled again, a long, self-satisfied sneer. "The God of All delivered it to my hands to help fulfill the prophecy."

"What prophecy?" Kelene demanded.

Zukhara disregarded the question and tapped the book with his forefinger. "I can read this, so do not try to trick me. I simply want to know how to use the magic to control these spells."

Glancing over her mother's arm. Kelene read the names of some of the spells in the handbook. Most were simple day-to-day twists of sorcery that took only basic skills and caused little harm, such as firestarters, spheres of light, easy transformations, household aids, and simple medications. But there were others that a man like Zukhara could twist to his own purposes: a spell to paralyze an animal or human, spells of destructive power, a spell to summon wind from a gathering storm, and others she would be loath to show him.

Control first, she thought to herself. She had never taught anyone magic; that had always been Gabria's duty. But it seemed reasonable to start at the beginning where every magic-wielder had to start and take it as slowly as she dared. Perhaps, given the help of the gods, she and Gabria could find a way to escape before Zukhara pushed his training too far.

She traded looks with Gabria, then closed the book and pushed it aside. "We will start here," she said, tapping her own forehead, and she launched into her first lesson. "Will is at the center of sorcery. With every spell you create you are attempting to impose your will on the substance of our world. Magic is a natural force that is in every creature, stone, or plant. When you alter that force, even with the smallest spell, you must be strong enough to control the effect and consequences. The forces of magic can destroy you if you cannot control them."

She paused and stared at Zukhara's dark visage. Unconsciously she had been repeating Gabria's old lesson that she had listened to for years before the words took on real meaning. "The strength of will is the most important trait of a magic-wielder. Therefore you must know yourself. every measure and degree of your own being, so you can recognize your own limitations and know when sorcery has begun to bleed substance from your life-force."

Zukhara's hand suddenly grabbed Kelene's right arm and pulled her wrist out straight toward him. He touched her embedded splinter so hard she flinched in pain. "Enough of your childish lectures. I have the will of the Living God; there are no limitations other than my own lack of knowledge. I will have a splinter in my wrist in ten days' time or I will remove your arm at the elbow. Are we clear?"

Kelene gaped, aghast at his monstrous arrogance. He had no comprehension of his own weaknesses and therefore dismissed any possibility of them in impervious blindness. Perhaps she and Gabria wouldn't have to escape; perhaps all they had to do was wait for Zukhara to destroy himself in his own overwhelming self-confidence.

She hoped he would hurry and do so soon. She didn't want to have to tell him there were no more diamond splinters. Gabria had used the last one only a year ago and had not yet found a new source for the special, power-enhancing gems.

Kelene yanked her wrist out of his grasp and said firmly, "Fine. Then we will begin with control." She held out her fingers and demonstrated commands for Zukhara's first spell.

The Turic watched avidly, then followed her instructions until he had formed a perfect greenish-white sphere of light. Late into the night the sorceress and her pupil practiced and discussed, manipulated magic and worked on simple skills, until Kelene was exhausted and Gabria drooped beside her.

Indefatigable, Zukhara ordered them to lie down, retied their hands, and departed, his back still straight, his step as forceful as always.

"Oh, Mother," Kelene sighed when he was gone. "What are we going to do? He's at least as strong as Sayyed, and he's learning fast."

"I was afraid of that when I saw him work. He burns with ambition. But what is he planning? Why is he so determined to have a splinter within ten days?"

Kelene sighed and closed her eyes. She was so tired, and there was nothing left she could say.

Gabria's questions passed into silence unanswered.

9

Zukhara slammed his hand on the rough table. "What tripe are you showing me? Why will it not work?" he demanded. Stewing in frustration, he tried again to form a simple transformation spell to change a cluster of grapes into a handful of plums. He focused on the grapes and spoke the words of the spell for the third time.

On the bunk behind him, Gabria wordlessly moved her fingers and used her own will to throw his magic astray. The grapes on the table wavered a few times, then burst under the pressure of the vying sorcery.

The Turic spat a curse.

"Be patient," Kelene told him coolly. "Concentrate on what you want. You have to know exactly what you intend to create or the spell will go awry."

"I know what I want," he ground out.

"Then perhaps you are not trying hard enough to control the magic. If you cannot master these simple spells, you will never be able to control the more complex sorcery."

They eyed each other across the table, Kelene stiff and her head thrown back; Zukhara tense and angry, the lines pulled tight around his mouth and across his brow. In the flickering lamplight, he reminded Kelene of a black-and-gold adder, its large, dark eyes glittering, its lean head poised to strike.

"All right, try something a little simpler," she suggested, pushing the dripping grapes aside and picking up a flask of water. She poured a small amount of water into a dish and placed it before the Turic. "With a minor spell you can turn this water to ice," she said and showed him how to do it.

Zukhara tried the spell and managed to create a film of ice on the water before the pottery dish shattered and spilled water across the table. Kelene watched him impassively, like a teacher helping a pupil who cannot quite grasp an easy concept. He tried spell after spell, and no matter how hard he tried, everything went wrong.

An hour later he was struggling to create a flame on a candle when Kelene suddenly lifted her head. From somewhere nearby came the sounds of boots scuffling on the ground, several soft thuds, and the mutter of muted voices.

Gabria didn't have to break the spell that time, for the disruption caused Zukhara to jerk his hand, and the candle sagged into a pool of melted wax. Muttering under his breath, Zukhara strode to the door, unlocked it, and stepped out.

Kelene followed him with her eyes and saw a dark-clothed man meet him just outside the door. "Counselor, we have found two more pilferers in the wagons," she heard the man say.

Zukhara looked at something out of Kelene's sight. "Get rid of them," he ordered. "But not here. More deaths will draw attention. Take them out past the oasis."

The callousness in his voice chilled Kelene with a hollow foreboding. It could so easily be herself or Gabria he so casually disposed of. The counselor climbed back into the wagon, dusting his hands as if ridding his palms of some dirty annoyance. He settled on his stool across from Kelene and almost negligently flicked his hand and set the wick of the melted candle burning. He stared at the tiny flame for a long time, his volatile expression lost in thought. The silence built around him, thick as walls.

In one sudden movement and without warning, he sprang from his seat and delivered a stunning blow to Gabria's jaw. The fury of the assault snapped back her head, with an audible crack, against the wooden wall.

"Get back!" he roared at Kelene when she jumped to help her mother. With fierce deftness, he retied Gabria's hands and stuffed the gag back in her mouth. Mute with suspicion, he sat down and repeated the transformation spell Kelene had tried to teach him. The cluster of split grapes turned into a heap of delicate purple plums. He tried every spell they had practiced that had gone wrong, and each one worked perfectly. Kelene watched him, too terrified for Gabria to intervene.

"So," he hissed. "You thought to dissuade me from my goal by ruining my magic." He turned his baleful glare on Gabria. She lay half-stunned, her face white and her body limp. Blood ran down her chin from a cut on her mouth. She attempted to focus on him, her frustration and anger almost as potent as his. "You cannot stop me. Understand, fools, magic is part of my destiny. It is one of the weapons foretold in the prophecy."

There was that allusion to a prophecy again, Kelene realized. "What are you talking about? How can a clan power be any part of a Turic prophecy?" she snapped, her tone made sharp by her nervousness.

Zukhara seemed to swell before her eyes. Tall as he was, he straightened his spine, threw back his long shoulders, and jutted his chin forward arrogantly. "Five hundred years ago when your paltry horse clans were still settling the plains, the Prophet Sargun wrote *The Truth of Nine* from his prison in the dungeons of Sarcithia, while it was still part of the Tarnish Empire. When he escaped and returned over the mountains to his homeland, he founded the city of Sargun Shahr and gave his book to his younger brother. The city has since vanished. We still seek it today, but *The Truth of Nine* is in Cangora in the keeping of the Holy Order in the great temple of Sargun."

Kelene felt her mouth drop open, not at the lecture, for most clanspeople knew the generalities of Turic history, but at the conclusion she drew from his rhetoric. "Are you saying there is a prophecy about you in that book?"

He leaned forward, his hands on the table, and his daunting figure cast shadows over her still form. "The sixth," he said as cold as winter. "'And the Gryphon shall rise to lay flame to the desert and feed on the blood of the unbelievers. Tyrants shall bow before him and nations shall fall at his feet.'" Zukhara's voice dropped to a low intonation, reciting the words of the prophecy as if breathing a prayer. "'By these signs will you know him. In his hand shall be the lightning of the north, and the wind of the Living God shall uphold him. Drought, pestilence, and famine will open his way, and the copper gate will fall before his mighty strength. Before the eye of his chosen handmaiden, he will stand in the light of the golden sun, and a bastard will sit on the throne of Shahr.'" His words dropped away, and he stood poised, his thoughts running ahead to the future and the fulfillment of his dreams.

For once Kelene could think of nothing to say. His audacity and conviction stunned her. The Gryphon. By the gods, she knew that name. "Fel Azureth," she whispered, unaware she had spoken loud enough to be heard.

Zukhara's head jerked up; his eyes glittered. "Yes, my lady. I am Fel Karak, the Gryphon, and the Fel Azureth is my sword. Already my plans are falling into place. There is but one weapon left to collect, and for that we shall leave the caravan tomorrow." He picked up the hair ropes, tied her hands behind her back, and steered her to the bed.

"Be glad, clanswoman, that you are here with me," he said softly. He touched her cheek, his fingers gently caressing. "Already the Gryphon sinks his claws into the north. When I gain the throne, I will claim the rich pastures north of the Altai for my own empire. With the lightning in my fingertips, your people will not withstand me. By year's end I will make *you* my queen and will lay the plains of Ramtharin at your feet as my wedding gift to you."

Kelene stared at him, her dark eyes enormous pools in her face. Although she could sense the stark power of his convictions through the touch of his skin on hers, she did not need her talent to grasp the reality of what she was hearing. "But I already have a husband," she said, too shaken to say anything more perceptive.

Zukhara's teeth flashed white against his black beard. "There is no law that says I cannot marry a widow."

With swift, sure movements he replaced Kelene's gag, cleaned the table, put out the light, and bid the women a good night.

Kelene listened to his footsteps pass away. Anger roared like a caged beast in her head, and she stared helplessly at the dark door, trying to bring her fear and rage under control. She wanted to shriek, to strike out at the man and his unshakable arrogance. She vowed to Amara, Sorh, Surgart, and Krath that she would find a way to stop him. There had to be something to thwart his plans. Not all prophecies come to pass as one would believe they should.

She turned her head to check her mother and saw tears leaking down Gabria's face. The sorceress had her eyes screwed shut and her pale face turned toward the ceiling.

Worry doused Kelene's anger as surely as icy water. As carefully as she could manage with her hands tied, Kelene used her long sleeve to mop away the blood on Gabria's swelling jaw and the tears that dampened her fair hair. Gabria forced a wan smile. Unable to talk, the two women pressed close and took solace in each other's company. Neither slept well that long, bitter night.

* * *

To young Peoren, the clatter of horses' hooves sounded unnaturally loud in the hushed twilight. He sat taller in his borrowed black cloak and tilted his head so he could hear the approaching troop. Beside him his picked men—two Dangari, Dos his guard, and six Shadedron—stiffened like alert hounds, their attention pricked to the approaching sounds of horses, hushed voices, and the softer chink and rattle of arms.

To all appearances the ten clansmen appeared to take no notice of the troop approaching them up the long hillside. They had built their fires with care and set them so the vanguard of the Turic raiding party could see them and identify them at a distance that would still allow the clansmen time to run.

Peoren smiled a slow, assured smile as the first Turics topped the rise. The scouts had reported the disposition of the raiders perfectly. Five point riders rode ahead of the main body of men. As if on cue, they reined their mounts to a halt and stared at the ten men, their tiny fires, and the ten clan horses. Peoren and his companions jumped to their feet, as if in alarm. The Turics whooped with glee. One yanked up a horn and blew a signal to the riders coming up behind.

With an appropriate display of fear, the clansmen scrambled wildly to their horses, mounted. and set off along the side of the high hill to escape.

The troop of raiders was a big one, numbering over two hundred mounted fighters. Some brought up the rear with strings of stolen horses and laden pack animals, but the majority drew their weapons and followed the escapees at a rush. After all, ten men were easy prey, and ten clan horses were a prize worth pursuing.

Led by a Shadedron guide, the fleeing clansmen raced down the back slope to the mouth of a valley that plunged deep into a range of plateaus and towering hills. They paced their horses at a gallop just fast enough to stay ahead of the chasing band of marauders. Down they swept into the valley, swung right along the streambed, then cantered swiftly upstream toward the cover of the tree-clad hills. The Turics pushed their horses harder to catch the clansmen before they escaped into the night.

Twilight darkened to a dismal gloaming, obscuring detail and washing out color in a thickening blue-gray haze. Mist rose from the creek in curling tendrils that gathered in the hollows and spread out over the low-lying patches of bog. Snow still lay piled in drifts in the colder shadows of the hills.

The clansmen pushed on behind the Shadedron, a hunter who knew the hills as well as he did his own tent. Peoren brought up the rear and lagged slightly behind to taunt the Turic into continuing the chase over the poorly lit trail. The hillsides climbed higher above the stream, and the remaining snow grew deeper.

The clansmen were almost in range of the Turics' crossbows when the valley curved sharply to the left and widened to form a fairly level open space devoid of trees and lightly drifted with snow. In the dense twilight the flat ground looked safe enough, and the Shadedron led his companions across to the foot of a high embankment. The Turics, coming past the curve, saw their prey's escape apparently blocked by a high bank and yelled their battle cries while they spurred their horses directly toward the milling clansmen.

In their excitement, the Turics did not notice a pale, luminous glow on the ground beneath their horses' feet. Camouflaged by the snow and the indigo twilight, the glow covered the entire level up to the base of the high bank where the clansmen waited with drawn swords. Atop the embankment in a cluster of brush and rocks, Lord Athlone watched the raiders and gauged his time. Gaalney and Morad, across the valley, watched too, and waited for the chieftain's signal.

The charging Turics raised their tulwars and prepared to overwhelm the small band of clansmen. In the blink of an eye, the earth sagged beneath their horses. The pale fluorescence they had never noticed flicked out with a wave of Lord Athlone's hand, and the hard crust the Turics mistook for soil dissolved into a quaking bog. The galloping charge turned into a thrashing, struggling, screaming quagmire of men, mud, and horses.

A few riders at the rear of the troop had not yet ridden onto the bog, but when they tried to turn around, a bright red wall of magic energy slammed into existence across the valley, blocking their way out. They reined to a stunned halt and watched over one hundred fully armed and vengeful clansmen silently rise from their hiding places and encircle the marauders.

The tribesmen still on firm ground guessed what their fate might be in the hands of the furious clans and chose to attack. They charged the nearest group of warriors and were brought down by arrows before they reached the first man. Another bunch at the front of the charge struggled toward Peoren and his men to cut them down. The Shadedron, sick with rage, met them hand-to-hand and killed several before Peoren stopped them. He looked into a square-jawed face with a scimitar nose and a killer's eyes, and he recognized the leader of the band that had attacked Ferganan Treld.

This was a prize too good to lose. Peoren bellowed to Lord Athlone and stood back from his opponent as the sorcerer lord dropped down from his vantage point and fired a burst of magic at the Turic commander. The blue force laid the man unconscious. Twenty more Turics were hauled from the mud and taken prisoner. The rest either drowned in the black, clutching bog, were crushed by the terrified horses, or were killed by the clansmen.

By the time night was full, the ambush was over. The clansmen rescued what horses they could, patched the injured Turics, and left the dead to the scavengers. They returned back up the valley, gathering the stolen horses and plunder-laden pack animals as they went. They set up camp by the stream and ate a robust dinner. They were tired and saddened by the tragedies that had forced their assault, but they had been victorious, and one band of vicious marauders had been destroyed without the loss of a single clansman.

After their meal, the men sat by their fires to sing and tell tales and celebrate their success, while their chiefs looked over the prisoners. Two guards brought the Turic leader first, his hands and arms bound and his dark eyes furious, to stand before the clan lords.

Peoren nodded once. "This is the man who killed my father."

"He was at Shadedron Treld, too," said young Hazeth.

The Turic stiffened defiantly and glared at his captors.

"I have seen the horses they stole and the goods they plundered," said Lord Wendern. "There is no doubt."

Lord Fiergan, the red-haired Reidhar, growled, "Who are you? Why did you attack our trelds?"

There came no reply. The prisoner shifted on his feet, his expression sullen and determined.

Lord Athlone rose to his feet with the slow, deliberate intent of a stalking lion. No hint of emotion altered his cold features; nothing distracted his merciless stare from the prisoner.

The Turic's eyes snapped to the sorcerer; he recognized the chieftain and knew his power. His swarthy face turned noticeably paler.

Wordlessly the chieftains watched Athlone walk to stand in front of the Turic. The guards moved away, leaving the prisoner alone with the Khulinin lord.

"You know the punishments we can mete out to vermin like you," Athlone said in a voice as smooth and penetrating as steel. "You will wish for any one of those to end your agony if *I* am forced to deal with you."

The Turic, who was nearly as tall as Athlone, tried to meet his gaze and failed. He edged back from the chieftain and looked wildly around to see if anyone was going to intervene, but the clansmen stayed where they were, mercy long gone from their thoughts. The Turic began to sweat in the chilly night air.

Athlone raised his right hand, his fingers inches from the man's face. The Turic stared in growing fear. "Now," the sorcerer continued, "who are you? And what can you tell us about the Fel Azureth?"

The Turic visibly blanched. Athlone's fingers dropped until they lightly touched the prisoner's forehead. "Talk!" he commanded.

* * *

By dawn Kelene and Gabria were wan and sore. It had been a miserable night, and the coming day that softened the black shadows and sent delicate beams of light dancing through the chinks in the wagon wall did little to lighten the gloom in the women's hearts.

Still dozing, they were startled alert when the door slammed open and Zukhara strode in. His features looked thunderous but, without a word, he laid out their breakfast, freed their hands, and stood aside as they climbed stiffly to their feet. Kelene was ravenous and ate well. Gabria only picked at her food. Her jaw was swollen and discolored purple and blue; her skin was terribly pale. Only her green eyes blazed defiantly at Zukhara as she sipped the wine he had brought her.

No sooner had they finished than the counselor replaced their bonds, tying their hands loosely in front of them. Kelene had little time to wonder why before he pulled a strange vial from the pocket of his robe. Striking like an adder, he gripped Gabria's injured face and turned it upward. He forced the vial into her mouth and poured its contents down her throat before she could overcome her pain and spit it out. Terror crossed her face.

"What have you done?" Kelene cried.

Satisfied, Zukhara replaced the stopper in the vial. "I have had enough of your disobedience. You would not take me seriously, so I offer you a new bargain. I have given Lady Gabria a slow-acting poison. If you obey me in all things, in ten days' time I will give her the antidote. If you do not, she will die a long and painful death." He paused and smiled a slow, malevolent smile. "Do not think to escape me and seek the antidote on your own. The poison is of my own making, and only I hold its cure."

Indifferently he turned to the Hunnuli and slathered more of the thick sedative on their rumps. Giving the women a slight bow, he left them and locked the door behind him.

Even as the lock clicked into place, Kelene climbed to her feet. Her ankles were still tied, but the ropes had loosened enough to enable her to shuffle the short distance to Demira's side. She grasped the hem of her tunic and tore a long, narrow strip off the bottom where it would not be immediately noticed. Bunching it in her hand, she rubbed the place on Demira's hip where Zukhara had smeared his potion. To her relief, a thin film of greenish liquid came off on her cloth. She knew she had not removed all the sedative and that it would be a while before Demira revived, but this was a start. She carefully wrapped the fabric in a wad, the green stain hidden in the folds, and tucked it in her waistband.

She turned slowly and faced Gabria. "I do not trust Zukhara to keep his word. If Demira can escape, she can find Father, Sayyed, or Rafnir," she said almost apologetically. She knew she was taking a big chance with Gabria's life.

The sorceress nodded, her resolution clear. "This man must be stopped," she said simply.

There fell a silence neither woman wanted to break. Gabria lay down on the pallet, too weary to stay upright. Kelene braced herself on the little bench and kept watch through the hours of morning as the wagon lurched and rumbled its way south in the wake of the caravan. The dust grew thick in the little room, and the air turned warmer.

It was noon, judging by the grumblings in her belly, when Kelene realized the van had noticeably slowed. The sorceress waited, scarcely breathing the dusty air. A moment later the van made a sharp turn to the right and dropped onto a rougher road. Kelene had to grab the small table for support, and the mares lurched sideways in their stall. Kelene noticed a ripple run through Demira's hide from neck to tail, and the mare stirred her head before slipping back into her stupor.

The van stopped. In the quiet that followed, Kelene could hear the distant sounds of the caravan, and she was not surprised that the noises were dwindling away. Zukhara had said they would leave the caravan. Several voices murmured quietly outside, their tones too soft to identify.

Kelene glanced at her mother. Gabria appeared to be sleeping, so she decided not to waken her. But looking at her mother reminded her of Gabria's conviction that someone had come after them. Kelene's heart sank. If that were true, if Athlone or Sayyed or Rafnir had followed the caravan to find them, how would the men know where this wagon had gone? They could follow the Shar-Ja all the way to Cangora, hoping to find Gabria and her.

She would have to leave some sign and hope, slim as the possibility was, that someone would find it and recognize it. But what? If she left something of magic, Zukhara could see it and know her intent. It could not be anything large either, since she had no way to get a big object out of the van.

The wagon jerked and started forward along the rougher trail. Kelene's hands flew to her braid and her red ribbon. It hung limp in her hands, bedraggled and dirty, but it was all she had. On her hands and knees she searched the floor of the wagon for a crack wide enough to push the ribbon through. Unfortunately, someone had rebuilt the bed of the old wagon, perhaps to hold the weight of the Hunnuli. There was not so much as a seam. She finally resorted to a fingernail crack in the wall beside the door. It was painstaking work to feed the limp ribbon through the crevice, and she prayed no one was riding behind the wagon. At last the red strip fell away and vanished to fall somewhere on the trail. Kelene's prayers went with it.

They camped that night along the trail, and Zukhara brought their food and drink as usual. He spoke not a word to them, but roused Gabria, watched them eat, and swiftly returned outside.

As soon as she was finished, Gabria went back to sleep. Kelene lay beside her, worried at her mother's lethargy. Sometime during the night, Gabria tossed in her sleep in the throes of a powerful dream. Kelene woke to her mother's voice calling low and insistently, "Sayyed!"

The dream faded away, and Gabria lay still, her breathing so shallow Kelene had to strain to hear it. Was this another of her mother's visions? Was it Sayyed who had come after them? That made sense to Kelene. He had the best chance of making his way through Turic territory. She dozed again, thinking of Sayyed and, most of all, his handsome, dark-haired son.

Zukhara's entrance startled Kelene awake, and she lay blinking in the morning light that streamed through the open door while he laid out their food, dosed the mares, and departed, all without a word spoken. As soon as the door closed behind him, Kelene worked her way to Demira's stall, and again she wiped off the thick sedative onto her rag. She put her hand on Demira's warm hide. Her probing mind immediately touched the mare's consciousness straining against the drug that imprisoned her body.

Ever so gently Kelene formed a spell that loosened the fabric confining Demira's wings. The Hunnuli, sensing Kelene's closeness, shifted restlessly.

Be easy, Kelene soothed. *Wait and be patient. When you are alert enough, fly and escape.*

No! Demira's resistance rang in Kelene's head. The mare was fighting the sedative with every ounce of her will. *I will not leave you!*

Please, Demira, you must! Mother has been poisoned. She will die if we do not have help. I think Sayyed has come to look for us. Find him! Bring him to us! You are the only one who can.

I cannot leave you, Demira repeated, but her thoughts were weak and confused.

Kelene leaned her head on the mare's rump. "Please try," she whispered. She returned to their table, roused Gabria, and tried to eat some food. Their breakfast that morning was simple—trail bread, dates, a wedge of cheese, and mugs of a sweet, red juice Kelene had never tried before. She eyed the juice suspiciously, wondering if Zukhara had slipped a poison or sedative into her drink. Thirst finally won over, and she drained the drink to the dregs. It was overly sweet but had a rich, fruity taste.

Gabria merely sipped hers and lay back on the pallet. Zukhara returned to gather the mugs and plates. He smiled his cream-eating leer when he saw Kelene's empty mug. "Did you enjoy the juice, my lady?" he asked pleasantly.

A warning buzzed in Kelene's mind; her eyes narrowed. "Why?"

"It contained a mixture I prepared especially for you." He moved close to her, trapping her against the wagon's wall. "If you are to be my chosen handmaiden, you must be receptive to my seed. I intend to father a dynasty of sorcerers with you." He brushed a strand of hair away from her face and softly kissed her forehead.

Kelene froze. The mingled smells of his clothes and the warmth of his body enveloped her; his tall weight pressed against her. She tried to struggle, but the ropes held her hands, and his strength trapped her helplessly against the wooden wall. "I can't have babies," she ground out between clenched teeth.

"You will," he chuckled close to her ear. "This is an old Turic midwives' remedy. It works well to light a fire in a barren womb."

"The better to burn your seed," she hissed.

Zukhara laughed outright. He stepped back and picked up the mugs. "Today we reach my fortress, where my last weapon awaits. There your work will begin . . . and our pleasure." Still chuckling, he left, and in moments the van jerked forward on its last leg of the journey.

Kelene could keep her anger down no longer. A raging scream tore from her throat, and she picked up the small bench and smashed it against the table. Both table and bench cracked and splintered into pieces. Outside, Zukhara's voice rose in derisive laughter.

The travel that day was long and difficult as the wagon lurched and bumped along a poor, unkempt road. Although Kelene had no idea where they were, the wagon seemed to be climbing ever higher. Hours passed. She felt the electrical energies of the coming storm long before she heard the muted rumble of the thunder.

The light in the wagon's interior dimmed to a grayish pallor. The wind began to pummel the vehicle's sides. Kelene could hear the crack of the driver's whip and the nervous neighs of the team. Voices shouted on both sides, and the thunder boomed closer.

In her stall Demira lifted her head. Her nostrils flared at the smell of the coming storm. "Patience," Kelene said to the mare.

The light was nearly gone by the time the wagon rumbled off the dirt road and clattered onto a stone-paved surface. The van made one final rush upward, then came to a stop. New voices called, orders were shouted, and Kelene heard the creak and thud of what sounded like a large door being opened. The wagon rolled forward a short distance.

Abruptly the door opened, and Zukhara climbed in. He untied their ropes and hurried both women outside. Gabria was hollow-eyed and groggy and had to lean on Kelene's arm. Kelene glanced quickly around. The storm was almost overhead, and the lightning cracked around them. She could barely make out a high stone wall with several dark squat towers, and to her left a long hall and a high keep.

"Bring the Hunnuli!" Zukhara shouted, turning to hustle his prisoners out of the storm. Rain splattered on the stone paving.

Suddenly a ringing neigh sounded above the wind's roar. There was a wild crash of hooves and a scream of terror. The Turic and the women whirled in time to see Demira rocket forward through a door in the front of the wagon. Hands reached to grab her halter, but she screamed and reared, flailing her hooves over the heads of her enemies. The fabric covering ripped and fell away; her wings spread like an eagle's, ready to launch.

"Catch her!" Zukhara shrieked. His words were lost in a crash of thunder.

The winged mare rolled her eyes at her rider. "Go!" shouted Kelene, and the mare obeyed. Like black thunder she charged the open gateway. Her legs were swollen from standing so long, her muscles were stiff and slow, and she was still slightly disoriented by the sedative. Yet carried by her desperation, Demira spread her wings and threw herself into the teeth of the storm. At once the clouds opened, and the rain poured down in blinding sheets. In the blink of an eye, the Hunnuli had vanished.

For one shattering moment Kelene thought she had pushed Zukhara too far. Quivering with furious passion, he turned on her and whipped out his dagger to press against her throat. His lean visage snarled at her like a wolf's.

"You didn't need her," Kelene forced herself to say calmly. "Like any horse, she will go home." She prayed he did not understand enough about Hunnuli to know they were not like any other horses.

Her cool words had some effect, for instead of ramming the blade into her neck, he spat a curse and dragged her inside the hall. She saw servants take Gabria away, but she had no chance to see where before Zukhara wrenched opened a door and flung her down a flight of stairs. Kelene scrambled to stay on her feet. The counselor's hand clamped more tightly about her wrist and dragged her down several more spiraling stairways that wound deeper and deeper into the subterranean depths of the fortress.

Silent and implacable, he hauled her on until her hand was numb and her legs were tired. At last he dragged her through a narrow archway and thrust her forward. She banged painfully against a low stone wall and had to grab at it to keep from falling.

A low, angry hiss filled the dark spaces around her. A strange smell lingered on the cold air. Zukhara snapped the words to a spell Kelene had taught him, and a bright white sphere of light burst into being. It hovered over their heads, casting its light over a huge stone ceiling that arched above.

"Down there is my weapon for the holy war I plan to launch. Unfortunately, it was injured during its capture. I brought you here to heal it and tame it to obedience. Do that, and your lady mother will get her antidote." Zukhara pointed down, over the stone wall.

Kelene turned. She saw they were standing on an overhang at the side of a large natural cavern. Slowly she let her eyes drop to the bottom, where a broad floor formed an amphitheater in the mountain's heart. Curled on the sandy floor, staring malevolently up at the light, was a creature unlike any she had ever seen.

"What . . ." she gasped.

Zukhara's anger receded before his pride. "That," he said, "is my gryphon."

10

"Father!" an urgent voice hissed in his ear. "Father, wake up!"

Sayyed stirred and groaned out of his stupor. He tried to move his arms until that same voice whispered, "No! Don't jerk like that. Stay still. Please, Father, try to wake up!"

The frantic urgency in that familiar voice penetrated Sayyed's groggy thoughts, and he closed his mouth and rested his aching limbs. Something seemed wrong though. Some strange thing had happened to his body that he couldn't understand. He could be wrong, yet he felt as if he were hanging upside down.

Sayyed opened his eyes. A brilliant morning sun illuminated everything around him with a clear, sharp light. The majestic mountains gleamed—upside down—in an endless sky of blue. Then he looked down, or was it up, and saw there was nothing beneath his feet but air.

The words he spoke were short and emphatic.

"Father!" hissed Rafnir's voice. "Please don't move!"

Sayyed's mind snapped fully alert, and he quickly recognized the precariousness of his position. He was tied back-to-back with Rafnir and hanging head-first over a very deep and very rocky ravine. Also, the rope that held them seemed dangerously frayed and was tied to a very fragile-looking wooden framework that overhung the edge of the chasm. And, he noted in increasing annoyance, his weapons and most of his clothes were gone. Lastly, he realized there were voices other than Rafnir's speaking behind him.

"I'm telling you, Helmar, these are simply Turics. Uphold the law and get rid of them," demanded a male voice.

"Turics or not, why waste two healthy men?" a female voice cried. This speaker sounded older and more insistent. "You know we need new blood if our line is to survive! These two are strong and can father children. Let them leave their seed in our women before you kill them."

Sayyed was so startled by the gist of the conversation that he did not realize for nearly a minute that the speakers were talking in Clannish. Not the

Clannish he was used to, but an old dialect combined with new word combinations and Turic phrases. He listened with both fascination and increasing anger.

"And what about you, Rapinor?" A third voice spoke. "You caught them. What do you say?" This third speaker was a woman whose voice was rich and self-assured.

Yet a fourth voice responded, "Lady, I don't know how to advise you. Yes, I found them in the Back Door, and they look and dress like Turics. But I swear they rode black horses bigger than any I've ever seen, and one man had a sphere of light."

"Are you sure it wasn't a torch he carried?" the first man said dryly.

"A torch on a night like last? No," the speaker said, the certainty clear in his deep, resounding voice. "The sphere was greenish-white like magic and went out when the man fell unconscious."

"There has to be a simple explanation for that," said the old woman irritably. "We all know magic is dead beyond the mountains."

Sayyed turned his head in an effort to see these people, and although he strained, he could not see around Rafnir. "What is going on here?" he said in Clannish.

His words caught the speakers' attention. "A Turic who speaks the tongue of the clans," said the first man. "All the more reason to kill them. They could get away and tell the clans."

Tell the clans, Sayyed wondered. Tell them what?

"Traveler," called the younger woman, "you were caught trespassing on land that is forbidden. Our laws automatically condemn you to death. However, we are having some doubts as to your identity. Who are you?"

Sayyed opened his mouth to answer, then closed it again. By the gods, how should he answer that? If he claimed to be Turic, these strangers would cut the rope and let him and Rafnir fall. If he said clan, they would probably do the same thing. His power itched to break the ropes that bound him and his son and set them on a more upright and equal footing with these people, but he decided to hold off exposing his talent until he absolutely had to. The speakers' opinion of magic was very unclear.

"We are looking for our family," Rafnir answered for him. "My wife and my wife's mother were kidnapped by someone we do not know. Yet the wagon that carried them came up into these mountains. We had almost found them when we were caught in the storm and lost the trail. If we trespassed, we did it unintentionally, and we humbly apologize."

The people remained quiet while they tried to understand Rafnir's unfamiliar dialect; then they burst into talk all at once in a babble of questions, demands, and angry opinions. Other voices joined in until Sayyed and Rafnir lost track of all the words.

"Who are these people?" Sayyed asked irritably. His head hurt from his inversion, and he was tired of all the arguing.

"I don't know. I can't see them either. They're just above us on a rock ledge," replied Rafnir.

Sayyed tried again to peer around his son and only succeeded in making their rope sway. He froze too late. He heard a creak and a snap, and in a sickening jerk, he and Rafnir began to fall.

"Lady!" the Rapinor voice shouted. "The rope broke!"

"Let them go!" yelled the first man.

Sayyed waited no more. He didn't care who those people were or what they were afraid of, it was time to show them that magic was very much alive and well. "I'll undo the ropes; you break our fall," he yelled to Rafnir.

The wind of their descent tore at his words, but his son heard them. Magic flared from Sayyed's hands, and the ropes dissolved into dust. With his arms free, Sayyed grabbed for Rafnir to keep him close. Rafnir's eyes closed as his lips formed the words to a spell he had used three years ago to catch Kelene in a terrible fall. The air thickened into a cushion beneath them. Their sickening speed slowed, and they tumbled gently onto a platform of wind and magic barely ten feet from the ravine's floor.

"Nice timing," Sayyed said, peering down at the boulders below.

"Gods," sighed Rafnir, "that was close. Let's get out of here."

"Not yet," Sayyed growled. He glared up at the ravine face where a group of people peered over the cliff's edge. "I want to know who *they* are."

He steadied himself on the platform of air while Rafnir carefully steered it up to the level of the precipice top. His arms crossed and his displeasure plain, Sayyed stepped off onto the stone and faced the group of people standing on the rocks. He looked them over and felt his anger begin to recede. He had never seen such a totally unanimous expression of astounded disbelief and awed surprise in his entire long and adventurous life. Not even the first and unexpected appearance of his magical talent had produced such stunned surprise. Every man and woman before him stared at him in speechless shock. As one their eyes shifted to Rafnir as he stepped beside his father and dissolved his spell; then they looked at one another.

Sayyed counted twenty-one men and women of various ages gathered on the cliff top, including the four in the forefront he assumed were the speakers they had not been able to see. All the people were remarkably fair-skinned, with light hair and blue, green, or gray eyes. Whoever they were, Turic blood had not been in their ancestry. In fact, if it were not for the location and their strange clothes, he would think they were clanspeople.

He decided to try something to break the barrier of tension and see what their reaction would be. His burnoose, outer robes, boots, and belt were gone. He had only his trousers and an undertunic left, so he pulled the tunic off and transformed it quickly and skillfully into a golden clan cloak. He flipped the cloak over his shoulders, stepped forward, and saluted the people as a whole.

"I am Sayyed, sorcerer and Hearthguard to Lord Athlone of Clan Khulinin. My son, Rafnir, and I have come to these mountains only to seek our kin."

He was gratified when a woman stepped forward and returned his salute. A tall woman, she stood before her people, proud and fearless. The bright light of morning flamed on a coiled mass of red hair and gleamed on her wide forehead, arched imperious brows, and wide, firm mouth. "I welcome you, Sorcerer. More than you know. I am Helmar, Lady Chieftain of the Clannad," she said in a clear, resolute voice.

She had a carriage of the head and a lancelike directness that reminded Sayyed of Gabria. And a woman chieftain? Gabria would appreciate that, too.

Sayyed bowed. "This was an interesting way to start the day, but I seem to remember we came with horses. May we return to them?" Despite his sarcastic choice of words, he kept his voice neutral, with none of the annoyance and mounting curiosity he was feeling.

As if a spell had been broken, the stunned silence evaporated into a flight of activity and astonished voices. Helmar gave a series of quick orders, and several people dashed away while others gathered around the two clansmen.

"This way," said a man Sayyed identified as one of the four. He was a giant of a warrior, muscular, burly, and softspoken. "I am Rapinor, swordsman and personal guard to the Lady Chieftain. Your horses are still in the back passage." He hesitated, his craggy face curious. "Are your mounts Hunnuli?"

"You have heard of those too?" Sayyed remarked. The more he learned of these people the more mysterious they became. How much did they know about clan magic?

"Softly, Rapinor," Helmar admonished. "There will be time for answers after we return the horses."

A thousand questions burned on the faces of all the people around them, but none gainsaid the chieftain as she led the strangers up a path to the crest of the ridge. There she paused and stretched her hand out to the west. "Welcome to Sanctuary."

Rafnir whistled softly, and Sayyed simply stared.

At their feet the ridge dropped away into a deep valley that lay like a green jewel in the cold heart of the mountains. Lush and verdant, it stretched for nearly five leagues east and west, nestled between three lofty peaks. Sunlight glittered on the waters of a small lake and a river on the valley's floor and picked out the white plumes of several waterfalls that cascaded down the western face.

"Look!" Rafnir said. His finger pointed toward the waterfalls, but it was not the water that gripped his attention. A huge ledge bisected the western face of the canyon wall midway up its height. On the ledge beneath a towering overhang was a cluster of buildings carved from the natural stone and sitting in eminence over the valley. Below, herds grazed in the meadows, and the tiny figures of more people could be seen moving about their tasks.

Helmar's eyes crinkled in her weathered face as she watched the reaction of the two clansmen. Her expression was calm but wary, and she studied the two men as thoroughly as they studied the valley.

Beside her, an older woman touched Sayyed's cloak. Small, bright-eyed, and quick as a bird, she was the only woman in the group wearing a long robe. The rest of the people, even the women, wore long, baggy pants, warm wool shirts, and leather vests or tunics. "Sorcerer, I am Minora, Priestess of the Clannad," she told Sayyed.

"Ah, yes," Sayyed said, flashing a smile. "The one who wanted to keep us for breeding stock."

Although Sayyed did not know it, he had a very charming smile that took any sting out of his words. Minora laughed, a ringing, delightful burst of humor. "And I still do. We are very isolated here. Good breeders are hard to come by."

He turned to look at the magnificent structure across the valley. "Did your people make that?"

The priestess lifted her chin to see his face. Short as Sayyed was, she barely reached his shoulder. "The ledge and the stone were there. We have simply worked it as we wished."

"We could certainly use these people at Moy Tura," Rafnir commented to his father.

A look too indescribable to understand passed over Minora's face, and the other people hesitated, their expressions still and hard.

"What is Moy Tura?" Helmar quickly asked.

But Sayyed sensed a nuance of familiarity in her tone that belied her ignorance. "An old ruin in our land. We are trying to rebuild it."

"Who—" she started to ask.

"My lady, you said no questions until the horses are released," Rapinor reminded her bluntly.

She chuckled, low and throaty, and led the group on a winding course along the top of the ridge and down a steep, tortuous trail to the tiny canyon where the stallions were trapped.

"When you entered the passage last night. we sealed the entrance," Rapinor explained. "We had no idea what we had caught."

Sayyed's fingers went to his throat. If his neck looked anything like Rafnir's, a blue and purplish bruise ringed his throat where the rope had hauled him off his Hunnuli. "Indeed," he said dryly.

Helmar cleared her throat in sympathy, and her lips twisted in a wry smile. "You must forgive our style of welcome. We do not usually allow strangers into our valley. If it had not been for Rapinor and his insistence that you were using a sorcerer's light, you would be dead already."

Sayyed shot a look at the burly swordsman. Stout as an oak, the lady's guard had not budged from her side since the two men landed on the ledge. Nor had his hand strayed far from the sword buckled at his waist. Another man, younger but more dour than Rapinor, stood on Helmar's other side. His heavy brows framed his eyes in a frown, and his thick lips were pursed with displeasure.

"How is it that you know so much about magic," Sayyed inquired, "what with your being so isolated in a realm that forbids its use?" And, his thoughts continued silently, why is it so important to you?

Lady Helmar cocked her head and gave him a wide, challenging stare from her green-gold eyes. "We hear things once in a while. We do not drop everyone over the ravine." She flashed a brilliantly disarming smile.

A short hike later, they reached the valley floor and trekked to the narrow entrance leading to the crevice where the stallions were trapped. Helmar and her two guards worked their way in, followed by Sayyed and Rafnir. They heard the horses long before they saw them, for ringing neighs echoed along the rock walls, punctuated by heavy crashes reverberating on something that sounded like wood.

The clansmen saw why a few minutes later. The high, narrow passage had been completely blocked by massive stone blocks fitted together to form a thick wall. The crashing sounds came from a wooden wicket gate set in the wall.

"The Back Door," Rapinor said. "Your horses obviously found it." He strode forward and, standing wisely aside, drew the heavy bolts. The door flew open, and Afer and Tibor charged through ready for battle. Their eyes glowed green with angry fire, their tails were raised like battle standards, and their hooves clashed on the stone.

Seeing their riders, both stallions stopped and snorted. *Where were you?* trumpeted Afer. *Who are these people?*

Before Sayyed could respond, Helmar stepped forward and boldly put her hand on Afer's arched neck. The stallion instantly stilled, his ears stiff and his nostrils quivering as he gently sniffed her arm and face. Tibor crowded over and smelled the chieftain from hair to belt, then nickered a greeting.

When she stepped back, the Hunnuli were satisfied and calmly went to join the sorcerers. A look of surprise passed between Rafnir and Sayyed.

Sayyed bent in the pretense of examining Afer's legs. "Are you all right?" he said softly.

I am and you are! And I am glad to get out of that crack. There was no grass in there, and I'm hungry!

As if she had understood what he sent, Lady Helmar bowed slightly to the two horses and the clansmen. "I would like to make amends for our poor hospitality. Would you care to stay the night with us and share our table?"

The dour young man beside her made as if to protest, until he saw Minora give him a hard look. He subsided, looking sullen.

Sayyed thought of the city in the cliff, of the hidden valley and the secretive people who inhabited it, of the veiled suspicion he saw in every person's eyes, and the gleam of excitement as if they could not quite believe what he and Rafnir had done. He thought of the Clannad's knowledge of Hunnuli, sorcerer's lights, and the "death" of magic beyond the mountains. These people with their pale skin and fair hair seemed different, and yet there was an undercurrent of familiarity he could not quite ignore. Surely one night here in this valley would make little difference in their search for Gabria and Kelene, and perhaps the Clannad could help by telling them where the wagon track went and how to find it again. He bowed to Helmar, and with Rafnir's consent, he agreed to stay.

The group rejoined the others waiting at the mouth of the passage, and everyone walked down a steep, narrow trail to the valley floor. Once there, they paused on a low rise at the western end of the valley and gazed at the land about them.

"Sinking River carved this basin," Helmar told her guests. "The waters come from the high peaks down those falls to the river, where it runs the length of our valley and spills into the lake." She pointed to the small lake that lay below the rise. Not much bigger than a large pond, the lake sat serene in a ring of slender trees and grassy banks. Clear water lapped its rocky shores and sank down into unseen depths. "The lake has no bottom that we have been able to find. The river is swallowed by the mountains."

The clansmen filled their eyes with the beauty of the valley. Having witnessed the bleak slopes of the rugged peaks and felt the fury of the Storm King, they could appreciate the lush serenity of this hidden realm where spring was in full bloom. Thick grass and vegetation carpeted the valley. Trees in full leaf grew in groves along the riverbanks and in scattered copses up the slopes to the towering valley walls.

A movement in the nearby meadow caught their gaze, and they turned in time to see a ghostly herd of horses sweep past a belt of trees and come galloping toward the rise. Both men drew their breath in wonder at the white animals that approached them. More than a hundred mares, stallions, and foals flowed like an avalanche up to the foot of the hill and neighed a welcome to the strangers.

Smaller than the Hunnuli, yet equally as graceful and beautifully proportioned, every horse was white, ranging in shade and intensity from dapple gray to the most brilliant snow.

A stallion and a mare cantered up the slope together. The mare, a starry white, went to Helmar with a greeting, but the stallion arched his neck, pranced to Sayyed and Rafnir, and sniffed them to familiarize himself with their scent. They rubbed his neck, which was the color of polished slate; then he went to

Afer and Tibor. The two blacks touched him muzzle to muzzle, nickering their greetings. Sayyed removed the Hunnuli's saddles, and together the three stallions galloped down to the herd. The people and the mare watched them go until the horses spread out over a broad meadow and began to graze.

"Your horses are incredible," Sayyed said to Helmar. "How did you manage to breed such a consistent color?"

"Fear, Clansman," she replied helpfully. With a graceful leap she mounted the mare's broad back, and an enigmatic smile touched her lips. "Bring them to the cliff, Rapinor. I shall go prepare a feast." The mare sprang away, as swift as a falling star. Minora chuckled to herself.

From the rise they walked down the valley to the waterfalls and the base of the great ledge. Rope ladders hung down the wall, connecting a series of small ledges, handholds, and narrow steps in several difficult trails up the cliff to the cave settlement. More people joined the group, their faces full of amazement and some disbelief at the arrival of the sorcerers. From somewhere above a horn sounded a summons. The sun was high by that time, and its warm light filled the valley from end to end, yet despite the business of the season, every person in the Clannad laid down their tasks and came at the call of the horn.

With a skill born from a lifetime's practice, the people clambered up the ladders to their home. Sayyed and Rafnir climbed up more slowly, and when they reached the top they were welcomed with the return of their clothes and weapons. The men were then led to a wide, circular gathering place near the edge of the cliff where a low stone wall had been built along the rim. A fire burned in the hearth at the center of the ring, and much to Sayyed and Rafnir's surprise, a real feast had been hastily prepared for their arrival.

Helmar's own handmaidens sat Sayyed and Rafnir beside the chief's seat and served them from platters of meat and fish, an interesting dish of cooked tubers, bowls of dried berries, and rounds of flat bread. Tall flagons of cooled wine and pitchers of ale were passed around.

As Sayyed gratefully ate the first hearty meal he had had in several long days, he let his eyes roam over his surroundings and the people around him. The settlement in the cliff was not as large as he had at first thought. While the buildings were large and numerous, the population was not. At a rough count he estimated there were about four hundred men, women, and children in the Clannad. Since he had not seen any other buildings, tents, or shelters within the confines of the valley, he assumed they all lived in this stone aerie.

The cliff buildings themselves were remarkable, some towering four or five stories above the floor level. From where he sat, Sayyed could see several artisans' houses, a gathering hall, what looked like a temple, and numerous multi-level dwellings, and while the buildings were not opulent, they looked comfortable and well maintained.

It was while he was looking at the narrow passages between the buildings that he made an interesting observation that only added fuel to his curiosity. Unlike a clan camp, this settlement had no dogs. Not a one, as far as Sayyed could tell. There were, though, cats of every color and age, lounging on windowsills, draped on walls, and padding along the walks.

One tabby boldly walked up to him and sprang into his lap. Pleased, Sayyed scratched her ears and the base of her tail, remembering Tam's cat waiting for him in Moy Tura. The cat settled on his knees and purred her song for him.

A soft laugh drew his attention, and he looked up into the green-gold eyes of Helmar. Now that he could see her close up, he saw that despite the similarities in character, there was little physical resemblance to Gabria. Helmar's face was square and strong-featured with a straight nose and an incongruous sprinkle of freckles. He guessed she had seen more than thirty summers, for years of sun, wind, and work had worn away the softness of youth. Her body was hard, too, from physical labor, and her hands were nicked and calloused from wielding a sword. She lounged on her fur-draped seat, as self-assured as any clan chieftain.

Unconsciously, he smiled back.

"You like our cats?" she asked.

"I have one at home. I miss her."

"Tell me about her."

And out of this simple, ingenious request came an afternoon of talk and tales and history. From the story of Tam's cat, Sayyed went on to tell his fascinated audience about Tam, the plague, and the clans. Rafnir took his turn, talking about Moy Tura, Kelene, and Demira. The people of the Clannad listened avidly.

When Sayyed described Gabria and her battle with Lord Medb, the people sat hushed and unmoving. Sayyed, looking at their faces, thought their interest went beyond mere politeness. In a whole afternoon, not one person left the gathering. Children napped in their parents' laps, elders dozed in their seats, but not one person walked away from the tales. When he was finished, a low buzz of conversation filled the circle. The sorcerer glanced around and was surprised to see the sun had gone behind the western peaks. Darkness filled the bowl of the valley.

The talking stopped as Lady Helmar rose slowly to her feet. She looked thoughtful and rather sad, but her voice was as firm as ever. "This Lady Gabria, this last Corin, is she the other woman you are trying to find?"

"She is Kelene's mother," Rafnir replied. "They were taken together."

"I should like to meet her. I think we will go with you to this fortress."

The younger guard beside her leaped to his feet and planted himself squarely in her way. "My lady, think again. It would be folly to leave the valley this time of year. Let them find the trail themselves."

Lady Helmar did not step back. Coolly she faced her guard and said, "Hydan, you forget yourself."

Jut-jawed and steely-eyed, Hydan pointed at the two sorcerers like a man flinging an accusation. "What if they're lying? What if all we have heard has been a tale to save their necks?"

Sayyed felt Rafnir tense and stir, and he laid a restraining hand on his son's arm before Rafnir jumped into anything unnecessary. Helmar, he could see, was equal to the confrontation.

Eyes blazing, she ignored the rest of the gathering and pushed herself close to Hydan to make her point very clear. "And I suppose they faked the sorcery they used this morning," she said fiercely. "Truth or half-truth, they are here and they are magic-wielders." She threw a wild gesture at the stone city behind her. "Do you want to live like this forever? If we can find this Lady Gabria, she will confirm the truth."

"If there is a Lady Gabria," Hydan muttered.

"If you doubt, Hydan, then ride with me and learn for yourself."

As quickly as he had flared up, the young guard subsided, having rammed his feelings against the wall of his chief's will. Helmar, obviously used to his tantrums, turned back to Sayyed without a pause. "You said the wagon had a red emblem of some sort and took the trail up around the Storm King? I know that path. It goes to a fortress owned by an old noble family."

"The old stone castle?" Hydan put in, as coolly as if he had never shown his temper. "The latest resident is one of the royal counselors, I have heard."

"His name wouldn't happen to be Zukhara?" Rafnir guessed. Hydan didn't even have to answer that. Zukhara's name fit the trail of clues and events they had been following since Council Rock.

"You know this man?" Helmar asked.

Sayyed nodded once. "A dangerous adversary." He lifted his eyes to her face and met her forthright gaze. He thought briefly of offering to leave alone— surely he and Rafnir could find the fortress with a few directions—then he dismissed the idea and bowed to the determination he could read so clearly in those expressive eyes. Yet he couldn't help but wonder why she was so willing to help two strangers that only hours before she had planned to drop down a ravine. And why was it so dangerous for the Clannad to leave their valley? These questions and many more trooped through Sayyed's thoughts. It was a puzzle with too many pieces missing.

At that point, men brought torches to the gathering circle. The fire was stoked, and several people fetched their instruments to strike up some dance music. Like their language, the Clannad's musical instruments were an interesting blend of old clan, Turic, and individual designs, and the music they played was rollicking, toe-tapping fun. The people danced late into the night, breaking only to listen to a harper sing ballads of the white horses, the Sinking River, and the valley they called home.

Sayyed and Rafnir enjoyed the evening and the pleasant company of the cliff dwellers. It was a frustrating evening, though, for try as they might they could not lead anyone into answering more than basic questions about their daily lives. Minora was more than happy to discuss her duties in the temple to the goddess they worshiped, but she neatly skirted any inquiries about the origins of the white horses and her insistence on keeping the two men for breeding. Rapinor, too, was closemouthed about anything except his duties as swordsman to Lady Helmar. And the lady herself, when asked a question, more often than not answered it with another question. Sayyed found himself talking to her for nearly an hour about his childhood with the Turics and his decision to join Gabria. In all that time she said nothing about herself.

At last the chieftain clashed the hilt of her sword against a gong hanging near her chair and ended the gathering. The people quickly split up, going their separate ways back to their homes. Helmar took Sayyed and Rafnir to quarters that had been prepared for them on the ground floor of a tall building and bid them goodnight.

When at last they were left alone, Sayyed drew a long breath and expelled it in a gusty sigh. "I still don't know who these people are," he said irritably.

They found pitchers of water set aside on a stand for washing and beds covered with woven blankets. The stuffed mattresses on the beds felt so delightful after days of sleeping on the ground, Rafnir threw himself on one and was asleep before Sayyed had removed his boots.

Bone-tired as he felt, Sayyed could not sleep yet. Too many things ran through his mind, whirling as fast as the melodies of the Clannad jigs. He thought of the clan cloak he had transformed earlier and remembered he had left it at the gathering circle. Barefooted, he walked silently through the darkened passages back to the open ring.

He took one step out from between the buildings and as silently drew back into the shadows. Someone was standing in the ring beside the cloak Sayyed had left flung over the place where he had sat.

He stared at the form, trying to see who it was. Night filled the huge cavern with velvet darkness, but beyond the stone walls a curtain of countless stars glittered their distant, silver light. The person turned sideways against the backdrop of stars, and Sayyed recognized the handsome, straight profile of Helmar. Ever so slowly she picked up the cloak and seemed to hug it tightly to her chest; then she turned and strode toward him. Sayyed pushed deeper into the sheltering shadow as she walked on past.

The sorcerer blinked in surprise. For just the wink of an eye, Helmar had been close enough for him to see her clearly, and in that brief moment, he had seen the shimmer of tears in her eyes.

Sayyed walked slowly back to his quarters deep in thought, and when he finally drifted to sleep that night, it was Helmar's face, strong yet sadly vulnerable, that colored his dreams.

11

Kelene crouched against the stone wall as far from the gryphon as she could manage and vehemently loosed a string of well-chosen words vilifying Zukhara's ancestry. Blood dripped from three long scratches on her arm, and a bruise spread over the right side of her face. She glared balefully at the gryphon, who hissed and glared back with equal ferocity.

"Stupid bird," she muttered to herself. Or whatever it was. Even after two days of being trapped in its vicinity, Kelene still wasn't sure if the winged creature was a bird or an animal. It was beautiful, she had to admit that. Its narrow head, wings, and the beaklike nose reminded her of an eagle, as did its piercing hunter's eyes and the bright gold fur that looked suspiciously like feathers covering its entire body. The legs. though, looked like those of a lion, powerfully muscled, sleek, and deadly. Its feet had large pads fitted with razor-sharp retractable claws. The beast had a long tail like a cat's, and Kelene had noticed that it used the tail to communicate its feelings much as Tam's cat did. It used its tail now, lashing it irritably back and forth as it lay on the floor and glowered at her. Its tufted ears lay flat on its head.

"Afraid of a few scratches?" Zukhara's voice reverberated through the cavern. The woman and the gryphon glared up with matching hatred at the overhang. That was one thing Kelene knew they had in common.

"The beast will not kill you," Zukhara called to her, the scorn clear in his loud voice. "It is chained and prefers the taste of horseflesh. You have had two days already, two days that your lady mother lies dying."

Kelene leaped to her feet, ignoring the gryphon's startled snarl. "How is she? Is she still alive?" she called anxiously.

"She is being cared for," the Turic said curtly. "And she is still alert enough to continue my training in sorcery. But you have only five days left until the poison completes its task." He lowered a basket to her and left, his words still echoing in her mind.

Five days, she thought miserably, and she was no closer to taming this gryphon than she'd been when Zukhara dumped her in the pit with it. On the other hand, she thought wryly, the company of a wild gryphon was certainly preferable to Zukhara and his plans for her.

She unpacked the food and a wineskin from the basket. He certainly was taking no chances that she go hungry. He had sent enough delicacies to last another day, and the skin was full to bursting with the same fruit juice he had given her earlier. She wrinkled her nose at the sweet smell. He had probably laced it with more of his midwives' remedy. For the briefest moment she hesitated and thought of her wish to have a baby. If this remedy worked, was it worth the chance? Could she rely solely on luck and her wits to keep her out of the counselor's bed? Then, almost fiercely, she changed the juice to water. She wanted a child desperately, but she wanted Rafnir's baby, not a child conceived in trickery and hate.

After she had eaten, Kelene repacked the basket and stood to stretch her back and shoulders under the wary gaze of the gryphon. As she moved, something fell out of her skirt to the cavern floor. She picked it up and recognized the wad of fabric she had used to wipe the sedative off Demira's rump. It had lain forgotten in her waistband for three days. Curious to see if the ointment was still damp, she unfolded the cloth, and the faint medicinal smell rose to her nostrils. The sedative, set in its oily base, had saturated the fabric through almost all the folded layers. Kelene grinned. If this hadn't fallen out when it had, she might have been drugged by the very potion she hoped to save.

She folded it again, wrapped it in another scrap from her already tattered tunic, and returned it to its hiding place. Unfortunately there wasn't enough to sedate the gryphon. It stood taller than a Hunnuli and probably weighed twice as much.

But she had other weapons for that beast. Kelene rolled up her sleeves. She had refrained from using more than a few minor spells in the presence of the gryphon for fear of injuring it further or scaring it beyond redemption. All she had received for her gentle concern were scratches, bruises, and snarling disdain. Well, time was too precious now to softfoot around this beast! She would have to take her chances with its sensibilities.

Kelene recalled the handbook of Lady Jeneve, and in her mind's eye she pictured the page she wanted and the words to the spell that paralyzed living creatures. She recreated the spell and released it, stopping the gryphon in midstride before it knew what hit it. It could still breathe, and its eyes glowed bright with fear and anger, but it did not move as Kelene came close.

Softly, gently, she spoke to the gryphon to ease its fear. She did not touch it yet; she merely walked around the creature to ascertain the full extent of its injuries. Fortunately most of the wounds were scrapes and scratches that were healing on their own. Only one long abrasion on the left hind leg looked swollen and festering.

Kelene fetched the water left in the wineskin and her healer's bag. The first night Zukhara imprisoned her with the gryphon, he had returned her bag, sent her new clothes, and provided a pallet for her comfort. Kelene had ignored the new clothes, preferring her own torn and dirty ones to the silk tunic and the form-fitting gown Zukhara had sent. She found a use for them now, taking delight in tearing them into strips to bandage the gryphon's leg. She laid out several jars of salves, a bowl of water, and the bandages. When she was ready, she took a deep breath. The gryphon, its huge eye rolling back to look at her, looked terrified by its inability to move. Laying a hand gently on the gryphon's warm side, Kelene closed her eyes and extended her empathic talent down her skin and into the creature's body.

Wild, hot, and fierce, the gryphon's emotions broke over her, making her gasp at the sheer force of its personality. At once she realized the gryphon was a female, young, barely of breeding age, and consumed with rage at her captivity. Kelene felt barbs of suspicion and bright red animalistic waves of fear. She probed deeper, soothing her way with calm thoughts and feelings of concern, toward the heart of the gryphon's emotions.

Ever so delicately Kelene let her thoughts touch the creature's mind. *Easy, girl,* she sent kindly. *You and I are in this together. Let us help one another.* She didn't know if the golden beast was intelligent enough to understand her thoughts and the concept of cooperation, but it was worth a try.

Much to her relief, the gryphon's vivid, tumultuous feelings began to settle down to calmer waves of wary curiosity.

I will not hurt you, Kelene continued. *I want only to treat your hurt.*

Her mental touch still lightly on the gryphon's mind, she began to clean the infected cut. Skillfully she salved it and bandaged the leg, all the while stroking the creature with her empathic touch.

When she was finished with the wound she added one more thought before she broke their bond. *I am a captive like you, and like you I have to serve the man. If you will help me, I will help you gain your freedom.* And with that she withdrew her mind and dissolved the paralyzing spell.

The gryphon shook herself and snarled irritably at Kelene, but although she still stood in range of the creature's powerful paws, the gryphon sat down, curled her tail around her feet, and contemplated the sorceress with eagle eyes.

"Think about it," Kelene said aloud, and she returned to her pallet to let the animal rest. Would the gryphon settle down and let her help? She didn't know, and she was too tired to think about it for long. Without intending to, Kelene fell soundly asleep.

The gryphon's growl woke her to darkness, and she bolted upright at the chilling sound. The sorcerer's light she usually maintained had gone out while she slept, leaving the cavern in impenetrable night. The gryphon growled again, low and full of menace. Her chains rattled in the darkness.

Kelene raised her hand to relight her sphere when a small handlamp flared to light in an entrance she had not seen before. A stone door, cunningly set in the rock of the cavern wall, creaked closed behind Counselor Zukhara. He set the lamp on a ledge and moved toward her pallet. Kelene sprang to her feet in alarm.

"I have been watching you and your progress with the gryphon. It is almost ready." Kelene said nothing and warily watched him approach. He paused an arm's length away and eyed her from head to toe. "You are not wearing the clothes I chose for you," he said levelly.

"I had other need for them," Kelene replied. Nervously she edged back, very much aware that Zukhara wore only a loose-fitting robe open to his chest and his ivory ward. Deliberately she turned to run and, under the cover of her more violent movement, she dipped her fingers in her waistband and palmed the wad of fabric.

Zukhara lunged after her. His hands closed on her shoulders and wrenched her off balance. Her tunic ripped across the back. Half-hauling, half-dragging her backward, he flung her to the pallet and pinned her down with the full length of his body. Kelene lay panting and wild-eyed. She struggled against his weight, and as she tried to heave him away, she clamped the rag with oily sedative against his upper arm.

To keep his attention on her, she screamed and fought with all her might and prayed the sedative would work. She could feel his passion exuding from him in a heavy cloying aura, and she desperately closed her mind to his touch, terrified of being overwhelmed by his need.

Zukhara forced his hand over her mouth and silenced her screams. In the sudden quiet, she heard the gryphon lunge against her chains. The beast's growl rose to a hair-raising cry that shivered to the vaulted ceiling of the cave.

Zukhara heard it and exalted. "Tonight, my chosen, we consummate our union in the presence of the sacred gryphon." Kelene lay still, her face marble-white, her fingers still fastened to his arms. "You are like the gryphon," he told her. "Untamed, fierce, and proud. I have waited a long time for this."

Kelene's eyes widened. Did his voice seem to slur a bit on those last words? No sooner had she thought that, than Zukhara's eyes rolled up in his head and he slumped over her, dead to the world.

The sorceress gratefully pushed him off. She wrapped the rag back in its cloth and grinned. The sedative was potent stuff indeed. She had no idea how long the drug would last, so she quickly went to work. First she tried the stone door, but as she had feared, it was locked with a powerful spell. Not that she was certain she wanted to escape yet anyway. She had no antidote for Gabria and no knowledge of where to find her mother, or Nara, or even a way out. Nor did she want to kill Zukhara yet, for those same reasons. There would be a better time to escape—a time perhaps when she could also free the gryphon. Instead she decided simply to play along with Zukhara's plans. Let the man think he had succeeded, she thought grimly; then maybe he would leave her alone for a while.

Setting one blanket aside, she mussed her pallet as if it had been vigorously used; then she draped the Turic's long body over the whole thing. Her fingers found the ivory ward, pulled it out, and she cracked it ever so slightly under her knee. The crack would weaken the ward's effectiveness, and if all went well, he would not notice the damage until too late. She pulled off his robe, averting her eyes in distaste, and dropped it in a pile with her own torn, dirty tunic and skirt. Then she transformed the spare blanket into a pair of riding pants and a thick, warm tunic similar to those she had worn before.

She looked around for a place to lie down away from Zukhara and was surprised to see the gryphon sitting at the end of her chain and regarding her with calm, friendly eyes. In fact, she was purring. She walked up to the creature, waiting for her perked ears to go flat, but the gryphon only lay down on her side as if inviting Kelene to join her. Kelene threw all caution to the winds. She curled up beside the gryphon's warm, furry-feathery side and waited for Zukhara to wake up.

She didn't have long to wait. The sedative was old and there hadn't been much to work with on the rag. In a matter of minutes, Zukhara stirred and sat up rather groggily. He looked around for her. Kelene huddled closer to the gryphon's side and tried her best to look like a wounded maiden. The Turic's eye roved from himself to the bed to their clothes to Kelene's miserable expression, and Kelene was rewarded by a flicker of confusion in the man's dark eyes. Finally he stood, donned his robe, and strode toward her. The gryphon's tufted ears snapped flat, and her warning growl stopped him in his tracks.

He lifted a sardonic eyebrow. "I see you have tamed the beast," he said to Kelene.

"She and I have something in common," Kelene retorted.

"She? I didn't realize." He smiled in pleasure. "How appropriate."

"I thought gryphons were extinct," she said, trying to keep the aggrieved tone in her voice while leading him to any subject other than what had *not* happened between them.

She needn't have worried. Zukhara's pride would never let him admit he didn't remember a thing. He thankfully accepted her lead to an area he could discuss with authority and assurance. "My hunters found one tiny pride so far back in the mountains it took days to reach them."

Kelene noticed the gryphon was paying close attention to their exchange, and she pondered just how much the animal understood. "Are the others still there?"

"As far as I know. I took only the one."

"But why? What use will she be to you?"

"You do not know the Turic religion," he said scornfully, "or you would understand. Gryphons are the sacred messengers of the Prophet Sargun. In our ancient tales, it was a gryphon who freed the prophet from his prison and carried him home. The gryphon is a powerful symbol to my people, and this one will be the vanguard of my conquest. When she flies, the people will know my armies are blessed by the Living God, and they will flock to my call."

Kelene merely nodded. She had given up being surprised by the scope of this man's plans. "And when you are finished with her, will you let her go?"

Zukhara's mouth lifted in a cold smile. He knew she was talking about more than the gryphon. "When I am finished, she may not want to go." He bowed slightly to them both. "Good day, my lady. Stay with the gryphon and be sure she will come at your call. Tomorrow we leave for Cangora."

Kelene jumped to her feet. "And my mother?"

"She comes with us." He laughed as he turned to leave. "And the antidote, too." He blew out his lamp, leaving Kelene and the gryphon in the darkness, and the door boomed shut behind him.

* * *

The Clannad mustered at daybreak in the meadow at the foot of the cliff settlement. Fifty warriors, men and women armed and dressed for battle, mounted their white horses and fell in behind their chieftain's standard. Sayyed and Rafnir, astride their Hunnuli, marveled anew at the beauty of the Clannad horses and their training. Except for simple saddlepads, the horses wore no tack of any kind, yet they obeyed their riders as well as any Hunnuli.

As soon as the ranks were mustered, Lady Helmar raised a gloved fist. She rode her star-colored mare that morning and wore a shirt of silver mail that glistened like water in the pearly light. Her bright red hair hung below her helm in a heavy braid that dangled over her shoulder, and a bow and quiver were strapped to her back. She gave a single piercing call that was answered by fifty voices in a shout that rang across the valley. In the city above, those who remained behind waved and shouted good-bye.

The troop trotted down the valley, sorting themselves into a single file as they approached the passage of the Back Door. One by one they rode down the narrow crevice and worked their way down the rugged glen beside the tumbling stream. Even in the light of a sunny spring day, the going was slow. It was nearly midday before the first of the troop came to a halt by the tall, grotesque pole of faces that guarded the faint trail.

"Do you know anything about that statue?" Rafnir asked the rider closest to him.

The man looked up the length of the pole and grinned. "Those things have been in the mountains since long before us. But this one was found many leagues away. My grandfather helped move it here to guard the Back Door. The local shepherds are terrified of it and stay away from the valley."

The clansmen fully expected to travel the rest of the afternoon. The day was clear and mild, the trails were drying, and the traveling would be easy. But to their astonishment, as soon as the last Clannad warrior reached the ancestor pole, instead of mounting and moving on, Helmar led her riders into the shelter of a thick belt of trees and ordered them to dismount.

"Because," she insisted when Sayyed demanded to know why, "we always travel at night. The only reason we left early was to traverse the glen in the daylight. But now we're out of our territory. Now we rest the horses and travel at night." And that was that.

Sayyed and Rafnir could only swallow their impatience and wait. The stallions didn't seem to mind. Sayyed noticed Afer and Tibor had taken a strong liking to the white horses and apparently found something amusing about their company. When asked, though, neither stallion would give a definite answer.

Sayyed scratched his beard and tried to relax. It was not easy. The afternoon wore slowly on while the horses quietly grazed, the warriors dozed, and the insects droned in the undergrowth. Finally Sayyed brought out his tulwar and the special stone he kept solely to sharpen the weapon, and he began to run the stone smoothly along the curved blade. After several strokes, he felt the tingling on the back of his neck he always got when he was being watched, and he looked up into Helmar's intent gaze. Her eyes sparkled, green and intense, the color of sunlight in deep water. She met his regard with frank interest.

"Are you as good with that blade as you are with magic?" she asked, her voice lightly teasing.

He lifted an eyebrow and kept working. "You have only seen me use one spell, so you cannot know whether I am good or not."

Beside the chief, flat on his back, Hydan chuckled at the remark.

"If half of what you told us is true, then you must be one of the finest sorcerers in the clans," she said.

"He is." Rafnir spoke up from his resting spot by the trunk of a tree.

A hiss of humor escaped Sayyed. "All of what I told you is true," he said shortly. "Now tell me a truth. Where did your people come from?"

"Over the mountains." She shrugged. "We have been in Sanctuary for generations."

"Why did you decide to save us when you learned we were sorcerers?"

"You saved yourselves. We couldn't very well argue with magic-wielders."

He grunted. "Where did you learn to speak Clannish?"

"We didn't know we were until you came along."

Exasperated, Sayyed put away his stone. He felt as if he were running into walls with every question he asked. Either they had a poor oral tradition, they simply didn't care about their ancestry or—and Sayyed was more inclined to believe this—they were deliberately concealing a secret they weren't ready to share.

He shoved his tulwar back in its sheath, crossed his arms, and leaned back against a tree, shutting his eyes to end the conversation. The Clannad would reveal their truths when they wanted, and until then he was not going to beat his head against their walls.

When night came, the troop ate a cold meal and continued across the mountain slopes toward the trail Sayyed and Rafnir had lost in the storm. The two sorcerers quickly acknowledged that the Clannad warriors were quite good at night travel and their horses were sharp-eyed and agile. But the darkness disguised details, drained color, and turned the world to shadow, and even the most seasoned traveler was slowed by night on treacherous paths in the mountain wilderness. Worse yet, the heavy rains of the storm two nights ago had washed out many sections of the trails they were trying to follow, and a huge, muddy landslide blocked one shortcut they tried, forcing them on a long detour out of one valley and up a traverse over a high, spiny ridge before they could find their way to the wagon trail. By dawn they were tired, muddy, and still leagues from the fortress.

When daylight painted the eastern horizon, the Clannad began to look for a place to shelter for the day. Sayyed, though, urged Afer close to Helmar's mare. "We can't stop now," he said bluntly. "Gabria and Kelene have been in that fortress almost three days. We have to get them out!"

"And we will," Helmar replied. "But the horses need a rest and we—"

"Do not travel in daylight. I know," he cut her off. "But we don't have that time to waste."

"I will not endanger my people for—"

"What is *that?*" Hydan exclaimed.

All eyes swept to the brightening sky in time to see something large and dark swerve toward them. A shadow swift as a storm cloud raced overhead and plunged out of the dawn light. The white horses neighed a warning.

Hydan's warrior instincts brought his hands to his bow and an arrow before he stopped to think. In a blur he nocked the arrow, raised the bow, and drew the string to his jaw.

"No!" bellowed Rafnir.

Tibor sprang forward and rammed into Hydan's horse, knocking the man's aim askew. The bow dropped, but his fingers released the string, and the arrow sang wildly into the group clustered around Helmar.

In the same second the downdraft from a huge pair of wings swept over the party and blew the shaft farther off course. *I found you!* trumpeted a Hunnuli voice.

"Demira!" Sayyed shouted in joy. Just as he spoke, the arrow pierced through his arm and into his side. Stunned, he looked down at the shaft that pinned his arm to his ribs, and a sickly smile twisted over his lips. "I knew I should have stayed in Moy Tura," he said and slowly sagged off Afer to the muddy earth.

Appalled, Helmar, Hydan, and Rafnir slid off their mounts and hurried to Sayyed's aid. While Tibor joyously welcomed Demira, the warriors carried the sorcerer into a copse of trees and laid him on the cloak Helmar had returned. There was no question now that they would have to stop.

Helmar snapped orders to her riders, and in moments every man and horse was out of sight in several scattered groves of trees. One man was a healer, and under his direction Helmar and Rafnir removed the shaft from Sayyed's arm. Fortunately that part proved easy enough, for the arrow had pierced straight through the muscle on the back of his upper arm. The difficulty came in removing the arrowhead from his ribs. Demira's wings had probably saved his life by slowing the arrow, but it still had struck with enough force to wedge between two bones. It took a long while to cut the skin, work the arrow free, and stitch the wounds. Although Helmar and the healer tried to be gentle, by the time they were through Sayyed was drenched with sweat and utterly exhausted. His hand reached out to grip Helmar's, and he thankfully passed out into healing sleep.

The lady stared down at his hand, still dirty from clenching the earth in his pain, and her fingers tightened around his.

Afer gently nosed her. *He will be all right.*

"I know," she murmured.

Rafnir looked up sharply. "What?"

She settled more comfortably beside the clansman, his hand still in hers, and sighed. "Just talking to myself."

Sleep, the healer's salves, and a warm meal soon bolstered Sayyed's constitution. As soon as he could stand without getting dizzy, he insisted on greeting Demira and making much over her return. The mare confirmed Gabria and Kelene were in Zukhara's fortress, and she told the men the sketchy facts she knew.

"Poisoned!" Sayyed said furiously. "Are you sure?"

That is what Kelene said, Demira replied. *She was certain someone had come after them, and she ordered me to leave.* Her mental tone still sounded aggrieved. *I have looked for you all over these mountains!*

Rafnir flung his arms around her neck, and that was all the thanks she needed.

The troop left the trees that night at Sayyed's insistence, but the loss of blood had left him weaker than he thought, and he could ride only a few hours that night. They stopped again the third day in a woods only a few leagues from the fortress. Sayyed was too tired to argue. Although his impatience pushed him on, his body would not obey. The puncture in his arm was healing well, but riding had pulled the stitches in his side. Blood oozed from his bandages, and the wound looked red and swollen. Sayyed knew he would be no good to Gabria and Kelene if he did not regain his strength, so he ate his food, swallowed a draught provided by the healer, and went to his bed without protest.

Just past midnight the next night, the troop climbed a rocky hillside and rode down into a steep ravine. There on a high plateau overlooking the ravine, they saw the stark outline of several squat towers and the high stone walls of a fortress. On one side of the castle the cliffs fell sheer to the ravine floor; on the other a pale road wound its way up the steep face to the entrance.

"Good gods," Rafnir breathed. "How do we get up into that?"

"By the front door," Sayyed growled.

He conferred with Helmar for several long minutes and, when they were agreed, the Clannad riders dismounted. Silently and nearly invisibly, the warriors began to work their way up the road toward the fortress. Demira pushed aside her fear of flying at night and flew a reconnaissance over the fortress.

It is lightly guarded, she reported when she returned. *And they are not paying close attention.*

Sayyed and Rafnir watched the descending moon and gave Helmar and her warriors another half hour; then Sayyed trotted Afer openly up the road toward the fortress gates. Rafnir mounted Demira, and she launched herself into the darkness.

Demira was right, the guards were very lax that night. Sayyed rode nearly to the top of the plateau close to the gate before a voice called out to challenge him.

Sayyed replied in Turic, "I have messages for the Supreme Counselor, Zukhara."

"Not tonight," grumbled a voice on the wall.

Sayyed shot a look over his shoulder to the dark, rock-tumbled edge of the road. A tiny flash, the reflection of moonlight on a dagger blade, signaled Helmar was ready.

"Sorry, but I really must see him now," Sayyed snapped, and he raised his good arm and fired a powerful blast of magic at the wooden gate. To his astonishment, the magic struck the wood and evaporated. The entrance was protected with magic wards!

This arcane defense was so unexpected, Sayyed stared in surprise. Shouts echoed on the walls, and feet pounded along the battlements. The sorcerer had wanted to surprise the garrison, and all he had succeeded in doing was rouse them all. He tried again with a more powerful bolt. That one shook the gate and boomed against the stone, but the wards were new and well made, and they held.

Sayyed took a deep breath. He was weaker than he imagined, and the thought crossed his mind that maybe he wasn't strong enough after all to break this gate. As if Afer had read his thoughts, the big stallion neighed, and someone slipped up beside the Hunnuli.

"Try again," Helmar cried to the clansman.

He pulled in all the magic he dared use, formed it into an explosive spell, and released it from the palm of his hand. Before he could even draw breath, a second bolt followed his across the night-dark space and exploded just behind his on the portals of the gate. The wards vanished in a clap of thunder, and the wooden gate cracked to ruins.

The Clannad warriors charged forward, their swords raised, their voices lifted in battle cry. Behind the walls, Demira came to land on the stone pavings, and Rafnir, in all the confusion, sprang into the hall to look for the women.

Sayyed looked down at Helmar, too startled to think of anything to say.

She smiled at him. "If you had been full-blooded, you might have learned that 'clannad' is an ancient clan word for 'family.'"

"Your ancestors were clanspeople?" he asked, feeling rather dense.

"A long time ago."

"But you have no splinter."

"There are no more," Helmar replied with a shrug. She touched his right wrist where his splinter glowed beneath his sleeve and ran to join her warriors in the fighting at the gate.

The garrison, undermanned and ill-prepared for a battle with sorcerers and sword-wielding warriors who came out of nowhere, quickly surrendered. As Sayyed and Helmar ended the assault and rounded up prisoners, Rafnir ran out of the hall, looking thunderous. "They're gone!" he shouted furiously.

Sayyed turned on the commander of the fortress. "Where is Zukhara? Where are the women he had with him?"

The Turic drew himself up in pride for his master. "The Gryphon flies, and Lord Zukhara rides to claim his throne."

"He did what?" asked Helmar puzzled. Sayyed had not gone into detail about the current unrest in the Turic realm. He assumed the Clannad knew.

"Lord Zukhara left this morning with the sorceresses," the soldier explained as if to a simpleton. "Soon he will call his armies and march on Cangora."

12

"A day!" Rafnir cried, totally frustrated. "We keep missing them by a day!" He paced back and forth in the hall of the mountain fortress, slamming his hand on a shield every time he passed it. The shield was a large one, hung on the wall for decoration, and it made a satisfying crash every time he hit it. "Why can't we leave now?" the young man demanded. "The Hunnuli could catch up with their horses.

He got no immediate answer. His father, Helmar, Rapinor, Hydan, and several other warriors sat around a long table in front of a roaring fire. A map of the Turic realm, unearthed in a storage chest by the garrison commander, lay unrolled on the table amid a scattered collection of flagons, pitchers, and plates. The rest of the troop rested, tended their horses, or raided the castle storerooms for food and drink. The fortress garrison kicked its collective heels in the dungeons.

Midnight had passed hours ago, and dawn would soon lighten the road, but Sayyed made no effort to move from his chair. There were too many forces in motion now to leap precipitously into action. He wanted time to think. He had already explained in detail to Helmar and her men what had happened at Council Rock and later in the caravan. They had been unpleasantly surprised. Still, in spite of their concern, Sayyed fully expected the mysterious Helmar to take her riders and return home now that their duty was done.

He was, therefore, startled when she spoke into an interval between Rafnir's rhythmic banging. "If you plan to go after Zukhara, you will need help."

A ripple of surprise passed through her men. Rafnir halted in midpace.

Instead of looking pleased, Sayyed's brows lowered in suspicion. "Why? It will mean leaving the mountains, traveling in daylight. Why do you offer that now?"

Helmar slowly rose. Her helmet had been laid aside, and her hair blazed red-gold in the firelight. She swept her hand over the map, then looked at her warriors one by one. When she spoke, her words were only to them. "For generations we have lived in Sanctuary thinking the world had abandoned us.

Now the world has come pounding at our door, and we learn it has changed while we hid in our mountain fastness. Knowing what we know now, do we want to continue to hide and let the world go by without us? Or do we ride forth and embrace the possibilities of the future?"

Her question fell to every man, and there was silence while each one considered his answer.

Rapinor spoke first, the loyal, staunch warrior who would follow his chief to the grave. "I go with you."

"Have you considered the consequences, Lady Helmar?" asked another man.

"For the past three days, Dejion. I have also considered the consequences if we stay home and turn our backs. As Minora keeps telling me, we have grown stagnant. Our bloodlines are dying from lack of new stock. If we go back, we could lose everything our ancestors tried to save."

"Then I will ride with you, and the gorthlings take the hindmost," the warrior laughed.

"I still haven't seen this Lady Gabria," Hydan grumbled. "But you make a good argument."

The others, too, agreed to ride with the clansmen, and Helmar nodded her satisfaction. "Then go. Talk to the warriors. Tell them why and say any who wish to go home may do so."

The men bowed and left, leaving Helmar with only her two guards and the clansmen. She pulled in a deep breath and sat down so quickly her sword clattered on the chair. "Does that answer your question?" she said to Sayyed.

He leaned back in his chair, his legs stretched out in front of him. His arm hurt and his side throbbed abominably, but he wouldn't go to his pallet yet. This night was too full of revelations. "What made you decide this?" he asked.

"The mare." Helmar nodded toward the open doorway where the Hunnuli rested in the courtyard. "When I saw her in all her beautiful living flesh, I knew you had been telling me the truth—all of it. I realized then that our stone walls would no longer be enough. It is time the Clannad shows its true colors."

Sayyed offered her a slow, conciliatory smile. "Will dawn be a good time to start?"

At that Rafnir's hands went up in annoyance. "Why wait until then? They like to ride at night; let's go now!"

"You may leave any time," his father told him, "because I want you to go back to the Ramtharin."

A bright flush swept over Rafnir's face, and he turned on his heel and stamped to the table.

Seeing the look on his son's face, Sayyed held up his hand. "I need someone I can trust to find Athlone. He said send a message, remember? Well, I'm sending you and Tibor. Get him to come south with the werods to help the Shar-Ja."

The audacity of such a suggestion took Rafnir's breath away. "You want him to bring the clans over the Altai? But the Turic will think they're being invaded."

"That's why I want you to go. With you at Athlone's side, you can tell the Turics you have been summoned by the Shar-Ja in accordance with the peace treaty."

"A treaty that was never signed!"

"A mere formality. Make a likeness of the Shar-Ja's banner. Dress like a Turic noble. Make it look official."

"What if the Shar-Ja doesn't want any help?" Rafnir demanded.

Sayyed rubbed his temples and said grimly, "I don't think he is in any position to argue."

Helmar had been listening to the exchange, her face thoughtful. "Can't you take your flying horse? It would be faster, would it not?"

Rafnir picked up a full flagon and put it down again, still too agitated to stand still. "No. She can carry me short distances, but I am too heavy for her to carry such a long way. Besides"—he cracked a crooked grimace—"I doubt you could get her any farther away from Kelene than she already is."

Helmar nodded as if she had already anticipated that answer. "Well, your journey back will be dangerous if you go alone across the open country." She traced a line north along the foothills of the Absarotans. "One of my rangers could lead you on mountain trails all the way to the border."

"Lady, that is generous, but I don't think your horses could keep up with a Hunnuli," Rafnir replied distractedly.

The lady chieftain laughed softly as if at a private joke. "On the mountain slopes you have not been able to witness the full talents of our white horses, young Rafnir. Be assured, the whites will match your blacks."

Sayyed pursed his lips and looked thoughtful. "And I suppose your white horses are descended from clan stock, too."

She nodded, her eyes merry. "Of course."

When she didn't add more, Sayyed bent forward, cupped his hands over hers, and said earnestly, "One day will you trust me enough to tell me the full truth of your history?"

Helmar's eyes fell to their linked hands, and something flickered in the back of her heart, that same heart she thought she had hardened to the attentions of men. "One day," she said and pulled her hands free.

Rafnir went back to his pacing, but this time he did not slam the shield as he passed—a good sign, Sayyed thought. The older sorcerer continued with his plans, letting Rafnir stew over his duty. "There is another favor I must ask, Lady," he said, and hesitated before he went on. "It could be very dangerous, but it is important to me and maybe to the Turics as well."

"Ask."

"I need someone to get word to my brother, Hajira, in the Shar-Ja's caravan. He is the sole guardian of the Shar-Ja's only living son. That boy has to be protected at all costs."

Helmar steepled her fingers. "I know nothing of this boy or the Shar-ja beyond what you have told us, but even that little shines brighter than what I have heard of this Zukhara. I will find someone willing to go."

"My lady, with your permission," Hydan said, rising to his feet. "I will go. I speak a little Turic, and I owe Sayyed a favor for shooting his arm and making us late."

The clansman looked around, surprised. He had not expected help from that quarter. "Can you find your way?"

"Hydan is one of the few who leave the valley on occasion to visit nearby settlements. He is a good man," Helmar added. "His only faults are a temper he can't control yet and an overreaching desire to protect what he values."

The swordsman's face turned red, but he did not waver when she asked, "You understand what you might have to face?" He nodded. "Then go with my blessing and ride safely."

After that was settled, Sayyed, Rafnir, and Helmar bent over the map again to finalize their plans. Although Sayyed had made most of the decisions to that point, he was very interested to learn Helmar had a quick grasp of the worsening situation and a sharp mind for tactics. She was the one who suggested sending other rangers out to gather news and who pointed out a rough trail over the Khidar Pass that would take them directly to the Spice Road and cut off leagues of extra travel.

One point confused her though. "What will we do when we catch up with this Zukhara? What if he's already joined his army of fanatics?"

Sayyed could only shake his head. The same thought had occurred to him with no brilliant inspiration to light its way. "I won't know until we get there," he admitted. "So if you have any ideas . . ." He yawned, too tired to finish.

The fire had burned low by that time, and everything that could be planned had been discussed. Sayyed's swarthy face had washed to a grayish pallor, and he moved with uncomfortable stiffness when he stood. Helmar took one arm and Rafnir the other, and they led him firmly to a bed. He was asleep before they had pulled a blanket up over his chest.

* * *

The castle bailey was bustling with activity when Sayyed woke the next morning. After a quick wash and a quiet moment for his morning prayers, he strode out into the sunshine in time to say good-bye to Rafnir and his guide.

Rafnir had not verbally agreed to leave the search for Kelene and Gabria, but Sayyed knew his son well enough to hope he would accept the reasons for this request. He stood out of the way, his arms crossed, while Rafnir buckled one of the Clannad's saddle pads on Tibor instead of the heavy Turic saddle.

"I'm trusting you to find Kelene," Rafnir said, his voice sharper than he intended. He modified his tone a little and went on. "I never fully understood how you could grieve for Mother for so long, but when I think what it would be like to lose Kelene, I begin to see." He clasped his father's arm and sprang to Tibor's back. "I will bring the Clans!" he vowed. He was about to go when he turned and tossed out one more observation. "Father! I think Mother would approve of Helmar." He waved, and in a clatter of hoofbeats, the black stallion and the white cantered out of the fortress and on their way.

"What was that?" Helmar asked, coming to stand by the sorcerer.

A quirk of a smile passed Sayyed's lips. "He said good-bye." He wasn't sure why Rafnir would feel inclined to say what he had, and yet he thought his son was probably right. Tam would have liked Helmar. A gust of wind flounced by, snapping his cloak and sending dust swirling around the bailey in tiny whirlwinds. The sky was achingly blue and cloudless, but the air this high in the mountains was thin and still chilly in the mornings. Sayyed shivered as a finger of breeze brushed past his neck. "Tam," he whispered. Then he glanced over at a straight nose, a dusting of freckles, and a pair of green eyes set in a frame of red-gold lashes—so different from Tam's delicate oval beauty—and he was glad Helmar was there.

Hydan left next, with Sayyed's message wrapped around Hajira's gryphon knife and tucked carefully in his shirt. He had scrounged some Turic clothes, including a shortcoat emblazoned with Zukhara's red emblem, and had saddled his reluctant horse with Rafnir's Turic saddle. He looked passable enough, if rather uncomfortable in the saddle, and he saluted his chief and trotted out in Rafnir's wake.

A short while later, Helmar led her troop out the fortress gates. To her delight and secret relief, every warrior chose to go with her on her quest to help Sayyed rescue the sorceresses. They took with them all the supplies and equipment they could pack on the backs of the garrison horses. Sayyed waited with Afer until the riders were out of sight; then he hurried down a winding stairs to the dungeon level. The prisoners crowded around the doors as he unlocked them.

"You have to the count of one hundred before this place is destroyed," he said calmly.

The Turics took one look at his face and fled the castle as fast as they could run. The clansman leisurely rode out the gates, counting as he went until Afer reached the bottom of the ravine. He turned and studied the cliff wall.

". . . ninety-eight . . . ninety-nine . . . one hundred."

Sayyed raised his good arm, pointed to the cliff at the base of the castle wall, and sent a long, steady beam of power into the rock. There were no explosions this time, just a rumbling sound that began beneath the beam and radiated rapidly outward. Suddenly an enormous chunk of the rock face slipped loose. Cracks appeared in the fortress walls; then the ground fell from beneath the structure. The hall, most of the outbuildings, several towers, and half the walls slipped down, tumbling and crashing in a cloud of stone, dust, and debris to the ravine floor. The remains of the fortress lay shattered, and the entrance to the narrow spiral staircase leading down to an empty cavern vanished in a pile of rubble.

Sayyed found the sight of the gaping ruins small satisfaction for all the trouble Zukhara had caused. Afer snorted in agreement. Swiftly they set off and soon caught up with the Clannad.

Now that the troop agreed to risk daylight travel, they made excellent time. They rode south at a brisk pace back the way they had come, and in less than two days they reached the back entrance to Sanctuary. Taking with her most of the packhorses and three of her warriors, Helmar left the others to rest and refresh themselves in the tumbled glen.

Sayyed did not know what she said to her people in the valley, but she came back the next dawn with twenty-five more riders and a glowing expression on her face.

"Minora sends her blessings," was all she would say.

She led her warriors up the slope of a high hill and stopped to watch them pass by. Sayyed paused beside her. The world before them lay bleak and unpeopled, the mighty peaks turbaned in cloud, the slopes mottled with forests and bare outcroppings of stone. Beyond the wild lands to the east where the mountains gave way to the arid plains, the horizon was swathed in mist, as if already obscured in the smokes of war. Behind the troop lay the narrow path to Sanctuary and all that name implied. Sayyed, who had seen for himself the beauty and security of the valley, marveled at the courage it took to step out of the protective walls and ride into a dangerous, troubled world. Some of the men, he knew, had never set foot outside their valley.

Overhead, Demira neighed to the people below and wheeled over the slower moving column, keeping a sharp vigilance from the sky.

That day and the next the Clannad rode in deadly earnest, first to the east to the less rugged and more open foothills, then south toward the Turic capital of Cangora, located on the fringes of the great southern desert. They rode hard, and for all their settled ways, they and their white horses endured as well as any nomadic band.

Their guide was an older man, a short, powerful warrior with the lively, quick glance of a curious child. While most men of the Clannad did not usually leave Sanctuary, a few trained as scouts or rangers and learned the mountains and the trails from tradition handed down from other rangers and from years spent exploring the great peaks. This man knew the trail Helmar had found on the Turic map and led his people unerringly on the shortest and safest route possible.

They saw smoke the second afternoon, a dark column of fumes that rose above the plains and slowly spread across the southern skyline. Demira flew to investigate, and when she returned, her message was dark and grim.

I saw a caravan, a big one, scattered along the side of the road for nearly a league. There were wagons burning and dead men everywhere.

Sayyed felt a cold fear grip his belly. "Can you describe any part of it? Was the Shar-Ja's wagon there?"

I did not see that wagon, but I saw dead guardsmen with his colors, and I saw other wagons I recognized from Council Rock. Her tone faltered, and she dropped her long lashes. *Even the plague camp did not look or smell so awful.*

Sayyed and Helmar exchanged a long look, but neither could ask about Hydan or Hajira or Tassilio. Even if their bodies lay in the dust of the Spice Road, Demira could not have distinguished them from her place in the sky. They rode on toward the smoke and hoped that somehow the two men and the boy survived.

On the third evening, one of Helmar's scouts found them as they rested the horses along the bank of a scraggly, half-dead stream. The rider trotted his sweat-soaked horse directly to Helmar and nearly fell off as he tried to dismount.

"The clansman was right," the scout said wearily. He was so tired he could barely stand. "I went down to the settlement at Khazar and talked to some of the merchants and shepherds. The news is spreading like locusts. They say the Fel Azureth have risen. The Gryphon has declared himself the true ruler of the Turic and has called a holy war to purge the land of unbelievers. Half the men in the settlement are leaving to join him, the other half are talking about fighting him. They say the Gryphon is marching on Cangora and that his forces massacred the Shar-Ja's caravan."

"Is anyone attempting to organize the resistance against him?" asked Sayyed.

"Not that I know of. I heard many of the tribal leaders who accompanied the Shar-Ja were killed in the massacre, along with most of the royal guards. The tribes are in confusion. The Shar-Ja's soldiers are leaderless, and no one knows what befell the Shar-Ja."

Sayyed leaned back against Afer's strong side. "By the Living God, this gets worse."

"Aye, it does," responded the exhausted scout. "They say the zealot's army meets no resistance because he carries the Lightning of the North."

"What is that?"

"I have never heard of such a thing. But I also heard a gryphon flies in the vanguard with a black-haired woman on its back. A woman reputed to be a sorceress."

Sayyed's eyes widened. "A gryphon? Do you mean a real one?" He whistled. "And Kelene on its back? No wonder the people won't fight him." His voice broke off, then went on. "Did you hear any news of the boy, Tassilio?"

The scout shook his head. "All I heard was that the caravan was on the road when fighting broke out in the ranks of the tribal levies, and before anyone knew what was happening, the entire caravan was under attack. They never had a chance."

"Do you think Hydan had time to reach them?" Sayyed asked Helmar.

She knew who he meant, but she had no reassurance for him. "I don't know."

His hand fell to the hilt of his sword; his sharp gaze turned far away. "Are you sure you still want to go? This has become far more than a rescue of two women from an unknown assailant."

"We have gone too far to turn back now. I will ride with you, Sorcerer." She lifted her hand, and he clasped it with his own, making a joined fist to seal their vow.

"Besides," she added with a grin, "in the words of Hydan, 'I still haven't seen this Lady Gabria.' "

* * *

Kelene gripped the gryphon's sides with her knees and dug her fingers into the feathery-fur down to touch the creature's warm skin. After a lot of practice, she had learned that the best way to communicate with the creature was through the same sort of mental link she could establish with the Hunnuli. It was difficult and tiring, but the gryphon was much more likely to obey that than a mouthful of nonsense words shouted in her ear. *Down, young one. It is getting too dark to fly.*

A growl issued from the gryphon's throat, but she finally obeyed and began to spiral slowly to earth.

Kelene sighed. Riding a gryphon was exciting, because unlike Demira, the animal had been flying since birth. Exquisitely graceful, as skilled as any bird, she read the nuances of the forever changing currents and flew as if her body were a part of the wind. But she was also willful, resentful, and still very wild under the weak link of obedience Kelene had established. Unlike Demira, who adored her rider, Kelene knew the gryphon only tolerated her and waited for the day she would be set free. The sorceress understood how she felt and tried to be as kind as possible, but that did not make riding the gryphon over these long, hot days any easier.

Kelene would have given almost anything to fly the gryphon away—almost anything but Gabria's and Nara's lives. The gryphon, too, would have to pay a price too high, for Zukhara had fashioned a collar spelled to release a killing bolt if she flew beyond two leagues of his position. Kelene did not know how the collar worked, but she was not going to find out by testing it. There had to be some other way she could take her mother, Nara, and the gryphon and escape from Zukhara. She just had to be patient and keep looking.

Kelene glanced down toward the ground. Already Zukhara's army had stopped and made camp along the Spice Road. She sighed again and fought down the despair that seemed to hover over her with increasing potency.

When she first heard Zukhara's plans, a part of her mind had dismissed them as the ravings of a deluded man, but in the past four days, everything had happened as he had said it would. The moment he stood before his followers at Impala Springs and proclaimed himself the new, true leader of the Turic tribes, men had flocked to his call. Kelene had no notion how he spread the word so fast—unless he had preplanned it—but true to his word, on the tenth day after he threatened Kelene, he called his holy war, and men from all over the realm arrived to answer his summons.

Thank the gods, Kelene thought, he had not fulfilled his threat to remove her arm for the diamond splinter. After Gabria had explained that there were no more splinters, and he had satisfied himself that the women's could not be surgically removed, he dropped the issue for the time being and contented himself by awing his followers with demonstrations of his power, until everyone knew Zukhara did indeed carry the Lightning of the North in his hands.

In the meanwhile, Zukhara commanded Kelene to fly the gryphon at the head of his ever-growing army as it marched south toward Cangora. Even from the air the sorceress had seen the awe and the fear the gryphon's presence wrought. Some people bowed low to the golden creature, others stared in stunned surprise, and still others fled at her approach. No one tried to withstand Zukhara's army. The force of fanatics, rebels, and supporters marched unopposed along the caravan road. There seemed to be no one willing to make a stand for the Shar-ja. Would it be the same in his own city?

The gryphon swept low over the parched grass. She was stiff and unwilling to land yet, so Kelene let her fly a few more minutes along the road. They had flown south only a short distance from the army when the gryphon's ears perked forward and her nostrils twitched at the warm breeze.

Suddenly a light gust swept by, and Kelene smelled it too, the heavy stench of rotting bodies. She almost reeled in her place. A sharp, piercing picture burst from her memory, an image of her return to the clan gathering during the worst of the plague. Her stomach lurched, and Kelene forced her memories back before they overwhelmed her self-control.

Ahead through the twilight, she saw several shadowy things on the verge of the road. She peered harder, and as the gryphon flew closer, the entire disaster became clear. Burned and broken wagons, vans, and chariots lay on both sides of the path for as far as Kelene could see in the dimming light. Their contents were scattered everywhere, already picked over by looters. Dead horses bloated among the wreckage, and wherever Kelene looked, in the trampled grass, by the wagons, in small or large heaps, lay the bodies of dead men.

Kelene quickly turned the gryphon away and, ignoring her annoyed hiss, told her to return to the camp. They came to land in a clear space near Zukhara's tent. Her hands shaking, Kelene fastened the gryphon's chains as Zukhara had instructed, gave her a heaping meal of goat meat, and strode into Zukhara's tent. Whatever she had intended to say was immediately squelched by Zukhara's sharp gesture.

"Sit!" he ordered and pointed to a smaller chair near his. The man was seated in a large, ornate, high-backed chair near the center of his spacious tent. Bright lamps lit the interior, and beautiful woven rugs covered the floor. Zukhara had dressed in black pants and a black robe embroidered with a golden gryphon standing rampant. The clothes were simple yet rich and on his tall, limber frame, very elegant. He sat composed, waiting expectantly with his officers on either side.

Kelene reluctantly perched on the chair he indicated. By Amara, if she had to swallow any more resentment, Kelene swore she would burst. She hated being put on display like this! Being the Gryphon's "Chosen" had a few privileges, but they were all heavily outweighed by the disadvantages. She could only be thankful that he had been too busy to force his attentions on her again.

She heard the tread of boots outside, and eight men crowded into the tent. All but one saluted and bowed low before Zukhara. Kelene gasped. The one man who did not, or could not, bow was the Shar-Ja. If he had looked old and sick at Council Rock, he looked near death now. His once strong face sagged with loose folds of grayish skin. His red-rimmed eyes were nearly lost in the sunken shadows of his haggard face. He barely had the strength to stay upright, yet he fought off any hand that touched him and through some force of supreme will managed to stand unaided before Zukhara.

"Good," the Gryphon said, a short, sharp bark of approval. "You caught him alive. And the boy?"

One officer stepped forward. "Your Highness, we have not yet found his body, nor the guard who was with him."

A flicker of anger passed over Zukhara's features, but he merely commanded, "Keep looking. I want no loose ends."

"And what of me?" the Shar-Ja said scornfully. His voice had a surprising timbre to it that demanded Zukhara's attention. "Am I a loose end, too?"

The lamplight fell in the Gryphon's eyes and turned to black fire in a face as still and cold as ice. "No, Shar-Ja Rassidar. You are a very important part of my plans. Do you know the Ritual of Ascension?"

The old man gave a fierce bark of laughter and somehow stood straighter until he towered over the men around him. Kelene had not realized until then just how tall he really was, or how proud. "I am aware of the ritual. It was abolished several centuries ago."

Zukhara's smile came, quick and feral. "Yes, and in the name of Twice Blessed Sargun and to the glory of the Living God, I intend to resurrect the old ways, beginning with the Ritual." He gestured to his men. "Take him to his wagon and keep him there. No one is to see him or go near him." The men swiftly obeyed.

When they were gone, Zukhara turned his burning glance to Kelene. "You have done well, my lady. You and the gryphon have flown as successfully as I had hoped. I have a gift for you."

Kelene flung herself to her feet. "Mother has but one day left! The only gift I need is her antidote."

He stood and walked to his table where a small tray of multicolored glass bottles stood shining in the light. He picked up a small vial sealed with wax. "As you have undoubtedly noticed," he said, coming close to her, "I am very knowledgeable in the arts of medicines and poisons." He pulled the sorceress close and pressed her against his chest with one arm. With the other he held the vial up to a lamp. "Not only can I design a poison to suit my purposes, I also create antidotes and partial antidotes that delay the effects of the poison."

Kelene's jaw tightened. "Do you fulfill your promises?" she said between gritted teeth.

"Partially, my lady." He chuckled and kissed her fully on the lips before he handed her the vial. "This will keep the poison in check for another ten days or so. Continue your exemplary behavior, and I will give her more."

"What about the antidote?" Kelene exploded. Would he keep this game going indefinitely?

"I hold it close," he replied, and he pulled out the chain that held his ivory ward. There, hanging beside the ball, was a small, thin silver tube. "When I feel you have earned it, the reward shall be yours."

Kelene clamped her mouth closed and averted her face. At least, she thought, he had not noticed the crack in the ivory ward.

He kissed her again, long and languorously deep, until Kelene thought she would gag; then with a sneer he pushed her toward the entrance. "Not tonight, my lady. Though the thought is sweet. I have too many things to attend to. Sleep well."

Kelene did not bother to answer. She gripped the precious vial, whirled, and fled.

13

The Gryphon's army rose at dawn to another clear sky and hot sun. They knelt in the dust for their morning worship and bowed low to Zukhara, the figurehead of their reverent zeal. Their fervor ran high that morning as they broke camp and prepared to march, for by evening they would reach the outskirts of Cangora and perhaps meet their first resistance from forces still loyal to the Shar-Ja. At least they hoped so. Their blood burned for battle and the opportunity to give their lives in service to the Living God and his servant, Zukhara. After all, Zukhara, the Mouth of Shahr, had told them all that such a death guaranteed their entrance to paradise.

At the sound of the horns, the men took their positions. The Fel Azureth, the fist of Zukhara, took the honored place in the vanguard, their highly trained units riding like members of the Shar-Ja's own cavalry on fleet horses. Behind them rolled the Shar-Ja's wagon with its prisoner under tight guard. Then came the other combatants, some in orderly ranks on foot, some in mounted troops, still others—mostly rabble and hangers-on who had come for the loot, the thrill, or motives of their own—marched in crowds at the rear. Behind them were the supply wagons, camp followers, and a unit of the Fel Azureth who kept a vicious order on the trailing mobs.

The army set out under Zukhara's watchful scrutiny and soon reached the wreck of the Shar-Ja's grand caravan. Several days in the late spring sun had wrought havoc on bodies already torn by weapons and the teeth of scavengers. The stench along that stretch of road was thick and cloying and as heavy as the clouds of flies that swarmed through the ruins. The men wrapped the ends of their burnooses over their mouths and noses and pushed on, paying little heed to the dead.

Overhead, on the wings of the gryphon, Kelene tried not to look at the carnage below. She felt bad enough having to forward Zukhara's cause with her presence, without witnessing the bloody results of his ambition. She prayed fervently he would not order her to use her magic against the Turics. So far, his own power had been enough to awe and terrify his people, and she hoped that his pride would prevent him from seeking overt aid from a woman. But who was to say? If the city of Cangora bolted its gates against him and his army had to lay siege to it, he might be angry enough to force her hand. His arcane prowess was growing by the day, but the power of a fully trained sorceress could open an unwarded city in short order.

Kelene patted the gryphon's neck. Rafnir, she silently cried, I need you. Where are you?

She had no way of knowing that on that day Rafnir was far to the north, across the Altai with her father and the clan chiefs, preparing the werods for war.

* * *

That same morning, leagues behind Zukhara's army, the riders of the Clannad crested a high ridge and looked down on the dusty, beaten path of the Spice Road on the flatlands below.

"This is as far as I can lead you, Lady," the guide said gruffly. "I have never traveled beyond these hills."

Helmar studied the road from one horizon to the other, as far as she could see. At that moment it was empty. "You have done well, thank you. The trail is clear now for all to see."

Rapinor looked skeptical. "You want us to go down there?" All the warriors stared at the open road as if it were a poisonous snake.

"Too long a solitude makes a heart of fear," Helmar responded, and she urged her mare into a trot down the hillside. The warriors did not hesitate further but followed after her straight, unyielding back.

They have been biding for so long, it has become habit, Afer commented.

"And how do you know that?" Sayyed inquired, still watching Helmar ride down the slope.

Helmar told me. I like her. Most of the Clannad are magic-wielders, you know. But she became chief because she proved herself to be the most talented.

"No," Sayyed said, almost to himself. "I didn't know. And did she also tell you how they came to be hidden away in the Turic mountains?"

Not yet, the stallion nickered. *But I could make a few guesses.*

"So could I," Sayyed replied thoughtfully. "So could I." He folded his golden cloak into a tight roll, tied it behind his saddle, and wrapped his burnoose around his head. If need be, he could pretend to be a Turic escorting new troops to Zukhara's war. He didn't know what they would find on the road ahead, and he did not want to give Zukhara any warning that more sorcerers were coming after him.

He glanced critically at Demira shifting impatiently by his side, and he realized there was no possibility of disguising her long wings. There was only one thing he could think of that might explain her presence.

A halter! she neighed. *That is humiliating!*

No more than this saddle! If I can wear tack, so can you. For Kelene! Afer told her severely.

So they left the mountains, a Turic on a big black horse, leading a winged Hunnuli mare. If anyone asked, Sayyed would tell them he had captured the mare and was taking her to the Gryphon.

Strangely enough, no one did ask that day, for though the road soon became busy, no one dared stop the strange troop of hard-eyed warriors jogging purposefully along the side of the road. Other groups of mounted or marching men traveled south toward Cangora, and a few refugees fled north. But not one person tried to join the troop or talk to any of its riders. They only stared as the white horses trotted by.

The sun was nearing its zenith when Afer, Demira, and the white horses flared their nostrils and began to toss their heads. An erratic breeze blew hot and dry from the desert, and on its skirts came the unmistakable smell of unburied dead.

In the open, nearly treeless land the riders saw the scavenger birds and the remains of the massacred caravan for a long way before they reached the first burned wagon and decaying bodies. A few birds squawked at the intruders and flew farther down the road to settle on another spot. Some of the dead had already been claimed and taken away for burial, but many more still waited on the sandy ground among the dead horses and scattered debris.

Helmar brought her troop to a stop. "We may not ever know if we do not look," she said to Sayyed, who was grateful for her concern.

They spread out in pairs along the long strip of road and carefully searched each wagon, body, and heap that belonged to the Shar-Ja's caravan. No one had a real hope that they would find Hydan, Hajira, or Tassilio among the wreckage, but if they found the bodies, at least they would know. Sayyed worked tirelessly in the search, since he and Afer were the only ones who could recognize Hajira and Tassilio, and while he saw a few faces he vaguely recognized, he found no one to match the description of the boy and his black-clad guard.

He reached the last cluster of wagons near what had been the front of the caravan and walked slowly among the ruined vehicles. Several of them had been stripped of anything usable by looters, but there was one on its side some distance from the others that looked familiar and still intact. He strode toward it, and suddenly two things happened at once. A horse neighed somewhere behind it, and a large dog leaped out of the interior and charged toward Sayyed. Its wild barking filled the quiet and drew everyone's attention. A warrior nearby drew his bow, but Sayyed yelled at him to put it away, and he held out his hands to welcome the dog. The big animal, whining and barking in delight, planted his paws on the man's chest and licked his face clean.

"Sayyed!" cried a familiar voice. A lean young figure burst out of the wagon's door and joyously flung himself in the embrace of the sorcerer. Between laughter and tears, Sayyed calmed down boy and dog enough to get a good look at them. They were both stretched tight with hunger and the shadows of fear, and Tassilio's face had lost what was left of its boyish innocence. But, the god of all be praised, he was unharmed.

He gazed up at the clansman with huge eyes, and every pent-up word came tumbling out. "Sayyed, you're here! I prayed you would come. And look at the horse with wings! Is that Demira? Did you find Kelene and Gabria? Who are these people? Where is—"

Sayyed raised a hand to stem his rush of wild words. "Tassilio, where is Hajira?"

The boy led him to the wagon, talking rapidly as he went. "Hajira knew it would happen, you know. A strange man told him just before it started. Hajira stayed close to the Shar-Yon's wagon, and the minute he realized we were under attack, he threw the driver off and drove as far as he could before we were hemmed in by the fighting; then he loosed the horses, tipped the wagon over, and forced me inside. He thought no one would bother the funeral wagon."

He scrambled inside. Sayyed stooped to look in the covered vehicle. The Shar-Yon's sealed casket had been respectfully covered with the royal blue hangings and pushed to the side that had once been the roof, forming a narrow space between the wagon floor and coffin. There on a makeshift bed lay his brother, a crude bandage on his shoulder, another tied to his thigh.

"He was awake a while ago," Tassilio said, his voice quivering. "But now he won't wake up." Despite his strength and growing maturity, tears filled his eyes, tears brought on by exhaustion, grief, and overwhelming relief. He swiped them away with a dirty sleeve.

A grimace on his face, Sayyed stood to call Helmar and her healer. She was already there behind the wagon, standing with a crowd of her riders by a lone white horse and looking stricken. Something long and very still, wrapped in a shroud of royal blue, lay on the ground at the horse's feet. Sayyed felt a hand on his arm, and he looked down at Tassilio's unhappy face gazing at the mound.

The boy cleared his throat and said, "I don't know who he was. He came that morning, looking for Hajira. They were talking when the fighting started. He stayed with us and defended the wagon when some of the Fel Azureth came after us." Tassilio paused to wipe his eyes again. Helmar and her warriors had turned to listen to him, and he met the chief's regard directly as if he spoke only to her. "He was very brave. He fought beside Hajira, and he saved my life, you know. He took a sword thrust that was meant for me. When the attackers went away, they thought everyone was dead. I helped Hajira into the wagon, but I couldn't help the stranger. I could only cover him and keep the vultures away. I don't even know his name." The tears suddenly came in earnest and slid unchecked down his cheeks.

The lady chieftain knelt on one knee in front of Tassilio and offered a cloth for his face. "His name was Hydan," she said softly. "He was my swordsman, and yes, he was very brave. Like you. I am glad to know he died well, and I thank you for taking care of him."

Her simple, direct words were what Tassilio needed to hear. He took the proffered cloth, giving her a tremulous smile in exchange, and vigorously scrubbed his face. When he emerged from behind the cloth, his tears were gone, and he looked closer to his normal self.

Sadly the Clannad riders tied Hydan's wrapped body onto the back of his horse. Helmar took the horse's muzzle in her hands and leaned her forehead against his to say good-bye. "Take him home," she murmured. The horse neighed once, a grief-filled, lonely call; then he trotted away with his heavy burden.

"Where is he going?" exclaimed Tassilio, astonished.

"He will take his rider home to be buried with honor," the chief answered, distracted by her own thoughts.

"How does he know where to go? Do you live close by? Who are you, any-way?" Tassilio was definitely returning to normal. He didn't even wait for an answer but grabbed Helmar's arm and pulled her to the wagon where Sayyed had returned to tend Hajira.

The Clannad healer quickly answered Helmar's summons, and willing hands moved Hajira out to a shelter rigged by the wagon box that gave the healer more room to tend the injured man.

After a thorough examination, the healer told Sayyed and Tassilio the good news. "His wounds are not dangerous. The worst of his malady is dehydration. He needs liquids and plenty of them. If he can get through the next few hours and stave off infection, he should be fine."

Tassilio whooped and danced around the tent with his dog.

True to the healer's word, Hajira revived under a steady treatment of water, honeyed tea, and finally broth. In the late afternoon, he surprised everyone by sitting up and insisting rather forcefully that Sayyed take him and the boy out of this stinking, fly-infested, pestilential wreck. The healer agreed, and the rid-ers very thankfully obliged. They built a makeshift cart for the guardsman out of several broken wagons, hitched it to a horse, and left the massacred caravan behind.

Sayyed rode beside Hajira part of the way and told him what had been hap-pening. The wounded man listened, his eyes half-closed, and when Sayyed completed the tale, his haggard face lit with amusement. "Only you, my brother, could go into those mountains to find two magic-wielders and come out with over seventy."

"Just not the right ones."

Hajira's mirth fled. "No. Not yet. This is worse than we feared." Ignoring the pain in his shoulder and leg, he pushed himself up against the back of the cart until he was propped upright. "Zukhara is using your women to help him fulfill an ancient prophecy from *The Truth of Nine* that he thinks applies to him."

"And you do not believe it?" Helmar asked.

Hajira snorted. He knew enough Clannish to understand her. "Prophecies are not exact. They can be bent to fit any number of events."

"What then is the Lightning of the North?" asked Sayyed.

"Where did you hear that?"

"From what little bit of news we have been able to gather. It is rumored Zukhara carries the Lightning of North in his hand."

Hajira shrugged that away with one good shoulder. "It must be Kelene and Gabria's sorcery."

Sayyed scratched his chin. That made sense, so he mentioned something else that had bothered him. "Did the Fel Azureth kill the Shar-Ja?"

"I doubt it. I saw them capture his wagon just before we bolted for the funeral van." He bowed his head to Helmar, who rode on his other side, Tassilio perched happily behind her. "Thank you for sending your man, Lady. He told me he had ridden day and night to reach us. I am sorry it was his doom to come at such an ill-timed moment."

She acknowledged his thanks and said, "There is one thing I would know. How have you two survived for two days?"

The Turic pointed a finger at the boy. "He is a most ingenious scrounger."

Tassilio blushed beneath his dark tan and blurted, "You would have done the same for me."

"True." Hajira's eyes crinkled with a smile then slid closed, and the man drifted to sleep.

Tassilio solemnly regarded his friend with something akin to adoration. "He wanted me to run away and leave him, but I couldn't do that! And he was right, too. No one came near the Shar-Yon's wagon after the battle. Many people came to loot or look for wounded or for the dead, but no one dared approach a royal coffin defended by a large dog and a horse as white as a ghost." The boy grinned at the memory and almost as quickly his smile slipped away. He sniffled, thankful that the worst part of his ordeal was over, and surreptitiously swiped a sleeve over his eyes.

Then his quick mind found another thought, and he reached back and patted the mare's white rump. "Hydan's horse was something special, wasn't he? He seemed so horribly sad at the death of his master, I could hardly bear it. I told him I was sorry and I thanked him, and you know the odd part, I think he understood."

"Most horses understand a kind heart," Helmar replied.

"Don't try to get direct information from her, boy," Sayyed warned him dryly. "She is as secretive as a clam."

"All secrets are revealed in good time," Helmar retorted. "And the reasons for them."

Weary and safe for the first time in a long while, Tassilio leaned against Helmar's strong back. "At least we'll be in Cangora soon. I hope my father is there."

The adults made no answer. No one knew what they would find in Cangora, and no one wanted to hazard a guess.

The Clannad rode for the rest of the daylight hours, following the beaten trail of Zukhara's army. Although they saw other Turics along the way, most of the people looked too suspicious or frightened to offer any further news of the Gryphon. The riders came to the last oasis on the Spice Road near sunset, hoping to find the army camped there, but the oasis was empty, and the tiny settlement close by was deserted. The reason for that dangled in the few tall trees around the four walls. Ten men of various ages, their hands bound and their robes stripped away, had been hung not more than hours before. An edict nailed to a tree forbade any man from removing the bodies until they rotted off their nooses.

"So the Gryphon deals with those who do not accept his will," Hajira said in a voice heavy with scorn and disgust. "The families who lived at this oasis were Kirmaz tribe. Their leader did not travel with the Shar-Ja's caravan. He is a stubborn man with a fierce sense of tradition who did not get along well with Zukhara. Once he knows about this"—Hajira jerked a hand at the hanging men—"he will be hard to hold back. The guard's words dropped off, and his face grew very thoughtful. "Cut them down," he said abruptly.

The lady chief started at his sharp voice. "What? Why? Would it not be better to let the families deal with the bodies? Do we risk the time?"

"It is probably already too late to catch the Gryphon before he reaches Cangora," Hajira replied, intent on his own thoughts. His piercing eyes swept the nearby foothills. The wells and springs of the Spice Road oases bubbled up from an intricate series of underground rivers and streams that flowed from the secret heart of the Absarotan Mountains. They were the lifeblood of the western half of the Turic realm and were granted for safekeeping—and often as favors—into the hands of the different western tribes. Even in times of drought, the oases usually had water. This particular set of wells was doubly important for its proximity to Cangora and its location along a prime road that led into high pastures in the mountains. It had been zealously tended by the Kirmaz tribe for several generations.

Hajira was familiar with their leader and knew his reputation as a firebrand. If he could get the man's attention, it could be worth the time spent. "The survivors are probably up there now watching us from that cover," he told Helmar. "They don't know who we are yet, but if we treat their dead with respect and leave a message for the Kirmaz-Ja, we just might earn a new ally."

Following Hajira's advice, the riders cut down the ten men, laid them carefully in a row in the shadow of a mud-brick building, closed their bulging eyes, and covered their bodies with blankets and then stones to discourage scavengers.

When the job was complete, Hajira hobbled to the mounds with Sayyed. "The families will return soon and can bury these men as they see fit, and they will know the Raid are not afraid of the Gryphon." The two men draped Sayyed's coat over the first mound where anyone coming to investigate would see the Raid emblem and understand.

After watering the horses, the Clannad continued their journey. They were not far from Cangora, and they wished to push on after Zukhara, in the hope that his army would camp before the gates and they would be able to find the women before the Gryphon entered the city. It all depended on whether or not Cangora would defend itself.

Yet the closer they drew to the capital, the more evidence they found of the Gryphon's brutal advance. An increasing number of small villages and farms were located along the road, and many had been raided to feed the voracious army. More bodies hung from trees or lay hacked in front of their abandoned houses. One building, a storehouse from the looks of its burned remains, had been blasted to splinters by what they all recognized was magic.

"Would Kelene do that?" Hajira asked, nonplussed by the amount of damage.

"If Zukhara held a knife to her mother's throat, she might," Sayyed said heavily.

"That is something I have wondered since you told me this tale," Helmar said. "Why don't Kelene and Gabria use their sorcery to escape? They've been held for days now, and we know they're alive."

"Zukhara has poisoned Gabria, but beyond that I do not know, and I have been thinking about it from the night we realized they were gone."

She is afraid of him, Demira sent. *I know that from her touch, but I do not know why. He kept me asleep for so long and then, when I woke, she made me escape.*

Sayyed shook his head. "So what hold does he have over her? Kelene has the courage of a lioness and the stubbornness of a badger. I hope she is just biding her time."

"And what will you do if Zukhara forces her to fight us?" asked Helmar in her quiet, husky voice.

"We will leave that to our gods," he replied, so softly she could barely hear him.

The road wound on along the treeless, rolling hem of the foothills. To the west the sun had dropped behind the massive ramparts of the Absarotan peaks. To the east a purplish haze settled peacefully over the flat, arid lands bordering the Kumkara Desert. Ahead of the troop where the road rolled south over a long, easy hill, the riders spotted the first gray clouds of smoke climbing on the still evening air. Soon they noticed a murmur as deep and threatening as thunder rumbling in the far distance.

The riders glanced uneasily at one another. Hajira sat up in his cart and strained to see ahead. The road was deserted now; the countryside was empty of life. A tension hovered in the air as palpable as the sounds that grew louder and more distinctive the closer the troop drew to the top of the hill. By now they could distinguish the din of thousands of voices raised in anger, the clash of weapons, and several large explosions.

The troop hurried forward to the top of the slope and there halted to stare down at the scene below. Cangora, the ancient capital of the Turic rulers, sat in a great bay in the sheltering arms of the mountains. Roughly equal in size to old Moy Tura, it climbed in gentle levels and terraces up the natural slope of the valley to a massive hump of rock that towered over the city and prevented attack from the rear. Cangora was also fortified with thick stone walls and high, domed towers that provided a solid line of defense across the bay. Its only large entrance was a massive gateway hung with the huge copper doors that gave the city its Turic name, "Copper Gate." After the vanished holy city of Sargun Shahr, it was the most important site in the Turic realm, a center of trade, religion, and art. Cangora had never been taken in battle.

The Gryphon's army had drawn up before the great city in shouting, seething ranks. They had no siege engines and not enough men to assault such a large fortification, but even from their position on the distant hill, the Clannad could see Zukhara's army would need nothing more than the one person who stood before the massive gates to open its way into the heart of the city. A distinctive blaze of fiery blue light seared from the person's hand toward the top of one of the towers. The dome exploded in a deadly blast of stone, melting lead, and burning timbers. Three other towers had already been destroyed.

"Is that Kelene?" asked Helmar in surprise and consternation.

Hajira leaned forward over the driver's shoulder, staring at the figure so far below. "No, by the Living God's hand," he answered. "That is Zukhara!"

A horrified hush fell over the watching warriors. The answers to so many questions fell into place.

"The Lightning of the North," snarled Sayyed. "It's not Kelene's sorcery, it's his!"

In spite of the darkness the watchers on the hill could see frantic activity on the walls. Weapons blinked in the torchlight, and people struggled to put out the fires before they grew out of control.

Just then a large, dark shape winged slowly over the city. Torchlight and the light from several fires by the front gate glowed on the golden wings of a living gryphon. On its back sat the figure of a woman, her dark hair unbound, her body unmoving.

Demira suddenly neighed in anger and would have sprung into the air if Sayyed had not seen the tension in her muscles and anticipated her intention. "No!" he bellowed and gave her halter such a tug, it yanked her off balance and into Afer's side. "No! Do not even think it. Not yet. Wait and see. We cannot rescue her in front of an entire army."

The mare neighed a strident peal of frustration. *Let me get her. I can outfly that thing!*

The black stallion snorted fiercely in reply. *No, you cannot. That is a creature born to the air. And if you will not think of yourself, think of Gabria and Nara!*

Demira pawed the ground. Her coat broke out in damp patches of sweat, and her tail swished a furious dance, but she accepted their logic and angrily clamped her wings to her sides—for now.

Another sound drew their attention back to the besieged city. The braying voice of a single horn echoed across the distance. The attackers fell quiet. The man in front of the gates blared out a thundering message. The troop could not hear his words, but they heard his exalting tone and knew what he demanded.

Nothing happened for a long while. The gryphon continued to cruise over the city; the army shuffled impatiently like a hunting dog waiting for the kill. Smoke swirled from the tops of the shattered towers.

At last another horn sounded, this time from the battlements of the city's wall, and the huge gates swung slowly open to allow a small contingent of men to exit the city. From their robes and the flat gold chains glinting on their chests, Hajira identified them as members of the Shar-Ja's council. They bowed low to Zukhara.

"That's it then," he growled. "If those men are negotiating, the city will surrender. I had hoped the governor would put up a fight, but they have probably killed him."

The words had no sooner left his mouth than the envoy turned to point to something, and two more men dragged a body out of the gateway and dumped it at Zukhara's feet.

A roar of triumph swelled from the ranks of the Gryphon's fanatics. They lifted their weapons high and crashed their shields together, making a cacophony of noise that filled the valley from end to end and shook the foundations of the city. The great gates opened wide. The Gryphon and the Fel Azureth entered Cangora in triumph.

14

A pall of mist shrouded Gabria's dreams. Dense and heavy, virtually impenetrable, it hung across her subconscious, obscuring the visions that formed in her mind. She struggled to get through the fog to a place where the air was clear and the light was as bright as the midday sun over the Ramtharin Plains, but there seemed to be no end to the clinging, gloomy mist. No beginning. No end. No life. Just dismal obscurity.

Then she heard a sound familiar to all clanspeople: the distant drumming of hoofbeats. A jolt of fear went through her. It had been twenty-seven years since the massacre of her clan and the inception of the vision of her twin's murder. She had suffered the same dream or variations of it several times since then, and it never ceased to cause her grief and pain. It always began in fog and always included the sound of hoofbeats. She half turned, expecting to hear her brother's voice, and found she was alone in the mist. No one spoke; no other sounds intruded into her dream. There was only the single beat of one approaching horse.

Gabria looked in the direction of the sound and saw a rider on a ghostly white horse materialize out of the mist. A Harbinger, her mind said. The immortal messenger sent from the god of the dead to collect her soul. Zukhara's poison had worked at last.

But her heart said no. Her heart still beat in her chest, faster now with growing excitement, and her thoughts, too, leaped at the vision coming toward her. Harbingers were male, as far as anyone knew, but the rider on this glorious white horse was a woman, and a magnificent woman at that, dressed for battle and bearing a sword. A helm hid her face, and the style of her clothing was unfamiliar, but behind her back, rippling like a chieftain's banner, flowed a cloak as red as Corin blood. The woman lifted her sword in salute . . . and vanished.

Gabria stirred restlessly on the bed. "They're coming," she whispered.

Ever alert even in sleep, Kelene roused and moved close to check her mother. "Who is?" she asked, but Gabria sighed and slipped back into deeper sleep.

The light from a candle by the bed flickered over Gabria's face and highlighted the sharp angles of her features with a yellow outline. Kelene bit her lip worriedly. Normally slender, Gabria had lost so much weight she looked gaunt. The poison in her system made her nauseated, and it had been all Kelene could do to persuade her to take liquids so she did not become too weak and dehydrated. Her long, pale hair, usually shining and meticulously brushed, lay in a limp and bedraggled braid. Her skin had taken on a grayish pallor, and her strength had ebbed, so she tired very easily. In fact, she showed so many of the same symptoms Kelene had noticed in the Shar-Ja, Kelene seriously suspected Zukhara had poisoned him as well.

Wide awake now, Kelene slid off the bed and walked across the room to a window seat set in a deep embrasure. She didn't like sleeping on that high bed anyway; it was too far from the ground. A warm pallet on the floor made more sense and was certainly easier on the back than those overstuffed feather mattresses the Turics saw fit to put on their beds. Of course, this room was meant as a guest room for visiting nobility, not clanswomen accustomed to tents and stone ruins.

Kelene cast a censorious glance around the darkened room and curled her lip. The whole thing was too big, too elegant, too overdone. Large pieces of ornately carved furniture, murals, thick rugs, and pieces of decorative art had been arranged in the room by someone, Kelene was sure, with a very tense and cluttered mind. The effort had been made to impress, not to make comfortable, and she found the whole effect annoying.

Suppressing a sign, she drew back the drapes and unlatched the glass-paned window. Glass was a rarity among people who spent most of their lives moving tents around, but Kelene liked the feel of the smooth, cool surface and the way light could pass through. If she ever returned to Moy Tura, Kelene decided to find a glassmaker who could teach her how to create the panes and the beautiful colored glass bottles, vials, and jars she had seen the Turics use.

She leaned out over the sill and drew a deep breath of the night air. Far below her the city of Cangora dropped gradually down street after street to the great copper gates that now stood closed for the night. The city was dark, brooding in silence after its easy defeat by the Gryphon the night before.

After the surrender of the city, Zukhara had taken up residence in the Shar-Ja's palace at the foot of the magnificent buttress of stone that thrust out from the foot of the mountain and formed the foundation of Cangora's defenses. Kelene could not see the rock formation from her window, but she had noticed it from the gryphon's back and recognized its unopposable might. The Turics had recognized that strength long ago and built a large temple on the top of the lofty stone. That temple, Zukhara had told her, was the main reason he had come to Cangora. Unfortunately, he had not yet told her why.

Thankfully she had seen him only once since he locked her and Gabria in the room near his quarters, and then it had been for just a brief time while he displayed her to the remaining members of the Shar-Ja's council. In the meanwhile, he had been constantly busy, swiftly solidifying his position in the city and spreading his war throughout the realm. The city governor's body had been hung in a gibbet by the front gates and was quickly joined by three more city officials who protested Zukhara's right to impose martial law on the population.

He set a nightly curfew for all city inhabitants, and the Fel Azureth patrolled the streets in squads to ruthlessly enforce his brand of civil law. The rest of the army, those who were not billeted at the palace, moved into several inns and a number of large homes around Cangora, throwing out the inhabitants and plundering the stores. Zukhara did little to keep them in check, and anyone foolish enough to complain found himself talking to rats in the city's prison. Those who did not profess their belief in the Gryphon's holy calling also found their way to the dungeons.

It was hardly an auspicious way to begin one's magnificent reign, Kelene thought sourly. She lifted her gaze beyond the night-cloaked city to the heights beyond where the caravan road came down from a broad, open hill. Although she could not see the distant landscape, she remembered it well.

"They're coming," her mother had said.

Who was coming? Was someone out there riding to their rescue? Or was it something she could not yet understand, something Gabria had seen only in a dream? Kelene studied the place where the hill should be as if she could penetrate the blackness and see what was there. Last night she had heard something—or thought she had. There had been a brief sound that called for just a moment over the roar of the army and the crash of its weapons. It had risen so faintly she still wasn't certain it had been there, but it sounded so familiar, so dear. Maybe it was just wishful thinking that she had heard Demira's voice on the hilltop beyond the city.

Leaving the window open, she returned to the bed where Gabria slept peacefully and pulled a spare cover onto the floor. She folded the blanket into a pallet and stretched out close to the bed so she could be near if Gabria needed her. Her eyes closed and her body relaxed, but it was a long time before she slept.

* * *

Because of her restless night, Kelene slept late the next morning and roused only when servants brought trays of food into the bedroom and set breakfast on a table near the open window. She bounced to her feet, having slept better on the floor, and maneuvered the servants out the door when they insisted on serving the clanswomen their breakfast. Kelene closed the door in their faces. "Overfed, interfering females," she said irritably.

At least they had had one good idea—they had brought a pot of freshly brewed tea. Kelene prepared a cup, laced it with milk, sweetened it with honey, and took it to her mother.

Gabria was already awake, and she smiled as Kelene sat beside her. Carefully she drank the hot tea, letting it settle her queasy stomach between sips.

"Do you remember the dream you had last night?" Kelene asked after a while.

The older sorceress looked blank; then she tilted her head in thought. "It is so vague. I feel as though I walked in a fog all night. But I do remember a white horse."

"A *white* horse?" Kelene repeated, alarmed. The color was unusual among clan horses because of its connection to sorcery and to the Harbingers' spectral steeds. "Was it a . . ."

"No," Gabria hurriedly reassured her. "I thought so too at first, but it was ridden by a woman."

"Who? And why would you say 'They're coming'?"

"Did I? I don't know. I don't remember anymore."

Kelene clicked her tongue. "Mother, some day, a long time from now, when you enter the presence of the gods, will you please ask Amara why your dreams are always so maddeningly unclear?"

The remark brought a smile to Gabria's face, and for a moment lit her dull eyes with humor. "I'll be sure to let you know the answer."

They were still laughing when their door banged open and Zukhara's major-domo walked into the room. A golden gryphon on his uniform identified him as one of the Fel Azureth, and the deep lines on his forehead and the chill black of his eyes marked him as a man of little humor.

Kelene glared at him and said coldly, "Were you born in a brothel that you do not ask to be admitted?"

He ignored her remark. His eyes slid over the room disdainfully and did not once look directly at her. "His Supreme Highness, Lord Zukhara, Ruler of the Faithful, expects your presence, clanswoman," he demanded in crude Clannish.

"I guess that means me," snapped Kelene.

"And he wants you in one of the gowns prepared for you."

Kelene spat her opinion of the dresses and stalked out of the room before the officer realized she was going. She still wore the clan pants and tunic she'd made in the cavern—that was good enough!

The officer hurried to catch up, his face a frozen mask. Without another word he led her to an airy room on a lower floor of the large and spacious palace, where Zukhara and several other older men and two priests in yellow robes stood together talking.

The Gryphon's distinctive eyebrows lowered when he saw Kelene. "I asked you—"

Kelene cut him off. "I am comfortable as I am."

The men looked shocked at her effrontery, but Zukhara snapped his fingers and spoke a brief spell. To Kelene's chagrin, she found herself clothed in a long blue gown with a bodice that clung to her form and a skirt that flowed like water to her feet. Silver embroidery decorated the neckline and the hem, and a silver belt tucked in her slender waist. Even her long hair was braided with silver ribbon and crowned with a simple coronet. She'd never felt so elegant, self-conscious, or humiliated in her life.

Zukhara suddenly broke into his charming smile. "You are lovely, my lady. And do not think to change it back, or you will stand before the city in nothing but your silky, pale skin."

Kelene swallowed hard. She had no chance to retort, for in the next minute a fanfare of horns blared close by. Zukhara took her hand. It was only then that she saw the magnificence of his clothes and realized he had arranged something important.

Heavy drapes were pushed aside by servants, and Zukhara, Kelene, and the other men walked out onto a large balcony overlooking the palace grounds. Crowds of Turics filled the huge, open space and overflowed down the promenade into the streets. Half of Zukhara's army was there, yelling loudly and prompting the sullen citizens into cheers. Fanatics began chanting Zukhara's name.

The usurper basked in the adulation before he held up his hands and commanded silence. The crowds gradually quieted to hear his words.

"Rejoice, tribes of the Turic, your salvation is at hand!" Zukhara shouted. "Long have we been led down paths of greed, sloth, iniquity, and corruption at the hands of the Line of Festith. See how we pay for their evil! Our wells run dry; our animals die; our women and children starve. The grain we plant withers for lack of water. There is no help for us! The Living God has turned his countenance away from our pleas. As long as we allow the last Festith to rule as Shar-Ja, Shahr will not deem us worthy of redemption."

A few hisses and boos followed those words, but most of the crowd remained silent.

"See what happened when the Shar-Ja tried to forge a pact with the infidel horse clans? His evil and greed were repaid with treachery and his only son murdered. That was our sign, my people! Sent by our god to show us the way out of our darkness. We must overthrow the perverted power of the Shar-Ja Rassidar and as foreseen by the Prophet Sargun, place the Gryphon on the throne of the Turic realm."

The men of the Fel Azureth burst into cheers.

Kelene stared, wide-eyed, at the man beside her. She knew he was capable of concocting lies, of twisting the truth to fit his purposes, and of deliberately misleading his own people, but he executed his speech with such fervor and sincerity, in a voice that boomed to the edges of the throng with just enough pleading in it to show sympathy and concern for his audience. She might have believed it herself if she had not been a witness to the truth of his cruelty and manipulations.

Zukhara's voice cried out once more. "Behold the heretic who brings such affliction upon us." He pointed downward and out from the main doors came four men bearing a chair litter. Tied to the chair, in his ceremonial robes, sat the Shar-Ja, still alive and furiously silent.

The city dwellers looked shocked as the Shar-Ja was paraded up and down in front of the palace. Zealots pelted the ruler with rotten fruit and worse, but the citizens drew back as if from a leper.

"Four days from today, on the first day of the month of Janas, I and the priests of Sargun will perform the Ritual of Ascension to formally kill the Shar-Ja and prepare the throne for a new dynasty. As ordained in the sacred texts of the rite, that day I will take this woman as my wife and be ordained Celestial Monarch and Sacred Ruler of the Turic Tribes. As it was written, so let it be done!" He raised his arms to the roar of approval from his followers; then he thrust Kelene forward to the edge of the balcony just long enough for the crowd to see her. He turned on his heel and strode back indoors, dragging Kelene with him. As soon as he slowed down, the sorceress yanked her hand out of his grasp.

"I will not marry you!" she yelled. "I am already married and no widow." She knew it would do her no good to argue, but her temper had grabbed the bit and run away with her common sense.

He flicked a hand as if to swat away an unimportant fly. "Your marriage as prescribed by your people under your heathen gods is considered invalid in our land," he replied, his arrogance unruffled by her fury. "To us, you are not united to any man, except me."

She crossed her arms, feeling stymied. "It will do you no good. I have not been drinking the 'remedies' you send with my meals. I am still barren and can do nothing to increase the blood of Valorian in your descendants," she threw out for lack of anything better to say.

He laughed then in delight. "Of course you haven't. You have been eating it ever since the night in the cavern when I discovered you had turned the juice to water. That was clever. But not clever enough. By the time we consummate our wedding night, the remedy will have completed its purpose."

"There will be no wedding night," Kelene said very slowly and distinctly, as if each word were a dagger to plunge into his heart.

His hand flashed toward her, caught her braid, and wrapped it tightly around his fingers. He wrenched her head back until her throat was exposed. "You are so beautiful when you are angry. Do not change. It will be such a pleasure to break that spirit," he hissed in her ear. His fingers caressed her neck where the blood surged under her skin. "There will be a wedding night, and soon you will forget that worthless man who never gave you a son."

This time Kelene reined in her hot reply. Nothing she could say would change his mind or alter his plans one whit, and all she wanted to do now was escape from his sight and think. Four days, by the gods, that was so little time! Her hands itched to snatch the chain around his neck and run, but what good would that do? Even if she managed to kill him, she still had to fetch her mother, find Nara and the gryphon, who were housed somewhere on the palace grounds, and contend with an entire army. She needed help, at the very least a good distraction, but a rescue force of several magic-wielders would be most welcome.

Zukhara kissed her lightly on her throat, and a chill sped down her spine. If something didn't happen soon to precipitate her escape, Kelene knew she would have to choose between her own honor and her mother's life. Clan society frowned on adultery; some women had even been exiled for promiscuous behavior. But what if the cost of fidelity was death for Gabria? More importantly, what would Rafnir think? How would he feel if she submitted to another man? Would he understand? She groaned, her teeth clenched, and prayed he would never be tested like that.

Zukhara laughed at her. Still holding her braid, he dragged her along the corridors back to her room and wrenched open her door.

Gabria, already dressed and seated at the table, stared coldly at the Gryphon as he shoved her daughter into the room. "My lord counselor," she said before Zukhara could leave. "A boon I ask."

He hesitated, curious, and because he was feeling generous at the moment, he decided to listen. Although he would never admit it even to himself, he harbored a grudging respect for this clanswoman who had survived so much in her life. He considered it an honor and an achievement to be the one who would at last kill her. "What do you wish?"

"I would like Lady Jeneve's book."

Zukhara shrugged. He had memorized every word and every spell in the little book. There was nothing in it the sorceress could use to thwart him and no real reason why he couldn't give it to her for a short while. "Why do you want it?" he asked.

Gabria pushed herself to her feet and walked to Kelene's side. "It is a part of a clan long dead. I would simply like it as a memento."

The Gryphon bowed. He could be magnanimous. "Then you shall have it. I will send it to you today. Good day, ladies." He swept out, and the door banged shut behind him. They heard the unmistakable hum of a spell, and when Kelene tested the door, she found it barred with a powerful ward.

She leaned her back against the door and ripped the silver coronet off her head. "Four days, Mother. That's all we have left."

* * *

The moment the Gryphon vanished from the balcony, the citizens of Cangora hurried back to their shops and homes. Disgruntled and fearful, they paid little attention to the beggar boy with the idiot's smile who crouched with his bowl and his mongrel dog near a column in the promenade. He laughed and chattered to someone only he could see with his great black eyes, and merely grinned all the wider when his bowl remained empty.

At last the court and the promenade had emptied of everyone but the many guards who watched the palace. One of them strode over to the boy and told him to move on. The urchin nodded extravagantly, his mouth hanging open, and he shuffled away with the dog at his side. The guard frowned, thinking Zukhara should do something about the riffraff in the city.

The "riffraff," meanwhile, continued his way down the streets and eventually reached the Copper Gate. A large contingent of the Fel Azureth commanded the gates, led by a giant of a man whose very appearance gave most men no thoughts of arguing with his decisions. Under his harsh eye, the guards scrupulously examined every cart and wagon going through, interrogated everyone, and refused entrance to anyone they thought suspicious. Undaunted, the dirty urchin wandered over to the captain of the guards and held out his bowl.

"Go on, simpleton," the man growled, too busy to deal with the likes of street rats.

The boy grinned wider, whistled to his dog, and trotted out the gate. The guards didn't give him a second look. He continued on, apparently aimlessly, up the caravan road, past the fields and a few outlying buildings and businesses until he reached the high hill. At the top he paused to look back; then a triumphant smile replaced his idiot's grin, and he sprinted out of sight of the city. Laughing to himself, Tassilio raced his dog along the road and, as soon as the way was clear, he angled left into a wide dale partially obscured from the road by a belt of wild olive trees. The Clannad had set up camp there in a scattered grove of trees while they tried to decide what to do and Hajira and Sayyed mended.

Tassilio could hear Sayyed even before he reached the outskirts of the camp. He waved to the outpost guards and ran directly to the healer's tent where the brothers stayed under the watchful eye of the Clannad healer.

"Where is that boy?" Sayyed was yelling. "He has been gone since sunrise."

Tassilio understood the sorcerer's sharp, angry pitch the moment he sauntered into the tent. Sayyed was on his side, his back to the entrance, his fists clenched, while the healer tried to clean the infected pus and flesh from the hole in his ribs.

"You're a good man," the clansman said through clenched teeth. "But on the whole I'd rather have Kelene as a healer."

Before he could stop himself, Tassilio blurted out, "I saw her! With Zukhara."

His unexpected voice caused everyone in the tent to startle, including the healer who accidentally poked Sayyed a little too hard in the tender flesh.

The clansman uttered a vile curse even Hajira had never heard. Ignoring his aching leg, the guardsman neatly collared Tassilio and pulled him to a seat near Sayyed. "Do not ever sneak up on a sorcerer who is in pain," Hajira warned. "He might turn you into a toad."

Tassilio's eyes widened. "Could you do that?" he asked Sayyed breathlessly.

Sayyed glared at him. "Don't tempt me. Where in the name of Sargun have you been? And what do you mean you saw Kelene?"

Before Tassilio could answer, Hajira limped to the tent flap and called for Helmar. The lady chief came quickly, slapping dust from her pants and hands.

She cast a sympathetic glance at Sayyed and an irritated one at Tassilio. "Heir or not, young man, you do not leave this camp without telling one of us first," she admonished. "We looked everywhere we could for you, and I will not allow you to add further to our troubles by getting yourself lost or killed or captured. Do you understand?"

Momentarily chastened, Tassilio hung his head and kicked his bare feet at the ground. He knew he deserved the reprimand—he had snuck out without asking—but he felt his news was worth the risk. His irrepressible good spirits came bounding back. "Yes, ma'am," he said, his face alight with his tale. "But I did see Kelene. And Father, too. He is still alive!"

Helmar knew a lost cause when she heard it. "Then you'd better tell us," she said with a sigh and sat down by Hajira.

Tassilio told them in excited tones how he had entered the city that morning, learned of Zukhara's proclamation, and mingled in with the crowds at the palace. He repeated Zukhara's speech almost word for word and described exactly what his father looked like and what Kelene was wearing.

"She is so beautiful!" exclaimed the boy who was obviously verging on manhood. "And her chin goes up when she's mad, and her eyes are thunderous!"

Sayyed, bandaged and sitting upright, chuckled at Tassilio's description. "So she has not been drugged or broken yet. That is a good sign."

"But four days!" Tassilio exclaimed. "Zukhara said he will perform the Ritual of Ascension then. We've got to do something to help Father!"

"What is this ritual?" Helmar asked.

Hajira grimaced at the memory of the texts he had read about the rites. "It is an ancient ceremony that is intended to purge the throne of one monarch to make way for another. Ritualistic murder. Zukhara intends to behead the Shar-Ja and burn his body. He then takes a wife that same day and begins his own line on the throne of Cangora."

"Where does Gabria fit into all of this?"

"My guess is she is being used as a lever against Kelene," Sayyed answered.

"I hope she is still alive," Helmar said.

Sayyed sighed so softly only Helmar heard him. "So do I," he said.

Something in his tone unaccountably pricked Helmar's feelings. There was more than mere worry in his voice; there was what . . . yearning? She mentally kicked herself for thinking such a thing, let alone letting it bother her, but her self-inflicted reprimand did little good. Immediately an unbidden, jealous pang insinuated itself into her thoughts and reminded her that Sayyed himself had admitted to loving this woman once. How many men put themselves in such jeopardy for someone else's wife without good reason? Helmar flung herself to her feet before her thoughts got any more ridiculous. She strode out of the tent without another word.

In surprise, the men watched her go. Only the healer, an old and trusted friend of the chief, thought he understood. "She has never been married," he tried to explain. "She does not yet understand."

"Understand what?" wondered Sayyed.

The healer shrugged his bony shoulders. "How she feels about you."

Stunned, Sayyed looked at his brother, then at the healer, and he felt his face grow hot. Despite having deeply loved two women and having been married to one for eighteen years, he had not understood either. He liked Helmar and respected her more than he thought possible, but he had never imagined she would feel the same for him. After Tam's death he firmly believed there would be no other love for him. Now he examined his feelings and, for the first time, he realized his desire for love had not died but merely slept within his heart. Could Helmar be the one to revive it? He suddenly smiled. It was like discovering a beautiful box intact in the ruins and not knowing what he would find inside. Intent on his own musings, he pulled on his loose tunic over his bandaged ribs and walked out of the tent in a direction opposite to the one Helmar had taken.

Tassilio grinned at Hajira and winked at Sayyed's departing back.

* * *

The sun shone hot when a lone horseman approached the Clannad camp later that day. At the first low-pitched warning signal, the riders grabbed their weapons and formed a line of defense at the perimeter of the camp.

The rider, a Turic on a chestnut horse, reined his mount to a halt and studied the warriors with approval. He held up his hand in peace. "I am Mohadan, the Kirmaz-Ja. I see by your dress and white horses you are the troop I seek," he said in Turic.

Hajira stepped out of the line of warriors and addressed the tribal leader as an equal. "I am Hajira al Raid-Ja, Commander of the Tenth. Why do you seek us?"

The stranger lifted an arched eyebrow and leaned his arm on the saddle horn. "These are hardly Turic soldiers, Commander, and as I heard it, most of the Tenth was slaughtered."

"Not all of us, Kirmaz-Ja. So we make do with what we have."

"And what are you planning to do?"

Hajira, who knew the tribal leader to be a man of honor, gave a short bow. "Perhaps you would like to join us. We could discuss possibilities."

The stranger dismounted and led his horse to the camp to meet with Hajira, Sayyed, Helmar, and Rapinor. The Clannad warriors stayed in position, relaxed yet alert while their chief led the Turic to the shade of several tall cedars. Cool wine and plates of cheese and dates were brought and served by Tassilio. The Kirmaz-Ja sat wordlessly, watching the preparations with a fascinated eye. He seemed particularly intrigued with Helmar and her obvious authority.

"I do not know of you, Lady," he said in rough but credible Clannish, "or your people. You are like clan and yet not clan. And how is it that a woman leads a troop of warriors? Some of whom," he suddenly noticed, "are also women."

"Swords and bows are not our first weapons," Helmar replied. "Strength of arms is not as important as talent to us."

The Turic narrowed his eyes. He had smallish eyes deep set behind a thin nose, but they were not piggish eyes, for his face was too hard and narrow, and his gaze glittered with intelligence and wit. He had a grizzled beard trimmed close to his jaws, and his knotted hair was iron gray. He shifted his eagle's glance from Helmar to Sayyed. "And you, you are Turic no longer. I would guess you are the half-breed who turned to sorcery."

Sayyed merely lifted his cup in reply, impressed by the man's knowledge and intuition.

"Are you here because of the women Zukhara holds?" Mohadan wanted to know.

Briefly Sayyed and Hajira told the Kirmaz-Ja the events beginning at Council Rock and leading up to their arrival at the outskirts of Cangora. Sayyed only touched on his time in Sanctuary and the Clannad's offer to ride with him, but Mohadan's sharp attention missed nothing, and he studied the warriors around him with keen interest.

When the narrative was through, however, Mohadan drove straight to the point that had brought him to see them. "I was told yesterday what your men did for the dead at the Saran Oasis. The families were grateful that you defied the Gryphon's edict to let the men hang until they rotted. So tell me now, will you join your forces to mine and help me bring down the Gryphon?"

15

Hajira shared a glance with Helmar and Sayyed before he turned to Tassilio sitting close beside him. "Is it your will, Shar-Yon, that we unite with this man and the enemies of the Gryphon?"

For the first time, Mohadan's expression registered real surprise. He had paid little attention to the boy who had served the wine, and now he focused all his fierce regard on the son of the Shar-Ja. "You are the sandrat? Rumor said you were dead."

The boy looked startled at the name by which Hajira had called him, but he collected himself quickly. "No, Kirmaz-Ja," Tassilio replied with every ounce of his father's dignity. "I am the Shar-Yon, and I am very much alive."

Mohadan, the traditionalist, the man sworn to honor the throne of the Shar-Ja, had never once considered the possibility of winning the throne for himself. He greeted the unexpected appearance of an heir with sincerity and relief and bowed low before the boy. His gesture sealed Hajira's decision.

At a nod from Tassilio, Hajira drew a dagger from a sheath at his waist and jabbed it into the ground in front of Mohadan. By doing so, he followed an old Turic custom of offering his services to another tribal leader. If Mohadan pulled the dagger free and returned it, he would accept Hajira's services in an agreement as binding as a blood vow.

The Kirmaz-Ja looked at the blade quivering in the dry grass. "I welcome your assistance, Commander, but I must ask, does this also include the sorcerer and the lady and her warriors? I have a feeling that without them, we will stand little chance against Zukhara's power."

Sayyed answered first. "I have already sworn to my own lord that I will do everything I can to return the sorceresses to the clans. To that end, I will help you for as long as the women are held captive."

"Fair enough, Clansman." He turned to Helmar who was sitting beside her guard. "And you, Lady?"

Sayyed was taken aback by the bold look of interest in the man's eyes when he looked at the chief, but Helmar seemed to pay no heed. Unaffected, she tilted her chin and replied coolly, "I made my promise to Sayyed to help free Lady Gabria and Kelene. We will do what needs to be done."

The man's jaw tightened, and his eyes hardened under a thoughtful frown, as if he had just made an unwelcome observation. He glanced at Sayyed then nodded to himself in decision. Without further hesitation, he yanked the blade free and passed it hilt-first to the royal guard. Hajira accepted it back with a thin smile.

"Now," said Mohadan, jumping to his feet, "if you will break camp and come with me, I have something to show you."

They followed his suggestion, swiftly and efficiently, and in less than an hour were riding in a column along the caravan road toward Cangora. They bypassed the city by a wide loop and trotted into the hills on the southern end of the broad valley. Mohadan led them into the first deep dale they reached and pointed them toward a long meadow where a large, bustling camp sat along the banks of a dry streambed. The yellow banner of the Kirmaz floated above one of the tents.

"Most of those men are my own," said the Kirmaz-Ja, indicating the camp with a wave of his hand. "Some are survivors from the caravan. Others have been coming as the word spreads. Not all goes Zukhara's way. There is fighting along the coast and in the cities of Hazereth and Shamani where the Fel Azureth have met resistance from several tribes—including the Raid. Perhaps two hundred men have gathered at my summons. More will come." He indicated a place in the meadow where they could erect their camp near his.

"If all goes as planned," Sayyed told him as they all dismounted, "there will be more men soon. My son is bringing Lord Athlone and the werods to aid the Shar-Ja as promised in their treaty."

A second look of surprise spread over Mohadan's face. Surprise, Sayyed thought, was not a common emotion to the hard-bitten leader, and today they had managed to shake him twice.

"They are coming to help?" Mohadan almost shouted. "We thought they had crossed the Altai to take revenge for the capture of the women and the raids on their trelds by the Fel Azureth."

"I sent for them six days ago."

Mohadan gave a great, gusty snort. "They crossed the Altai yesterday. A messenger bird brought the news from a cousin of mine this morning."

"Yesterday." Sayyed looked thoughtful. "Then they are four or five days away—if they ride like the wind and no one stands in their way."

"I will see that no one does! I will send an escort and a safe-pass for the men of the clans."

"Kirmaz-Ja, that is an excellent idea, but may I suggest we send the safe-pass and an urgent message with the winged mare? Only she is swift enough to reach them quickly."

I heard that and the answer is no! Demira bugled before anyone else could respond. The mare pranced to Sayyed, her big eyes alight with anger. *I am not going away from Kelene again!*

Mohadan could not "hear" what she sent telepathically, but he understood what she meant well enough from her stiff-legged stance and her flattened ears. He gave a noncommittal shrug. "Perhaps it would be better—"

Helmar cut him off by throwing an arm around Demira's neck. The mare rolled her eyes at the chief but did not pull away. "If you were not the best choice to reach Kelene's father, we would not ask you," she said in soothing tones. "If Hajira were healed and able to ride that far, he could go, though his horse could not travel fast enough. Some of my men would go, but they are not Turics and would be in constant danger. You have your glorious wings to fly swiftly above the trouble and reach Lord Athlone in time. Please understand. To have any chance at all of saving Kelene and Gabria, we need more men to attack the city."

The Hunnuli twisted her neck so she could regard Helmar with her star-bright eye. *Could I come back as soon as I find them?*

"As fast as you can," the chief promised.

Then I will take your message to Lord Athlone and Rafnir. She tossed her mane. *The sky is clear, and the road is open. I will try to fly all night.*

"She will take the message," Helmar said, relieved.

Satisfied, the Kirmaz-Ja hurried away to obtain what he wished to send to the clan lords, and the Clannad put up their shelters and ate their evening meal. Sayyed and Helmar made much over Demira, brushing her glossy coat, wiping the dust from her nostrils, and feeding her tidbits until the Turic leader returned.

Mohadan brought a rolled scroll and a yellow banner tightly wrapped in cloth. "Give these to Lord Athlone. They will clear his way along the Spice Road to Cangora. And tell him to hurry," he said to Demira and awkwardly patted her neck. He was not accustomed to talking to horses.

They fastened the banner and the scroll to Demira's back and watched as she lifted slowly into the deepening blue of the evening sky. When she was gone, a tense anticipation settled over the camp. There was nothing left to do but wait.

The next day came hot and dry, as had most of the days before it. The arid wind that blew from the desert sucked what little moisture there was from the ground and left the hills parched and brown. After morning prayers, the Turics spent their time readying for war. They repaired their tack and battle gear, checked their weapons, and practiced swordplay and archery in the scattered splotches of shade under the few trees. Most of the Clannad stayed to themselves out of nervousness and hesitancy, for they had never been in the company of so many strangers. A few wandered over to satisfy their curiosity and before long were drinking Turic ale, admiring strange weapons or ornaments or other objects that were new to them, and fumbling through clumsy conversations.

No one remained idle throughout the day. A regular rotation of guards kept watch on the perimeters of the valley and on the camps. Scouts rode to watch the trails and the caravan road. A steady stream of men traveled the roads around Cangora that day. Most rode on to the city to join the Gryphon's holy war, but word of Mohadan's resistance traveled as fast as Zukhara's proclamation, and a constant trickle of reinforcements flowed into the Turic camp all day.

After noon, Helmar, Rapinor, Sayyed, Hajira, and Tassilio joined the Turics in the shade of Mohadan's big striped tent, and they discussed with the leader and his officers everything that came to mind concerning Zukhara, his intentions, the layout of Cangora, and their plans.

"Is it true, Lady," Mohadan said to Helmar, "that all of your riders are magic-wielders? Why couldn't you blast your way into the city and bring it down around Zukhara's ears?"

The lady chief drank some water from a cup before she took a deep breath and answered. "We are, but not all of us have the same strengths. Some of my people rarely use magic. We have been isolated for so long, our ways have become stagnant and our bloodlines are weakening."

Rapinor started to protest, and Helmar laid a hand on his arm. "You know it's true. That's why you came. It isn't just our horses or our livestock that are threatened. It is us." She turned back to Mohadan. "Yes, we could open the gates with our magic and wreak havoc on your city, and we will do so if there is no other choice. But I would prefer to wait for the clans. It would be better if we had an army behind us to distract the Gryphon's forces while we try to save the clanswomen and confront Zukhara. Besides," she said, winking at Tassilio, "I do not want to be the only one to shoulder the blame for damages to the Shar-Yon's city."

The Kirmaz-Ja nodded at her wisdom and cracked a hard smile. "I understand. It would be better for us as well if we rode together. We have little hope of defeating the Gryphon alone."

"Exactly." She returned his smile with one of her own, her eyes crinkling at the corners above the constellations of freckles. She lifted her cup. "To cooperation and allies. Something we have not had in generations."

More ale was brought, along with honeyed wine and ewers of precious water. The talk went on while several of Mohadan's men outlined a map of Cangora for the strangers, describing the streets, the palace and its barracks, and the pinnacle with its huge temple.

"Could we try infiltrating the palace in a small group?" Sayyed suggested.

Tassilio looked dubious. "The palace and the grounds are heavily guarded, and soldiers are everywhere. The guards at the gate check everything and everyone. I don't know how you could get past and still find Kelene and Lady Gabria. That palace is huge!"

"I still think a lightning attack is our best hope. We strike fast, ride to the palace, and stop Zukhara before the ritual," Mohadan stated emphatically.

"And what if he kills the women or the Shar-Ja before we get there?" Hajira asked.

The Kirmaz-Ja sighed heavily. "That is a chance we take no matter how we approach our attack."

The talking went on while each person had their say about tactics and ideas. Although Tassilio listened closely, Sayyed thought he looked rather thoughtful, and the clansman wondered what scheme the boy was hatching in his active mind.

At the same time, scouts brought reports from the city, and new arrivals brought news from other regions of the realm. Fighting had spread across the country as the few surviving tribal leaders, appalled by the massacre of their contemporaries, struggled to organize resistance against the Gryphon's rebels. Those tribes without leaders were riddled with strife and confusion. Mohadan had hoped other leaders would join him at Cangora, but as the time passed and more news filtered in, he had to accept that he would have to fight alone.

By the time the sun crawled to its rest beyond the western mountains, the Turic and the Clannad alike were weary and ready for the cool of night.

The second day followed much the same course of heat and talk and preparation. The loyalists struggled to strengthen their numbers, and the Gryphon worked tirelessly to tighten his hold on Cangora and his bid for control of the fifteen tribes. Tension's grip grew tighter over everyone while they waited for the first day of Janas.

Sayyed, especially, festered in his worry and impatience. Questions crowded into his thoughts almost unceasingly, like crows harrying a hawk. Would the clans arrive in time, or would the Clannad and Mohadan's small army have to go, alone, up against the big city, which was well defended by a host far larger than their own? How was Zukhara treating Kelene? Had Gabria died of the poison? Would he and the Clannad be able to reach the women before Zukhara killed them? That fear terrified him the most and kept him awake late into the night, debating ways to get to them in time.

The third night, after another hot, interminable day, Sayyed crawled from his pallet and left the tent he shared with Hajira, Tassilio, and the healer. The darkness embraced him in a cool breeze and laved his fevered thoughts in quiet serenity. He walked barefooted away from the camps, out into the meadows where the horses grazed. The white Clannad horses were easy to see in the starlight, but it took him a while to find the black shape of Afer, standing like a shadow close to Helmar's mare. Their tails idly swished at a few stubborn flies, and their heads hung in peaceful rest.

At Sayyed's approach, both horses lifted their muzzles and nickered a welcome. Gratefully the sorcerer pushed his anxieties aside and crowded in between the two horses, where their warmth and companionship were the balm he needed for his spirit. Unwilling to disturb the silence, he leaned against Afer and sought out the stallion's favorite itchy places. He rubbed and patted and scratched until the big stallion quivered with delight. A soft nose nudged his elbow, and without thinking, Sayyed turned around to caress the mare. He discovered quickly that she liked her back and withers scratched, and he dug in with all ten fingers to massage her itchy skin.

The mare stretched her neck, her eyes half-closed, her ears flopping. If she had been a cat, Sayyed mused, she would be purring.

Oh, that is wonderful, a light feminine voice sighed in his mind.

Sayyed grinned. He had suspected as much. "How about here?" He moved his fingers to the end of her mane, where the ridge of her withers rose under her silvery coat.

Yes, came the voice again. The mare leaned into him. *I like that.*

"So why didn't Helmar tell me you were Hunnuli?" Sayyed asked casually, still scratching her back.

The white mare stilled, then gave a snort of amused annoyance. *Well, it is too late now to play dumb. Do you know how hard it has been to keep quiet around you?*

"Why did you?"

Helmar told us all not to talk to you. Not until she was sure.

"Is she so afraid of me?"

Not of you. Of the clans.

"Why?"

I will save that, at least, for her to explain.

"All right." Sayyed chuckled. "But if you are Hunnuli, why are all of you white?"

The horses turned their heads and whickered a greeting to someone else. Helmar walked out of the darkness. She wore only a light, loose-fitting tunic that rippled around her thighs in the soft breeze. She leaned over the mare's back, her expression unreadable in the night.

"They're not true whites, Sayyed. Only their hair is white. Our ancestors took the color of the lightning and covered over the black. If you look under their hair, their skin is still dark as night." She patted the mare and stallion and softly chuckled her husky laugh. "Marron, my beauty, you stayed quiet longer than I thought you would."

He was scratching my back, the mare offered as an apology.

"Is the lightning still there?" Sayyed asked, fascinated.

"Yes, if you look closely enough." Helmar pushed in by Sayyed, parted the hairs on Marron's right shoulder, and said, "There, you can just see the outline."

The sorcerer eased close to her and peeled at the place she indicated. Faintly in the darkness he saw the pale line of white skin beside black. In the days that followed, Sayyed never could decide if what happened next was deliberate or accidental—and Afer would never tell him. Just as he straightened, Afer and

Marron shifted closer together, knocking into Sayyed and throwing him off balance. He took a step to catch himself and banged into Helmar. Her strong arms went around him to steady him. His wounded arm hit her shoulder, and by the time the pain ebbed and he realized what had happened, they were standing wrapped in a tight embrace.

Neither moved. They were so similar in height, their hearts beat against one another, and their eyes stared at each other's from only a breath away. They hesitated, both surprised by the sudden intimacy of their position. Helmar's hands trembled against Sayyed's back, and Sayyed felt his skin grow hot. In a flash of unspoken consent, their lips met, and they kissed so long and deep it left them gasping.

Marron playfully reached over and nipped Afer. The stallion stamped a hoof, his neck arched, and he nipped her back. In a flash of phantom white, the mare leaped away, her tail held high like a flag. Afer galloped after her, and the two people were left alone in the meadow. The velvet night closed softly about them.

They stood, neither wanting to say a word, neither needing to. Sayyed's hands untied the strip of leather that bound Helmar's thick braid and gently worked her hair loose until it floated in a waving mass down her shoulders and back. He inhaled her scent, a warm blend of leather, horses, sun, wind, and a special fragrance all her own. He buried his face in her hair while her arms pulled his hard body against hers.

They kissed again, and all their questions and worries were cast to the winds until there was nothing left to think about but the warm grass and the wonder of a love unlooked for that had found them both.

Beyond the darkened meadow at the edge of the Clannad camp, a slim figure and a shaggy shadow slipped out of the healer's tent and worked their way around the perimeter guards. Silent and unseen, they crept over the hill and disappeared toward the valley of Cangora. By dawn they were sitting at the city gates patiently begging and waiting for the day to begin.

* * *

Afer and Marron came back just before sunrise and woke the lovers in time to return to camp. The four of them walked back together, feeling very pleased with each other. Helmar and Sayyed stopped near the tents, not willing yet to end their time together. This was dawn of the first day of Janas. There was no more time to save the Shar-Ja or Kelene and Gabria. They had to attack Cangora today, with or without the clans, and the gods only knew how the day would end. Arms entwined, they looked to the east, where a pale gold band of light illuminated the flat horizon.

They were so engrossed by the beauty of the coming day, they did not see a dark shape come swooping out of the west. An eerie, shattering cry broke over the predawn's hush, and suddenly the valley was filled with the screams of terrified horses. The two camps awoke to stunned life. Guards came running; men tumbled out of their tents.

Sayyed and Helmar whirled in time to see a huge creature dive from the sky, its wings folded, its talons extended. Howling, it dove among the Turic horses, and with a sweep of its big paw broke the necks of two animals. The rest fled in a maddened stampede away from the horrendous beast. They charged in a panicked mass up the valley and, blinded by their own fear, plowed directly through the Kirmaz-Ja's camp. The thundering of hooves and the screams and shouts of men filled the valley.

The gryphon growled with satisfaction. Hooking a dead horse in her claws, she flew heavily away, back toward Cangora and the man who had summoned her.

The valley was left in chaos. Through the dust kicked up by the stampeding herd, Sayyed and Helmar could barely make out the shambles of the Turic camp. The hazy forms of men ran through the pale light. Others lay motionless on the ground.

Helmar took one long look and became a chief again. She quickly squeezed Sayyed's hand and ran into their camp, shouting for Rapinor and her warriors. Snapping orders, she quickly organized them into parties and led them across to the Turic camp.

Sayyed watched her go. She was so different from his quiet Tam, and yet the two women shared the same strength of character, the same ability to coolly handle a crisis. He thought for just a moment about their night and the box in his heart he had opened. The contents had turned out to be something he would treasure for as long as he had left to live. He put his hand on Afer's shoulder. "Go," he commanded. "Gather the Hunnuli and round up those horses. Zukhara started the hostilities this morning, but we are going to finish them."

Afer and Marron neighed their agreement and galloped away to do his bidding. Hajira found him then, and the two brothers hurried to the Turic camp to do what they could to help. In the middle of the wreckage stood the Kirmaz-Ja, unharmed and punctuating his shouted orders with fierce gestures. Mohadan was in a towering rage that turned his dark eyes to black fire and his face to a mask of insulted fury.

"He thinks to stop us," the Turic snarled to Sayyed and Hajira, "by driving off our horses and occupying us with disaster. But I will attack Cangora today if I have to crawl there on my hands and knees!"

The dust slowly settled, and the Turics and the Clannad worked to bring some order to the chaos. They were relieved to find there were not as many dead and wounded as they had feared. The first cry of the gryphon had alerted most of the tribesmen, who had managed to get out of the way of the stampede in time. In all only six bodies were placed together under a tree for burial, and fourteen men had to be treated by the healers for abrasions, lacerations, and broken bones. A broad swath of the camp lay in trampled ruins, and it took several hours to sift through the debris for enough clothes, weapons, and battle gear to equip the men able to ride. The sorcerers helped as best they could to repair or transform the needed equipment, but it still used more time than they had to spare.

The Hunnuli soon calmed down the Turic horses and herded them back to the mouth of the valley. Eager warriors brought their mounts in to the picket lines and began to saddle them.

As order slowly returned, Mohadan calmed down. A cold, deliberating anger replaced his earlier temper, and he gathered his officers, Helmar, Hajira, and Sayyed for a meeting.

"There has been no word from the clans," he said bluntly. "We must assume they cannot arrive today. Yet this is our last day to save the Shar-Ja. By sunset he will be dead, and Zukhara will sit on the throne. We are all that stands between that madman and the power of the crown. Do we attack today or wait until the other tribal leaders join us and the clans arrive?"

"Today," Hajira said forcefully.

"Even with the reinforcements and the Clannad, we number barely eight hundred. The Gryphon has amassed closer to seven thousand, and he holds the fortifications."

"We know that, Kirmaz-Ja," said one of the officers. "But I would rather die attempting to save our rightful ruler than sit by and let that usurper murder him."

Mohadan glanced at the lady chief. "Are you still willing to ride with us?"

Dirty, disheveled, and still dressed only in her light tunic, Helmar's authority and self-confidence shone as clearly as any accoutrements of war. "Of course. Our objectives may be slightly different, but our destination is the same."

"So be it," the Kirmaz-Ja stated. "We ride within the hour."

A sudden clamor made them all jump. "It's coming back!" a guard bellowed just before several horns blared a warning. Everyone froze, their eyes searching the sky.

"There!" shouted Hajira.

Faster than an eagle, the gryphon had circled around to attack the camp from a different direction. She dove on the picket lines, screaming her ear-piercing cry. The horses erupted into a rearing, pitching panic.

"The horses!" shouted Mohadan, and his men shook themselves from their motionless fear and awe and raced to defend their animals. Archers armed their crossbows with the short, barbed quarrels that could pierce armor. They fired a deadly flight, but the gryphon swerved at the last minute and roared her derision at the puny missiles. She swooped again over the meadows and harried the horses into terrified flight. Only the Hunnuli ignored her attempts to panic them and steadfastly tried to hold the frightened herds together.

The gryphon saw the white horses and understood what they were doing. She stooped low, her wings humming in the speed of her dive, and sank her claws into the back of one white Hunnuli. Before she could get it off the ground, three others and Afer charged her. The black, larger than the others, bared his teeth and drove his hooves into the gryphon's shoulder.

Hurt and furious, the gryphon let go of her prey. She crouched, ready to pounce on the black that had hurt her when another force hit her in the side and knocked her off her feet. Her baleful eyes sought the source of this new hurt, and she saw a man fire a blue blast of magic at her. Catlike, she twisted to her feet and sprang into the air. She was all too familiar with the effects of that powerful force. More bolts chased her into the bright sky.

Helmar and other Clannad magic-wielders joined Sayyed, and together they kept up a barrage of magic that forced the gryphon to circle higher and higher above the camp.

One rider, tears running down his face, ran to help his wounded Hunnuli.

Meanwhile, the Turics and the Hunnuli calmed the other horses enough to get them saddled and ready. The gryphon still circled the valley, but as long as the magic-wielders continued firing at her, she did not dare approach any closer.

"God of all," Sayyed gasped when he paused to wipe the sweat from his forehead. "That creature is strong. The Trymmian force hardly rattles it."

Helmar agreed. "It will be tough to shake it if it chases us all the way to Cangora."

"The Turics will be ready soon," Sayyed pointed out, eyeing her inadequate clothing. "You'd better prepare the Clannad."

She graciously accepted the hint, kissed him on the cheek, and took half the warriors with her. They came back shortly, dressed in mail and fully armed, and sent the rest back to do the same. By the time the Turics were mounted and ready to ride, the Clannad had whistled in their Hunnuli and waited to join them.

Sayyed looked around for Hajira to say good-bye. Hajira had chosen to keep Tassilio in the camp, despite the boy's pleas, and Mohadan had wholeheartedly agreed. A city consumed in desperate fighting was not a good place for the Shar-Ja's last son. But Hajira came running out of their tent, hurriedly buckling on his sword and looking so mad he could have spit lightning bolts.

"He's gone! And that mangy dog with him!" the guardsman yelled. He grabbed a saddle and threw it on the nearest spare mount with such force the frightened horse jumped out from under it, and Hajira had to calm it down before he could try again.

"What do you mean? Wasn't he here earlier?" Sayyed demanded.

"I thought he was, but things were so crazy, I don't know now. His bed is empty, those rags of his are gone, and he and that dog of his are nowhere in camp. I'll wager my next ten years of life he has gone to Cangora." Hajira's voice was laden with both anger and frantic concern. He managed to settle the skittish horse and mount without too much difficulty. "If the Fel Azureth don't kill him, I just might," he growled and kicked his horse to join the others.

Flanked by the magic-wielders, the Kirmaz-Ja led his small army out of the valley. The gryphon, seeing them leave, dropped close to harry the column, but the sorcerers drove her back with oaths and spheres of blue energy.

Hajira, Sayyed, and Helmar joined Mohadan at the front. "The Copper Gates will probably be enspelled with wards and be the most heavily guarded," Sayyed said. "But the straightest, quickest road to the palace and the citadel runs from there."

The Kirmaz-Ja nodded, his grizzled beard jutting from beneath his helmet. "We'll attack there." He glared at the sun, now nearly overhead. "Damned gryphon. It delayed us too long. We had no time to get anyone inside, and now it's almost noon. The Ritual of Ascension was always begun when the sun reached its zenith. We have very little time to fight our way through. At least it is a long ritual."

"And we probably do have someone inside," said Hajira irritably. "For what little good it will do us."

The column left the valley behind and trotted down the hills to the broad vale where the level fields rolled up to the foot of the city's wall. The gryphon wheeled and screeched overhead. The sun beat on the men's armor. The column spread out into a long line, eight horses deep, and moved forward at a canter. The yellow banner of the Kirmaz-Ja floated over the head of his standard bearer.

Sayyed hesitated a moment; then he unrolled something he had brought with him. A gold clan cloak spread over his knees. He fastened it on, glad at last to be able to wear it openly and proudly before the Turics. A flash of color caught his eye, and he turned his head to see Helmar pinning a cloak to her own shoulders. The cloak did not surprise him, since the Clannad had been clan at one time, but its color did. Bright and bold and fiery red, Helmar wore the color of Clan Corin. He gaped at her, wondering why she had chosen that color; then she drew her sword in a signal to her riders and yelled a piercing war cry that was immediately echoed by a bellowed Turic command.

The horses, Turic and Hunnuli alike, stretched out their necks, pinned back their ears, and sprang forward into a gallop straight toward the gates of Cangora. Horns blared on the city walls. The tribesmen and Clannad answered back with horns of their own that sang a challenge that reverberated throughout the city. The Turics lifted their voices in a wild, high-pitched ululation that sent chills down Helmar's back. The polished gates, already closed and barred, gleamed like a beacon in the sun.

The Clannad warriors, those most talented, drew together behind Sayyed and Helmar. Others spread themselves along the charging line. As the horses thundered closer to the city wall, the magic-wielders drew on the omnipresent magic and shaped it to their will. At Helmar's command, they fired as one at the massive Copper Gates and at selected places along the wall.

The wards Sayyed had predicted were in the gateway, and they were even more powerful than the sorcerer had feared, yet they had never been meant to withstand the sustained power of so much magic. The wards groaned and sparked and held for several precious minutes until at last, in a thunderous explosion, they gave way, and the attackers' magic blew out huge sections of the towers on either side of the gate. The copper doors themselves sagged and slowly toppled to the ground in a resounding boom. Other sorcerers breached the wall in two more places, opening new entrances into the city.

The Kirmaz men roared with triumph and charged to the breaches. The Clannad followed more slowly. They had expended much strength fighting the gryphon and destroying the wards, and they were starting to tire.

Stunned by the blasts, Zukhara's forces hesitated a few vital minutes, allowing the attackers to gain a foothold just inside the wall. The Fel Azureth, already accustomed to Zukhara's sorcery, recovered first and rallied their forces into action. Men from every quarter of the city rushed to beat back the invaders at the wall. All too soon the Kirmaz-Ja's charge bogged down under the overwhelming numbers of rebel troops that surrounded them. The warriors were forced to dismount and fight hand to hand in a vicious, bloody struggle to maintain their positions. Archers fired down on them from sections of the wall and buildings nearby. Swordsmen charged their defenses. A small mangonel was brought down the main avenue and used to batter the Kirmaz-Ja's force with chunks of rock and deadly spiked balls.

Only the sorcerers of the Clannad kept the tribesmen from being decimated. They were spread out among the three attacking groups along the wall, and they desperately worked to deflect missiles, provide cover fire, and protect the loyalists as best they could with defensive shields of energy. But the magic-wielders were tiring from the unending struggle. A few had already had to stop and rely on their swords for protection; several had already been killed.

In the Kirmaz-Ja's troop, Sayyed felt his energy flagging. He had not imagined the Gryphon's forces would be so relentless. They pushed forward, regardless of the cost, and slowly but steadily wore down the loyal Turics. Try as they might, the Kirmaz could not move forward or backward. They were trapped in a steadily shrinking circle that could end only in death.

16

The war song of the horns soared up the mountain's bay, carrying farther and longer and louder than any other sound from the battle at the city wall. The citizens heard it in the streets and in their houses. Some answered the call and marched down to join in the fighting on one side or the other; some listened to it and barred their shops and homes.

One boy, dressed as a beggar, lifted his head for the blink of an eye, the mindless grin on his face slipping to reveal a shining flash of excitement. Clutching his bowl, he ambled up the road, closer to the palace.

The music soared on ever higher and lapped against the high walls of the palace where the Gryphon's guards heard it and readied themselves—just in case.

Zukhara paused once in his preparations and recognized the horn music for what it was. The puny loyalist force had somehow evaded his gryphon and come knocking at his door. Let them knock, he sneered. His army and his gryphon would soon annihilate them. He had more important things to do this day of days.

In her room high in one of the palace wings, Kelene flung open her window and leaned out on the sill. "Listen, Mother!"

Gabria joined her on the window seat. Her smile lit even her dark-ringed eyes. "They're coming," she murmured.

Kelene stared down toward the gates, hoping to catch a glimpse of something or someone, but all she saw were the sandstone buildings marching down the slope to the distant wall, where smoke drifted above a few rooftops. A winged shape floating over the lower city caused her to catch her breath, and her fingers gripped the sill. "The gryphon. He's set the gryphon on them," she cried, torn between her fear for the attackers and for the gryphon. She hadn't seen the wild creature since Zukhara locked her and Gabria in their room, and Amara only knew what he had done to the beast since then.

"She will be unharmed," Zukhara's voice said from the doorway. "I would not endanger a thing so precious without some protection."

Kelene spun around, ready to heap four days' worth of frustration and anger on his head, when she saw him and nearly choked on her words. The counselor stood in the doorway in front of a retinue of priests, officers, and supporters. He wore ceremonial robes of royal blue velvet tipped with white fur and decorated with handsewn pearls and silver threads. A silver mantle draped his broad shoulders, and a simple crown ringed his jet-black hair. Tall, slim, and elegant, he looked to all who beheld him the quintessential monarch. Only the icy glitter of his impersonal eyes gave any hint of the cruelty beneath.

"Are you ready, ladies?" he said without preamble. He held out his hand to Kelene.

Kelene forced back her temper and did not demur. She was dressed now in a red gown trimmed in gold, ready for whatever would come. The sorceresses looked at one another in silent understanding, and Kelene gave her mother an almost infinitesimal nod. She ignored Zukhara's hand and took Gabria's arm instead to help her mother out the door. They walked down several flights of stairs and to the south end of the palace, where the throne room sat in sunlit splendor.

The room was part of the oldest wing of the palace, built nearly three hundred years before Zukhara's time. Its architect had used white stone to build the walls and designed the floor into a mosaic of tiny tiles of lapis lazuli, agate, and marble. Delicately carved buttresses held up a vaulted roof tinted black and ornamented with paintings in blue, white, and silver to represent the firmament—from whence came the name, the Celestial Throne. Between the buttresses were long, narrow windows that had been thrown open to the morning sunlight and wind. Light poured in brilliant bars into the room, reflecting off the gleaming floors and shining on the great sun throne of the Shar-Ja.

Hunkered over a broad dais, the heavy wooden seat was covered entirely in beaten gold that reverent hands had polished to a brilliant sheen. In the wall behind it was a huge, round stained-glass window that depicted a golden sun. Blue hangings were draped above the throne, and two men, dressed in the blue of the Shar-Ja's personal guard, stood beside it. It wasn't until Kelene had passed through the shafts of sunlight and stood at the foot of the throne that she realized the two guards were dead and merely propped there before they accompanied their slain ruler to his grave.

She closed her eyes. She didn't know if the clan gods would be present among a people who did not believe in them, but she prayed fervently that Amara could hear her plea. "Help me find the right moment," she silently begged the mother goddess.

Zukhara's voice startled her out of her reverie. "Welcome, Shar-Ja. Come, sit on your throne."

Three men entered from the big double doors. Two were garbed in the black and gold of the Fel Azureth, the other was the Shar-Ja, struggling to stay on his feet. They hustled the old man up the steps of the dais, set him on the throne, and tied his arms to the armrests.

The priests with Zukhara set quickly to work, lighting pots of incense and sprinkling the throne with water and sand to bless the proceedings in the name of Shahr, the Living God, and his prophet Sargun. Their chanting filled the room with their low pitched voices.

A small crowd of servants, Fel Azureth, and spectators from the city began to gather in the throne room near the entrance to witness the ancient rites. No one paid any attention to the boy in the stolen shirt and baggy pants who slipped into the rear of the crowd to see what was happening.

The priests ended their prayers and blessings for the throne and paused before beginning the next rite to purify the Shar-Ja for death. In that brief moment of aching silence, Kelene strained to hear something, anything, outside that could help her choose her moment to act. Her heart skipped a beat. She tried not to react, but her fingers tightened around Gabria's arm. The chanting began again and drowned out anything she could have heard on the wind. But it had been there, she would swear to it. Faint and far away she had heard the unmistakable clarion call of the Clan horns.

* * *

The horns sounded again, although Kelene did not hear it that time, on the heights of the caravan road above the valley. Pure and sweet and powerful as the north wind, their music rolled down the dale and washed over the city wall. Those on the battlements and in the towers heard the horns and hesitated. Those on the ground locked in the wild melee could not hear the song over the clash of weapons, the frenzied shouts of fighting men, and the screams of the dying.

But Afer heard it. His great head went up and his ears swept forward. He neighed a trumpeting call over the noise of the fighting. *They come!* he cried to all who could understand.

Sayyed and the warriors of the Clannad took heart and passed the word to the Turics. "The clans are coming!"

High on the fortifying wall men shouted, and several horns blew a warning. Surprised, the Gryphon's army hesitated and drew back a step to see what was causing the uproar. Nearly everyone who could snatched that pause to look out through the gaping holes in the wall.

A dark line of horsemen stretched across the valley, coming at a breakneck gallop. The sun glittered on their spears. Their numbers were obscured by the dust that billowed up from the horses' pounding hooves, but Zukhara's forces did not need to count. The colorful banners of the clan chieftains in the forefront and the four black Hunnuli horses in the lead were enough to make them blanch.

"Back!" bellowed Mohadan to his men. "Get out of the way!"

Frantically the Kirmaz and the Clannad grabbed their horses and their wounded and scrambled to get out of the way of the charging clan werods. The Fel Azureth pulled back too, and rallied their men to barricade the streets.

Abruptly the air reverberated with the heart-stopping war cries of all eleven clans. The ground trembled under the hooves of the horses. With lightning precision, the line lowered its spears and split into three groups, one for each breach, and pounded through the gaps in the city wall. Lord Athlone and Rafnir led the horsemen through the ruined gateway and smashed head-on into the defenders' lines. The Fel Azureth could not hold. Although the clansmen were fewer in numbers and weary from days of relentless travel, their ferocity and momentum carried them irresistibly over the enemy. The spears gave way to swords and battle-axes, and the battle was joined.

Mohadan gave a shout to his men, and the Kirmaz plunged back into the fight. The Clannad, weary from the magic they had wielded, followed close behind.

Many of the Gryphon's volunteers broke and ran under the combined assault of tribesmen and clansmen, but the trained fanatics of the Fel Azureth had their master's orders: hold the city at all costs. They begrudgingly fell back before the werods and the Turic loyalists. They regrouped, fought, and regrouped again, struggling against every step they took backward. Yet even they could not withstand the power of the clan sorcerers for long. Backed by the riders of the Clannad, Lord Athlone, Rafnir, Gaalney, Morad, and Sayyed pounded their way slowly but steadily up the streets of Cangora toward the Shar-Ja's palace.

Helmar rode with the clan sorcerers for a short while as the fighting swept into the streets; then gradually she began to fall back. A strange sense of fear and urgency settled in the pit of her stomach. She shot a look up the broad avenue that she knew led toward the palace. Lady Gabria was up there—a woman she had never met, but the only woman left in the entire population of clanspeople who was of direct lineage to the Corin Clan. She was also a link in the tragedy of the Purge that had massacred so many magic-wielders. To Helmar, that link was vitally important.

She glanced up the road again. The clansmen were moving steadily closer to the palace, but not fast enough. Someone should get there faster in case Zukhara panicked and disposed of his prisoners. A shadow swept over the ground, and she saw the gryphon winging toward the upper levels of the city where the palace lolled at the feet of the massive stone bastion.

Demira, Helmar remembered. Where is Demira?

"Marron, can you call the winged mare? Is she close?"

There. She is above the walls, responded the white mare. *She follows the gryphon.*

Helmar followed Marron's directions and saw Demira not too far away. "Call her! Tell her I need her! Please, my beauty. She can carry me above the fighting to Kelene and Gabria."

Marron understood and obeyed. She neighed a pealing call that reached over the battle and caught Demira's ear.

Helmar cast an apologetic glance at Sayyed, who was fighting by Lord

Athlone's side, and swiftly ducked Marron down a side alley that was momentarily clear.

No one saw her go but Rapinor. Startled by her abrupt departure, he turned his horse to follow. From out of an open window, a man leaned out with a cocked crossbow and fired it wildly into the struggling men below. The swordsman, intent on following his chief, did not see the quarrel until it embedded in his chest. He looked down at it, feeling rather silly, and slowly toppled from his stricken Hunnuli.

Helmar went on, unaware of Rapinor's fate. She and Marron found an open square wide enough for Demira to land. As soon as the mare touched down, Helmar explained what she wanted. Demira's reply was immediate. The chief climbed onto her back, grabbed a handful of mane, and held on while Demira cantered forward into her take-off.

Marron watched the direction they went. Helmar had not told her to stay or go, so she scudded after them like a cloud blown on a stormy wind.

* * *

In the celestial throne room of the Shar-Ja, the spectators were growing restive. The breeze that wafted in the open windows blew a faint clamor of war from the city below that disturbed the sacred dignity of the rites. Only the Shar-Ja and Zukhara seemed unaware of the increasing din.

The ceremony had reached the moment that signaled the death of the current monarch. The sword for the beheading had been blessed, and the priests stood by with a basket for the head and wrappings for the body. A soldier stepped behind the Shar-Ja's throne and pulled Rassidar's head up and back to expose his neck.

Zukhara grasped the hilt of the sword with both hands. It was a two-handed broadsword of great weight and antiquity, yet he handled it as skillfully as a master. His eyes on the Shar-Ja, he walked to the throne and raised the sword over his shoulder.

A boy, of no more than thirteen years, darted around the crowd. He drew back his arm and, with the accuracy earned from months of practice, fired a rock from a slingshot at Zukhara's head. The missile missed the Gryphon's temple by a mere inch and hit instead just above his right eyebrow. The man staggered from the surprise and pain of the blow; the sword fell from his hand and clanged on the floor.

Swift as a striking hawk, Kelene snatched the moment. She took two steps away from Gabria, gathered the magic around her, and aimed a sphere of energy at the ivory ward beneath Zukhara's robes. The power hit him hard and knocked him into the dead guard by the throne, but it wasn't quite enough to break the ward. Furiously he lashed back, sending a fistful of stunning blasts at Kelene and the boy. The people in the crowd screamed and ran for safety.

The first blow took Kelene in the chest before she could defend herself and sent her spinning against the wall. She sagged to the floor, unconscious. Gabria choked on a cry and ran to her side. A second ball of energy caught Tassilio and threw him skidding across the floor.

The priests and the guards looked at each other uneasily. Zukhara spat a curse. Blood dripped down his face from a cut on his forehead. He yanked out his dagger to stab the Shar-Ja, and another rock cracked into his arm.

Tassilio knelt on the floor, looking very much alive and very aware of what he was doing. He pulled a knotted piece of rope out of his shirt and jiggled it tauntingly at the Gryphon.

Zukhara recognized it for what it was. His face grew livid. "Sandrat!" hissed Zukhara.

"That's right!" Tassilio yelled fiercely, sliding another rock into his sling-shot. "A bastard, just like you! But now I am Shar-Yon and that is my father, the rightfully ordained ruler of the Turic. You are nothing but a traitor, Zukhara, and I will see you dead!"

The Gryphon raised his hand to strike down the loathsome boy. With surprising strength, the Shar-Ja twisted his body and lashed out with his foot. He caught Zukhara on the back of the knee and knocked the leg out from under the usurper. The Gryphon fell heavily down the stairs. He pushed himself upright, shaken but uninjured, and glared malevolently at the old ruler.

"They're coming," a hollow voice intoned close by.

Zukhara spun around and saw Gabria standing upright and staring blankly at the large double doors. From somewhere in the corridors came the sounds of screams and the hard clatter of approaching hooves. He wasted no more time. He dashed to Kelene and lifted her over his shoulder. Gabria was too weakened by the poison to fight him off, and a backhanded blow knocked her to the floor. In a daze she watched him go behind the throne and disappear; then hoofbeats pounded outside the room and the doors crashed open.

A red-haired woman in full battle dress and wearing a red cloak rode in on a black winged Hunnuli. Gabria smiled through her tears. The horse wasn't white, but Demira was quite good enough.

The remaining priests and Fel Azureth must have thought so, too, for they took one look at the furious sorceress and fled, leaving only Tassilio and the Shar-Ja with the two women. Tassilio ran to his father and used the dagger to cut him free. Demira skidded to a stop on the patterned floor and Helmar slid off.

Her heart in her throat, the chief ran to Gabria's prostrate form. The older sorceress stared at the stranger as if she were still a vision. Her hand grasped the red cloak. Helmar was shocked by Gabria's thin body and shadowed face. Blood oozed from a cut on her cheek, and her hands trembled. But anger smoldered deep in Gabria's jewel-green eyes, and she managed to push herself to a sitting position.

"You," Gabria gasped. "By Amara's grace, where did you come from?"

Helmar steadied her and helped her rise to her feet. "Out of the past, Lady Gabria."

Kelene! Where is Kelene? Demira neighed. She clattered around the room to look for her rider.

Tassilio guessed what she wanted. "He took her out that way," he cried and pointed to the hanging blue drapes behind the throne. He hurried around to show her the door and found it closed and locked.

The Shar-Ja leaned his frail weight heavily on the throne and told them, "It leads to the courtyard outside and the path to the temple. He probably had horses waiting to take them up to the pinnacle."

Tassilio tried to work the lock; Demira tried to kick in the door. But it was wasted effort. The door was solidly barred. Frustrated, the mare took another circuit around the room and saw there were no more doors and the windows were too narrow for her bulky wings. Before anyone could gainsay her, she suddenly turned and cantered out the double doors to find another way to reach Kelene.

"He's taking her to the citadel," Gabria said fiercely. "She needs more help than Demira can give her."

The sounds of fighting had grown nearer since Helmar's arrival, yet it had not lessened in intensity. The Fel Azureth fought like wolves and still had the slight advantage of numbers and familiarity with the city streets. It could still be a while before Lord Athlone or Sayyed or Rafnir could subdue them enough to come and help, and that might be too late.

"Take me up there," Gabria pleaded.

Helmar exhaled sharply. "But, Lady, you are too weak. If you tried to use magic—"

"I am too weak to destroy him. Not to distract him."

More hooves pounded in the hallway, and Tassilio's dog bounded into the room just ahead of Marron. Barking and wiggling, the dog leaped delightedly on the grinning boy.

"Cal, I told you to stay outside," the boy laughed.

Well, you did not tell me to stay, Marron huffed to the chief. She was breathing heavily and hot with sweat.

"And glad I am I didn't," exclaimed Helmar. "We must still try to free Kelene."

"A *white* Hunnuli," Gabria breathed. She held her hands out to the mare and let Marron sniff her hands and face.

Helmar snapped her fingers. "Nara! We need her. Is she still alive?"

"Zukhara may be many things," replied the Shar-Ja dryly, "but he is not wasteful of things that are valuable to him. I heard he has the black Hunnuli under guard in the palace stables."

Marron stamped a hoof. *I will get her. I saw the stables on my way up here.*

"Pity the guards who stand in the way of that horse," the Shar-Ja said in wonder as he watched her go.

Tassilio ran out then and came back with a pitcher of water. "It was all I could find," he said, offering some to the women and his father.

The Shar-Ja took a sip of the proffered drink and smiled at his son. "By the Living God, where have you been? Zukhara told me you were dead, too."

Tassilio blushed at the warmth in his father's voice, and for once the voluble boy was tongue-tied. He grinned and shifted from foot to foot. "I was helping my friends," was all he could say.

The Hunnuli mares came back, sooner than the women expected. *The guards were gone,* Marron explained. *The palace is almost empty. Everyone has either left to fight or to hide.*

Nara said nothing but pushed close to Gabria, sniffing her all over and whickering her joy and relief. Whatever sedative Zukhara had given her had worn off, and she looked thin but fit. Gabria threw her arms around her mare's neck, burying her face in the black mane. With Helmar's help, she climbed onto Nara's broad back.

"When Sayyed and the others reach here, tell them where we went," Helmar told Tassilio.

The boy nodded fiercely. "Take the first left hallway, go to the end, and turn right. There are doors there that lead outside."

A quick salute and the sorceresses were gone, their Hunnuli's hooves echoing away down the corridors. Tassilio softly closed and locked the doors behind them and returned to wait with his father.

Helmar led the way along the opulent hallways. She noticed Marron was right—the palace seemed deserted. No one tried to stop them as they trotted the horses through the corridors.

Tassilio's directions proved accurate, and the women found themselves out in the bright sunlight on a broad, grassy esplanade. In front of them the towering bastion of stone soared high into the blue sky. On its top, like a red and green crown, sat the temple of the prophet Sargun.

Built originally as a citadel, the redstone buildings had been consecrated as a monastery and a temple a few generations after the death of the holy prophet. It housed a magnificent library, gardens, the royal crypt for the Turic shar-jas and a population of perhaps one hundred contemplative monks and active priests. It was used by the Turics only in times of the most sacred rites. A narrow road rimmed by a stone fence zigzagged its way up the steep face to the top. There was no sign of Zukhara or Kelene anywhere, and nothing moved in the sky but a few wisps of clouds.

Marron and Nara hurried off the esplanade and found the beginning of the temple road at the end of a long courtyard. Together they trotted up the steep way.

Kelene was too groggy to understand what was happening. All her whirling mind could recognize was the pain in her chest and stomach and the difficulty of breathing. She concentrated on her lungs and the effort of pulling in the air. Her chest seemed so sluggish, even heavy, as if something were pressing it down. Her stomach hurt from something that pushed into it, making her nauseated. She seemed to be moving by some outer volition, certainly not on her own feet, and her head felt strangely heavy and swollen.

She opened her eyes and looked at something fuzzy and dark brown. Her vision rocked sickeningly, so she closed her eyes, took a slow breath, and tried again. This time her eyes focused a little better, and the brown, fuzzy blur became clearly a horse's belly. With that understanding came full realization. Zukhara had thrown her over a saddled horse and was leading it somewhere uphill.

Struggling did little good because he had tied her to the saddle. Those same Hunnuli hair ropes, Kelene thought sourly. She lay still and tried to soothe the pounding in her head while she waited to see what he would do. It wasn't easy. Zukhara seemed to be in a desperate hurry. He rode a second horse and cantered the mounts as often as he dared up the steep grade. By the time they reached the top of the incline, both horses were blowing and lathered in sweat. He urged them through a strong-looking gate and brought them to a rough stop in the cloistered courtyard at the main entrance to the citadel buildings.

Leaving the horses where they stood, he ran back to close the gates. Kelene could not see what he was doing, because he had his back to her, yet he seemed to take an inordinate amount of time just to lock a gate. Finally he came back, tugged Kelene off her mount, and carried her over his shoulder into the forecourt of the front entrance. Several priests ran to meet him.

"Where is the Tobba?" he roared at them. "Bring him to the Chamber of Unity."

Kelene's mind whirled. What did he intend to do? Didn't he realize his cause was lost? The Shar-Ja was still alive. Cangora was falling into the hands of the loyalists, and his fanatics were being defeated. "What are you doing?" she said aloud.

The Gryphon heaved her over onto her feet and held her bound arms in an iron grip. "I failed to kill the Shar-Ja today, but without the antidote, he will die shortly anyway. The throne will still be mine. I am Fel Karak, the Gryphon, the anointed servant of the Living God!" he ranted. "And you are still my chosen wife." He wrenched her forward and dragged her with him through the corridors of the outlying buildings toward the inner sanctum of the temple grounds.

The sorceress struggled to bring her thoughts under control. It was time to act, to fight back, but her head and chest hurt so much from the earlier arcane blow that her wits felt addled and her vision was still blurry. She could hardly form a single coherent thought, let alone a strategy to defeat a sorcerer with a functioning ward. She staggered after Zukhara, paying little attention to where they were going.

After what seemed a very long time to Kelene, Zukhara pushed open a door adorned with vines and wooden roses and tugged her into the Chamber of Unity, the chapel used by members of the royal family for marriages and betrothals. Zukhara did not bother to explain anything to his captive, he simply placed her in front of a tiny, wizened old man and wrapped his fingers around her wrist.

The old man, the Tobba, was the spiritual leader of the community of priests and monks at the temple. He was very familiar with the Gryphon and his methods, and he did not even murmur a complaint at the hasty and unorthodox arrival of the man and his intended bride. He stretched out his skinny arms and lifted his voice in supplication to Shahr as set forth in the ancient texts of Turic matrimony.

Kelene did not need a translator to tell her what the priest was doing, nor a witness to interpret the self-satisfied smirk on Zukhara's face. She had to get away from him now, before she became married to him in the eyes of Turic law. She glanced around the room, hoping for some bit of inspiration. She knew she was not strong enough to fight Zukhara physically. He was a powerful, athletic man who could overpower her all too easily. Nor could she use spells against his body as long as he wore the ivory ward. Perhaps, she thought, she could manipulate something around him that would give her a chance to slip away. She knew him well enough by now to know he would come after her, and she hoped he would. She still wanted the antidote hanging around his neck. She needed time only to untie her hands, clear her mind, and perhaps get some help.

The Chamber of Unity, she noticed, was more like a garden than a room. The walls were hung with pink silk handpainted with delicate white roses. Living roses grew in pots in every corner, along a small ornate altar, and in hanging baskets around the ceiling. To the right, wide doors sat open to the sunny warmth of a magnificent rose garden where rosebushes of every color filled the air with a sweet, heady fragrance. In the quiet of the afternoon, Kelene heard the gentle hum of bees.

A slow smile tickled the corners of Kelene's mouth. A spell came to mind, a simple, ordinary, everyday spell from Lady Jeneve's book: a spell to attract bees to a new hive. She breathed the words to herself and worked the magic into a gentle spell; then she shifted just enough to let her fingers touch the edge of Zukhara's ceremonial robes.

The magic worked faster than she thought it would. The Tobba had just finished his first set of prayers and was laying a strip of linen over their joined wrists when a bee whizzed into the room and settled on the Gryphon's cheek. He brushed it away only to have ten more suddenly buzz about his head. All at once the room was filled with honey bees whirling in a cloud around Zukhara.

The Tobba fell back in a panic. The usurper yelled, waving frantically with his free hand at the determined insects. His flailing arm angered them, and they flew at him aggressively. He pulled his hand off Kelene to slap at several bees crawling down his neck, and she hoisted her long skirts and bolted into the garden.

Zukhara's furious shout rang out behind her, but he was too occupied with the bees to give immediate chase. She raced down the grassy paths between the raised beds of roses until she was completely out of sight of the chamber before she slowed a little to take stock of her position. She had entered not just one garden but an entire complex of landscaped gardens of every variety, lovingly tended by the monks of the monastery. The rose garden was but a small part of a natural labyrinth that covered a large area of the temple grounds. The temple itself was not far away.

* * *

At the top of the road leading up to the citadel, Marron and Nara came to a stop in front of the closed gates. Helmar grunted her exasperation and slid off her mare. Two heavy wooden gates barred with iron hung from high stone pillars attached to very solid walls. There was no way around the gates or over them. Helmar stalked to the middle and yanked on them. The gates didn't budge.

"They've been sealed with magic," she called back to Gabria.

Marron sidled up beside her. She stretched out to sniff the gates just as Helmar initiated a spell to break the arcane seals. The mare's nostrils suddenly flared. *Helmar! No, don't—*

She never had a chance to finish her warning.

The gate exploded in their faces.

* * *

From the sunlit gardens of the temple, Kelene heard the muffled boom. She cocked her head to listen, hoping the sound meant help was arriving. When nothing more happened, she decided the muffled explosion was probably part of the fighting in the city. She hurried on.

She saw several good places to hide in the small groves of trees, heavy clumps of shrubbery, or in sheltered nooks scattered throughout the gardens. But she knew they could be only temporary. Her instincts sought a high place. Somewhere above the grounds where she could watch for Zukhara, or where she could see the city below. Perhaps she could see the fighting in the streets and learn who had attacked the city. Maybe, by the grace of Amara, Demira had brought Sayyed and Rafnir and they were already looking for her.

Kelene took a precious moment and paused just long enough to turn her talent inward on her throbbing head. Her magic eased the pain enough to enable her to see clearly and to run without worrying that her head would split open. As an afterthought, she also took time to change the red dress to pants and tunic, which gave her more freedom of movement. Then she went on quickly, moving through the maze of flowerbeds, vegetable gardens, fruit trees, and shrubbery as fast as she could move. She headed toward the tallest edifice she could see in the citadel complex, the great Temple of Sargun.

The temple was unlike anything Kelene had ever seen. It was built in levels that rose ten stories high around a towering central sanctuary. On the exterior, on every level, were hanging gardens of foliage plants and brilliant flowers. From the ground it looked like a verdant pyramid rising in steps to a crown of reddish stone.

Kelene hurried to the temple's base. She heard shouts behind her and the furious voice of Zukhara. He had managed to banish the bees and come after her as she had predicted he would. A hot fury surged through her, fed by the days of misery, worry, and anxiety. That man had threatened her, hurt her, poisoned her mother, tried to rape her, and forcibly taken her and Gabria away from their home and loved ones all for his own selfish greed and ambition. He had called the dance for all those days. Now, Kelene thought fiercely, let him pay the piper.

She reached a broad stairway leading up to the first level of the temple and flew up on racing feet. She caught a glimpse of men running toward her through the gardens and ran along the outside walkway to the stairs going up to the second story. The steps were broad and solid and easy to navigate, but they were staggered along the side of the temple rather than climbing in a straight line up to the top.

A sudden blast of the Trymmian force exploded on the steps beside her. Kelene stumbled up to the next level, turned, and stared down the stairs.

Zukhara stood on the level below, glaring up at her. His hand was raised to fire again. "Come down, my lady. There is no escape."

Kelene did the only thing she knew he could not tolerate. She laughed at him.

His eyes ablaze, he fired a sphere of the Trymmian force directly at her. This time a red shield of defensive energy crackled into existence in front of her. The blue sphere ricocheted off into a wall. The sorceress turned and ran to the next set of stairs, her shield still intact and hovering close behind. Zukhara hurried after her. Temple guards came up behind him, but he waved them back. The sorceress was *his* prey.

The hunt continued up the side of the temple, like a crackling, booming thunderstorm. Kelene led Zukhara on, taunting him into using his power. Zukhara was strong, Kelene knew, virtually invincible as long as he wore the ward. On the other hand, he was arrogant and inexperienced. His ward would be little protection against his own magic if he lost control of his spells.

On the fifth level she slowed down and shot a few bolts of power at him, which he easily dodged. Sneering, he instantly returned a barrage intended to shatter her shield. Kelene gritted her teeth and intensified her defenses, then rushed on ahead of him. She climbed up and up, ever higher along the sides of the temple, past the hanging garden boxes full of ferns, flowers, and tiny trees. She was panting by the time she climbed to the ninth story. Her legs hurt after so many days of inactivity, and the pain had returned to her head. She hoped Zukhara was as tired as she felt, but when she looked back, he was striding up the stairs at the same relentless pace. Kelene stopped to catch her breath, and she waited at the foot of the last staircase for the Gryphon to reach her level.

He bared his teeth in a wolfish smile when he saw her. "There is nowhere left to go, Clanswoman. Submit to me before I am forced to break you."

"I'd rather break this," she retorted and pointed her hand toward him. Instead of firing at him, though, she released a blast at a huge plant box hanging over his head. The wood exploded in a hail of shattered fragments, dirt, and bits of plant. Zukhara was knocked backward by the shock of the blast.

Instantly Kelene lowered her aim and sent a sustained, specific beam of energy toward his chest, where his ward lay concealed. She felt a pressure there, fighting against her power, and she concentrated, forcing her magic deep into the intricate curves of the ward to find the crack and break it open. Blinded by the shower of dirt, Zukhara struggled to regain his balance and fight off her assault with a shield of his own.

Something shifted beneath the pressure of Kelene's spell. The ivory ward, although designed to resist intense amounts of magical energy, had been weakened by the crack in its surface, and now it wavered in the force of Kelene's power. The crack widened.

Zukhara hunched over, his arms wrapped around himself to protect his ward as he tried to form the shield. Kelene pushed harder. She imagined her hand closing around the pale white ball, the feel of its delicate weight on her palm, and the satisfying crunch as she crushed it in her fist.

There was an audible pop. In disbelief, the Turic pulled the silver chain out of his robes and gaped at the shattered bits that fell out onto his hand.

Kelene stared avidly at the small silver tube that still hung on his chain. She did not want him to take revenge on the loss of his ward by destroying the antidote, so she moved quickly to distract him. "Sorcerer!" she sneered. "Ha! Now we're even. No false protection. Only our own skills. Try to break me now." And she dashed up the stairs to the very top, the roof of the temple.

Her ruse worked. Zukhara dropped the broken ward and sprinted after her. They came off the stairs onto the large flat, tiled roof. There were no potted plants growing up here. It was bare and unadorned and open to the vast sky. A small altar faced the east, and several stone benches sat along the low wall that framed the roof placed there for the priests who came to study the stars. The view of the mountains was breathtaking.

Kelene ran to the far end to look for another set of stairs in case she needed an escape. Instead of stairs, she discovered that the end of the temple edged the rim of the rocky pinnacle. From the temple's lowest floor, the ground fell away in a precipice that dropped nearly a thousand feet to the valley floor. Kelene sucked in a lungful of air and whirled to face Zukhara. He had finally completed his shield and stood across from her, enclosed in a dome of glowing energy.

Kelene pursed her lips. He was showing his inexperience. A full dome of shielding required a great expenditure of strength and concentration to maintain and was hard to move about. Kelene had learned that a simple shield, even one as small as the battle shields carried by warriors, was easier to use and needed less attention to keep intact.

Her thoughts stopped short with a jerk. What was that? Something, a presence, nudged her awareness. Not Demira. Then a high-pitched screeching cry sounded overhead, and a large golden shape wheeled over her. The gryphon. The creature screeched again in a jarring, nerve-racking tone that sounded both angry and annoyed. She curved her wings and gracefully back-winged onto the roof between Zukhara and Kelene. Crouched there, she hissed at them both. Her ears lay flat, and the hairs rose on the back of her neck.

Kelene stared at her, outraged. "What have you done to her?" she cried to Zukhara.

That the gryphon had been abused was obvious. Her ribs poked out of her golden sides; her coat was matted and dirty. Raw wounds encircled her legs where she had fought against her chains, and red, oozing welts covered her face and shoulders. Worst of all were the singed circles on her sides where someone had used the Trymmian force against her. Kelene remembered seeing the gryphon earlier, flying over the city wall when the fighting started, but if any sorcerers had been with the attackers, she doubted they had caused the damage to the gryphon. The burn wounds looked several days old and were already crusted over.

Something else looked different, too. The gryphon wore a new collar, intricately woven in knots. A ward, Kelene decided; Zukhara had sent the gryphon out with a ward.

As if to confirm her suspicions, Zukhara snapped a command in Turic to the gryphon. She snarled, a low menacing sound of fury. He shouted again and raised his fist. The gryphon winced away. She looked at Kelene, and if there was any recognition in her slitted eyes, it died when Zukhara evaporated his dome and fired a blast of magic at the creature.

The gryphon screamed, more from fear than pain since the collar protected her from most of the blast, and she pounced at Kelene, her talons extended and her teeth bared. The sorceress dove out from under her.

"No, girl," Kelene cried. The sorceress held out her hands to signal peace, but the gryphon jumped toward her again. Kelene swerved sideways too late. The animal's paw caught her back, and she fell sprawling near a corner of the low wall.

Zukhara laughed, a low sound as full of menace as the gryphon's growl. He formed spheres of the Trymmian force and fired at Kelene to drive her into the corner. She scrambled back until her legs banged into the stone wall. She flicked up a shielding dome against Zukhara's bombardment and the gryphon's teeth, and tried desperately to think of some way out of the trap. She could not stand there forever holding up an arcane shield, yet she could not fend off the gryphon and fight Zukhara at the same time. She did not want to hurt the gryphon either, unless she was forced to.

The creature snapped at the red power, then ripped her claws over the length of the small dome. Her breath hissed. Her lips curled back from her long incisors. She paced around, staying well away from Zukhara.

All at once another dark shadow scudded across the roof. Kelene shot a look at the sky and saw Demira silently stretch out her long forelegs and dive directly at the gryphon. The winged beast half turned, startled by the mare's appearance, and caught a kick on her face from the horse's back hooves. The kick did not injure her since Demira had no real force behind such a maneuver in midair, but it hurt, and it infuriated the already angry gryphon. She sprang off the roof and streaked after Demira.

"Oh, gods," Kelene panted. She knew the Hunnuli had only a slim chance to evade the flying predator. For one desperate and blind instant she turned her gaze to follow Demira's escape and forgot about Zukhara.

He lashed out instantly with a spell that did not touch her or even her shield. It landed on the square of tiles beneath her feet and transformed the slate to a sheet of glaring ice. Caught unprepared, Kelene found her feet slipping on the sheer surface. She fell, smashing her head against the low wall.

Two blows in one afternoon were too much, her mind thought through a haze of pain and whirling bits of light. Her shield faltered and went out. She knew she should renew it, but at that moment she could not remember how. Zukhara's face swam in front of her. It smiled at her with such a gloating smirk that it would have made her queasy if she weren't already feeling very ill. She felt his hand on her face and sensed her death in the hatred and fury that steamed from his touch.

"Zukhara!"

Kelene blinked in surprise. She hadn't said anything.

The Turic flinched as if something had struck him. With an oath, he jumped to his feet and faced Gabria. The sorceress stood at the top of the stairs, looking like one of the plague dead. Her hair hung loose, as wild as any hag's. Her face was ghastly white and streaked with dark rivulets of blood. More blood smeared her torn and tattered skirts.

Zukhara, in his arrogance, rejoiced. Gabria could not fight him; she was too weak, yet she could watch her daughter be crushed beneath his power. He would not kill Kelene's body; he still wanted that for breeding. He would destroy her personality, the spirit that made her so unique. He leaned over Kelene again and lowered his hand to her face.

The little silver tube hanging loose on its chain dangled forgotten from his neck. It twisted and danced in a gleam of sunlight and shone like a tiny sun in Kelene's blurry vision. It beckoned to her hand to reach for it. Just as Zukhara's fingers touched her cheek, Kelene grasped the tube and yanked hard. The chain dug into the man's neck and broke with a snap.

He yelled in fury but, before he could snatch the tube back, Gabria formed a spell—a simple, devilish one that required little strength from her failing body—and flung it at him. A small green ball of power flew through the space between them and smacked into his shoulder. It clung there like a bur. Immediately tiny tendrils of green energy burst out of the ball and skittered over his torso like streams of angry fire ants.

Zukhara arched backward, stunned by the itching pain of the magic. He scratched frantically at his arms and chest and back; he pulled at the little green bur, and all his efforts only made the burning stings worse. He staggered back from Kelene to the wall and screamed for the gryphon.

Free of his weight, Kelene grabbed the stones by her head and hauled herself to her knees. She was just high enough to peer over the low wall and see the ground below, where the gryphon crouched close to the temple wall, flanked by two furious Hunnuli mares. Demira had been clever enough to realize she could not outfly the winged predator. As soon as she saw her mother, Nara, approaching the temple, she had landed and sought the older mare's help. Now the gryphon had two large and powerful horses to contend with, and she was discovering they were not such easy prey. At Zukhara's bellow, she bounced into the air and beat her way up to the top of the temple.

Kelene saw her coming. Summoning all her strength, she willed her hurting body to walk toward Gabria. Her mother stumbled toward her. They met in the middle, and their arms went around one another.

Zukhara finally pried the green bur off his shoulder. He threw it to the ground and stamped on it. "Kill them now!" he shrieked at the gryphon. The creature wheeled, reluctant to obey the man's demands. She hissed at him and slowly came to land near the women. "Kill them I said!" he screamed again.

Kelene snatched at the one chance she had left. Letting go of Gabria, she threw herself at the gryphon and caught one of its long legs. Surprised, the animal jerked back, but Kelene held tight to the warm, furry limb. Her fingers clasped tight against the skin. Using her empathic talent, she reached into the gryphon's turbulent mind to touch the bond of familiarity she had forged during their time together. The gryphon growled a rumbling note.

It's all right, beautiful one, she sent softly, reassuringly. *It is me. I will not hurt you. I promised to help free you, remember?*

The creature's growl slowed and faded. Her nose sniffed Kelene's scent.

"No!" Zukhara yelled at her. "You are mine! You will do as *I* say. Now kill them both." Overcome with embittered rage, he lashed out at the gryphon with a whiplash of fiery magic.

Without the ward the spell would have killed her. As it was, the lash caught the gryphon on the haunches like a flick of lightning. She reared up, breaking away from Kelene, and screamed a shivering cry. Her wings beat the air; her eyes burned with white-hot fire. In one powerful leap she sprang at the man she hated above all other men.

Zukhara's arrogance proved his undoing, for even as he saw her come he could not believe the gryphon sent to him by his god would turn on him. By the time his brain thought to react, her powerful talons had ripped into his stomach. He screamed once before she crushed his head.

Kelene turned her eyes away. She walked back to Gabria, and for a time they simply stood together in utter exhaustion. Relief, release, and happiness formed a potent brew of feelings that began to revive Kelene's battered form, and she became aware of several details. The first thing she pointed out was the blood on Gabria's face and clothes.

"Most of it is not mine," Gabria said unhappily. "It is Helmar's and Marron's." She held up her hand to forestall Kelene's questions. "The tale is too long to explain now, but as soon as you're able, please go to them. Zukhara booby-trapped the citadel gate, and it blew up in their faces."

Kelene nodded. "There is only this; then we will go." She held up the silver tube she had torn from Zukhara's neck. "The antidote."

Years of aging dropped away from Gabria's face at the touch of a brilliant smile. With shaking hands she took the tube, unscrewed the top, and swallowed half the contents. "I will save the rest for the Shar-Ja," she said. "I could tell just by looking at him that he had been poisoned the same way."

"I hope it is enough. Amara only knows if there is any more."

A grumbling sound drew their attention back to the gryphon. Demira and Nara came clattering up the stairs, and the gryphon crouched, snarling at their presence.

Kelene skirted the remains of Zukhara's body and calmly patted the wild gryphon. Even hungry as she was, the creature had not tried to eat the man's corpse. Gently Kelene unfastened the collar on the gryphon's neck. Stroking her back, Kelene extended her magic into the gryphon to ease the pain of the animal's burns and injuries. *Thank you,* she told her. *That is twice you have saved me. I keep my promise. Go home and find your family.*

The gryphon's tufted ears snapped up and, without a backward glance, she leaped off the roof into the afternoon. Wild with joy, she called once and flew faster than the wind toward the western peaks. They watched her for a moment, until her golden shape disappeared in the distance.

Silently the sorceresses mounted their Hunnuli and left the temple roof, where Zukhara's trampled body lay alone and unmourned.

18

While they rode back to the front gate, Gabria told Kelene the little bit she knew about Helmar.

"A red cloak?" Kelene said in amazement. "Where did she come from? Do you think she is a Corin?"

"I don't know. All I can tell you is that she and her Hunnuli risked their lives for us, and I don't want to lose her now." Gabria's reply was iron-firm, a sure sign that her strength was starting to return.

Kelene said nothing else. She worked instead on her own condition to clear her battered mind, still the pain, and bolster her energies. By the time they reached the cloistered courtyard, her headache had eased from blinding agony to a dull ache that was tolerable, and her limbs felt strong enough to deal with what she had to do.

A small group of yellow-robed priests clustered under the shade of the arched cloister near the remains of the gate. Gabria went to them and gestured to Kelene.

The young sorceress slid carefully to the ground. She patted the mare, delighted beyond words to have her back. "Demira, I must ask one more favor. Please go back to the palace and find my healer's bag in our room. Third floor, west wing. And see if you can find Rafnir, too."

I will look for Sayyed, as well. I think he loves Helmar.

Kelene barely had time to register that surprising remark before Demira sprang aloft and dropped over the rim of the citadel's wall. Kelene hurried to help Gabria.

Priests from the temple had brought the unconscious woman to a resting place on a low cot out of the sun. They had been afraid to carry her any farther. A healer skilled in the arts of surgery and medicine had already begun the difficult task of stopping the bleeding from lacerations on her head, neck, and chest. Kelene looked at the bloodied face and marveled that the woman was still alive.

The healer said something in Turic, and Gabria made an understandable reply. The healer nodded to Kelene. She knelt down by Helmar's head and set to work. Although she did not speak very much Turic and the healer knew no Clannish, they were able to meld their efforts into a swift, efficient treatment. Kelene removed the wooden splinters and debris and cleaned the wounds while the healer priest deftly stitched the worst lacerations closed before the chief lost too much blood. It was a long, difficult process.

Helmar roused once and tried to twist away from the healer's sharp needle, but Kelene laid her fingers on the woman's forehead and eased her gently back to sleep. The Turic healer nodded with approval. They were nearly finished when Demira returned from the palace with Kelene's bag in her teeth and Tassilio on her back.

"Hajira and Mohadan are with Father, so I came to help," he announced, hopping off the mare's back. "Demira told us what happened. Lord Athlone, Rafnir, and Sayyed are on their way up."

Kelene smiled her thanks. "A gift for your help, Shar-Yon." She handed him the silver tube of antidote.

Recognition ignited Tassilio's face into an incandescent grin, and he quickly handed the precious vial to one of the priests. "Give this to my Father at once!" he commanded. "Tell him I will come as soon as my work here is done."

Kelene gratefully took her bag back to Helmar's bedside. Most of the immediate work to save Helmar had been done, but the woman faced a long siege before she could fully recover. Shock, blood loss, dehydration, and infection were side effects she would have to battle in the next few days. Fortunately she had suffered no broken bones, and as far as Kelene could tell, no internal injuries. Even so, neither Kelene nor the Turic healer who had helped her knew if Helmar would survive the devastating blast. Only time and her own strength could help her now.

To improve her patient's strength, Kelene brought out a carefully wrapped packet. Using some warm water brought by a monk, she made an infusion from a special combination of herbs that she always kept prepared and readily available in her bag. The recipe was an old one she had found in the ruins of Moy Tura, and its invigorating potency had helped restore many people to health. With Tassilio's help, she explained to the healer what it was, and he watched with interest while she mixed the tea with honey and dribbled it between Helmar's lips.

Kelene glanced around the courtyard for her mother and saw Gabria kneeling by something on the other side of the gate. Oh, gods, she had forgotten about the Hunnuli. She passed the cup to Tassilio and went to check on the horse.

Gabria had treated many wounds in her life, but she was the first to admit she was not a healer. It was apparent to Kelene as she joined her mother that the older woman felt overwhelmed by the extent of Marron's injuries. With one hand Gabria pressed a strip of cloth torn from her skirt over a gaping wound in the mare's chest and with the other tried to stem the flow of blood from a gash on the mare's neck.

Dismayed, Kelene dropped her bag and knelt beside the bloodied horse. The priests, assuming the mare was dead, had left her where she had fallen after the gate blew up, and she lay on her side, bleeding slowly into the dust from dozens of punctures, slashes, and abrasions.

"I don't think we can save her," Gabria said in a voice thick with tears. "She reared up and took the full force of the blow to save Helmar."

Kelene touched the mare's gray muzzle where the black skin showed through the short white hairs. The skin was warm and her eyelids flickered, but Marron was dangerously close to death. And if she died, Kelene knew Helmar would probably die, too.

"We need water, lots of it. Cloth, blankets, and a big bucket of hot water." She pointed to her bag. "If that tea helps humans, maybe it will help a Hunnuli, too."

Gabria fought down her worry and went to gather the things they would need. Demira and Nara stood close by Marron, their noses almost touching her. Kelene leaned forward to rest her cheek on the mare's face and said, "Marron?"

A flicker of consciousness flared in Kelene's mind—not the vibrant, alert thought of a healthy Hunnuli, but at least it meant Marron was still alive and, on a subconscious level, still aware. Kelene probed deeper into the horse's mind to reach her understanding. She extended her power over Marron's body, lessening her pain and soothing her fear.

Marron. I am Kelene, Demira's rider. Helmar is alive. Do you understand? The Hunnuli's thoughts burst brighter in recognition. *She is alive. But you must stay alive, too. Do you hear me? If you die, she will lose her will to fight. Please stay with us! We will take care of both of you.*

The mare's thoughts sparkled a weary acknowledgment, then slowly faded into the dim, pulsing glow of deep sleep.

Kelene heard horses approach, and she lifted her head to see one of the most welcome sights she would ever remember in her life: her father, her husband, and her father-in-law on their Hunnuli cantering almost neck and neck toward the citadel gates. Their three stallions slid to a stop, and the men dropped off in one unbroken movement.

Kelene stood up, took one step forward, and found herself engulfed in her husband's arms. She buried her face in his shoulder and held him as if she would never let him go. His clothes were filthy, spattered with blood and coated in dust, reeking of sweat and smoke. A dark beard framed his jaws, and his face was too thin, but Kelene thought she had never seen him look so wonderful.

Sayyed paused long enough to see she was safe; then he looked closely at Marron, and his face turned a sickly paste color. He ran into the courtyard to find Helmar. Afer joined Nara and Demira in their vigil over the white mare.

Lord Athlone came out of the gates, helping Gabria carry the water, buckets, and bandages. His clothes were as bad as Rafnir's, and his hair and beard were unkempt. His face was lined from days of worry, and his expression was sober after seeing Helmar. But underneath it all, like a light burning in a worn and weathered tent, glowed a joy too bright to mask. It was matched in its luminosity only by the happiness in Gabria's eyes. He set down his burdens and silently hugged his daughter. Words would come later when the wounded were cared for and the most immediate tasks were done.

With Gabria and Rafnir close by to help, Kelene settled down to the task of repairing Marron's torn chest and shoulders. She felt sometimes as if she were piecing together a shredded blanket of black skin, white hair, and too much red blood. It was a wonder the horse's jugular had not been punctured. The gods, Kelene decided, had kept their hands over Helmar and Marron.

When at last she was finished, Kelene felt worn to a single thread. Her hands shook as she slathered Marron's wounds with an ointment made to fight infection and keep the skin soft so the stitched wounds would heal without crippling scar tissue. If Marron survived, she would always carry scars, but Kelene wanted her to heal as unimpaired as possible.

Since they could not leave the mare lying in the road, the sorceress gradually roused Marron out of unconsciousness. Ever so gently, Afer and Nara nudged her onto her stomach, then helped her ease to her feet. Standing on either side of the swaying mare, they propped up her weight as she tottered into the citadel to the shady cloister near Helmar.

At Tassilio's insistence, the priests agreed to allow the chief and her Hunnuli to stay in the cloister where they could be close together. Straw was brought for Marron, and she lay down again, her eyes closed and her muzzle near Helmar's shoulder.

Kelene steeped a bucket of the restorative for the mare, leaving it where she could reach it without difficulty. She also fixed cups for herself, Gabria, and the three men. They all drank it gratefully.

Sayyed sat, like a man in a daze, beside Helmar. He wiped her face with a cool cloth and slowly fed her sips of her tonic, but a haunted shadow grayed his face, and his limbs were tensed with a terrible anxiety.

Gabria watched him worriedly. He had had that same look in the plague tent when he watched Tam die. She had no idea he had fallen so deeply in love with this woman—perhaps he hadn't either until now. But gods above, Gabria sighed, how would he survive if he lost another love? She leaned into the embrace of her own dearest husband and thanked Amara with all her heart for their reunion.

As soon as Helmar and Marron were as comfortable as they could be, Kelene found the nearest place to sit down and began to shake. Tears filled her eyes. Her strength was gone; her will was depleted. Her head pounded like an overworked drum. She had nothing left in mind or body but a strong desire to lie down and cry. Rafnir scooped her up in his arms. The last thing she remembered for a long time after that was the softness of a bed and the warmth of Rafnir's body as he held her close and comforted her to sleep.

She roused late in the afternoon of the following day in a chamber she soon learned was in the citadel. Rafnir had left, but Kelene was delighted to see a new clan tunic and skirt draped over the foot of the bed and a tray of stuffed meat rolls, cheese, grapes, and wine on the table. Kelene discovered she was ravenous. As soon as she had dressed and eaten, she hurried through the corridors to the front entrance. No one was there but Sayyed and his patients under the cloister. Twenty-four hours had brought little change to Helmar or her horse, and if Sayyed had left her side once, Kelene saw no sign of it. He still wore his filthy, rumpled clothes, and dark shadows circled his eyes from the lack of sleep.

Kelene kissed his forehead. "Thank you for coming after us," she said.

He cracked a semblance of a smile. "You led us on a merry chase."

"Tell me," she asked as she bent over the chief. So while Kelene examined Helmar and Marron and made more of the tea, Sayyed told her about the long journey from Council Rock. Once he got started, he seemed compelled to keep talking, and he told her everything about Sanctuary, the Clannad, Hajira, the ride to Cangora, and most of all, like a man astonished by what he was saying, he talked about Helmar.

Kelene listened quietly. Her father-in-law was not usually so verbose; in fact she had not heard him talk so much in years. She knew it was a measure of his fear for Helmar that made him confide so much of his feelings, and a measure of his love for his daughter-in-law that he chose to share his thoughts with her. Kelene was more grateful than words could tell.

After his tale had wound to an end, Kelene stayed with him. She brought him food and tea and made sure he ate it. She gave him clean clothes. She tended Afer and Demira, who stayed close by, and she conferred with the Turic healer to find the best ointments and pain relievers for her patients.

Lord Athlone and Gabria had returned to the palace, where Gabria and the Shar-Ja were slowly recovering from the effects of the poison. Rafnir had gone down to help Athlone, but he came back in the evening full of news.

"The last of the Fel Azureth surrendered this afternoon," he announced with deep satisfaction. "Mohadan's men routed them out of an old storehouse. The Gryphon's army in Cangora has been completely destroyed."

Kelene looked involuntarily in the direction of the temple. "And what of Zukhara?"

"The Shar-Ja ordered his body brought down from the temple and hung on a gibbet at the front gate. He is spreading the word that the Gryphon died a traitor's death."

The sorceress thought of the golden gryphon and the faith and loyalty she symbolized to the Turics. "He did," she replied shortly.

Rafnir glanced at his father. "Hajira has been restored to his command with full honors. He is reorganizing the survivors of the Shar-Ja's guard. Tassilio told his father everything, and the old man is so grateful to have his son restored to him, he would give Hajira the world if he asked for it."

Sayyed only nodded a reply.

A hush settled over the courtyard. The evening sounds became subdued and distant in the tranquil peace before sunset. The cloister basked in the last of the day's glow.

Helmar's gasp came as a surprise to all three of them. Her mouth opened and closed; then her eyes widened in surprise. She held up her bandaged arms and felt the stitches on her face. "Sayyed?" her voice croaked.

He took her hands in both of his and tenderly pressed them to her chest.

"Don't try to talk," Kelene advised. "Your face is still bruised and swollen, and there are stitches on your jaw and along your forehead. Just rest, and we'll tell you everything later." She fixed more restorative tea for Sayyed to give Helmar, this time laced with a dose of poppy juice to help her sleep.

When Helmar slept again, Sayyed looked more hopeful. "This is the first time she has tried to talk."

"That's a good sign," Kelene told him in all sincerity. "She is strong and healthy. She knows you are here, too. That will help."

Kelene was right. At sunrise the next morning she went out to the courtyard and found Marron lying on her belly, her legs tucked neatly under her, nibbling hay from a pile under her nose. Helmar lay awake, her eyes fastened on Sayyed's sleeping face.

Her alert gaze followed Kelene around while she checked Marron's stitches, changed her bandages, and fed her a small bucket of bran mash.

"Will she be all right?" Helmar whispered anxiously in a voice dry and raspy from disuse.

"As right as you," Kelene replied softly. She examined Helmar's wounds, too, and gave the chief a reassuring smile. "It was not your day to die. The Harbingers must have been too busy to catch you. Both of you were badly injured, and you will carry the scars. But your wounds are clean and healing well. I think you'll be able to go home soon."

"Home," Helmar echoed. Her eyes followed Kelene back into the building before they returned to Sayyed's face. "Home," she repeated, but the happiness she should have felt at such a thought was missing. There was only uneasiness and the fear of impending loss.

Two days later the Clannad carried Helmar on a litter down the road to the palace. Accompanied by the clan magic-wielders, she was escorted to a chamber beside a quiet garden where Marron was settled comfortably on a soft green lawn of grass. It was then the chief heard of Rapinor's death and learned the casualties of her troop. Fifteen riders had died in the battle at the gates; twenty more had been wounded. Helmar turned her face to the wall to hide her tears.

From that day on she had a constant stream of visitors, from the Shar-Ja and Tassilio to Lord Athlone and the clan chieftains who had come with him. From all her visitors she began to piece together the full tale of the past days.

"Now let me see if I have all of this," she said to Sayyed one evening. "Lord Athlone captured a raiding party of the Fel Azureth and learned about the Gryphon and his plans."

"Right. Zukhara had sent his fanatics to cause trouble on the border, hoping we would do just what we did—call for a council. We walked neatly into his trap, bringing Kelene and Gabria with us. Once Athlone learned what was going on, he convinced the other chiefs to support a move over the Altai to help the Shar-Ja. He had already gathered the werods of five clans before Rafnir found him. With those and the men from Council Rock, they rode here in less than four days."

"Four days," she breathed, awed by such a feat. "And is Mohadan doing well?"

"He is in his element." Sayyed laughed. "The clan lords have been staying out of the way and leaving restoration of the government to Mohadan and the Shar-Ja. Mohadan is making himself indispensable. He's already brought news that the extremists' rebellion is failing. Without Zukhara there are no other leaders to take firm command, and word that the Shar-Ja is recovering and has announced a new heir has strengthened his position. There is still a deep loyalty and respect for the Shar-ja."

"Will he fully recover?" she asked.

"It looks as though he will. He and Gabria both grow stronger every day."

Helmar leaned back against her pillows and sighed. Through the open doors of her room she could see Marron grazing, and she winced at the red lines that crisscrossed the mare's white neck, chest, and shoulders. Helmar hadn't seen a mirror lately, but she imagined she looked equally as rough. Her eyes turned back to Sayyed.

He had hardly left her side the past few days, except to clean off the grime of war and deal with his own needs. The rest of the time he had stayed with her, changing her bandages, feeding her broth and tea, telling her stories and news, or just keeping her company in the quiet hours when she rested.

Anyone else spending so much time with her, she probably would have thrown out, but Helmar found she craved Sayyed's company. She missed him horribly when he left, and she cherished every moment he spent with her. Kelene had told her about Tam and Sayyed's vigil at her dying, and Helmar realized he was terrified of losing her, too. The knowledge strengthened her will to recover and forged her feelings for him into an abiding passion.

As the days rolled into the hot Turic summer, Helmar rapidly improved under the care of Sayyed, Kelene, and the Turic healers. One morning she felt strong enough to walk around the garden with Marron. The walk was glorious, but it made her realize how weak she had become. She began to walk every day, exercise with her sword, and retrain her muscles to regain her former strength and agility. The day the stitches came out she celebrated by going for a ride. Afer offered to carry her, since Marron was not yet ready to carry a rider, and Helmar delightedly rode the big stallion around Cangora to see the sights.

Much of the damage caused by the fighting had been repaired by city builders and the Clannad riders whose magic helped speed things along. Rafnir helped, too, learning at the same time much about construction and architecture. He and the other sorcerers had rehung the copper gates and rebuilt the walls.

Zukhara's body had been taken down by that time to be burned and his ashes thrown to the winds. A few of his officers languished in the dungeons awaiting trial.

A month passed in peace and growing optimism. At last the time arrived when Lord Bendinor and the other clan lords prepared to leave for the Ramtharin Plains and the summer gathering. Lord Athlone decided to postpone his return until Gabria and Helmar were strong enough to travel. Savaron, he knew, was quite capable of taking the Khulinin to the gathering.

Two days before the clansmen were due to leave, the Shar-Ja called for a council to be held in his audience chambers the next day. When Helmar heard of it, she asked to speak to Lady Gabria alone. Gabria came, bringing Lady Jeneve's book and the red cloak. They talked for several hours, and what they had to say to each other they kept to themselves. As soon as Gabria left, Helmar called her riders. She brought them all into her room and talked with them for several hours more. When they had said all there was to say, she bid them go to the Shar-Ja's council.

The council began at midmorning in the large, airy chambers off the celestial throne room. It was quite crowded, for the Clannad riders, the clan chiefs, the Kirmaz-Ja, a unit of royal guards, the Shar-Ja's newly appointed counselors, and Kelene and Gabria were there.

The Shar-Ja entered with his son and sat on a chair at the head of the room. The antidote and days of activity and optimism had worked a miracle on the Turic overlord. His pride and vigor had returned, bringing health to his poison-wracked body and energy to his work. His skin had lost its pallor, and his eyes gleamed with intelligence and wit. Part of his healing had included finding his oldest son's body and bringing it home to Cangora for a royal funeral. The grief for his dead son still lingered, but the pride he felt for his intrepid younger son went leagues to heal his aching heart.

He rose and bowed to the assemblage. Standing tall, his white hair uncovered and his head unbowed, he expressed his gratitude to all who had helped preserve his throne. "Especially I owe my deepest gratitude to the people of the Dark Horse Clans and the Clannad, who rode to help a neighbor when no obligation was owed and no oath of fealty had been given. To you, the lords of the clans, I offer you this—better late than never at all."

A scribe stepped forward with four rolled scrolls and handed them to Lord Athlone. He passed the extras to Lord Jamas, Lord Wendern, and Peoren, then opened one and read it aloud to those around him. Written in both Clannish and Turic, the scrolls bore word for word the treaty they had completed at Council Rock. At the bottom of each scroll was the official seal and signature of the Shar-Ja. Quills were passed around and each chief signed his name to the scrolls. Lord Athlone returned two copies to the scribe. He bowed low to the Turic overlord.

"You rode a long way to get those," Rassidar said with a touch of humor. "I did not want you to go empty-handed. And you, Peoren," he said to the young Ferganan. "I was not so befuddled by Zukhara's poisons that I forgot my promise to you. I will pay your compensation in horses, stock animals, cotton, and spices to be delivered at a date of your choosing. Will that be sufficient?"

Peoren bowed to the Shar-Ja, his face red with pleasure. "That will do well indeed, your majesty, and I will call off the blood feud. May this be the end of any hostility between clan and tribe."

Lord Athlone said, "Shar-Ja, our offer still stands to help if we can during this drought."

"Unless you know a spell to bring rain, you have done more than I could ever have asked for. But we're not in the dire straits Zukhara led us all to believe. He and the Fel Azureth had been stealing and hoarding grain for the past two years. We have found enough to keep the people fed for a little while longer than we'd hoped. Perhaps you could ask your gods to send us some rain." He turned to regard the crowded room and saw the Clannad standing in a quiet group near the back of the chamber.

"Lady Helmar," he called and waited until she came forward. "You came out of our mountains like a legend. No one has ever reported your colony or any people like you in our midst. I hope you will not disappear again into the misty peaks. I have heard a great deal about you these past days from those who have gotten to know you, and because of what I have heard and what you have done for us, I would like to grant the Clannad perpetual ownership of the valley you call Sanctuary, to keep and hold as you see fit with no obligation or debt owed to the throne of the Shar-Ja."

The Clannad riders stayed strangely silent behind their chief, creating a quiet unified support for Helmar as she turned at an angle to look at both the Shar-Ja and the clan lords. Her voice rang out through the chambers so every person could hear. "Some of you have probably guessed how the Clannad came to be in the Turic mountains, but for those of you who do not know us well, I will tell you. Generations ago, during a summer clan gathering, my ancestress Lady Jeneve received a secret message that the magic-wielders had been slaughtered at Moy Tura." She paused when a gasp of surprise and understanding spread from the crowd around her. Only Lady Gabria watched her quietly and bent her lips in a knowing half-smile.

Helmar continued, "Lady Jeneve guessed what would happen if the murderers reached the gathering, so she took her family, her pet cats, a few friends, and their Hunnuli and fled south into the Turic mountains. They found Sanctuary by the grace of the gods, and for two hundred years we have slowly multiplied and lived in terror that someone would find us and give away our settlement to the clans. We did not know until Sayyed and Rafnir stumbled into our back door that sorcery had been resurrected by Lady Gabria. Shar-Ja, if we may wait to accept your generous gift, I would like to talk to my people and to the chiefs about returning the Clannad to the Ramtharin Plains. My lords," she said directly to the clansmen, "we would like to go home."

The clan chieftains stared at her. Some looked shocked; some appeared pleased. "But where will you go?" Lord Fiergan asked sharply. "Do you wish to join a clan or start a treld of your own?"

"Well, we can talk about that later I suppose—" Helmar started to say.

Sayyed began to grin as the possibilities lit a fire in his mind. "My lords," he said, cutting into Helmar's reply. "The Clannad could come to Moy Tura. They are used to living in buildings, and we are in desperate need of help." He winked at Helmar, and she beamed back. She had hoped he would make such an offer.

"I must talk to the rest of my people," she said firmly, "but I think that is a suitable solution."

"Then I will accept your answer whenever you decide," the Shar-Ja told her. "And I will count you as a friend wherever you go."

Kelene whooped with delight.

The clan chiefs left the next day with the Shar-Ja's treaty and Helmar's petition to rejoin the clans. They promised to take the news to the gathering and encourage the clanspeople to accept. Sayyed went with them. Although he wanted to stay with Helmar, he felt he would be a good advocate for the Clannad at the gathering, and Lord Athlone agreed.

Before he left, though, he presented Helmar with a betrothal gift of a bracelet woven from hairs taken from Afer's and Marron's tails. "It is just a simple thing," he explained, "to remind you of me until you say yes."

She kissed him, grateful that he did not demand an answer yet. How could she decide until she knew where her people would go? She watched him ride away over the foothills back to the plains of the clans, and her heart ached to go with him. Oh, Amara, she wondered, what will I do if the Clannad says no?

Ten days later Lord Athlone, his men, Lady Gabria, Kelene, Rafnir, Helmar, and the Clannad riders bid farewell to the Shar-Ja and Tassilio and Hajira. Their farewells were long and pleasantly sad and full of promises to visit. They trotted out of the city, onto the Spice Road, and turned north toward the mountains and the valley of Sanctuary.

Kelene turned back just once to look beyond the pinnacle and its green and red temple to the peaks beyond, hoping, foolishly she knew, for one last glimpse of the gryphon. Then she sighed and cast a sidelong glance at her husband.

"Do you know how many people are in the Clannad?" she asked, her tone deliberately innocent.

"Yes, about three hundred and eighty-two. Or so Helmar said," Rafnir answered.

"Good, then if they come, we will have three hundred and eighty-three new inhabitants in Moy Tura."

He was slow to catch on. "Three hundred and—" His voice caught, and he stared at her. The delight blossomed on his face. "Are you sure?"

She grinned then, shining like a star. "Yes! Zukhara's midwives' remedy actually worked! And that," she said, her spirit exalting, "is my best revenge!"

EPILOGUE

The following year proved another turning point in the history of the Dark Horse Clans. Bards marked its events in the Tale of Years; clanspeople talked about it for seasons afterward. It became known as the time of the Return of the Dead Clan.

That summer, a season marked by plentiful rains both north and south of the Altai, Sayyed and Rafnir decided to go to the clan gathering and take their people with them. They were one of the last groups to arrive, but they had planned that deliberately to honor their chieftain, Lady Helmar, and the three hundred and eighty-two members of the Clannad that would attend a clan gathering for the first time in over two hundred years.

The other clans crowded along the rivers and on the hillsides to watch them come. The Khulinin waited near the big council tent. Lady Gabria sat on Nara and felt the tears stream down her face, but she didn't bother to wipe them off. She thought of her father and her brothers and the other Corins who had died twenty-eight years ago. She wished fervently they could have been there to watch the return of the Clannad.

The first riders came over the distant hill from the north, and Gabria recognized Kelene, who rode with her baby daughter bundled in a carrier on her chest, and Rafnir. Behind them rode Sayyed close beside his wife, Helmar, on her star-white mare. Just to their right, bouncing along like a puppy on stilts, was Marron's month-old colt, a handsome baby Hunnuli with a black coat, the white lightning mark and, like an omen from the gods, a white mane and tail.

Then came the others, in a trailing column of carts, horses, and excited people—each and every one of them wearing the red cloak of Clan Corin.

The main body of the clan rode to the old Corin campsite along the Isin River, but Helmar, Sayyed, Rafnir, and Kelene trotted their Hunnuli to the council grove and greeted the other eleven clan chiefs.

Lord Bendinor stepped forward and spoke so all could hear. "Do you, Lady Gabria, as last surviving heir to Lord Dathlar and the line of Corin, acknowledge these people to be descendants of Lady Jeneve, daughter of Lord Magar of Clan Corin?"

Gabria looked up into Helmar's shining face. "I acknowledge them with all my heart."

Bendinor nodded to several people by the tent and, as Gabria watched through her tears, the scarlet banner of the Corin clan was raised for the first time since the massacre and took its rightful place among the twelve clans of Valorian.

A Brief Glossary of the Dark Horse Clans

The Clans	Chief	Cloak Color
Corin	none	Red
Khulinin	Athlone	Gold
Geldring	Hendric	Green
Wylfling	Jamas	Brown
Dangari	Bendinor	Indigo
Shadedron	Wendern	Black
Reidhar	Fiergan	Yellow
Amnok	Terod	Gray
Murjik	Geric	Purple
Bahedin	Ryne	Orange
Jehanan	Sha Tajan	Maroon
Ferganan	Tirek (Peoren)	Light Blue

Hearthguard: A chieftain's personal bodyguards. These men are the elite warriors of the clan and are honored with this position for their bravery, skill, and loyalty.

Hunnuli: Magical black horses that can communicate mentally with their magic-wielding riders.

Meara: The king stallion of the clan's herds, one that is chosen for its ability to defend the mares and foals.

Treld: A clan's permanent winter camp.

Valorian: Ancient hero of the Dark Horse Clans.

Weir-geld: Recompense paid in the form of gold or livestock to the family of a person who was murdered or killed in a personal duel.

Werod: The fighting body of a clan. Although all men are required to learn the rudiments of fighting, only those who pass certain tests make up the werod.

Wer-tain: The commander of the werod. These men are second in authority only to the chieftains.

About the Author

Mary H. Herbert started writing fantasy in high school and continued during attendance at the universities of Montana and Wyoming, and at the Center for Medieval and Renaissance Studies in Oxford, England. Her first four novels in the Dark Horse series were national chain bookstore best-sellers.

A Brief Glossary of the Dark Horse Clans

The Clans	Chief	Cloak Color
Corin	none	Red
Khulinin	Athlone	Gold
Geldring	Hendric	Green
Wylfling	Jamas	Brown
Dangari	Bendinor	Indigo
Shadedron	Wendern	Black
Reidhar	Fiergan	Yellow
Amnok	Terod	Gray
Murjik	Geric	Purple
Bahedin	Ryne	Orange
Jehanan	Sha Tajan	Maroon
Ferganan	Tirek (Peoren)	Light Blue

Hearthguard: A chieftain's personal bodyguards. These men are the elite warriors of the clan and are honored with this position for their bravery, skill, and loyalty.

Hunnuli: Magical black horses that can communicate mentally with their magic-wielding riders.

Meara: The king stallion of the clan's herds, one that is chosen for its ability to defend the mares and foals.

Treld: A clan's permanent winter camp.

Valorian: Ancient hero of the Dark Horse Clans.

Weir-geld: Recompense paid in the form of gold or livestock to the family of a person who was murdered or killed in a personal duel.

Werod: The fighting body of a clan. Although all men are required to learn the rudiments of fighting, only those who pass certain tests make up the werod.

Wer-tain: The commander of the werod. These men are second in authority only to the chieftains.

About the Author

Mary H. Herbert started writing fantasy in high school and continued during attendance at the universities of Montana and Wyoming, and at the Center for Medieval and Renaissance Studies in Oxford, England. Her first four novels in the Dark Horse series were national chain bookstore best-sellers.